THALIA

Also by Larry McMurtry

The Last Kind Words Saloon

Custer

The Berrybender Narratives

Hollywood: A Third Memoir

Literary Life: A Second Memoir

Rhino Ranch

Books: A Memoir

When the Light Goes

Telegraph Days

Oh What a Slaughter

The Colonel and Little Missie

Loop Group

Folly and Glory

By Sorrow's River

The Wandering Hill

Sin Killer

Sacagawea's Nickname: Essays on the American West

Paradise

Boone's Lick

Roads

Still Wild: Short Fiction of the American West, 1950 to the Present

Walter Benjamin at the Dairy Queen

Duane's Depressed

Crazy Horse

Comanche Moon

Dead Man's Walk

The Late Child

Streets of Laredo

The Evening Star

Buffalo Girls

Some Can Whistle

Anything for Billy

Film Flam: Essays on Hollywood

Texasville

Lonesome Dove

The Desert Rose

Cadillac Jack

Somebody's Darling

Terms of Endearment

All My Friends Are Going to Be Strangers

Moving On

In a Narrow Grave: Essays on Texas

By Larry McMurtry and Diana Ossana

Pretty Boy Floyd

Zeke and Ned

THALIA

A TEXAS TRILOGY

Larry McMurtry

LIVERIGHT PUBLISHING CORPORATION
A DIVISION OF W. W. NORTON & COMPANY
Independent Publishers Since 1923
NEW YORK LONDON

Printed in the United States of America
First Edition

Manufacturing by Quad Graphics, Fairfield
Book design by Lovedog Studio
Production manager: Anna Oler

ISBN 978-1-63149-375-1

Liveright Publishing Corporation
500 Fifth Avenue, New York, N.Y. 10110
www.wwnorton.com

W. W. Norton & Company Ltd.
15 Carlisle Street, London W1D 3BS

1 2 3 4 5 6 7 8 9 0

To James and Curtis, Texas troubadours

Contents

Introduction

Life and art alike are filled with accidents. The big one in my career was the discovery, by chance, of William Butler Yeats, the great Irish poet, and his famous epigraph:

> Cast a cold eye
> On life, on death.
> Horseman, pass by!

Had I not stumbled upon those words, I have often wondered whether I would have written *Horseman, Pass By*. It was, for me, the key that turned the starter to my journey as a writer. I went home to Archer City in 1958, the summer after I graduated from North Texas State University in Denton, Texas, to cowboy on my father's ranch while I wrote the book.

I had little previous experience in writing fiction, but I jumped right into *Horseman*. The novel grew out of a short story I had written in the only creative writing class I attended while at North Texas State, which was about the decline and death of a famous Panhandle cattleman. It was probably my first intimation of Charles Goodnight, the great Panhandle cattleman himself. My father's own family produced nine cattlemen, who were sprinkled all over the Texas Panhandle. In all, I did five drafts, written at a five-pages-a-day pace. Once my fluency was established, I occasionally doubled that pace, but the five-pages-a-day is the one that has served me throughout most of my writing life. I finished *Horseman* about a week before I left Archer City for Houston, Texas, where I was about to enroll at Rice University as a graduate student in English.

Looking back, I realize that completing *Horseman, Pass By* marked the end of my direct contact with the myth of the cowboy—or at least, the myth carried throughout their lives by the cowboys I knew. My father was one of those cowboys. I myself have carried that myth through more than forty books. I didn't know where the completion of that first novel might lead, but I did know, once I finished it, that my life was to be spent with words.

Leaving Cheyenne, written a few years after my first novel, is, in my estimation, a vast improvement over the occasionally pleasing lyricism of *Horseman, Pass By*. At the very least, I like to feel that in *Leaving Cheyenne*, I had matured as a writer. It tells the bittersweet story of a longtime love triangle among a rancher, his cowboy, and an appealing countrywoman who loves them both. It might be generous to call it my American version of *Jules et Jim*, Francois Truffaut's lively masterpiece that tells the same story in French.

The Last Picture Show, the third book contained in this Thalia trilogy and originally published in 1966, was written while I was teaching freshman English at Rice University in Houston. It was written in order to teach myself how to write fiction in the third person. I wrote it in the first person and then painstakingly translated it into third person. *The Last Picture Show* is mostly known by the brilliant movie (written mostly by me and Polly Platt) directed by Peter Bogdanovich. Polly, Peter's wife at the time, had read the novel, loved it, and then pestered her husband to read it and consider adapting it into a film. She had multiple roles on the movie, including production design, makeup, and helping Peter find its brilliant cast. Polly and I remained close long after the film ended and up to her death in 2011.

The novel takes place in a small town in 1950s Texas I called Thalia, much like the small town where I grew up, but that small town might live anywhere within the vastness of this great United States. The movie house in Archer City burned down in the 1950s, when the population was less than two thousand people—the same census number today. The closing of the picture show in a place already isolated from the outside world would undoubtedly intensify, both intellectually and emotionally, that sense of isolation.

After World War II, much of America began an exodus from the small towns to the cities. And so the myth of the cowboy grew purer, because there were so few actual cowboys to dispel it. While writing these three novels, it was clear to me that I was witnessing the dying of a way of life, too—the rural, pastoral way of life. And in many of the books that I've produced, it has taken thousands of words to attend, as best I could, to the passing of the cowboy as well: the myth of my country, and of my people, too.

—Larry McMurtry

HORSEMAN, PASS BY

HORSEMAN, PASS BY
is dedicated to my parents,
W. J. and Hazel Ruth McMurtry,
with gratitude and love.

Prologue

LONNIE:

I remember how green the early oat fields were, that year, and how the plains looked in April, after the mesquite leafed out. Spring had come dry for seven straight years, and Granddad and the other cattlemen in Dry Bean County had had to watch the bare spots widening in their pastures. But that year the month of March was a long slow drizzle, and when it ended, the bare spots shrunk again and new grass carpeted the flats. When I rode out with him on Saturdays, Granddad would sometimes get down from his horse, to show me how the grass was shooting its runners over the droughty ground; and he told me that nature would always work her own cures, if people would be patient enough, and give her time. After school on the weekdays, riding the long road home through the ranches in the old yellow school bus, I watched the range change. I watched the whole ranch country shake off its dust and come alive.

At night, when the milking was done and the supper eaten, we sat on the east porch, in the late spring dusk, resting and talking about the day. On the warmest nights Grandma came out too, and rocked for a while in the cord-bottomed porch rocker, sometimes crocheting doilies to spread on the living room chairs. Even Hud might sit on the steps a few minutes, brushing his red suède boots before he left for town. But soon he would leave in his rag-topped Ford, and Grandma would get too cool and go back to her radio. Granddad and I sat on the porch alone, through the best hour—that last little while when he and I watched another day turning into night.

Just before full dark, the bull bats came out from somewhere and swooped around the lilac bushes; and the horses clopped past the yard on their way to the dark grazing flats below the hill. A highway ran alongside the horse pasture, a mile to the east of our house, and from the porch we could watch the cars zoom across the plains—north to Amarillo or Raton, south to Dallas or Houston or Fort Worth. The big Diesel trucks growled through the thick prairie dusk. The railroad was just the other side of the highway, and about sundown the Katy freight chugged by, pulling its string of oil and cattle cars. During the shipping season the cars were full of calves, their bawling a lonesome sound at twilight. Sometimes the bawling stirred Granddad: reminded him of other times he had heard it, and of men he had heard it with. Then he might tell me stories of his days on the big ranches, or of cowboys like his dead foreman Jericho Green. I sat below him, flipping my pocketknife into the soft dirt of Grandma's lilac beds, taking in every word he said.

Granddad was an old man then, and he worked hard days. By eight or eight-fifteen he was tired of sitting up. Around that time the nightly Zephyr flew by, blowing its loud whistle to warn the station men in Thalia. The noise cut across the dark prairie like the whistling train itself. I could see the hundred lighted windows of the passenger cars, and I wondered where in the world the people behind them were going night after night. To me it was exciting to think about a train. But the Zephyr blowing by seemed to make Granddad tireder; it seemed to make him sad. He told me one time that it reminded him of nights on roundup, long years ago. On quiet nights he and the other cowboys would sit around the fires, telling stories or drawing brands in the dirt. Some nights they would camp close to a railroad track, and a train would go by and blow its whistle at the fires. Sometimes it scared the cattle, and sometimes it didn't, but it always took the spirit out of the cowboys' talk; made them lonesomer than they could say. It made them think about womenfolk and fun and city lights till they could barely stand it. And long years after, when the last train would go by, Granddad got restless. He would stretch, and push his old rope-bottomed chair up against the house. "Train's gone, son," he said to me. "It's bedtime." Then he took his coffee-can spittoon over to the yard fence, stood there long enough to piss, and went into the house.

With that Granddad's day ended, and my night really began. I went to the windmill and let the faucet run till the coldest deep well water came gurgling up through the pipes. After I drank I sometimes went over and sat in the rope swing that hung from the biggest sycamore limb, to drag my feet in the sandy dirt and watch Granddad through his window as he got ready for bed. When he had his nightshirt on he usually came to stand awhile by the window screen, looking into the dark and scratching the scarred old leg that he had almost torn off in a roping accident. Then he would turn his back on the night, and go to bed.

When I knew Granddad was in bed I went back to the windmill and stopped the blades, so I could climb up and sit on the platform beneath the big fin. Around me, across the dark prairie, the lights were clear. The oil derricks were lit with strings of yellow bulbs, like Christmas trees. The lights were still on in the kitchens of the pumpers' cabins, the little green-topped shacks scattered across the plain, each one propped on a few stacks of bricks. Twelve miles away, to the north, the red and green and yellow lights of Thalia shimmered against the dark. I sat above it all, in the cool breezy air that swept under the windmill blades, hearing the rig motors purr and the heavy trucks growl up the hill. Above the chattering of the ignorant Rhode Island Reds I heard two whippoorwills, the ghostly birds I never saw, calling across the flats below the ridge.

Sitting there with only the wind and the darkness around me, I thought of all the important things I had to think about: my honors, my worries, my ambitions. I thought of the wild nights ahead, when I would have my own car, and could tear across the country to dances and rodeos. I picked the boys I would run with, the girls we would romp; I kept happy thinking of all the reckless things that could happen in the next few years. Some nights it stormed out on the range, and I watched the little snake-tongues of lightning flicker against the clouds. When it was clear enough, I could see the airplane beacons flashing from the airport in Wichita Falls.

Later, I climbed down and drank from the faucet before I went to bed. I tiptoed through the kitchen, across the patches of moonlight that sometimes lay on the cool linoleum, and climbed the stairs to my room under the roof. On nights when I was wide awake I lay on top of the covers and read a paperback until I got drowsy, or until I heard Hud coming back from town. I was always ready to sleep by the time he came in. In the summers I slept with my head toward the foot of the bed, so I could see the moon and the yard trees out the window. That way I got what breeze there was; and that way, too, I only had to raise up on one elbow in the mornings to watch the lots, and see Granddad and the cowboys catching their horses for the new day. I didn't always sleep the hours a growing boy was supposed to, but the nights that spring were a field that I left well sown.

One

FOR DESSERT THAT NIGHT HALMEA MADE A BIG FREEZER-ful of peach ice cream, rich as Jersey milk and thick with hunks of sweet, locker-plant Albertas. It had for me the good, special flavor of something seasonal, something you have waited all winter to taste, like early roasting ears or garden tomatoes. I ate three big helpings and still couldn't get enough. When the freezer was almost empty I went in to get the dasher, but Hud shoved me out of the way and took it himself. We dished the last peachy drops of cream and took our bowls out on the porch to scrape them dry.

Granddad had taken his last helping of cream and gone out before us, and his empty blue saucer was sitting by his elbow when we came out. He sat on the bottom step of the porch, whittling on a cedar stick he had picked up that day. He whittled it down patiently, setting his knife in the reddish wood just so; and while I scraped my saucer I watched the thin slivers curl off the stick and drop between his legs. Eighty years old and more, Granddad was then, but the sandy hair on his head was still thick as ever, and his gray eyes were still steady and clear. He pulled the thin blade of the case knife in toward him, his mouth loosening as he worked. For a few minutes he went on smoothing the stick, and nothing was said. We all sat enjoying the quiet evening. Then Granddad looked up from his whittling and nodded toward the three empty bowls.

"Why don't you take them bowls in to Halmea?" he said to me. "She might want to get her dishes done."

"Then let the nigger bitch gather 'em up herself," Hud said. He sat on the edge of the porch, picking his teeth with a sharpened matchstick. He had on his suède boots and a new pearl-buttoned shirt, but he didn't seem to be in any hurry to leave for wherever he was going.

"Let her work a little," he said. "She sits on her butt all day."

"She ain't the only one," Granddad said, rubbing his fingers over the smooth length of stick. "It won't hurt Lonnie to move once in a while. He's young and supple."

"Young and simple," Hud said, spitting. He smirked at me when he said it, a lock of his dark crow hair falling over his forehead.

I got up and grabbed the three empty bowls and took them in with no argument. Hud was thirty-five to my seventeen, and my best bet was to pay him as little mind as possible. Everybody in the county, even Granddad, took a little of Hud's sourness, and nobody felt quite big enough to do anything about it. Granddad kept him on partly because he was a stepson, I guess, and partly because, when Hud was interested and cared to be, he was as good as the best and more reckless than the wildest of the thousand wild-ass cowboys in the Texas cattle country.

When I went in with the bowls, Halmea was sitting by the kitchen table reading *True Romances*. The supper dishes were piled on the washboard, and the ice-cream freezer still stood in the sink. Hud was right about Halmea sitting on her butt nine tenths of the time, but she could afford to. She was the only one of us who could keep Grandma in a halfway good humor.

"You better get those dishes washed," I said. "Granny'll have kittens."

She looked up from the magazine, grinning her lazy, big-mouthed grin. "Few kittens jus' what she need," she said. "She worried so 'bout goin' to de hos-pital, she ain't gonna mind no dishes tonight. Get on an' let me read."

I sat the saucers in the sink and went down the darkened hall to the bathroom. When I came out, Grandma was standing by her bedroom door, looking for someone to pester.

"Lordy ain't it hot tonight," she said. "Help me out on the porch and I'll sit awhile. My kidneys don't give me a minute's peace."

I took her arm and led her out to the rocking chair, but then I went back to the kitchen to keep from having to listen to her gripe. Halmea had laid her magazine down and was giving her toenails their daily coat from a bottle of nail polish she kept in the cabinet. Her big tan-soled feet were bare, one of them propped on the churn stool so she could reach her toes. She looked up suddenly and caught me glancing at her where her floppy blue dress was lifted off one leg; she just gave me that slow grin of hers and went back to dipping the toenail brush. "Tend you own rat-killin'," she said. I fiddled with the water pitcher a minute and decided I'd be just as well off listening to Grandma after all. Sometimes Halmea was too unconscious even to pester. I set the pitcher down and went back to the porch.

Grandma was wadding her calico apron between her hands and rocking like sixty, talking a blue streak to keep time with her rocking. "I never had no kidney operation," she said. "I hate to just lay there knocked out an' not keep up with what they're adoin' to me. I ought to be the one to say."

Over to the east, I saw a pickup pull off the highway and start across the dirt road toward us. "Here comes Jesse," I said. "I guess he got 'em unloaded."

He was a new hand, Jesse. Just a week before he had stepped off a cattle truck and come walking up to the ranch house with nothing but a saddle and a paper sack full of clothes, looking for a job. Hud was against him from the minute he came through the gate, but Hud was against hiring anybody, and Granddad took Jesse on anyway. He was coming back from hauling a few dry cows to a new pasture; coming home to cold supper and no peach ice cream.

"I swan," Grandma said. "It's a pity an old woman like me has got to be cut into afore she dies. But it ain't aworryin' you-all one bit. They could cut off my nose an' nobody but me 'ud miss it. It's awful when an old woman can't get no sympathy from her own kinfolks."

"You're gonna get your bills paid, though," Hud said. "If I could accomplish that, they could have my nose." He laughed lazily, without looking at Grandma, and she began to daub at her eyes with the apron. I walked over to the north edge of the porch and looked off toward Thalia. Around us, under the last daylight, the plains lay clear. To the east purple was spreading into the sky, but west of me the trail to the lots was a lane of dusty gold light. I saw three crows pass over the willow thicket behind the barn and go cawing off into the blaze of western sky.

"Looks like the Lord would think it was trial enough, keeping me sixty-five years in this hell on earth," Grandma went on. "But I ain't the one to say."

"More than likely you ain't," Granddad said, looking up from his stick. "Scott, was you figurin' on getting into town tonight?"

"Thought I would," Hud said. "I didn't dress up to sit out here an' listen to Ma bitch."

"Now, Huddie," Granny said, changing her tune. "You just stay here tonight. There's a storm warning out from ten o'clock on."

"Fine," Hud said. "Maybe it'll rain an' green up this desert a little. If I sat around an' waited for ever little piss cloud to turn into a tornado, I never would go nowhere."

Granddad laid the stick on the steps and folded up his knife. "What time're you an' your mother plannin' to get off in the morning?" he asked.

Hud shrugged lazily. "Early enough," he said. "About four-thirty or five."

"I just wondered," Granddad said. "The doctors wanted Jewel to be in the hospital by dinnertime. If I was gonna make that long a drive I'd want all the sleep I could get."

"Hell," Hud said. "I ain't a hunnerd years old, like you. I don't need a week of sleep to be fresh."

Granddad didn't answer. The pickup rattled across the cattle guard to the south of the house, and Jesse waved at us as he drove on toward the barn.

"Say," Hud said. "Why don't you call the hide-and-rendering plant and have 'em come an' get that heifer. She just died this evenin'; she's still fresh enough to make soap." Hud and Lonzo had found the carcass on their way in that afternoon. Neither one of them knew what killed her, and Granddad hadn't gone out to take a look.

"Oh, I don't believe I will," Granddad said. "Fore I go to bed I'll call Newt Garrett and get him to come out and take a look at her in the morning. I'm kinda curious about what killed her. Lonzo's out there now keepin' off the buzzards."

"That's the stuff," Hud said, swelling up. "Call in some horse's ass to take your money. Don't never bother asking me what I think about anything."

"Well," Granddad said, "Newt ain't no what-you-say, and you ain't no authority on cattle diseases. I ain't either. This may be something I need to know about."

"Why, sure it will," Hud said, laughing his hard sharp laugh. "It'll be just bad enough he'll have you vaccinate ever head you own. And Newt's a vaccine salesman." He spit again, into the flower beds.

"That don't automatically make him dishonest," Granddad said, giving Hud a steady look. "You just concentrate on getting your mother to the hospital all in one piece, and I'll tend to my cattle."

"Sure, boss," Hud said, grinning down at Granddad. He swung himself off the rail and stood up, stretching his long arms above his head. Just then the dogs began to bark, and Jesse came around the corner of the house. The three of them hadn't quite got used to him, and they sniffed around his pants legs. Jesse was dragging his game leg a little, looking dead tired.

"Why, hello, wild horse," Hud said. "Lose your crutch?"

Jesse gave him a tired, uneasy grin, and didn't try to say anything. Hud's style was strange to him, and around Hud he never knew quite what to say.

"You might get you a roller skate . . ." Hud started, but Granddad cut him off.

"Get 'em turned out all right?" he asked. "I hated to work you so late, but I didn't see no other way to do it."

Jesse took off his mashed-up straw hat and fingered the shaggy black hair on the back of his neck. "Why, yes," he said. "I got 'em unloaded all right." Actually, Hud exaggerated about Jesse's gimpy leg. As cowboys go, he was in good shape.

"Son, go in and get Halmea to scare Jesse up some supper," Granddad said. "He looks like he needs to graze a little."

"I could sure eat a bite," Jesse said. "I believe I'll go get me a drink of your well water to warm up on."

"Well, where's your manners?" Grandma snapped, her loud old voice surprising us all. "You ain't even got the politeness to say hello to me," she said. "I been sittin' here waitin'."

"Why, excuse me," Jesse said. "My goodness, I didn't even notice you, Miz Bannon."

"Go on an' get your drink," Granddad said. "It don't make no difference." I could tell he was about to get out of snuff with her and her son. Jesse ducked his head toward her as politely as he could and stepped back around the house.

"Good riddance," Grandma said. She had gone to fanning herself with an old Sunday-school fan she kept under the cushion of the rocker. "Help me back in the house, Lonnie," she said. "This night air's gettin' too cool."

"Let the boy alone, Jewel," Granddad said. "If you can't get in an' out under your own power just stay where you are awhile."

That made her fan a little faster. "I ought to know better than to ask a Bannon," she said. "Help me in, Huddie."

Hud laughed his quick, crow-caw laugh. "Hell, Momma, I can't," he said. "I'm just aworkin' from the shoulders down. If Homer Bannon says for you to get in by yourself, that's the way you better get in." His open-top Ford sat in front of the yard gate, and he stepped off the porch and strode lazily across the darkening yard. "Don't you folks lock the storm cellar," he said. "I may come aswimmin' in." He kicked one of the dogs back through the gate, shut it, and slipped under the wheel of his car. The Ford had a special horn, a cattle-caller, and Hud gave it a long scary blow as he gunned away. He kept the car in second for a mile or more, the rough, blasting sound of his mufflers loud in the evening stillness.

Grandma got up without saying a word and went into the house. In a minute there was a loud blast of static, and then the moany sound of a gospel song seeped out through the open screen door. Granddad looked like he'd just as soon be by himself, so I went around the house, meaning to see about Jesse's supper.

He was standing under the windmill, his Levi's unbuttoned. He had taken his soaked shirttail out of his pants and was letting the cool night air dry the sweat on his stomach. We could still hear the fading sound of Hud's mufflers as he squealed onto the highway and off toward Thalia.

"He drives that thing, don't he?" Jesse said. "Is the old lady still pretty mad?"

"Not at you," I said.

He ran his fingers through his thick black hair. "I never could get along with old women," he said. "My own grandma give me hell as long as she lived. So did Ma. I had one aunt I could kinda be easy with, but I lost track a her."

"You ready to eat?" I asked him.

"Let me get my shirttail in," he said. "Your grandma might come in the kitchen and catch me." He quickly lowered his pants and smoothed down the wet tails of his heavy khaki shirt, then buttoned the Levi's again. "Lord, I need a haircut," he said. "Been a month or more since I had one."

When we got in the kitchen, Halmea was back with *True Romances*, but the ice-cream freezer was gone from the sink, and the dishes had at least been stacked in the red dishpan. She laid the magazine down when she saw Jesse, but he just grinned at her. I snatched the magazine before she could pick it up again, and began to thumb through it myself.

"Weak readin'," I said. "How about gettin' Jesse some supper?"

"Just Mistah Jesse?" she said, "Nothin' fo' you?"

"Might set me a plate," I said. "I can eat a few beans."

She got up, grinning timidly at Jesse, and went to the cabinet. Jesse was someone Halmea hadn't felt out very well, and she walked easy when he was in the kitchen. I plopped down at the table and opened the magazine, while Jesse went down the hall to wash. Through the open door to the dining room I could hear Grandma's radio blaring—when she listened to preaching the whole household got a sermon. "*Keep on*," the preacher said. "*Keep on adrinkin' your liquor, apitchin' your parties. . . .*" I got up and kicked the dining room door shut. Halmea was standing all spraddle-legged, reaching in the icebox for a jar of pickles, and I tried to give her the hip when I went by. But she straightened up too quick. "Go on," she said, "befo' you wets you didy." She had heard Granddad tell me that one time, and she thought I'd be real insulted to hear it from her. "Don't tear up my storybook," she said. "I ain't done with it yet."

Jesse came in then, his sleeves rolled up to the elbow, his thin neck red from the scrubbing he had given it. He sat down across the table from me and began to fiddle with his fork, a little impatiently. Halmea put a platter of cold roast beef on the table first, then a bowl of red beans in thick, brownish gravy, a little plate of fresh-washed radishes and carrots, some plum-sized tomatoes, and a few sliced onions in a bowl of vinegar. Jesse took some of everything and went to eating, not waiting for his tea. I just dished out a few beans, and an onion slice or two.

"Light bread's all gone," Halmea said. "Kin you-all make out on carn bread tonight?"

"That'll hit the spot," Jesse said, looking up from his plate. "Could you spare me a glass of buttermilk to go with it?"

"Spare you a gallon of it," she said. She fished a slab of coarse yellow corn bread out of the oven and set it where we could help ourselves, then got the big pottery crock of buttermilk out of the icebox and poured us each a glassful.

"I believe I'll have a glass a dat myself," she said. "If you gentlemens don't mind."

Jesse had his mouth full, but he nodded for her to sit down, and she went to the cabinet to get a glass. He was almost through eating already, and I had barely finished a small plate of beans. He ate as if he expected someone to snatch his plate out from under him before he got enough.

"Where's old Lonzo?" he asked, wiping his mouth. Before I could tell him, we all heard the loud moaning whistle of the train, coming across the plains from the south.

"He's out watching that carcass," I said. "Granddad wants the vet to look at it before it gets scattered."

Halmea had pulled up a chair, and was busy crumbling the cold yellow corn bread into her buttermilk. When she had enough crumbled up, she stirred it around with her spoon. "You-all hollah when you need somethin'," she said.

"I went by and seen Hank Hutch for a minute," Jesse said. He reached in his frayed shirt pocket for a package of cigarettes. "That feller's working himself to death."

Hank was our neighbor, a young cowboy about thirty years old who lived just across the highway. He worked for Granddad when there was a lot of work to do. When there wasn't, he cowboyed for other people, pumped a little oil lease the other side of Thalia, and picked up whatever work he could shoeing horses for the ranchers. He had a wife and three little girls, and was just barely keeping his head above water. He and I got along fine what little we were together.

Jesse wadded up his napkin and dropped it in his plate. "That's a hell of a way to live," he said. "I hate to see an old boy scratchin' at two or three jobs thataway, never knowin' nothin' but work and want. I believe I'd just as soon throw a life away as work it out like he's doing. Hard on him an' hard on his kids and womenfolk. Makes me glad I ain't married. Least there's one worry I ain't got."

Halmea snorted, her mouth half-full of corn bread and milk. A few drops of milk worked out of the corner of her mouth and trickled down her brown chin, but she wiped the stream away with her wrist.

"Dat's one worry you need," she said, giving him one of her slow, half-sassy looks. I saw she had gotten over being uneasy of Jesse in a hurry. I was so surprised by what she said I almost had to leave the table. She was always coming out with something strange in front of strangers. But I guess it embarrassed me more than it did Jesse, because he just drug on his cigarette and shook his head. He even gave her a tired grin. I saw them sit there looking at each other, beginning to get friendly, and in a way that made me feel alone and restless and let out. It's a way older people have: without even meaning to they let people younger than them know they aren't in the same club. Halmea leaned her elbows on the table and drank her buttermilk, halfway ready to laugh at me and Jesse both; there were beads of sweat on her face, and her heavy nigger breasts pouched out her gray dress. She chuckled to herself about something, a quick chuckle I always got a kick out of hearing. Jesse had tilted his chair back against the way, and was looking at Halmea through the smoke of his cigarette. There was something sad about Jesse, it was just on him, like his washed-out Levi's and frazzled khakis. All the time I knew him, I never really saw him look comfortable. Something in him would need to brood, like something in Halmea would chuckle.

For a minute, nobody said a word. Then Halmea raised her glass to take a big swallow of buttermilk, and I saw the dark, sweaty wad of hair under her arm, and part of her stretched white brassière. While the two of them sat there looking so relaxed, I had to sip my buttermilk and squirm, thinking about Halmea. Once when I had the dogs up in the barn loft looking for rats, she had walked out in the weeds below me to a hen nest. I barely looked her way, but the minute I did she hiked her dress and squatted in the green broomweeds to pee. She went on gathering her eggs and never saw me, but I never did forget that glimpse, and if I happened to pass behind her while she was working at the sink, and saw one of her dark loose breasts when she raised her arm for something, it got to me worse than if all the girls in high school had shown up in the study hall naked.

Finally Jesse looked up and stamped out his cigarette. "I don't see it," he said. "A poor boy like me's got to be lucky to get along, just like it is, and if he's got a family he needs to be two or three times as lucky. So far I ain't even been lucky enough for myself."

Halmea was getting surer of Jesse by the minute, and when she got surer she just got more audacious. "Sheew," she said, "don't tell me. A man by himself just like de fishline without de hook. He ain't gonna snag on nothin', dat away."

Jesse smiled, but he didn't laugh. He looked like he just didn't have the energy for more than a smile.

"Go on," Halmea said. "I knows about menfolks, or I ain't know anything."

Then we heard the tap of Granddad's boots as he came down the hall toward his bedroom. The sound of the radio had stopped, so Grandma had already gone to roost. Granddad stopped by the kitchen door and looked in at us, his coffee-can spittoon in one hand. "It's bedtime for us old folks," he said. "Jesse, that vet won't be here very early, I don't imagine. We don't need to get up till six or so."

"Okay," Jesse said, reaching under the chair for his hat. "If I'm awake I may get up and work that colt a little. I couldn't sleep late if you paid me to."

"Do what you want," Granddad said. "If the vet gets through in time we may try to fix a little fence. Good night." He started to go to his bedroom, then turned back. "You-all might keep an eye on the clouds," he said. "Jewel thinks it's goin' to storm."

When he had gone on and shut his bedroom door, Halmea got up and went quickly down the hall. I finished my buttermilk, and got up to walk Jesse to the bunkhouse. Halmea caught us about the back door and handed Jesse an armload of sheets and towels. "I fo'got dis mornin'," she said.

“Much obliged,” Jesse said. “That bunkhouse gets pretty dusty. Enjoyed the supper.”

“You welcome,” she said. “Now you-all shoo.” We were going anyway, but it was a good thing. Sooner or later every night Halmea would decide it was cleaning-up time, and when she did it was a good policy to stay out of her way. I had picked up her magazine as I went out, just to devil her, and before I got off the porch steps she hollered at me to bring it back. I took it back in and pitched it on the table, to tempt her. On the cover it had a picture of a bride crying into her veil, and under it it said MAMA, SET ME FREE.

“When you gonna be a bride, Halmea?” I said as I went out. I knew she had already been one a time or two, and I liked to tease her about it. I heard her deep bubbly chuckle after I slammed the door.

Jesse was waiting for me in the yard. He had just been on the ranch a week, but I was already in the habit of trailing him down to the bunkhouse every night. He stopped by the storm cellar to light a cigarette, and in the flicker of the match I saw his thin, hungry-looking face. The dogs were giving his pants legs another sniffing.

“Ain’t that a fine old sycamore tree,” he said, nodding toward it. The big tree stood just a few feet from the back door, and some of its longest limbs waved over the house. When I was at the Tarzan age I had practically lived in it.

“Lord I wish I had me a place with a few trees like that ’un on it,” Jesse said regretfully. He started down the thin foot trail toward the bunkhouse, and I tagged along for the conversation. “It’d be an accomplishment,” he said. I got around him and opened the bunkhouse door for him, then switched on the lights. He set the bedclothes down on an empty cot. The house was just one long bare room, with five or six steel cots in it, and a little partitioned-off lavatory and shower bath down at one end. There were a card table or two, a few chairs, and a couple of shaving mirrors on the wall. Lonzo and Jesse had taken about three mattresses apiece and piled them on their cots to make the sleeping a little softer. Their beds were rumpled, and the sheets on them gritty with the blown-in sand. What few clothes they had hung on the ten-penny nails that Granddad had driven into the wall years before. Neither Jesse nor Lonzo stayed in the bunkhouse any longer than they had to, and neither bothered to clean it up. Spider webs hung in the ceiling corners, and the floors were as gritty as the sheets.

Jesse sat down on his cot and began to pull off his tight-fitting dusty boots. "And you're just seventeen," he said, surprising me.

"Not for long," I said. "My birthday's in September."

But I don't think Jesse was even thinking of me when he spoke. "My God," he said. "When I was seventeen I never got enough of anything." He set his boots carefully under the cot and began to unbutton his khaki shirt. "Summer I was that age, I was workin' on a hayin' crew around Chillicothe," he said, looking regretful, like he would. "You'd think pitchin' them big old bales of alfalfa up and down all day woulda been enough exercise, but not then it wasn't. I had an old boy named DeWayne working on the same crew with me, and we bought us a '27 Chevy and kept it tied together with bailin' wire all that summer. We made ever square dance and rodeo and honky-tonk in the country, and I don't know which we run the hardest, that car or the country girls that showed up at the dances." He hung his dirty shirt over the back of the chair. "Boy, boy," he said. "I do-ce-doed and chased them girlish butts around many a circle that summer."

I could listen all night when Jesse got to going back over his life, but the story never lasted long enough, and it always ended with him getting tireder and more sad. He sat on the edge of the cot, stratching his lank, white stomach, and arching his feet to get the boot-stiffness out of them.

"But, hell," he said. "You're big enough to get out and do your own rarin' and tearin', without no pattern a mine. Just so you get all the good you can outa seventeen right now, because it sure wears out in a hurry. Or did for me." Then he leaned back on the cot, still wearing his Levi's and socks. "What I need is about eight hours on this squeaking cot. Turn out that light for me, will you?"

I was in such a listening mood that I hated to leave, but I could see Jesse was worn to a nub. I went to the door, and switched off the light. "See you *mañana*," he said. "Lord, I'm tired."

I guess he had reason to be worn out, but when I went out the door I felt like I wouldn't ever need to sleep. What little Jesse had said about his running around just made me a little more restless than I usually was, and I was usually crazy with it. I wished I had something wild and exciting to do. But I didn't have an old wired-up Chevy, and it was too late to go anywhere in the pickup, and if I had taken it and gone there would just have been Thalia to go to, just an empty courthouse square to drive around. I went to the windmill, but instead of climbing up to the platform I got a drink and sat down in the thick cool yard grass, leaning my back against the wooden frame. I thought about the three nights I had got to spend in Fort Worth, the summer before. Granddad had gone down to buy some cattle, and at night he sat in the lobby of the big hotel, talking to another old cowman, and let me do pretty much as I pleased. He thought I was going to picture shows, I guess, but instead I wandered up and down Main Street, that one long street, under the city lights. I went way down to the south end of the street, to where they have the gospel missions and the Mexican picture shows, where the wild-looking people were as thick as crickets under the yellow neon. Pretty soon I discovered that I could slip in the hillbilly bars, into one of the dark booths, and get them to serve me all the beer I wanted. I sat there gripping the cold sweaty bottles and listening to the laughter, the shuffling dancers, the sad hillbilly music. But what I got in Fort Worth was just a taste, just a few mouthfuls of excitement; and leaning against the windmill, I couldn't think of anything I wanted more than to go back for another swallow or two.

In a few minutes the back door slammed, and Halmea came across the dark yard, on her way to her little house for the night. She was looking down, and didn't notice me, so when she got almost to the gate I gave a loud hiss, like a bull snake makes. She jumped and dropped her magazine, then stood there scared to death, twisting her neck around. She saw me then, but she still wasn't sure about the snake.

"Deys a snake in dis yard," she said, not making a move. "I stay right here an' watch him, and you see can you slip aroun' easy and get the flashlight an' de hoe." I guess she actually thought she had the snake spotted; she never took her eyes off the ground.

I flopped back in the grass and hissed again, laughing before I finished the hiss. "I might know," she said. In a few minutes she'd be boiling, but right then she was so relieved she just snatched the magazine and went on out the gate.

"Ou-la, Halmea," I said. I knew she wouldn't get snake off her mind for days. I could just see her, tiptoeing down the path, taking about half an hour to make it to her house. Every time she stopped she'd hear an old bull rattler sliding through the grass. And if she didn't find him in the grass, she'd look him up in her horoscope.

When Halmea was out of hearing. I lay back in the long, uncut Bermuda, and wondered about what all Jesse had said. It still made me itch to be off somewhere, with a crowd of laughers and courters and beer drinkers, to go somewhere past Thalia and Wichita and the oil towns and Sno-Cone stands, into country I'd never seen. I was glad Jesse had come: he could open things up. Granddad didn't talk to me much any more, and anyway, Granddad and I were in such separate times and separate places. I had got where I would rather go to Thalia and goof around on the square than listen to his old-timy stories.

In a little while the sand ants began to sting my wrists, and I got up. I went around behind the smokehouse to piss. In my grade-school days we had hung carcasses in the smokehouse, beeves and hogs that Granddad and the cowboys butchered on frosty mornings in November. For a while then there would be cracklin's, and salty smells, and the dogs would be fighting over the pigs' feet. But now the beeves and hogs were in the locker plant in Thalia, and the smokehouse only held broken lawn mowers and spades and pieces of harness. I heard a dog yapping, stranded somewhere out in coyote country. As I went in the house I noticed the lighting flickering off to the southwest, and saw that the stars were blotted out in that direction. But in June in our part of the country, clouds and lighting were no novelty, and I didn't pay them any attention.

When I got upstairs I didn't feel very sleepy, so I got out *From Here to Eternity* and read over some of the scenes with Prew and Maggio in the New Congress Hotel. I thought it was about the best book ever to come to our drugstore newsstand, and I kept reading some of the chapters in it over and over. Those parts about the dances in the New Congress reminded me a lot of my nights in Fort Worth; the people in the book seemed a lot like the ones I saw. Then I read thc part where the sergeant got her the first time, and put the book back in my suitcase in the closet. I turned off the light and stretched on top of the covers to sleep, smelling the green dewy ranchland through the screen.

Two

HUD DIDN'T HAVE TO RUN FROM ANY TORNADO, BUT HE must have got in some kind of a storm because he didn't come in till six-thirty the next morning. Jesse and I were eating breakfast when we heard the convertible slide up to the back gate. Grandma had been up and ready to go to Temple for two or three hours, and she run into the kitchen to give him an eating out; but Hud looked so red-eyed and wild she just went on back to her room and began to gather up her hatboxes. I finished my breakfast and went down to the barn and drove Granddad's Lincoln to the house so we could load it. Granny had packed enough stuff for an arctic expedition.

Jesse and me were admiring the car when she came tapping out the back door, all powdered and painted, wearing a big green hat with a veil on it. She might have been going to the fair she was in such a good humor. Granddad brought out the first load of suitcases, and Jesse and I hurried in and got the rest.

"Well, I'm ready," Grandma said. "Where's Huddie? I don't intend to wait no longer. If I got to go be cut up I'm ready right now." Granddad helped her into the car, and stood by the door to try and keep her from jumping out again for some foolishness. Hud came out in about five minutes, fresh-looking enough to have slept for a week. He pitched his canvas army bag in the back seat, and got under the wheel.

"Now be careful, Scott," Granddad said, one hand still on the car door. "If you get tired, why, stop and sleep." He took out his checkbook and fountain pen, and used the hood of the Lincoln for a desk as he wrote out the check. He folded it carefully and handed it across the car seat to Hud.

"That ought to take care of the hotel and such," he said. Hud already had the motor running, and for a minute I wished it were me who was driving away. Granddad patted Grandma on the shoulder. "Jewel, you get on back here as soon as you can," he said. "We're liable to need you."

Grandma was looking straight ahead, impatient to be off. Her eyes were snappy as a bird's, and she wanted no conversation. "Don't be ahurryin' me home," she said. "You just tend to your ranch. I'm gonna take my time with this operation."

"We're gone," Hud said, throwing the car in gear. "Watch out for the kids and the cripples, and don't buy no vaccine factory." The wheels spun a minute in the thin gravel of the road, and the car jerked away.

Jesse said he had to go where he could get the leverage on his bowels, and Granddad told me to start loading a few posts in the pickup, so we could fence a little when we got the veterinary business done. I backed the old white pickup up to the post pile, and had loaded about ten or twelve of the smallest cedars I could find when I saw Newt Garrett drive up to the house in his muddy blue De Soto. Granddad was still in the house, so I left the posts to go tell him Newt had come. About the time I got to the back porch, Granddad came out.

Old Newt was still sitting in his car, with the motor still running. He hated to walk worse than any man in the country, and wouldn't unless he absolutely had to. He was an old-timer, nearly as old as Granddad. Once he had been a Texas Ranger, and he had enough pension to keep him alive, and enough oil money on top of it to make him about half-rich. He spent most of his time playing moon in the Thalia domino hall, but he still did a little horse-doctoring for the people he liked. He had lost his voice box in a cancer operation, and had to talk by pressing an electric buzzer against his throat. For the last few years he had been so contrary that nobody but Granddad would have anything to do with him, and Granddad just called him in once in a while when some heifer was having a hard time squeezing out her first calf. Granddad shook hands with him through the window of the car.

"Get any rain?" he asked. That was always the first question.

Newt took out his buzzer and stuck it to his throat. "Sprinkle," he said. "Late last night. Nuff to wash the dust off my chickens." Newt was a funny old fart anyway, and the dry way he buzzed out his words tickled me to death.

"Kill your motor and get out," Granddad said. "We'll go in my pickup. I don't believe we could get across them roads in that car."

Jesse came up about that time, and when Newt finally got out, Granddad introduced him. Newt shook his hand, and then pointed at the De Soto.

"Ain't no automobile," he said. "See. It's a slide. It ain't no higher than a slide." He got his bag of instruments out of the back seat and started for the barn.

Jesse and I tagged them down the trail and got in the back of the pickup, on my twelve little cedars. Just as Granddad was about to drive off he remembered Lonzo, out there without any breakfast, and he drove back up to the house and sent me in to fix a plate.

The minute Grandma left the house Halmea must have unplugged the living room radio and carried it to the kitchen. When I came in the back door, it was on the cabinet, blaring rock 'n' roll, and Halmea was putting on a dance all by herself.

"Listen at it," she said, slapping her hands together and slide-stepping in front of the sink. The song was "Honeylove," and the loud honky saxophone practically curled the wallpaper. If Granddad hadn't been a shade deaf he would have heard it from the pickup. But old juicy Halmea just grinned and snapped her fingers at me and went on dancing. Then she got tickled at me or at herself or something and giggled till she could barely keep from falling over. Finally the song stopped, but even then she kept on shuffling a little to a tune of her own.

"Cut it off," I said. "Fix me a plate for Lonzo right quick. Granddad's waitin'."

She already had a plate in her hands, and was crossing to the icebox. “Dat Mistah Bannon,” she said. “Dat man hurry himself too much. He ain’t got no slowdown to him, whut’s de trouble.”

“He’s made it eighty-two years without relaxing,” I said. “Couldn’t you get any hillbilly this morning?”

“I ain’t dancin’ no hillbilly,” she said, piling cold roast and sausage and boiled eggs on the plate. “I’m just *dancin’* dancin’, dis mornin’.” When she had a good pile, she covered the plate with aluminum foil and set it on the cabinet for me. I started for the door, but she stopped me. “Mistah Lonzo needs some coffee,” she said. The radio had started up a Fats Domino song, and she was slow-dancing across the room with the percolator.

“If you drop that coffee your ass is mud,” I said. Then I almost dropped it myself, corking the Thermos. When I went out the screen door I could hear her bare feet slapping the linoleum as she went on with her lonesome, happy dance.

Newt was sitting with his voice box in his hand, so I knew Granddad had been getting a lot of dry conversation. I handed Newt the lunch to hold, and climbed in the back. Jesse sat with his back against the cab, smoking a cigarette and looking glum. I told him about Halmea cutting up, but it didn’t make much impression on him. “Some girl,” he said. Watching him, as Granddad crept along down the feed road, I thought what a strange man Jesse was. In no time he could turn so gloomy and sad it made you uncomfortable to be around him. He looked out across the pastures with a disappointed expression on his face. When we came to the gate leading into the west pasture I jumped out to open it, but it was a hard gate, and he had to come and help me hook it shut.

We had to go about four or five miles across the big pasture to get to where the heifer was. I sat back against the endgate, enjoying the clear blue sweep of sky, and the early, grassy smell of the range. Finally Granddad stopped the pickup on top of a little ridge, and we got out. Newt looked kinda contrary. He was so famous for his laziness that I wondered how far Granddad could get him to walk, especially across the wet pastures. It was later than it should have been, and getting hot.

"She's over this way a little piece," Granddad said. "I better not try and drive any farther. Can you walk it?"

"Oh yes, oh yes," Newt buzzed. "Go ahead." Jesse and I followed them, not feeling very useful.

"We might as well astayed an' fenced," Jesse said. "I don't know what help we'll be here."

We waded through a patch or two of high prairie weeds, getting our Levi's damp almost to the knees. It had come the heaviest dew I'd nearly ever seen. We topped a little rise and saw Lonzo sitting under a big mesquite tree about fifty yards away. He was asleep, a twenty-two rifle laying across his lap. The carcass of the heifer lay about twenty or thirty yards to the south of him, and there must have been fifty buzzards sitting in the trees around it. As we came in sight one of the buzzards flopped to the ground, and began a slow, cautious waddle toward the heifer. The others stayed in the trees, nodding their scabby bald heads now and then, and raising their wings.

Lonzo woke up when he heard us coming, and he tried to pretend he had just been possuming, to get the buzzards to come down. He began to shoot, working the little pump-action gun as fast as he could, six or eight shots before he ran out of bullets. Most of the shots kicked up grass stems and little puffs of dirt on one side of the bird or the other, but at least one shot hit him and knocked a wad of tar-colored feathers from his back. He took off anyway, rose gradually, turned and flew right over us, not more than fifteen feet high. I could almost have jumped up and grabbed his scaly feet. All the other buzzards rose too, taking off from the limbs like springboard divers; only they sprung upward into the air, and swirled up to where they looked like flies against the blue pane of sky.

Lonzo stood up and began to reload his twenty-two. He was a tall, lank, gangly boy from Oklahoma who had been working for Granddad nearly two years. He claimed the only thing he'd ever got enough of his whole life was work, and that when it came to food or pussy or beer he always came out on the short end. He was easily satisfied, though, and if he couldn't get any of those other things, he would settle for lots of sleep.

"Look at them cowardly sonsabitches," he said, waving the gun at the buzzards. Newt stepped behind Granddad when he did that. He thought Lonzo was crazy and dangerous.

"Would you look at them chickenshits," Lonzo went on, his Adam's apple jerking in his thin neck. "You couldn't keep 'em scared off with artillery." It surprised some people that Granddad kept Lonzo on, because he didn't know beans about cowboying, and didn't show much talent for learning. Hud said right off that Lonzo only knew how to talk and eat and fuck and fist-fight and chop cotton, and that the only thing he was a top hand at was eating. "See there," he said, pointing to where three buzzards lay dead on the ground. "Pretty good shootin' for a twenty-two. I'll get some more if they ever settle down."

"Easy now," Jesse said. "Leave a few to keep the country clean."

I handed Lonzo his plate and Thermos, and he started over to his bedroll to eat, but Newt stopped him. Newt had been eying the dead buzzards, and he got his talk-piece out.

"Broke the law," he said. He really thought he was putting Lonzo in his place. "Big fine for killing buzzards."

Lonzo had picked a hard-fried egg off the plate and was gobbling it down, the twenty-two dangling carelessly from the crook of his arm. He had his mouth full when Newt buzzed, and he took his time answering.

"No shit?" he said finally. He got a kick out of Newt. "Is there really a law like that?"

"Oh yes," Newt buzzed. "Oh yes."

Lonzo squatted on his heels and chewed another egg. "Well," he said, "I was raised in Oklahoma. Up there they don't have as many foolish laws as they do other places." He looked up and grinned at Newt. "I had an old boy tell me once, he was a highway patrolman, that the law was meant to be interpurted in a leenent manner. That's what I try to do, myself. Sometimes I lean to one side of it, sometimes I lean to the other." He laughed at himself, or at Newt, and uncorked the Thermos of coffee. Newt acted insulted and went over to the carcass, where Granddad was. Lonzo poured hot coffee into the Thermos cup, the smoke rising from the glass rim of the bottle. He winked and blew on the coffee to cool it. "Looks to me like them boys in Austin oughta have something better to do than make laws about a lot of goddamn buzzards. Don't it look that way to you?" He took the three last pieces of sausage in his hand and slung the paper plate over his shoulder into the mesquite. Then he ate the sausages in about three bites. "I had to hump to keep them bastards off," he said. "I finally propped my flashlight so it shone right on the heifer, an' whenever one stepped into the light, I let him have it." He stood up, picking his teeth with his thumbnail.

We went over, then, and watched old Newt poke around on the heifer. For about five minutes he didn't do anything but squat in front of her head and look at her, working his lips like he was making conversation. Granddad squatted down beside him. He had taken out his pocketknife and was whittling on the dry stem of a ragweed, shaving off the thin brittle bark. The lines in his face were deep, that morning, like ruts in road, his whiskers snow white against his brown face. He looked at the heifer curiously, but he didn't seem too disturbed. He had lost a lot of cattle at one time or another in his life, and one dead heifer didn't discourage him much.

The heifer was laying on her side, her two top legs sticking out in the air. She was swelled up with bloat, but there was no smell to amount to anything. Hud said she had just died when he found her. She wasn't cut, or crippled-looking, and there was no swelling on her that could have meant a snakebite.

Finally Newt stood up and fiddled for his buzzer. "I don't know," he said. "I don't know. Beats me. We might look in her stomach."

"Now's when we all need clothespins," Jesse said, rolling up his shirtsleeves. We moved the heifer like Newt wanted her, and he took a long knife and opened her up. There was stink enough then, but so far as we could tell, it was just work wasted. "Beats me," Newt buzzed. His old, burnt, freckledly face looked solemn. He left the heifer and walked over to the good shade tree where Lonzo had his bedroll. The rest of us followed him over.

"Homer," Newt buzzed. "Homer. Get on the telephone, call up the state vet. He might know."

That surprised us all, but it like to floored Granddad. It was the first time anybody had heard Newt Garrett recommend another veterinary; and a state vet on top of that.

"Why, what in the world?" Granddad said. "Is it all that complicated? I never have much doings with them fellers if I can help it."

Newt didn't back up a step. "Better call," he said. "Might be something serious. I don't know. I can't tell. Homer, better call."

"I never figured on havin' to call in the government," Granddad said. "I ain't sure I want to, just for one heifer." Granddad had got so he would walk a mile rather than involve himself with the government offices, and even so, compared to Hud he thought they were little darlings. Hud plain hated the mention of government. One of the worst things between Hud and Granddad was that Granddad had let him go in the service when he could have kept him out.

"Play safe," Newt buzzed. "They may all get sick if you don't."

"What makes you think so?" Granddad said.

But old Newt had his private stubborn streak, and he wouldn't volunteer a word. Granddad hummed and hawed with him a little longer, then Newt got mad and stuck his buzzer in his pocket and headed for the pickup. Granddad waved for Jesse and Lonzo to come over.

"He wants to get to the domino hall," he said. "Jesse, I guess you better stay out here awhile. I'll take Lonzo in with me and let him snooze a little. Come on to the pickup and get the water can, so you won't parch."

Jesse went with us to the pickup, and carried the gray metal can back through the weeds. As we were driving away we heard the quick pop of the twenty-two. It was hot in the back of the pickup, and Granddad was just poking along, driving as slow as he could and stay in high gear. Lonzo didn't care. He took off his hat and let the wind dry his sweaty head. "I got the best end of the deal after all," he said. "He ain't gonna kill no buzzards in the daytime. Them cowardly bastards are too smart."

2.

After dinner Halmea filled some empty ice-cream cartons with beans and meat and tea, and I put them in an empty vaccine crate and carried them out to Jesse ahorseback. Some of the tea sloshed out, but I got there with most of what I started with. I was hoping Jesse would be in a talking mood, so I could stay awhile; but it turned out just the opposite. He looked hot and down-in-the-mouth, and acted like he didn't much want me around. I left him right away, and rode home across the still, weedy pastures, wondering how to spend the afternoon.

When I got to the lots I loped out to the big tank that stood about half a mile north of the barn. I wanted to water my horse, and check on the bullfrog crop. It was a big, deep tank, with a gravel bottom. There was a nice stand of cottonwoods, and the bank had a good covering of Bermuda grass. Halmea and her colored friends loved to fish in it. There were some nice catfish in it, and a lot of croppie, but about all I ever caught were the little five-inch perch. My life's ambition was to get Halmea to go in swimming with me some time, but so far she wouldn't even wade.

I unsaddled, and decided to give it another try. She was in the living room, flopped on the satin-covered divan that was Grandma's pride and joy. She was laying on her stomach, humming and filing her fingernails.

"Let's go swimmin'," I said. "The tank's like bath water."

"I ain't no paddler," she said, barely looking up. She had kicked her red sandals off, and they lay on the living room rug, about ten yards apart.

"You could be," I said. "With feet like yours."

"Sheew, my feet's just barely do to walk on. We might go fishin' though."

"Too much trouble," I said. "I'd have to scrounge up bait."

Then she sat up, pushing her heavy, kinked black hair off her forehead, tucking some behind her ears. "Let's do go fishin'," she said. "I been in dis house too long. We got some liver fo' bait."

I hadn't thought of the liver, but I knew I wasn't going to sit around pulling out those worthless perch all afternoon, when all I really wanted was to see Halmea in the water. At least I wanted a chance to duck her a time or two.

"It's too windy to fish," I said. "Don't be so scared of the water."

She looked surprised, and then she gave me the slow grin. She had on a loose floppy dress, and her breasts rolled against it like cantaloupes when she sat up. "Sheew," she said, grinning. "Me scared a watah?" Then she fell back suddenly on the satin couch and haw-hawed, the deep careless laughter coming clear up from her guts it sounded like. "I got yo' number," she said.

"You got my nothin'," I said. "I just thought you might like to swim awhile, you look so bored."

"Who you foolin'?" she said. "Honey, it ain't Halmea." She laughed as if the funniest thing possible had just occurred to her. It was the laughing fit of her life, I guess, and she had to wipe the tears out of her eyes and off her cheeks. "Sugah, you plain as day," she said. "You don' want no fishin'." And she picked a copy of *Life* magazine off the floor and began to look through it, still laughing her rich, teasing laugh. I couldn't even get her interested in fishing, after that. "Go on, Mistah Tightpants," she said, giggling.

Finally I gave it up and went outside. Granddad had been after me for a week to cut the goat-heads in the chicken yard, so I sharpened my shovel and went at it. I worked like a demon, and in thirty minutes or so I had cut about ten thousand and only had a million or two to go. Halmea came out of the house, on the way to her little shack. She leaned on the chicken-yard fence a minute, grinning, the wind blowing her floppy dress against her legs.

"Can't you find no bait?" she said. She laughed and went on down the trail, and I got after the goat-heads, the sweat running down my face and into my eyes.

3.

Granddad had gone to Thalia, to see about the vet. When he came back he was silent and blue, and in spite of all we could say he went out and stood a turn watching the heifer. "You drive," he said to me, after supper. "I'm going out an' spell Jesse awhile." So I drove the pickup through the late, dusky pastures, and he looked out of the window at the bunches of cattle as we passed them. He didn't say two words. The sun had about thirty minutes to go when I parked the pickup on the ridge and we got out. That time of day the prairie smelled rich to me, stingy and sappy and green.

Jesse was stretched out on Lonzo's bedroll, resting. The buzzards were in some low mesquite trees, two or three hundred yards away.

"Why, I can stay out here tonight," Jesse said, surprised to see us.

"No, you go in an' eat an' rest awhile," Granddad said. He walked over and looked solemnly down at the heifer. The green flies were buzzing and crawling in the open gut. Granddad had on a Levi's jacket against the night cool, and his mashed-up brown Stetson was pulled down over his forehead. "The other vet's comin' in the morning," he said. "Maybe we'll be done with this before much longer."

Jesse and I went on back to the pickup, and I drove us home across the darkening pastures. Jesse was in a better humor than he had been that afternoon, and I hit him up to go to the picture show. He was agreeable, so while he ate cold supper for the second night in a row I went to the bunkhouse and routed Lonzo out. He had flopped down asleep the minute he got through the door, without even taking off his Levi's or his heavy khaki shirt, and of course he was lathered in his own sweat. I got him awake enough to convince him he wanted to go with us, and he dripped a little shower water on his head and put on some fresh clothes. He was still drugged and gloopy, and didn't say a word. We went out and set on the fender of the pickup, where it was cooler, and in a minute Jesse came out of the house and stopped to light his after-supper cigarette.

We got in, and I drove down the dark dirt road to the highway, swung on, and gigged the old pickup for all it was worth toward the lights of Thalia. Lonzo sat next to me, still half-asleep. One minute the town lights would be just ahead of us, bright against the dark sky, and the next minute we'd hit a little dip and they would fall out of sight. There was just the lights and the highway and off to the west a few stars overhead.

"Lonesome old night," Jesse said. I glanced over at him, and the tired lines of his face were softened and hidden by the dim light from the dashboard. A big lonesomeness hung over Jesse all right. "Better slow down," he said. "You'll run plumb through town before you can stop."

But I roared on into Thalia, fifty miles an hour right up to the square. I slowed down a little and circled it, parked in front of the lightbulbs and cardboard posters of the picture show. The pickup rolled against the curb hard enough to shake Lonzo out of his drunken stupor, and we got out and went in. When I was a kid in grade school Thalia had had two picture shows, but in those days the oil-field activity was big, and Thalia was a wild, wet sort of half boom town. Pretty soon the oil production fell off and the oil people took their cars and their dirty scrappy kids down the road to another field. The people who stayed voted to close the beer joints then, and after that there wasn't any place to go at night except the picture shows and the all-night trucker's café. A year or two later one of the shows closed up and they started using the billboards to run advertising for the one that hung on. That night there was an old picture playing, *Streets of Laredo*, with Gene Autry and Smiley Burnette. We all got popcorn and sat down to watch the previews. By the time the main show came on, Lonzo was wide awake and full of sass.

"Look at that silver mounted saddle," he said, snickering. "You couldn't lift that bastard on a horse with a goddamn crane."

"I met Gene Autry once," Jesse whispered. "Two years ago at the rodeo in Houston. Seemed like a strange man."

I don't know how he would be at the rodeo, but in the picture he was his chubby fat self, knocking the bad guys over like dominoes. Between Lonzo's snickering, and the little kids chasing themselves up and down the aisle, I could barely hear the picture. When *Streets of Laredo* was over they had one of those silly comedies where you were supposed to sing along with the bouncing golf ball. Lonzo wanted to sing with it, but he couldn't read fast enough to keep up with the ball, and everybody in the show got to laughing at him. I poked him in the ribs to make him quit, but he clipped me under the chin with his elbow, not noticing, and I had to sit and hold my breath for a minute, till my teeth stopped rattling. I kept forgetting how strong Lonzo was. Finally there was a newsreel showing the New York Yankees trotting across a baseball field in Florida, and it was time for the previews to start around again.

We left the show and drove down to the drive-in so I could get a hamburger. Lonzo had missed his supper, so he got three. I offered to buy Jesse a root beer or something, but he just sat and smoked. I went up and put a quarter in the outdoor jukebox, played "Folsom Prison Blues" and "I'm in the Jail-house Now," and we all sat and listened while the hamburgers cooked.

"What do kids do for fun around here?" Jesse asked, watching the carhop hurrying around between the cars. She was making up to a carload of roughnecks, fixing to go out on the night's tower.

"Whatever there is," I said.

"What the hell is there?" Lonzo said. "About a dime's worth is all I can see."

Actually we didn't do an awful lot. There was the pool hall, the snooker and eight-ball tables. But most of the time we just rode around and talked, or hunted up girls to court. Once in a while we drove to the county line and bought some beer.

"I guess kids out here have to make their own," Jesse said. "It ain't that way in the cities, what I've seen."

"Lonnie oughta go to Oklahoma," Lonzo said. "Hell, we had some big times up there when I was growing up. All the girls put out."

"Put you out, you mean," Jesse said. He flipped his cigarette out the window. "But I guess this ain't so bad. Many a one grew up with less."

"Hell, they grew up in the wrong state if they did," Lonzo said. "They oughta tried Oklahoma."

I saw some of my buddies over in another car, and I wished for a minute that I had left Lonzo and Jesse at home. If I had been by myself I might have got with the other boys and scared up something. I figured I'd try it the next chance I got. We got the hamburgers, and all the songs played, so we drove on back to the ranch. We flipped to see who would go out and replace Granddad, and Lonzo lost. He drove off, and Jesse and I stood a minute at the yard gate.

"Enjoyed the picture," he said, "but say, listen. When you get to wantin' to go make whoopee on your own, just say so and me and Lonzo'll catch up on our sleep. I don't like to see nobody in a cramp." He was quiet a minute, and then he went on. "I remember when I was about nineteen," he said. "I had been on my own, and I had to go back and start helpin' Dad. We had a cotton patch in Throckmorton County, right next to the highway that run in to Fort Worth an' Dallas and no tellin' where-all. I spent all my time following a couple a work mules around that field, and all day long folks would whiz by in their cars, going places I wanted to go. Don't think I wouldn't a given that whole run-down piece a land to a jumped in one a them cars and gone whizzing by some other pore bastard that had to work.

I never could stand to be cramped up after that. I hate to see anybody in a cramp." He patted me on the shoulder, and strolled off through the darkness to the bunkhouse. I felt tired out. I went to my room and flipped through an old magazine or two, but when I saw the lights of Granddad's pickup coming along the prairie road, I pitched the magazines down and went to sleep.

Three

I HEARD GRANDDAD'S STEPS ON THE STAIRS OUTSIDE MY door as I turned over. He came in and laid his hand on my shoulder. "Lonnie boy," he said. "Breakfast time." Then he went out of the gray room, and I knew that getting up was my responsibility. It looked misty outside, and I lay on a minute, my face nuzzled into the cool pillow. Then I heard the faraway slam of the screen door as Halmea came in to cook breakfast, and in a minute I heard "Let the Lower Lights Be Burning," the early theme song, coming from the kitchen radio. Jesse and Granddad were talking, standing on the porch just below me. When I heard them I swung my feet to the bare piny smoothness of the floor.

The light in the yard was timid yet, but I could see the heavy glisten of dew on the Bermuda grass, and smell the dampness of the gray range in the early breeze. While I was buttoning my stiff clean khaki shirt I heard the raspy voice of the radio announcer, bringing the five o'clock news. I put on my socks and went downstairs to the bathroom, my boots in my hand. I didn't feel woke up at all, and I remembered one bad morning when I had come downstairs with my eyes half-shut and got into the kitchen closet by mistake and pissed sleepily on the brooms.

When I came into the kitchen Halmea was standing by the stove, flipping grease over the eggs she was frying. She had on a clean blue dress, and looked too cheerful to fool with.

"Wish I could sleep till dinnah like you does," she said.

"Fry your eggs," I said, dragging a package of Post Toasties from the cabinet. Granddad and Jesse were already sitting at the table, eating eggs and bacon and sipping coffee from their saucers. I missed Lonzo, and remembered he was out on the range again. I poured milk over my Post Toasties, and began to read the advertising bullshit on the back of the box. I had read it a hundred times, but there was nothing else handy. By the time I got to biscuits and syrup Granddad and Jesse had carried their plates to the sink and gone out, and I had to sop up my sorghum in a hurry and follow them.

When I stepped off the back porch the sun was just coming up, striking all kinds of colors against the low mossy clouds that still hung in the west. My regular job was to scatter hay for the horses, so while Granddad and Jesse milked I climbed up in the high loft and kicked down a few dusty bales. By the time I had them in the racks the two full milk buckets were waiting to be carried to the house and strained. The milk was hot, and the foam on top fizzed a little as I lugged the buckets to the back porch. Halmea came out and helped me fix the cheesecloth on the blue milk strainer, and I slowly poured the two bucketfuls through. When I got back to the lots Granddad and Jesse were at the big water trough, trying to unstop a faucet. I went over, but I was just in the way.

"I believe here comes our man," Jesse said, looking up. A black Chevrolet was bumping down the rough road toward the barn; there were two men in the front seat.

The driver stopped the car beside the water trough, and the man riding got out. He was a short man, not as tall as I was, and he had a medical badge of some kind pinned on the front of his gabardine jacket. He came toward us holding out his hand, and looked friendly as could be.

"I'm Jimmy Burris," he said. "Good morning to you men. Looks like you-all need a plumber, not a vet."

"Oh, just a faucet clogged," Granddad said. The vet shook hands with all three of us; he nodded for his driver to get out, but the man sat behind the wheel and made like he hadn't noticed the nod. We all stood around a little stiff for a minute, everybody trying to think of what to say next. I wondered why the man in the car was so unsociable.

"Well," Granddad said finally. "I guess there's no use in us standing here till dinner. I imagine you've got other things to do today, and I know good and well I have. Let's go look at that carcass."

"Do we go in my vehicle or yours?" Mr. Burris asked.

"Let's go in mine," Granddad said. The vet waved for his driver to kill the motor, and the man got out. He was a big surly-looking man named Thompson; he just nodded when Mr. Burris introduced us. The vet got his bag, and we left.

For some reason, Jesse got in the pickup cab with Granddad and Mr. Burris, leaving me in the rear with Thompson. He chewed on a match, and didn't say anything. His face was red, and full of little chicken-track blood vessels, and his eyes didn't seem to quite match. When we got to the hard gate I was hoping he'd get out and get it, but he didn't make a move. I got it open all right, but I had a terrible wrestle shutting it. I was afraid somebody would have to come and help me, and keep me in the doghouse all morning. I managed, but I skinned up one hand good and proper.

"By god, you did get it," Thompson said. "I thought you was gonna have to leave it open. Didn't you have no Wheaties this morning?" I didn't say a word to him.

When we got to the heifer that morning, there was no time wasted. Lonzo was mad because we hadn't brought him breakfast, but there wasn't anything we could do about it. Granddad walked over and stood looking down at the heifer, and the veterinary followed him.

"There she is," Granddad said. The heifer smelled pretty bad, and the green flies were getting what the buzzards couldn't. Mr. Burris squatted by the heifer's head, looking at her shrunken jaws. He pursed his lips.

"Who cut this carcass open?" he said.

"Newt Garrett," Granddad said. "Was that the wrong thing to do?"

Mr. Burris didn't look up. "It could have been the very worst thing possible," he said. "I'll have to see." He put on some rubber gloves and got a knife out of his bag. While we stood watching him, careful not to get in his light, he cut out the heifer's tongue and put it in a bottle he had in his bag. He didn't look nearly as cheerful as he had when he stepped out of his car that morning.

"I wouldn't have believed this if I hadn't seen it," he said. "I'm not sure I believe it anyway. But we'll see." He stood up then, and faced Granddad. "Mr. Bannon, I'm afraid you may have something bad."

"I was kinda afraid of that myself," Granddad said. "Reason I had you look. I couldn't figure a heifer just dropping dead like that. Do you know for sure what it is?"

"Well, yes and no," the vet said. "Here, we might as well get away from this stink. I've got all I need. Let's go to the shade and talk cool. I'd like to find out a few things if you've got time."

"I've always had more of that than anything else," Granddad said. He didn't seem half as worried as Mr. Burris. He walked over to the big tree and squatted on his heels by Lonzo's bedroll. While Mr. Burris was taking off his rubber gloves, Granddad found him a little stick and began to whittle. He always did that, if he was still for two minutes. Squatting there with his brown hat pulled way down over his forehead he looked awful small and old, but awful determined. We went over and squatted too. Lonzo lay down on his quilt. Thompson stood with his arms folded, just in the edge of the shade. He acted like none of it was the least concern of his.

"Mr. Bannon," the vet said. "Have you by any chance bought any Mexican cattle in the last year or two? If this is the disease I think it is, it very seldom comes this far north."

Granddad looked up, not especially surprised. "It's been almost three years ago," he said. "I bought two hundred head of cows from a ranch down near Laredo. But I don't believe that heifer yonder was out of one of those cows."

"Oh, that wouldn't make any difference," Mr. Burris said. "I was just trying to line up some possibilities in my mind. I was hoping maybe we could trace this thing down, but if it's been that long ago I don't guess it's worth the trouble." He was tapping one fist against his knee. "Mr. Bannon," he said, "how long would it take you to get your cattle together?"

"My cattle?" Granddad asked, surprised. "You mean the ones in this pasture, or all the ones I own? I could have this pasture here by sometime after dinner."

"No, I think we ought to at least look at them all," Mr. Burris said. "We're going to have to make an inspection, and the sooner the better."

"For what?" Granddad said. "Inspection for what?"

Mr. Burris was picking at a little scab on the back of his hand. For what killed that heifer," he said. "Mr. Bannon, I hope I'm wrong, but I'm very much afraid you've got the worst kind of trouble a cattleman can have. I think that heifer died of hoof-and-mouth disease. Now my opinion isn't the final verdict, but just from the looks of things I think we better get to investigating this situation."

"Oh me," Granddad said. He kept his eyes on the stick. "I never thought it would be nothing like that."

For a minute nobody said anything. I was thinking of Hud, of how wild he would be when he got wind of it. Hud had done everything he could to keep Granddad from buying the Laredo cattle—he hated the whole South Texas area, and especially the Mexicans that were in it. He had picked out a bunch of cows in Colorado that he claimed were a whole lot better than the ones Granddad bought, and he never let Granddad forget it.

"I wish you'd tell me a little more about this," Granddad said. "I'd like to know what-all we got ahead of us."

Mr. Burris seemed a little nervous. "That's hard to say," he said. "The first thing, you've got to send somebody out here with a can of kerosene to burn this carcass. I'd like to kick Mr. Garrett's butt for cutting that animal open. It was the very one thing he ought not to have done. Then you-all better get your cattle together. If you could get them all where we can see them in the morning, it sure would help. We've got to take a lot of samples."

"What kind of samples?" Granddad said. He was watching the vet awful close.

"Samples of this germ," Mr. Burris said. "You see, there's three kinds of this hoof-and-mouth, or anyway, three diseases that look an awful lot alike. One kind just works on cattle, and that's what we hope you haven't got. Another kind works on horses and cattle, and another kind on swine and a few other animals. All of them are bad enough, but of course the cattle and sheep variety is the one where there's the most danger of an epidemic. What we'll have to do is bring a few sheep and a horse or two and some swine and try to give them what this heifer had. We may have to infect a few of your cattle artificially; then we just have to wait and see what happens."

"Well, Mister Burris," Granddad said. "Supposing it turns out to be this epidemic kind, then what? What do you do for it?"

Mr. Burris licked his lips. "I was hoping you knew that," he said, "so I wouldn't have to tell you. I was thinking you'd probably read about some of the other epidemics they've had."

"Oh, I guess I have," Granddad said slowly, his eyes on the stick he was whittling. "But it's been several years ago. I ain't tried to keep up. You mean they still kill cattle for things like that?"

"If it's hoof-and-mouth they do," the vet said. "They don't have any choice. Oh, in European countries they try to stop it with a quarantine, but over here we don't dare do that. In the last bad epidemic in the United States, if I remember correctly, the government had to kill about 77,000 cattle, plus almost that many sheep and goats, and even something like 20,000 deer. It's a terrible thing."

"You mean there ain't no vaccine?" Granddad said. "Ain't you college fellers figured out no better method than killing, in all this time?" He sat with his knife still in his hand, waiting.

"Mr. Bannon, we don't make miracles at college," the vet said. "We don't even know for sure what causes this disease, and you nearly have to know the cause before you can find the cure."

"Then tell me this," Granddad said. "How long will it take to find out just which one of these diseases killed this heifer?"

"If we get to work tomorrow, it shouldn't take longer than a week for the symptoms to begin to show up in the animals we infect. If they don't show up in the horses or the swine in that length of time, then we'll know."

"I see," Granddad said. "Now suppose it is this worst kind, but suppose just a few of my cattle have got it. What then?"

"I'm sorry," the vet said. "One or all, it would still require the same treatment. And incidentally, while we're making the experiment diagnosis, we'll have to insist on a very strict quarantine. No animals of any kind ought to leave this ranch, and no new animals will be allowed to come on it. This disease spreads like a grass fire. So far as we know, we may have it on our clothes right now, or the wind may have blown some of it fifty miles away since Garrett cut that heifer open. Actually, one animal can infect a whole area. And the sad thing is, the disease itself will hardly ever kill an animal—I guess that heifer was one exception—but just let there be a hint of it and you have to kill every head of cattle that's had any contact with it."

"And you're convinced, are you?" Granddad said. "You think that's what killed her?"

"Yes, sir, I do," the vet said.

Granddad stood up and slowly knocked the dust and the mesquite shavings off his pants legs. "Well, sir," he said, "I'll tell you something right now. I'll have my cattle together by tomorrow, as many of them as I can get. I'll help you examine 'em, I'll quarantine 'em, I'll work with you ever way I can. But I won't let you kill this herd, disease or no disease. I'll fence up tight and hold the quarantine as long as you want me to, but I won't let you drive these cattle into pits and shoot 'em, like they do in Mexico. I know, I've heard about it, and what's more I've seen it done. And I don't doubt an epidemic is a terrible thing. But the cattle I saw killed were sick, an' my cattle ain't. Oh, a few of 'em may be, but not many, and it'll take more than a telegram from Austin to convince me they are. I don't doubt I'm contrary and old-fashioned, and wrong about a lot of things, but I don't intend to have my cattle shot out from under me on account of no school-book disease. I don't believe in shootin' healthy animals. There's few enough as it is."

The man Thompson laughed when Granddad said that. He seemed to think it was pretty funny. Granddad turned to him, his old neck set.

"What kind of a smart aleck are you, mister?" he said. Thompson's laugh died off, and we all stood there uneasily. Finally Mr. Burris stood up and lifted his bag.

"Well, I don't think we need to talk any more about it today, one way or the other," he said. "I hope it turns out to be one of the minor varieties myself, so we won't ever have to talk about it any more." But it was easy to see he didn't think it would. Going back, Jesse rode with me and Thompson, and he got out to help me shut the hard gate.

2.

When we got back to the barn, Granddad went up to put in a telephone call to the hospital, to see how Grandma was getting along. He sent Jesse and me over to Hank Hutch's place, to see if Hank could help us round the cattle. If we were going to have all the stock in the horse pasture by night, we would need a lot of help, and a fair amount of luck to boot.

I drove, and Jesse slumped over against the door, fiddling with a package of cigarettes. He hadn't shaved that morning, and sweat was shining under the scraggly stubble on his thin cheeks. We were half-way to Hank's before he said a word.

"Looks like I landed in the goddamn wrong place agin," he said sadly. "Trouble's my middle name."

"I don't think it'll turn out so bad," I said. I didn't. Granddad wouldn't let people do anything on his ranch that he wasn't willing to allow.

Jesse sighed. "You got more cherry in your cheeks than I have," he said. "Shit, I can see it building. I oughta stayed on that truck and let it haul me clear to Wyoming."

I turned the pickup off the highway, across the shaky wooden cattle guard, and drove up to Hank's front door. There wasn't a fence, and there wasn't any yard. We saw Hank around to the side of the house, tinkering with an old tractor he'd swapped for somewhere. He waved at us, and came over. He was a tall, red-headed man, built heavy. The paint had worn off the old farmhouse where he and his family were living, and the whole place looked like it was held together with baling wire. There was a broken tricycle standing in the bare flower beds. One of its pedals lay on the porch, with a couple of cracked sawdust dolls.

"I tell you," Hank said, when Jesse had told him what was coming off. "I got one little piece of fixin' to do on a well. It won't take me fifteen minutes. You-all go on and leave me a horse in the lot. I'll catch up with you. I'm ready to start right now." When he wasn't in a hurry, Hank was a lot of fun to fool around with. He turned to the house. "Mama," he said loudly. His wife came then and stood in the door, a thin blond-headed woman with a feed-sack dishcloth in her hands. Hank's three barefoot kids, all of them little girls, hung back behind her, too timid to show themselves while we were in the yard. "I'll be seeing you tonight," Hank said. "Homer's got some work to do, so I guess I'll eat over at the big house." Mrs. Hutch looked like she was worn nearly out; besides the kids she had her mother to take care of. The little girls were as quick to hide as lizards.

"You-all come in an' have some ice tea before you go off in the hot," she said.

"Naw, we can't, Mama," Hank said. "Homer's got about three day's work to get done by sundown." He started for his pickup. "I'll go in mine," he said. "See you fellers in the pasture."

As I started back up the road I could see the three little blond-headed girls standing on Hank's front porch, watching us drive off.

"Ain't that a hell of a way to live?" Jesse said. "I pity that pore woman."

I couldn't understand why Jesse was so depressed. It seemed like he always felt sorrier for people than they felt for themselves. I guess he was probably feeling the sorriest for himself, all the time. Hank and Janine had a pretty hard time of it, all right, but they always seemed fairly cheerful, and acted like they got along pretty good. Hank was as jolly as the next man, poor or not. But Jesse sat in his corner, silent and sulking about it, while I drove home. I turned on the radio a minute and heard "Driftwood on the River" before we came to the ranch. When we drove through the cattle guard we saw Granddad and Lonzo standing down at the lots. They had their chaps on and their horses saddled, ready to go. Jesse came out of it a little.

"That sure is a nice pony your Granddad rides," he said. He meant Stranger, Granddad's pride and joy. Halmea was out in the back yard hanging out a washing—when I honked at her she dropped a couple of clothespins. I parked the pickup in the shady hallway of the barn, and we walked out into the hot dusty sunlight, to catch our horses and begin the round.

Four

WE SPENT THE REST OF THAT MORNING RIDING THROUGH the hot, weedy pastures, pushing the cows and calves out of the shady places where they were resting. It was after eight o'clock when we started—a bad time of the day to be working cattle, hot as it was—but we took it as easy as we could. Granddad had four little pastures, and one big one. His old cows had been fed all winter and were gentle as they could be; it was just a matter of finding them in the brush and throwing them together. Once we got them in bunches they were easy enough to handle. Hank Hutch caught up with us before we had the first pasture rounded, and with him helping we got along a lot faster. As we loped through the high weeds in the valley pastures the weed pollen swirled up around us and started us sneezing.

By dinnertime we were driving the cows from the third little pasture up the hill toward the house. Our horses were lathered from the morning's ride, and all the cattle were too hot. The little calves had their tongues out, dripping long white strings of slobber into the dust. Every minute or two the old cows would try to stop and graze. We were about as hot and droopy as the cattle, our Levi's sweated through, and our khaki shirts looking like they'd come through a washing machine without being wrung out dry. The cattle drifted into the big horse-pasture tank, and we rode to the barn. "Let's turn these ponies loose," Granddad said. "We'll start fresh this afternoon." We pitched our saddles in the shade and watched the horses roll around, scratching their sweaty withers in the dirt.

When we got to the house, a washpan full of cool water was sitting on the porch table, with a cake of lye soap beside it, and a handy towel.

Lonzo washed up first and sat down on the concrete steps to clean his fingernails. In a minute Halmea called us in to eat.

Granddad was slow coming up from the barn. He came in after the rest of us had already sat down at the table. "Take your time an' eat," he said. "You may not get another chance to rest till after dark." He looked shaggy and solemn, and pretty tired.

So we ate. Halmea had earned her money that morning, if she never did again. She had beans and steak and flour gravy, tomatoes and onions and lettuce and radishes from the garden, some fried okra, some hominy, hot rolls and butter, and cherry cobbler for dessert. It looked like an awful lot of food when we set down to it, but with Lonzo and Hank sitting across the table from one another it sure melted away. The rest of us ate our share, but we were just amateurs compared to them. When we were done all the bowls were empty, and the cherry cobbler was just a red stain in the bottom of a piepan. Halmea poured another round of ice tea, and we loosened our belts. Granddad got up the minute he was finished and carried his plate to the kitchen.

"You-all drink your tea and rest a minute," he said. "I got to make a phone call."

"He shore looks down in the mouth," Hank said, when Granddad had gone on out of hearing. "You don't reckon they'll really come in here with the guns, do you?" He looked at Jesse.

Jesse let a thin cloud of smoke ease out of his nose before he answered. "I've heard of it happenin'," he said.

"If a man come on my land and told me something like what that vet told Mister Homer, there'd be a quick war," Lonzo said. "I remember when they first started this cotton measurin' business. Some old boy come out an' told Pa he couldn't plant but so much cotton. Pa said he'd plant what he pleased, and the feller kept on him till he finally went and got the shotgun. The old boy left, but it didn't do Pa no good. He ended up just plantin' so much cotton anyway, and the fuckin' grasshoppers ate two thirds of that."

Granddad called for us to come on, and we all got up. I was just a tiny bit stiff from the morning's ride. We picked up our straw hats and stepped out into the yard, where the sky was white with sun and heat. I stepped under the sycamore tree a minute, to adjust my eyes.

"This evenin's gonna be a regular bitch," Jesse said, pulling the brim of his hat down a little farther. He had got in the habit of dreading things. We left the cool sycamore shade and went down to the lots to catch our horses. I led mine to the big water trough and let him drink his fill. He was a worthless, long-legged bay horse that I didn't much like. The water in the trough was deep and black near the bottom, with little green patches of mossy scum floating on the surface. When we mounted, the sky was high and white, with just a few thin milkweed clouds scattered near the horizons. The horses were sweating before we had gone a mile.

But the rounding that afternoon went better than any of us had expected it to. We were lucky in the big pasture, and found most of the cows in one place, so we didn't have to waste so much time prowling in the heavy mesquite thickets. They were standing around in the shade, but we stirred them up and pushed them down the brown sandy trails to a tank. The old cows waded in up to their bellies, while the big half-yearling calves farted around on the banks. When we got them all started toward the house Granddad sent Hank and me off to look for those that were missing. I rode my bay hard for a couple of hours, trotting along the brown shelving ridges and shoving through the thick weeds and the blooming green mesquites in the flats. I found two little bunches of cattle and managed to get them to the main herd before it left the pasture, so I felt fairly proud of myself. By five o'clock we had them trailing into the horse-pasture tank. Granddad sent Hank and Lonzo to get a pickup load of hay, to scatter for the cattle, and he and Jesse and I got fresh horses and loped down the road a couple of miles to the little Idiot Ridge pasture, the last one we had to round.

The pasture was open, not many trees on it, and compared to some of the others it was easy gathered. It was our bad luck that all the cattle were on the far side, standing around the windmill, so we had a long drive to make by dark. It was beginning to cool off a little, but Granddad kept his oldest cows in the Idiot Ridge country, and with them we couldn't make much time. Right at sundown we were driving them along the high ridge toward headquarters, with another mile and a half to go. In front of us the red sun was dropping cleanly down the last few feet of sky, falling into the gold thicket of mesquite on the far hill. There was not a cloud near it, nothing to break the clear spread of light. The pasture lay under the quietest, stillest light of day; it looked as perfect as some ranch picture on a serum calendar. The old cows walked slowly, their red coats gray to the flank with dust, their heads low. Now and then they stopped so a calf could suck a swallow or two of milk before we prodded them on. Some of them still carried their calves. Their sides bulged like barrels, and streams of yellow piss trickled down their hindquarters into the grass and dirt. The little calves waddled along stiff-legged, bawling for their mothers to stop. The old Hereford bull and the two longhorn steers, the cattle that Granddad kept for old time's sake, were in the herd. The two rangy, brindle steers walked in the front, following the trail down the long slope to the lots. The old bull slouched along behind, twitching the black buzz flies off his back. We all fell back to the rear and let the cattle follow the steers—they knew where they were going as well as we did. The evening air was cool, but heavy with the smells of dust and cattle piss and prairie weed. The grass was already browning under the long days of sun. Before us the trail ran downward like a slack lariat rope, ending at the big water trough.

Granddad was tired; he sat loose in his saddle. "I swear," he said. "I wonder if the government's gonna inspect them two longhorns of mine. They're gonna have a time adoin' it. Them big horns'll never go through a chute."

"Where'd you get them two?" Jesse asked.

"Raised 'em," Granddad said. "I been keeping 'em to remind me how times was. Cattle like them make me feel like I'm in the cattle business."

"Hell, I'd let 'em go back in the brush," Jesse said. "Then if the government wants 'em, let the government go find 'em."

"Well, I don't know what to think yet," Granddad said. "I ain't gonna try to decide till I find out for sure what's wrong with my cattle." He spit tobacco juice into the grass. "Don't do no good to worry ahead," he said. "Anyway, I guess I know now what's the matter with that case of sore-foot we got up in the hospital trap. I didn't think that looked much like the foul-foot."

Then we drove the tired cattle through the twilight, and he said no more. We got them to the tank just about the time the new moon lifted its rim above the highway to the east, a big swollen grapefruit of a moon. The cows walked out into the water, but the two big steers stopped and began to tear and shake the blocks of hay that Lonzo and Hank had scattered. We left them there, drinking and eating, pushing in with cattle from the other pastures, and I thought of how much work it would take to get them all separated again. That was enough to put me down on the government myself. After I unsaddled I left Granddad and the men to make plans for the morning, and went on to the house. I wanted to clean up as quick as I could, and get into Thalia for a little while, to shoot some pool. I thought maybe if I got to Halmea when nobody was around, she could help me come up with an excuse.

Halmea turned out to be a help, all right. She figured up what groceries we needed, and it didn't take much to persuade Granddad to let me go in after them. I bathed and put on some clean Levi's and a T-shirt before I ate; then as soon as I was through eating I got in the pickup and drove away from the ranch, through the cool night. As I left I saw Jesse and Lonzo sitting on the steps of the bunkhouse; I didn't much want them to go, and I didn't figure they much wanted to, so I didn't ask them. I drove slow till I got out of the horse pasture, so as not to bump the old cows that stood in the road.

When I got to the highway I turned my little window in and let the cool air swoosh on me as I gunned the old pickup toward Thalia. Just inside the city limits I braked and swung off the pavement onto the crunching gravel driveway of the highway grocery store. I thought I had better get the groceries first, before the old people who ran the store went to bed. A couple of old women were rocking on the porch, in front of the R. C. Cola thermometers and the Garrett snuff signs. I bought some bread and sugar, picked myself up a new pair of work gloves, twirled the paperback rack a time or two, and went out. I had the night to play around with, what there was of it between then and getting-up time.

Thalia was a still, quiet place at night. I drove slowly through the one long main street, now and then hearing a snatch of fiddle music out some open window. Some of the folks were out watering their lawns or visiting with the neighbors. In the summertime, in that country, evening is the peaceful time of day.

I parked on the square and got out. In front of me, under the big courthouse mulberry trees, a few old men were sitting on the wooden benches, talking and whittling and spitting as the night came down. Those old men were always there. On Saturday afternoons when I was younger I used to dirty up my clean weekend Levi's, sitting on the ground in the mashed mulberries, listening to the old men swap stories and yarns. But after a while their talk got old. All they knew were stories about old times, and I could hear better ones than they could tell from Granddad. They sat there then, they sit there now, I guess, whittling, spitting, nothing for them but the benches and the mulberry mush, the whittle sticks and the Brown Mule. But it was getting later, and I knew that pretty soon they would wobble home to their daughters' back rooms and leave the square to we boys.

There were a lot of kids in the pool hall, standing around the eight-ball tables at the back, Cokes and cues in their hands. My buddy Hermy Neal was at one table, shooting eight-ball with a cousin who was visiting him from Oklahoma City. I skirted around the money tables, where the reckless-ass oil drillers were shooting nine-ball at a dollar a throw. They were studs, those drillers: all they cared about was their cars and their work, and now and then their gambling. Dumb Billy, the stupid orphan kid who made what living he had shoveling shit at the local stock pens, was standing by a snooker table. He liked to watch the balls roll across the smooth green felt. Lem the Lion, the old nigger who ran the pool hall, was slipping around with his rack waiting for the games to be over so he could take in money.

"Hey, man," Hermy said. "You got your pickup?"

"It's on the square," I said. "Who's takin' the winner?"

"Winner's ass," he said. "Let's got get some beer while we got transportation." He was a tall blackheaded kid, fairly devil-may-care. He was a pretty good athlete when he wanted to be.

I hadn't meant to go out of town that night, but the more I thought about it the better idea it seemed. And I didn't really ponder it long. Granddad would be too sound asleep to know when I came in. He hardly ever knew anyway.

"I'm game," I said, watching Hermy's four-eyed cousin draw a bead on the four-ball. He hit it head on and missed the pocket about a foot and a half.

"Table's off level," he said. "Look at it wobble."

"You fucked up," Hermy said. He grinned and bradded in the eight-ball. His cousin drug a dime out of his pocket and pitched it on the table for Lem the Lion. Then he and I and Hermy and a couple more boys cut out and piled in the pickup.

"Make the square a time or two," Hermy said. "We might scare up some pussy."

"You're dreamin', man," his cousin said. His cousin thought Thalia was a shitheap of a town, and he was always putting up Oklahoma City. "You could circle this goddamn square a thousand times and not see a good-lookin' girl," he said.

"Who said good-lookin'?" Hermy said. "I wouldn't back away from a gentle heifer, not tonight." He wouldn't, either. It hadn't been long since half the boys in the town had had a wild soiree with a blind heifer, out on a creek one cold night.

But it turned out the cousin was right. I blew out of town and we flew down the road toward the county line, laughing and fighting in the cab, weaving all over the road sometimes. We were all too young to buy beer, but that didn't matter. If no cops were around the clerk would sell to a six-year-old, and if some were close by you had to look like Granddad even to get inside the store. Hermy's cousin was the littlest fart in the pickup, but we made him go in. He had to prove he wasn't completely worthless. Actually, the man would have sold him the store if he'd had any money.

On the way back to Thalia we tore into the six-packs. Hermy was an expert at opening the cans so they'd spew right in somebody's face, and he gave his cousin a regular beer bath. His cousin was so excited he didn't mind. We were living it up for once, talking about where we might find some girls when we got back.

But when we got there the drive-ins were closed, and the only person awake in the whole town, it looked like, was old Buttermilk, the night watchman. He was sitting on the curb in front of the grocery store, talking to his scroungy brown dog. There was nothing to do but make the lover's lanes, and then drive around the square and the two business blocks while we finished the beer.

"Shit, let's get out, man," the cousin said. We were all tired of riding, so we took the rest of our beer and went over to the courthouse benches to drink it. In a few minutes Buttermilk shambled over, beginning his rounds. "You boys ain't jackin' off, are you?" he asked. That was his favorite question. We hurrahed him a little and he went on. The moon was high and the courthouse lawn was white with light. We watched the one stoplight turn from red to green, from green to red, from red to green, and on and on.

"I'm horny," Hermy said. He was sitting in the grass fiddling with an empty beer can.

"I wish we could go someplace," I said. "I'd like to go to Fort Worth or someplace like that."

"I don't want no Fort Worth," Hermy said. He was trying to bend the can between his hands. "I just want some pussy in the next half hour or so."

His cousin snorted. He was getting pretty drunk, and his glasses had slipped way down on his nose. He looked like he was going to get sick on the beer.

"You boys don't know what it is," he said. "You oughta live in Oklahoma City. Man, up there you have to fight to keep your pants on." He thought he was pretty much of a cocksman.

"Is that how you got so rough?" Buddy said. Buddy was a little guy, but he always acted mean and hustly. If he got his bluff in on somebody he'd run them ragged.

"That's how," the cousin said. "How you been making out with the milk cows?" He was a little drunk and a good deal excited "Man, this town is nowhere," he said. "Nowhere, U.S.A. Deadass County, Texas." Everybody had been pestering him for days, and he was getting back.

"By god, I wondered how you got so tough," Buddy said.

"I'm not the roughest," the cousin said, pushing his glasses back up in place. "But I know damn well I can whip your ass," he said, taking his glasses off.

We all perked up a little. It wouldn't be much fight, but at least something would be happening.

"You got it to whip," Buddy said.

Both of them were too full of beer to have good sense, and too far gone to back down. They went out in the moonlight to fight, being careful to pick a spot of lawn where there weren't any water faucets to trip over. When they found one they began to stand and look at one another, with their fists doubled up.

"Start it, you chickenshit," Buddy said. He was in his Golden Gloves crouch, but he didn't move toward the cousin.

"You start it," the cousin said. "I'll end it."

Hermy was so disgusted with the whole thing he didn't even get up off the grass. I felt kinda sorry for the two, actually—it was half funny and half sad, the way they kept walking around and around one another in the moonlight. Neither one was mad at the other, really, and they must have both been wondering how they ended up in such a fix. Finally Buddy got his nerve up enough to run in and hit at the cousin, and they had a little shove fight that lasted about ten shoves. Then they separated and stood there, trying to get chummy so they wouldn't have to fight any more.

Hermy got up off the ground and knocked the dirt off his ass. "I'm going home before I get killed," he said. I took him and the cousin home and left Buddy and the others on the square, to talk over the fight. As I drove out of town I noticed the rodeo flags waving in the breeze: the Thalia rodeo was less than a week away. I felt blue as I drove out the empty highway. The silly fight had put me in a lonesome mood, and I couldn't get the funny, beery feeling out of my stomach. I turned on the radio and got some hillybilly music, but it didn't cheer me up. I wouldn't have minded going with Hermy's cousin to see what it was like in Oklahoma City, at least it would be a change. Thalia was okay, I really liked it, but I just didn't want it for all the time. The old cows bawling in the horse pasture kept me awake till nearly morning, and I lay in bed with my eyes open, thinking about all the girls I knew in Thalia and those in Oklahoma City I didn't know, all of them with night gowns on, asleep somewhere and breathing in the night.

Five

THE EARLY SUN SHONE ON STRANGER'S SORREL COAT, AND when he moved his head to look at Mr. Burris, the curb chain on the bridle jingled a little. Granddad had gotten off, to talk, but the rest of us were still on horseback, waiting for orders. The sun was less than half an hour high, but we had already made a circle of the horse pasture, and all the cattle were milling and stirring up dust in the big pen. Mr. Burris stood in front of us, slapping his gloves against his leg. He had shown up that morning in a station wagon, with four men besides Thompson, and a lot of veterinary equipment.

"I think while you've got 'em all penned I'll just have you run 'em all through the chute," he said to Granddad. "If it won't be too much trouble. That way we can kinda get an idea of how many's infected, and how far along they are. Then we can get what specimens we need without any trouble."

"I see," Granddad said. He had shaved that morning, and had on a clean shirt and a fresh blue pair of Levi's. "That'll be fine with us. When you-all get done with 'em we may work a few of these calves, if that ain't against the law."

"No, sir," Mr. Burris said. "You do what you want to with 'em. We're ready to get to work if you are."

We all turned our horses and rode into the dusty lots. First we separated into two lines of horsemen and let the cattle trickle between us, so we could count them. Then we cut them up into groups, the cows that had calves in one place, the drys in another, the yearlings someplace else. Hank and Jesse and one or two of the neighbors went on with the separating, while Lonzo and I tied our horses and began to run the oldest cows through the squeeze chute so the vets could work on them. Cecil Goad, one of our neighbors, would run a few cows into a little crowding pen, and then it was up to me and Lonzo to put them on in the chute. The vets were waiting. They were all dressed in gray coats, and had a whole conglomeration of bottles and jars set out beside the chute. They turned out to be a quiet, hard-working bunch; they handled their end of it a lot quicker and smoother than Lonzo and I handled ours. It was a mean, tiresome job, any way you went at it. The chute was plenty big enough for calves, but it was a pretty tight squeeze for some of the old cows, and we had the devil of a time getting them to take it. We couldn't get but ten or twelve in the pen at one bunch, and then they spun and kicked and bellered, started in the chute and backed out, stuck their heads in the corners and wouldn't move, turned and snorted, did ever aggravating thing they could think of to do. In a few minutes Lonzo and I were covered with dust, and hoarse from yelling at the old cows. The sun got high and the dust rose in a cloud from the sandy pens as the cattle milled and bawled. Granddad was working at the head of the chute, letting the cattle out when the vets were done.

It was past the middle of the morning before we had a real breakdown, but when it came it was a good one. Three cows got to crawling on top of one another in the chute and busted one fence to smithereens. Once it was busted there wasn't anything we could do but stop and fix it, and that took till nearly dinnertime. So when we went up to eat we hadn't even finished with the cows, and had all the calves and yearlings to work that afternoon. We ate quick and started in again, in the white heat of twelve-thirty. I was loggy, too full of ice tea and pie, and it got me into trouble. We had the crowding pen almost empty, just one old cow left in it. She was a thin line-backed hussy, with one horn broken off and a long string of foamy slobber hanging from her chin; nothing we could do would make her take the chute. We surrounded her and finally she stuck her head in like she meant to go. When she did I run up behind her to shut the gate. Then she turned back through herself like a bobcat and went charging down the west wall of the pen. As she went by me she threw out a big cracked hoof, and I spun away from it like I had from a thousand others. Only I spun a fraction too slow, and it caught me on the hip. All I felt was a shove, and a splat on my chaps. When I tuned in on things again I was outside the pen, sitting with my back against the red plank railing of the scales, and Granddad was wiping my forehead with a piece of wet cotton he had got from one of the vets. Inside the pens the dust was still swirling.

"You all right, son?" Granddad asked me. He poured some cold water over the cotton and rubbed my head. "She kicked you into the fence," he said. "You skint your head a little on the pipe."

He seemed to think I would survive, because he handed me the cotton and went back to the head of the chute. My head was throbbing a little, but my hip wasn't sore. While I was trying to make up my mind to get up, Mr. Burris came and knelt down by the water can to pour himself a drink.

"Boy, you caught a lick," he said, smiling at me. "That woulda killed an old man like me."

I didn't feel very talkative, so I just nodded and gave a kind of sickly grin. He sat there a minute, trying to be friendly, but neither of us could think of anything to say. Finally he put the lid back on the water can and left, and I got up and went back to the crowding pen. I knew the cowboys would be on me for a week if I quit work because of a little skint head.

And I could have worked anywhere but in that crowding pen, heat or skint head or not. It was about two o'clock in the afternoon, hellish hot weather, and all of us were sweat and dust over sweat, and more sweat trickling through the fresh coat of dust. Little branches and creeks and streams of sweat ran out from under our shirtsleeves and hatbands, and there were dark muddy brown spots in the circles of dirt under our eyes. The pen was like a sand pile with a monstrous fan in the bottom, blowing the sand up into our faces; then when it got so high the hot south wind blew it back down our necks. We were working the heifers by then, all of them scary as antelope and about as wild. Lonzo had got his hands on an electric hotshot, and the way he was jobbing the heifers could have got us all killed; it just made the cattle spin and kick that much worse. After about an hour of sucking in dirt and spitting mud I got sick to my stomach, and while we were bringing in a new penful of calves my dinner came up in a burning gush, most of it through my nose. I gagged and gagged, and my head kept throbbing, the sweat that stung the raw place just making it worse. I started to go back in the pen, and then I thought fuck it and went to the house, the weak trembles so bad in my legs I was afraid I was going to flop in the path, right there in the red ants and chickenshit.

When I hobbled in the back door, Halmea was in the kitchen rolling out a piecrust. She took one look at me and came over and grabbed my arm.

"Honey, you's white as a sheet," she said. "Sit down heah."

"Leave me alone," I said. "No wonder I'm white, you got flour all over me."

"Okay," she said, turning me loose. "Go splat on de flooah, see who picks you up." I saw her brush her hair back with one hand, leaving a white streak of flour across her forehead. I went on up the stairs and flopped on my counterpane, feeling sick and sleepy. My room was hot as a cookstove, and in a little while I came out of a doze, lathering in a pool of my own sweat, my head about to crack open. In the white, still heat I could hear the cattle bawling from the lots. I thought how much better it would have been if we'd ridden that day—at least, riding, there were breezes along the ridgetops, and the sweat cooled as it trickled down your ribs. In the bed it was close and sticky. I dozed again, still conscious of the oven of heat, and the constant pulsing in my temples. Then I looked up and Halmea was in the room; she was setting something on my little bedside table. I saw her through a dozy haze, standing over me, the white band of flour on her forehead moistened with sweat and running a little. She said something that

I didn't understand, and stooped to feel my forehead with her cool hand. When she stooped I saw part of her breasts. I didn't say anything, and in a minute she left the room. I raised up and found a big glass of sweetened lemonade on my table, the sugar just settling to the bottom. The cold glass was sweating, and the lemonade was pale, full of thin chips of ice. I sat up and drank it slowly, sipping the sweetened juice and spitting the white seeds across the room in the direction of the wastebasket. Then I fished out the thin, melting slivers of ice and sucked them one at a time, to make them last. I thought how much nicer it was to be drinking Halmea's lemonade than to be chowsing cattle in the dusty pens. Halmea was good about some things; she was good, period. If she was in the mood she would take care of you whether you wanted her to or not. Right then I liked her as well or better than almost anyone I knew. As I sucked the ice, I thought of her in my room, remembering the white on her forehead and the dark slope of her breasts against her seersucker dress. When I had finished the ice I let the sugared water in the bottom of the glass slide over my tongue, and then I sat the glass on the table and slept again, a longer, cooler sleep.

2.

Granddad's hand on my shoulder woke me. The yard was shadowy with twilight, and at first I thought I had slept on through the night. "Don't you want some supper, son?" he asked. He was sitting on the thrown-back quilt that lay across the foot of my bed. From the mask of muddy dust on his face I knew he had just come from the lots. "Get up an' wash an' eat a bite," he said. "You'll feel better." His voice was tired and slow, but powerful with feeling, and he lifted one of his stubby hands from the quilt and ran it through his stiff dusty hair. I looked out the window, into the evening. Three scissortails were chasing a raggedy-winged old crow across the sky. The horizon to the west was still rosy, but the sun was long gone for that day. Granddad stood up, and I saw that the sweat of the long day had soaked through his Levi's and darkened the leather of his wide, hand-made belt. "Pretty evenin', but it was a shitter of a day," he said. "Hud and his momma ought to be in before too long." He left, and I sat up in bed, tired from sleeping too long.

By the time I got downstairs, full dark had come to the plains. I stood on the back porch a minute, smelling the grassy evening smells of the country. Jesse and Lonzo were eating when I went in. They were too worked down to do much more than nod. Halmea came in with a stewer full of cold apricot preserves. "You alive, or is you a ghost?" she said.

"I bet his appetite'd be the last thing to die," Granddad said. I was pretty hungry, but I didn't feel like talking. Lonzo was so tired he kept dozing off with his coffee cup halfway to his mouth, and sloshing coffee on his wrists. He stumbled off to the bunkhouse right after supper, but me and Jesse went out and set on the cellar while Jesse smoked.

"You pretty tired?" I said.

"You better believe it," he said. "I can't take work like I used to, Rodeoin' so long got me outa shape for anything else. I'm too tired even to sleep. Maybe if I sit here a minute I can get up the energy to go to bed."

"How is it rodeoin'?" I said. "Isn't it pretty excitin'?"

He lit another cigarette and shook out the match. "For a while it's excitin'," he said. "Then it just gets to be work. It ain't like workin' out here, plain cowboyin', but it's still work."

I was hoping he'd go on and tell me about some of his high times, but he didn't seem like he wanted to talk. Jesse was that way. Whenever I was just aching for him to talk, he wouldn't say two words. It was when I'd just as soon be quiet and think that he thought of so many things to tell. I guess we coulda been wonderful friends if we coulda got together at the right times a little more often.

We sat on the sloping stone roof of the cellar and were quiet. The moon was above us to the southwest, like a round white slice of pear. I could hear rock 'n' roll music from the kitchen radio, just loud enough that I could enjoy it without especially listening. In a few minutes the light clicked out in the kitchen and I heard the slap of Halmea's loose sandals on the concrete of the back porch. She stopped in the yard and stood in front of us, still tapping one foot to the turned-off music.

"You-all come play me some checkahs," she said. "Some marble checkahs. Come on, Lonnie, you fresh outa anything to do."

"Okay," I said, standing up. "Sure, I'll come clean your plow." She asked Jesse to come too, but he stomped out his cigarette and shook his head.

"I couldn't even see the marble holes, I'm so tired," he said. The three of us walked out of the yard, down the trail toward the bunkhouse. The trail was a pale rope of light between the dark patches of weeds. The old cows had been driven back to the pastures, and there was no bawling that night, just the singing crickets.

"Last time I played checkers was before my Grandpa died," Jesse said.

"I enjoy playin' dis Chinese," Halmea said. She was afraid of snakes, walking so close to me that she stepped on my heels about every yard or so. "I gets tiredsome workin' all de time."

We weren't even to Halmea's cabin when I heard the roar of a car on the dirt road. "Whoa," I said. "Guess who's comin' now?" I could almost see Hud gunning the Lincoln over the graded road. Granny would be sitting up straight as a poker in the seat, waiting to tear into us.

"I might know," Halmea said. "Be no checkah playin' tonight. I bettah least get de coffeepot on." She turned and started quickly back toward the house.

"Maybe the operation will slow the old lady down a little," Jesse said. "Make her ease up."

Up the trail, Halmea heard what he said, and her quick deep laugh came back to us through the darkness. "She didn't have any operation," I said. "It was all just in her mind to begin with. She complained so much Granddad decided to send her down for a put-up treatment. All they did was put her to sleep and take a few fake stitches. She's no worse off than she's ever been."

"Well, I've heard 'em all, now," Jesse said. "I sure nough better get some sleep."

I stood in the dark, listening to the sound of the car. I heard the pipes on the cattle guard rattle; Hud must have hit it doing about sixty-five. The car lights lashed against the trees in the back yard, and he hit the brakes and burned gravel right up to the gate. By the time I got to the car Hud had Grandma out and was carrying her through the back yard, her fussing ever step of the way. I loaded myself with boxes and kicked the car door shut; the radio was still on, but I would have had to set my load down to turn it off. Hud met me at the back door, his old self. He was chewing a toothpick to splinters, and his tangled black hair looked like it hadn't been combed since he left.

"Time you got here," he said. "Ma wants a nightgown outa one a them boxes; you better take it to her. She thinks she's done a hard day's work, sittin' on her butt talkin' a blue streak for three hundred miles."

I stumbled on into the kitchen with my load, but I almost dropped it when I saw Halmea. She was bent over the kitchen table, crying, the tears running down her wrists and dripping onto the white oilcloth. I was so surprised I didn't stop, I went on to Grandma's room, wondering what in the world had happened to spoil Halmea's good mood. Granny was sitting on the edge of her bed, fanning and talking out loud to herself.

"Sit them luggages down," she said. "Get me my blue sleepers outa that yeller box. I got to get still befo' this heat an' all gives me a relapse." She was tickled to death to have me to talk at. "Never in my life was I in anything like that hospital," she said. "Them places is just one sin right after another. A person'd be better off just to stay home an' trust in the Lord." I wasn't finding any blue sleepers, and I was wanting to go see what had happened to Halmea. Granny never let up.

"One a them nurses, tryin' to undress me bare as a baby with menfolks in the room, I told that hussy. Shame an' disgrace." I finally found a gray nightgown in another box, and I pitched it to her.

"Where I told you to look in the first place," she said.

Halmea was still sitting at the table, wiping her eyes with a soggy paper napkin. She was holding her breast with one hand. When she saw me come in she dropped her hand and looked down. Every second or two her chest would jerk, like she had the hiccups. There was beans and meat on the table for Hud, but he wasn't there.

"What's the matter, Halmea?" I said. "You want me to go get you anything?"

She shook her head, her eyes filling up and her mouth quivering. "If dey was, it'd be a gun," she said, her voice shaky. She wouldn't say another word. I saw she just wanted me to get out, so I left.

There was a light flashing in the front yard and I went around to see about it. It was Hud, poking around under the hood of his convertible with the big flashlight. He was whistling "The Wabash Cannonball," and fiddling with his fan belt.

"Here," he said. "Hold this light a minute. I want to check them batteries."

"Did you see what was the matter with Halmea?" I said. "She wasn't crying when you-all came in, was she?"

"Let me have the light," he said. When I handed it to him he suddenly shined it right in my eyes, so I had to turn my head. Then he slammed the hood with both hands.

"Naw, she wasn't bawlin' when I went in," he said. "I gave her a little tittie squeeze. I guess you're old enough to know how that is, ain't you? A man gets to wantin' a little chocolate milk." He got behind the wheel and began to turn the engine over.

I walked around to his window, feeling helpless and mad at the same time. "Goddamn you," I said. "Don't you do that no more."

He snickered. "Fuck off," he said. "You ain't got no private milkin' rights."

He leaned his head out the window and let his motor idle. Neither one of us said anything. "Let me tell you something," he said in a minute. "I heard about this big cattle inspection you-all had today. Me an' that Grandpa a yours is goin' round and round one a these days, and I ain't gonna be the one that get's dizzy." He threw the car in gear suddenly and whipped out onto the road. Before he drove off he laughed and gave me the finger.

I went to the Lincoln and drove it into its shed. Then I got out and set on its back fender awhile, trying to decide what to do about Halmea. I wanted to cheer her up some way, but I probably couldn't manage it if I tried. It wasn't such a dark night, but a lot of small clouds were racing beneath the stars like greyhounds, pushed along by the high south wind. I was half in the mood to go to Thalia, but I didn't.

Finally I walked down to Halmea's shack. It was dark inside, but I didn't figure she was asleep. I stood in front of her door for a few minutes, hoping she would see me through the screen and say something. When I saw she wasn't going to, I walked around to her window. Ever minute or so the moon would come clear between the sliding clouds, and the moonlight shone pale and floury over the shack wall and the whole ranch yard. Her bed was pushed right up against the window screen, and I could make out the whiteness of her cotton nightgown. Ordinarily it would have set me on fire, seeing her on a bed, but then I didn't feel that way. "Halmea," I whispered. I whispered several times, but I had to say it louder before she heard me.

"Who out dere?" she said.

"Me," I said. "I'm sorry I woke you up."

"What you want?" she said. She didn't sound particularly friendly.

"Just to say much obliged for the lemonade," I said. That hadn't occurred to me till that minute, but it sounded good, "That was all."

She didn't say anything for a minute, and then she chuckled and rolled over. "Okay," she said. "Much oblige fo' you goin' on about you rat-killin' and lettin' me sleep."

I did. I went to my room, but it was a long time that night before I went to sleep. I read a little of *From Here to Eternity*, and then lay on my bed wide awake in the darkness, my head full of old sights and half-dreams, some nice and some uneasy. I remembered something Hud had told me once about my daddy: how he had killed my real grandmother. Hud said a snake had crawled up on the cellar, and Daddy shot at it and the bullet ricocheted off and hit Grandmother in the head. Granddad was off in the pasture, and she died under the sycamore tree before he got home. I never had the nerve to ask Granddad about it. But I knew that the ranch wasn't as cheerful as it had been. Hud and Granddad had too many bad arguments, and now there was the cattle disease and all that to worry about. Sometimes reading about Karen Holmes would make me wonder about the army, but I didn't think I would feel like Prew did about it, and I didn't intend to go off the deep end in that direction. Then there was Jesse's gloom and Halmea's crying and a lot of things that didn't look good.

Sometime late at night Hud came roaring in in his Ford. He stopped it under the shade trees by the back fence. His radio was on good and loud, and from where I lay I could hear Carl Smith singing "The Bonaparte's Retreat." Hud switched the radio off in the middle of a line, and went on singing it himself. He sounded like he had whisky in his voice. I raised on my elbows and watched him stand by the water house cleaning his boots. It was Hud's one good habit, cleaning his boots every time he wore them.

I don't remember seeing him go into the house at all: he may have cleaned them all night. I dozed off about that time, and I dreamed that Granddad and I were out together, riding in the early morning. The sun was just up, and the breeze cool on us as we rode across the high country. We stopped our horses on the edge of a hill, a high, steep hill, maybe it was the cap rock, and rested, our legs across the horses' necks. There below us was Texas, green and brown and graying in the sun, spread wide under the clear spread of sky like the opening scene in a big Western movie. There were rolling hills in the north, and cattle grazing here and there, and strings of horses under the shade trees. Then above us the little gray clouds began to slip away toward the north like coyotes in the pastures. We could see creeks winding across the flats, dark green oak trees growing along their banks. The green waving acres of mesquite spread out and away from us to the south and east. I saw the highways cutting through the bright unshaded towns, and I kept expecting Granddad to say something to me. But he was relaxed, looking across the land. Finally he swung his feet into the stirrups and we rode down together into the valley toward some ranch I couldn't see, the Llano Estacado or the old Matador. . . .

Six

THE NEXT MORNING GRANDDAD WOKE ME UP TO SEE IF I wanted to go into Wichita with him, to a cattle sale. He had bought some milk cows from a man the week before, and had agreed to get them at the sale. Now that the quarantine was on he couldn't bring them on the ranch, but Hank Hutch had agreed to buy them if Granddad would haul them to his place. I jumped into some clean Levi's and got down to breakfast in a hurry, but it was hurry wasted. Hud decided out of contrariness that he wanted to go, and while we were waiting for him to change clothes Grandma got in a preserving mood. The upshot of it was that we all ended up working in the garden till almost ten o'clock, bosses, hired hands, and all. She even had Hud out picking peas in his floosy pants. When we left she and Halmea had a wagonload of produce to put up.

It was past dinnertime, still and hot as could be, when we got to the auction barn. I had planned on stopping off in Wichita and seeing a picture show, but Granddad vetoed that. He said he might not stay long, and he didn't want to have to hunt me up. He was looking tired and depressed, like he wasn't feeling very gay. I figured Hud would give him hell about the cattle and the vets on the way in, but Hud didn't. When we got to the sale Granddad went off to prowl among the pens, looking for the man who had the milk cows, and Hud got with some of his gambling cronies and disappeared into the beer joint next door. I was left by myself to watch the sale, like I knew I'd be.

For a while it was enjoyable. There was a little row of padded seats around the auction ring. They were for the privileged buyers to use, the men who represented big feed lots and packing concerns. They were a mean, crooked lot to my way of thinking but they were fun to watch. They sat around in gray shirts and $10 straw hats looking proud of themselves. They talked and cussed and guzzled the cold beer the waitresses kept packing in from the stockyards café; but in spite of all the chatter they never missed an animal that came through the ring, and nine times out of ten it was one of them that made the buy. The auctioneer was auction-talking in a steady stream, leaning over the rail with a microphone in his hand, his pearl-buttoned shirt sweated through. Behind the big buyers, wooden grandstands sloped up to the ceiling. The little men sat on them, the small ranchers, talking stock to one another and the dirt farmers in yellow flat-brimmed hats and blue overalls come in maybe to sell a milk-pen calf. I saw a big operator wall around the ring, a beer bottle in one hand and a little snap-tail whip in the other. He had on white pigskin gloves, and he stopped all the way around the packer's ring to slap people on the back and interrupt their conversations. The cattle poured through the ring in ones and twos and tens, ever color and ever kind, the loud song-talk of the auctioneer meeting them when they came in and following them as they went out.

After I had been watching nearly an hour and a half—plenty long enough to have seen a good show, anyway—I saw Hud walk up and slip his arm around one of the waitresses. He patted her about belly level, almost making her drop a tray of beer bottles. When she saw who it was she just laughed and slipped on by him. He spotted me and came over.

"Homer seen you?" he asked.

"Not since we got here," I said.

"He's ready for you to load them milk cows," Hud said. He pushed his straw hat off his sweaty forehead. "Good milk cows," he said. "We oughta keep 'em and let the fuckin' government go to hell. Get 'em at chute number five. I got to see a feller right quick."

I went out into the dusty heat of the parking lot, to the pickup. The door handle was so hot I had to put my gloves on to open it, and the cab was like an oven. I drove around to the loading chutes, hoping not to have to wait, but a farmer in a new International was getting him a few scrawny Brown Swiss at the chute I was supposed to use. I sat in the cab, broiling in my own juice for fifteen minutes, while he got his business done.

As soon as he left, I backed up. While I was fixing my endgates a kid a little younger than me came walking up the chute. He just looked like a city high-school kid, ducktails and flowery shirt, but he had a piece of rubber hose in his hand, like the yard men used.

"You want some cattle?" he said. "We'll load 'em for you. That's all we do, load cattle." Old Andy, the regular loader, came up right behind him, and I told them both who I was and what I was after.

"I know 'em," Andy said. "Come in here last night from Cache, Oklahoma." He slouched back down the dusty alleyway after the cows, but the kid never moved.

"I'm Marlet," he said. "I coulda gone and got 'em. I knew where they was as good as Andy." He swung the piece of water hose back and forth. "Shit," he said, "I been working in these yards ever time I get a day off, helpin' 'em load cattle. I don't care whether they pay me or not, I still come an' help."

"Damn, why?" I said. "You couldn't get me out in this heat and dust to work for nothin'."

He slapped the board fence with his hose. "I don't mind it hot," he said. "We used to live on a farm an' work all the time, till Ma and Pa separated. Then we moved up here. I work for the Dr. Pepper bottlin' company ever day 'cept Sundays and Tuesdays."

"Do you have a horse?" he asked, looking at me closely out of his marbly black eyes. He asked like I was guilty of something bad. I told him I had three, all of them no-count.

"Someday I'm goin' to," he said. "I'll come over here an' chase ever one of these cattle out of the pens, ever fuckin' one. They make wienie sausage out of 'em, did you know that?"

About that time the three Jersey cows came up the chute, with Andy following them. I got behind the endgate out of sight, but Marlet stood right where he was, right in the way. He had an unlit cigarette in his mouth, and he just stood there looking at the cows. Of course they turned back down the chute, and Andy had to jump around like crazy to keep them from going by him.

"Goddamnit kid, you're in the way," Andy yelled, waving his punch pole at Marlet. The kid didn't look at Andy at all, but he climbed up on the fence, and the cows came running up the plank and into the pickup. As the last one went underneath him he reached down and hit her as hard as he could with the piece of hose.

"I like to hear it pop," he said, the cigarette still between his lips. "Did you know they make wieners out of 'em?" He sat on the fence, cooler than I was, while I fastened the endgate and hooked the chain behind it.

I had to wait for Granddad and Hud, so I pulled the pickup over in the shade of the auction barn and opened both the doors. I was going to lay down in the seat, but Marlet came and got in on the other side. He still had his hose.

"The police told me not to go with no more girls," he said. "They said they could put me in jail if I did. It's about to strangle me." He looked at me with such a serious expression on his face that I felt like I had to at least turn and face him. I really wished he would go back to the lots, so he'd be in Andy's way instead of in mine.

"I got a theory," he said. "I didn't get it from nowhere, not from no Nazis or no Communists or nobody. It says it's all right to get it. It's what God wants you to do." He leaned forward in the seat, thinking about his theory. "I'm going to make a song about it and get it on the radio," he said. "That's the way to get rich. It goes: 'It ain't no siiinn to geet iiiiit . . . !'" Then he lowered his voice. "I never got it but seven times," he said. "There used to be a whorehouse on Ohio, but the politicians closed it down for the elections." He tapped me on the knee, his eyes like black marbles. "I never got it from a blue-eyed woman once," he said. "Ever time from a brown-eyed woman. Ain't that terrible? I mean, you know?" Then he went on. "I used to go with a girl named Rosalind Chatteau, but now she won't let me go with her. I was over at my cousin's house the other day and he had three women there. They ever one had brown eyes." He looked around at the chutes, where Andy was yelling at some cattle. I thought he was going to jump out and go help, but he changed his mind. "You know what sugar dibetus is?" he asked. I nodded that I did. "I got that," he said. "There's three kinds of insulin you got to take. They get me so messed up it's about to strangle me."

He stopped talking, and we sat in the hot, noisy loading yard for about five minutes, not saying anything. He took the same unlit cigarette from his shirt pocket and put it between his lips. "Ma cleans over at the hide-an-renderin' plant," he said. "We live over there." Suddenly he got out of the cab and stood looking at the chutes, popping the water hose against his leg. "You-all have a ranch?" he asked.

When I said yes, he shook his head as if he'd known it all along. "I wish we did," he said. He took a couple of steps toward the pens, and then came back and looked up at me. "Take it easy," he said. "Or any way you can get it."

I thought he was the strangest kid I'd ever met. I sat there thinking about him and his strangling, until finally Granddad and Hud came out of the auction barn. Hud came around to the driver's side and motioned for me to scoot over. His face was wet with sweat. "Look at them shittin' Jerseys," he said. "Let's get out of this oven." I scooted over in the middle, where it was hottest, wishing the long drive home was over.

We were going right into the sun all the way. In the distance I could see the heat waves rising off the brown, burning land, and there was always a watery patch of mirage on the pavement ahead of us. With three people jammed into the cab, it was blistering; the sun was just dropping level with the windshield. The cloudless sky was still pale with heat. Granddad was inspecting the sales slip on the cows when he got in; he folded it carefully and tucked it into his billfold. His mind seemed to be on something far away.

"I wish you'd a cut loose from fifty more dollars and got tinted glass in this buggy," Hud said. "I'm fryin' in my own grease."

"Tinted glass wouldn't help," Granddad said. "Besides, I might not a had it to cut loose from."

"Oh, but you did," Hud said. "Fifty times fifty."

Granddad said nothing to that, and Hud fell silent as we drove through the big ranch country. The rush of air through the little window whipped the black locks of hair on his forehead back and forth. He nor Granddad neither one seemed in a bad arguing mood, but sitting there between them, I began to feel uncomfortable, like I was riding a horse along a high slippery ledge when it was raining. One splash of words in the wrong place and I didn't know where we'd be. For the first time, then, I noticed how much fresher and more powerful Hud looked than Granddad. Granddad was tough and steady, but he was looking awful tired and old.

"I saw you talking on the telephone for a good long while," Hud said. "Talkin' to the vet?"

"I talked to him," Granddad said. "But I didn't get a whole lot of information out of him."

"Hell, did you expect to?" Hud asked. "When a government son of a bitch wants you to know something he'll call you, or else send you a telegram."

"I reckon that's right," Granddad said. "He said they were watching the test animals pretty close, but hadn't nothin' showed up yet. I guess it'll be a few days yet before we know anything."

Hud took a toothpick out of his pocket and began to pick his teeth as he drove. I couldn't figure why he was keeping so quiet about it all, and I guess Granddad couldn't either.

"What's your idea on all this, Scott?" he asked. "What do you think we'll have to do?"

"Why I don't know nothin'," Hud said, grinning suddenly. "You're the boss, you must be the one who knows if anybody does. I just work from the shoulders down, myself." We had heard that line of talk a thousand times, and Granddad just waited it out.

"I agreed to the long quarantine," he said. "Don't you reckon that'll satisfy 'em?"

Hud spit his toothpick out the window. "Shit," he said, "they don't need you to agree to nothin'. They're the law. They'd just as soon do something you didn't agree to. You can agree with 'em till shit quits stinkin' for all the good it'll do you."

"These fellers ain't that bad," Granddad said, his eyes squinted almost shut against the direct light of the sun. "You ain't met these fellers. The boss seems to be as nice as he can be."

"I'm just here drivin'," Hud said. "Just workin' with my hands."

"Goddamnit, now, I'm asking you," Granddad said. "You been adyin' to be asked. Do you think they'd come in an' liquidate?"

Hud took his eyes off the road and looked at Granddad; he wasn't grinning any more. "Hell yes, they'll liquidate," he said. "But let me tell you something. Don't be abotherin' to ask me now. You done missed the time for that. You missed about fifteen years."

Granddad sighed. "Now what the hell do you want?" he asked. "I don't doubt I treated you hard, and I don't doubt I made some mistakes. A man don't always do what's right. But that was over an' done with years ago. It ain't got nothin' to do with this."

"You just think it ain't," Hud said. "It may be over, but it ain't done with by a long shot. Not none of it." Hud was talking slow, and watching the road, but the words he said came spurting out in the close cab like blood from a chicken's neck. "You're too old to know what I want," he said. "You always were. Not only too old, but too blind an' stingy an' contrary." Granddad listened without changing his face or saying a word. "You never thought I wanted more than you was a mind to give, did you?" Hud said. "You let that bronc fall on you an' mash you up so you thought you was goin' to die, and you got Ma to nurse you, an' she thought the same thing, an' you ended up marryin' her. Then you got well an' found out she wasn't such a bargain, and I was just part of it, just another muscle-head for you to boss around. You thought I oughta drive that goddamn feed wagon for you, instead of goin' to college. Yeah. You held on tight then, but you sure let me go in a hurry when the draft board started lookin' for somebody to go do the fightin'. But hell, you were Wild Horse Homer Bannon in them days, an' anything you did was right. I even thought you was right myself, the most of the time. Why, I used to think you was a regular god. I don't know more."

Granddad seemed to have quit listening to him. "It ain't hard to look behind you an' see mistakes," he said, after a minute. "This here's a different day, an' I don't see what drivin' that feed wagon has got to do with this hoof-an'-mouth. But I guess if they try an' liquidate we can hold' em off some way, lawyers maybe." He looked out the window.

Hud looked over at him and laughed his hard, slapping laughter. "Lawyers my ass," he said. "Fuck a bunch a lawyers. Now you asked me, I'll tell you what I'd do. I'd get on the telephone tonight and sell ever breed cow you got. They ain't got no chain on you yet, and we could ship the old bitches out before you finish them tests."

We both looked over at him like we thought he was crazy, but I knew he wasn't. He just always came out with the first scheme that popped into his head, however crazy-sounding it was.

"You mean try an' pass this shittin' stuff off on some old boy who wouldn't know what he was getting'?" Granddad said. "I'd have to be a whole lot worse off than I am to do that."

"Hell, no," Hud said. "Sell 'em to someone stupid enough to buy 'em knowing what the situation was. There's a many of 'em dumb enough to do it, just on the gamble."

"Oh, I don't doubt there's some that would," Granddad said. "But that ain't no way to get out of a tight."

"Well, let me tell you somethin' else," Hud said. "I'll tell you what all this has got to do with the feed wagon, you don't see it yourself. Someday I'm gonna have your land, Mr. Bannon, and right here may be where I get it. You're the old senile bastard who bought them Mexico cows, and you're the one better get us out of this jam, if you don't want to end up working from the shoulders down yourself."

"I believe you're locoed," Granddad said. "What in hell do you mean?"

"Oh I ain't figured it all out perfect yet," Hud said, "but I can give you an idea. The main thing is you, old man. You're too old to cut the mustard any more. Ain't that how the song goes?" He slapped me on the leg suddenly, like we had a big secret between us. "Liquidate or not," he said. "When this is over you might as well just get you a rockin' chair, so you'll be outa my way."

Granddad looked at him like he couldn't believe his ears, and Hud pushed his hat back off his head and went on talking, the old-time wildness in his voice. "I'm gonna have this ranch a yours," he said. "Someday I am. I'm gonna give the orders on it. I ain't got it figured out perfect yet, but you can put that much down in your book right now. I may get it now, and I may have to wait a few years, but I'm gonna get it."

"How do you figure you could get it now?" Granddad said.

Hud kinda laughed. "Someway," he said. "When a man your age goes off an' buys a bunch a sick cows, it means he's too old an' daffy to operate any longer. My mamma's got an interest here that needs protectin'. You got a lot of this stuff after she married you, and some of it's hers. You got the incompetence, and hotrod here's too young to take over. Them lawyers you was atalking about might figure it so I ended up with the power of attorney. I don't know. But if I don't get it one way, I'll get it another."

"Why you're badly mistaken about all this," Granddad said. "I'll be the only one runs this ranch while I'm above ground. After that you might get some of it, I don't know. But you can't get my power of attorney no way in the world."

"Pity I can't," Hud said. "You just don't make no bets on that. What I said was, I was goin' get your land."

"You ain't even consistent," Granddad said. He kept looking at Hud like he couldn't believe his ears.

"Who gives a shit," Hud said. "I'm gonna be boss." A shiny blue Cadillac passed us, and he pounded his fist against the pickup door. "Look at that blond head, would you," he said, pointing at the dressed-up woman who was driving. "How'd you like to crawl in with that?" he said, slapping my leg. Granddad frowned, and Hud laughed.

"I guess I better watch my language," he said. "I don't want to corrupt no minors." He chuckled. "But don't you know, if a man could get her in the back seat she'd make some cat tracks on that ceiling."

We drove on, forty miles an hour all the way home. Granddad and Hud got silent, both of them thinking of the times ahead, I guess. When we got to Thalia the sun was low in the west, and it was beginning to get cool. The merchants were closing up their businesses and walking home to supper. Old Man Hurshel Jones was out watering his lawn, and he waved when he saw our pickup go by. He was an old ex-cowboy who put in his days in the domino parlor; he had worked for Granddad at one time. We crossed the railroad tracks and saw the switchman's little girl out wading in a mud puddle, where the water main had leaked. "Wet plumb up to her Adam's apple," Hud said. He drove on out of town, past the junk yard, and past the cotton gin that had never ginned a bale that I could remember. The sun was a big red ball, sitting about a foot above the horizon; it wasn't hot and white any more. Hank hadn't got in yet, so we just left the milk cows in his pen and told his wife. We drove across the highway, and up the dirt road between the mesquites. When we hit the cattle guard the dogs came running out to bark at us, and wag their stub tails. No one was on the porch, but there was already a light in the living room. Halmea was in the back yard, wrestling a big rug off the clothesline.

Hud stopped the pickup by the yard fence. "I got something to do that can't wait," he said. "You-all take it from here." He walked to the fence, put one hand on a post, and jumped over.

"Oh me," Granddad said. "I wish I could move like that. I believe I'll get out too. You can take the pickup on to the barn."

He got out, and shut the pickup door carefully. Seeing Hud jump the fence reminded me of the years when he cared to be an athlete. He rodeoed a good deal, and in the summertime he caught for the local ball team. Some of the Thalia sports got enough money together to run a string of lights around the ball field, and for a few years after that, night ball games were big affairs. Hud would catch with just a mask and a glove for protection. Half the time he wouldn't even use the mask. One night he almost got his thumb torn off by a tip, but he got him a can of kerosene and soaked the thumb between innings and went on catching. He would cuss the batters till they got so mad they'd swing blind. "Stick a fork in him, he's done," he used to say.

I drove on down to the lots and put the pickup in its shed. Jesse was in the horse lot, unsaddling Granddad's young horse. He had decided to enter him in the cutting horse contest at the rodeo, just for the experience, and he was working him pretty hard. I turned on the water in the big trough, and sat on the iron edge while it filled up, sloshing my hands. I could see the round white moon reflected in the water, with little bits of green moss floating over the reflection like thunderclouds. I dipped one hand and tried to slosh out the moon, but it kept rocking back and forth. Seeing it made me think of Marcia, my cousin. When we were kids we used to float kindling ships back and forth across the tank to one another; I didn't even know what had become of Marcia. The day had left me tired in a strange way, and I was about in the mood to skip supper and lay down in the short grass and rest, lay there and watch the white moon move across the sky. I bet Marlet had never fiddled around a water tank, sailing boats with a girl like Marcia. I flipped a stick into the tank and watched it bob on the rising water. It made me think of an old hillbilly song by Moon

Mulligan, called "I'll Sail My Ship Alone." With all the dreams I own. Sail it out across the ocean blue.

"Better turn that water off," Jesse said. "It's sloshin' over." He was going to supper, and I walked up to the yard with him, listening to him brag on Granddad's colt. He seemed real quiet, but friendly, and in a good mood. When we got to the gate we met Hud coming out, dressed in his rodeo clothes.

"Gimme room," he said, grinning. "I'm going up to Burk to the rodeo. You honchos wanta go?"

I was so surprised I didn't say anything, but Jesse grinned and shook his head. "No thanks for me," he said. "I'm gonna stay here and scare up a checker game."

"I guess that is about your speed," Hud said. He got into his convertible and left, with us standing there watching him.

"That's the first time in my life he ever asked me to go anywhere," I said. "I wonder why he did it."

Jesse took a package of cigarettes out of his pocket. "Lonesome, I imagine," he said. "Just tryin' to scare up a little company."

"Him lonesome?" I said. "Why he can get more women company than anybody around here."

"That ain't necessarily much," Jesse said. "It ain't necessarily company, neither. Women just like to be around something dangerous part of the time. Scott ain't so mean but what he could get lonesome once in a while."

"You shoulda heard him this afternoon," I said. "You'd think he was mean." I sat down on the steps and began to clean my boots, and Jesse went on in to wash up for supper. When the time came, I turned out to be hungry after all.

Seven

Maybe it was Marlet, at the auction, or maybe it was Hud's wild talk on the way home, but whatever it was caused it, I had the blues that night, and everything I did made them get worse. After supper, Halmea went to her cabin, and I wandered into the living room looking for a new magazine to read. Grandma and Granddad were there, each one sitting by a separate radio. They disagreed over the programs so much that they couldn't get along with just one. "Fibber an' Molly'll be on in a minute," Granddad said. "Sit down an' listen." The wallpaper in the room made the light seem yellow as sulphur. Granddad's face seemed thinner than it had; he hadn't shaved, and the short silver whiskers looked ragged against his skin. He wasn't being as clean about his tobacco chewing as he usually was. Neither one of them paid much attention to me, and I leaned on the mantel and read an old copy of the *Cattleman*. Grandma was listening to *Break the Bank*, and the two programs blaring so loud against each other made me want to grit my teeth. It gave me the terrible feeling that things were all out of kilter, all jumbled up. But I couldn't seem to leave them, the two old ones. I sat down by the mantel, under the picture of my folks, and read through the old magazine. I wished I could get Granddad out on the porch, into the cool night. In a minute he turned the radio dial to another station, but it turned out that Fibber and Molly had gone off the air for the summer, or maybe forever. Granddad kept fiddling with the dial, trying to find a program that suited him, and I got up and left the room, more depressed than ever.

My room didn't do much to cheer me up. I read in about half a dozen books, but I couldn't get interested in any of them, and I finally fished out a couple of old *Playboys* and went through them, looking at the shiny, naked girls. But whatever I did, that night, I just seemed to get more and more restless; it was like an itch there's no way to scratch.

Sometime late in the night I woke up, and for a minute I was all right, cool and fresh. For a while I lay on the bed enjoying the breeze, but then, when I couldn't slide back into sleep, my restlessness came back, stronger than it had been before. The longer I lay there the worse it got. The house was quiet, but I figured it must be nearly morning. I dressed and went downstairs, meaning to go out to the windmill. But when I was on the back porch I got another idea: I found a flashlight, a twenty-two, and a box of hollow-point shells.

I decided to go shoot things, shoot anything I could find. About halfway to the barn I stepped off the trail and walked carelessly through the high weeds, not caring how many rattlesnakes I stepped on. I was wishing I had a frog gig, I was in a mood to gig things. You gig things you got them. But I went on through the dark brush anyway. The first thing I did when I came to the tank was step on a big cottonmouth. He slid on by me to the water. I waved the flashlight around till I spotted a big bullfrog, sitting on the bank about twenty feet away. Then I sat down on the Bermuda grass, so I could hold the light on the frog and aim the gun across my knees. I hit him, heard the hollow-point splat into him, but before I could get him he flopped into the water. "Smart aleck," I said. "Now the turtles eat you." I shot five or six more frogs, some of them pretty long shots, but they all flopped into the water. Then I shot a turtle and splattered his shell. I missed a moccasin and hit a couple more frogs, and my gun was empty. I felt like shit, like all the bullets had been hitting me. I thought of Marlet, and I wished I could have shot him, the crazy little bastard. A rabbit came hopping up on the dam and I shined my light and blasted him. He kicked and died. "Tonight I may shoot everything," I said. Then I shot another big frog and got him before he flopped. I held him up by the legs and let him kick. "See what good it does you," I said. Then

I threw him out in the tank. “Feed the turtles,” I said. “Frog a day keeps the doctor away.” I was shaking all over, and I had frog blood on my pants leg where the big one had flopped against me. I went over and picked up the rabbit and threw him as far out in the water as I could. “Eat hearty,” I said to the turtles. “I hope you get rabbit poisoning.” Then I went out in the darkness, the sunflowers and milkweeds up to my chest. A sunflower scraped my wrist and I dropped the flashlight—I went on and left it shining up through the weeds. Then I went back and picked it up. Suddenly the high weeds and the darkness made me feel like Marlet, like I was strangling, “Oh me,” I said. “I wasted all those frogs.”

I guess the shooting woke Halmea up, because there was a light in her cabin. But before I could get there to calm her down it went out, and I went on to the house and put up the gun. I got scared and sad about what I'd done, especially about walking through all those snaky weeds. I could still hear the bullets plop into the peaceful, sleeping green frogs. The night around me was still and heavy as a blanket, and I knew I didn't want to lie down beneath it, not then. I felt like you do sometimes in a high fever, when everything goes out of focus and gets far away, and your hands feel the wrong size. I heard the little gray moths tapping against the porch screen, and I went out again. All the stars were lost in cloud. West, behind the barn somewhere, I heard the hot farting roll of thunder. The dogs had dug holes in the cool dirt where the water tank overflowed, and I stepped over them going to the windmill. I knelt by the faucet and laid my cheek against the cool iron of the water pipe. The water ran over my feet, slow at first, then coming out of the pipe in cold white spurts. I made it run slowly; on my hot back and shoulders it felt like ice. In a little while I felt too cool, and I turned it off and started to climb up to the platform. But I stopped halfway up the ladder. It was lonesome on the windmill. The rig lights were far away and dim. I thought of Halmea, of seeing her light on, and I thought how good it would be if she were still awake, so we could sit and talk awhile.

The thicket of clouds was moving westward, the moon hidden somewhere in it. It was so dark I almost stepped on an old hen that was squatting in the trail. When she squawked I jumped a foot. Then for the second night in a row I stood by Halmea's window screen and listened to her breathing. But she must not have been sleeping very soundly. When I scratched on the screen and whispered, she came right away awake.

"What you mean, nigger?" she said.

"No, it's me agin," I said. "I thought you were awake."

"Lonnie?" she said. I guess she remembered the night before. "You gettin' crazy sleepin' habits." Then she turned over on the bed and laughed so you could have heard her in Thalia. "You beats a goose," she said, laughter spilling out around the words. She sounded relieved, and I paid the laughing no mind.

"Maybe I better stay out here," I said.

"Whut fo'?" she said. "Come in here, you wants to talk so bad." I could barely make out the white of her nightgown as she got out of bed. "If it ain't dark I don' know whut it is," she said.

She shoved a chair where I could feel my way to it, then went back to the bed. "Set down," she said. "Nobody gonna swallow you." The old bedsprings squeaked when she flopped back on them. Now that I was in the room with her, I began to get nervous.

"You a crazy one," she said. She seemed tickled about something, but she changed her tune when I told her about the shooting.

"You done dat?" she said. "Dat scared de livah outa me."

"I don't know why I did it," I said. "I didn't have nothin' else to do, for one thing."

"Sheew," she said, "dat's no reason. You had de blues about sometin', I seen dat at suppah."

"I'm just sick of all this," I said.

Suddenly she clicked on the little lightbulb at the head of her bed, and the yellow light spread over the room, as welcome as the sun. "Sick uv whut, honey?" she said. "Tell me little more." She looked at me out of her calm black eyes, smiling the least little bit. I got tight and embarrassed when I saw her, I couldn't help it. Her breasts sagged heavy against the nightgown, her bare legs tucked up under her as she watched me.

"Things used to be better around here," I said. "I feel like I want something back."

"Pity," she said. She picked up her pillow and held it in her lap. "You mighty young to be wantin' things back," she said.

"If Granddad and Hud could get along a little better it would be okay," I said.

She grinned a little, and then a solemn look came on her face. "If an' if an' if," she said. "You if yourself crazy. I been ifin' aroun' lot longah dan you have, an' whut it get me? Just whut I eats an' whut I wears out."

We sat quiet for a minute; Halmea had a faraway, solemn look on her face. Her lips were puffed a little. "Ain't much talk, is it?" she said, and I nodded. Outside, the chickens were squawking, and the chicken house was a shadow in the first gray light. Halmea was picking the flaky brown paint off the bedrail, pursing her lips like she wanted to whistle. It was peaceful and nice for a while: I had quit thinking about anything. She clicked off the lightbulb, and we sat in the dim gray room.

"I just work while I ifs," she said. "When I get dat done I works a little mo'." She stood up, yawned and stretched her back. "My back gonna quit me first," she said. "Den I guess I just if." She went to the screen door and looked out into the grayness. "Cloudy," she said. "Now you get on. You got mo' kinks in you dan I got in my back." She stood in the doorway, scratching one leg through the white gown, while I walked up the path in the cool of morning. She would be going to the house, to cook breakfast, but I knew it was almost an hour away, so instead of going up to my room I went quickly to the lots and took my bridle from a nail in the harness shed. Then I went to the oatbin and scooped some yellow oats in a bucket. I took the oats and the bridle and walked back through the dewy grass toward the tank, hoping to meet the horses on the way.

2.

They weren't at the tank, but I stood on the dam and watched them coming out of the brush to the north, trailing to the lots for their morning feed. The fish were making dawn breathings on the gray sheet of the water. When the horses got close enough I shook the oat bucket at them, and they filed over to me one by one. Each one stretched his neck and took a mouthful, afraid of being caught. When Stranger came up I set the bucket on the ground and let him nose it; while his head was down I slipped the reins around his neck. I bridled him, and poured the rest of the oats in little piles for the other horses. A covey of bobwhites whistled behind the dam; I waited a minute and saw them trail down to water. I hung the empty oat bucket on a snag.

Stranger let me slip on his bare back, and we trotted off toward our big valley pasture. When I got through the gate, the dewy grass stretched away in front of me, almost six miles to another fence. The dawn breeze stirred in my face: the sky to the east was brightening. Idiot Ridge was a mile away, breaking the levelness of the plain. I touched Stranger into a steady lope, so we could get there and wait for the sun. Dozens of feeding jack rabbits broke before us, but as we went past they zigzagged off to the side and stopped, their long ears folded against their heads. A big, brown-winged prairie hawk sat on the limb of a dead mesquite, watching for quail. Once Stranger jumped a small mesquite bush when I wasn't looking, and I almost slid off his slick back. When we got to the ridge I slowed him down, and he picked his way through the loose gray rocks to the top.

On the north edge of Idiot Ridge I stopped and slid off. Headquarters lay to the northeast, where the sun was about to come up. The whole long line of sky behind the house and barn was orange and red; the wind was driving the layer of summer clouds out of sight to the northwest. I could see the horses we had left at the tank, filing up to the lots for their regular feed. In a few minutes Jesse would tend to them. Farther down the ridge two hawks were gliding low over the rocky hillside, dipping and swooping, then almost steady in the air. Stranger whinnied, then bent his neck and began to graze. The sky was a country of changing colors, like the land: red in the east, still deep night blue in the west. The moon was fading out of sight. Across the thread of highway, in a neighbor's pasture, an old bull bellowed, the hoarse sound barely reaching me. I could see a few of Granddad's cows on the flats to the south. Suddenly Stranger raised his head and snorted. Two young dog coyotes were trotting along the edge of the ridge, coming right toward us. When they were about fifty yards away, I whistled and they stopped, their gray heads cocked and alert. Then they loped off the slope over the edge and I lost them among the rocks and chaparral. Fingers of sunlight crept up the ridge, crept over us, and made Stranger's sorrel coat shine like fire. I watched the light brighten the rangeland a minute; then I got back on and touched Stranger with my heels. I turned him directly toward the barn, so I wouldn't have to stop and open the horse pasture gate. Sliding off the steep ledges I was afraid to give him much slack, but once we hit bottom, with only level pastureland between us and the homeplace, I let him go. In a hundred yards he went from trot to lope to dead, tearing run, till he was stretched out low to the ground, with his red legs blurred beneath him. I couldn't see for the wind tears in my eyes, and I was afraid every second I would fall off, but I let him go. It seemed like I had been waiting a week for the thrill and excitement of his speed. We went over the gray-brown grass like it was a race track, Stranger running for all he was worth and me leaning over his neck hanging on to his flying mane. Suddenly, out of the corner of my eye, I saw a fence and knew we were nearly there and must stop. It was the fence that led to the lots, I remembered that the lot cornered, that Stranger would whip around it, and I started to slow him down. But it was too late, he was turning without me, slipping away from between my legs, already turned and gone, the reins burning through my hands, the ground somewhere below or behind me. Then I hit it, I was rolling, a rock bumped my hip, there was nothing to grab, then no more rolling and I sat up, wondering if I were hurt. Suddenly Jesse had ahold of my shoulders and was trying to push me back down. "Be still," he said. "Be still. You may have something broken." But I wanted to stand up, I felt too good to be still.

"I'm okay," I said. His face was pained, like he was the one who was hurt. It must have been a terrible fall to watch. Stranger stood by the lot gate, the bridle reins trailing in the dirt. I grinned, and Jesse's face relaxed a little. He gripped me under the arms and helped me up.

"It looked like both your legs would break off," he said.

My hip was sore from the rock, but otherwise I didn't seem to have a scratch on me. I led Stranger through the gate and slipped the bridle off as he went by me to the hayrack.

"He runs like an antelope," Jesse said. "All the years I followed rodeo I never seen a harder-lookin' fall."

"It wasn't as hard as it looked," I said. Walking to the house for breakfast, I felt as good as I had in weeks. I was even hoping there was a day's work ahead.

3.

By the time I had finished my Post Toasties, everybody else was nearly done eating. Hud had his mouth full of biscuit, and was pouring a dark stream of sorghum over a lump of butter that lay in his plate. He had on slacks and a white shirt, dressed up to go somewhere. Granddad was saucering his coffee, not paying much attention to the breakfast-table conversation. When breakfast was over he got his hat and went out the back door. I ate as quickly as I could and started to the lots, but Halmea stopped me.

"You in no hurry," she said. "Help me strain dis milk."

The two big buckets of milk Lonzo had brought up stood on the back porch; the yellow layer of cream had already risen to the top. Halmea handed me a piece of cheesecloth, and I spread it over the top of the old milk strainer. She lifted one of the heavy buckets and slowly poured the milk through the cloth into the clean straining basin. The milk ran through in a swirling white stream, leaving the little flecks of dirt and manure stuck to the damp cheesecloth. Clear beads of sweat stood on the black dark skin of Halmea's throat and neck.

"Watch what you doin'," She said. "You let dat rag slip an' we got it all to do ovah."

When we were finished I got my hat and went down to the lots, to see what the day's assignment was. Granddad was in the tool shed, sharpening the blade of his shovel.

"What do we do today?" I asked. "I feel almost like workin' for a change."

"Goodness, I wish I had a job for you," he said, cleaning the file against his pants leg. He put his weight on the shovel handle, to hold the blade steady against the bench, and sharpened a little while he was considering.

"Oh, son, I wasn't gonna do much today," he said. "I'm just gonna cut a few weeds here around the house. I guess this mornin' you better go with the boys and help 'em patch some of that fence on the west side. I don't guess we'll do much this afternoon. Kinda hate to waste work until I find out a little more about the cattle." The rasp of the file drowned out conversation for a minute, and I stood there watching. Seeing him sweat over the shovel, I wished I could stay and cut weeds with him. I didn't feel right about leaving him to work alone.

"You ain't worried about that scheme of Hud's, are you?" I asked. He laid the file down and tested the edge of the blade with his finger.

"Hud?" he said. "What scheme? Oh lordy, I got so many things lined up to worry about I ain't come to that. I imagine Scott was talkin' not too serious. I don't think he's got much of a scheme in his mind." He shook his head and picked up the file. "If I don't get a bill of health on these cattle there won't be much ranch for him to run," he said.

"Aw, I don't really think they'll liquidate these cattle," he said, after he had filed a minute. "But I ain't young enough to count on what I think bein' right, either, an' I ain't fool enough to figure on things turning out the way I expect 'em to." He put up the file and started off around the barn. Jesse hollered at me then, and I went over to the post pile and helped him and Lonzo load the fencing tools.

4.

None of us worked very hard that morning. There didn't seem to be any reason to strain ourselves. By eleven-thirty we were sitting on the back porch, waiting for Halmea to call dinner. While we were waiting, Lonzo and Jesse got to talking about the towns they knew. Lonzo's travels didn't take long to tell—after he named the times he'd got drunk in Lawton or Ardmore or Oklahoma City, he was about through. But Jesse could have talked all afternoon and on into the night and not have scratched the surface of all the things he'd seen and done. He got to talking about places he'd been on the rodeo circuit, and just hearing the names was enough to make me restless. He'd been to practically ever town in Texas, big or little, Lubbock and Amarillo and Houston, Fort Worth and Dallas and San Antone, Alpine and El Paso, Snyder and Olney, Vernon and Dumas and Newcastle and a hundred more, and then on into New Mexico and Colorado, to Tucumcari and Clovis and Gallup and Cimarron, Raton and Walsenburg and Denver, on up to Cheyenne and Pendleton and Pierre and Calgary, over to St. Louis and Sioux City, Chicago and Kansas City and New York, and a hundred more I couldn't even remember. I could tell by the way he rolled the names around in his mouth that he must have liked rodeo, or at least have liked seeing places. But he wouldn't admit it.

"That's no life," he said. "You boys think stayin' in one place is tiresome, just wait till you see that goddamn road comin' at you ever mornin'. And still comin' late that evenin' and sometimes way into the night. I run that road for ten years and never caught up with nothin'."

“I’d like to run that bastard,” Lonzo said. “Long as I could chase down a piece of pussy now and then, to keep me goin’.”

“If you stayed on it that long, you must a liked it?” I said. He shook his head and spit.

“Oh, it gets in your blood like anything else you do,” he said. “For a while it’s right excitin’.” He fanned a fly away from his face. “I just wonder, when it’s all said and done,” he went on, “who ends up with the most in this scramble. Them that go in for big shows and big prizes and end up takin’ a bustin’, or them that plug along at what they can kinda handle. Home folks or show people. They’s a lot a difference in ’em.”

“Which are you?” I said.

“I kinda split the difference,” he said. “I missed out on the good things a both kinds, loose-horsing like I have.” The way he said it, I couldn’t help noticing how sorry he felt for himself. “I still got some loose horse in me,” he said.

Halmea called us then, and we went in and ate. After dinner, while everyone was heading for their napping spot, I went out in the front yard and set down under the cedars. I leaned back against one and let the hot wind blow in my face. Sticky cedar sap was oozing out of the trees, and I caught the burning summery smell of the lilac bushes. I thought about all those rich names Jesse had rolled off his tongue, and about what little I had to compare with them myself. Except for trips to the county-line beer joints, those few nights in Fort Worth were all I had. I guess they just amounted to a few evening walks downtown, when the city lights were flashing. But they had seemed like something rich to me. I had left Granddad in the hotel lobby, and prowled through the drugstores for a while, spinning rack after rack of shiny-covered paperbacks, and listening to jukebox music. Gradually I would work my way south, to the beery end of Main Street, where all the weirdos walked around. Old hobos would zigzag along the sidewalk, carrying bottles of wine in brown paper sacks, or else they stood under the yellow lightbulbs of the Penny Arcade, waiting for the rowdies inside to flip out cigarette butts. In the shooting galleries the tough sharpshooters with tattoos and ducktails shot the quiet white ducks that went around and around through years of bullets. Once in a while some ace would hit the bell above the ducks, and a loud *piiinng!* rang out, mixing with the honking and the talk. About every two doors there would be a bar, dim and dark inside, but pouring loud talk and hillbilly guitar music out on the sidewalks of the town. I walked in one once where three hillbilly musicians in straw hats were standing behind the bar making music for everyone. The guitar player was picking as loud and fast as he could, till finally the bar girls and drillers and truck drivers and wild cowboys, and all the men and women beering and loving in the cool, dim leathery booths turned their heads to listen and clap. Everybody went to laughing and yelling and slapping down silver on the tables, and on the dance floor the dancers hugged and whirled in the blue darkness and the smoke. The only ones who weren't having a good time were a few lonesome-looking boys at the bar. When the musicians went off to drink beer, the jukebox flared up and played hillbilly dance music the rest of the time I stayed. It played old songs by Hank Williams and Ernest Tubb and Kitty Wells, and it was cold, cold hearts in the darkness with dancers bumping into each other and going on to dance some more. Those that didn't dance sat in the booths and drank from the sweaty bottles of beer. It was no more work and no more lonesome and all the honky-tonk angels living it up. I slipped out and went on past a few more bars, and past the mission and the shouting preachers, and past the pawnshops with their windows full of switchblades and guitars, all the way down to the Mexican picture show. Next to it was a tattoo parlor where I saw a soldier getting a big blue eye tattooed right in the middle of his forehead. By the time I felt ready to start back to the hotel, it was late, and the street wasn't so friendly. The colored men would whisper to me from the steps of the run-down hotels, whispering about women upstairs. Some of the hobos I had seen on my way from the hotel would be sitting spraddle-legged against the buildings, coughing. The lonesome boys that had been in the bars would be leaning on telephone poles or standing by their cars, no one to go to and no one coming along. The bars were quieter, but the same sad music, Kitty and Hank and Ernest, reached out of the doors to pull the boys back in. I saw a few fights, saw cops running into bars, once saw blood on the sandy sidewalk, where a boy had been stabbed. But I even enjoyed the shatter of those nights: things were moving around me, and it was exciting. One night a blonde girl in a pink rodeo hat ran by me and jumped in an Oldsmobile convertible, but her boy friend jumped in and grabbed her before she could get away. He jerked her hand off the ignition and shook her till her hat fell off and her white blond hair was tossed and tangled. "I'll coldcock you, you're just beggin' me to," he said. "Carl, don't, gimme my purse," she said, and he shook her some more. "I'll stomp that bastard's ass," he said. I walked away, back toward the hotel. That same night a crowd of rich city kids came out of a fancy eating place and laughed at me. The boys had flowers on their white coats, and the girls wore long lacy evening gowns. "Cowboys are darlin'," one girl said. That's all right, I thought. They were too silly even to bother giving them the finger. I went on to my room and went to bed. When I turned over I could see the city lights, still red and green and yellow, blinking through the blind; and later, after I had slept awhile, I heard the far-off sound of an ambulance screaming through old Cowtown's morning streets.

It wasn't like what all Jesse had seen, but it was something. I raised up on one elbow under the cedars and looked over the pastures south, toward Fort Worth. Heat waves rose off the land, so that the cars on the highway were blurred. A loose wire was rattling on the yard fence. The front door slammed, and Granddad came out to empty his tobacco can. When he went back in the house he held on to the porch pillar a minute, to steady himself. I got up and brushed the dirt and the cedar needles off my pants. I was thinking that some night I would talk Granddad out of the Lincoln, and Hermy and I and a few other boys could take a quick trip to Fort Worth. If we left early we could make it down there by nine or ten o'clock, and be back by sunup. That would leave plenty of time to do more than we had ever done.

Eight

THE RODEO PEOPLE BEGAN TO MOVE INTO THALIA THE day before the show actually began. That day they brought in the rodeo stock, and the contestants came to town, some of them off the circuit, and some just off the ranches. The poor boys came with nothing but their rigging and a change of clothes, but the winners drove in in big white Lincolns, with fancy horse trailers hitched on behind. The cowgirls came too, wearing big hats, and britches that fitted them like skin fits a snake. I don't guess they ever slept from the time they hit town until the rodeo was over four days later. During all that time there was nothing but beer drinking and rodeo talk, courting and dancing, and even the merchants in Thalia came out in Western wear. Rodeo was the one big get-together of the year.

Since it all came like Christmas, only once a year, I was careful not to let any of it pass me by. The morning of the day before the show I got up before anyone and slipped out of the house and took off for town in the pickup.

I didn't eat any breakfast, so my first stop was Bill's Café. When I got there the place was already full; there were twenty or thirty cars parked out front and more driving up all the time. People were milling around like cattle in a pen. The sun was starting its long climb, the gold rays flashing on the shiny chrome of the cars. From across the highway there was the wet grassy smell of the pastures that surrounded the town. Cowboys in Stetsons and sleeveless shirts were coming out of the café, and others just like them were crowding in. I wandered around among the cars for a while, thrilled with the sound and the people and the cool morning. I walked by a muddy pink Oldsmobile,

'50 model, and saw a girl I knew sprawled like a doll in the back seat. Her long black hair hid her face, and she still had a can of beer in one hand. She heard my feet on the gravel and raised up, her gray eyes blank. "Sugah?" she said. "Why dint you take me in?" She didn't recognize me, but I opened the door and sat down by her a minute. "Throw this out," she said, handing me the beer can. "I'm full." Her name was Irene. She slumped against me and went back to sleep, and I eased her down in the seat and got out. I could hear music from the café, high, loud jukebox music, and I wanted to go inside.

I was lucky to get a seat at the counter. All the booths were full and running over. Everybody was finding friends they hadn't seen for years, or running into people they had seen the night before, and whichever it was, they sat down and talked old times. There were a few thin cowboys at the counter who didn't look so happy; they reminded me of Jesse, or the lonesome boys in the Fort Worth bars; none of it was very exciting to them. I ordered coffee and eggs, and sat there swinging back and forth on my red-topped stool, listening to the music and the roar. Ever time I swung I saw my reflection on the shiny milk machine; my cowlick was sticking up, and I knew if Hermy had seen it he would have kidded me and sung about Jeanie, with the light brown hair like mine. The big jukebox was never quiet, the voices of Slim and Roy and Kitty and Ernest and Hank helping the cowboys grieve or celebrate. The waitresses in clean morning uniforms wove through the tables with gallons of coffee and big platters of eggs. The cowboys in the booths talked the sleep and the beer out of their voices, telling each other about the ride or the women or the long year's work just done. They laughed and whittled toothpicks out of matches. One cowboy with a little too much spirit had brought his rope in with him, but when he started to make a loop his buddies swarmed over him and got it away from him before he could do any damage. When they carried him out he was laughing so hard at himself that he couldn't see. I wished it was rodeo more often, so there'd be more wild breakfasts and strange crowds. I fiddled with my eggs to make it last. A cowboy near me picked his girl up and carried her outside; she laughed and kicked so much her blue shirttail came out of her rodeo pants. When I got outside he was trying to stuff her through the window of his Mercury, and a lot of other fellows were standing around giving him advice and encouragement. He got her in and stood there laughing about it, his hands in his pockets. Then she rolled up the car windows right quick and locked him out.

I went on down to the rodeo arena, to watch them unload the bulls and the bucking stock, but I was a little late. By the time I got there the old humpbacked bulls were standing by the hayracks, pulling out long strands of prairie hay. There were a couple of young guys in rodeo clothes sitting on the fence watching the bulls. I climbed up by them and made their acquaintance. They had come from Cimarron, New Mexico, to ride the bulls.

"Shit, we can't ride no closer to home," one of them said. "If my old man found out my ass would be mud."

The one that said that was a quiet-looking kid. He didn't look much like a bull rider. The other one's name was Sandefer, and he pretty well thought he was it.

"Wait till I get on one a them big bastards," he said. "The fur's gonna fly."

"Whose fur?" the other one said. He didn't really look too thrilled at the prospect of getting on one of the old surlies, and I didn't blame him. Sandefer popped him on the arm to cheer him up. To the right of us, across the arena, the concession people were moving in their popcorn machines and Sno-Cone stands. Some carpenters were hammering behind the chutes; a couple of bulls had got to fighting and torn the gate down. The old gray and black bulls looked lazy and tame as milk cows out there eating hay, but they wouldn't look so gentle when you got 'em crowded into a chute.

I liked to watch the bulls, but I got pretty tired of Sandefer talking like he was Jim Shoulders or Casey Tibbs. I left them on the fence, speculating about which bulls they would draw. There weren't very many people around the arena, and I went to the grandstand and climbed up to the top seats and sat down to watch. I could see beyond the rodeo pens and watch half of Thalia waking up. I saw a woman stagger out to her clothesline in a bathrobe, to hang out an early washing. In the arena below me a cowgirl was loping her paint horse around and around in circles—she acted like it was the only thing she knew how to do. The sun was getting high enough to make my scat uncomfortable, and I got up to go. Even in the mornings I was restless. Below me, in the parking lot a cowboy was trying to get his girl to come through in broad daylight. But she wouldn't. She nearly would, but she wouldn't. Kids were coming down the road to watch the men and horses; they always swarmed around the rodeo people like flies, trying to find someone who would let them ride a horse. I watched the cowboy in the Chevy awhile, and then went down and bought me a plain Sno-Cone before I went back to the ranch.

2.

"Telephone's ringin'," Willie said. "Mistah Hack." We had just finished dinner, and were sitting around the table drinking the last cool swallows of ice tea and listening to the radio. Granddad smiled when he heard Willie come on the air.

"Hack-berry Ho-tel," Willie said. "Willie speakin'."

"Dat niggah," Halmea said.

"It's just a program," I said. "How do you know he ain't a white man?"

"Hell," Hud said, "a white man don't sound that worthless." He was sitting on the wood box picking his teeth. "Turn it over to Fort Worth and get the cattle market."

"Too late," Granddad said. "Nothin' left but the cotton quotations by now."

"That's all right," Hud said. "I'd just as soon hear cotton markets as listen to a nigger jabber. I might go into the cotton business one a these days." He stretched his arms and got up to go to the bathroom. While the program was going on we heard a car rattle the cattle guard and come around to the back of the house. I went to the back door to see who it was.

"It's Mr. Burris," I said.

"Have him come in," Granddad said.

Mr. Burris came to the back door, and I held it open for him. "You missed dinner," I said. "Your timin's off." He nodded and grinned at me, but it was easy to see he was under pretty much of a strain. He didn't walk as light and reckless as he had that first morning. When he got to the dining room he had to go through a little routine with Granddad: Mr. Burris saying he'd had plenty to eat, and Granddad trying to feed him anyway. Hud came in and Granddad introduced him. He said howdy, but he gave Mr. Burris a pretty hard looking over.

"Well, if you won't eat, we may as well move out on the porch," Granddad said. "I believe it's a little cooler out there. I guess you got something to tell us or you wouldn't be here."

Mr. Burris rubbed the back of his head and managed not to say anything. Lonzo slipped off by himself, out the back door, but the rest of us filed out and arranged ourselves on the shady porch. Granddad made Mr. Burris take the rocking chair. We all sat and chewed toothpicks awhile before anything was said.

"Well, I guess the tests are done," Granddad said, finally. He fished in his Levi's for his pocketknife.

"No, sir, actually they aren't," the vet said. "Not completely. It will be at least one more day before we can say for sure what your cattle have got. But we've got a pretty good indication now, and the way things were looking, I thought I ought to run out and talk to you. There hasn't been a sign of sickness in the horses and swine we vaccinated, but a couple of the cattle have already developed blisters. I'm afraid it's going to mean that you've got the worst thing you could have."

Granddad shook his head, and winced a little. He reached out and cut a twig off one of Grandma's hedges, and began to trim it with his knife. "I guess I mighta knowed that," he said. "I guess it didn't make sense to me how a herd of cattle could look as good as mine does and still be half dead."

"I know it's strange," the vet said. "But your cattle aren't half dead, you see. Even if the disease hit ever animal you've got it might not kill over thirty per cent, but the thing is, it might get out and kill thirty per cent of the cattle in the whole area. And the ones it didn't kill wouldn't be worth keeping." He stopped and looked out over the pastures. Hud was watching him, the match still in his mouth.

"And there's no cure atall?" Granddad said.

"None we know of," Mr. Burris said. "It's like a bolt of lightning. It don't hurt you till it hits, but then it hurts a lot."

"Oh me," Granddad said. "I was hopin' it wouldn't come to this. And you don't think there's much chance of anything changing the picture?"

"Very little," the vet said. "I'm afraid it's all but settled now. Technically, we have to wait another day, but I can't offer you any hope."

"Then it's like I said before," Granddad went on. "I'll try an' cooperate with you any way I can, short of killin' my cattle. Just anything. You let me know, and I'll do my best to get it done. If you got any new vaccines you ain't tried out, you're welcome to use these cattle to experiment on, even if it kills ever one of 'em. That way you got a chance a doin' some good. But just drivin' 'em in a pit an' shootin' 'em I can't abide that."

"I know it's a terrible thing," Mr. Burris said, facing Granddad. "Even to think about."

"Yes, it is," Granddad said. "I imagine thinkin' about it's all you ever done, ain't it? Well, sir, I've seen some of it first hand, durin' the depression, an' it's a sight worse to see than it is to think about." Granddad looked small and grizzled and determined, but his voice wasn't as final-sounding as it usually was. He sounded a little old and shaky.

Mr. Burris waited politely till he was through, and then he went right on with what he was saying. Hud watched him, but he never opened his mouth. "I'm sure you're right about that," Mr. Burris said. "I'm sure it is worse to see. But, Mr. Bannon, none of that changes the situation. You got to act how the situation lets you, and in this case you and I are both helpless so far as doing what we'd like to do is concerned."

"Maybe so," Granddad said. "I know there's a lot a times when a man is helpless—I've been in plenty of 'em. But a man's got to go on and do what he can, that's the only way he's got a finding out whether he's helpless or not. In this case I ain't convinced I am. I got a lawyer lookin' into the legal side of this, and he may turn out to know a thing or two you an' I don't."

Mr. Burris was quiet a minute. "I'm afraid you'll be disappointed if you expect much help from the law," he said. "Of course you were right to go see about it. But the law on this has already been argued a good many times, and unless it's something pretty recent that I don't know about, the lawyer will just have to tell you what I'm telling you now. The only thing you can do is liquidate."

"I can't have that," Granddad said. I looked at Hud and noticed a kinda tight grin stretching his mouth. What he was thinking was beyond me to guess.

"But, Mr. Bannon," the vet said, "you may have to have it. Your cattle are public enemies now. Bad enough for you to lose your herd, that I'll grant. You'll be paid a top price for every animal killed, you know that. I imagine it will be something like $300 or $350 a pair. But whatever it is it won't pay you for all the years it took you to breed these animals and get them as good as they are—we both know that. But better you lose them, breed or no breed and pay or no pay, than to have this thing spread and eventually have to kill 75,000 cattle, like they did the last time it got out. It could sure happen, and it probably will unless we handle this thing quick; it probably will."

After that, the conversation died down for a while. Granddad sat hunched over, like he was straining to get something out. The rest of us were just waiting. Granddad looked up, and let his eyes play over the hot noontime pastures, the gray grasslands stretching before him to the east. Finally Mr. Burris decided to try another tack.

"But at least you will be paid good money," he said. "I mentioned that. And after all, Mr. Bannon, you're getting up in years. You can afford to slow down for a year—that's the period of quarantine." Granddad looked up, a little surprised, but Mr. Burris went on. He was trying hard. "Rest won't hurt your grass," he said. "It'll be just that much better for the herd you or these young men put on it. While it's empty you might sell a few oil leases or something. A ranch is more than just the cattle that's on it."

He should have kept quiet, but he didn't know. Granddad leaned back and closed his pocketknife. "Oil," he said, looking down at his hands. "Maybe I could get some, but I don't believe I will. If there's oil down there these boys can get it sucked up after I'm under there with it. Something about this sickness, maybe I can't do much about, but the oil-field stuff I can. I don't like it an' I don't aim to have it. I guess I'm a queer, contrary old bastard, but there'll be no holes punched in this land while I'm here. They ain't gonna come in an' grade no roads, so the wind can blow me away." He looked up again, across the land. "What good's oil to me," he said. "What can I do with it? With a bunch a fuckin' oil wells. I can't ride out ever day an' prowl amongst 'em, like I can my cattle. I can't breed 'em or tend 'em or rope 'em or chase 'em or nothin'. I can't feel a smidgen a pride in 'em, cause they ain't none a my doin'. Money, yes. Piss on that kinda money. I used to think it was all I was after, but I changed my mind. If I'd been in this business just for the money I'd a quit an' started sellin' pencils or something back before you were born. I still like money as well as any man, nearly, and I done with it an' without it as much an' more than most people have, and I don't ever intend to let on I don't want a big share of it. But I want mine to come from something that keeps a man doing for himself."

He stopped, and Mr. Burris sat quietly, looking helpless and nervous. There wasn't much more he could say.

"We're much obliged to you for comin' out an' tellin' us how the tests were goin'," Granddad said. "I wish they were goin' different, but I don't think we'll quit hopin' just yet. Maybe when we get the final word we can get together an' do what's right."

"I'm sure we can," Mr. Burris said, standing up. Granddad walked around to his car with him, and they talked a little more. I stayed with Jesse. Hud disappeared into the house without once opening his mouth.

"Don't sound good," Jesse said. "That talk about lawyers, I guess that's just bluff." We sat on the porch, waiting for orders, but we didn't get any. When Hud came out again he went straight to his car.

"See you rannies," he said. "Don't get sores on your butts."

"Where that feller's going, nobody knows," Jesse said.

Nine

The next day Granddad went to Wichita, I guess to see his lawyers. Lonzo took a notion to enter the saddle-bronc riding contest and hitchhiked into Thalia to sign up. He had an old car, but nine tenths of the time it didn't run. Hud hadn't come in the night before, and nobody had any idea where he was. It looked like such a dull day that I went into town about nine in the morning and shot pool till dinner. The whole town had a rodeo look already, paper cups and beer cans everywhere, and piles of horseshit drying in the street. I shot bank shots until I got tired of leaning over, and then went home to dinner.

The minute we got through eating, Halmea was on Jesse and me to play checkers. She looked kinda worn down, but she claimed to be dying for a game. Jesse kept talking about how he hadn't played in thirty years, but since it was just Chinese checkers, she talked him into coming along.

"Dat's all right," she said. "I always does de best after I lays off a little while."

"Thirty years is a bare bit more than a little while," he said.

We went into her room and she pitched her stack of movie magazines off the card table onto the bed. She had a variety-store picture of Lana Turner on her dresser, and an old lumber-yard calendar with a picture of Jesus holding a lamb, hung on the wall. It was two years old.

"I'll just kick off dese floppy shoes," she said. She shoved them under the bed with her bare feet. We scooted the card table in front of the window, so it would catch what breeze there was.

"Your calendar don't keep very good time," I said.

“It do very well fo’ me,” she said. “It just runs a day a two off.” She got out the Chinese checkerboard and laid it on the old green table. I dropped the marbles in their slots. We decided to play two at a time instead of three, and Jesse elected to watch the first game. He tilted his chair back against the wall. I began to jump Halmea’s marbles right and left.

“Hellation,” she said. “You movin’ too fast.”

“I never played that kind,” Jesse said. “I used to play the other kind a good deal, when Granddad was still alive. I remember once we lived outside of Mineral Wells, down close to the Brazos River. It was a wet winter, and all us kids had to stay inside a lot. I did more checker playing that winter than all the rest of my life put together. Anyhow, it kept Granddad in a good humor, the pore old soul.”

I was moving into Halmea’s triangle with my marbles, in spite of all she could do. She sighed. “I guess I had a grandpappy somewher’,” she said. “But I may not, I don’t know.”

“I remember mine well,” Jesse said. “He got killed that same winter.” I was about as interested in Jesse’s talk as I was in the checker game, but it didn’t take much concentration to beat Halmea. “We were eatin’ breakfast one mornin’,” he said, “and Grandpa wasn’t around. He was always getting up early and going down to a little grocery store, on the highway, right by the river, and we didn’t pay it no mind if he was gone a few minutes. It was a cold, foggy river that morning, and I was on the side a the table away from the fire, about to freeze. Then a feller that worked in the store came running in and took Pa outside and told him Grandpa was dead, down on the highway. That Brazos River fog was pretty thick, and he was walkin’ along too close to the pavement, and some feller from Arkansas came along in a Chevrolet and hit him without ever seein’ him. Knocked him about a hundred feet off the road, and ’bout drove the man who was drivin’ crazy. That was about the time Pa moved us to Lamesa, just before my oldest bud left home.”

Halmea shook her head and twisted her feet around the chair legs. “Sheew,” she said. “White folks families beats me. I ’member seein’ my own pappy just six, seven times. Dey no tellin' where dat man is now. He may be dead as you grandpappy."

"Don't you keep up?" Jesse said.

"How you gonna keep up?" she said. "A gal can't tag him aroun'."

And they went on that way, talking back and forth, while I beat Halmea four or five times. After a while they got on the differences between white folks parties and colored folks parties, and Halmea got tickled remembering all the funny things she'd seen, till she couldn't hold the marbles for giggling and laughing about them. The marbles began to pop off and roll around on the floor, and she kept on laughing, and so finally Jesse had to take her place. He wasn't as bad about laughing, but he was more interested in the talk than in the checker playing, so when it was all over, about three o'clock, I was the undisputed Chinese-checker champion of the ranch. Halmea and Jesse were in about the best mood of their lives, and all the chuckling and fine friendly talk and the games I won made me feel good too. Finally Halmea had to go hang out a washing, and I went to the house and flopped on the living room couch, feeling loose and lazy. I felt good about Halmea and Jesse, and I dozed off to sleep.

2.

About four-thirty or five that afternoon, Halmea woke me up to tell me she was going off to a fish fry with some colored boy. I said okay, and thought no more about it. She said our supper was in the stove. Then about six-thirty, when I was dressing to go to the rodeo, Hud came home. Granddad was still gone, and I couldn't leave till he came home. Jesse had taken the colt into town in the pickup, and I would have to use the Lincoln. I was in the downstairs bathroom when I heard a car door slam, and I thought it might be Granddad. But when I opened the bathroom door and heard all the slamming and banging in the kitchen, I knew it must be Hud, and nobody else.

When I went in he was yanking out the kitchen drawers, and pawing in the breadbox. His shirt was open all the way down his stomach, and he looked like he hadn't shaved in a week. A bottle of Hiram Walker sat on the kitchen table; it was better than two-thirds empty. Hud looked about the meanest I'd ever seen him, his hair all tangled, and his face tight and wild. It scared me a little, just seeing him.

"Where's that nigger?" he said. "I want supper an' I don't want no hesitatin' about it."

"She went to a fish fry," I said. "The supper's in the stove."

"Well, if that ain't a fragrant pile of shit," he said. "A fine bunch around here. Payin' her money to run off to a fish fry when I'm starvin' to death. I'd like to get ahold a that bitch." Granny must have heard him all the way to her room, because she came hobbling in. She looked pretty scared herself.

"There's plenty here," she said. "I'll fix you some. You sit down."

"Screw it," he said. "Sit down yourself. When I come in from a trip I want my meal on the table, not waitin' to be fixed. If this ain't a homecomin'."

"Where all did you go?" she asked.

"What's it to you?" he said, picking up his whiskey bottle. "Wait an' be surprised like the rest of 'em."

He was too wild-acting to fool with, and we both shut up. He was shifting back and forth on his feet, like a bull that had been crowded too close. "Well, get it on the table," he said. Granny began to jump around like she was twenty-five years old, and I left them and went out on the porch. I wanted to go to town, but I didn't have a way to leave. I stood on the porch and watched the cars go flashing across the land. I was wishing I had one. Then there were steps in the living room behind me, and Hud came out. "She's got tea to make yet," he said, sitting down on the steps. He had his whiskey bottle.

"Gettin' dark," he said. His voice was a little looser, but still mean. "I'll tell you, I like lots of light. I was over there in the jungle and had to lay out one night by myself, dark as hell and Japs all around me. Ever since then it's been piss on the dark."

"I got a deal goin'," he said. "It's gonna knock some people on their asses, an' you might be one of 'em."

"Wouldn't take much to knock me," I said.

"Sure as hell wouldn't," he said, grinning, "Get your ass outa here. I can't think good with you around."

I didn't argue. I decided I'd go see if I could get Lonzo's Hudson started; he didn't care for me using it if I could. He must not have tried it himself, because it started right off for me. On the way to Thalia I met Granddad, driving along the highway as slow as the big Lincoln would go. He knew he was getting pretty old to be driving, and he took it pretty easy. When I got back to the ranch myself, eight hours later, I had seen the first night of the rodeo. It was a slow, dragging show, but I had a lot of fun fooling around behind the chutes, talking to Hermy and the other boys. I even found a girl to take to the dance, and we stayed till it was over. When I got home I was pretty well worn out. The house was dark, and my sheets were hot. I went to the bathroom and got a glass of water and sprinkled them down, but the night was sultry hot, and they didn't stay cool.

3.

I was sitting up in bed. A wild yell woke me. At first I was groggy, and I thought I had dreamed it, but then I heard it again and I knew it was Hud. It was bright moonlight outside, but I couldn't tell where the yelling was coming from. I got out of bed and felt around for my clothes. I thought he had been staggering around drunk and got on a rattlesnake. As soon as I found my boots I hurried down to the kitchen and put them on. Then I got the big flashlight out of the pantry, and the twenty-two out of the gun closet. But it was so light in the back yard I really didn't need the flashlight, and I shoved it in my hip pocket. The dogs were standing by the yard gate, listening and growling. Then I heard Hud's voice again, loud and rough in the still night. He wasn't yelling any more he was just talking loud. He was in Halmea's room. The light was on. I heard his voice again, and I started for the room. I saw the yellow patch of light that fell on her wooden steps. My legs were trembly, and I put a shell in the chamber. I knew what I'd see when I got there, but I didn't know what I could do. When I was halfway down the trail I saw Jesse step quickly into the light and go inside; he just had on his pants and undershirt. Then I heard Halmea crying and trying to say something, but her voice got mixed with Hud's, and the sound they made was very loud against the stillness of the pastures.

I didn't go to the door, like Jesse had. I went to the window I could see them as plain as day, not two yards from me, Hud and Halmea. They were on the bed, and Hud had wrestled her part way under him. Halmea's face was turned toward me, she was trying to curl toward the wall; her eyes were shut, and the squeezed out tears wet her cheeks. She was trying to jab at Hud with her elbow, to roll away from him, but he wouldn't let her. He had made her naked from her feet to her breasts, and he was laying across her brown twisting legs, trying to catch her hand. He had his cheek against her side, but he raised up, and I saw that he was grinning his old wild grin. He kept shoving at Halmea's white nightgown, trying to shove it over her head, but it was all wadded up around her breasts. I couldn't see Jesse anywhere, and I raised the twenty-two and pointed it at Hud. Then Hud laughed, his teeth white and strong in his whiskered face. "Now, you bitch," he said, and I knew I ought to shoot him and I knew I couldn't. Halmea's eyes were still shut and her mouth was twisted, but she didn't try to holler. "Just rest easy," Hud said. He smothered her arm against his chest and brought his hand over her shoulder and hit her with the heel of it, hard in the face, like he might hit a mare and she grunted with the hurt of it, and gritted her teeth as if she thought he was about to hit her again. Blood came in the corner of her mouth, but she was still trying to roll and kick. "Wild bitch, ain't you?" Hud said, grinning again. He turned her, then, and jammed his big knee down between her naked legs, and he laughed. The blood was pounding through my head so I could barely think. I wanted to shoot Hud and not be afraid of him any longer, but I couldn't think to, I just stood there watching. Then Hud slipped his hand up under the wadded white gown and caught and squeezed one of Halmea's breast, and then mashed it and she groaned when he did. She said, "Oooah," and I shot the gun. I shot and the bullet tore through the screen above them and thunked into the wall on the other side of the room. I couldn't shoot to hit him; I guess I thought just any shot would end it. He rolled off Halmea and I saw her brown body twist as she turned toward the wall. Then I cocked the gun and went around to the door, but even before I got there Hud was out and grabbed me, yanked at the screen and shoved me inside, into the yellow light. He was still grinning. "You little fucker," he said. "Come in where you can watch the show." I stumbled on the linoleum, and he was behind me, he shoved or backhanded me, I was on the floor, up against the wall, half under the card table, my eyes still open, the gun on the floor at the foot of the bed. Jesse was laying on the linoleum, by the bed, not moving. Hud shook the tangled hair out of his eyes, his hands at his Levi's buttons; he was looking at Halmea—he didn't even glance at Jesse or me. Halmea was curled right against the wall; there was a long raw scratch on her naked back. "Turn over here, nig," Hud said, grinning; he grabbed one of her ankles. "Here's half the menfolks on this ranch come to help you," he said. "The other half's slower and lazier. I guess they'll be along in a minute. I'll stack 'em up two deep 'fore I'm done with you." I sat against the wall, a ringing like a seashell in my head. I wondered where Granddad was, if he was up. Halmea uncurled and began to kick at Hud with both feet; her eyes were open and her bloody lips squeezed tight together. But Hud leaned over and slapped her on the gut with his open hand and the air whoosed out of her mouth and he grabbed her other ankle and pulled her around him while she tried to get wind. Halmea turned her head toward me, and when she did Hud put both hands on her face and held her down while he shoved and shoved, and I could hear her choking for wind and I could hear Hud's breath, but not my own and not Jesse's, and I could see the dark blood from Halmea's mouth trickling down the sheet toward the part of her that was under Hud. I didn't move or blink, but then Hud was standing up grinning at me; he was buckling his ruby belt buckle. "Ain't she a sweet patootie?" he said. He whistled and began to tuck his pants legs into the tops of his red suede boot. Halmea had curled toward the wall, and the blood on the sheets was smeared.

"Now let that be a lesson to you," Hud said. He was calm and loose-looking. He was talking to Halmea, but he held out one hand to me, as if he wanted to help me up. "You keep gallivantin' aroun' without tellin' me, I'll sure as hell do it agin. Cause now on, I'm the boss. Not Homer Bannon, not fantan there, not Ma. Me. Mister Scott. The boss." He turned and went out the door without looking back. Before I could move, Halmea jumped off the bed, her face wilder than Hud's had been.

"Where dat gun?" she said. She grabbed it off the floor and went to the steps and shot three times into the darkness. She quit, and I heard Hud laughing. She shot twice more and clicked the gun two or three times before she knew it was empty; then she dropped it on the steps and went back to the bed. We heard the rough roar of Hud's mufflers, the last time I ever heard them.

Halmea was wiping the blood off her mouth with the sheet, and I began to get up. She squatted down and bent over Jesse, rolled him on his back. When she did he put out a hand like he wanted to be helped up, but his eyes were still shut. I saw a big reddening spot on his jaw. Halmea sat down and propped his head on her leg.

"Honey, if you okay, wet me a rag," she said, not looking up. I found one hanging over the lavatory, and dampened it for her. When she rubbed Jesse's face he began to blink a little, but he wasn't conscious.

"He got hit bad," she said. "Just as he come in de do'."

I wet the rag again, and finally we got Jesse to open his eyes. He didn't say a word; he sat against the edge of the bed and put one hand up to shade himself from the yellow light. Halmea went to the lavatory to wash the blood out of her mouth. When she came back we helped Jesse stand up.

"Can't clear my head," he whispered. I let him lean on me. "I need to lie down awhile, I think I'd be all right," he said. Halmea took one arm and I took another and we managed to ease him down the steps. He seemed a little steadier then, and she went back. He held onto me and I helped him across the dark chicken yard to the bunkhouse. "I'm gonna lose my beer," he said. "Can't get my head back on right." When I got him to his cot he began to pull off his undershirt. "Much oblige," he said. "Oh me." He lay back and I turned off the lights and went out into the cool. My own head was throbbing and my neck was stiff, but I felt clear.

Halmea hadn't turned the light out in her cabin, so I went back to see what I could do. She was laying on the bed where Hud had just had her, her face in the crook of one arm. She snuffled something when I spoke at the door, and I went in. She didn't look around, and I didn't know anything to say. I sat down on the edge of the bed and waited. I could see the wetness glisten on her wrists and hands. In a minute she felt me on the bed and looked up, her eyes red and puffed.

"Ise sho down," she said.

"It's over," I said, patting her lightly on the shoulder. I saw three or four cut places on her shoulder and side, where Hud had scratched her in the scuffle. Blood was sticking to her cotton nightgown.

"Oh, it oveh," she said. "Lot a good dat do."

"He was just so drunk," I said.

"Shit," she said, and she sat up suddenly, her lip turned down so I could see the gash on its underside. "Don't gimme dat drunk talk. Mistah Hud wasn't drunk. An' drunk don't mean he can come in an' do dat to somebody."

Her face was beginning to puff where he had hit her, and it occurred to me that she might be hurt really bad. I went and got the washrag for her—it was all the medicine in the cabin—but she was too mad and stirred up to use it.

"Should I take you to town?" I said. "Do you need a doctor?"

"Hush," she said. She stood up, looking so beaten and raw and tired that I didn't know what to do. "I'm gonna wash dem cuts," she said, not noticing the clean rag I had just wet for her. She got another one, but she couldn't reach the cut on her back. I took the rag from her and daubed it clean, while she held her nightgown up.

"I bettah get my suitcase," she said. "I leavin' in de mornin'."

"But you don't need to go," I said. "The law can take care of Hud."

She frowned at me, still raw and angry. "Hush about de law," she said. "No law gonna hear about dis, you see dey don't. Tell de law, dey have it my fault befo' you turn aroun'. I seen dat kinda law befo'."

"But don't run off," I said. "He'll leave you alone."

She snorted. "You see him leave me alone," she said. "He leave me alone good aftah he done wit' me." Then she softened up and began to cry. "Heah, I helpless," she said. "Dat gets me. He come in heah aftah me an' do what he did. Nobody stop him dis time, nobody gonna stop him next time. I seen him come in de do'. Dere I is, I knowed it too. He done told me he'd be dere, plenty times. I thought, dat's just Mistah Hud, he ain't gonna come. But he do come, an' dere you is. Next time he come to dis girl, he gonna have a long trail to follow, I know dat."

"Halmea," I said. "Halmea, don't you go off and leave us. We need you around here. I sure do. I want you to stay."

But she looked farther from me than she ever had. "You get along okay," she said, and it wasn't me, her old honey, she was saying it to. "You see," she said. So I left her and picked up the gun and the flashlight and took them back where they belonged.

I went up to my room and undressed and got in bed, but I didn't even think about going to sleep. My head had started aching, and I felt a little sick at my stomach. I kept seeing Halmea stretched on her bed naked, and Hud wrestling her under him. I knew he didn't do it because he was drunk. He did it because he wanted to get her down and job it in her. I knew he wanted to get Halmea; he'd told me so plenty of times. I remembered how she was crying that night he got home from Temple; how he had caught her in the kitchen and pinched her teats. What bothered me was I had wanted to do pretty much the same thing to Halmea. I didn't want to do it mean, like Hud did everything, but I wanted to do it to her. I was shaking, lying there in bed. And Hud would always do the thing he wanted to do, whether it hurt anybody or not; Hud just did what he intended to do. Watching him screw Halmea, I should have killed him, but didn't. I stood back and I waited. Wanted to watch. I was shaking more, lying there. I did like Halmea so much; she was one of the best people there ever was, and I could see her so many different ways when she was the Halmea I liked. But now I could only see her naked, pinned there on the bed, like a heifer Hud had thrown down to work over or to splay; I could see her haunch and her breasts and Hud grabbing at her ankles. It made me feel sorry for her and yet want to watch at the same time; and I got more miserable, turning over and over trying to get comfortable. Finally I shoved open the screen and vomited down the side of the house. I was thinking how I wanted to do good things for Halmea and never do a mean thing to her, but I couldn't get over wanting to wallow her. I thought of her that day she brought the lemonade and set it by my bed when I felt sick; and I remembered the streak of flour had been white on her forehead. I wanted to thank her for that and do something nice for her on account of it. But even thinking about the lemonade, what I remembered most, more than the tall sweaty glass or the icy juice or her cool fingers on my forehead, was the dark tight tops of her breasts as she stooped over. Thinking of all that made me want to cry, and I turned over again and wished I could find a way to get peace. I wished I could get together with Halmea somewhere way off from the ranch, where we could just talk. If we could, I might think of a way to let her know all the different things I thought about her that night; maybe she would have known what was silly about them, and what was right and good. Anyway, we could have talked. Finally, my head eased a little ,and I quit tossing and turning and worrying so much. The moon was still high up in the west, shedding its faint white light over Granddad's pastures, and I lay with my face to the window watching the night till I fell to asleep.

4.

Halmea cooked breakfast in her town clothes the next morning. We were a tired-looking bunch, all of us except Grandma; she was as full of energy as ever. Hud wasn't there, and Jesse was feeling too bad to eat much. Granddad took it all in, but he didn't ask any questions while we were eating. We were drinking our coffee when Halmea came in and gave notice.

"I needs to be leavin' today," she said. "If Mistah Lonnie or somebody kin haul me inta town. I can stay till somebody else comes if you-all just have to have me, but I needs to leave today."

"Why goodness," Granddad said. "Why you quittin' us so sudden? Ain't we been treatin' you right?"

"Some is," she said, not looking at him. "But I needs to go."

"Now I wouldn't do that," Jesse said. "I think things will be all right. No use you worryin'."

"I ain't worryin'," she said. "Ise just quittin'."

She washed the dishes and I drove her into Thalia. Grandma took on about it some, but Halmea didn't pay her any mind at all. During the ride in, we both kept pretty quiet. She seemed awful far away, still blank and raw outside and in.

"What you gonna do?" I said finally. "Just sit home?"

"I get me a job someplace," she said. "I'm gonna take a trip, de first thing. I spect I go see my sistah in Oklahoma City. Might just stay up dere an' work."

Every day the Trailways Bus stopped in Thalia, and it had Oklahoma City on the sign in front of it. But to me it was just another of those unseen towns down the highway, a place where some roads ended and others began. I couldn't imagine Halmea living there.

I pulled up in front of the little unpainted house where her aunt lived, and helped her carry the few bags and boxes up to the porch. Her aunt was in the side yard, hoeing her garden; she was chopping the tomato plants along with thc goat heads and weeds. She was so blind and deaf she didn't even notice us all the time we were moving the boxes.

"Ain't she a sight," Halmea said. "She choppin' dem pea vines like dey wus weeds." She stood on the steps, and I stood below her in the brown, clean-swept yard, my hands empty. She kept fiddling with the belt on her blue-and-white dress.

"You tell you grandpa I sholy sorry to leave," she said. "Specially to leave so quick like. But I just needs to go. Help him out, he gettin' old an' feeble now. He your job all de time." She seemed so blue and sad, and I knew she wished I'd go on home; but I was choked up and I hated to leave. "You get into town, why, come an' see me." she said. "You be welcome."

"When you leavin'?" I asked.

"Leavin' where?" she said.

"To go to Oklahoma City."

"Oh lawdy," she said, "I just said dat. I may not go anywhere. An' den I may. I be here awhile." She grinned a puffy grin at me and stepped up on the old board porch. "Go on to work," she said. "Don't be lazy."

"Well, I'll see you," I said. "You take it easy."

She nodded, and I got in and drove on to town, to the pool hall. I intended to put in the morning shooting, but the place was empty except for Dumb Billy. I didn't feel like practicing, so I went on home.

I didn't figure Granddad would have anything to do, but my figuring was off. It turned out to be a good thing for me that the pool hall was empty. When I got to the ranch my horse was saddled and tied to the feed rack, and there was a note fluttering from the note pin on the lot gate. It didn't take long to read:

> LONNIE—
> Come on to the West pasture. We got to round the cattle up again. Get you a big drink, it will be a miserable day.
> YOUR GRANDDAD

When I was mounted, I noticed the bulldozers. There were eight or ten of them, sitting out in the old grown-over field we never used. By the time I was a mile from the barn they had cranked up, and you could hear them all over the prairie. Huge clouds of dust began to roll out of the fields, and I knew they must be scraping out pits. Even so, I didn't believe it. I didn't believe Granddad had given up, and I still didn't believe it when I saw him.

But whether he had or not, he was right about the day. We rounded them all up again, and worked till after dark to do it. Only this time, when we came in worn out and hungry, there wasn't any Halmea to serve us steak and beans and cherry pie.

Ten

THE ROOM WAS STILL DARK WHEN I FELT GRANDDAD'S hand on my shoulder. "Time to get up, son," he said. I turned over, but I didn't think I could possibly get up and work without a little more sleep. There wasn't the least sign of morning in the yard; the moon hung somewhere over the house, still covering the pastures with dim milky light.

I was asleep, but I got up anyway and staggered around dressing. When I got downstairs, Granddad was standing by the stove, frying eggs, and the men were just coming in the back door. Hank Hutch was with them, and he began to help Granddad with the cooking. The bawling that had gone on all night was sparser now, the old cows finally bedded down. I drank some milk and began to put away bacon and eggs. Granddad finally left the stove and ate, without saying a word. Hud was not there.

Granddad was the first one through with breakfast, and the rest of us had to hurry our coffee and follow him out of the house. Dawn was still aways off, but a timid grayness was coming in the eastern sky. We caught our horses in the dark lots, and led them out to be saddled. Then I saw several sets of headlights coming across the pastures; the drivers were honking, trying to get the old cows to move out of the road.

"Here they come," Graddad said. "At least they'll be on time." He sighed heavily, fiddling with his flank girt. "I'd rather take a beatin'," he said.

There was nothing to do but mount up and start the cattle toward the pits. It was just light enough then that I could see the brush, and make out the cattle, where they stood in bunches in the early mist. I went on the very outside of the pasture, right next to the fence, and shoved the cattle down to the inside men. The horse pasture was only a section, and it didn't take very long to go around it. The line of men inside shouted and yelled, to keep the cattle moving, and the cows moved off in strings toward the big tank. Behind me the rim of the plain was reddening, the sun creeping close to the surface. I topped a little ridge, the highest ground in the pasture, and saw the whole drive spread out below me. The first red streamers of light were dusty and brilliant on the green mesquite. Banks of mist rose from the dewy grass and hung gray around the bellies of the moving cattle. Hank was next to me; Jesse next to him; then Lonzo, popping the reins of his bridle against his chaps; Cecil Goad and his boys farther away; and Granddad, small and farthest of all, sitting on the other side of the tank watching his herd come down to water. I could hear Cecil yelling at the cattle: "Commence agoing." When we got to the tank the cows and calves walked into the shallows, splashing the clean gold sheet of the tank. They were already slinging slobber over their shoulders at the flies. Less than a mile away the pits were waiting. It was like a picture: me, the men, the fresh leafy range, the Bannon herd trailing into water, Granddad watching. I rode on to the tank and let my horse splash in among the cows. Granddad sat above me on the dam, his hands folded on the saddle horn, his horse standing quiet. The sun flashed on Stranger's bright coat, and showed Granddad burning clear. Then he waved at Hank and Jesse, and I whirled to the drive. Horses and cattle stirred the water to foam. We left the tank, and in no time were almost to the pits. Granddad dropped out of the drive when we went past the barn. I figured he went after the two longhorns and the old bull. He had shut them up the night before. But he came back with just the two milk cows. With all the help we had the cattle were easy to handle. Then the pits were in front of us, gaping in the old rocky field, each pit with one end sloped and one end steep. The cattle paid them little mind; they went right on down the sloped ends, curious to see what they'd find at the bottom.

I was stationed at the slope end of the next to last pit west. I was supposed to keep anything from coming back up. Cecil Goad's boy held the pit next to mine. The cattle were standing quietly in the bottom, the calves sucking, the cows licking themselves and their calves. Then one of the state men came up behind me and stepped to the edge of the pit. He had a clip-action rifle in his hand; a thirty-ought-six.

"Hi, son," he said. "I hope this won't shy your horse."

"It may." I said. "I never shot off him atall."

He was a short gray-headed man, as nice as his job would let him be. "Ride off a little piece when I start shootin'," he said. "Won't nothin' come outa this pit." He spread a rag on the ground and laid several extra clips on it, glancing ever minute or so at the cattle. "Fine bunch a cows," he said.

Then the first shot sounded behind us, and my horse jumped and reared. The man dropped on one knee and began shooting, and the hungry young heifers fell. In a second I couldn't hear anything for the sound and the bawling; all I could do was fight my snorting horse as close to the pit mouth as possible. The guns went off constantly, and the horse was crazy with scare. Finally he hung his head and stood quivering, every muscle tight. Dust rose from the pits so thick it was a miracle the gunners could see to shoot. The cattle below bunched tight together, bellering and milling in a welter of dust and blood. Nothing did them any good. The man with the gun was deadly. The second one clip emptied he had another one in and was leveling the gun. The biggest old cows fell like they had been sledge-hammered; they kicked a time or two, belched blood into the dust, lay still. Not one in my pit got up. A calf dashed toward us and the man swung the gun and knocked it back on the body of a horned cow, its hind legs jerking. The old cows rolled their eyes and spun around and around. Not for a minute did the dust or noise settle. Finally the last animal in the pit stood facing us, a big heifer. She was half hemmed in by the sprawled carcasses. She took one step toward us, head up, and the man fired, slamming her backward like a telephone pole had bashed her between the eyes. She lay on her side, one foreleg high in the air. The man took out his clip and went quickly to another pit, to help. I was as tight as my horse; I was sick of the heat, and of the dust smells and gunpowder and thin manure. I tried to spit the putrid taste out of my mouth, and couldn't. The flies were already buzzing around the hot carcasses, the shit bugs swarming on the green puddles. The Goad boy was vomiting all over a young mesquite bush, but I didn't feel sick that way; I just felt suffocated by the dust and sound, like my throat was filling up with sand. I saw Granddad, sitting on Stranger at the head pit. He pointed and some gunner sent another bullet into some straining animal. The noise began to scatter, just a finishing shot or two. Granddad was sitting still, his hands on the saddle horn. For a second all I could hear was the scraping bolts, as the gunners cleared their magazines. Then it was silent and hot.

Jesse was on his horse, at the third pit; he was talking to Hank Hutch. I rode by him on my way to the barn, and heard him talking in a watery voice, but what he said got away from me. Hank loped up beside me before I got to the barn, and we rode in together.

"Didn't take long," I said.

He was the quietest I'd ever seen him. "Don't take very long to kill things," he said. "Not like it takes to grow."

The rest of the men rode up behind us. They tied their horses and we all walked over to the water trough to drink. The two old steers and the old bull stood in the little feed pen, lazily pulling oat straw out of the hayrack. Mr. Burris and his driver walked up while we were drinking the cold water, and I offered him a cup. He drank and handed the cup to Thompson. In a minute Granddad tied Stranger and came over.

"Well, I was agonna keep them three," he said, pointing to the old cattle. "But I guess it wouldn't do much good; they'd just get lonesome. Three head ain't much of a herd."

"And they ain't none a them cows," he added, pulling off his gloves.

"They make good animals to have around," Hank said. "They remind you of the time when the government didn't have to run a man's business for him."

Granddad shook his head. "Hell," he said. "If the time's come when I got to spend my time lookin' back, why, I'd just as soon go under. I ain't never got much kick outa my recollections. Maybe I'll learn, I don't know."

"Goddamn," Thompson said. "We missed three. You-all stay here I'll take care of 'em." He started toward his car.

"Where do you think you're agoin', Mister," Granddad said. Thompson stopped and looked at him, unsure.

"To finish this job," he said. "Somebody needs to."

"You just come back here," Granddad said. "I'll kill them three myself, seein' as I raised 'em. Get me the rifle, son," he said to me.

But Thompson fidgeted. He didn't quite have the nerve to go on after his gun, but he wanted to awful bad. "There ain't no guarantee you'd do it," he said.

"I just said I would," Granddad said.

"Shit," Thompson said, turning toward his car.

He had his hand on the door when Mr. Burris came awake. "You get in that car," he said. "We're going down and see about burning these carcasses, and then we're leaving. Mr. Bannon can take care of the rest of this without us bothering him."

I stepped to the pickup and got the thirty-thirty we kept behind the seat, to use on coyotes. There were shells in it, but I got a box out of the glove compartment, just in case. Thompson got in the Chevy and said no more, but Mr. Burris still stood by the water trough, looking uncomfortable. He was twisting one of the leather buttons on his jacket. We could all feel him straining for something to say.

"Now you go on, Mr. Burris," Granddad said quietly. "I know this here ain't your doin's. I imagine you got enough worries without takin' on any a mine. I'll last over this here. You just see about the burnin', and then get that feller there off my ranch."

"Well, all I can say is I'm sorry," Mr. Burris said. "I'm sure sorry."

"So'm I," Granddad said. "Things are just put together wrong. There's so much shit in the world a man's gonna get in it sooner or later, whether he's careful or not. But you go ahead, we ain't mad at you." He held out his hand, and he and Mr. Burris shook.

"Well, I'll be back to see you about the payments," Mr. Burris said. He got in and they drove off, dust hanging over the car.

"He ain't such a bad feller," Granddad said. "Just got a shitter of a job." He came over and took the gun from me. Then he went to the feed pen, Jesse and Hank and me following. The two old outlaws stood across the lot from us, as far away as they could get, the bright morning sun flashing on their horns. The old cherry-backed bull still stood by the hayrack, his eyes shut, chewing the yellow oat straw slowly. Tiny sprigs of hay clung to his white dewlap.

"They'll never grow stock like them old fieries agin," Hank said. Granddad stood with one hand in his pocket, the other holding the gun.

"I never will," he said. "Lord, but I've chased them two steers many a mile." His voice was even. "I don't know if I can kill 'em," he said. "But I guess I can. Goddamnit. I'll just do it right here and you fellers can tie onto 'em an' drag 'em down about the hill somewhere to burn 'em. You-all go to the pump and draw me three five-gallon cans a gas, so we can burn 'em quick. I'll handle this end of the operation."

The other men were sitting around the corner of the barn, not saying much. We didn't speak to them as we went by.

"I don't think he'll kill those cattle," I said to Jesse. "He's had 'em too long." We found some cans in the smokehouse and went to the pump, all of us listening for the shots.

"Yes, he will," Hank said. "He'll do it for sure."

Then, with two cans full and the third filling, we heard the first sharp shot, and its echo bouncing back off Idiot Ridge. All the bloody smells of the morning came back on me, and I got the weak trembles. I imagined the old steer in the lots, knocked to his side, the old horns closer and closer to the dust. And Granddad, as old as the steer, sighting down the bright barrel. I sat down by one of the gas cans, on the short dusty grass.

"I told you he would," Hank said.

Jesse watched the gas pump and didn't say anything. Then the second shot came, and there was only one to wait for.

"Just the bull left," Hank said. "Piss on it, we might as well go back."

Old Domino left then, still standing at the hayrack eating the yellow hay. Then I saw that Jesse and Hank were gone, and I got up to follow. Hank had taken my can.

We got to the water trough and two shots came; came fast as the gun could lever, and their echoes bouncing off the ridge as one. The four of them were in the lot, Granddad squatting by the fallen bull, his hands clasped between his knees, his old felt hat pulled down. The rifle leaned against the hayrack.

"Took two shots," Hank said. "Them old bulls is hard to kill."

I trailed one hand in the water, wetting my shirt sleeve. I thought he might as well be dead with them, herd and herdsman together, in the dust with his cattle and Grandmother and his old foreman Jericho Green. Then Granddad came out of the lots, the gun in his hand. The steers and the bull lay where we all could see them, the flies free at last to crawl on their unmoving heads. All of us stood by the fence: Jesse and Hank, Lonzo, Cecil and Clement, Silas and John. "Burn the sonsabitches," Granddad said. He handed me the thirty-thirty, and turned to the neighbors. "Much obliged, you fellers," he said. "Until you're better paid." Then he walked to the house.

Eleven

I WENT INTO TOWN THAT NIGHT, HOPING THE SECOND rodeo performance would be better than the first. I asked Granddad if he wanted to go with me, but he just shook his head. He hadn't said two words to anybody since the killing. Right after supper both he and Granny went to bed. The killing seemed to take as much starch out of Granny as it did out of the rest of us—or maybe what did it with her was having to cook for a change. She drove into Thalia to hire somebody, but she hadn't found a girl that suited her.

When I got to the rodeo arena a long line of people were filing by the ticket office. As I walked through the hundreds of parked cars I saw the cowboys beginning their night. They stood in groups by the open turtlebacks, drinking cans of cold beer. The girls stood with them, shaking their combed heads and peeping at themselves in the rear-view mirrors. The contestants who were really in rodeo for the money were squatting on the ground checking their rigging; but most of the boys were just there for beer and excitement. I saw Irene talking to a bunch of girls, and thought maybe I'd hunt her up later on in the night. I wanted to get the ranch completely off my mind.

I already had my ticket, so I walked in and headed for the bucking chutes. I knew most of the boys would be there, sizing up the bulls and talking. Riding a bull was the kind of thing you did to prove you didn't give a shit. Going past the Sno-Cone stand I ran into Hermy. We stood there a minute watching a couple of drunk cowboys try to date the pretty black-haired woman who was making the hot dogs. Hermy hit me on the shoulder.

"When you-all movin' out?" he said.

I was watching the cowboys, and I didn't understand him. "Hell, I just came in," I said.

"Naw," he said. "I mean Hud's deal."

"You got me," I said. "I don't know what you're talkin' about."

"No shit?" he said. He began to fiddle with his belt buckle and kick his boot toe in the dirt. "Maybe I shouldn't be spreadin' rumors," he said.

"What'd he do?" I said. "Is he in jail?"

"Not by a long shot. He's around on the north side of the arena, sittin' in a new Cadillac. And he ain't the only one sittin' in it."

"Who else?" I said.

"The prettiest bitch you ever saw," he said. "Truman Peters' wife."

I just shook my head. I didn't doubt it for a minute. "Yeah," Hermy said. "This'll knock you on your ass. They say he screwed Truman some way and sold him part of your Granddad's ranch. Won a lot of money off Truman in a card game and went and bought the car and came back and got Truman a little drunker and sold him some kind of crazy option on the ranch."

"Aw, I don't believe that," I said. "He couldn't a sold anything. Even Truman Peters wouldn't fall for anything like that." Truman was an oilman, a multimillionaire, reckless as hell with his money. His wife had been a movie star before she married Truman.

"A lot of 'em say it wasn't legal," Hermy said. "But some of 'em say Hud's just slick enough to get away with it."

"Naw, it couldn't a been legal," I said. But knowing Hud, I didn't feel too sure. When he was running wide open he was a hard man to stop, and with Granddad so discouraged over the herd, and old anyway, I didn't know if he could set Hud down again.

"Anyhow," Hermy said, "Hud's supposed to a won $80,000 dollars from Truman just playin' cards."

"I'm going around an' see him," I said. "Come go with me."

"No," he said. "I got a bull to ride in the first go-round. Better be careful. They say Truman's gonna be after Hud with a gun for runnin' off with his wife."

"You be careful," I said. "You're the one's gonna be on a bull."

It didn't take me long to find the Cadillac. It was a long cream-colored job, parked right next to the bandstand where the little high-school band was warming up. Hud and the woman weren't even facing the arena.

"Hey," I said. "Can I talk to you a minute?"

He turned from her and squinted at me. "Why hello, hotrod," he said. "What's with you?"

"I won't bother you long," I said.

"You goddamn sure won't," he said. "Come around here and get in."

I got in the front seat, beside them. The car was dark and cool on the inside, smelling of new leather upholstery and whiskey. Hud was smooching the woman, but he broke off when I got in.

"You remember his dad, don't you, Lily?" he said. "Dan Bannon. The pride a the fuckin' prairie." She and I looked at each other through the dimness. She was an awful pretty woman, I thought. Her long blond hair fell down past her shoulders, and she looked at me without smiling. Hud had unbuttoned the front of her red dress, and I could see the tops of her breasts and the white cups of her brassiere, the rodeo lights from above us throwing a strange glow across her on her hair. She had grown up in a little town near Thalia.

"Aw yea," she said. "I remember Dan. Me and him was sweethearts about two weeks one time." She laid her hand on Hud's leg. Hearing her mention my father made the hair bristle on my neck.

"If you're pissed off, get your ass out," Hud said. "No, I ain't really sold the ranch, but I got some money for it. When I do get it from Homer, then I'll see whether Truman can have it or not. The nice thing is, don't nobody but me know what I've done." The woman's dress was wadded up in her lap, and Hud was rubbing her long bare leg, his hand sliding up and down.

"You moving us off?" I asked, and he leaned back and laughed.

"You ain't that lucky," he said. "Hell, no. If I do ever sell Truman the land I got a deal rigged where I can lease it back. It's the funniest goddamn thing you ever heard. By the time they get this deal unraveled I may be as old an' worn out as Homer Bannon. Nobody knows whether the place is mine or Truman's or Homer's."

"Hon, you could sell Truman heaven if you got him drunk enough," the woman said. She turned toward Hud, and the strange gold glow from the lights fell on the soft tops of her breasts. She put her mouth against Hud's shirt and giggled. "You better watch little Dan," she said. "He thinks you're mean."

Hud squeezed her against him and winked at me over her head. "Hell, I am mean," he said. "Didn't you know that?" She looked up and kissed him, and I got out and walked away.

I thought I ought to at least go out and tell Granddad what was going on. Hud was acting so crazy it wouldn't hurt Granddad to be on his guard. When I went back behind the chutes I saw Hermy, still peeping through the board fence at the bulls. He looked nervous.

"I kinda wish I'd stayed outa this bull ridin'," he said.

"You'll never learn any younger," I said, I thought a little hurrahing might cheer him up. "Maybe you won't have to ride very far."

"Eat shit," he said. "I don't feel too good."

I thought Jesse might want to go to the ranch with me, and I asked a couple of cowboys if they'd seen him. He wasn't any trouble at all to find, because he was at the concession stand, eating an orange Sno-Cone and talking to the pretty blackheaded woman. It didn't take field glasses to see that he wasn't getting any encouragement to go on talking.

When he saw me he reached out and put his arm around me; he was drunk enough to be a little extra friendly.

"Did you hear about Hud's deal?" I said. We walked over to the arena and leaned on the fence.

"I heard about ten versions of it," he said. "Looks like somebody showed their ass, but I don't know who." The way he was acting made me a little mad. He had entered the colt in the cutting horse contest to give him some experience, and now he was getting too drunk to ride.

"Look at that boy get busted," he said, watching the show. I couldn't even see the show; I kept seeing the woman's white breasts, and Hud's hand on the heavy part of her leg.

"I'm going out to tell Granddad," I said. "You do what you want to."

"No, I wouldn't go worry that old man," he said. "Don't add no more load on him right now. I don't believe Scott actually sold anything anyway."

"I better go tell Granddad," I said, but Jesse just wasn't paying me any attention.

"I need a can a beer," he said.

"Are you goin' get drunk before you ride?" I said, and he laughed. It was a painful kind of laugh, like something has stung him, or torn inside him.

"I can ride when I'm drunkest," he said. "Some a these nights I'll have to tell you about a ride or two I made."

He wasn't talking to me, really, and I walked off from him. I felt like I was smothering in the crowd. The lights and the giggling and the kids with Sno-Cone on their chins and the drunk cowboys—all of it made me feel like I was strangling. Jesse hanging on the fence half-drunk depressed me, and Hermy about to risk his ass on a bull he knew he couldn't ride depressed me more. It looked like Hud was the only one doing any good for himself. I got in the pickup and drove out of town, and when I was moving down the dark highway, moving on like the song said, I didn't feel so hemmed up and I kinda relaxed. Driving could do that for me a lot of times.

The ranch house was dark, and I knew it had been dark ever since I left. Granddad would be sound asleep, and it would be a hard job waking him up and getting him to understand the news I brought. Standing a minute in the kitchen, I missed Halmea. I wished I had her to tell it all to, so I wouldn't have to wake up Granddad. But I was there, and I went down the hall and into Granddad's room before my nerve failed me. Moonlight from an open window fell in a white puddle on his floor. It lay across the old chifforobe, and touched the silver-edged picture of Grandmother that had stood there since I knew the room. Granddad lay in darkness on the bed. I could hear the heavy whistle of his old man's breath. He was laying on his back, one hand upon his chest.

I came close to him. "Granddad," I said. "Granddad, wake up." I shook his arm gently, and he raised up on one elbow, his eyes open. "That you, Annie?" he said, and for the second time that night my neck hair stood up. He had asked the question to Grandmother. "What is it?" he said, rubbing his eyes with one hand.

"No, me," I said. "Lonnie. I want to talk to you a minute."

"Oh," he said. "Let me get my boots on."

"You don't need to get up," I said. But he got up anyway, scratching himself through the cotton nightshirt.

"We got to light the lamps," he said, moving slowly to the dresser. "We can't do no talking in the dark." We had electricity, but he had an old kerosene lamp on his dresser that he still used when the power went off. He got it and lit it. The yellow light didn't fill the room; it left high shadows on the walls.

"Sit down, son," he said. "Get you a cheer." He reached in his pocket for his tobacco, but he had on his nightshirt, and it wasn't there. In the yellow lamplight he looked a thousand years old. He was thin-armed, and his eyes set back in shadows. I wished then that I had left him asleep.

"What have you done?" he asked me.

"Not me," I said. "Hud did it. He's trying to sell the ranch."

"Huddie?" he said. He leaned his good ear to me. Just the way he said it made me have to swallow, because I could tell that for some sudden reason he wasn't with me, he was back in another time. I could tell he thought I was my father.

"Hud," I said. "He's tryin' to sell the ranch."

"Is he?" he said. "Oh no, Huddie couldn't sell it. I'm glad you're not in no trouble, Dan. Your ma worries about you some."

"No, Granddad," I said. "Hud is trying to sell it to Truman Peters. Really trying to sell it."

Granddad smiled at me as if it were a joke. "Huddie's a wild one," he said. "His mother's the same way. Ain't nobody ever got no rope on him." He looked at the lamp, and the light made his lined cheeks look yellow. For a minute I think he was with me, in the right night. "He can't sell it," he said. "This here land is mine. I may decide to let him run some of it awhile, I don't know. Right now I just feel like throwing in the sponge and giving up."

That was what I had wanted to hear. "Okay, then," I said. "I'm going on back to the rodeo. You sleep good." I thought maybe he just hadn't been awake at first, but then I knew it wasn't that.

"That's all right," he said. "Just don't worry your ma; she's got enough." He sat on the edge of the bed, smiling at me. Then he took the lamp back to the dresser and blew it out. The moonlight fell back into the room, and Granddad's shadow moved across it. The springs of the old bed creaked. "Just the boy," he said, and the room was quiet.

The talk had been too strange and sad. I thought maybe Granddad had been in a dream, and had stayed in a dream through it all. I saw that the supper dishes were still in the kitchen sink, and for a minute I thought about washing them. But I was feeling like I had in the rodeo crowd, only just the opposite. I wanted to get out of the dark old house with its dreams and ghosts. Granddad was on the other side of a high barbed fence, with each wire a year of life, and I couldn't go over it and I couldn't crawl through. But anyway, I had eased myself a little, and I felt like when I got back to town I could enjoy the rodeo. Only, the worst of all, I wanted Halmea. I wanted to talk to her for a little while. I wasn't as worried about Granddad as I had been; he seemed to be where Hud couldn't hurt him. But driving through the dark alleyways of mesquite, I thought of Halmea, and wished there had been some-way to keep Hud from doing what he had. Then I remembered seeing

Irene in the car seat, the morning before the rodeo, her hair spread like a scarf. I knew she was at the rodeo, and I decided to try and find her. She wasn't as exciting as Lily, sitting in the Cadillac, but she was who I would look for. After the show was all over, after the dancing and the fiddle music, when the gay riders had all gone off to bed, Irene and I might ride out into the heavy-smelling fields, and stay there awhile. Her black hair would be all the cover we'd need.

Twelve

THE NEXT DAY WAS THE LAST OF THE RODEO, AND I DIDN'T much care. The whole crazy circle of things got so it tired me out. When I woke up that morning I could see Jesse down in the lots, moving around, and I got up to go talk to him. I had looked for him the night before, after the dance, but he wasn't around, and I guess he got home on his own.

There was nobody to cook my breakfast, and I didn't feel like cooking it myself. I ate a bowl of cereal and did without anything else. When I got to the barn, Jesse was dragging around cleaning out the horse stalls. A friend of ours who had a little pasture in town was keeping the colt during the rodeo. Jesse looked pretty puny.

"Seen Granddad?" I asked him.

He stopped raking hay and leaned on his hull fork a minute. "He's up an' gone," he said. "He saddled up about an hour ago and rode off west."

"Didn't say where he was going?"

"No, he never," Jesse said. "He said a few other things, though. Said he'd have to let me and Lonzo go. He don't plan on having much work to do for a while."

"Did he mention about Hud?" I said. "I came out an' told him last night."

"Naw, he never," Jesse said. "He said he was sorry he couldn't afford to keep us till times got better. I didn't expect he'd be able to. He ain't allowed to run no cattle for a year."

I remembered how Granddad's mind had strayed into the past the night before. "Did he seem all right this morning?" I asked. "He acted last night like he might be slippin' a little."

"Well, he didn't seem very spry," Jesse said. "But I didn't notice nothin' else."

I left him to his raking and went up to the house. Grandma met me at the door and lit into me to take her to Thalia, so she could look for some help. She had taken herself the day before, whether she could drive or not, but she wasn't in the mood to try it again. I finally had to take her. She went to see a lady who had cooked for us years before, and the lady told her of a girl who might help. We chased the girl down and got her to agree to move out the next day, so Granny was satisfied. I wasn't so happy about it myself. She was a lazy, fattish-looking white girl, and she acted dumber than a turkey.

When we got back, Granddad was sitting by his radio. I asked him where he'd been, and he said he had just wanted to ride around and have a look at his grass—see how much he had. He talked as sensible and reasonable as he ever had, only he was awful blue and depressed.

"I don't know if I got the energy to start it over," he said. "I don't know if I've got the time. Right now I just feel like I've finally wore plumb out. I couldn't hardly drag a saddle this morning. I may just have to sit here till I rot."

"I guess this was the worst thing that ever happened to you, wasn't it?" I said.

He rubbed one hand through his hair, and shook his head. "Oh no," he said. "Not the worst by a long shot. Your grandmother getting killed was a tragedy. Aw, I can get over this here if my health don't go to failing me."

I tried quizzing him about Hud, but he just said he'd have to see him before he'd know anything. He mentioned firing Jesse, but he said he had about changed his mind and decided to keep Lonzo around a little while, if he could. He had decided to build some new fences. Finally Granddad got to where he was paying more attention to the radio than he was to me, and I went upstairs to read. When I came down a little later to eat a bite, I noticed how stiff Granddad got around. It was like his leg joints were sticking on him all of a sudden.

2.

When I left for the rodeo that night, Hud still hadn't come home. There had been no sign of him, or of the Cadillac, and we had no way of knowing whether Truman Peters had caught up with him or not. Jesse and Lonzo went into town together, in Lonzo's old car, so I was left with the pickup.

I was way late getting to the show. On the outskirts of town, like in that song, I saw Buddy Andrews stopped beside the road. He had had some kind of a breakdown, and was out fiddling under his hood. He was as pissed off as he could be. Something had gone wrong with his generator, and he had a hot date for the rodeo. I tied on to him with a chain and pulled him into Thalia, but of course when we got there it turned out all the mechanics had gone to the rodeo, and weren't to be found. Buddy was in the worst mood of his life. We spent about an hour tracking down a colored mechanic, and then another hour getting the car and the mechanic to a garage where he could go to work on it. When I finally left them, Buddy had got his clean clothes greasy, and was trying his best to get the man to hurry. The final performance of the Thalia rodeo was almost over before I even got to the parking area.

I could tell there wasn't much show left, because the musicians were already over on the concrete slab, tuning their fiddles and guitars. The people who didn't like rodeo and just came to dance were filing out of the grandstand and heading for the slab. I went on inside, anyway. The cutting horses were in the arena working, and our colt wasn't with them. I stood by the fence and watched. While I was standing there a kid named Pin came up to me; he was wearing a big black Stetson, and he had a can of beer in one hand. He looked like the rodeo, about nine tenths done.

"Hey, cowboy," he said. "Did you see Hermy?"

"Not tonight," I said. "I just got here. I been helping Andrews fix his car."

"Oh, goddamn, you shoulda been here," he said, belching. "A bull stepped on Hermy. God, he was hollerin' and cussin'."

"No shit?" I said. "Did he get hurt bad?"

Pin nodded and tried to look solemn, but he was enjoying having a story to tell. "The bull stepped right in his stomach," he said. "He wasn't out, though, he was yellin' his fuckin' head off. They say he was broke all to pieces inside. Shit, you ain't gonna see me on one a them bastards." He left, tossing his beer can on the ground with a thousand others. I noticed he had a canvas contestant's sticker pinned to the back of his shirt.

YOUR ATTENTION PLEASE, the announcer said. WILL JESSE LOGAN REPORT TO THE ARENA AT ONCE. LAST CALL FOR JESSE LOGAN. WILL YOU PLEASE BRING YOUR HORSE TO THE CUTTING ARENA AT ONCE. IF NOT, YOU WILL BE SCRATCHED. YOUR ENTRY WILL BE SCRATCHED. LAST CALL FOR MR. LOGAN.

I ran around behind the chutes, wondering where in the world Jesse was. Surely he hadn't gone off without making the final performance. Then I found the colt, saddled and ready, tied to the fence. But no Jesse anywhere. I was almost ready to ride the colt myself, when I heard the announcer scratch the horse. I left him tied and walked on around the arena, figuring Jesse might have got in a fight or got kicked or something. Somebody yelled at me and I saw Hud and his new woman coming out of the grandstand. He was leading her along by the arm.

"Well, now where's your fine feathered friend tonight?" he said.

"I wish I knew," I said. "Granddad fired him this morning, he may be gone. The colt's back there tied."

"Homer fired him? The hell he did." He pulled Lily to him and snickered something in her ear. She smiled at what he said. Hud was wild and messed-up-looking, like he hadn't changed clothes since the card game, his shirttail out of his pants; but Lily was wearing a gold and white dress, and her long honey-and-butter hair curled like a colt's tail down her back. She looked even prettier than she had in the Cadillac.

"Well, the sonofabitch just wasted an entry fee," Hud said. "Tell him he better not forget he's fired. If I run into him I may take that entry money out in skin."

"Carry me back to the car, honey," the woman said. "I can't wade through this cowshit." Hud picked her up like she was a doll, and she put her face against his neck.

LADIES AND GENTLEMEN, the announcer said, THIS CONCLUDES OUR SHOW FOR TONIGHT. LET ME REMIND YOU ABOUT THE BIG DANCE OVER THERE ON THE SLAB, STARTING RIGHT NOW. FREDDY HILL AND HIS POST OAK VALLEY BOYS WILL BE THERE FURNISHING THE MUSIC, FROM NOW TILL ONE O'CLOCK. ADMISSION IS JUST FIFTY CENTS A HEAD, SO YOU FELLERS GRAB YOUR FILLIES AND GET ON OVER THERE. THANK YOU, LADIES AND GENTLEMEN, AND WE HOPE TO SEE YOU ALL BACK WITH US NEXT YEAR. OH, EXCUSE ME, he said. WILL YOU KEEP YOUR SEATS JUST A MINUTE? I HAVE SOME NEWS THAT YOU-ALL WILL BE ANXIOUS TO HEAR, THE YOUNG MAN WHO WAS INJURED TONIGHT IN THE BULL-RIDING CONTEST IS NOW BEING TAKEN BY AMBULANCE TO THE HOSPITAL IN WICHITA FALLS. THEY WERE UNABLE TO TREAT HIM SATISFACTORILY HERE. I KNOW YOU'RE ALL HOPING AND PRAYING THAT THE YOUNG MAN IS ALL RIGHT, AND WE SURE ARE TOO. IF ANY MORE NEWS REACHES US WE'LL GIVE IT TO YOU AT THE DANCE. THANK YOU, AND GOOD NIGHT.

It made me feel weak in the stomach to know that Hermy was bad hurt. Right then, they were racing him across the dark highway in an ambulance. The next morning I would get loose and go visit him, but first I had to find Jesse.

The dance slab was filling up fast. Over the voices and the shuffling, I could hear the band playing "Your Cheating Heart," and the boot soles scraped the concrete in time to it. I passed by a fist fight and stopped a minute to watch. "You're a hot-check-writing bastard," one of the boys said, and they slugged away. I went on. Fist fights would be easy to find. I pushed my way onto the dance floor, and it felt like the whole ranch country was in on it with me. The old men bunched together near the corners, and the little kids, boys and girls both, were out on the dance floor whooping and running. I saw one little boy sound asleep on a bench, with a couple courting right beside him. The rodeo contestants and their girl friends made up a good part of the crowd. Now that the show was over the boys were drunk and excited, hoping the nooky was going to come after the dance, and they really lived it up. The grown-ups two-stepped and single-footed right along to the rock and roll numbers that the band had to play. Now and then there would be a polka or a square dance especially for the old folks. But it wouldn't be long before the old ones would trickle out, and the musicians wouldn't have anyone but the kids to please. Then the dance songs would last longer and go faster. "Hit it there, Leroy," the bandleader said.

I eased my way through the crowd, looking for Jesse among the sorrowful stag cowboys on the sides. I went around twice without finding him, but I knew he would have been easy enough to miss. Then I ran into a girl I knew, and we danced awhile. She was so looped she barely knew me, but it didn't matter. The cowboy vocalist laid down his fiddle and came to the mike to sing. He sang a new song, one I had only heard a time or two before. It was called "Fräulein."

Far across the distant waters
Lived an old German's daughter,
On the banks of the old River Rhine . . .

I locked my hands and dropped them on the girl's butt, and swayed along with the music and forgot Jesse for a minute. The people were quieting down a little, and the singer was crying into the mike about the girl him and all the other soldier boys had left alone across the waters. "That's too slow," Charlene said, looking up at me. "I want somethin' fast, make a little whoopee, don't you?" But she got quiet again. The mournfulness of the song was getting to me, but before I had really caught it bad they switched to a polka and I led Charlene to the side. While we were watching the old folks jig around, a tired-looking cowboy waltzed up to us with a blonde. "Here, you can have this one," he said, holding out the girl's arm. "I don't want her no more; I'll take yours." I told him he was welcome to all I had, and walked away. They were all too drunk to know what became of me.

Since I wasn't finding anybody in the dance, I went outside and walked through the parking lot awhile. The pickup wasn't very far from the dance floor, and I went to it. There was a wagon sheet in the back. I got in and unrolled part of it and stretched out on my back. I thought maybe Jesse might come by, and waiting would be the quickest way to find him. The band was playing one of those songs of Hank Williams', the one about the wild side of life, and the music floated over the car tops and touched me. I felt lost from everybody, and from myself included, laying on a wagon sheet in a pastureland of cars. Only the tune of the song reached me, but the tune was enough. It fit the night and the country and the way I was feeling, and fit them better than anything I knew. What few stories the dancing people had to tell were already told in the worn-out words of songs like that one, and their kind of living, the few things they knew and lived to a fare-thee-well were in the sad high tune. City people probably wouldn't believe there were folks simple enough to live their lives out on sentiments like those—but they didn't know. Laying there, thinking of all the things the song brought up in me, I got more peaceful. The words I knew of it, about the wild side of life, reminded me of Hud and Lily, but more than that, the whole song reminded me of Hermy and Buddy and the other boys I knew. All of them wanted more and seemed to end up with less; they wanted excitement and ended up stomped by a bull or smashed against a highway; or they wanted a girl to court; and anyway, whatever it was they wanted, that was what they ended up doing without. That song ended, and another one began, and it ended, and then I got up and went back into the dark arena to untie the colt and take him to his pen. I thought maybe I would come back to the dance and honky-tonk a little myself.

3.

Before I got near the horse, I heard Jesse talking. He was sitting spraddle-legged against the fence, talking to the horse. There were three or four empty beer cans scattered around his feet.

"Everbody's gone home but me," he said. "If anybody's left it's always me."

When I squatted down beside him he didn't seem a bit surprised.

"Hello," he said. "I had her, but she got away."

"Who got away?" I said. I had a pretty good idea.

"That pretty little woman," he said. "We were in somebody's car, just talking, and I took a little nap, dozed off a few minutes. I woke up an' she wasn't there." He sighed, and started to get up. "But I been left many a time," he said. "I didn't wake up in time to ride the colt, either. I just fucked up."

"It don't make too much difference," I said.

"Makes a little," he said. I saw that he wasn't really drunk, he was just trying to be, or wishing he was. "Oh, the colt wouldn't a won," he said. "But it woulda made a little difference to me. Reason I came up here in the first place, I got drunk an' fell off a cuttin' horse. In the San Antone show. Ladybug went one way and Jesse went the other."

"Hell, so what," I said. He was feeling real sorry for himself about something. "Falling off a horse ain't much of a crime," I said.

"No," he said. He was fiddling with the colt's reins. "Fallin' off wasn't no crime. It wasn't even a disgrace. My boss didn't think so either. He give me three hundred dollars and told me to haul Ladybug home. But you know," he said. "I never done it. I got to thinking about it and got drunk agin, and went up the road about sixty miles an' turned the trailer over an' broke that little mare's neck. That was the crime of it. Third best cuttin' horse in the nation, an' she was just a five-year-old. Let's go to the dance," he said. "I want to watch them pretty girls whirl."

I told him I'd meet him there. I got on the colt and took him to the pen and unsaddled him. The dance wasn't but a half a mile away, and I walked back through the cool quiet streets. I could hear the music plain as a radio, and I wasn't all hemmed-up in the crowd. When I got back, Jesse was leaning on the wire fence, looking in.

"Let's stay till the music stops," he said. "This here fascinates me."

The music was slower by that time, with just a couple of dozen couples pushing themselves around the dance floor. It was after one o'clock, and the bandleader was ready to quit. Some of the cowboys weren't tired, and they wouldn't let the bandleader stop. Jesse stood there nearly thirty minutes, nodding his head to the slow music. I sat on the fender of somebody's car. After they had played "Good Night, Ladies" three times the cowboys gave up and everybody straggled out.

"We might go get a bite to eat," Jesse said. "I ain't goin' back out to you-all's place. Found a trucker, an old boy I used to rodeo with. He said he'd give me a ride to New Mexico early in the mornin' if I'm here. Guess I better sleep in the truck, so I won't miss it."

We went to the pickup, and I drove. Jesse leaned against the door with his head on his arm as we followed the slow line of cars back through town. He looked awful low and sad, and I couldn't think of anything that would cheer him up. I hated to see him just go off down the road, with nothing to take with him and nowhere to go. In a minute I heard him singing the verse to the soldier song:

Far across th' dis-tant waters
Lived an ol' German's daughter,
On th' banks of th' ol' Rivah Rhiiinnne . . .

"Ain't that tune pretty?" he said. He looked out of the pickup window at the dark houses. We were on the edge of town, then, and could see the yellow lights of a big oil derrick, standing on the prairie miles away.

"Fräulein, fräulein, look down from your window an' be mine," he sang. "That the way it goes?" He sighed and slumped back in the seat. "I never will forget that tune," he said.

I pulled in at Bill's, and we followed a group of cowboys inside. When the last performance of the rodeo was over, the people all left for another town, so the café was almost empty, just a few tired rodeo hands eating a late meal before starting their long drives home. We took our pick of the booths. I ordered coffee and cherry pie, and Jesse just ordered coffee. He went on talking.

"I knew this mornin' I was gonna do all this," he said. He looked up and smiled when the ugly, waddle-assed waitress set the coffee in front of him. "I guess I done had it planned," he went on. "Because I don't intend to ride in another arena agin. Only reason I go to rodeos is to chase after the prettiest tail I can find, and I know beforehand I ain't gonna catch that." I ate my pie slowly, not looking at him very often. He looked terrible, sick and worn out, dark scraggly whiskers on his cheeks. He kept nibbling at the tag of his Bull Durham sack.

"Ain't no fräulein ever looked down on me," he said. "Not unless it was to ask for money. Some fellers just belong in whorehouses, I don't know why."

"I halfway wish I was going someplace," I said. "I ain't doin' any good around here."

"You just think you ain't," he said. "You better stay till your Granddad gets back on his feet a little. That's a lot a good you can do. After he kinda gets over this it might not hurt you to see the world some."

"I don't know how long that will be," I said. "May not ever be. Granddad sure looks worn out." Somebody had put money in the jukebox. It was Ernest Tubb, singing "Rainbow at Midnight." His deep voice carried over what little talk there was in the café. The waitress was going around mopping off the dirty yellow tabletop with a dripping rag.

"You probably ain't got any money to leave on, anyway," Jess said.

"Two hundred dollars calf money," I said. "That'd last me awhile."

"Yeah," he said, setting his coffee cup down. "About a week. But you're the boss." He rubbed his fingers into the corners of his eyes. "It don't hurt to take a little look around," he said. "Just don't turn into an old loose horse like me. You're better off to stop somewhere even if it ain't no paradise. I could have myself, many a time. I had the chances any man has." He wiped his lips with his napkin, and dropped the napkin in his coffee cup. "I guess I was too particular, for too long, what's wrong with me. I went all over this cow country looking for the exact right place an' the exact right people, so once. I got stopped I wouldn't have to be movin' agin, like my old man always done. But that's going at it wrong. I shoulda just set down an' made it right wherever the hell it was.

"I ain't agoin' to now," he said, and he blew smoke out of his mouth with a weary breath.

"Granddad made something good," I said. "Look at him. It didn't stay made."

"Look at him," Jesse said, his voice sharp. "He lost something all right, but by god he's still got something too. I know a lot a people in worse situations than your granddad's in."

"Well, I guess he did make something he could keep," I said.

"I'd say so," Jesse said. "I'd say your granddad made it." His hands were clasped together on the table, and he looked shivery and shaky, like he'd just fallen in a cold winter river and pulled out to a place with no fire.

"Some folks do," he said.

Thirteen

JESSE HAD QUIT TALKING, AND WE SAT LISTENING TO THE jukebox. It was Wayne Rainey, singing

Why don't you haul off
And love me, like you
Used to do . . .

Why do you treat me like a worn-out shoe, and on like that. My pie was eaten, except for a few crumbs, and I pushed them around with the red prongs of my fork. Finally Jesse got up. "Let's go," he said. "If you can run me back to the pens I'll find that truck and catch me a little nap."

He paid the ticket, and we went out. There were only five or six cars in the parking lot—one of them had its back doors open and a cowboy's legs stuck out one side. There were two or three beer cans under his heels. I drove Jesse back to the pens. The lights were out and the whole area was dark, but there were still a few cowboys around, sleeping in cars, or on blankets and sleeping bags spread behind the chutes. We found the truck, and I helped Jesse girt his saddle to the sideboards. He stood on the high running board, looking down at me.

"Well, I guess I better try an' snooze awhile," he said. "Much obliged for the ride an' all."

"Oh, you bet," I said. "You're welcome."

"Tell your grandpa I enjoyed working for him what little I did," he said. "I imagine I'll be running into you somewhere, one a these days."

"I hope you get a good job," I said.

"Oh, I guess I'll get by," he said. "It's hard times and dusty roads."

He said to be careful, and I said so long, Jesse. That's the last I'll ever see of him, I thought. I drove back through Thalia, under the fluttery rodeo flags that would have to come down for another year. The highway to the ranch was deserted, and all I could get on the radio was gospel singing and commercials from the station in Del Rio. I felt like I was losing people every day. If there had been anyplace open in Thalia besides Bill's, I would have gone back. A coyote ran across the road in front of me, yellow in the headlights, his eyes shining like marbles. I slammed on my brakes and grabbed for the thirty-thirty, but he had already scooted under the fence and disappeared.

2.

When I turned off at the cattle guard, I noticed a pair of headlights coming up behind me as fast as ambulance. Before I had gone a half mile across the pasture the headlights were about a foot from my rear bumper, and I could see the Cadillac grille reflected in my rear-view mirror. Hud was right on my tail, and I started to pull to the right, so he could get by. But when I flashed my lights on bright I saw something. I saw somebody crawling and I was almost on him. Granddad! He was just in front of me, down on his hands and knees at the side of the road. I braked and swerved to the left and my car lights were right in his face and then they were on the empty road and the Cadillac jarred my rear end. Then I was bouncing over the left-hand bar ditch and into the pasture, the pickup almost spinning over, so I was thrown against the far door and hung to the wheel with one hand, all the time seeing Granddad crawling toward me in his nightshirt, with blood on his chin. The high weeds and little mesquite bushes slowed the pickup enough that I stomped the pedals and got it stopped. I jumped out and ran back, but I didn't see Granddad. Hud was out in the road in front of his car, wiping blood off his nose. The grille of the Cadillac was caved in and one headlight broken, and Hud standing in the light of the other one slinging blood off his nose. For a minute I thought I had dreamed Granddad.

"Goddamn you," Hud said. "You little piss-ant. What the fuck did you stop for? You got your life's work ahead, paying for this car."

"No, didn't you see him?" I said. "He's out here, Granddad. He was crawlin' in the ditch."

"The hell he is," Hud said, turning toward the bar ditch. He threw a bloody handkerchief down, and in the stillness we heard Granddad say, "Jericho," real loud. He was in the ditch behind the car, still moving on his hands and knees. Hud knelt down and stopped him.

"Hud, who is it, hon?" Lily said. She was in the back seat.

"Oh, snakeshit," Hud said. "Run get that pickup an' point it this away, so we'll have light. I can't turn mine aroun' in this road. I may a run over him."

I ran to the pickup and backed it around, paying no attention to stumps or bushes. In the dark Granddad didn't look too bad hurt, and I wasn't quite as scared as I had been. I just couldn't figure it out. I turned off the pickup lights before I thought, but Hud yelled and I switched them back on. Hud was holding Granddad in his lap, trying to keep him from moving. All Granddad had on was his old nightshirt; he didn't even have shoes. But he recognized Hud.

"Don't hold me back, Huddie," he said. "I fell. I was going out to look at the cloud, see if it was time to get the men up." His voice was hoarse and slow. "We got to get to work," he said. "Turn me loose now. I'm okay." I thought he was. I could see blood on his hands and knees, where the rocks and gravel had skinned him up, and there were grass burrs in his arms and in his nightshirt, but I thought he was all right. I thought he must have fallen off the porch or something and knocked himself silly, was all, like he might from a fall from a horse. But Hud wouldn't turn him loose, and when he wouldn't Granddad began to fight him, and to whine down in his throat.

"Lily," Hud yelled. "Lily, get up." Blood was dripping from Hud's smashed nose and dropping on Granddad and on his shirt.

"Annie, you help me," Granddad said. "Got to get up now and get these men started. Wake these men up. I can't lay here no more. A man ain't to crawl."

"Shit, this old man's hurt bad," Hud said. He lifted Granddad's nightshirt, and I suddenly saw a jagged end of bone protruding from Granddad's side above his hip. The sight made me turn weak.

"Lily, goddamnit, get up an' start that car," Hud said. He yelled at her and cussed her as loud as he could. Instead of starting it the woman got out and came around to us. When she saw Granddad she grabbed onto the fender of the Cadillac. She didn't have anything on from the waist up, nothing except a brown sweater she had pulled over her shoulders and buttoned in front. Her stomach was bare.

"Huddie, won't you let me up?" Granddad said. He was trying to get his hands loose; he was looking up at Hud, but he didn't see me. "It ain't no bad cloud," he said. "We got to get these men up an' get to work. Move stock." His voice was cracking, and he was whining when he breathed in air. Hearing the whine and seeing his throat jerk the way it did made tears come in my eyes. It seemed all of a sudden like Granddad was someone I had forgotten about for a long time, and hearing the deep hurt sound of his whine brought back all he was to me.

"Lie still, Granddad," I said. I couldn't think of any way to help. But Hud seemed to be thinking, he seemed to be in his right mind, and I just set there, holding Granddad's good leg still, waiting for Hud to decide what to do.

"Lily, take this car an' go to the house," he said. "Telephone's in the hall. Call for an ambulance and tell 'em to get here quick, the road through Bannon's horse pasture. Tell 'em we got an awful sick man. We'll try an' keep him quiet."

"Goddamn you, now don't hold a man down," Granddad said. His throat swelled, and he strained to get up. For a minute it was all the two of us could do to hold him, but then he went weak all of a sudden and lay back. All we could hear was him harking and coughing, and the Cadillac motor turning over.

"Knew it," Hud said. "Sonofabitch won't start no way. Five-thousand-dollar car, and it ain't no more use than a wagon. Ain't as much." I was on my knees, trying to pull some of the burrs out of Granddad's arms, but he wouldn't hold still. Hud was looking more wild-eyed and desperate, and Granddad just lay there weak, harking, and Hud's wrists were trembling as he held him still.

"Honey, I can't start it," Lily called. "The goddamn thing, I can't start it."

"Come on here," Hud yelled. "Bring that whiskey. It's in the seat." She came wobbling out on her high heels, the heavy bottle in one hand.

"See if we can get a little down him," Hud said. "Might help." I held Granddad's leg still, and Hud held his hands, and the woman squatted down and leaned over Granddad. She tried to tilt his head back and make him take some whiskey; but Granddad was trying to talk again, he was mumbling and trying to talk to the old people, to Grandmother and to Jericho Green, and the brownish whiskey bubbled off his mouth and ran in a stream down his chin and neck. It made a sharp smell, sharper than the dust smell of the road.

"Honey, I can't make him drink this stuff," the woman said. She had put her arms in the sleeves of the brown sweater, but it was loose in front and her breasts had fallen out. "I'm just wasting it, all I'm doin'," she said, and she kept trying to pour with one hand and hold the sweater together with the other, and I didn't like her for that.

"Keep pourin'," Hud said. "You're doin' all right." Finally Granddad took a little and gagged it up.

"You-all," he said. "You-all, don't make me drink that." Lily took the bottle away then and pressed her hands to her jaws, like she had the toothache.

"Look here," Hud said. "Yonder's a car coming out of Thalia. I just seen the lights up the road. Look now. Lonnie, he's a long ways up there yet. You run out to the road and flag him down, you can beat him. Tell him we got a dyin' man here. If he's got a big car make him come over, if he ain't make him telephone. Now hurry."

"I'm scared he'll die," I said. "He might while I'm gone. Can't we take him in the pickup some way?"

"Get on, or I'll promise you he'll die," Hud said, frowning at me. Blood from his nose had dripped and smeared all over the lower part of his face, and he looked terrible.

"He's sufferin' agony," Hud said. "You stop that car."

3.

I ran down the dark dirt road as fast as I could, fighting the darkness with my arms and legs. Hud had said Granddad was dying, and I could remember the bone tip protruding from his side. The darkness shut in around me, and two or three times I ran off in the brush and weeds, stumbling into the bar ditch and out again on the soft, graded road. I began to give out in the legs, and I had to slow down, but anyway I got across the cattle guard and onto the pavement with the car still a good mile up the road toward Thalia. I stood at the edge of the pavement and waited, the longest wait, and the lights came on toward me. They disappeared beneath some little ridge, and then came in sight again and the car swept down the slope my way. I got in the middle of the road and waved my hands and hat, and the man hit his brakes. It was a big Olds, and I was thinking we could load Granddad into the back seat and take him to the hospital in it. The driver kept slowing down, and I stepped off the road so I could talk to him. But the minute I did the motor roared and the car went zooming by, the fender just under my elbow in the dark. The man who was driving wasn't even looking at me. I yelled for help, but by that time he was gone, doing sixty or seventy miles an hour. I guess he was afraid I'd hijack him.

And then I was alone, standing on the edge of the pavement in the darkness, thinking of how Granddad was hurting, how he had whined.

Hud said he was suffering agony. I walked up and down the highway, I don't know how many minutes, trying to think of something I could do. I knew I ought to do something. I looked for another set of headlights, anywhere, in any direction, but none were in sight. It was between two and three o'clock, about the deadest hour of the night, and I knew there might not be another car along for half an hour. I wished I had run the other way, to the ranch house. It would have been farther, but there was a telephone there, at least. That hadn't occurred to me in time, and it hadn't occurred to Hud either. I wanted to start back. It seemed like I had been gone for an hour, and that Granddad might be a lot sicker, might even be dying. Or Hud might have decided to try and move him in the pickup after all. I was walking around on the pavement, my head down, and when I looked up I almost hollered. I saw another car, another set of lights coming from Thalia. It was a good ways off, but I got in the middle of the road and waited. If the car got by it would have to run right over me, or else go into the bar ditch, and I would have a chance to yell. The lights were only a few hills away, and I was hoping it would be another big car, big enough to move Granddad in. Then I looked up the road, and the lights weren't coming. I walked a little ways up the road while I waited for them to come over the ridge, and they didn't come. I walked and waited till I knew there wasn't a chance. The car must have turned off; it must have been somebody from Thalia going home. Or else the driver just pulled off the road to go to sleep. I was almost sick at my stomach from waiting and walking the highway and worrying about Granddad. I looked toward the pastures, and I could see the faint light above the mesquites, the pickup lights. It seemed out of place, and I looked again and discovered I had walked nearly a half mile up the road from the cattle guard. Seeing the lights made me think of Hud and Granddad, there in the bar ditch all that time, Hud wild, and Granddad suffering and dying, and the butter-haired woman with her breasts hanging out of the sweater. I began to run back, to run down the pavement toward the cattle guard. When I got there I stopped just a minute, to take one last good look up and down the highway. But I didn't see any lights, and I went on to the cattle guard. I was going across it when I heard a woman's voice, pretty faint, but like a yell, and then a bang, a gun shot, and the long cracking echo off Idiot Ridge. It could have been the Cadillac starting; it could have been a backfire. But the sound and the echo had been too much like sounds I had heard before, and I remembered the coyote gun. After I saw the coyote, I hadn't taken time to put it back behind the seat. I remembered trying to keep it from bouncing off when Hud had knocked the pickup across the road.

I left the cattle guard and started back, but I went slow, like I had gone to Halmea's cabin that last night. Before I got very far I could hear the roar of a big truck coming toward Thalia. It was far away, miles away maybe. I walked on toward the one shadowy spot of light in the mesquite. I didn't know what to think at first. Then I thought Hud must of shot the woman; he must have killed her for some reason. That was why she screamed. And then I knew he wouldn't shoot her, and I thought it must have been Truman Peters. Truman must have been waiting for Hud at the ranch. He must have seen the light and come down the road and found them, seen his wife with her naked teats and Hud had had to shoot him. I knew he couldn't shoot Hud, I got scared and began to walk faster. I wanted to be out in the light. Then I heard the woman crying something at Hud, and I didn't hear anything else.

4.

When I came into the light, Lily was bent over the turtleback of the big car, crying into her elbow. Hud stood by the fender of the pickup, talking to himself. The bottle of whiskey was sitting on the fender, and the rifle leaned against the pickup door. I saw the ejected shell laying in the dirt road, the brass shining in the light. Hud was talking, to himself, or to Lily, I never did know. Then he drank, his head jerking quickly back.

My granddad lay in the bar ditch. He lay still. An old Levi's jacket, the one we kept behind the pickup seat, it had been thrown over his face, so I couldn't see what he looked like, or see his head at all. Lily's dress, the fancy one all white and gold, was stretched over Granddad too; it covered up his side. Just his two bare legs struck out from under the dress, one straight, and one bent crooked, and scarred up besides from that rope tear years and years before. I knew it was before. I knew it was Granddad there dead, but I kept thinking it wasn't. I saw some blood puddle in the gravel by the Levi's jacket, and I choked and gagged. But I didn't get sick. I went over and squatted down by Granddad, by the good leg I had tried to hold. Seeing the Levi's jacket over his face made me remember all the things I had meant to buy him and give him, sometime or other. I had meant to buy him a blanket-lined jacket, for one thing.

I heard a whiz. Hud's arm swung. There was a whistle, and the whiskey bottle hit the ground somewhere in the pasture. "Whiskey, ain't it," Hud said. His voice wasn't loud. I saw there were still grass burrs in Granddad's legs. In a minute I felt Hud come and stand behind me. I couldn't feel any of Granddad there with us; it was just Hud and me. I looked up at him and he was looking off into the dark. I felt like I would gag again, but inside I was all dry and hot, like I had fever. Hud was looking into the pickup headlights, stretching his hands out toward them like the lights were a fire and it was winter.

"Lonnie," he said. "No shit, it was the best thing. The pore old worn-out bastard."

"But he woulda been," I said. "It woulda been all right, he woulda got well. I needed him." I started to pull the jacket off and look at Granddad's face, but I didn't. Hud came around in front of me and squatted down. I knew he wanted me to listen to him. He looked right at me, and didn't do it to scare. I saw sweat on his cheeks, but his voice seemed easy for once, not mean or rough.

"You listen to me," he said. "No shit, it was best. I ain't lyin' now. Homer wanted it."

"But he wasn't so bad," I said. That was all I could say. If I could have felt Granddad was there, I could have felt something to say. But it was just Hud and me.

"Hell, I had to," he said. "He was bad off, Lonnie. You wasn't here. You wasn't acoming, and he got to spittin' blood and tryin' to get up, an' hurtin' himself. Tryin' to get to them goddamn dead people a his. I thought if he wanted to get to 'em so bad I'd just let him go. He always liked them better than us that was alive, anyhow."

"But he was Granddad." I said.

"He was all fucked up," Hud said. "He was throwin' up blood, and that leg like it was. Worse than it was the first time he hurt it. He was just an old worn-out bastard. He couldn't a made it up no way in the world. He couldn't a made it another hour."

Then Lily come over an' hung on Hud's shoulders, mumbling something about Truman in his ear. But he didn't even look around at her; he was still talking to me.

"But what will I do?" I said. "Granddad was always . . ."

"You'll do without, like the rest of us," he said. "Lonnie, no shit now, he was ruined. He wasn't ever gonna be no good agin, he was just gonna lay somewhere an' rot. I took an' shot him cause he needed me to."

"Honey, don't just squat there talkin'," Lily said. She was trying to get Hud to stand up. "Hud, put him in the car," she said. "Let's go let people know. Somebody's gonna come along."

I just squatted there, looking at the Levi's jacket and the stickers in his legs, and trying to feel something of Granddad, so I'd know something to do. I saw Hud looking down at Granddad too. Only Hud looked easy and peaceful someway, like he was finally satisfied for the first time in his life.

"You don't know the story," he said. "Me and him fought many and many a round, me and Homer Bannon. It's hard to say, though. I helped him as much as he ever helped me, I believe that."

I dried up then. I felt like I didn't have anything else to say, to Hud or anybody, ever. I wasn't down on Hud. I didn't even think about him. I was just pushed back in myself like a two-bit variety-store telescope.

Finally Hud stood up and told the woman to get in the pickup. Then he went over and put the gun behind the seat, where it belonged.

"You take his feet," he said, when he came back. "Let's lay him on the wagon sheet. It ain't gonna hurt him none now. We can take him on to the hospital; maybe they'll clean him up a little."

"Don't they have to see it?" I said. "The sheriff and the law?"

Hud kinda smiled, and shook his head. "If they won't take it the way we tell 'em, let 'em do without," he said. "Ain't nobody gonna lie." He grinned his old, strange grin, and I didn't know at all. I had believed him. I thought at first that he shot Granddad to stop the hurting. But seeing that wild blood-smeared grin, I didn't know. It could have been for kindness or for meanness either, whichever mood was on Hud when he held Granddad in the ditch.

We lifted Granddad and laid him in the back of the pickup, on the wagon sheet I had used when I listened to those songs. Hud made me drive, and he sat back there and held Granddad from bumping till I could get to Thalia. And when the hospital had took Granddad away, Hud made me drive Lily to the hotel, so she could get some sleep, and he borrowed a car from one of the doctors and went and woke up the sheriff and the justice of the peace and told them about it.

Fourteen

All the next day I sat in the barn loft, thinking and trying to figure things out. Some of the people from Thalia came down to the lots to look for me, but I kept quiet, and none of them thought to climb the ladder. I knew they had found the place where Granddad fell off the porch and hurt himself. So anyway, that part of it was settled. The high loft door was open, and I could watch the people around the house come and go, like they did all day long. I sat with my back against some bales of alfalfa and looked out the loft door at the sky. There must have been at least a thousand white clouds that crossed the sky that day. I wasn't crying or hurting or worrying much. I was just watching the people and the thunderclouds. Once in a great while I would wonder where Granddad was. I would wonder if there was any part of him watching it all from someplace. I had heard the song about the ghost riders, and I wondered if there could be anything of Granddad riding that big sky, in the thickets of cloud. Sometimes I felt for a minute like there might be, and other times I thought it was a silly thing to think.

There were a couple of police cars around the house most of the day. I saw the deputy sheriff out in the back yard looking around a time or two, but he didn't come to the barn. Late in the afternoon Hud and Lily and Grandma came out in the back porch and stood awhile, and then Hud and Lily got in the Cadillac's and drove away. The Cadillac's grille was still all mashed in, but Hud had managed to get it running. Hud looked okay, and he acted like he was running things. I tried to decide for myself why he really killed Granddad, but I couldn't. I never could tell why Hud did things; he was too much a mystery to me. But I could sure tell that he was in control, and that Truman Peters, or the law, or anybody else wasn't going to get him stopped for a while. I knew they'd probably have some kind of a trial about Granddad's killing, but they wouldn't give Hud much trouble. I had watched a good many trials in Thalia, and I'd seen a lot dumber people than Hud get away with doing a lot worse things than he had done. Even if they hung a sentence on him it would be suspended. With Granddad gone, nobody would slow Hud down.

During the heat of the day the loft was like an oven, and I had to sneak down to the water tank a time or two to drink. Finally I wet my shirt and spread it under me for a pallet, but I didn't go to sleep. Cars kept driving up to the house, and I watched the people go in. Most of them were womenfolks, bringing things to eat. Later in the afternoon, when it began to cool off, they really came thick, and a lot of people were milling around in the back yard. The sky was the same big sky I had always known, the same blues and whites and grays, and the same hawks circling around in it. About dark I climbed down and went to the house. The people tried to make a fuss over me, but I told them I didn't feel good, and I went to my room and changed clothes. There were piles of food in the kitchen, and I was hungry, so I went back down and ate a little. It turned out the food was mostly cakes and potato salad. Nobody paid much attention to me, because a carload of Granny's kinfolk had come in about that time. When I was full, I slipped out of the back door and left in the pickup.

It was Halmea I wanted to talk to, and I drove to her house first. I felt like Halmea would have heard all about it, and would be waiting for me to come and talk. When I drove up to the house there were a few colored boys and a couple of girls standing in the street. They were laughing and hugging themselves and pushing each other around for the fun of it. I saw one girl who was Halmea's friend. It seems like her name was Eunice. I went over to them and they all quit laughing, and I asked them if they knew where I could find Halmea.

"You too late," Eunice said. "She done left fo' Dee-troit. She been gone since yesterdy."

"Already left?" I said. I felt silly and disappointed. It was an awful letdown, and for a minute I didn't know what to say.

"She tol' me you'd be comin' aroun'," the girl said. "But she didn't say why she goin', and she didn't leave no 'dress with me. You might get it from Aunt Beulah."

But the address wouldn't have given me what I wanted, and I didn't waste any time trying to explain it all to the old deaf woman who was rocking on the porch. If Halmea was gone, they were all gone, and Thalia might as well be empty. I was so disappointed I almost turned around and went back home, but finally I drove down to Hermy's. I thought there might at least be some news about him. Sometimes rodeo performers aren't hurt as bad as it looks like at first, and I thought he might even be home from the hospital.

Hermy's little sister met me at the door. She said her folks were still at the hospital, and that she'd been left at home with the littlest kids. She was about sixteen, and her name was Grace. I had dated her once or twice, but I'd known her so long, and Hermy and I were such close buddies, that we didn't accomplish much together. She said she didn't know anything. She thought Hermy was still pretty bad off. I found out which hospital he was in, and left. I meant to go see him as soon as I could get away. When I left Hermy's house I went downtown and made the square a time or two, but it was Sunday night, and only one night after the rodeo, and nobody was there but old Buttermilk and his dog. I began to feel like I was the only person left in the country, and it was a shitty feeling. On my way home, though, I stopped in at Bill's a minute for a hamburger and ran into Buddy Andrews and another kid or two, and we sat around and fed the jukebox until it was pretty late.

2.

There didn't seem to be a soul there when I came up to the church, and that suited me fine. It was Monday afternoon, right in the hottest part of the day. I had taken all I could stand of Grandma and her kinfolks, and once I was dressed up there wasn't anyplace to go but to the church house. When I saw there wasn't any cars parked out in front I felt better, and I hurried up the steps. Inside it would at least be cool and quiet and peaceful, not like the ranch house.

But when I opened the doors I saw that I had been mistaken. They must have just driven the hearse away to gas it up. I stood inside, on the thick carpet, and the black coffin set right in front of me, below the pulpit. I didn't want to sit in the family section that they had marked off with blue ribbon, so I sat down close to the back. I picked up a songbook to hold in my hands.

Two of the funeral people were there waiting: the man from the home, and Old Lady Singer, who played the piano. The minute I sat down Old Lady Singer began to play "Abide with Me," and she kept on playing it for hours it seemed like, all the time the people were coming in. The piano didn't sound too well in tune, and the old lady wasn't too good at playing it, either. I squeezed the songbook in my hand and made it bend. The man from the funeral home was one of the sorriest shits I had ever seen. Watching him, I wasn't so sad, not even with the sorrowful music the old lady was playing. He made me feel cold, and scornful, I guess. I had seen him the day before at the house, late in the afternoon. He had been whining around Granny about providence, when all he wanted was to get both hands in somebody's pocket. He was really spruced up for the big occasion, wearing a tar-paper-black suit and black shoes with flashy wing tips. There were a lot of big springy piles of flowers around the coffin, and he was arranging them. Once in a while he sneaked a glance at me or the old lady, to see if we appreciated his labor. The little black button of his hearing aid stuck on the side of his head like a woman's earring.

I wanted to go up and see Granddad someway and have my good-by over with, but all I could do was listen to the sorrowful music, and squeeze the songbook. I squeezed it and squeezed it until I thought the notes would drip out and splash on the floor.

But anyhow, it was dark in the church, and the deep-blue glass windows were cool as shady water. I always liked those blue windows, and I liked the rich brown wood of the church seats, wood that was the color of Halmea's breasts. But they had a sweety-sweet picture of Jesus over the choir booths that I didn't like at all. Jesus looked like he was a Boy Scout, waiting to get his twenty-first merit badge from the head Scout Master.

I was trying to decide to leave, when the people began to come through the church doors. A world of ranch people came. The bosses were there from all the headquarters, and a lot of hired hands with them, and a few that were just loose cowboys. A good many of them had worked for Granddad at one time or another, and nearly all of them had worked with him. Then the old ladies from Thalia trooped in, whispering to one another and shaking powder on the aisles. I could hear them whispering how Granddad had gone to a better place. They could think so and go to hell; I didn't believe it. Not unless dirt is a better place than air. I could see Granddad in my mind a thousand ways, but always he was on the ranch doing something, he wasn't in any loaf-around eternal life. I could see him riding, enjoying his good horses; or I could see him tending the cattle; or see him just standing in the grass, looking at the land and trying to figure out ways to beat the dry weather and the wind. Those were good places to me, and any one of them was a damn sight better than being in a church house, in a coffin, with a chickenshit snooping around you and a lot of old ladies talking. They could talk Bible till they were blue in the face, and end up dirt too someday. The longer I sat and watched it—the man, the old ladies, the little girls coming in fluffed up like cotton candy—the colder I got, and the worse I hated it all. More people came than Granddad would ever have dreamed of having: store people and businessmen and oil drillers and strangers by the swarm. People were at the funeral that Granddad hadn't ever seen. Some were there that he'd forgotten, and some that he hated and despised. Their wives were with them, all wearing slick black dresses, with little veils hanging down over their eyes and white gloves on their hands. In a little while the whole church was full, except for the two rows they saved for Grandma and her people. The funeral-home man put some of the late ones to bringing in chairs from the Sunday-school rooms, so they could fill the aisles.

Finally I saw Grandma and one of her sisters go by, and I knew it was fixing to start. Grandma didn't look at me. Then somebody took hold of my arm, and I saw Hud. He was wearing a new, expensive-looking suit, and a necktie with it.

"You come on," he said. "You got to sit with us."

I didn't want to move, so I didn't say anything. But Hud squeezed my arm till I felt his fingers pinching the bone, and I knew I had to go or be dragged. I got up, but I kept the songbook in my hand.

He sat me down so close to the front that I could see the glass cover of the coffin, and the satin padding around the inside rim. Seeing it made me feel weak. Two of the ladies on the row behind me were sniffling, and hearing them made me cold again.

Then Old Lady Singer stopped playing for a minute. When she did, the choir trailed in, and the two preachers right behind them. One of the preachers was Brother Barstow, and the other one I didn't know. They sat down without saying a word. Then the choir got up again, and began to sing "Rock of Ages." When they got to the line about the water and the blood I began to shiver, and I couldn't stop myself.

When the song was finished, the preacher I didn't know got up and went to the pulpit. He leaned on it for a long time and looked down at us without saying anything. He took his handkerchief out of his coat pocket, and I thought he was going to cry like the old ladies. But he just cleaned his glasses. When he got them clean, he fished a little card out of his pocket and began to read about Granddad.

He read his name to be Homer Lisle Bannon—born in Texas in 1868, and died there 1954. Died the last day of July. He told how Granddad had come to the Panhandle when he was just a boy, and how he had been a cowboy and a cattleman all his life. He told about him marrying my real grandmother, and when she died; and he told about when my daddy was born, and when he died; and he told about Granddad marrying Grandma, and he mentioned me. Then he went on and told a lot that wasn't true, about Granddad and the church. He told some more that wasn't true about Granddad's being respected and loved by people all over the state. There wasn't hardly anybody cared much for Granddad. Some liked him and some were scared of him and a good many hated his guts. Me and a few cowmen and a few hands and an old-timer or two loved and respected him some.

Hud hadn't changed expression the whole time, but Grandma had quit sniffling and was sitting up looking proud. The tears had rutted out the powder on her cheeks until her face looked like wet plaster. Then Mrs. Turner, the lady who sang the high parts for the choir, came down to the piano to sing a solo. She sang solos for everything, but she practiced her singing, and was good at it. The song she sang was "Yes, We'll Gather at the River," and she sang it too fine for me to stay cold. Yes, she sung, we'll gather at the river, the beautiful, the beautiful river. She sang out, and I could see the cords quivering in her throat. While she was singing I wasn't mad, and my eyes got hot and I had to wipe the wetness away with my fingers. She made the song go higher and higher, and as long as it lasted everything was different, and I thought again that Granddad might be moving above the pastures. I saw the river, running down the canyon and out under the trees, with cattle standing in it, and horses watering at the pools. It was a sight Granddad always loved, a flowing river. But Mrs. Turner finished too soon, and sat down, and I knew she wouldn't sing any more by herself. I lost the river, and heard the women sniffling, and I knew Granddad was done with flowing water for good and all.

Brother Barstow got up, then, to do the sermon, and I got dry quick. Brother Barstow was Grandma's crony, and Granddad's mortal enemy. He was a big man, proud as a peafowl, always gossiping with widow women, and trying to get something on everybody, just in case. Grandma used to have him out to the ranch a lot, to devil Granddad. The first time he came, Granddad was polite enough, but he told the preacher plain as day that he had got along without churches for a good long while, and that he didn't intend to start with them so late. Then one day Brother Barstow came out, during a revival week, and tried to get Granddad to say he'd go with Jesus. He didn't explain where. Granddad thought it was ignorant talk, and told him so. But Brother Barstow kept on about it till he made Granddad mad, and Granddad run him off. Granny had him back, but after that Granddad stayed out of his way.

When he got to the pulpit he took out his handkerchief and wiped his forehead and his eyes. Then he looked up at the ceiling, and stuck the handkerchief back in his pocket. "Let us pray," he said.

"Our dear Heavenly Father," he said. "One of our beloved neighbors has been called up to dwell with Thee. We that are left here with our anguish and loss pray that You will receive him into Glory, and feast him, and keep him in Your holy Love, throughout Eternity. Homer Bannon was one of Your faithful servants. He was a herdsman, and he tended his flocks and Yours well; and we know that You will grant him his reward. We bow our heads to You, oh God, and put our trust in Thy love and Thy mercy. And we won't fear for Homer Bannon, because we know he is with You. But for those of you Your children who must remain longer in this place of trials and sorrows, we pray You will send strength. We pray that You will plant Your rod, that we may lean on it and grow strong, so that when the day comes for us to lay down our earthly husks, as Brother Homer has, we may come humbly and penitent to Thee. Be with us now, and give us courage, as we ask these things in the name of Thy son our Lord, Jesus Christ. Amen."

Granny and her kinfolks and the old ladies were crying like they were all about to die, and Brother Barstow stood looking down at them, calm and shiny-eyed, like they were just little kids with skint knees. He waited till they got a little quieter, and then he began to turn through his Bible. He acted like he had lost his place, and he kept turning pages, looking for it. Then-all he found the place he wanted, and he bent over it and nodded. The people got quiet, and he raised his head and popped the Bible shut.

"Good people," he said, "we have gathered here in this holy place today to mourn the closing of another great book of life. Brother Homer Bannon, whom we all knew and loved, has at last been called to his rest." Hud leaned over then and whispered in my ear—it was the only time he moved during the whole sermon. "Called, my ass," he said. "It looked to me like he was driven."

Brother Barstow went right on.

"As his good friend and pastor, I knew Homer Bannon well, and in his declining years I visited him often. We grew to know one another, and as our friendship ripened, Homer and I often sat and talked about the day when he would be going to his reward.

"And so, my friends, my own heart was as grieved as yours to hear of Homer's passing. This morning it grieved me so that I couldn't sleep. I got out of bed and went out on my porch, and I watched the night turn to morning. And when I saw God's sun come up, when I saw it shed the message of His glory over the world, I thought of Homer Bannon, and I was reassured."

He stood there a minute, solemn, and he opened his Bible and began to read. I wished I could have laughed out loud at all he said. I wish I could have laughed and laughed and laughed. Or I wish Hud would have done it. But we didn't.

"In the Book of Genesis, Fifth Chapter, Twenty-fourth verse, it says: 'And Enoch walked with God; and he was not; for God took him.'" He closed the Bible again and leaned on it with his elbow.

"And friends, that is how it was with Homer Bannon," he said. "He walked with God, and God took him. Homer raised his horses and his cattle on God's earth. He watched over them like a good shepherd, and because he did, God made his life a Glory.

"Homer was a friend to God, and God gave him a long life. He gave him material abundance, and He gave him a loving family to watch over him in the days of his feebleness. And now God has taken him, taken him where he will never have to labor in the sun and the sleet again. He has taken him to a range it is not ours to trod, where the grass withereth not, and neither does the water fail. Homer made a date with God, an appointment, and he kept it. Many's the time, before the days of his infirmities, when I have seen Homer Bannon riding out to tend his herds, and I have thought: 'There is a good man. There is a man for God.' And now, he has not perished, he has merely kept his contract with God, and ridden on. And we who are left have a contract with God also, and if we follow Homer's example we will someday be granted our appointment. When that appointment comes, when we get to that place, that land beyond the river, richer than even this land, finer than even this land, we will find our friend Homer Bannon there ahead of us, ranging on Eternity. 'And Enoch walked with God; and he was not; for God took him.'"

When he finished my legs were jerking. I was thinking of how Granddad really did feel about land, how he was always studying it. A lot of people in the church were crying. As soon as Brother Barstow sat down, the choir got up again and sang "Whispering Hope." Mrs. Turner sang high and splendid all the way through it, and I was shivery again. Then Brother Barstow got back up and said: "Now dear people may the grace of our Lord and Saviour Jesus Christ rest and abide with each now and forevermore, Amen." In a minute the pallbearers came down to the front and stood there looking awkward while the funeral-home man fiddled with the coffin. He made them all stand back, so he could be the center of attention for a while. Then they picked the coffin up and carried it toward the back of the church, and I thought they were taking it away. The funeral man came over and stood by Grandma and motioned for us to stay seated. "The mourners are looking now," he said. I looked around and saw the coffin sitting right in the door of the church. I saw a man lifting his little girl up, so she could see Granddad.

Then the man motioned for us to get up, and I followed Hud out of the aisle. I could see the coffin again, and it seemed as big as a boat. It was much too big for Granddad. He was just skin and bones. The silver rim around the coffin shone like fire, and when I got closer I saw that all the inside of it was lined with pink satin. Granddad was laying there in it, what was left of him. He had never been in anything as showy as that before. I stopped by the side of it, and then I knew that he was really dead and gone forever; I may not have known it before. They had a slick black suit on him, and a white shirt and a vest, and a dark red necktie with a little gold bird on it. His hands were on his chest, as white as paint. I squeezed the songbook when I looked at his face. They had put paint on him, like a woman wears, red paint. I could see it on his cheeks, and caked around his mouth. I could see slick oil on his hair, and some sticky stuff like honey around his eyes. I wished I could have buried him like he died; he was better that way. I stood there too long, I didn't want to move away from him, and finally Hud pulled me a step or two. He held my arm.

"Come on," he said. "Let 'em take him to the graveyard an' put him down. Let's get this shit over with." I went with him to the edge of the people, and we stood there while Grandma looked. She was the last one. Then the man shut the lid so nobody could see, and I was glad. The pallbearers lifted the coffin and set it in the back of the hearse.

"Come on," Hud said. "You got to ride with us to the graveyard."

But before he got hold of me I turned and jumped back into the people. I slipped through them and got clear and ran way around to the back of the church. I wasn't going any farther with that crowd, Hud or no Hud. He didn't seem to be following me, and I fell on the ground behind a hedge.

Then I heard the cars begin to drive off. The church got quiet, and I sat there in my good clothes, on the ground. I felt like crying a little then, because the day was so bad, because they had finally hit at Granddad when he couldn't hit back. But my eyes were dry, and I was hot as if I had fever.

I opened the songbook and began to look for the song about the beautiful river, but I couldn't find it. I hummed a little of it to myself, and then I remembered how Mrs. Turner sang it, how fine it sounded when she sang the words about the beautiful, the beautiful river. It made me remember Granddad, like he was before the cattle sickness, in those days when he had some laughing in him. I remembered a lot of things about him that I hadn't thought of in a long time: how I used to sneak out of bed early in the mornings and watch out the window as he passed by on his way to the pasture, the wild cowboys following behind. I was always wondering what horse he would take—he might take a bronc or not. Once after he'd been sick he made the cowboys wire him on with baling wire, so he wouldn't get weak and fall. I looked down at the bare ground behind the hedge, the bare brown ground, and I remembered that they had taken Granddad to put him in it. I guess he had passed me finally and for good, to go to his land. It began to seem like they hadn't hurt him so much, after all—anyway, he had stayed with the land, like he always intended to do. The coffin and the paint wouldn't matter once he was deep in the land. I decided then that I wouldn't need to worry a lot about keeping his ranch, or about losing it, either, because whatever I did about it would just be for me. He had always held the land, and would go on holding what he needed of it forever. I got up then and walked around to the front of the church, looking at the green grass on the ground, and watching the white clouds ease into the sky from the south. I went in the church and laid the songbook on a seat. Then I went back outside and stood on the walk in front of the church house, looking at the grass, at the skim-milk clouds, at those blue church-house windows, thinking of the horseman that had passed.

Epilogue

The next afternoon I left Thalia, and nobody but Hud knew I was going. I told him I wanted to go visit Hermy, and that I might go somewhere else and work awhile if I could happen onto a job. He said it would be all right with him, but that they'd probably want me to come back when all the legal business about the killing came up. He said that might be a good while. Hud seemed calm and fairly friendly, and he didn't act depressed at all. They were going to try to indict him for murder without malice, but he said he didn't think they'd ever do it. The worst he could get if they did was five years, and that was nearly always suspended. I knew he'd probably come out of it on top. He told me to keep in touch, so they could locate me in a hurry if they needed me.

I took a few clothes and a few of my paperbacks and drove to town in the pickup. I drew my money out of the bank, and left the pickup parked in front of the courthouse, where Hud could find it easy. But it was the middle of the afternoon and hot as fire, and I didn't feel like just striking off down the highway. I fiddled around the drugstore awhile, and then went to the pool hall and shot snooker till almost dark. I even won about six bits. When I came out it was dusk, and the four street lights around the square were lit. I stood on the curb by the pickup. They had sprinkled the courthouse lawn, and the water and grass and hot day made a good smell. I got my suitcase and decided to make a start. A red cattle truck was stopped by the filling station, and the driver was out checking his tires. I walked over and stood watching him.

"Felt like I had a flat," he said, coming around the truck. He grinned at me. "Guess I'm feeling things."

"Where you headed?" I asked. I felt a little silly.

"Raton, New Mexico," he said. "Goin' all the way, an' comin' back through here sometime tomorrow night. I truck outa Fort Worth."

"Could you let me ride to Wichita?" I said. "I got to get there tonight."

"Why sure, hell yes," he said. He was a short blackheaded guy with a pot belly and a crazy grin. He waved for me to get in the truck. "I been lonesome as a hound-dog all the way," he said. "My name's Bobby Don Brewer."

I crawled up in the high, bouncy cab, and set my suitcase between my legs. "I'm Lonnie Bannon," I said, and we shook hands. "A buddy of mine got hurt bull-ridin' the other night, an' I thought I'd go see him."

Bobby Don ground the truck in gear and we started off. "I used to ride them bulls when I was a young fucker," he said, spitting out the window "But I got me two boys now. Mama don't let me rodeo no more. Sometimes I miss it, you know." He slapped the seat with his hand, and honked at a gasoline truck, looking a little saddened. "I had me some good times, rodeo-ing," he said. "Runnin' aroun', drinkin' beer an' all that. Knew some good ol' boys I don't get to see no more. All of us out scratchin' for a livin', I guess."

"Say?" he said, "Bannon, you say? Kin to Homer Bannon?"

"I'm his grandson," I said. "You know him?"

"Hell, yes, I know him," he said. "I trucked many a head a cattle off his ranch. Hell, I remember you now, remember you now, remember seeing you. How is Mister Homer?"

I didn't want to get in a long conversation about it.

"Mean as he ever was," I said.

He grew quiet, and we rode through the outskirts of Thalia. The sun was going into the great western canyons, the cattleland was growing dark. I saw the road and the big sky melt together in the north, above the rope of highway. I was tempted to do like Jesse once said: to lean back and let the truck take me as far as it was going. But I wanted to see Hermy, and I knew Bobby Don wouldn't have any time to waste. I saw the lights of houses as we flashed by in the darkness, the little houses, the ranches and the farms I knew. Bobby Don hummed some old song whose tune I had forgotten, and I sat thinking about Thalia, making the rounds in my mind. At home it was time for the train to go by, and nobody was sitting on the porch, But for a little while, as the truck rolled on across the darkened range, I had them all, those faces who made my days: Jesse and Granddad, Halmea and Hud.

"Goddamn," Bobby Don said, turning to me. "It's sure too bad about your buddy getting' hurt. Them bulls can be bad business, I know that."

The cab was dark and the dash light threw shadows across his face, so that when I looked at him, and saw him pull down his old straw hat and face the road, he reminded me of someone that I cared for, he reminded me of everyone I knew.

LEAVING CHEYENNE

My foot's in the stirrup,
My pony won't stand;
Goodbye, old partner,
I'm leaving Cheyenne.

The Cheyenne of this book is that part of the cowboy's day's circle which is earliest and best: his blood's country and his heart's pastureland.

L. M.

I

THE BLOOD'S COUNTRY

South of my days' circle, part of my blood's country,
rises that tableland . . . clean, lean,
Hungry country. . . .

I know it dark against the stars, the high lean country,
full of old stories that still go walking in my sleep.

JUDITH WRIGHT, from *South of My Days*

One

When I woke up Dad was standing by the bed shaking my foot. I opened my eyes, but he never stopped shaking it. He shook it like it was a fence post and he was testing it to see if it was in the ground solid enough. All my life that's the way he'd wake me up—I hated it like poison. Once I offered to set a glass of water by the bed, so he could pour that over me in the mornings and wake me up, but Dad wouldn't do it. I set the water out for him six or seven times, and he just let it sit and shook my foot anyway. Sometimes though, if he was thirsty, he'd drink the water first.

"Get up from there," he said. "If you're big enough to vote, you don't need to sleep past daylight. You do the chores today. I'm gonna trot off down in the pasture and look around. One of them scrawny heifers might have calved, for all I know."

And off he went, as usual. The last time Dad done the chores was when I was twelve years old, and the only reason he done them then was because I had let the ax slip and cut my foot nearly off. I never did know what he done down in the pasture every morning; by the time I could get the horses fed and the milking done, he'd be back.

For once though I was kinda glad he woke me up. It was election day, and my sly friend Johnny had worked it around somehow so that he and Molly got to watch the ballot box during the first shift. There was supposed to be at least two people to a shift. What he figured was that nobody would be there to vote till after dinner, so he could do a little courting with Molly on the government's time. Only I didn't intend to let him get away with it. I never liked to see a man cheat on the government.

I DONE the chores a little too quick. By six-thirty I didn't have a thing left to do, and I knew there wasn't any use getting to the schoolhouse before about eight o'clock. It was just over on Idiot Ridge, about a ten-minute ride. If there's one thing I can't do at all, it's wait. So I got a rag and polished the saddle a little, and that was a mistake. It was a pleasure to polish a saddle like that; the mistake was that Dad walked in and caught me.

"You needn't jump," he said. "And you needn't try to hide it. I found it day before yesterday anyhow. It's a nice saddle. Why ain't you been using it?"

I had put the saddle under a tarp, way back in the dark end of an empty oatbin. But you couldn't hide nothing from Dad.

"Because it ain't mine," I said.

"Hell it ain't," he said, a little surprised. "What'd you do, steal it?"

"You aggravate the piss out of me," I said. "I never stole a penny in my life, and you know it."

"Plenty's waited longer than you to start. Whose is it then?"

"Didn't you see the name plate?" I said. "It's sterling silver looks like you'd have noticed it. I had this saddle made for Johnny, and I just haven't got around to giving it to him yet."

For once Dad was flabbergasted. I knew he would be, but didn't see no sense in lying to him.

"Giving it to him?" he said. "You're giving a hundred-and-fifty-dollar saddle to a thirty-dollar-a-month cowboy. That wouldn't make sense to a crazy man. And it sure don't to me."

"Well, I can't help it, Dad," I said. "Johnny did me a big favor which I ain't at liberty to talk about. Nobody ever did me that much favor before, and I may live to be older than you without nobody doing me that much favor agin. Johnny never owned a quality piece of equipment his whole life. I had the money and just thought I'd get him something he could use. There's nothing wrong with that."

Dad had real black eyes, and when he wanted to look fierce he didn't look it halfway. He looked fierce then.

"Giving a saddle like that to a McCloud is like pinning a diamond stud pin on a goat's ass," he said. "Favor or no favor. And besides, whatever money you had come from me."

"Johnny ain't sorry," I said. "Being poor don't make him no-count. I worked plenty hard for the money I spent on this saddle, and if you think I'm overpaid, hire you another hand."

"Settle down," he said. "I ain't gonna whip you, you're too old. Let's go outside . You can polish his saddle some other time."

We went out and stood by the water trough and looked at the cattle grazing down in the Field pasture, just this side of the River. I washed the saddle soap off my hands.

"Ain't this a good ranch?" Dad said. "I put a lot of work and a lot of years into it, but by god I've got it all back in money and satisfaction."

"Go on and bawl me out," I said. "I've got some pretty urgent business to get to this morning."

"You sure have," he said. "You've got to rush over to the schoolhouse and see if you can keep your good friend Johnny from getting in Miss Molly's pants. If you can keep him out, you figure you'll eventually get in. Well, suppose you just sit here and listen about five minutes. You might learn something."

"I don't like the way you talk about my friends," I said.

"Pity," he said. "I'm gonna have to leave this ranch to you some day; now I want you to get to taking that serious. I ain't mad about the saddle. But you took off and left, right in the middle of the calving season. You never gave me no warning or nothing, and you took that McCloud kid with you. And you've never said one word to me about where you've been or why. That don't add up to very sensible behavior, and I ain't too happy about leaving this ranch to somebody who ain't sensible, I don't care what kin he is to me."

"Well, I'm sorry as I can be, and you know it," I said. "But there ain't nothing I can tell you about that. I just had to leave."

He set there and looked off down the pasture. Dad was getting quite a bit of age on him.

"Nobody ever did me favor enough in my entire life for me to waste two hundred dollars on them," he said. "I guess by the time I'm dead ten years you'll have thrown away what I spent fifty years making. Old age is a worthless damn thing."

"Oh, hush," I said. "By the time I've run this ranch for ten years it's liable to be twice the size it is now."

"Yeah and I'm liable to flap my arms and take off from here and fly like a buzzard any minute now," he said. "That sure is a good saddle. I'll tell you one thing, Johnny McCloud ain't no favorite of mine."

"Well you ain't no favorite of his either, that I know of," I said. I went and put the tarp back over the saddle, and Dad went up to the house to eat.

Of course things never worked like I planned. Dad had found a sick yearling that morning, but he never took time to doctor it himself, so I had to catch a horse and go hunt it up and doctor it before I could go to the voting place. It was after nine o'clock when I got there, and Johnny and Molly had been there since eight. I hated it so bad I could taste it.

They were sitting on the schoolhouse steps when I loped up. She was letting Johnny hold her hand, and they were both grinning. Oh me, Molly looked pretty. She had on a blue and white polka-dot dress, and her long black hair was whipping around in the wind. There wasn't another soul around. Johnny was looking wild and reckless, so no telling what had went on. Molly was just a sucker when it come to Johnny.

"Look who's here," he said. "What happened, you ain't but an hour early? Where's your friend Ikey?"

"I been working," I said. "Hello, Molly." I knew he'd bring Ikey up, but I didn't intend to talk about it. Ikey was a nigger, but he was a nigger that could vote, and he was supposed to be partners with me to watch the voting box. Molly had already promised she would stay awhile with me after Johnny's shift was up, so what I had to do was figure out a way to get rid of Ikey quick. Johnny knew just what I was up to, of course, but it wasn't gonna do him any good.

"Get down," Molly said. She grinned at me, as sweet as ever, but Johnny still had ahold of her hand, and she never made him turn loose.

I couldn't think of too much to say, so I took my horse over and tied him to a mesquite. I went in and was going to vote, but they had been so busy spooning around they hadn't even unpacked the ballots, and I had to do it. I never voted though, I forgot about it. I don't think I voted in that election at all. Molly had finally got her hand loose, and when she stood up we all went over to the cistern and got a drink.

"What's that I smell on you, Gid?" Johnny said. "Smells like screw-worm dope. You ought to taken a bath before you come to work for the government."

"You don't smell like no prairie flower yourself," I said. "Been trapping any skunks lately?" When Johnny was just a boy the McClouds had had to sell skunk hides to keep going. They wasn't the only ones, of course, but Johnny hated skunks worse than anything. His folks had finally got better off, but they still just had a little two-section place.

"Not lately," he said, but it kinda irritated him.

Molly, she never taken sides when me and Johnny argued. She would just stand there and grin her pretty, friendly grin, and curl a loop of her hair around one finger. She was pretty as a picture when she done that.

It didn't seem like I'd been there no time when Ikey come. He had an old brown mule that was about half-crippled; he rode the mule bareback wherever he went. We seen Ikey coming and Johnny began to grin. He always had some trick to play on Ikey, and most of them were funny.

"Looky there," he said. "Here he comes, riding that three-legged mule. I tell you what, Gid, some day let's saw that crippled leg off. That way it won't drag and slow Ikey down."

"You hush that," Molly said. "How'd you like to have one of your legs sawed off?"

"I might like it," he said. "You want to saw one off for me?"

"That's no way to talk. Make him hush, Gid." She sidled over toward me just a little bit.

Johnny just looked that much more devilish.

"What he needs is his damn head sawed off," I said. "That's the only kind of sawing that would do him any good."

Ikey arrived about then, and got off his mule. "Good mornin', Mis' Molly," he said. "Mornin', Mistuh Johnny, mornin', Mistuh Gid." The thing that worried me about Ikey was that he was so proud of being good enough to watch a ballot box like the white folks that he probably wasn't going to be in too big a hurry to leave. But I figured I could persuade him.

"Morning, Ikey," Johnny said. "Whyn't you shoot that pore old mule and put him out of his misery?"

I had to grin at that. Ikey was as surprised as if Johnny had asked him to shoot his wife. He thought he had one of the best mules in the country.

"Shoot dis mule?" he said, looking at it real close. "Den how'd I get aroun'?"

"Don't pay any attention to him," Molly said. "He's crazy. Come on in and vote, Ikey."

I was all for that, so I went in and fixed him up a ballot. I thought if we made a big enough thing of him voting Ikey might be satisfied and go on home.

"Boy, this is a big election," I said. "They say every vote is gonna be important. Think it over good, Ikey. Don't be in too big a hurry."

"Naw, don't excite Ikey," Johnny said. "He might stab himself with that pencil. It ain't worth the trouble, Ikey. The man with the most money's gonna get it anyway. It always turns out that way."

"It don't, do it?" Molly said. She never liked to hear anybody run down politics. I guess it was because her old man had been commissioner for our precinct one year; everybody criticized him so she had to take up for him twice as hard as she usually done. He was the most thieving commissioner there ever was, besides the most lazy, and Molly knew it. She just never would admit it, to herself or nobody else. Her daddy didn't get elected because he was the man with the most money; he got elected because he was the man with the most whiskey to give away. There weren't but twelve people in the precinct able to vote, and he gave ever one of them a jug of whiskey and still only won by one vote. The man that was running against him was too decent to vote for himself, and Old Man Taylor wasn't, so he won it. Afterward he got hold of the ballots and found out who voted against him and went around and got his jugs back from those. I know that's true, because one of the ones that voted against him was Dad, and the jug was damn sure all he got back. I guess Molly was the only person in the world who ever liked that old man.

Ikey, though, he never paid any attention to what we were saying to him. He was set up so he could just pay attention to one thing at a time, and right then he was paying attention to voting. He got out his spectacles that he was so proud of and polished them on his pants leg and put them on and adjusted them so he could see over them. It's a damn cinch he couldn't see through them. It would have been like looking through a pair of stovelids. After he got them set so they wouldn't interfere with his vision, he began to read the ballot. That took so long that me and Johnny had to go off behind the schoolhouse to pee before he got through. We left Molly there to help Ikey read.

"You sneaky bastard," I said, when we got out. "How long was you'all over here before I come?"

"Why, I'm ashamed of myself about that," he said. "Don't you think I've got a pretty girl, though?"

"I think Molly's a pretty girl, all right," I said, "but you ain't got her by a long shot. Why don't you take after Mabel Peters, anyway?"

"Why, Mabel's crazy about you," he said. "Watch where you're pissing. You get it on these gabardine pants and your name's mud. I mean it."

Actually I just splattered a little on his boots. "It's about time you were going home, ain't it?"

"Why, yes," he said. "I'll go get Molly."

He went, but he never got her. I went too. She walked out the door with him and he had her hand agin, but she must have told him she had promised to stay awhile with me. He didn't look too cheerful. I went on in to help Ikey.

He was sitting there licking his pencil, and after he'd done that about five minutes, he voted.

"Good lord," said. "I just remembered something. I was supposed to cut a big patch of cuckleburrs today. Down on the River. Dad's been after me about that for two weeks."

"Well then, why don't you go cut them?" Johnny said. "I'll stay here and do your turn at the voting box. You just go right ahead."

"Oh no," I said. "I wouldn't want nobody to do that. That's my responsibility."

"Don't worry so much," Molly said. I guess she was so sweet it never occurred to her what I was really worrying about. It damn sure occurred to Johnny.

"He better worry," he said. "I wouldn't want Mr. Fry mad at me. I think his best chance is just to forget about this voting and go do his work."

"Well," I said. "Since you're so anxious to help, I wonder if you'd like to lope off down there and cut them for me. It wouldn't take more than four hours."

That got into his quick. "Hell no, I wouldn't like to," he said. "I'm a cowboy, I ain't no damn cuckleburr chopper."

"Well, Ikey, what all do you have to do today?" I said. "Maybe I can hire you to do it. I'll give you two dollars, and you don't need to worry about watching this voting. Miss Molly's gonna stay here a little while and she'll be glad to do your part for you."

Ikey didn't give any argument at all. I wasn't much expecting him to: his normal wage was about a quarter a day.

"I'll cut 'em an' be glad," he said. "I'll jus' be glad." I gave him the two dollars and that settled it. That much money was such a shock to him that he couldn't hardly get it in his pocketbook. Then he folded up his ballot real slow and careful and looked kinda sad about having to drop it in the box. One thing about him, he really liked to vote. Then he got up and put away his spectacles.

"Well, I'll go cut 'em, Mistuh Gid," he said. "I sho enjoyed de elecshun day, Miss Molly. I hope we have anothuh one soon as we can."

Molly kinda laughed. "We will," she said. "We'll have one in November. You be careful, Ikey. Don't chop off your foot, and don't get on no snakes."

Ikey got on his mule and went off. Johnny just grinned and winked at Molly. It was hard to get his goat.

"I wish I was well off enough to hire my dirty work done," he said. "But I ain't that lucky. I always have to do my own."

"I never noticed you doing much," I said. "Besides, I felt sorry for Ikey. I'd like to see him get himself a better mule."

"If that ain't a lie I never heard one," he said. "Ikey's gonna spend that money on whiskey, and you knew it before you gave it to him. And you'll probably talk him out of three-quarters of that. You can't fool me."

"Why, Gid, I heard you quit drinking," Molly said. "I didn't know you started agin."

"I haven't," I said. "Johnny's just spoofing you."

"Well, I got to be going." Johnny said. He'd done all the damage he dared do. "Don't you'all take no bribes under five dollars."

That made Molly mad, so he was smart to leave. She was kinda patriotic, and never liked to hear people hint about crooked government. It was because her old man was so crooked himself.

Anyway, Johnny got on his horse and loped off, and there we were. It was about ten o'clock, and I didn't figure we much needed to worry about anybody coming to vote before dinnertime. Voting is the kind of thing most people like to put off as long as they can.

I looked at Molly, and she was looking at me and grinning. I guess she knew good and well what I was up to, rushing Ikey off.

"Well, Mr. Fry," she said. "You sure was in a big hurry to chase everybody off. That wasn't very sociable."

"I ain't very sociable with crowds," I said. Specially not crowds with Johnny in them." I kinda reached for her hand, but I missed. She laughed and stepped out the schoolhouse door. The wind begin whipping her hair up around her face.

"You're grabby," she said. "Grabby Mr. Fry."

"Don't call me that," I said. "And don't put on thataway. Let's go around to the cistern."

"Okay," she said, "let's do. Only you're so unsociable. I might just better go home."

I got her hand after all and squeezed it and she squeezed back.

"I'm a lot more sociable where you're concerned," I said.

I got my big slicker off my saddle and spread it out by the cistern so we could sit down without the grass and the chiggers eating us up. We got on the shady side and leaned up against the rocks and just set there. It was right on the hill, high enough that we could see anybody coming a long time before they would notice us. Molly let me put my arm around her, and she kind of slumped against me, and talked about this and that. I mostly listened. After a while my arm went to sleep, but I didn't dare move. Her hair was in my face. She must have washed it that morning, because it was real clean and I could still barely smell the vinegar she rinsed it in.

"It's a nice day for election," she said. "Look at the way the grass waves. I bet we can see nearly all over the county from here."

I kept wishing she'd turn her face around, but she wouldn't do it.

"Gid-ing-ton," she said, "what are you doing back there where I can't see you?" She called me that somctimes; she thought Gid was too short a name. I was agreeable.

"Don't you wish I'd turn my face around, so you could kiss me?" she said. "Now don't you?"

"I could stand it," I said. "You won't, though."

"You think I should let a boy kiss me on election day?" she said, and then she turned around anyway, and let me. Some of her hair was between me and her mouth; I didn't care. Only after a while she began to giggle and squirm.

"Let me fix it," she said. "Who wants to kiss hair?" she sat up and turned her back, and all I could see was black hair and her polka dot dress. Then she rolled over on the slicker and propped up on her elbows.

"Let's quit," she said. "Let's just talk. What if Johnny was to come back?"

"What if? It ain't none of his business what we do."

"He thinks it is, though." I made her let me kiss her again, but she kept giggling and wouldn't get serious about it. "Johnny thinks it's all his business," she said. "He keeps asking me all about us."

"Well, he can just cut it out," I said. "I'm not going to put up with much more of him. You're my girl now, ain't you?"

"Am I?" she said, looking up at me through her hair, half-grinning and half-serious. "I think I'm too silly for you."

"No you ain't. Why, I'm worse that way than you are."

"No you ain't," she said, and she wasn't kidding. "You're not even as silly as Johnny, and he's not as silly as me. Eddie's the only one who is."

"If you mean he's the only one who's dumb, you're right," I said. I hated that sorry Eddie. “At least I’m a little smart. I’m smart enough to know you’re the prettiest girl there is.”

I made her let me kiss her agin, and finally it shut her up and she got real quiet and sweet. Once you get Molly quiet she’s the warmest, sweetest girl in the world.

“I still think you’re my girl,” I said.

“Maybe I am,” she said. “Lay down here and hush.”

She hugged me real tight, and just about that time we heard Ikey’s mule. I could tell that mule a quarter of a mile away.

“Damn it all,” I said. “Ikey’s coming back. I’d like to wring Johnny’s neck. I know damn good and well he put him up to it.”

“Let’s just lay here,” she said. “Let’s don’t get up. Maybe if Ikey sees us he’ll go on away. Or we could run hide.”

“No,” I said. “Damn Johnny anyway. I’ll get even with him. I don’t want Ikey to see us, and it’s silly to hide. I ain’t gonna do that.”

She got up and I folded the slicker.

“Brush the grass off my dress,” she said. “I got off the slicker.”

She turned her back and I brushed her off. She didn’t really look mad, and she put her arm around me and let me hold her hand even while Ikey was coming up. But she kept looking off across the pasture, off down Idiot Ridge.

“Where did you get that dress?” I said. “It’s awful pretty, Molly.”

“I made it. Thank you.” She looked up then and seen I had grass on my cheek, and she brushed it off with her hand. “You just ain’t very silly, are you?” she said.

Two

JOHNNY NEVER WOULD ADMIT HE SENT IKEY BACK; HE WAS too stubborn. But I knew he was the one responsible. I finally got Ikey sent off agin, but it was too late. Ikey wasn't hardly out of sight the second time before Dad come, of all people.

Dad made out like he come to vote, but he never: he just come to see what I was doing. He knew I was there with Molly, and he just thought he'd come and spy a little. I hated it like poison when he did something like that. Molly, she never minded. She always took up for Dad, and I guess he liked her for it; he always treated her like she was the prize of the world. Except when I got to talking about marrying her—then he got mad.

"Don't be a damn fool and marry young," he said. "Specially not to no poor woman. Work about thirty more years and make you lots of money. Then go off somewhere and marry a rich widow. Don't never marry somebody who's as broke and ignorant as you are; marry somebody who knows a little about it. Then you might have a chance to enjoy yourself a little."

That was Dad for you. I didn't pay him much mind. He never could understand that he wasn't me.

What I knew was that Johnny McCloud had two things coming: one was a good saddle, and the other was a good whipping. I guess he thought I had a whipping coming too, because he started it all.

About a week after election day, Old Man Ashtoe, the feller Johnny was cowboying for, sent him up to Henrietta with a little bunch of cattle he wanted delivered. Johnny delivered the cattle, all right, but then he bought some whiskey from somebody and got drunk and insulted a deputy sheriff or two and got put in jail. Soon as he got home Old Man Ashtoe fired him, and Johnny was so broke he had to take a job with a harvesting crew. The first day he worked with them was the day they were finishing up harvesting our oats. Dad had me out helping them, of course.

"Ain't this hell?" Johnny said, when we were going out that afternoon for another big load of shocks. "A cowboy oughtn't to do work like this. This here's clodhopper work. It's a kind of disgrace, ain't it to you?"

"Not to me," I said. "I don't have no choice about it. It's a real disgrace where you're concerned, though. If you'd have behaved right, you could be horseback right now."

"I never asked for no sermons," he said, grinning at me. "You've got just as much oatseed in your hair as I have. Where you want to work, on the wagon or on the ground?"

"On the wagon," I said. "You're such a good hand with a pitch-fork, I don't want you to get out of practice."

We worked for about an hour, I guess. He threw the shocks up to me with his fork, and I stacked them on the wagon. The wagon was stacked up pretty high.

"I just need eight or ten more," I said. "Let's hurry, then we can take a rest."

He stuck his fork in a big shock, and I noticed him stop to look at it pretty close. I figured there was a rattlesnake under it; we had killed five or six that day. Oatschocks were a great place for rattlesnakes, because so many rats lived under them.

It was awful hot, and I started to take my gloves off to wipe my face. Then Johnny picked up the shock and got ready to heave. I seen it coming and reached out to catch it, but just before I got my hands on it this big snake head came right up between my hands and hissed in my face. It scared the piss out of me and I went to running backward for all

I was worth, but the shock kept right on coming till it looked like the snake was going to fall right on my face. I kicked like hell and went off the wagon backward, fighting with my hands to keep the snake out of my lap. I never seen where it went, because I hit the ground like I had fallen off a cloud. I never rolled an inch. In a little while I heard a lot of people laughing and one of them was Johnny. I looked around and Johnny and three or four of the harvesters were about to bust their guts laughing. Then I seen the snake sliding off the wagon wheel: it was an old brown bullsnake was all. It was mad, too, but not no madder than I was. I had to lay back down; I was seeing spots before my eyes.

"We better help him up," one of them said. "He might have busted something."

"Hell no, he'll be up in a minute," Johnny said. "You better get back to work or you'll be the one with something busted."

I propped up on my elbows and looked at him. "You're a damn bastard," I said. "What if that had been a rattlesnake?"

"It couldn't have scared you any worse," he said. "Besides, I seen what it was."

"Well, you better take a good look at the world," I said, getting up on my hands and knees. "You won't be able to see much when I get through with you."

"Goodness me," he said. "Maybe that'll teach you not to fiddle with my girl."

I was beginning to feel the blood coming back from wherever it went to when I seen that snake. Johnny was standing about ten feet away, leaning against the wagon wheel and grinning.

"She's no such a thing your girl," I said.

Then I went for him, and we had it out right there. I nearly got the best of him right off, but then I got to missing ever time I swung at him. I guess the fall had thrown off my aim. Pretty soon I got tired and he did too, but we just kept standing there, pounding the piss out of one another. Finally we both stopped for a minute.

"When you've had enough, say calf rope," I said. "I don't want to put you in no hospital."

"Calf rope, your ass," he said. "You're going to bleed to death if we don't quit."

"Hell," I said. "My nose always bleeds in the summertime."

"Let's quit anyway," he said. "Get a drink of water. You quit first."

"Nope."

"Then we'll just have to stand here till you drop," he said. "I never seen such a stubborn bastard."

We might have stood there till dark, I don't know. Finally the boss harvester noticed us and came over.

"Damn boys," he said, "why don't you fight with the pitchforks next time? There won't be so much blood that way."

"He started it," I said.

"Load the wagon," he said. "You can fight some more tonight if you want to."

So I wiped off a little blood and Johnny got his pitchfork, and we finished making up the load. He never threw up no more snakes, either. Finally we got all the oats we could haul and went to the barn. Johnny rode on the seat with me.

"Shit-fire," he said. "I'm quitting this job. I ain't no damn clodhopper, and I ain't gonna let no fat-ass like that give me orders."

"What are you gonna do for money when you quit?" I asked.

"I been thinking about that." he said. "You know what, Gid, I think I'll go to the Panhandle. This here country ain't no place for a cowboy. It's all right if you got your own ranch, like you have, but if you ain't, it's no good. I'd like to go up on the plains, where them big ranches are, and do some real cowboying. I'm tired of sitting around here listening to my old man bitch at me. I think I'll just strike out."

"I wouldn't mind going with you," I said. "Hell, working for Dad's worse than being a hired hand. He thinks he has to tell me ever move to make."

"Then let's go," he said. He was excited about it. But I knew I never would be able to get away from Dad. There was too much that needed doing around the place that he couldn't do. Besides, we had done been gone two months, to that hospital. I pulled the wagon over in the shade of the barn, and we got down.

"Let's go over to the horse trough," I said. "Wash this blood off." I figured if he was going off to punch cattle, I had better give him his saddle. Even if I was still mad at him.

"Well, you coming with me?" he said. Then he bent over and ducked his head plumb under the water and came up shaking it like a wet dog.

"I don't reckon so," I said. "I guess I got too much to do here."

"Too much cowboying or too much courting, which one?"

"You better watch out," I said. "I ain't going to take no more off you today."

He slapped his hat back on without even drying his hair. "Hell, I ain't eager to go off and leave Molly, either," he said. "But a man's got to get out and see a little of the world in his life. I guess they'll be some pretty sweet girls up there."

"Not that sweet," I said. "Let's unload the hay."

"I may not go after all," he said.

But stacking those damn itchy oats in the hot oatbin almost got us down. I guess we was both weak from the fight.

"Oh hell," he said, when we finished. "Piss on this. This here'll kill a good cowboy in a week. It takes weak-minded bastards to stand this kind of work. I'm quitting."

"I don't blame you," I said, and I didn't. It would be the real life, up on the plains, with all those big ranches and cow outfits. I just couldn't manage it, though.

"Come around here," I said. "I got something for you."

We went around in the hallway of the barn, and I drug out the saddle. He never knew what to make of it.

"That's a beauty," he said. "Whose is it?"

"Yours," I said. "I thought you ought to have it for going to the hospital with me and taking care of me all that time. If you're going off to cowboy, you'll get some use out of this."

"Why, my god," he said. "You don't mean it! Why, ain't it a beauty. That's as nice a saddle as I ever seen."

"Yeah, it ought to last you a long time."

"Well damn, sure much obliged, Gid," he said, feeling of the leather. "This here's something to be proud of. I never had nothing this well made in my life."

"Let's try it out," I said. "It's too late to haul oats today."

We caught a couple of horses and went for a ride. I never saw Johnny so tickled over anything, or so excited. He rode it awhile and then I rode it awhile, and it rode like a rocking chair. It was a little creaky and new, but he would ride that out of it in a hurry.

We got back to the barn just in time to start the evening chores. Dad was out fiddling around in the lots, watching the milk-pen calves.

"Well, this settles it," Johnny said "I ain't wasting a saddle like this on this part of the country. I think I'll leave in a day or two. Sure wish you'd go with me."

"Can't make it," I said. "You better wait till them eyes get better. Ain't nobody going to hire a blind man."

"Blind, my ass," he said. "What about your nose?"

"It ain't very bad squashed. It'll straighten out."

Dad finally come poddling over and looked at the saddle some.

"Well, I see you boys been beating on one another," he said. "Too bad neither one of you had any sense to beat into the other one."

"Oh, we wasn't out for blood," Johnny said. Dad got a big laugh when he told him about me reaching out for the snake. Johnny could tell things so they sounded a whole lot funnier than they were.

"What do you think about my new saddle, Mr. Fry?" Johnny asked.

Dad just grunted. "I think it's a better one than I ever had," he said. "And I'm four times your age and several times your smart." He walked off toward the house. Johnny winked at me and I grinned. Dad never got Johnny's goat quite, and it tickled me.

Two days later Johnny rode to Henrietta and pitched his saddle in the caboose and took the train north. That left me and Molly with the country to ourselves, but I was kinda sorry to see old Johnny go. He was a good buddy even if he was a smart aleck, and I felt lonesome whenever he wasn't around.

Three

I GUESS DAD HAD BEEN HOPING I'D CHANGE MY MIND AND KEEP the new saddle for myself. When Johnny actually took off and left the country with it, it put Dad in a such a bad humor he never got over it for a month. And when he was in a bad humor he could think up a million mean jobs for me to do. I spent the last part of July and the whole damn month of August digging corner postholes and cleaning out sewer lines and cutting devil's claws and plowing. I hated the plowing the worst. And all the time I was down in the field, eating dust and yanking on the damn contrary mules, Johnny was up on the plains, riding his new saddle and living like a cowboy should. I got so tired of thinking about it that one day I just come right out and told Dad I was pretty much in the notion to go up there too.

"The hell you will," he said. We were riding one of the River pastures, looking for screwworms, and Dad rode up on a hill and stopped his horse long enough to tell me off.

"You'll just stay right where you are," he said. "And if I tell you to plow, by god, you plow."

"But I ain't no damn farmer," I said. "Why don't you hire your farming done? Why do I have to waste my time doing it?"

"I am hiring it done, and you're the one I'm hiring," he said. "Why pay somebody else to do something we can do ourselves? That ain't no way to get rich."

"I see a few cattle down toward the southwest corner," I said. "What makes you think I want to be rich anyway?"

"Because I bred you," he said. "I know damn well I couldn't breed a boy with so little sense as to want to be poor. You got enough sense to know it's better to be rich than poor, ain't you?"

"That ain't what the Bible says," I said.

He just looked at me. "I ain't responsible for what the Bible says," he said. "If it says that, it's wrong. And I never asked you for no preaching, either. I know there's fools in the world who say poverty is holy, but you let them go without shoes some cold winter, like I did when I was a kid, and then see how holy they think it is. Being poor just makes people little and mean, most of the time. It's a damn degrading thing."

"All right," I said. "Hold your horses. I don't want to be poor. But you can not want to be poor and still not care whether you're rich or not."

"Yes, and them's the kind of people that never accomplish nothing," he said. "They're just damn mediocre. If you're gonna try at all, you ought to try for something big."

"Well, I'll never get nothing big from plowing that worn-out field."

"You might," he said. "You might plow up a diamond, you don't know. I count twenty cattle in that corner."

"I just counted eighteen. Let's go get them."

"I ain't finished telling you what's good for you yet. Now you got the itch to go up on the plains and cowboy, just because Johnny McCloud's up there. Now I'll tell you about Johnny McCloud. He's a good cowhand and he ain't scared of nothing. I'll admit that. But that's the limitation of him, right there. He'll never be nothing but a damn good cowhand. When he dies he'll own just what he's got on and what he's inherited. And that saddle you gave him, if he don't lose it in a poker game first. He'll fiddle around his whole life working for wages, and never accomplish a damn thing."

"That don't make him bad," I said.

"Course not. It don't make him bad at all. I've known a lot of fellers like him, and some of them I liked a lot. The point is, you ain't like that. You've got too much of me in you. Punching somebody else's cows never would satisfy you. But you might waste a lot of time before you figure that out. The man that gets the farthest is the man that wastes the least time and the least energy he possibly can. You ain't old enough to know that yet, but I am. If you can just learn to listen to me, you'll save yourself a lot of misery."

"I guess you know everything in the world, don't you?" I said. "I don't guess you was ever known to be wrong, was you?"

"Oh yes, I've been wrong. I've been wrong more times than most people have been right. But that ain't no significance. I've also done forgot more than most people ever know.

"But anyhow," he said, "it don't take much sense to figure out that you and Johnny are two different kinds of people. Let's go look at them cattle."

We doctored a few worms, and was riding home down the lane, late in the afternoon. It was close to sundown, and Dad had worn down a little around the edges.

"Gid," he said, "now there's no need for you to go around feeling sorry for yourself for two months just because you have to plow an oat field once in a while. Before you're my age you'll have had all the cowboying you need. A man that's training himself to run a ranch has got to be able to do all kinds of things."

"You can say all you want to," I said. "I still wish I'd gone to the Panhandle. I ain't training to be no oat planter. I intend to enjoy my life."

"If that ain't a fine ambition," he said. "Why, any damn fool can enjoy himself. What makes you think life's supposed to be enjoyed anyhow?"

"Well," I said, "if you ain't supposed to enjoy it, what are you supposed to do with it?"

"Fight it. Fight the hell out of it." And then he got to talking about the cattle and the screwworms, and about how dry it was. He said he'd like to build some new tanks if he thought he'd have the pleasure of living long enough to see them full; we didn't argue no more. In a way I wanted to go, and in a way I didn't. Old as Dad was getting, and as much work as there was to do, I wouldn't have been too happy about going off and leaving him. There would be too many times when I'd have to think about him making the rounds by himself, and that would have spoiled the fun. When it come right down to it, Dad and I got along pretty well. All that time I was in the hospital I kept thinking about him home working, and it bothered me worse than the stuff itself. Johnny and me *was* different that way. His dad was just as old and had about as much to do, but it never bothered Johnny to go off and leave him. Course Johnny's mother was still alive, but he just figured his dad could take care of himself.

"If I did stay home it wouldn't make no difference," he said. "Daddy would be out working himself to death anyway, only he'd be working me to death along with him. I can't see no profit in that."

He was right, I guess. It's just all in the way you feel about a thing like that. Me being home never slowed Dad down either, but at least if I was there I didn't have to fight no guilty conscience.

ONE GOOD THING about having old Johnny out of the country was that I didn't have to watch Molly so close all the time. I knew there wasn't nobody besides me and him she cared much about; not unless you wanted to count Eddie White, and I never. Eddie was a shiftless old boy about my age; he worked around the oil patch whenever he felt like working, and when he didn't he hung around Thalia playing dominos or running his hounds. He was too no-count for a girl like Molly to pay much attention to. I think she just mentioned him once in a while to keep me and Johnny uneasy.

I guess the best time me and her had all the time Johnny was gone was the day I took her fishing. We had shipped a carload of calves to Fort Worth just to try out the market, and Dad had gone with them, to sit around the stockyards a day or two and watch them sell. When

Dad took a big vacation like that he always come back wanting to do all the work in sight in the first half-hour, so I thought I better take me a little time off while I had the chance.

It was late September then—a nice warm day, but not too warm. We had had our first little norther about four days before; it cooled things off to where they were just about right. I waited around the house till nine or ten o'clock, then caught my horse and rode across the west pasture and up the hill to the Taylor place.

Old Man Taylor was there of course. He was sitting on the cellar, sharpening his pocketknife and drinking his morning whiskey. He was a terrifying sight. Along his cheeks his beard was white, but all of it that was underneath his mouth was a kind of muddy yellow from all the tobacco juice and whiskey he had dripped on it.

"Clean your feet before you come in this yard," he said. "I don't want none of your damn cowshit in my yard."

That would have been funny if he hadn't said it in such a mean voice. His yard looked like a slaughterhouse anyway. The old man done everything he had to do in the yard, and it showed it: there were bones and chicken heads and empty whiskey jugs and junk iron and baling wire and old shoes and pieces of plank and mule harness and horse turds and slop buckets, and I don't know what all else scattered everywhere. Molly said she tried to clean the yard up once in a while, but the old man wouldn't let her: anything that was there, he said, was there because he might need it. The miracle of it was that such a sweet, nice girl like Molly could have grown up in such a nasty place.

I scraped my feet on the fence wire and the old man never said another word to me.

Molly was in the living room, trying to kill a stinging lizard that had run in one of the woodboxes. She was dressed like a boy, in an old shirt and a pair of pants that had belonged to one of her brothers; they had all left home. But she looked like a girl; I wanted to grab her right there and kiss her, but if the old man had come in there would have been hell to pay.

"Let's go fishing," I said.

"Guess what?" she said, grinning and looking happy. "I got a postcard from Johnny last week. Want to see it?"

"No, I don't want to see it," I said. "I want to go fishing with you. Now do you want to go or don't you?"

"Yes," she said, "let's go right now. I just thought you might like to read Johnny's card. He mentioned you in it too."

I did want to read it, but I wasn't going to admit that to Molly. No telling what an idiot like Johnny would write on a postcard.

"Your dad don't look in too good a humor," I said.

"Get the poles out of the smokehouse and I'll wrap up some bait," she said. "Dad won't bother us. He likes catfish for supper."

I got the poles and propped them against the fence and went down and saddled Molly's horse. The old man was still drinking and sharpening his knife; he never even looked up. In a minute Molly came out with a lunch sack and a bait sack. She went up to the old man and hugged him a little with one arm and whispered to him and kissed him on one cheek and then come on out to me. She really liked that old bugger—it always surprised me to see it. He looked up at the lunch sack, but he didn't say anything.

"Want to go to a tank or to the River?" I said.

"Let's go to the big tank," she said. "South of the hill, in you-'all's place."

It was my favorite tank too, but it was better for courting than for fishing. I never caught nothing there. There was a lot of Bermuda grass around it, though, and shade trees and nice places to sit.

Molly was riding a little gray horse her old man had cheated a feller out of two years before. I was riding old Denver; we named him that because his momma come from Colorado. We loped nearly all the way to our fence before we pulled up. I let Molly go in front of me. Her hair was flying all over the place, and her shirttail come out. She rode good though. There wasn't no cattle around the tank when we got there, and not a ripple on the water, except once in a while when some dragonfly would light on the tank for a minute. We used liver for bait, and I put enough on the hooks to last awhile and stuck the poles in the mud. Molly sat down on the Bermuda grass, in the shade, and I sat down by her and held her hand. We were all set to fish.

It was about a perfect day. The sky was clear, and the sun felt warm like summer while the air felt cool like fall. We lolled around on the Bermuda grass and courted and ate lunch and fished all day. We caught three fish too, two croppies and one nice little cat; I guess we could have caught more if we had tried. We got a lot of nibbles, but Molly was so good to be with that day that I quit paying attention to them. I held her down and told her it was just turtles gnawing at the bait. She knew how inconvenient it was to catch turtles.

Sometime in the early afternoon, when we were over under the big shade trees and not even pretending to fish, I finally asked Molly to marry me for the first time. There wasn't much grass under the trees, and we were laying on the slicker. We had been kissing a good deal and she seemed to like me so much that I didn't see why not to ask her. I was crazy about her.

"Molly," I said, "say, Molly. We're sweethearts anyway, why don't we go on and get married? Wouldn't that be the best thing to do? I sure would like to marry you."

She kinda grinned to herself and wouldn't look at me.

"Don't you want to at all?" I said. "You're the one for me, I know that for sure."

"You're my favorite," she said, and sat up and kissed me. "Gid-ington. But what in the world would we do married?"

"Why, what everybody else does, I guess. We ain't so different."

"Maybe you ain't," she said, "but I am. I don't want to get into all that stuff yet. It ain't near as much fun as things like we're doing today."

"How do you know?" I said. "You ain't been married. It might be more fun."

She got kinda mad. "Don't tell me that," she said. "I don't want to marry you or nobody else. Girls who get married just to do a lot of things with boys ain't very nice. I don't like it. I'd just as soon do all those things and not be married, and I mean it. I ain't gonna marry till I have to because of having a baby, and I mean that too. And I wish I didn't even have to then."

Well, that shocked me as much as anything I ever heard, Molly saying that. It was just like her though. She never cared what people thought about her. I guess she never thought she was very respectable anyway, growing up with the daddy she had. I knew a lot of people around Thalia who didn't think she was nice, either, but they didn't mean anything to me.

"Honey, don't talk that way," I said. "I'm crazy about you and I just want you for a wife, that's all."

She looked sorry then, but she looked kinda wild, too, and we lay there and hugged one another for a long time before she would talk agin at all.

"I'm crazy about you too, Gid," she said, hugging my neck. "You're the best to me of anybody. But I ain't going to marry, I mean it. I'll do anything you want me to but that. I'll do everything else if you want me to right now," and when I kissed her she was trembling like a leaf. But we never managed it, somehow: it was my fault. I guess I was too surprised at Molly, and I couldn't quit thinking about it. She practically took her shirt off and that was something, but I couldn't quit thinking about it, and I knew it wasn't right, so I made her quit.

"Now we got to quit," I said. "You know it, Molly. Why can't we get married?"

Then she got real cool and mad at me, but I was pretty mad too, and I didn't back down.

"Let's go swimming, Gid," she said. "It's so hot. Then we can talk about it some more." She was cool as ice when she said that.

"You hush," I said. "There ain't no use in you teasing me, and you know it. I ain't no damn kid. We got nothing to go swimming in, so how can we go?"

"We got skin," she said. "I didn't know you was such a scardy-cat. Why do you want to get married if you're scared of girls?"

"Now listen, Molly," I said. "I told you to quit teasing me and you better do it before I shake the hell out of you. I'm sorry. But I ain't scared of you. I just know what's right and what ain't, and you ain't gonna talk me out of it just because you're mad. And if you don't like it, you can just stay mad."

"Don't ask me to marry you any more," she said, only she wasn't mad then, she was kind of quiet. "Get off my shirt, honey. You're too sober, I never could get along with you. You didn't know I was like this, did you?"

I grabbed her and made her let me hold her, even if she didn't want me to.

"I may be too sober," I said. "I guess I am. But I'm not going to get stampeded into doing something crazy even if we do both want to. You got to be a little careful about some things."

"Okay," she said. "You done said that. Shut up about it. Let's fish or ride or do something. I'm tired of sitting here being so careful. I guess you're so careful you won't even want to hold hands with me no more, will you?"

But after a while she got in a good humor again and we walked around the dam and rode horses some and finally went home about five o'clock, just when the shadows were beginning to stretch out. The old man was gone when we got there and I cleaned the fish for her. She cooked them and made biscuits and gravy and we each ate one of the croppie, bones or no bones. We left the catfish for the old man.

After supper we went out on the porch and swung in her porch swing and she was real warm and sweet agin and we kissed all we wanted to. I don't guess things could have been any nicer, except that I had already begin to feel mad at myself for not taking better advantage of the afternoon. But she acted like she'd forgot about it. She teased me a little about Johnny.

"I know why you don't come see me as much any more," she said.

"It's because Johnny's gone. You don't really care much about me, do you? You just like to spite Johnny."

She was wrong about that and we both knew it, but it was true that I got a little extra kick out of being with Molly when Johnny was around to notice it. It would have probably been the same with him if he'd been in my place.

I made up with her for the afternoon, only she wouldn't hear a word about marrying. I had to drop that for a while, but I didn't care. She gave me a big kiss just before I got on my horse and held on to my hand until I had to turn loose and ride away. And she stood on the hill and watched me go.

Later I got awful mad at myself for being such a sissy down at the tank. I must have been either scared to death or crazy, I couldn't figure which. At least we could have gone swimming, that wouldn't have been no great crime. The more I thought about it the worse it got, and it was all I could do to keep from riding back over that night. But I figured the old man would be back, so I never.

I guess I always did think things over too much, at least where Molly was concerned. She was a special girl. Johnny, he would have done it and then thought it over later, but I always did the thinking first. The next time I got the chance I decided I would try his way.

But things never worked out too good. Dad rode in the next morning with about a month's work lined up to do, and I had to stay mad at myself all the time I was doing it. By the time things loosened up enough that I could get back over to see Molly, why it was the middle of October and Johnny was home agin, so I had him to worry about. If there was one thing I learned that day, it was not to miss no opportunities. I just wish learning it had done me a little more good.

Four

I GUESS IT WAS BEING SO MAD AT MYSELF OVER MOLLY THAT caused me to run off one night and court Mabel Peters. I knew at the time I didn't have no business doing it. In the first place it was on a Friday night, and I never got off work till after dark, and I knew I would have to start agin before sunup. And it was nearly six miles over to Mabel's house; I could have gone over and seen Molly with a lot less trouble. But I was still kind of ashamed of the way I acted around Molly; I didn't want to see her that night. Mabel wasn't the kind of a girl I could get excited about in no permanent way, but every once in a while she was the kind I could get real excited about in a temporary way. Her folks were so poor and they lived so far off from everybody that none of the boys courted Mabel much. She was right pretty in a neat, timid kind of way, but she never had no real boy friends, and I knew she was so anxious for a sweetheart she would do most anything. So I wasn't very proud of the reasons I went to see her, but I went, anyway.

Mabel's ma and pa were pretty old and usually went to bed early; except for one or two of the younger kids, Mabel was nearly always up by herself. I rode up to the yard gate in the dark and sat on my horse till the dogs kind of quieted down. One thing I hated about visiting the Peterses was them barking dogs. There must have been six or eight; I never knew Old Man Peters to keep no less. In a minute Mabel came out and stood in the door.

"Who's that out there?" she said.

"It's just me, Mabel," I said. "I'd get down but I'm afraid these dogs would eat me."

"Gid?" she said. "Hush up, Pete, hush that." I guess Pete was the boss dog, because he went running over to her, and in a minute they all quieted down. Then I got off my horse and tied him to their mailbox.

"Have you been to supper?" she said. "Come on in and I'll fix you some."

But I never let her get me in the house. Their little old house always nearly suffocated me. It was an old chickenhouse, was what it was; Old Man Peters had just kinda rebuilt it. It never had but four little tight rooms, and they were so small and squeezed up and had such low ceilings that I couldn't hardly breathe when I was inside. I don't see how they lived through the summertime; it would have been like living in an oven.

Mabel knew I didn't like it, too, and it always embarrassed her. She wanted me to come and see her, but then when I did come she didn't have no nice place where we could go, and that preyed on her mind. Mabel was awful pretty in the face; I was just kinda awkward around her because it took me twenty or thirty minutes each time to get over feeling sorry for her. She'd worked and wanted her whole life, and she always looked like she'd do just anything for somebody who'd give her the chance to have some fun.

"Aren't you going to come in awhile?" she said. "We can't just stand out here on the steps."

"No," I said. "I feel like moving around, how about you? I thought you might like to take a little walk with me. It's such a bright moonlight night we wouldn't need no lantern." That was true. The moon was big and white that night, sailing up over the pastures.

The Peterses' house didn't have a porch, just front steps and back steps, because it was propped up on bricks, but Old Man Peters kept his wagon back behind the barn and I figured that would be our destination. It was a good big Studebaker wagon, and he kept his wagon sheet in it.

Mabel was agreeable enough to the walk.

"That'd be nice, Gid," she said. "Where will we walk?"

"Just here and there." She grabbed my hand herself and held on to me tight. I guess she was afraid of snakes. She walked so close to me I was afraid to move my feet for fear of stepping on her. I went dumb then; I could have kicked myself. I couldn't think of one thing to say. And I was a little snake-shy myself; nobody's very anxious to get rattlesnake-bit. But Mabel didn't mind the quiet; she walked along sort of humming to herself.

"It's sure nice to see somebody," she said. "I swear Ma and Pa have been about to bore me plumb to death."

"Dad bores me a good deal sometimes too," I said. I was beginning to get a little excited from her walking so close to me that way. I never could understand how a little thing like Mabel could get me so excited, but she sure could. She was so thin you wouldn't even notice her if she was standing sideways to you, but once she got near you she sure did make herself felt. We sashayed around by the postpile a time or two and the pigpen once or twice and then I sidled over toward the wagon. I didn't need to sidle. When I asked her if she wanted to sit down awhile she just nodded, and it wasn't two minutes till we were kissing like old sweethearts. Mabel never pulled back a time; it was always me. At first I was kind of wishing it was Molly that was there, but then I quit caring so much, and I guess we'd have done the whole works without no conversation or nothing if I hadn't made the mistake of stopping to ask.

"You can if you want to, Gid," she whispered. "I don't care. And then we can get married and start having babies. That's what I've always wanted to do. You'll be the best husband in the world."

She just barely whispered that in my ear, but it hit me like a bucket of ice water.

"Goodness, we can't do that, Mabel," I said. "Dad would raise too much Cain, and your dad too. Let's go ahead anyway."

She didn't get mad, or say a word back to me, and she kissed me a whole lot more, but it never meant anything then. She had put on all the brakes. I was so mad at her I could have stomped her for a minute, but she kept on acting sweet and happy and never seemed to notice. She did notice, though; she was just too sly to let on. That was the big difference in her and Molly. Molly was wild, but she was warm, and she wasn't sly. Mabel wasn't really a bit wild, but she was really cold and sly. Mabel's little brain was cold as an icicle.

You couldn't guess that from the way she acted in the wagon. She cuddled up with me on the wagon sheet just as long as I wanted to stay, and I did stay a good while, hoping she would change her mind. But she wouldn't change her mind any more than the moon would change its direction. She sure did want to get married.

Finally I helped her out of the wagon and we walked back to the house. She never talked at all; she knew she couldn't do any good talking. But she kept close to me; I practically had to crawl out from under her to get on my horse.

It was just when I was about to ride away that she began to look real sorry. She had one hand on my ankle, and I was afraid she was fixing to cry.

"Come back to see me," she said. "I get awful bored around here, and I don't like for nobody to come to see me but you." And before I could get away, I was feeling sorry for her agin. I decided on the way home I would have to come back and give her another try. It had been worth it anyway.

Only next morning I wasn't so sure. I hadn't been asleep but two or three hours when Dad came in and started shaking my damn foot to wake me up. That was sure a long day.

Five

Johnny got back from the Panhandle on a Sunday night and went to work for us on Monday morning. He rode over about breakfast time, to see how I was doing, I guess. It was branding season and we were getting in some new cattle, so when Dad got back from his morning ride he asked Johnny if he wanted to go to work on a day basis, and Johnny said he did.

"And when I say work, I mean work," Dad said. "I ain't gonna squander no dollar a day for you to sit on your butt."

"I ain't never run from no work yet," Johnny said. "Of course there's some kinds I'd rather do than others. But you're probably that way about it too, aren't you, Mr. Fry?"

Dad grunted. He didn't like much conversation out of Johnny. "The kind I like best is none," he said.

I thought working up on the big ranches might have given Johnny a little responsibility, but it never. He was just as wild and crazy as he'd always been. One thing I noticed, though, he must have done a lot of riding. His new saddle was broken in to where it was comfortable as could be. He let me ride it a time or two, and I liked the way it rode.

He asked me right off if I had been taking good care of his girl.

"Mabel, you mean?" I said. "You bet, ever chance I get."

"Much obliged," he said. "Only she wasn't really the one I meant. I don't guess you know who that would be?"

"I don't guess. Not unless it's Annie Eldenfelder."

We carried on and kidded one another a lot. I was glad to see Johnny get back, really. Things were a good bit snappier with him around.

HE HADN'T been working for us a week when me and him got into a real scrape with Molly's dad. We never meant to, either, because we both knew how she felt about him, and getting into a scrape with him was the best way in the world to get crosswise with her. But sometimes you don't have much control over what happens to you.

A couple of our yearling steers had crawled through a busted water gap into Old Man Taylor's pasture. Dad seen their tracks going through when he was out on his early morning lookaround, and when he got back to the house he sent me and Johnny over there to get them out. Which wasn't no trouble to do. We found them with the old man's milk cows and drove the whole bunch down to our gate and roped a yearling apiece and drug them through the gate where they belonged. It was still early then, and chilly, with mist hanging over the ground nearly high as a horse's belly. We was glad for a little action to warm us up.

It was when we were going to fix the water gap that we got in trouble. The first thing we done wrong was to ride down toward the creek on the Taylor side of the fence. We knew the old man would raise hell about that if he caught us, but we did it anyway, just to spite him. Then Johnny spotted a coyote. He loped through the fence about a hundred yards ahead of us, and Johnny said he saw him squat down in the grass and stop.

"Hell, let's rope that sonofabitch," he said. "I ain't never roped a coyote, have you?"

"Naw," I said. "Reckon we can catch him?" But I was already making me a loop. I had always wanted to rope one, and I figured this was my chance. Johnny, he couldn't throw his rope in the creek, so I never worried about him catching it. He made a loop big enough for a dinosaur to go through.

"I tell you now," he said. "I can't see him, but he's right over there between them two big bunches of chaparral. Let's sneak up on this side of him, so he can't dodge back through the fence. That way we can chase him clear to the north side if we need to. He ain't gonna sit forever, so when we get past that third post let's charge hell out of him. You ready?"

"He's practically roped," I said. "If you miss your first loop, haze him over my way so I can get a good throw."

We held our ponies down to a slow walk till we got past the post: then we jobbed the spurs to them and away we went, holding up our ropes and yelling like mad. I lost my hat before we even seen the coyote, and Johnny lost his a minute later. In about two seconds we was to the chaparral and up Mr. Coyote come; he jumped plumb over the bushes and it looked for a while like he was running along on top of the mist, two feet off the ground. Me and Johnny was right on his ass, and Johnny was done swinging. I swung to the side to give him room. Johnny had a damn good roping horse, he run right up by the coyote and leaned over, so all Johnny had to do was drop on the loop, but Johnny threw too late and missed about twenty feet, only this throw turned the coyote and it cut right under my horse while I was running full speed. I yanked to the right and went to spurring for all I was worth. Old Denver turned on about fifteen cents and was after the coyote agin before Johnny even got pulled up. By then we hit a strip of mesquite brush and I thought we had lost him, but then I decided to ride like hell and try to chase him through the brush and out into the clearing by the Taylor horse tank, so I could get my throw. Into the brush we went, with me about twenty yards behind the coyote and Johnny somewhere back of me. I ducked and spurred and the mesquite limbs flew. Only if Johnny couldn't rope, boy he could ride. By the time we were past the middle of the brush he went by me on the left just a-flying, waving his rope and his horse jumping trees and bushes and limbs busting like crazy. The coyote was still ahead though, sailing along on top of the mist. I spurred a little harder and we all three hit the clearing about the same time. In a second we were at the tank. I beat the coyote to the water about two steps and turned him over the dam, and Johnny was right there to keep him from ducking back so he went over the dam and down on the other side and I went right over with him and threw while we were still half in the air: caught him clean as a whistle. Old Denver fell then and nobody could blame him; I went rolling off to one side and the coyote to the other. But when we all got up we had a big dog coyote on the end of the rope.

"Good throw, by god," Johnny said. "I thought you was gonna turn a flip off that dam."

"It's a wonder I didn't," I said. I was too out of breath to say much. Johnny got his rope on the coyote too, and we had him where he couldn't do any harm.

"I wish Dad was here," I said. "I bet he never roped one." One thing I could do, and that was rope.

We were about to knock the coyote in the head and get the ears so we could collect our bounty when Old Man Taylor walked up on the tank dam from the other side. He had his .10-gauge shotgun in one hand and a couple of dead squirrels in the other—probably they were going to be Molly's breakfast. When he got up closer I seen his beard was wet, so I guess he had him a whiskey jug hid off in a stump somewhere.

"Goddam you boys," he said, "Goddam trespassers. What are you little sonsofbitches doing on my place?"

We never said a word, but we didn't like it. People can't just come up and cuss you without you getting mad.

"Well, the cat got your tongues?" he said. "Answer me when I ask you something. Didn't your folks teach you no manners?"

"We had to come over and get a couple of our yearlings and fix the water gap on the river," I said. "Then we accidentally run on to this coyote and roped him. That's all, Mr. Taylor."

"Oh you did, did you?" he said. Boy he looked mad. "Young farts ought to have your asses kicked."

We were getting about all we could stand of it, but we didn't know quite what to do. For one thing, we still had the coyote on the ropes, and the old man noticed it.

"Turn that coyote loose," he said. "That there's my own coyote anyway. I don't ever want to catch you roping my coyotes agin. Turn the sonofabitch loose."

That was the silliest thing I ever heard of, claiming that coyote.

"No sir," I said. "We caught him coming out of our pasture, and we'll just have to take him back." I thought I could be just as silly as he was.

"Oh you are, are you?" he said, stuffing his squirrels in his hip pocket. "Now what about you, little McCloud? You get down and turn that coyote loose."

Johnny was half-tickled by it all.

"No sir," he said. "I would, only I'm scared to. I'm kind of a coward when it comes to getting one of my hands bit off."

The old man got madder and madder, but he shut up and just stared at us. That's when I really got uneasy, and I don't know where it would have gone if Dad hadn't rode up about that time. For once in my life I was glad to see Dad. Old Man Taylor was just crazy enough to have shot us.

I guess Dad had missed me and Johnny and come to see what kind of mischief we was in. When Dad was impatient to work it never took him long to miss a person. He rode up like there wasn't nothing unusual about the gathering at all.

"I see you boys been fiddling around," he said. "I thought I told you to come on home when you got them yearlings out. How are you today, Cletus?"

"No damn good," the old man said. "Looky what them boys done. I wisht you'd make them turn that coyote loose. I don't like boys roping coyotes of mine."

Crazy old fart.

"Aw, you didn't look close enough, Cletus," Dad said. "That's my coyote. See that earmark I put on him. Hell, I never even knowed he was out. It's lucky these boys found him. Once your coyotes get off in the brush they're hard to find."

I was flabbergasted and so was Old Man Taylor. Johnny was just tickled. We all looked, and sure enough the coyote did have a piece of his ear missing. And I don't know yet whether Dad was really responsible for it being gone or not. I imagine it was just chewed off in a fight, but you can't tell about Dad. Old Man Taylor like to swallowed his Adam's apple.

"How do you mark your coyotes, Cletus?" Dad asked, solemn as a judge. "I never noticed. If you'll show me, I'll have these boys run what they find of yours back in your pasture."

But Old Man Taylor was a pretty sly old bastard himself—you couldn't hem him up for long. He walked over and grabbed the coyote by the snout and looked at his ear.

"By god, it is yours," he said. "I come off without my spectacles this morning.

"Say," he said. "I like the looks of this coyote, Adam. How much will you take for him?"

That even surprised Dad, only he never much let on. He got out his plug and cut himself off some tobacco; then he offered the plug to Old Man Taylor and he cut off a bigger chew than Dad's. All the time Dad was thinking it over. I bet he thought it was funny as hell.

"Oh, I don't know, Cletus," he said. "I ain't been watching the market too close. I'd have to get about three dollars for him, I guess."

"By god, that's fair," the old man said, and I'll be damned if he didn't take out his pocketbook and pull three one-dollar bills out of it and hand them to Dad. Dad folded them together and stuck them in his shirt pocket. That was a dollar more than the ears would bring in bounty money.

"Good trade," the old man said. "Wonder if them boys would help me a minute, Adam. I might as well earmark him while I got him caught."

"Sure," Dad said. "You boys get down and help Mr. Taylor mark that coyote."

The old man stood back and opened his pocketknife, and there wasn't nothing for it but for us to do the dangerous work. I went up one rope and Johnny up the other, and we managed to get his snout without being bit too bad. I muzzled him with my piggin string and we threw him down and hogtied him with Johnny's. Then the old man cropped his ear and the job was done.

"Much obliged, boys," he said. "Now I'll know the bastard next time I see him.

"Can I borrow your piggin strings and just leave him tied awhile?" he asked, real friendly. "Tame him up a little. After a while I'll send that girl of mine and get her to lead him up to the house. She ain't got a damn thing else to do."

The thought of Molly having to drag that coyote to the house made me fighting mad. But Dad was ready to go.

"Let's get home, boys," he said. "We got all them calves to brand. Much obliged, Cletus. Take care of yourself. Hope he makes you a good coyote."

"Oh yeah," the old man said. "He'll do."

"WELL, THAT was a damn good trade," Dad said. "Three dollars always comes in handy."

"Hell, we caught him," I said. "We ought to get a little of it."

We come to the gate and Dad stopped and waited for one of us to get down and open it. Johnny did.

"Oh you think so, do you?" Dad said. "Well, I don't. He was my coyote to begin with. All you done was rope him. If you was to rope one of my calves, that wouldn't make it yours, would it?"

"What made him yours?" I said. "You wasn't serious about that ear-mark business, was you?"

He just kept riding and never answered.

"Shit-fire," Johnny said. "I believe I'll quit, Mr. Fry. I better go back and untie that coyote before Molly has to come drag him to the house. I don't want her fiddling with that big bastard. He might bite her hand off."

"I'm with you," I said. "Let's turn him loose. We can get back in plenty of time to do the branding."

"The hell you will," Dad said. "I just got you boys out of one scrape and I ain't got time to get you out of another. Cletus is just waiting for one of you to come back so he can get that extra dollar out of your hide. He'd get it too, don't think he wouldn't."

"Dollar," I said. "You made three."

"Yeah, but Cletus will get two back when he sells them ears to the county. Why, he ain't gonna keep no coyotes. He just spent that money to keep from backing down."

Me and Johnny couldn't hardly believe it.

"You mean a poor man like him would spend three dollars just for that?" I said.

"Who's a poor man?" Dad said. "Cletus Taylor ain't poor. He's just tight. Just because he don't spend money don't mean he ain't got any. I don't spend much myself, and that's one reason I got so much more than most people."

"Well," Johnny said, "if I was a man and I had money, I believe I'd at least buy myself and my daughter some decent clothes to wear. I wouldn't go around dressed disgraceful. I believe I'd spend a little of it enjoying life."

"Most young fools would," Dad said. "That's why most young fools are broke."

Me and Johnny shut up. There was no use arguing with Dad. And he was right about one thing. Just as we crossed the Ridge we heard the .10-gauge go KLABOOM, like a damn cannon.

"One less coyote," Dad said. "And that many more frying chickens I'll get to eat next spring. I'm glad you boys have finally learned to rope."

Six

Old Man Taylor got his damn revenge anyhow, only he took it out on Molly instead of us. I could have killed him for it.

Two nights after the coyote roping they were having a big harvest-time square dance over in Thalia. It was about the biggest dance or get-together they had between the Fourth of July and Christmas, and I had an agreement with Molly that me and her would go. I asked her the day we went fishing, while Johnny was still up in the Panhandle. He was mad enough to bite himself when he found out I had done asked her. He ended up having to take Mabel Peters, and it served him right.

Anyway, I got all spruced up and was going to use Dad's buggy. I drove over to Molly's just about dark, and I was sure excited. I didn't care too much about the dance, but the thought of getting to ride all that way with Molly sitting by me was something to be excited about.

But when I got to Molly's the house was completely dark. It surprised the devil out of me. There wasn't no light on of no kind. For a minute I thought Johnny must have pulled some kind of a sneak and taken her off already. I didn't know what to think. It was a still, pretty night, and not a sound to be heard. Finally I hitched the horses and walked across the yard and up on the porch. Still not a sound. I hesitated a minute before I knocked on the door—I decided her old devil of a daddy was hiding in there someplace, waiting to jump out and give me hell about the coyote. I walked around on the porch for a few minutes, hoping somebody inside the house would finally hear me and say something. Molly could have lain down to take a little nap and rest up for the dance.

But nobody said nothing.

"Hell-fire," I said, finally, and went up and knocked on the door good and loud.

"I can't go tonight, Gid," Molly said, and it like to scared me to death. She had been standing just inside the door all the time, but off to one side of the screen, so I couldn't see her.

"You'll have to go on without me," she said. "I ain't feeling good."

"My goodness, Molly, you scared the daylights out of me. Why don't you turn on some kind of light."

"I don't want to," she said, and her voice was trembling. "I just want to be in the dark, Gid." And then it was real quiet, and I knew she was standing there crying, even if I couldn't see her. Molly cried the quietest, she never made a sound at all. Then I heard her move off in the dark and bump into a table or something and run down the hall, and things were quiet agin. The only sound I could hear was the windmill creaking.

I didn't know what to make of it. Something was bothering her pretty bad for her not even to ask me in. One thing I knew, I wasn't going to no dance without her. She could forget about that.

But that didn't solve the problem of what to do. I had to get to talk to her, and the only way to do that was to go in the damn dark house and find her. I wished I had had enough sense to ask her if her dad was there. If she was the only one home, I was all right. But I could just imagine that old man, standing in the living room with a club, waiting for me. The more I thought about it, the madder it made me. I remembered how he had cussed me and Johnny when he found us with that coyote. Finally I opened the screen door and doubled up my fists and clobbered on in. About three steps inside I stopped and crouched over, watching for him.

But he didn't come. If somebody had come in with a light, I would have looked silly as hell. Pretty soon I knew damn well he wasn't there. Molly wouldn't have let me walk into no bad situation without warning me. And the old man wouldn't have waited for me to come in: he would have come out. Besides, if he had been there I would have smelled him, he was such a fragrant old bastard.

So I went on down the hall to Molly's room and didn't give the old man another thought. Sure enough she was in on her bed, crying. The moonlight was coming through the window. I went over and sat down on the edge of the old creaky bed and put my hand on her arm.

"Now, honey," I said, "don't lay there taking on. Turn over and tell me where you hurt and I'll see if I can find some medicine." It was strange, because Molly wasn't the kind that went around being sick.

She wouldn't answer me, though, and for a few minutes I just had to sit there, holding her the best she would let me. She moved over under my arm and acted like she was glad to have me there, but she wouldn't look up. She wasn't crying loud, but she sure wasn't happy.

In a little while I fumbled around and found some matches and lit the lamp. The minute I had the light on I seen what it was all about. Her face and throat and the front of her dress was all wet from tears, but the trouble was, she had a black eye. It wasn't a bad one. In fact it kind of made her look prettier or older, in a way, but you could tell she had one. I knew who done it, too.

"Don't you say a word against my daddy," she said. "I know what you're thinking. He wouldn't have done it if I hadn't been so mean."

That was a lie, but I never said a word.

"I sure am sorry about it," I said in a minute. "But it ain't bad, Molly. It ain't no reason to stay in the dark all the time. By tomorrow you won't even be able to tell it."

I wanted to cuss the worthless old bastard good, but that would have just messed things up.

"I know it, Gid," and the tears were pouring out of her eyes. I sat down and hugged her again. "But the dance is just tonight," she said. "And you're all dressed up and look so nice, you ought to go on. I had my dress all fixed, too. I'd been looking forward to it for I don't know how long. Why does it have to happen at such a bad time?"

I could see how it was a pretty big disappointment. To a girl, especially. Molly never got to go places very often. In fact, it was just very very seldom that she went any place. When you come right down to it, she didn't like much being as cooped up as Mabel Peters, only there was so much more of Molly to coop up.

"Now hush, sugar," I said. "It ain't such a great calamity. This ain't the only dance there'll ever be. We'll get to go to plenty more."

"No we won't," she said. "I don't care." She pulled up the counterpane and wiped her face, but there was still a little puddle of tears in the hollow of her neck. She looked at me kinda mad and I got out my handkerchief and wiped her throat. She was so pretty, black eye or not.

"I wish there never would be another one," she said. "Then I wouldn't have to be so disappointed. I know I won't get to go, even if there's a hundred dances. I guess I'm just too mean."

"Oh hush that up," I said. "You ain't mean, and you ain't hurt, either. We can have just as much fun right here as we could have at the dance."

"But I don't want to stay here. I stay here all the time, Gid. I wanted to go where there were a lot of people having fun."

"Okay," I said, "let's go. It ain't late. That little old shadow on your eye ain't no reason to stay home."

But that just made her cry more. I never knew girls had so much crying in them. Missing that dance didn't amount to a hill-of-beans in the long run, but Molly acted like her heart was broken.

"Now you hush," I said. "This is a silly damn way for you to act. If you want to go, why get up and dry your face and let's go. Hell, by the time we get there everybody will be so drunk they wouldn't notice if you had three black eyes. And if you don't want to go, why hush anyway, and let's go in the living room and pop some popcorn or something. Crying all night won't do any good."

Finally she did hush and just lay back against me. I held her until I was sure she had calmed down.

"That's better," I said. "Have you decided yet?"

"We'll just have to stay here," she said. "I don't want to go to the dance unless I can go looking nice, and I can't do that with this eye. Besides, my dress is all wet. But you ought to go. Just think of all the girls you could dance with."

"I don't know," I said. "Me and you may dance a little ourselves, before the night is over. Johnny can take care of all them other girls."

"He said he wouldn't. When I told him I had already promised you, he said he intended to go to the dance drunk and not dance a single time, just to spite me."

"Sounds like him," I said. "But what he says and what he does are two different things. You know that, don't you?"

"Not when it comes to me, they ain't," she said.

"Where's your dad tonight, anyway?"

"He was out of whiskey and had to go to Henrietta. He may not be back for two or three days."

"Let's go in the living room then," I said.

WE DID, but we never popped no popcorn. I had had a big supper anyway. We built a big fire in the fireplace; it was the only light we had. Molly started to the kitchen to get something and I caught her in my arms and swung her around a time or two and kissed her.

"Now ain't this dancing?" I said. "Ain't this better'n dancing in a big crowd, anyway? If you ask me, that black eye is the nicest thing about you tonight."

"I wish you'd take off that stratchy necktie," she said. "It's about to rub a raw place on me."

"Boy, I will," I said. "It was choking me anyway." I took it off, and my wool coat too. But I never let Molly get to the kitchen.

"Now let's dance," I said. "Just us two. Let's round dance. You hum the music."

She put her head on my chest and hummed a little bit of some song. I hugged her against me real tight and we moved around the living room floor, in the shadows of the fire. "Let's just imagine the music, Gid," she said. "I can't remember what I'm humming half the time."

"I ain't got that much imagination," I said, but we kept dancing anyway; we danced real slow. Molly's hair had a good smell. I got to wanting to kiss more than I wanted to dance, so I stopped and made her tilt her face up and let me. We stood there so long I expected the sun would be coming up. But it was still dark and shadowy.

"I want to make up to you for the other day," I said. "I sure do love you."

She kept standing there against me with her eyes shut, and didn't say anything, but when I kissed her agin she seemed real glad.

"It's okay then? If I make it up to you tonight? I've been worrying about it a lot."

"Yes, I want you to," she said, "but let's stand here a little while longer. Let's not think about anything."

So we stood there and kissed some more and got closer and closer together and finally moved on down the hall to Molly's room, where we had been at first. When we got there I remembered something and left her for a minute and went and latched the screen doors. I went back and she was crying.

She grabbed me and I held her tight. "Where did you go?" she said. "You never needed to leave me and go nowhere."

"Just to latch the doors," I said.

She got fighting mad all of a sudden. I had to hold her to keep her from hitting me. "Don't ever leave me like that agin," she said. "I don't care if the doors are latched or not. Next time you leave me, just keep going." And she actually bit me, she was so mad or hurt or something. I almost shoved her down I was so surprised. But I held her in the middle of the floor till she got real quiet and we were close together and kissed a long time agin. I never wanted to leave her, that's for sure. What I couldn't figure was, how I was going to get my boots off without stopping the kissing for a minute.

"Let's sit down, Molly. These new boots are killing me."

"Poor Gid," she said. "Here, sit on the bed. I'll help you take them off."

And in a minute she had, and I was holding her agin. Then I accidentally tore her pretty dress. I thought that would cook my goose, but it never. She put her hand on my neck and kissed me. I started to tell her I was sorry but her mouth kept stopping me. "Don't talk no more," she said, "don't you say another word tonight."

I WAS the first one awake. I guess I expected Dad to be shaking my foot. But there was just Molly; she was lovely. In a minute she woke up too and yawned and saw me and giggled and snuggled over and kissed me. It was purely delicious. Only I had begun to realize that Dad's buggy and horses were still hitched outside, and that it was past daylight and he was wondering where I was.

"Good god, I said. "Dad'll skin me alive. I ought to woken up and gone home."

"Scardy-cat," she said. "Let's stay here all day. That will show them they ain't the boss of us. I'd like to stay right here, where it's nice and warm and just us, wouldn't you? Can we?

"Oh lord, I'd like to too," I said. "But Dad is the boss of me, I guess. I better skedaddle."

"Well, I wish we could stay," she said. Then she sat up and grinned, without no covers or nothing. "But I'll cook you some hot biscuits, anyway." And in a minute she had kissed me and crawled over and got out of bed. She was poking around in a drawer looking for some Levi's, with just her behind pointed at me.

If it didn't bother her, I didn't see why it ought to bother me. I loved her and I didn't figure I'd have too much trouble persuading her to marry me, after we'd spent the night. Only when I looked down at the bedsheets I couldn't figure it out.

"Hey, sweetie," I said. "Ain't you normal? I thought you was supposed to bleed all over the place."

"Why, didn't you know no better than that?" she said, turning around and grinning at me. She had a pair of Levi's in her hand, but she hadn't put them on. "You're the funniest boy, Gid." The morning light was coming in on her through the windows; she pulled on a shirt and never buttoned it, and her hair was down over her shoulders. I thought she was the prettiest thing I had ever seen.

"You didn't have to worry," she said, innocent as daylight. "You only bleed like that the first time."

I was absolutely flabbergasted.

Seven

IT MADE ME PRETTY DOWN IN THE MOUTH, FINDING OUT that I wasn't the first feller ever to spend a night with Molly. I couldn't think straight for a while, I was so upset. But there wasn't much I could say about it, because she got up just happy as a lark, and not the least bit down in the dumps about anything. She fed me some awful good biscuits for breakfast, too. But I never enjoyed my food. All I could think about was wanting to get married to her as soon as I could.

Of course Dad raked me over the coals when I finally got home. He seen me unhitching the buggy, and here he came.

"Well, at least you ain't eloped with her," he said, looking at the buggy to see how stratched up it was. "But I bet it wasn't because you didn't try. Your good buddy Johnny's been down there digging postholes for three hours. Get on down there and help him."

"He ain't my good buddy," I said. "I guess I can change clothes before I go, can't I?"

"I'd just as soon you worked in them you got on," Dad said. "If you dirty them up, you won't be running around so much at night." And I had been out two nights in a month, and one of them he never knew about.

Johnny, he was sweating his whiskey out. But I wasn't in no mood to sympathize with him.

"Where you been?" he said. "Why wasn't you'all at the dance? Hell, I waited for you till one o'clock."

"We got lost and never made it. How'd you and your sweetheart Mabel get along?"

He leaned on his diggers a minute. "Why, she'd be a darling if she wasn't such a bitch," he said. "I had to run backward all night to keep her from proposing to me."

He would have chattered all day if I had let him, but I grabbed my diggers and walked off a hundred yards or so and went to digging. I wasn't in a talking mood.

WELL, I THOUGHT about it and thought about it, and I couldn't come to no decision. It had to be Johnny that done it, but he never acted the least bit guilty about it, and Molly never either, so I had no way of knowing. The only thing that made me doubt it was Johnny was him not bragging about it. He just naturally bragged a little if he had done anything to brag about. Anyhow, I didn't think it was right for two fellers to have spent the night with a sweet girl like Molly and not either one of them have married her. The more I thought about it, the surer I was about that, and something had to be done about it. If Johnny had been there first, then he ought to have the first chance at marrying her, and if he didn't want to, why I damn sure did. And the way I seen it, Molly could have her choice of me and him, but that was all the choice there was to it. She couldn't go running around single much longer, that was for sure.

All the same, I couldn't help being mad at myself, because I kept wanting to go right back over and spend another night. And I would have, too, if her damned old man had ever left agin; I snuck over several times to check, but he was always there. I hadn't forgot about him giving her that black eye, either.

Finally me and Johnny had it out about her, when we were going to Fort Worth, of all places. About the middle of November, Dad decided to ship the rest of his calves, but he didn't want to go along and fool with them, so he sent me and Johnny.

"I guess I'm a damn fool for sending two idiots when I could just send one," he said. "But maybe if I send two, one will be sober enough to look after the cattle part of the time. I want you boys back here on Sunday, and I don't want you to give them cattle away. If you see any yearling steers worth the money, you might buy me about a hundred of them and bring 'em home with you."

Of course it was the biggest lark in the world to me and Johnny. We struck out early one morning, with a norther blowing cold as hell, and drove the cattle to Henrietta and put them on the railroad cars for Fort Worth about night that same day.

"Them cattle are safe," Johnny said. "Let's go wet our whistles. My damn throat's full of dust."

Mine was too, and we bought some whiskey and went to washing out the dust. About that time we went into a little honkytonk there by the railroad yards and run into the deputy sheriff that had arrested Johnny the last time he was in Henrietta. Only he wasn't a deputy no more and was a good bit drunker than we was, and had two of his drinking buddies with him. Johnny asked me if I'd back him up, and I said sure, so he went over and called the feller a sonofabitch and the other feller called him one back and they went outside and had a fist fight in the street. Me and the other fellers went too, but we didn't fight. The ex-deputy bloodied Johnny's nose, but I think Johnny had a little the best of the fight.

"That'll show you, you bastard," Johnny said. "Next time just try and arrest me."

"Sonofabitch," the man said. "Want me to whip you good?"

That was funny, because they had already fought for fifteen minutes. Me and Johnny walked over to the pens and climbed around on the cars awhile, and the cattle looked all right to us, so we went to the caboose and went to sleep. Sometime during the night the train come and hooked onto the cars and off we went, I don't know just when. The caboose was awful bouncy, and it woke me up about Decatur. Johnny was sitting up holding his jaw; I guess it had bounced against the floor. There wasn't but one other passenger, a damn greasy oil-field hand, who looked like he'd got on the train about Burkburnett. He was asleep on the bench.

"Hell, let's go outside," Johnny said. "I can't sleep in this rickety bastard. Let's go out and look at the country awhile."

"I'm ready," I said.

We put on our jackets and walked out on the little porch of a thing at the tail-end of the caboose. It was a clear, starry night, but cold as hell. The norther was still blowing, and we was getting it right in our faces. We set down with our backs to the door of the caboose and watched the country go by in the dark.

"I sure like riding trains," Johnny said. "Lots faster than going some place ahorseback."

I watched the rails come out from under the car, and they didn't seem to be coming so fast. But they came awful steady; I kept halfway looking for them to end, and they never did. We went through some little old town, I never have known the name of it, and all it had in it was grain elevators. It was the most grain elevators I knew of this side of Kansas. We could see the shapes of them in the moonlight. It was real exciting to be going someplace.

"This here's where they make all the oatmeal," Johnny said. "Boy, I'm glad I ain't no farmer. There ain't nothing that can compare with a cowboy's life, if you ask me. You don't have to worry about a damn thing."

"It just depends," I said. "What if you own the ranch you're working on? Then you got to worry about making money and taking care of the cattle and all that kind of thing."

"Then you ain't a cowboy, you're a rancher," he said. "I never said I wanted to be a rancher. Damn, I wish I'd brought my sheepskin coat. I didn't figure it would get this cold in November."

"It's because we're moving so fast." My ears were getting numb, but it was a lot nicer ride out on the end than in that bouncy caboose.

"What you ought to do," he said, "is to forget all that ranching. And forget about marrying, too. Then one of these days we could go up on the plains and really have us a time. When the ranch gets to be yours, you can sell it and not have it worrying you all your life."

"That's just like you," I said. "You ain't got no more responsibility than a monkey. That ain't no way to amount to nothing."

"Responsibility ain't no valuable thing to have, necessarily," he said. "Listen at you. It depends on what you want to amount to. I want to amount to a good cowboy."

"Talking about marrying," I said, "that reminds me of something I've been meaning to talk to you about. Something pretty serious. I guess I got to admit you got first claims on Molly, but what I want to know is, do you really intend to marry her or not? One of us has got to, that's for sure, and if you ain't going to, I am."

He looked at me like I was crazy. Finally he laughed, but he was kind of uncertain about it.

"You needn't snicker," I said. "I found out all about it. I know you laid up with her. I done it too, of course, but you was the first, so she's really your responsibility. Now one of us has got to do something."

"I believe you're serious," he said. "And I know you're crazy. What in the world are you talking about?"

"It's simple as mud," I said. "You sweet-talked Molly into letting you spend the night with her. Okay. Hell, I don't blame you, I done it too. Anybody would want to. Only the first one has the most responsibility. It ain't no way to do a good-hearted girl like Molly, and you know it. Now is it?"

"Why, you beat all I ever seen," he said. "After being in that whorehouse and all that mess we went through in Kansas getting you cured, and you still sit there and talk like a damn preacher."

"Now you better watch it, or you'll get a real fight, Johnny." I said. "I ain't talking like no preacher. I'm just talking about doing what's right about Molly."

"I wasn't meaning her," he said. "I was talking about you. She's as nice as they come, I wasn't calling her no whore. But you ain't no more of a lily-white boy than I am."

"I know it," I said. "I just want to get this settled. It's been bothering me for two weeks."

"What I'm trying to get you to understand, there ain't nothing to settle. Molly ain't done nothing to be ashamed of. We've always treated her nice and she likes both of us. You're just ashamed of something that ain't shameful."

"Maybe so," I said, "but I'm pretty crazy about her, and I imagine you are too. But one of us ought to take care of her, and it'll be a shame if one of us don't that's all I meant to say. You was first, so you get the first chance."

"But that ain't even right, Gid," he said. "I wasn't first, no such thing. I always figured you was first. You was, and you know it. So why try to put the blame on me. I wouldn't do a thing like that to you."

That confused me. "The hell you wasn't first," I said. "Molly told me herself—she wasn't thinking what she was saying, I guess—that I wasn't the first one. Why are you trying to get out of it if you ain't ashamed?"

"Because I wasn't first," he said. "If you wasn't, then somebody else was. Not you nor me. Hell, I never stayed with her a time till last summer. When did you start?"

"The night of that harvest dance," I said. It flabbergasted us both. We never said a word for about fifteen miles, I guess. My ears like to froze off.

"Well, I guess we caught her," he said, finally. "I swear. I always figured it had been you. I wonder who the hell it was."

"It can't be just anybody," I said. "She's too sweet a girl. Who have we overlooked?"

"Aw hell," he said. "We ought to thought of it sooner. It must have been that damn Eddie."

"Not that worthless bastard, I can't believe that." But I remembered one time she said he was the only one silly enough for her her. I guess she meant it.

"He's the very one," Johnny said. "He ought to have the shit kicked out of him. What business does he have fiddling around with Molly anyway? That hound-running sonofabitch has probably got fleas plumb up to his middle."

"Yeah, that shit-ass," I said. "Evertime I see him he's greasy to the elbows. What would she want to take up with somebody like that for?"

"Aw, Molly's crazy," he said. He didn't sound too happy, and I wasn't either. Neither of us could stand that goddamn Eddie. "She don't think like other girls," he said. "Her trouble is, she's too nice. She's lived with that no-count bastard of a daddy so long she can't tell worthless people from them that's got something to them."

"That's about it. That old man's the cause of it all."

"I guess she figures she don't have no chance of being a nice girl anyway, growing up around him. That's probably why she took up with Eddie."

"Maybe there's somebody else," I said. "I'd rather it be nearly anybody than him."

But we couldn't think of another soul.

"Anyhow," Johnny said, "now you see that neither one of us has got to marry her. We don't need to have no guilty conscience. If he done it first, he's the one ought to marry her."

That shocked me worse than anything he'd said the whole night. "My god," I said. "You think I'd sit by and watch Molly marry a worthless sonofabitch like him. Why he ain't got nothing but a few hound dogs and a pair of roughnecking boots. He'd just drag her to one oil patch after another all her life."

"Serve her right, by god," he said. "She oughtn't to taken up with him in the first place."

"I know," I said. "But it don't make no difference. I'll just marry her anyway, even if I am third man. I ain't going to let her marry Eddie."

"Looky there," he said. "Ain't that a sight? I never knowed we was this close."

I looked, and there were the lights of Fort Worth. You never saw so many lights in your life. It was hard to imagine living in a place that big, but it sure was exciting to see all the lights at once. The train blew its whistle.

"That's cowtown," Johnny said.

"It's too early for anybody to be up," I said. "I wonder what they need with so many lights."

"I guess they just leave them lit so jackasses like us can tell when we're coming to a real town."

We stood up and looked, and pretty soon there were houses all around us and we went back in the caboose awhile, to warm up. The oil-fielder was still asleep. We decided he was drunk.

"I tell you what," Johnny said. We took off his shoes real careful and hid them over in a corner and got his shoelaces and tied his ankles together with them. We left a little play in the laces, but we tied about a dozen real hard knots and then spit on them to make them slippery.

"It'll take him a solid hour to get loose," Johnny said.

"It serves him right. It's what he gets for being an oil-fielder." We thought that was a pretty funny trick.

Pretty soon the train slowed down and stopped at the stockyards, and then the fun stopped too, for a while. We didn't know up from down about the stockyards, or what we we're supposed to do or nothing, and we got out and stood around in the cold and the dark for about an hour, waiting to unload the cattle. There were a lot of stockyards fellers moving around with lanterns and punchpoles, and a lot of railroad men too, but they never said nothing to us and we didn't bother them.

"Hell, maybe we ought to ask somebody," I said finally. "What if the train goes on and takes our stock with it?"

"I don't know," Johnny said. "My damn hands are froze. I hate to bother any of these men, don't you?"

I hated to too, so we stood awhile longer. Then the train blew its whistle, and that scared us enough that we found a Mexican and asked him. But he only knew Mexican and we only knew white man, so we finally had to ask one of the stockyards men.

“Goddamn, boys, you’all look about frozen,” he said. We told him our problem, and, by god, if they hadn’t already unloaded our cattle and taken them to a pen way off across the yards. We had been so cold we never noticed and had got by the wrong railroad car, one full of cattle that was going on to the slaughterhouse.

“Well, I guess we can go get a hotel room, can’t we?” Johnny said.

“Not till we find them cattle,” I said. “What if somebody tried to mix them with another bunch? Dad would have a fit.”

So we struck off across the yards looking for them, and just had an awful time. We had to crawl over about a hundred fences, and we couldn’t see well enough to tell if any of the bunches of cattle were ours or not. There must have been a thousand bunches of cattle, each one in a different pen. Finally by mistake we got in a pen with a couple of damn boar hogs. We didn’t even see them and thought the pen was empty till we got about halfway across it and heard one grunt as he come for us.

“Goddamn,” Johnny said. “Run.” We took off and hadn’t take two steps till another hog jumped up in front of us. He squealed and come at us too, but we jumped him before he got to his feet good and hit the fence and went up it.

“Shit,” Johnny said, “you can look for them cattle if you want to. I’m going to the hotel. I ain’t no hog fighter.”

The old boars were grunting and squealing around below us like they really wanted blood. I wasn’t a hog fighter either.

“Goddammit,” I said. “They oughtn’t to taken them cattle out of the cars without asking me. I’m the one responsible for them, ain’t I? Now I guess they’re lost.”

“Well, if they are, we just won’t go home,” Johnny said. “We can work around here for a few days and then catch a train up north. If them cattle are lost, I don’t never want to see Archer County agin.”

We finally found our way out of the yards and went through the big Exchange building. On the other side of it was the street. We walked down it and came to a lot of honkytonks and hotels; the honkytonks were closed, and the hotels didn't look too lively, but we finally come to one called the Longhorn, and an old feller came out dripping chewing tobacco on the rug and gave us a room for fifty cents apiece. I was worried about the cattle. I figured if I had lost them, I better go farther away than the Panhandle. I better go at least to Canada.

Johnny, though, he wasn't worrying; they wasn't his cattle.

"Me for some shut-eye," he said. "I wonder if that roughneck ever woke up."

It was an awful small, bare room we got, without no bathroom and with one of the littlest beds you ever saw.

"You mean we paid fifty cents apiece just to get a little old bed like that?" I said. "Hell, I slept in a bigger bed than that when I was a baby."

Johnny could sleep anywhere; he pulled off his boots and lay down. "Which you want," he said, "top or bottom? There ain't room enough for sideways."

But I thought I'd look at the street a minute, and when I let the windowshade up I seen it was daylight.

"Why, it's morning," I said. "Get up and let's go look for those cattle."

But he was done asleep and I went on without him. I figured I could do as well by myself anyway.

When I got back to the yards things looked a lot more cheerful; the sun was up and the cattle were bawling and people were charging around everywhere. They had big wide planks nailed on top of the fences, so you could just walk around above the pens and see the cattle without having to get down in the cowshit. I found my cattle in about ten minutes, and was I relieved. There was even a feller with them filling up the hayrack with hay. Them yards was really run right. The hay feller turned out to be a sourpuss.

"Howdy," I said. "I sure am glad to see those cattle."

"You're the Fry boy, ain't you?" he said.

"Gideon Fry. I'm glad to meet you."

"Why'd the hell you sleep so late?" he said. "You done missed two good chances to sell these cattle already. Your dad, now, he was always out at the yards by daybreak."

I never cared much to take a chewing out from an old fat hay hauler in a corduroy cap, so I asked him which way the buyers went. He got up on the fence and pointed one out to me, way across the yards. He bought for Swift & Armour, it turned out. I went over and introduced myself, and I'll be damned if he didn't buy the cattle right there, for a dime a pound. He took me right on in the Exchange building after the cattle were weighed and gave me a check. So that was that. I was so surprised I felt lightheaded; I had expected a hell of a day's work selling them cattle. It was just an hour after sunup and they were already sold.

There was a little lunch counter over in one corner of the big rotunda of the Exchange building, and I went over and bought myself a cup of coffee and set down with it. I just set there, feeling good, drinking the hot coffee; I felt like I could handle anything.

By then it was seven o'clock on a Monday morning, and the floor of the Exchange building was swirling with people. There was a big blackboard over on one wall and two men were at it all the time with chalk and erasers, marking up reports of prices and the number of cattle and whatnot at all the other big markets, Chicago and Kansas City and Omaha and I don't remember where else. The big cattlemen were stomping around the lobby, making deals and ordering people around. You could tell them right off from the just plain cowboys, even if they dressed alike. The cattlemen were the ones giving orders and acting like Dad acts, and the cowboys were taking orders and going off every which way to carry them out. I heard one feller, he was standing about ten feet from me make a deal for over a hundred thousand dollars' worth of cattle and he was just standing there drinking coffee, like me. Watching them big operators made an impression on me. They acted like what they were doing was important, and they did things like they meant them. Nobody was ordering them around, like Dad done me and Johnny. They was their own bosses—they weren't nasty about it, you could just tell. I guess it was independence. Anyhow, I went and got another cup of good strong hot coffee and set down to think about it. Dad had probably been right about me. Johnny, he could go off and cowboy if he wanted to; I might enjoy going along for a while, but it just wouldn't suit me for long. I wanted to amount to what all them big boys amounted to.

In a little while I went down the street a few doors and had breakfast at a little café. I started to go get Johnny, but I decided I might as well let him sleep. I felt like I'd wasted too much time in my life, and that cattle money was burning my pocket. There was all them cattle out in the yards, just waiting for somebody to buy them and make money on them. I intended to go make a little.

So I went back and spent the day on the yards. I kept expecting Johnny, but he never come, and I didn't have time to go get him. I had over eight thousand dollars of Dad's money when I started buying and trading and fooling around. Right off I bought a little bunch of steers and sold them not an hour later for a dollar a hundred profit. Boy, I felt like I was on the way. Only then a damn scoundrel from South Texas sold me another bunch too high. I guess I was tired or something and didn't look at them good. It was the ruination of me. I had made six hundred dollars on my first little deal and I figured I'd make that much more on the steers. Then I could buy some real good steers to take home to Dad, and I would still have made money. But, by god, if the last bunch wasn't the worst bunch of cattle I ever bought in my life. When I finally took time to really look them over, I seen how sorry they was, full of pinkeyes and foul foots and crips of one kind and another; looking at them from up above had fooled me. I spent all afternoon trying to sell them: I didn't dare go home with them. Finally I sold them back to the bastard I bought them from, at a four dollar a hundred loss. I lost twelve hundred dollars right there. During the afternoon I did buy some good steers and arranged to ship them to Henrietta, but that didn't make up for the twelve hundred dollars. It was just gone. I seen right then I was going to have to pay better attention if I was ever going to make a cattleman. Only I just gave up for that day. Losing that money kinda made me sick. I wanted to whip that South Texas bastard, but I didn't have a legitimate reason to. He had skinned me fair and square. It just left a bad taste in my mouth.

ABOUT AN HOUR before dark I went through the Exchange building and walked on back to the Longhorn Hotel. It was getting cold agin, and I felt sleepy and lonesome and plumb depressed with the world. Who I really wanted to see right then was Molly, in the worst way. Fort Worth didn't look like a very cheerful place any more. In fact, when I looked at it close, it looked like the dustiest, ugliest place I'd ever seen, except that town in Kansas where the hospital was. I would have given another twelve hundred dollars to have been back home, eating supper with Molly and listening to her talk.

But I wasn't there, and I had lost the money, and that was all there was to it. I sure did feel blue. I went up the stairs to our room, intending to get Johnny up so I could lay down and sleep, but when I opened the door I seen he wasn't there. And it was such a cold lonesome ugly little old bare room that I didn't feel like going to sleep in it, even if I was about to drop. The bed never had nothing on it but a little thin green counterpane anyway, and that wouldn't have kept a midget warm.

So I went back down stairs and out on the street. The street lights were done on, and they made the town look yellow and full of shadows. I figured Johnny was at the nearest honkytonk, but he wasn't; I had to go in eight or ten before I found him. Finally I seen him, way back in a bar, sitting at a table with some old feller I didn't know. They couldn't hardly see one another for the beer bottles stacked in front of them. Then I recognized the feller he was with: I had heard Dad tell about him. His name was Sam, and he was kind of a stockyards beggar, I guess; he had one real leg and one pegleg, and he wore a boot on the peg just like he did on the real foot. In his younger days he had been a cowboy on some big ranch and had got his leg pinched off between two boxcars, loading cattle one day. Johnny looked in high spirits.

"Hello partner," he said. "Where you been all day? I had me a good nap."

"I stayed out on the yards and traded a little," I said. "Wish I hadn't. A sonofabitch got the best of me and I lost a lot of Dad's money. I don't know what I'm going to do now."

"Drink a beer and don't brood," he said. "Hell, don't never brood. Sam can show us where and we'll go lose our virginity; then we can go home plumb busted."

"I can show you, sonny," Sam said. "Call that waitress over here. I'm strangling of thirst."

The waitress was a big fat woman in a red skirt; she was too ugly to look at if you could help it. I drank a couple of bottles right quick, but they didn't improve my spirits none.

"I wished you'd have come out there," I said to Johnny. "I needed you. What kind of a hand are you, anyway?"

"One with sense," he said. "And I ain't drunk, either, so quit frowning at me. I wouldn't get drunk before you did; it wouldn't be polite. Hell, if I had come out the way I was feeling today, we might have lost everything and really been up shit creek."

"I lost enough for both of us." I said. "Goddamn the luck."

"That's what I say, sonny," Sam said. "Goddamn the luck. I been saying that for years. Call that waitress over here, I could stand a little more beer, couldn't you' all?"

We stood a hell of a lot more of it. I don't guess we left the place till ten or eleven o'clock, and by that time the table top was full of beer bottles and we had set so many on the floor we were practically surrounded. We left a little alley for the waitress to come through, between me and where Sam was laying. He had slid off on the floor and went to sleep earlier in the evening and was stretched out nice and comfortable with his pegleg boot propped up on one rung of the chair. They had tried to drag him out, but me and Johnny felt like we ought to protect him. We would have fought like hell if anybody had grabbed him.

About that time, it was funny as hell: we both drank so much beer we got so we couldn't taste it. I don't know whether it was being tired or what, but it got so it didn't taste like beer, it tasted like real good water. And we were both awful thirsty, so we just kept pouring it down and ever now and then peeing some of it out.

"This is the best damn beerwater I ever drank," Johnny said. "How's yours taste?"

"Fine," I said. "Just fine. It goes down like twelve hundred dollars."

"Quit that damn brooding," he said, standing up all of a sudden. "Let's go to the whorehouse so you won't brood. Let old Sam sleep, we can find it. He don't need no pussy anyhow."

"Let him sleep," I said. "He don't need none."

I got up too, but then I fell down. I guess I stepped on a damn beer bottle; anyway, down I went. I fell right in about a hundred bottles, and Johnny he reached down meaning to help me and he fell too and there we were, rolling around in the bottles. At first I wanted to cuss, but then we both got tickled; it was kind of fun to lay there knocking empty bottles over, and we just sort of rolled and laughed and knocked the bottles every which way till I happened to notice we wasn't inside no more. It was colder and there wasn't any bottles and we were laying behind somebody's damn automobile.

"Hell, they threw us out," I said. "Did they throw you out too?"

He was up on his hands and knees laughing like mad. "Hell yes, can't you see me? They threw us both out."

"Want to go attack them?" I said. "Get back in the bottles?"

"Naw. Let's find the whorehouse."

I had forgot about that. Then the next thing this fat streetcar man was shaking me. "You boys need to sleep, go to a damn hotel," he said. "I've carried you far enough."

We were standing on a brick street, not very far from the courthouse, and the norther was blowing right down the street at us. Brother, it was cold.

"There's the courthouse," Johnny said. "Want to go there?"

"No," I said. "There ain't no whores in the courthouse, you damn fool."

"Might be some in jail," he said.

"I guess so," I said.

Then we ran into a damn drunk and he took us right to the whorehouse. He was so drunk he couldn't walk straight; he walked all over the street.

In the house there was a nice-looking redhead and I was going to be friendliest with her, only when we come in she said, "Here come two cowshits," and that made us so mad we didn't go near her. The carpet was so deep it confused me; my boots didn't make no noise; I thought I was barefoot.

Johnny just about fell over the banister going up stairs.

The girl in my room was blond-headed and I seen her turning back the counterpane on a big white bed. I watched her do that awhile and then I noticed we were laying on the bed and I didn't have my pants with me, just my socks and shirt. But she didn't have nothing on at all and she was getting out of the bed instead of in it; I seen her big floppy fanny going across the room and then she hiked up one leg and washed herself at a little dishpan of a thing.

"That was real nice, sweetheart," she said. "Now be a darling and help me make up this bed."

"We ain't through already, are we?" I said.

"Why sure, sugar," she said. "Can't you tell by your equipment?"

I wished then I hadn't drunk all that beer. Johnny was done downstairs when I got there and we went out.

"How do you feel?" I said.

"Horny," he said.

"Let's catch that streetcar, I'm about to freeze."

Of course we missed the train we was supposed to catch, so the new cattle got to Henrietta about twelve hours earlier than we did. That shrunk them a little. It was dark when we got there; we spent all night and till nine-thirty the next morning driving them home. We kept getting in thickets all night and like to froze to death, too; both of us looked like Ned when we finally got the cattle home and penned. Dad was in the barn loft when we penned them, and he come down and looked them over.

"Well, they ain't the worst cattle I ever seen," he said. "How'd the other cattle sell?"

"Good," I said. "Only I never got home with all the money. I got to cattle-trading and made a little money and let a damn feller skin me and lost all that and twelve hundred dollars besides. Maybe I can work it out in a few years."

I expected him to blow up, but he just kept walking around, inspecting the cattle.

"Got you in a little trading practice, did you?" he said. "Good. You may learn yet."

And he put us right to work, branding the new stock. I was so surprised at Dad that I never even minded the work. Dad was one man I never learned to predict.

Eight

It took us till past the middle of November to recuperate from the trip to Fort Worth. Johnny, he swore off beer drinking forever, but his forever usually just lasted about a week, and this one wasn't no exception. I couldn't enjoy myself much for worrying about when Dad was going to come down on me about the twelve hundred dollars. He just seemed to forget it, and Dad wasn't the kind to forget that much money.

One pretty warm fall day we worked like hell dipping cattle and hadn't much more than got to bed when somebody come riding up to the back gate just a-screaming. I jumped up and grabbed my pants and run out; Dad was done there. It was one of Mabel Peters' little brothers.

"Daddy says come tell you our house is on fire," he said. "Grandma burned it up."

We took his word for it. Dad yanked the kid off the horse and told me to take it and get on over there, he would follow and bring the kid in the wagon. So I grabbed a Levi's jacket off the back porch and went.

When I got there it was just a nice campfire left; an old chickenhouse don't take long to burn. The Peterses were all out in the yard, squatting around patting the dogs and crying: it was the only time in my life I ever saw that family all in one place, and I was surprised at how many of them there was. Six kids younger than Mabel, her momma and dad, and her grandma.

"Well, she's gone, Momma," the old man said. "Now we'll just have to trust in the Lord."

The grandma was taking on the worst; she had started the fire. She was about ninety-five. One of the boys said she had sloshed some kerosene out of a lamp onto the tablecloth. Mabel's mother was hysterical because she missed the boy they had sent to our place and thought he was burned up in the fire. There wasn't any fire fighting to do at all, and it was pretty miserable standing there watching the Peterses try to figure out what they had to go on living with. The old man had run out on the back porch and took out the milk strainer; it probably wouldn't have burned anyway. One of the boys had grabbed a Montgomery Ward catalogue and let the Bible burn, and Mabel had brought out a dish of pecans that was sitting on the new chair. The chair was the only new thing in the house, but nobody ever thought of grabbing it, and the two littlest boys had already eaten about half the pecans.

"Well, son," the old man said, coming over to me, "we're burned out."

"Dad's coming," I said. Then I went over and got Mabel and made her squat down close enough to the fire that she could at least keep warm. She was barefoot and never had on very warm clothes.

Pretty soon people that had seen the fire began to come. Dad was the last one there, but he had filled the wagon up with quilts, coffeepots and stuff to eat, so he done the most good once he come. We raked off a little of the fire and made some coffee, and gave each of the Peterses a quilt.

"Ain't it a mess, Gid?" Mabel said. Her teeth were chattering. "Now's when I wish I was married," she said, looking at me; the fire lit up her thin little face. She was pretty as could be in the face.

"If I was married," she said, "it wouldn't be so bad. We could all go over to my husband's house and live."

That about made my teeth chatter. I felt sorry for the Peterses, but nobody would have wanted all them kids and old folks swarming into their house.

"I wisht I'd got the chair," she said, starring to cry agin. "Why didn't I get the chair? Instead of the pecans."

Dad told Mr. Peters that if his family would all get in the wagon and wrap up real good in the quilts, I would drive them to Thalia. Mrs. Peters had a sister there, and they could stay with her a day or two, whether they liked it or not.

Everybody went home and Dad caught one of the Peterses' mules and went home himself, and I started down the road to Thalia with the biggest wagonload of sad people you ever saw. A norther had come up; I didn't have on a shirt under my jacket, and like to froze. All the Peterses went to sleep, but about halfway into town Mabel woke up and came up on the seat by me. She let me have a little of her quilt.

"We're much obliged to you, Gid," she said. "You're the nicest one that came tonight.

"Some of these days I'll marry you and make it all up to you," she said. "You see if I don't."

I started to tell her that I didn't want her to get her hopes up, but she squirmed over and kissed me and was like that all the rest of the way to Thalia. I could barely drive. It livened up the ride a whole lot.

"You remember what I said," she said, when we were coming into town. Her face was all white and excited, and neither one of us was particularly cold any more.

I got the job of going in and waking up Mrs. Peters' sister. Everybody else was afraid of the dog, but I beat him off with the wagon whip. When the lights came on all the Peterses climbed out and clobbered into the living room, looking like some Indian nation in all their quilts. The lady took them in, and I got ahold of two quilts and started back. Before I could get off, Mabel ran out and wrapped around me for about ten minutes. "Come and see me," she said. "I'll get awful lonesome in here."

After that, the Peterses had a real hard time of it. The sister kept them a week, and then they moved into the firehouse, and finally ended up back at the place living in their barn. People scraped up for them and gave them preserves and bacon and old clothes and a little money to get started on. But the old man never had the energy to start, and the boy had the energy but not enough sense. They were the poorest folks in the country, and Mabel felt disgraced. Finally they all left but her and went to some little town in Arkansas, where they had kinfolks. Mabel got a job in a grocery store and a room in a widow's house and stayed and tried to make herself well thought of. But she was still the poorest of the poor, and it was a long time before she got over it enough to have any prosperous boy friends.

Nine

As much as I worked around Dad, it looked like I would have been able to figure him out. A man as set in his ways as he was ought to have been more predictable. But he could always keep about a jump ahead of me.

We had three fair rains in October and a damn good slow three-inch rain the second week in November, and all our country looked good. We had more grass than we had cattle for, and it didn't look like it would be too hard a winter. I figured Dad would stock some more calves; that would have been the logical thing for a cattleman to do. One morning he sent Johnny off to check the water gaps, and told me to hitch up the wagon, we were going to Thalia. That was okay with me.

"Well," he said, once we were started, "I think I'll let you plant a little wheat this year. See what kind of a wheat farmer you are. Thought we'd buy some seed today.

"And don't go getting red in the face," he said. I was. "You ain't got no say-so about it, so just keep your mouth shut. I got the damn toothache this morning anyway."

"A toothache ain't got a damn thing to do with it," I said. "If you ask me."

"I never asked you. What I mean is, I can't stand no long conversation with my tooth hurting this way."

I got all nervous. It's terrible to be in a wagon when you get mad; you can't make it go no faster or anything. You just have to poke along when you feel like whipping and spurring.

"Well, I don't intend to do no farming," I said. "Your tooth can stand that much. You're crazy anyway. We ought to be buying cattle."

"Knock hell out of that mule," he said. "Keep him out of the ditch. He don't need to graze all the time.

"I figure it's gonna get dry," he said. "We've got some dry years coming. We might need this grass next summer more than we need it now, so I ain't gonna stock very heavy. It won't hurt you to try a little farming."

I began to get the Panhandle on my mind when he said that. It would take something drastic to bring Dad to his senses about me. Maybe if I run off for a little while it would do it.

We got to Thalia and got the wheat seed, and while I was loading it and fooling around the feed store trying to bargain with the feller for half a load of cottonseed hulls, Dad went up and got the doctor to pull his tooth for him. It must have had roots plumb down to the collarbone, because Dad spit blood all the way home.

"That was three dollars throwed away," he said. "Next time one wears out you can pull it."

"Okay," I said. "I'll do it for two and a half and save you the trip besides."

"I wish it would quit coming these damn cold northers," he said. "My blood's getting thin."

We didn't say much going home till we got to the place where the road went over Idiot Ridge. When we got there we could see the Taylor place across the long flat on the other hill, and off to the west of us we could see the Peterses' barn.

"Which one of them damn girls do you reckon you'll marry?" Dad said. "We may as well thrash that out while we're thrashing."

He beat all. "Why, I may not marry at all," I said. "I can't see that it's too much of your business, anyway."

"Oh, I guess it is. I was just curious as to which kind of trouble you mean to get yourself into."

"Well, if I marry either one it will damn sure be Molly," I said. "You couldn't get me to marry Mabel with a thirty-thirty."

"That's so," he said, spitting. "He said not to, but I think I'll chew a little tobacco. I'm bleeding to death through the head."

So the rest of the way he split blood and tobacco juice, instead of just blood.

"Okay," he said. "Mabel ain't the kind of girl you want; she's just the kind of girl that wants you. Molly, she don't want you."

"She damn sure does," I said. It made me mad. "What makes you think you know so much about her? Me and her get along real well."

"Oh, of course," he said. "I never meant to say you didn't. But you ain't gonna catch her, and your buddy Johnny ain't either, that's plain as day. And it's a damn good thing. She'd run you ragged if you did."

"How'd we get to talking about this, anyway?" I said. "I may not even marry. But if I do, it'll be Molly."

"Don't make no bets," he said. "And don't be sorry if you don't. If you stay loose from her, she'll make you the best kind of friend you can have. If you do marry her, you'll have ninety-nine kinds of misery. And you remember I told you that. A woman is a wonderful thing, goddamn them, but a man oughtn't to marry one unless he just absolutely has to have some kids. There's no other excuse."

"Well, you married, didn't you? You survived it, didn't you?"

"Yes," he said, "but your mother didn't . And I'm surprised I did. It like to done for us both."

"Anyhow, you're wrong about Molly," I said. "I can tell you that."

He kinda grinned at me. "You might tell me the time of day," he said, "if you had a better watch than mine. That's about all you can tell me. Of course if you marry the Peters girl, that'll be hell too, but at least you won't lose no friend."

"I swear I can't talk to you," I said. "You don't no more know me than the man in the moon. You think you know everything about me and you don't really know a damn thing."

"You're probably right," he said. "Maybe I'll improve." He got tickled at something and set there popping the reins on the mules and laughing to himself for the next mile or two.

"Did you mean you think I ought to marry Mabel instead of Molly?" I said. "I'm just curious."

"Oh no," he said. "I told you already I didn't want you to marry till you were forty or fifty years old. By then you might have enough judgment to marry right. Only I can see already you ain't gonna have enough judgment to last that long. I just mentioned it to see how much you knew about yourself."

"I'm sure you know more about me than I do," I said.

Dad sighed. "People are the hardest animals in the world to raise," he said. "And it's because nobody ever got them to breeding right in the first place."

"You don't breed people," I said.

"No, and it's a damn pity," he said. "I can take me a bull and get him with just the right cows at just the right time, and I won't have to worry much about the calf crop. But the chances of anybody getting the right man anywhere near the right woman are as slim as chances get. That's why I don't mind so bad being old. If I was young agin, I'd probably mess up even worse than I did."

Dad said that in a pretty sad way. It bothered me to hear him.

"That's a pessimistic damn thing to say," I said. "Why, I think life's a damn sight more fun than that."

"You ain't lived one," he said. Then he told me how much work we were going to get done that winter.

Ten

DAD KEPT ME SO BUSY WITH ONE THING AND ANOTHER that it was after the first of December before I got over to Molly's to ask her to go to the Christmas dance with me. One afternoon I got off early, though. Dad decided it was going to come a storm, and he wanted to leave the cattle alone till it was over. Johnny never come to work that day anyway; his old man had kept him home to help him kill their hogs. Dad said he didn't need me, so I saddled up and got my sheepskin coat and rode over to the Taylors'. It was cloudy and cold and looked sleety back in the northwest. I seen a big flock of geese going over. I hated the wintertime; it sure made the cow-work mean.

Molly was hanging out clothes when I rode up. She had on an old red flannel shirt and a pair of overalls and was actually barefooted out in that cold. I guess it was a habit. The Taylor kids hardly ever put on shoes before Christmas, and they had them off agin by Washington's birthday. She looked as pretty as ever. When I walked up she put her hand on the back of my neck, and it was cold from the wet clothes.

"Don't you hope it snows?" she said.

I kissed her right quick and made her let me help her hang up clothes. It was so cold they practically froze while we were getting them over the clothesline. There were scraps of burned tow sack floating around the yard, so I figured the old man had let the windmill freeze and Molly had had to thaw out the pipes.

Molly's cheeks were red and her hair all blowy, but she didn't seem to mind the weather. "Dad said he might kill a goose," she said. "If he does, maybe you can come over and eat some of it."

"Maybe I'll kill one myself," I said. "Let's go inside for a while."

I got the bushel basket the clothes had been in, and she caught me by the hand and led me in the house. The kitchen was nice. It was so warm the windows were fogged over. Molly had made some cookies that morning, and we sat down at the kitchen table and ate them.

"It's about time you came," she said. "I been missing you so much." She reached her foot under the table and kicked me with her toes.

"Dad's been working the daylights out of me. By the time I get loose from him I ain't fit company for a pretty young lady."

"I guess I could stand you," she said. "Ain't these good cookies? I feel so good today now that you showed up."

I pulled my chair around by hers, so we could sit close together. I decided I would start taking more afternoons off.

"Johnny comes by a lot," she said. "He said you'all had a pretty big time in Fort Worth. I wouldn't mind seeing Fort Worth sometimes."

"Maybe we'll go there on our honeymoon," I said.

She looked at me, half-grinning and half-serious; part of what was in her eyes was mischief and part of it wasn't. She had my hand in both of hers.

"I told you about that once," she said. "I don't intend to get married till I'm going to have a baby."

"Oh, now hush," I said. "That's silly. We'll get married by next summer, I don't care what you say."

She shook her head and thought about it to herself for a while, and wouldn't look at me.

"Anyway, don't go getting no black eyes week after next," I said. "We don't want to miss another big dance."

"I'm sorry about that, Gid," she said. "I knew that was why you come over. I already told somebody else I'd go with him."

That knocked a hole in my spirits. But when I thought about it a minute, it didn't surprise me. Johnny rode within two miles of her place every day; it was no wonder he'd asked her.

"Well, I guess he deserves to take you to one dance," I said. "Anyway I'll get to dance with you a lot. Johnny won't care about that."

"Oh, it wasn't Johnny," she said. "He asked me a long time ago. I promised Eddie I wouldn't go to dances with anybody but him any more."

I didn't have no idea what to say to that. I couldn't believe it.

"Are you plumb crazy?" I said. I started to bawl her out, but I seen she was sitting there about ready to cry. I held up.

"Well, has he asked you to this dance?" I said. "I haven't seen him lately. He may not be in this part of the country."

"No." She didn't let herself cry, but her eyes spilled over once. "I guess he's in Oklahoma," she said. "He ain't been here in a month. But I promised him anyway."

"But, sweetheart," I said. "He may not even be back in time for the dance. You don't want to miss it, do you?"

"No," she said. "You know I don't. But he told me not to go unless he was here to take me. So I better not."

"That beats anything in the damn world," I said. "I ought to spank you right here. What kind of a feller is he? That ain't no way to treat a girl." But I hugged her anyway, and her face was all wet against my neck.

"He's not any count," I said. "You know that, Molly."

"Sometimes I wish I hadn't promised him," she said. "But I did. You're my favorite."

We set in the kitchen for a long time, kissing and not talking much. She wouldn't say another word about Eddie or the dance. I didn't care. It was a comfortable time, and I didn't think much about the dance.

"Stay for supper with me," she said. "We butchered the milk-pen calf, so we can have beef. Dad may not be coming home to day, I don't know."

So I decided to stay, and I meant to make it all night if she'd let me. I milked and done her chores for her and chopped enough wood to last her through the cold spell. I even put my horse in the barn. Then we ate and got real cheerful. We found some popcorn and went in the living room to pop it in the fireplace. The living room was neat, so I knew the old man hadn't been there for a while. When he was around it was always full of junk and whiskey jugs.

"Wouldn't you like to get away from here?" I said. We were sitting on the floor close to the fire. Molly had unbuttoned her shirt a little and I was watching the firelight on her throat and chest.

"Why no," she said. "I couldn't leave here. This is where I intend to live. Anyhow, who'd look after Dad?"

We salted the popcorn and buttered it and ate it, and when Molly kissed me after that she tasted like warm butter and salt; I'll always remember that.

"I sure do like you," she said. "You can come stay with me anytime you want to, you know that, don't you? It doesn't make any difference about the dances."

She lay down with her head in my lap, and I looked down at her.

"I sure do like you too. But it makes a difference to me. You're the one I want and I don't want no other fellers around you."

She grinned and sat up and gave me one of those butter-and-salt kisses. The firelight lit up our faces. And just that minute we heard the back door kick in and the old man stomped into the kitchen. We heard him stamping around trying to get his overshoes off.

It made us both so sad at first we didn't even move. Then we sat up, and by the time he came into the room we were eating popcorn, just as innocent as you please.

"We're in here," she said. "It's Gid and me."

"Oh it is is it?" he said. He turned and went back to the kitchen and we heard him getting a glass out of the cabinet. When he came back he had a glass of whiskey in one hand and his bottle in the other. It was the first time I ever saw him drink out of a glass. He still had on his big sheepskin coat and his old dirty plaid cap, with the earflaps still pulled down over his ears and tied under his chin. He didn't look in too good a mood; it kinda scared me, actually. I kept on eating popcorn.

"Go get some firewood," he said. "It's a goddamn cold night."

I didn't know whether he was talking to me or Molly, but I got up and went to the woodpile and got an armful of wood.

"Put it over here," he said. So I dumped it right by his chair and he took his gloves off and picked out a chunk and leaned over and pitched it in the fire. Sparks and ashes flew everywhere, and Molly had to jump to keep them from getting on her. It made me mad.

"Good way to catch the house on fire," I said. "Let me do it for you, Mr. Taylor."

"Hell no," he said. He sat the glass down on one side of the chair and drank out of the bottle. I never did see him drink out of the glass agin.

"All right," I said. I didn't want no argument with him. "It's dangerous though."

"Danger-rus, my ass," he said, grinning at Molly like he was fixing to tell her some big joke. "This here's my house anyway, if I want to burn it down then by god I'll burn it down. Never asked you nohow. Get on out of here and go home. Who asked you over here in the first place?"

"He's just visiting a little," Molly said. "He ain't doing any harm, Daddy." She said it kinda timidly.

He gave her a hard look. "I never asked you to take up for him," he said. "A little licking wouldn't hurt you, sister. You ain't fixed my supper, so what are you sitting here for?"

She looked hurt and sad: I think she was really scared to death of him and didn't know it herself. She picked up the popcorn bowl and went to the kitchen without saying another thing.

I stood up and put on my coat and went over to the fire to warm my hands a minute.

"Get away from there," he said. "Don't stand between me and the fire, don't you know better than that? A little licking wouldn't hurt you none either, you damn coyote roper."

I didn't see why I needed to take any more off an old surly bastard like him.

“You ain’t gonna lick me,” I said. “You’re too drunk.”

He grinned, but it was a pretty mean grin.

“And quit trying to court my girl,” he said. “I’d chop her in two with an ax before I’d let a feller like you have her.”

“You’re so damn tough my teeth chatter,” I said. “I’m a good notion to stuff you up this fireplace right now.”

That was the first time in my life I ever said anything bad to a person older than I was. It scared me a little, but the old man just took another drink.

“You’re a little piss-ant,” he said. After that he just stared at the fire, and I left him to his bottle.

Molly was in the kitchen crying and stirring stuff on the stove.

“Don’t argue with Daddy agin,” she said. “Please don’t, Gid. I won’t like you any more if you do.”

I went up behind her and hugged her. “Yes you will,” I said. “I sure hate to go off and leave you tonight, you know that, don’t you?”

She turned loose of the frying pan a minute and turned around and kissed me, but we were both uneasy because the old man was so close by.

“You’re my girl,” I said. “You’re the only one I’m ever going to have.” I let her go then and started to leave, but she shoved the frying pan off the fire right quick and went out the back door with me, into the cold. And she still didn’t have no more clothes on than she had that morning.

“I’ll go help you get your horse,” she said. “Dad’s done forgot about supper, and he won’t think of it till I remind him.”

I hugged her up against me as close as I could. “What made him so mad?” I said. “I wasn’t doing anything wrong.”

“Hush,” she said. “Don’t talk about Dad. I don’t want you putting the blame on him.”

I shut up, but it still seemed an awful way for a girl’s daddy to act.

“I don’t think he’ll lick me tonight,” she said. “He was just talking.” Molly was funny. She didn’t seem to realize there was much wrong with him licking her.

The wind was singing down off the plains cold as ice, and by the time we got to the barn, Molly was about froze. I made her take my sheepskin while I caught the horse and saddled him. We lit the barn lantern and she held it so I could see what I was doing; even so the barn was mostly shadows and the horse didn't like it. When I got through I set the lantern down and rubbed her hands to get them warm.

"You'll probably take pneumonia," I said. "You ain't got many brains to be so sweet."

She put her cold hands on my neck. "I just came out so you could kiss me goodnight," she said. "It ain't much fun in the kitchen when somebody else is around."

I did, and it was funny: she was so cold on the outside and so warm underneath it all. Molly was always the warmest girl I knew. I blew out the lantern and led her and the horse out into the cold. I put her in the saddle in front of me, where I could hold her. The moon was up, and the little thin cold clouds were whipping across it, going south.

"I'd hate to be the moon," she said.

At the yard gate I got down and helped her off. But I held her up against the horse for a minute, so he could warm her on one side and me on the other.

"Come on to the dance with me," I said. "If Eddie bothers you about it, I'll stop him."

She kissed me for a long time then, and kept changing from one foot to the other. I guess they were about to freeze. Then she pulled back and looked at me.

"You ain't the only kind of good person," she said. "How do you know you're any better than him?"

"The same way you know it," I said. "Only you won't admit it. Come on and go with me."

"I can't, honey," she said. "I done promised. But I'm so glad you come over. Come back and see me a lot, Gid."

"You'll see a world of me before it's over," I said. "That's a promise I can make."

She held my hand even after I was on the horse; then we remembered she had on my jacket and she took it off and gave it to me.

"Now get on in before you freeze," I said. "I'll see you pretty soon."

"I wish you could stay," she said. "I hate to see you go off. You're liable to freeze."

But she's the one who would have frozen, if I hadn't turned and ridden off. I don't think she wanted to go back in very bad. I know I sure did hate to leave. I rode off about twenty steps and stopped to button my coat. "Don't get lost," Molly said.

"Go in, honey," I said. "It's awful cold," I guess she just grinned, I don't know. The last time I looked she was still standing there by the fence, with the wind blowing around her.

Eleven

JOHNNY AND ME TALKED IT OVER AND DECIDED WE WOULD go to the dance anyway, and not take no girls. Neither one of us wanted to take anybody but Molly.

"Course I might take Mabel home," Johnny said. "If she comes. But I ain't going to take her both ways."

"She won't go home with you," I said. "Mabel's got more pride than that."

Neither of us could understand why Molly would make a promise like that to a no-count like Eddie. But we knew it had to be stopped.

"I think we better whip him," Johnny said. "You and me can fight over her in our own good time."

"Naw, we better not fight him," I said. "That would just make her feel sorry for him. I guess that's why she goes with him anyway. I'll just tell him to stay away from her."

"He won't pay a damn bit of attention to you," he said. "Hell, I don't pay much attention to you myself."

AT LEAST it was a pretty night for a Christmas dance, and not too cold. When we crossed Onion Creek we both got the real dancing spirit, and we loped the rest of the way into town. But we sure weren't the first ones there. Half the horses and buggies in the country were hitched outside the dancehall, and there were even quite a few automobiles.

I wanted an automobile myself, but Dad was too tight to buy one. Johnny said he wouldn't have one of the things.

We came in right in the middle of a square dance and didn't have any way to get in on it, so we stood around patting our feet. The hall was nearly full, and the people were stomping and drinking a lot of eggnog and having a real good time.

"There they are," I said.

Molly was dancing in a set just across the floor from us. Her black hair was flying around her shoulders, and she looked her rosiest. Eddie had on his roughnecking boots, so you could hear him all over the hall when his feet hit the floor. He wasn't dressed up or nothing, and he looked like he was already drunk. It made me so damn jealous I could hardly stand still. Once when him and Molly met to do-ce-do he swung down and kissed her big before he went to the next girl; she never seemed to mind. I guess she was having such a big time being away from home that she forgot herself.

"Why do you reckon all these old folks want to get out there and dance?" Johnny said. "It's just making a spectacle of themselves, if you ask me."

I thought so too. The whole town was there. All the little kids were running around screaming and chasing one another and talking about what they were going to get for Christmas; their mommas and poppas weren't paying any attention to them at all. Everybody that could move danced. Fat ones and skinny ones and ugly ones and pretty ones. Of course there were a few bachelors off in the refreshment room, emptying the eggnog bowl and talking about the war, but there wasn't over a dozen of them. I even seen a preacher dance one set, and that was a pretty rare sight.

"I think I'll partake of a little eggnog," Johnny said. "Then we'll see what we can do about Molly."

I let him go. I didn't intend to drink much myself till after the dancing was over. I had a hard enough time dancing as it was.

When the set was over I started across to Molly, but it was crowded on the floor, and of course about fifty people stopped me to shake hands and ask how I was and wish me Merry Christmas and ask how

Dad was and how the cattle were and all that, so that they started a round dance before I could get over to her, and Eddie hugged her up and was dancing with her. It made me so mad I could have bitten myself. I didn't see how she could breathe he was holding her so tight.

I was right on the spot when that dance was over, though. Johnny was across the hall, talking to Mabel and some feller she was with. Eddie was grinning and red in the face and his cowlick was falling down in his eyes. He was in an awful good humor.

"Howdy, cowpuncher," he said, "dance with my girl awhile. I got to have me a drink. This dancehall is hot." He handed me Molly's hand and went outside; I guess he had him a bottle somewhere.

"Merry Christmas, Gid," Molly said. "I'm glad you'all finally got here. Guess what? Eddie's bought him a car."

I never asked her the story on it; it made me blue enough just to hear it. It was just the kind of thing that crazy bastard would do. He never owned a shirt in his life that didn't have fifteen patches on it, neither. We found out later he got the car secondhand for forty-five dollars. I guess he made the money roughnecking.

The next one was a round dance too, and we danced real slow. Molly had on a dark blue dress, and she had little tiny shadows under her eyes, like she hadn't been getting enough sleep. Her neck smelled like lavender. But her breath smelled a little like whiskey; I guess Eddie got her to take a drink. I wanted to say a lot of things to her, but she laid her head on my shoulder, and we didn't talk. Then I let Johnny dance one with her; I told him it was his Christmas present. I danced one with Mabel; she talked a blue streak.

After that I got to dance a good square dance with Molly, and that was fun. Eddie come in in the middle of it, but he had to sit down and wait. I figured I would give up on it for the night and get drunk myself. As I was leading Molly off the floor I told her I had her a Christmas present.

"Let me come over and get it," she said. "Dad hasn't been in too good a mood lately."

Eddie grabbed her and hugged her; he was about five degrees drunker than he had been. Johnny was getting drunk too; he spent most of his time with Mabel.

"Old Josh is going to take her home," he said. "I asked. But she said I could come by later and she'd make me some hot choclate. You know how I am about hot choclate."

I went in and took after the eggnog pretty heavy. I liked to sit and listen to fiddle music, so I sat down by the refreshment table and listened to "Sally Goodin," and "Four Little Ladies," and "The Texas Star" and all the others.

Then all of a sudden Molly run in and squatted down by me and whispered in my ear. I seen she was crying.

"Go stop them, Gid," she said. "It's such a nice dance; I don't want them to fight. Eddie gets so mean. Tell Johnny I won't never like him agin if he fights."

"What happened?" I said. "I been drinking too much. Where'd they go?"

"Outside," she said. "Go stop them, Gid."

Most of the people still seemed to be dancing and having a good time. Usually when there was a fight a lot of the men would go out and watch.

"They went off behind the cars," she said.

When I stood up I didn't feel so drunk. "I doubt if I can stop them," I said. "But I'll try."

The cold air felt real good after the dancehall, and my head felt clearer. Sure enough, they were over behind the cars. I guess they had already fought a little, because Johnny had a nosebleed. It didn't mean much; I think his nose bleeds just from excitement. Six or eight of the bachelors were standing around watching; they had turned some car lights on, so everybody could see better.

Eddie had one fist doubled up and his arm drawn back, and Johnny was just standing there watching him; he had his thumbs hooked in his pockets. Johnny was drunk as a bat; they both were.

"You're a damn oil-field hound-running coward," Johnny said. Johnny looked happy about it all; he never minded fighting. But Eddie was serious about it; he kept his fist doubled up. Eddie was a coward, that's why I wouldn't have wanted to fight him; somebody that's scared of you can really be dangerous. Johnny never noticed things like that.

I started to say something to Johnny, but decided not to. They were going to fight anyway. Eddie kept standing there, holding back his fist and sneering that mean sneer of his, and all of a sudden Johnny made a run at him and they went to the ground. Johnny was a quick bastard when he started. They went to rolling and bumping on the ground, each one trying to get a choke hold and neither one doing the other much damage.

"Hell, them boys ain't fighting," a man said. "They're just wallowing on the ground. Get up from there and fight, boys, if you're gonna fight."

They did, and that was Johnny's mistake. Eddie got him off balance and knocked him down and went to pounding on him. Then Johnny nearly got up agin and Eddie jumped on him and began to pound him against an automobile.

"Now that's fighting," the feller said.

I was getting nervous. It looked like we were going to be disgraced. Johnny couldn't get his balance, and Eddie kept pouring it on. Finally he got Johnny down agin, only he didn't go down with him. He stood back with his fist doubled up. I guess he thought he had won, because he kinda laughed.

"You goddamn cowpunchers, you can't fight," he said. "Hell, it takes a roughneck to fight."

And that was Eddie's mistake, thinking Johnny McCloud would quit fighting just because he was beat on a little. I knew damn well Johnny wasn't done with the fight because his eyes were open; Johnny never quit nothing while he still had his eyes open. I guess he was resting. Eddie sneered and Johnny come up and stayed up. Eddie tried to kick him back down, but Johnny got the leg and set Eddie down himself. And while he had his leg he managed to yank off one of the roughnecking boots and he threw it out in the darkness as far as he could throw. Then he run Eddie against an automobile. They were out of the light then; I don't know exactly what happened. Somehow Johnny got Eddie up on the hood of a car and shoved him clear off on the other side. He ran around the car right quick and we did too, but the show was over. Eddie was holding his neck and spitting and wouldn't get up or say anything; I think he had bitten his tongue when he hit. Besides the sheriff came out about that time.

"These boys ain't hurting one another, are they?" he said.

"Naw, they're just fighting, Gus," a feller said. "I guess they're about done."

Eddie stood up, but him and Johnny were both too tired to say much. I motioned at Johnny to keep quiet but he didn't see me. The sheriff didn't mind fighting, but he couldn't stand nasty talking.

"So you leave her alone," Johnny said. "You horse's butt you."

Eddie walked off to look for his shoe, and the sheriff turned around and took hold of Johnny's arm.

"I don't like that filthy language," the sheriff said. "Who started this fight anyway?"

"I did, by god," Johnny said. "And by god I finished it, too. And I'd whip you too if you didn't have that damn badge on."

That was just the kind of crazy thing Johnny would say. The sheriff started off with him. "Taking the Lord's name in vain is one thing I won't stand for," he said. "Not even at Christmastime. What if a lady had heard you say that?" And off they went.

"Don't think that Gus won't arrest them," the feller said. "He won't stand for no goddamn cussing, and I don't blame him."

"No, but you know something," another feller said, "he'll never get elected in this damn county agin. That's just how goddamn sorry people are getting."

I danced a round dance with Molly and told her it was okay.

"They wasn't neither one hurt," I said. "Eddie will be back when he finds his shoe. I guess I better take Johnny's horse up to the jail and see if I can talk the sheriff into letting him out."

Molly felt a little better when she was satisfied there was nobody killed.

"I wish I could take you home," I said. "Even if he has got an automobile."

"It makes me mad the way you talk about Eddie," she said. "Working in the oil field ain't no crime, is it?"

"No, and you're too sweet to argue with." We walked off the floor and I got my coat.

"I hope they let Johnny go," she said. "Tell him to come and see me when he can. I'm sorry he got in trouble on my account."

She wouldn't go outside with me, even for a minute—afraid she would bump into Eddie, I guess—but I made her promise to come over and help us with the hog-killing, the next week. I figured I could give her her Christmas present then. I sure did hate to leave her at the dance.

The sheriff of course wouldn't let Johnny go. I guess Johnny cussed him all the way to the jail. He was a funny sheriff. He never got mad and he never got tickled, either.

"That boy talks too nasty," he said. "I ain't gonna have that nasty talk around where there's ladies. Why, that would be a disgrace to the county."

"I know it," I said. I thought I better agree with him. "If you'll let me have him, I'll take him out of town quick, so there won't be no danger."

"No, I'll keep him tonight," he said. "Just put his horse in the barn. Be a good lesson to a boy like that. Besides, I want to give him a good talking to before I let him go, and he's done asleep."

So I went on home, eighteen miles by myself.

Twelve

The Wednesday before Christmas, Dad decided it would be a good time to kill the hogs. We had four big shoats to butcher; more hog meat than me and Dad could have eaten in two years. Dad had done made arrangements to sell three of the carcasses, though; the fellers he sold them to came over to help us. Dad had gone over special and asked Molly to come cook for the crew, and Johnny was there, of course, mostly just getting in the way. When you took Johnny off of his horse he was the worst hand in the world.

Me and him did the actual killing, shooting, and sticking, while Dad and the other men built the fires and got the water ready. Dad, he wouldn't have wallowed around in the hogpen mud for half the pork in Texas. Johnny worked the gun and I worked the butcher knife, and we laid them low. Then we got our horses and drug the carcasses up to the fire one at a time.

Johnny bitched around so much while we were scraping the carcasses that Dad finally sent him off down in the River pasture to drive in a yearling he thought was getting sick. Actually Dad must have liked Johnny; he let him get away with a damn sight more than I ever got away with.

About nine-thirty Molly come riding up; she had on her red mackinaw. Just seeing her made me feel so good I could have jumped six feet. I never realized how lonesome I stayed till I got close to Molly. Not even then. When I realized it was when I had been close to her and one of us was leaving. Then for a day or two the world would look twice as bad as it really was.

I took her down to the barn and put her horse where ours wouldn't kick hell out of him. I got her back in the hallway, out of sight, and gave her a kiss.

"Silly," she said. "Who ever heard of kissing in the morning?"

She wouldn't let me hold her hand when we got outside because she was afraid everybody would tease us. She was right; they would have.

It was a good day. We got the hogs butchered without no trouble, and Molly cooked a big dinner and everybody enjoyed it and complimented her on it, and that made her feel good. Johnny even made it back in time to eat; for once he showed pretty good manners. In the afternoon we made soap and cracklins and the other fellers loaded their pork and went home. It was nearly suppertime before we got all the kettles cleaned, so Molly decided to stay and fix supper, too. Johnny went on home. Dad gave him a quarter of pork for a Christmas bonus and he told us all Merry Christmas and went off with it tied to his saddle. Watching him leave made me blue for a minute; it was strange. I knew right then he'd never get Molly to marry him, only for a minute I wished he could have. It would have been nice for him if he could have.

"Well, we done a good day's work," Dad said. "Let's go inside where it's warm. I could stand some supper."

We went in and the kitchen was nice and warm. The lamps were lit. Me and Dad sat at the table and watched Molly working around the sink and around the stove, not paying us much mind; it was a treat for us just to watch. Me and Dad had batched for nine years, and we thought we got along pretty well, but having Molly in the kitchen eating supper made the way we usually done it seem pretty flat and dull. The house was just so much fuller with her in it. I guess Dad felt it too.

"Sure do appreciate your coming over to cook," he said. "This here'll beat Christmas."

Molly turned and looked at him a minute; she had a pan of biscuits in one hand and a gravy bowl in the other, and I don't think she even heard him. She just smiled and went on cooking, and Dad never repeated it. He was looking too tired, Dad was. He hadn't been feeling too good, I didn't think. Course he never said a word about it.

Molly fed us beef and beans and biscuits and gravy and pie, and we ate plenty of it. I couldn't take my eyes off her, and I couldn't keep from wishing I could get her to marry me. Then we could have her around all the time. She sat down at the other end of the table and drank her coffee, not saying anything but perfectly content. We were all quiet, but it was a real easy quiet.

Finally Dad got up and said he had to go to bed. He offered to pay Molly something, but of course she wouldn't take nothing. So he gave her a quarter of pork and some cracklins and told me to ride home with her to see that she got there all right.

Then it was just me and her in the kitchen.

"Let's go over to my house, Gid," she said. "Dad's gone to Wichita. You and him won't bother one another tonight."

"Okay," I said.

When we got there we built up the fire in the fireplace and sat in front of it a long time. I gave Molly her Christmas present, but I wouldn't let her open it, and we sat there not talking much or kissing much or anything, just resting together. Then she leaned forward and took some pins loose and shook down her long hair and lay back against me so the firelight shone on her face and eyes and mouth. I was half-sick, I loved her so much and was so excited by her. In a minute I was all wrapped around her. She wanted to go in the bedroom, and pulled her shirttail out as we went down the hall. It was cold as ice until we had been under the covers for a while, and then it got toasty warm and only Molly's fingers were cold. And there wasn't no old man to worry about, so we could go ahead. Only I was so excited about her I didn't do no good; I don't guess I knew enough about what I was doing.

"Oh hell," I said. "Dammit. I wouldn't blame you for marrying somebody else."

"Be still and hush," she said, and kissed me.

"I don't see why you put up with me," I said.

"You're my favorite," she said. "You ain't done nothing wrong. You just enjoy me a whole lot, I can tell that. And that's what I want you to do. Go to sleep, sugar."

And I did: it was the best sleeping in the world. When I woke up I could hardly believe I'd slept so good. Molly was still asleep and I was holding her. It was pure enjoyment. Finally I woke her up because having her asleep made me feel lonesome. We hugged and talked awhile. But she wouldn't say she'd marry me.

"That would be wrong," she said. "I don't love you that way." And then she leaned over and looked me right in the face, with her hair touching my chest. "But you love me that way, don't you?" she said, as if she had never thought of it before. "You do love me that way, Gid," she said. "That's going to be so sad. I don't love anybody that way." And she lay with her face tucked into my neck a long time, so I could feel her breath on my Adam's apple.

About daybreak we got up and had a real good breakfast and were cheerful as we'd ever been. I went home and worked and was all right that day. But the next day when I woke up I was so lonesome for her I was sick. All I could see that day was her face leaning over me, and her hair.

Thirteen

It didn't seem like I was going to be able to stand not having Molly around more of the time. Every time I thought about her I got bluer and bluer. And if that wasn't trouble enough, Dad had me farming. It was a warm January and looked like it was going to be warm all winter. Johnny was doing most of the cow-work, and Dad was just mostly piddling around; he still wasn't feeling good. So for four days in a row I had to go down and follow them worthless mules around that worthless field, thinking about Molly all the time and wondering when I'd get to see her.

Then one Monday about the middle of the morning Johnny come through the field on his way to the League pasture. He was jogging along looking pretty discouraged, and I waved at him to come over. I was tired of kicking clods around anyway, and he got off his horse and we set by the plow awhile.

"Don't you get tired of this?" he said.

"Naw, I love it," I said. "I'd like to do this for the rest of my life. What are you so down in the dumps about?"

"Oh, Molly, I guess. I wish I wasn't so damn sweet on her. Hell, I oughtn't to be. She don't care nothing about me. At least not like I want her to. She just ain't got no sense."

"She's got the wrong kind of sense," I said. "Anyhow, what's she done now?"

"Nothing she hasn't done before," he said, looking real sour. "I rode all the way over there to visit her last night and the first thing I saw was Eddie's damn automobile. I never even went in."

"See 'em?"

"I looked through the kitchen window. He was sitting there eating vinegar cobbler and she was waiting on him just like he owned the place."

That made me plain sick. We sat there for about ten minutes, neither one of us saying a word. I couldn't think of one hopeful thing.

"Shit on the world," I said. "Let's go someplace. I'll be damned if I'll plow my legs off while she cooks cobbler for somebody like Eddie. Let's just go to the Panhandle and show them all."

"All right," he said. "You going to leave the plow here?"

I DID. I rode in on one mule and unharnessed. Dad was up at the house, sitting by the fireplace trying to shave a corn off his toe. He looked pretty tired, but I wasn't in no mood to sympathize.

"Dad," I said, "things are just going wrong. I've had enough of this country. Me and Johnny are going up on the plains for a little while. I hope you can hire you a little help."

"Going, are you?" he said. "That oil-fielder running you off?"

"Not by a damn sight," I said. "I'm sorry to leave you."

"Oh, I guess I can do the work," he said. "I always have."

I seen he wasn't gonna act nice, so I didn't say any more to him.

"Let me hear from you now and then," was the last thing he said.

So we rode to Henrietta that night and arranged with an old boy to take the horses back to Archer County for us. We got good and drunk, and along about midnight we caught the train north. Our spirits weren't too good, but we were the only passengers, and we each got a bench and went to sleep. I dreamed that Dad was out terracing in the moonlight. When I woke up Johnny was still asleep and I had a headache, so I went out on the porch of the caboose. I guess we were about to Childress then; anyhow we were on the plains. The cold air kind of cleared my head. It was exciting to see all that country stretched out around me, but I felt pretty sad, too. I was split: I was glad to be where I was, and yet I wanted to be where I had just left. Looking down the rails, I couldn't help but think of the people at home, Dad and Molly mostly.

Thinking about them, I got lonesome, and went in and woke Johnny up. We stayed awake the rest of the night, talking about all the different big outfits we could work for. It would be the JAs most likely, or maybe the Matadors, depending on where we decided to go from Amarillo. We had about fifteen dollars apiece, cash money, and our saddles and saddle blankets, so we felt pretty well off.

We got off the train at the big brick station in Amarillo, and it was like getting off at the North Pole. The wind whistled down those big streets like the town belonged to it, and the people were just renters it was letting stay.

"Goddamn," Johnny said. "I never realized it was this cold up north in the wintertime."

We got a hotel room and decided to take the day to look around. Only the hotel room was so toasty and warm we stretched out and slept till almost six o'clock. When we went outside the lights were on and the streets were plumb empty, like the wind had blown everybody away. We found some saloons, though, and the people were in them.

"Let's celebrate before we go to work," I said.

He was agreeable, and boy did we celebrate. I wished we'd eaten supper first. I guess around home we never drank enough to keep in shape. We found some girls, too, even if they wasn't no raving beauties. We would have kept them for the night but they said our hotel was too respectable for them. They wouldn't take us to their places, so we went back to the saloons and drank some more and did without.

When we finally got back to the room we agreed we'd have to get up at four o'clock and look for a job. Boy, it was a bad night. If the hotel hadn't had a bathtub, we would have ruined the place. I brought up a good gallon, myself, before morning, and I wasn't nothing to Johnny. He made twice as many trips as I did. About the time it got light I seen him on his way to the bathroom agin, only he was crawling.

"What are you doing crawling?" I said. "Can't you even walk?"

"I might could," he said, and crawled on in anyway. I thought that was pretty funny.

"Hell, I can at least walk," I said. He was in asleep on the bathroom floor.

We never made it up at four, but we did get downstairs by about six-thirty. I had got emptied out and was feeling okay, but Johnny wasn't. I made him eat some breakfast, though, and he kept it down.

"That'll make you good as new," I said.

"I'll never be that good agin," he said.

By the time we got our hotel bills paid it was after sunup. The wind was still cold as ice.

"How much money you got?" I said.

"Oh, few dollars," he said. "Enough to last."

But, by god, when we counted, we had three dollars between us. Where the rest of it went I'll never know.

"We better go to Clarendon," he said. "That's the place to get jobs. Hell, we'll be broke by supper."

So we got railroad tickets to Clarendon; they cost a dollar apiece. Johnny went to sleep right off, but I sat up and looked out the window. That old plains country sure did look cold and gray to me, and I wasn't so sure I liked it. We ought to have waited till springtime to leave home. But still, it was a good feeling to be loose like we were; it was a kind of adventure, in a way, and it didn't too much matter about the cold. It mattered more about Molly and Dad. I was just glad Johnny was along. It wouldn't have been much fun by myself. I couldn't figure out what had happened to all our money.

They put us off in Clarendon about one o'clock. Johnny was all refreshed, and we turned up our collars and went walking down the street to see the town. It would have been a nice walk if it hadn't been for carrying the saddles.

I guess we were lucky; the first thing we struck was a horse auction. They were auctioning off a couple of hundred broncs some fellers had driven in from New Mexico. A lot of cattlemen were there. After we watched the bidding awhile we saw a funny-looking old man who didn't look like he could be very important, so we asked him if he knew where two cowpunchers could get a job. He was pretty friendly.

"You boys cowpunchers?" he said. "What else can you do? Can either one of your ride broncs?" He was a grizzly old feller and didn't have but half an ear on one side of his head.

"Both of us can," Johnny said. Which was a damn lie; he couldn't ride a bronc if all four of its feet were hobbled. He was an awful good hand on a horse, but he wasn't no hand to make a horse, so I contradicted him.

"I can ride broncs and he can do everything else," I said.

"My name's Grinsom," he said. "I could use a couple of hands myself. I'm gonna have a bunch of horses to drive home when this is over, and then somebody's gonna have to break them, I damn sure ain't. You boys come along and I'll try you for a week. I'll give you a dollar apiece to give these broncs a good ride, and If we get along with one another it'll be fifteen a month and bunk and board. That suit you?"

It didn't seem no great amount of money to me, and I couldn't figure a little dried-up feller like Mr. Grinsom owning much of a ranch, but Johnny thought it was fine, so we hired on. It turned out Mr. Grinsom owned thirty-eight thousand acres. He bought nineteen broncs and offered me and Johnny our pick of them to ride to the ranch.

Since Johnny had spoke up about being a bronc rider, that was pretty funny. He got throwed four times on the way to the ranch. I only got thrown once, and that was an accident. I was looking around and not paying enough attention to what I was doing.

"You ain't gonna break no broncs that way," Mr. Grinsom said to him, after the fourth buck-off.

Johnny was about half-crippled by then, and too mad to lie. "Hell no, I ain't no damn bronc rider," he said. "Gid can break these horses; he likes that kind of stuff. I'm a cowboy. I like to ride a horse that already knows something, so I can get work done. You keep me a week, and if I don't turn out to be the best hand you got by then, why by god just fire me."

Mr. Grinsom got tickled. He had pretty much of a sense of humor, at least about some things.

"My boys may give you a little competition," he said.

IT TURNED OUT he really meant *his* boys, too. He had a big fat good-natured wife and seven grown sons. He had two hired hands, too, but he never worked them half as hard as he worked his own boys. All the boys' names started with J: Jimmy, Johnny, Jerry, Joe, Jakey, Jay, and Jordman. I never could tell them apart, but they were nice enough old boys. They had a great big bunkhouse, and me and Johnny and the two hired hands and the seven boys all slept in it. We ate supper at the big house, and Mrs. Grinsom explained to us that after they'd had the fourth boy it had got too noisy in the house and they'd put them out in the bunkhouse with the cowboys when they got big enough to get around. I don't know where all the noise went; the only words I ever heard them say were: "Thank you for the supper, Momma, it sure was good." Each one of them said that to Mrs. Grinsom after their meals.

Me and Johnny thought it was a pretty strange family. But the other two cowboys, one's name was Ed and the other's name was Malonus, they *really* thought so. They were so glad to have new hands around that wasn't in the family that they just about hugged us.

THE NEXT MORNING the old man asked me if I really wanted to break the horses. I said for a dollar apiece, like he offered, I'd give them a good first ride.

"How many do you want to ride a day?" he said.

"Oh, I ought to be done with them by three o'clock," I said. "There ain't but eighteen left. I rode one yesterday."

He acted like he didn't believe me. He sent Johnny off with the boys and the other hands and stayed around the lots all day, doing little chores and watching me out of the corner of his eye.

I didn't care. I felt real good that morning. The cold didn't even bother me. I made a good strong hackamore and went after them broncs. By dinnertime I only liked six being done with them and I got the six in another three hours. I even saddled up a few of the worst ones and rode them agin, just so the old man would really get his money's worth. By that time he was sitting on the fence. I bet he chewed a whole plug of tobacco that afternoon. When I got done and turned them out in the horse pasture, he walked off to the house without saying a word. But I didn't care about that, either. I had been throwed seven times and was stiff and sore as hell, but I felt like a million dollars. I felt like I could have ridden fifty horses if I'd just had somebody to do the saddling for me.

That night the old man did a strange thing. He paid me at the supper table.

"By god," he said, after supper. "Now, Mother, make these boys be quiet." None of the boys had made a sound anyway. "I want you all to notice," he said. "This here's one feller that can do the job. He rode eighteen wild horses today, I seen him myself. And one yesterday." I was real embarrassed. The old man got up and stomped off to the bedroom and came back jingling a sack full of money. "I'll pay you right here," he said. "It might put some ambition into these boys of mine." And he counted me out nineteen dollars, mostly in silver money. There wasn't a sound in the room but the money clinking. Even after I gathered it up and put it in my pockets, there still wasn't a sound. Later that night Ed told me the old man never paid the boys atall, just give them a dollar apiece at Christmastime. That didn't surprise me much. Mr. Grinsom wasn't the first tight feller I'd ever seen.

We worked pretty good for about a week. Me and Johnny never had no trouble matching the other hands; by the time the week was over Johnny wasn't in no danger of getting fired. The old man was funny. He treated us like friends and his own boys like hound dogs.

But there were two things I couldn't get over: one was making nineteen dollars in one day, and the other was being homesick. If I could make nineteen dollars in one day, I was stupid to work a whole month for fifteen. And besides, I remembered the time in Fort Worth when I'd made four hundred in about two hours. Cowboying was fun, but it wasn't near enough fun to make fifteen dollars a month worth while. I knew I could beat that.

The homesickness was the worst part of it, though. I didn't mind the work, and I didn't mind the company; I didn't mind the country, or even the cold weather. I just minded feeling like I wasn't where I belonged. Home was where I belonged, but tell that to Johnny and he would have laughed like hell. He didn't feel like he belonged to any certain place, and I did. He was born not five miles from where I was, too. When you came right down to it, Dad was right: me and him was a lot different. I couldn't get over thinking about Dad and Molly and the country and the ranch, the things I knew. The things that were mine. It wasn't that I liked being in Archer Country so much—sometimes I hated it. But I was just tied up with it; whatever happened there was happening to me, even if I wasn't there to see it. The country might not be very nice and the people might be onery; but it was my country and my people, and no other country was; no other people, either. You do better staying with what's your own, even if it's hard. Johnny carried his with him; I didn't. If you don't stick with a place, you don't have it very long.

Me and Johnny argued for ten days. I just plain wanted to go back, and he just plain didn't. I got so I couldn't sleep; I would wake up and lie awake for hours. Then one Saturday, Johnny was in Clarendon and run into a man who had a ranch out near the New Mexico line; he wanted a cowboy or two to look after it through the winter; it was so dull he couldn't stand the winter there himself. He offered double what we were getting, and said besides he had a pretty little Indian woman who would stay out and do the cooking. So Johnny hired on for both of us, but he told the man we had two more weeks to go for Grinsom. I told him right off I wasn't going any farther west or north, but he thought I'd change my mind. Then on a Tuesday, Mr. Grinsom sent us out in one of his big pastures to look for sicklings—that was all he had for us to do—and I just decided I was through. I pulled up and stopped.

"Hell with it," I said. "I'm going to Archer County. There ain't no use in me loafing around here any longer."

We turned our backs to the wind and watched it whipping across the high open flats. He tried to talk me out of it. "Don't do nothing rash," he said. "Wait till we get on the new job. Think of that Indian woman."

"You go on out there," I said. "I don't want to spend no winter in New Mexico. What would I want with an Indian woman when Molly's just three miles from home?"

"Yes, but Molly's crazy," he said.

"I never stopped to argue," I said. "You coming or staying?"

He hunched his neck down into his collar and frowned. "I hate to see you miss a good winter," he said. "What'll I do for company if that woman don't talk English?"

But he was staying. "There ain't as much at home for me as there is for you," he said. "This here's more the life for me."

And I was crazy enough to want to stay with him, even when I knew I was going home. We were pretty good buddies.

"Well, I hate to run off and leave you," I said. "But I got to go. You'll be coming home next summer, won't you?"

"Oh sure," he said. "I just don't feel like going that direction right now, Gid. I hate to be stuck off out here with no company, though."

"Well, write me once in a while," I said. "I believe I'll lope on back. I might could get to Amarillo tonight."

"Say hello to the country for me," he said. "Give old Molly a big kiss and tell her she's still my girl."

"I'll sure do it," I said. "Don't let no crazy horse fall on you."

"Oh hell," he said. "Won't nothing hurt me unless I freeze to death. You watch out yourself."

I guess we should have shook hands, but we never. He kinda nodded, and turned and tucked his head down and trotted off into the wind, headed north. I set there a minute, watching him cross the windy pasture. Then I loped back to the ranch, gave notice, and talked the old man into loaning me a horse to ride to Clarendon.

"Why you running off?" he said. "Too dull? I may buy some more broncs in a week or two."

"Oh no," I said. "I just guess I'll go run my own ranch."

It was a pretty lonesome trip home. I had to wait till way after dark for a train out of Clarendon, and was the only one on it, then, so I didn't have a soul to talk to. I never slept a wink all night, I was too excited about going home. Only I wisht old Johnny had come; train riding was dull without him. I got off in Wichita Falls about ten the next morning and found a man with a wagon going to Thalia. We drove in about an hour before dark, and the first person I saw was Mabel Peters, coming out of the dry goods store where she worked.

"Why, if it ain't Gid," she said. She had put on a little flesh and was dressed nice and looked real cheerful. In spite of all I could do, she made me go home and have supper with her at the boardinghouse. All the boarders were there, so she didn't dare ask me up to her room, but she followed me out on the porch after supper and hung on to me for an hour, she was so glad to see me. She asked me four or five times if I would come back and see her.

It was so late when I left Mabel that I had trouble finding anybody to borrow a horse from, but I finally got one and rode home. I was practically sick at my stomach I was so glad to be going home. It was good to ride over some familiar country. I even went by Molly's, but there wasn't no light; I sat on my horse by the back fence a minute, thinking about her.

Our place was dark too. When I got in the first thing I did was tiptoe down the hall to Dad's door, to listen a minute. He was snoring like he always did. Once I heard him cough and hawrk. I was glad he was asleep. I guess I was afraid I would find him out in the moonlight, plowing that old oat field.

Fourteen

THE MORNING AFTER I GOT HOME I REMEMBERED DAD came in my room real early, but he never woke me up. I was about half-awake and I seen him standing inside the door. But I guess he figured I needed the rest, because he went on out and I stayed in bed till nine o'clock.

When I finally got dressed and outside he was down at the lots filling up the hayracks. It was a cold morning, with a big frost on the ground.

"Well, how's the Panhandle?" he said. "I guess you got rich quicker than I thought you would, or else you went broke quicker. Which was it?"

"Aw, I just got homesick," I said. "How's ever thing here?"

"Run down and wore out," he said. "Specially me. Why don't you get the horses up? A couple of them need their shoes pulled off, and I ain't had the energy."

Dad sure looked bad. He hadn't hired no help at all; I knew he wouldn't. But he wasn't lying when he said he was worn out. He didn't have much flesh on him any more, and he had been a big fleshy man. When I first got home I thought it was from working too hard, but it wasn't. He was just sick; he didn't have no wind any more, nor much grip in his hands. But he wouldn't go to a doctor for love nor money.

I felt real bad about having gone off and left him so long. I know it wouldn't have made any difference to his health if I had stayed, but it would have made some difference to me.

"Hell, you ought to go see a doctor, Dad," I told him. "You probably just need some kind of pep-up medicine. Why do you want to be so contrary?"

"I ain't contrary," he said. "I just don't want to pay no doctor to tell me what I already know. There ain't no medicine for old age."

"You're just tight," I said. "You oughtn't to let a few dollars stand between you and your health."

"I am tight," he said. "I'm rich, too."

"You don't live like it," I said.

"No, because I want to stay rich. The best way in the world to get poor is to start living rich."

I couldn't do a damn thing with him. He kept on working, day in and day out, warm or cold. And the thing was he wasn't much help any more, only he didn't seem to notice it. I was doing nine-tenths of the work, and it kept me busy and worn out and tired. It was just miserable old hard cold work, no fun to it, like loading cake and hay and feeding cattle and building fence and all kinds of winter work like that. I'd been home three weeks before I ever seen Molly.

But then she come over to see me one day and cooked us supper, and I guess she seen right off how Dad was. I think it worried her, but she was real cheerful that day and never mentioned it to me. But she started coming over two or three times a week and cooking for us. Sometimes she even got there in time to ride a pasture with me, or help me with the chores. It was real good of her to come; I was crazier about her than I had ever been. I was pretty lonesome anyway, and worn out and worried about Dad, and it was awful nice to have somebody warm like Molly to be with once in a while. But no matter what I said or how I said it, she wouldn't marry me.

"I know you want me to, Gid," she said. "But it might be bad if I did. You might be sorry you ever asked me," she said.

"That ain't true," I said. "I wouldn't be."

She thought a minute, and grinned, but a sad grin. "Then I might be," she said. "That would be just as bad."

One night after Dad had gone upstairs to bed we sat by the fireplace awhile, and we got to talking about him. Molly was the best person there ever was for sitting by the fire with. Every time she came over we got off by ourselves a little while, and those were about the only times I got unwound.

"You better make him go to the doctor," she said. "If you don't, I think he's going to get real sick."

"He's too damn contrary," I said. "He just won't go."

"Don't talk bad about him," she said. "He's a real good man. He treats me better than anybody I know, you included." I don't know what that had to do with it, but it was true. Dad always let Molly know he thought she was about tops.

"I don't reckon he'll die," I said. "You don't, do you?"

She hugged me then. "He might, Gid," she said. "He's just getting sicker and sicker."

I thought that over for a while and it really scared me. I couldn't imagine Dad not being around to give the orders. Even sick he was just as active as he could be, and never missed a thing. It was hard to think of Dad being any other way than alive.

"Dad couldn't keep still long enough to die," I said. Neither one of us thought it was funny, though.

"I sure am glad my dad's healthy," she said. "I guess he'll live to be a hundred. If he was to die, I think I'd just plain go crazy."

"I don't guess anybody lasts forever," I said. "Funny thing, I've always been sure Dad would outlive me. I just never thought of it any other way."

We sat for a long time, thinking about it. But I couldn't believe it would happen. I guess I knew it had to sometime, but I just couldn't believe it. Not even in my brain.

"Well, if he'd just quit working and set around and rest up a little," I said. "I think he'd get all right. He stays on the go too much."

She shook her head. "That ain't his trouble. I think that's good for him. If your dad had to die, I'd want him to do it working, wouldn't you? Just to go on working till it happens. That's all he loves to do. If he was to sit around in a rocking chair, he'd get to feeling useless, and that'd be worse than being tired."

I kissed her and we sat on the couch for another hour or so. I meant to ride her home, but I was too tired, and she wouldn't let me.

"Much obliged," I said. "Come back whenever you can. We sure are glad to see you."

"Why, I enjoy it, Gid," she said. "Next time Dad goes off I'll come over." When she rode off into the wind it reminded me of Johnny, up there on the plains. I missed having him around.

LIFE IS JUST a hard, mean business, sometimes. Here we were worrying about my dad, and three days after we had that conversation Molly's own dad staggered into his smokehouse drunk, looking for some whiskey, and picked up a jug of lye by mistake and drank a big swallow of it and it killed him. He never even got out of the smokehouse. Eddie and one of his cronies was over there at the time; he had been drinking with the old man, and he went out and found him. It was a windy, dusty evening. And the first thing Molly said to me when I got there was, "Well, Gid, my poor old daddy never lived to be a hundred after all." And she just about did go crazy that night.

It was the end of any respect I ever had for Eddie White. I guess he was just scared of dead people. Anyhow he sent his damn oil-field crony over in the car to tell us. Dad had gone to bed, and I didn't wake him. I left a note on the kitchen table, where he'd see it in the morning. And then I saddled up and got over there on the run, and when I got there Eddie and his buddie were just driving away. I don't know where they were going in such a hurry, but they left Molly by herself with her dad, and there wasn't no excuse for that, drunk or not. I rushed in and she was in the kitchen, bawling her head off—she didn't even know Eddie was gone; the old man was dumped on a bed in his bedroom, with just a quilt thrown over him. I never mentioned Eddie and she never either; maybe she was so torn up she forgot he had been there.

She wanted me to do something for her daddy, clean him up a little; but she didn't want to go in the room with me and I didn't want to leave her by herself for fear she'd get to taking on agin. I made her drink some coffee, and I got a towel and wiped her face and kinda dried her eyes, and then we washed the dishes. There was a lot to wash; I guess she had cooked supper for Eddie and his friend. Washing them calmed her down some. When we had the kitchen good and clean I made her hold the lamp while I went in and straightened the old man out the best I could. He looked terrible, and I didn't know a thing about what I was doing, but I got his boots off anyway, and got him wiped up some and laid out and covered up neater than he had been. It was a mistake for Molly to come; it made her sick at her stomach. She vomited in the bedroom first, and then I carried her to the bathroom and held her head while she finished emptying her stomach. She was awfully white and shaky. I walked her down to the bedroom and made her take her clothes off and put her nightgown on and get in bed, and she laid there and cried while I went back and cleaned up in the bathroom and the other bedroom. Then I left the lamp on the kitchen table and got in bed with her. She thought some people might come; she thought Eddie must have gone to tell some, when she remembered him. But I didn't expect him to tell a soul that night, and he didn't.

"But what will I do, Gid?" she said. "You know I can't do without Dad."

"Hush, sugar," I said. "Let me just hug you tight. Let's don't talk for a while."

And I did hold her. For maybe half an hour her eyes were wide open and she was stiff in the bed, but then she got warm and relaxed and her eyes shut and she was asleep. I stayed awake just about all night, holding her, and she never moved or turned over till morning. She was lucky to be able to sleep, I thought. She was so helpless, in a way. And when it got light and she woke up I was watching her and still holding her. I saw just as plain as day when she remembered what had happened, and I thought she would get bad again, but she never. She looked real serious and then she pulled my head down and kissed me and got up and put up her hair standing by the bed, and she never cried at all until later that morning, when Dad and the other people begin to come.

Fifteen

DAD FINALLY DID GO TO A DOCTOR, IN FACT HE WENT TO five of them, but he had been right all along. They never done him no good. One of them kept him in the hospital for two weeks, though, and that threw ever bit of the ranch work on me. It was around the first of April before I got Johnny off a letter, and then I never said much.

DEAR JONATHAN:
I know you love that name so much I thought I would just use it on you.

Well, how was the winter up there? I guess you have got a family of half-breed kids by now, or did that deal ever turn out? Let me know, I am sure curious.

I guess the big news down here is about Molly's old man. He drunk lye last month and died, it was awful hard on Molly but I think she is over the worst of it now. She is getting sweeter all the time, and I mean it, I think I am going to get her in the notion of marrying me one of these days, then when you come back you will really know what you've missed. But I guess you will bring your Indian sweetheart home, so you won't mind too much.

Eddie is acting sorrier than ever, I may have to fight him yet.

Well, I wish you would come home, we could sure put you to work, we might even give you a raise. Our steers wintered good but the calf crop is pretty puny. If we don't get some rain the grass will all play out by June.

I guess that's all the news I know of. If you see Old Man

Grinsom, say hello for me and ask him if he thinks I can ride or not. I have got a new sorrel horse by the way, he can foxtrot like nobody's business but he ain't no cowhorse yet. He's just a four-year-old though. I give thirty-five dollars for him.

Write me sometime and send me the news from New Mexico.

Your friend,

Gid

I guess old Johnny must have been sitting at the table with his pencil licked when he got my letter, because I got one from him in less than a week's time.

Dear Gid:

I would use the rest of your name too, but I ain't the kind that has to get even with ever mean trick that's played on me.

Well, this is the life for me, and I don't mean maybe. This place I'm at is the rancho grandy for sure, there ain't no damn mesquite to get in your way, but I do kinda wish it had a few more windbreaks in it. It like to blown us all away in Feb. and March, them was just fall breezes you got when you was up here. Jelly, she made a big wool bandanna to keep my neck warm.

Jelly ain't her real name, but that's what the boss called her so I use it too. He wasn't kidding when he said she was pretty. Boy I never would have made it through the winter without her.

Well, tell Molly I'm awful sorry about her trouble. I'm just sorry for her, I ain't gonna miss the old bastard personally, are you? I wish I had been there though.

If you do fight Eddie, don't let him get the first lick. Get the first one yourself, with a two-by-four if one's handy.

I ain't losing no sleep over you and her getting married, I know she ain't that far gone.

We had quite a bit of snow in early March, never had much before that. It's all the moisture we've had. This here ain't a very big ranch, really, and it's a good thing because there's just me to take care of it. The coyotes have got six calves so far, I even seen one Lobo but didn't get a shot at him. There ain't a decent horse on the place.

Well, write me agin. I like to hear the news. I may come home one of these days if I don't get lost in the sandstorms. Tell Molly I'll be seeing her.

Your friend,

JOHNNY

Sixteen

WE HAD A GOOD RAIN IN EARLY FEBRUARY, AND IT looked like that would be the last we'd ever have. We never had a sprinkle in March, and by the middle of April the pastures were looking like they usually looked in July. It never helped Dad's disposition, or mine either. We had to feed the cattle, and it was such hard, hot work Dad just couldn't do it. Between the dry weather and Dad being sick, I wasn't in a very good humor.

One morning I run into Eddie. I was down in the River pasture, feeding. The cattle could hear me well enough, but it was hot and they didn't want to come to the wagon. I hollered around for an hour and only got sixty-five or seventy. I was just about to go ahead and feed them when three damn floppy-eared turd hounds come loping up through the brush, barking like hell. The cattle took off in about ten different directions. I got down and chunked the dogs and went on and got most of the cattle back together agin, and I'll be damned if the dogs didn't come up and run them off agin. My horse was tied to the back of the wagon, so I got on him and took my rope down and went after some dogs. I didn't rope them, but I whipped the shit out of two of them. The other one was too much of a dodger. When I was trotting back to the wagon, coiling my rope, I seen Eddie slouching across the flat. I might have known they was his dogs; nobody but him had time to run hounds that time of year. He had on an old khaki jumper and some patched pants and some roughnecking boots and looked like he hadn't seen a razor in about ten days. Both of us were mad.

But I didn't start off unfriendly. "Howdy, Ed," I said.

"Goddammit, Fry, that ain't no way to treat dogs," he said. "No telling where they are now. I been looking for them all morning, and now I got it to do over agin."

"I'd been after these cattle they run off a good while, myself," I said. "I guess the dogs will come home when they get hungry, won't they?"

"But maybe I don't want them home," he said. "I might want to hunt some more."

"Listen here," I said. "I don't give a plugged nickel what you want, if you're asking me. But what I want is for you and them dogs to get out of this pasture. And the next time they scare off cattle of mine they ain't gonna get off so easy. Next time they're gonna get the shit drug out of them."

"I'm a notion to whip your butt, right now," he said.

I got off my horse.

"Have at it," I said. "I hope you brought your lunch. You may need it before you're through."

"Aw, hell no," he said. "Then I'd have to carry you to the hospital. But let me tell you, you got one coming. Write it down in your little book."

"Don't wait till I get too old," I said.

"Another thing," he said. "Stay the hell away from my wife. I don't even want to see you on her place."

"Stay away from your what?" I said.

"My wife!" he said. "Just leave her the hell alone."

It was like lightning had hit me, only not fast lightning but a real slow bolt that slid all the way down me. By the time it got to my feet I was plumb numb. I couldn't have said boo.

"Why, you look surprised," he said. "I guess that shows you, now don't it. You and your long-legged buddy, too. Hell, we been married three weeks, and she's a real dilly. Me and her we really take after one another. I never had a woman so crazy about me.

"Well, ain't you gonna congratulate me?" He winked and grinned.

I got back on my horse and went on back to the wagon, and he went off after his dogs. A good many of the cattle had come back, and I fed them.

THAT AFTERNOON I went out with the posthole diggers and the wire stretchers, but I didn't do no fencing. I went down to the far tank and sat under a big shade tree, watching the mockingbirds and the killdeers fly around. There were a lot of bubbles on top of the water; I should have fished. I just couldn't understand Molly doing it. I wouldn't have cared if lightning *had* struck me. There didn't seem no reason left to work or nothing. I got to wondering if I would ever see her agin, and I couldn't think what I'd say if I did. There wasn't no clouds to look at, just water and sky, so I watched the water awhile and then I watched the sky. I didn't do much thinking; I just sat there feeling tight and sick. About sundown I rode home. Dad noticed there wasn't no dirt on my diggers, but he was tired too, and he never said nothing about it. We had cold steak and cold potatoes for supper, and I made the coffee too weak. It wasn't such a good supper.

Seventeen

IT LOOKED LIKE THE WORLD WAS GOING COMPLETELY TO pot. Dad was getting worse instead of better, and three or four days after I found out about Molly I got another letter from Johnny.

> DEAR GID:
> Well, I've got so much time to kill now, I thought I would write you again. I have been in a real scrape, it's what I get for riding sorry horses, I ought to know better. I was off riding line and my horse buggered at a damn skunk and off I went, only I got caught in my rope and he drug me about half a mile. I guess I am the most skinned-up person you ever saw. Besides, my hip was broke, and I was about ten miles from home; it was a pretty hard crawl, I tell you for sure, I was out lost all one night. If it had been cold the coyotes would have ate me by now.
>
> Jelly she got me into town and now they got me cemented up so I can't turn over. It's pretty tiresome, so don't ever break no hips if you can help it.
>
> The horse come in, so I ain't lost the saddle.
>
> These doctors are no-count, they give me a lot of trouble. I guess it will be June before I'm worth anything agin.
>
> Wish you was up here, we could play some cards and talk over old times. Write me when you get time and let me know all about Molly and you dad and what's happening down that way. I ain't had much news lately.
>
> Your friend,
> JOHNNY

So he wasn't having no luck, either. I didn't know what to write him, all the news was so bad. I wished I could have gone up and stayed with him like he done with me, but it just couldn't be managed. Finally I wrote him a note.

Dear Johnny:
We are all sorry to hear about your trouble, that's a cowboy's life. I would come and stay, only Dad's pretty sick now and there ain't nobody but me to run the ranch.

Molly has married Eddie, I guess that's the end of that. I haven't seen her. He is too sorry to talk about.

We haven't had no rain, either.

I wish you would come on home when you get well, we could sure use a good hand.

Your friend,
Gid

Dad was looking low. I would have given anything to talk to Molly about it, but the times when I could talk to her were over and gone. I did go in and see Mabel Peters a time or two. She was a nice old girl, but she wasn't much help. She was after me to marry her, and I was half a mind to. I didn't see how I could be no worse off than I was. At least we'd have somebody to do the cooking and the housework. I wanted to hire somebody, but Dad wouldn't let me.

"Hell no," he said. "A hired woman would get the best of me in no time. We'll just get along by ourselves."

One day me and him drove a little bunch of cattle down to the League pasture. On the way back we stopped on the Ridge and talked and rested awhile. It was a pretty day. The mesquite was leafed out, and everything smelled like spring. Dad had got down to pull up a devil's claw, and said he didn't feel like getting back up right then; we sat under a post oak and talked. I had got where I liked to talk to Dad; it taken me a long time. From where we were sitting we could look off west and see halfway across the county, to the little ridges above Onion Creek, where Dad's land ended.

"I got a good ranch," he said. "That's one thing that cheers me up. The best land in the county."

He was right, I guess. To me it didn't seem like much consolation.

"The nice thing is that I'm a damn sight nearer worn out than this country. I'd hate to get old in a worn-out country."

"You ain't worn out," I said. "You're just damn pessimistic. If you'd stay in the hospital awhile, you'd get well."

He didn't say nothing for a minute.

"Well, it's too bad she married him," he said, looking across the country. "She'll make a good one. But just let me tell you something, son, a woman's love is like the morning dew, it's just as apt to settle on a horse turd as it is on a rose. So you better just get over it."

"Aw, I ain't hurt much," I said. "Why in the world did she want to marry a bastard like that? It just don't figure."

"Well, she's got a lot of sense when it comes to taking care of herself," he said. "A lot more than you have. She'll make it."

"Why, she ain't got no sense, when it comes to taking care of herself," I said.

Sitting on the ground, you could smell the spring coming right up through the grass and into the breeze. It was sad Dad felt so awful at such a pretty time of year.

"It's my fault you don't have more," he said. "You've always had me to give you orders. I never put you on your own enough. She's been on her own since she could walk.

"But there's no use in you sitting on your butt sulking," he said. "Sulking never made a dime nor kept a friend."

"We better get on home," I said.

By the time we got to the barn it was late evening, and the last of the sun was shining on the weathervanes above the barn. Dad was tired. He drank some buttermilk and went to bed. He had seemed a little bit worried about me.

"Anyhow you're stubborn," he said. "Stubbornness will get a feller through a lot of mean places."

The next morning he never woke me up, and there was a note lying on the table when I come down.

Dear Gid

Miserable night. There's no profit in putting up with this.

I think I'll go out on the hill and turn my horses free, or did you ever know that song? It's an old one.

Take good care of the ranch, it's a dilly, and don't trust ever damn fool that comes up the road. Always work outside when you can, it's the healthiest thing.

Tell Miss Molly I appreciated her coming and helping us, just tell her much obliged until she is better paid.

Well, this is the longest letter I've written in ten years, it is too long. Be sure and get that windmill fixed, I guess you had better put in some new sucker rod.

Your Dad

The rifle wasn't in the closet, so I knew that was that, and I sat down and held my head. I wisht old Johnny had been there, or Molly, but they wasn't. Directly I went outside and turned off the windmill and went on down to the barn and hitched the wagon and put the wagon sheet in it and headed off across the hill. He was right on the west side; he had on a clean khaki shirt and Levi's and had taken his hat off and was laying on his back on the grass. Once I seen him I wasn't so scared, for some reason. He just looked natural, like Dad, and comfortable. I put him in the wagon and took him up to the house and laid him on the couch in the living room and got a counterpane to cover him with. It was worse in that cool darkish dusty old living room than it had been out in the sunshine. I hated to be the one to start treating Dad like a dead person. It was a long time before he seemed dead to me. For three months after that I would wonder in the morning why he hadn't come to wake me up.

I guess Dad had been better known than I thought; there was a big funeral and a lot of talk about what a pioneer he had been. It never done him much good, or me either. The worst of it all was seeing Molly. After I went into town to the undertaker a lot of people came out to visit me and bring stuff to eat. Molly, she came too, and brought a cake, and it was so awkward I got a headache from it. I knew she was remembering when her dad died and wishing she could really help me, but she couldn't. All those people were there trying to cheer me up, and it just made me bluer. Every once in a while I would see Molly looking at me from across the room, and she would be crying and looking so sad I wished I could have gone over and hugged her and told her it was okay. Finally I did talk to her just a minute.

"Molly," I said. "One of the last things Dad did was tell me to thank you for helping us last winter. He sure appreciated it."

"I hope you'll come and see me sometime, Gid," she said. "When all of this is over." Right after that she left. I seen her at the funeral, but just at a distance. Eddie was even there. I guess old Johnny was the only one that wasn't. I wrote him a card and told him a little about it, but he never answered. In September, after he was back, we had a kind of little funeral ourselves: we took Dad's old white saddlehorse that he called Snowman out on the hill and let him loose in the pasture; nobody ever rode him agin. We left Dad's saddle hanging in the harness shed. Sometimes when I'm doing the chores early in the mornings, I wonder if Dad and that old pony aren't still out there, maybe, slipping around through the misty pastures and checking up on the new calves.

Eighteen

One afternoon about ten days after Dad died I decided I ought to look over the ranch. Of course I had been over every inch of it a hundred times, but it had been Dad's ranch then, and not mine. It was a nice sunny day, with a few white clouds in the sky, and not too hot; the week Dad killed himself we had a two-inch rain—it was just his luck to miss it—and the country looked wonderful. We had lots of grass, and the weeds weren't too bad yet. Dad had about ten thousand acres; he had had the whole county to pick from, and he picked careful. There was a creek to the southeast and a creek to the northwest, and the River down the middle, so if there was water anywhere in the country, we had it. And of course he had built good tanks. I saddled old Denver and started off east, through the Dale pasture and rode down our east fence plumb to the southeast corner; then I cut back across Westfork and rode west between it and the River, winding through through the brush till I got nearly to the west side and then turned north and rode up on the hill in the south pasture and rested awhile. The whole south end of our land was brushy, mesquite and post oak mixed; the farther north you went, the more mesquite and the less post oak. Dad said when he first saw the country there wasn't a mesquite tree anywhere, or a prickly pear. Then I crossed the River and rode northwest till I hit Onion Creek, and turned and came back southeast agin along the top of Idiot Ridge. There wasn't no mesquite on the Ridge; it hadn't got that far north. The north end of our land was still prairie, but you could look south off the Ridge and see the brush coming. Our headquarters sits southeast of the Ridge, on a long hill. Finally I rode back through the League pasture to the barn and turned old Denver loose. I sat on the lot fence awhile, resting and thinking. It was about an hour before sundown, and I didn't much want to go up to the house, since there wasn't nobody there. At least the milk-pen calves were a little company.

For a day or two after Dad died I had actually been in the mood to sell the place, just dump it, and go where I wouldn't have to be reminded of Dad all the time, or of Molly. But I got over wanting to do that. For one thing, I got so I liked being reminded of Dad. Of course I didn't like to think of Molly and Eddie, but it would have been pretty yellow-bellied to let them run me out of the country. Most of the time I hadn't paid much attention to the country; Dad had done that. But what I saw that afternoon looked pretty good to me.

I didn't think no more about moving; but even staying took a lot of thinking about. One thing for sure, I wasn't no solitary owl. I couldn't stay on the place by myself; in about a month I would have been dead of lonesomeness. So I figured the best thing to do was marry Mabel. She was the best girl left in the county, and I figured I could get along with her okay. She would be so grateful to me just for marrying her that she shouldn't fuss none for about fifteen years.

Then if Johnny ever come back, I could hire him to help me run the place. I wanted to buy some new land if I could; I didn't intend to stop with what I'd inherited; that would have been pure laziness. Of course Mabel and Johnny wasn't too fond of one another, but I figured that would iron out once me and her was married and he quit trying to get in her pants.

I sat on the fence and never even noticed sundown. I happened to notice the moon's reflection in the milklot water trough. The house looked so lonesome I just didn't go in, I caught old Denver and rode to Thalia without even eating supper.

When I stepped up on the boardinghouse porch I could see Mabel hadn't gone to bed. She was sitting in her chair, patching a quilt. I felt sorry for her. When I knocked she had to put on a bathrobe before she let me in.

"Why, come in, Gid," she said. "I was just thinking about you.

"You look kinda blue," she said. "Want some hot chocolate?"

I said no. Her bedroom was neat as a pin.

"I guess I am a little down in the dumps," I said. "You want to sit out on the porch awhile? It's a real warm night."

"Okay," she said.

We got in the glider and rocked, and she snuggled up against me, warm as a hot-water bottle. We seen the moon, way up there, and I wondered if its reflection was still down at the ranch, in the water trough.

"Honey, let's get married," I said. "I'm sick of this living alone."

"Why, I am too," she said, and she squeezed my hand right hard.

I hugged her and kissed her and stood up, thinking she'd go in and get her clothes on, so we could wake up the J.P. and get it done and go on home, but boy she fooled me. I never seen her run backward so quick.

"Why, I couldn't hold my head up if I got married that way," she said. "What are you thinking about?"

She talked like it would take us two weeks, just to get married. I never knew she was that silly about things before. She wouldn't even let me spend the night with her. I ended up having to pay fifty cents to spend the night in the damn hotel.

But I didn't back out. There wasn't nothing to be gained from that; not that I knew of. Only I told her the next morning that I wasn't going to wait around no two weeks, I had too many other things to do. She said I'd have to at least ride back to the ranch and get my good clothes; I had just come in like I was. So I done it. While I was gone she quit her job and packed her suitcases. And when I got back to town I hunted up a feller I knew and just bought me an automobile. I figured if Eddie White could afford one, I could too. He showed me how to drive it and I got it to the rooming house and put Mabel's stuff in it. Then we walked over to the Methodist preacher's house. It was a pretty day and Mabel was dolled up like a hundred dollars; I had on a wool suit and was about to cook. Anyway, the preacher called his wife in to witness, and he married us. I gave him three dollars. Mabel hung on my arm all the way back to the rooming house, and I guess everybody in town knew what we'd done. I sure was hot and embarrassed, but Mabel didn't even want me to take my coat off till we got out of town. It took a lot of wrassling to get that damn car home, no better roads than there were; I wisht a hundred times I'd never bought it. But we finally made it, and I yanked the car stopped by the back gate.

"Well, here we are," I said. "Man and wife." And I started to get her stuff out of the rumbleseat.

"Gid, you ought to be ashamed, ain't you going to help me down?" she said. "I see I'll have to do a little work on you." And she never wasted no time starting.

Nineteen

THE FIRST MONTH WE WERE MARRIED, I DON'T THINK WE saw a living soul but one another. I guess I must have run into a few other people, here and there, but I sure didn't say much to them, and I didn't give them the chance to say much to me. If there was one thing I didn't feel like putting up with, it was jokes about newlyweds. Just being one was joke enough.

Of course, it really wasn't that Mabel was so bad herself. She was a good person, a real good person, I guess, and she damn sure wasn't lazy or anything like that. She did her work, and she looked after me a damn sight better than I had been looking after myself. And there was a many a time when I was awful glad to have her around.

Still, it never changed the facts, and the facts was that I had done an awful ignorant thing. When I first realized just *how* ignorant, I was flat embarrassed for myself. A ten-year-old kid could have showed as much judgment as I showed. I guess Dad had been right when he said I didn't know anything about taking care of myself.

Mabel was a big surprise to me, of course. I thought I knew her to a T before I ever went in to marry her. I hadn't been married to her two weeks before I knew that a blind idiot could have found out more about her than I managed to. For one thing, she was a lot prouder of herself than I thought she was, and for another, a lot less proud of me. I soon found out that she didn't consider me no particular prize, but I had better be sure and let her know that I considered her one. She seen herself as the belle of the county; nobody was going to talk her out of that view. I soon gave up trying; she could see herself any way she wanted to.

It come down to two things: the first was that Mabel just wasn't a very generous person. I guess she never had anything to learn to be generous with. For every nickel's worth of her she put out, she wanted a dollar's worth of me. And got it, too.

The second thing was that I was still crazy about Molly. What few little times I'd been with her meant more to me than a lifetime with Mabel could have. I had feeling for Molly, and didn't for Mabel. And Mabel had none for me.

It wasn't very long before I was hanging around the lots till dark for a plumb different reason. It used to be I didn't want to go to the house because nobody was there; pretty soon I was working late because I didn't know what to do at the house when I got there. I seen the moon in the water trough many a time, and I seen it in the sky, and if one thing was for sure, it was that the moon didn't care. What I did didn't make no difference to it, or to nothing, or to nobody, I felt like. I did get a card from Johnny, but I didn't have the guts to answer it.

I never was bluer than I was that first month. If a feller has to be lonesome, he's better off being lonesome alone. But I'd kicked that advantage away forever, and there was no use sulking about it. It was done and that was final; I would just have to make the best of it. Only it didn't look like a very good best.

It reminded me of something Old Man Grinsom had said one time; it was the day we first run into him in Clarendon. Just to make conversation I asked him how long he had been in the Panhandle.

"Since '93," he said. "I come here with nothing but a fiddle and a hard on. I've still got the fiddle." And when we seen them seven boys we knew where the other went. My case was a little different. I got married with a ranch and the other, and I still had them both. And to be right honest, I guess it served me right.

Twenty

It was late April when we married, and May was the month we stayed by ourselves. By June I knew I had to do a little better than that for myself, someway. I was getting where I didn't even enjoy my work. One morning I had to fix a little fence on the northwest side, and when I got that done I decided it was time I went and checked up on my neighbors. The closest one was Molly.

When I rode past her barn I didn't see no automobile, and that was a great relief. It took so much nerve to get me there I would have hated to have to ride away agin. But Molly, she was there, out in the back yard hanging the washing on the line. There was a good breeze, and the sheets were flapping, so she didn't notice me riding up. She looked like the same old Molly, only more so, wearing Levi's and an old cotton shirt with the shirttail out; she had a clothespin in her mouth and three or four more in the shirt pocket. Her shirttail was damp in front, where the sheets had flopped against her. And her hair was loose, hanging down her back and getting in her face now and then; I seen her brush it out of the way with one hand. I thought she just looked lovely.

I got off and tied old Willy to a mesquite tree; then I walked into the yard and stopped behind her, at the windmill. I didn't know if I could talk.

"Hello, neighbor," I said. "How are you getting along?"

She turned around with a tablecloth in her hands; I thought she was going to cry. She had those little dark places under her eyes. She dropped the wet tablecloth in the grass, and I went over to pick it up.

"My, Gid," she said. "You scared me."

For some reason I was real embarrassed; I squatted down and picked up the wet tablecloth and was going to try and wipe the grass off it. But Molly squatted down too and put one of her wet hands on my neck, and then there was her face and she kissed me. I shivered clear through. But her face against mine was as warm as sunshine, and I had to sit down in the grass and hug her.

"Now ain't this some way for old married folks to be acting?" I said.

She grinned, but it was just half a grin, really, and her mouth quivered.

"It's nice, though," she said. "I'm so glad to see you. Let's go in the house."

I helped her up and put my arm around her; we let the tablecloth and the clothespins lie where they fell. I asked her if she wanted to finish hanging out the washing, and she shook her head.

"No, but let's sit on the cellar awhile," she said. "It's too pretty to go in; I just don't like to sit on the dewy grass."

The cellar was stone, and the sun had warmed it up. She held one of my hands.

"Where's Eddie?" I said.

"Just relax," she said. She knew what I was thinking. "He's gone to Oklahoma, working in the oil fields."

"Good lord," I said. "He's a strange feller. I don't see how he can stand to go off and leave somebody like you."

She snickered. "That's because you ain't Eddie. He ain't the married kind. He'd go crazy if he couldn't get off and run around."

I wanted to ask her why in the hell she married him, then, but I bit my tongue and didn't.

Molly was in the sweetest, happiest mood. She kept glancing at me and smiling and she rubbed my hand between hers.

"Well, I'm just so glad to see you," she said, and in a minute turned around and kissed me. I held onto her for a long time, and then I figured I better tell her something for her own good. Only she knew what was on my mind agin.

"Don't be so scared," she said. "That no way to make me happy. It's just us here, you know."

"I know," I said. "And you're the sweetest woman I ever had hold of, I don't mind saying that. But now listen. We got to get something straight. I'm married and you're married, and I ain't the shy old kid I used to be."

"Good," she said, grinning. "What's shy got to do with it?" She reached up and pulled a thread off my shirt collar and rubbed my neck with her hand.

"It's got a lot," I said. "This kissing and hugging is just inviting it. The state I'm in, it's whole hog or nothing."

"That's so nice," she said. "One thing I've always hoped is that you'd come over here some day ready to be whole hog in love with me. I hoped sooner or later you would."

That just flabbergasted me.

"Honey, good lord," I said. "I been whole hog in love with you for the last ten years. Maybe more. Surely you know that."

She looked me in the eye for a long time, a little sad, with one corner of her mouth turned up just a little. "I know you think so," she said. "But you haven't, Gid. You ain't even this morning, yet."

"Well, what do you mean, whole hog?" I said. It seemed to me, looking at her with her face so close to mine, that it was impossible to love a person more than I loved her, and the way she sent that cool look up at me made me mad. I could have hated her. It was a bad feeling; I felt myself getting mad, and I didn't want to.

"I mean just you loving me," she said. "And nothin' else. Just pure me and pure you. But you're always thinking about Johnny or Eddie or your ranch or your dad or what people will think, or what's right and what's wrong, something like that. Or else you're thinking about yourself, and how much you like me. Or else you just want to get me in bed. Or else you just like to think about having me for a girl. That ain't loving nobody much. I can tell that."

"Why, goddamn you," I said. "That's some way for you to talk." I was thinking about her marrying Eddie.

"That's the way I've always talked to you, darling," she said. "You ain't thinking about me, you're thinking about Eddie." She reached up her hand to my cheek and smiled, but I was too mad then to care; it was like my blood vessels had busted. I yanked her back across the cellar, I seen later where it skinned her leg, and held her down and kissed her. It's a wonder she didn't get fever blisters. And for a long time we stayed that way, and she kissed back, only I knew it wasn't working somehow, it wasn't convincing her of anything. I let up and looked at her: she felt warm but she still looked cool, and there was a terrible strain inside me; I didn't know what to do or how.

"Molly, what do I have to do?" I said. "You drive me half-crazy, don't you know that?"

"I wish I could drive you all the way," she said, holding my hand against her chest. I could feel her breathing.

"I didn't know you were like that," I said. "Why do you want to hurt me that way?"

"Oh Gid," she said, and tears come in her eyes, "I don't want to hurt you. I just want you to turn loose of yourself for a minute, so you can hold *me*. That's the only thing I want."

She got upset then and cried and I was ashamed of myself for getting mad. At the same time I was still mad. I didn't see how she could go marry Eddie and then expect much of me. But I didn't want her sad.

"I just don't guess I know how to do that," I said. "If I did I would."

She sat up and wiped away the tears and smiled at me, her cheeks still wet. "I know you don't," she said. "But maybe I can show you."

She took me in the house then, and it was nice and cool and shady, after the sunshine. I made her let me put some iodine on the big skinned place on her leg; it burned like the devil. I felt silly, to have done a rough thing like that. But Molly never mentioned it. I was all nervous and tense and jumpy and nearly sick, and she kind of loved it all out of me, like a fever. I was so upset that for a long time after we had done it I couldn't go to sleep or be still in the bed, but she stayed with me, I remember her face, and I finally did sleep and slept good. When I woke up the afternoon sun was pouring in the windows and the room was hot. Molly was still with me and was holding my hand against her chest. She had thrown all the covers back.

"You're a good sleeper once you get to sleep," she said. "You slept four hours without even turning over."

I pulled her down so my face was right against hers. "I'm not going to let you go," I said. "I'm going to give you everything I've got to give; you're the only person that's worth it. I don't know why you wanted to take up with somebody worthless like me agin, but it's too late for you now."

She swung her head back to get her hair out of her eyes, and it fell all over my face. I lay for a hour, I guess, smelling her and listening to her breath; I could tell she was pleased about something. She was a mystery to me, but I was glad I had finally pleased her someway. After a while the sun moved and the sunlight came right on the bed, so we were laying in a shaft of it, with a million little dustmotes in the air above us. Things looked lovely and funny for a change.

"I swear you smell like a gourd, Molly," I said. "I never noticed that before."

"Maybe I never smelled that way before," she said. "I'm starving, you stay here and let me get us something to eat."

I was pretty hungry too. Only not hungry enough to get up; I never felt so good and lazy in my life. Maybe I would just stay there in Molly's bed for a month or two. That would have set people on their ears. Molly crawled out and wound up her hair, standing by the bed with the sunlight across her stomach.

"You're a shapely hussy," I said.

She snickered and pulled on her Levi's. I must have dozed off agin for a little while. When I opened my eyes she was sitting on the bed cross-legged, with just her Levi's on, eating a piece of cornbread and drinking buttermilk. There was some for me, with a couple of pieces of cold chicken, sitting on a chair by the bed. It wasn't there long. When we finished there were cornbread crumbs all over the bed and Molly had buttermilk on her upper lip. I wiped it off with a corner of the sheet. I wanted her to lay down agin, but there were so many cornbread crumbs in the bed that it wouldn't do, so we both got up and I put on my pants and we went in the living room and sat on the couch and hugged and talked awhile.

"When I come over here today I was going to ask you a lot of questions," I said. "Like why you married him, and all that. But I've just about forgot the questions, and I don't guess I really care about the ones I remember. What do you reckon caused that?"

"Me, I guess," she said. She was eating a piece of stick candy she had found somewhere, and was slouched back against my arm without nothing on but her pants, just as relaxed as she could be, and in a perfect humor. She wouldn't let me have any of the candy, but when I kissed her now and then I got her taste and the candy's too.

"One thing I do want to settle, Molly. What do you want to do about these people we're married to? Do you want us to go off somewhere or anything like that?"

"Do you want to go?" she said.

"No," I said. "That's kind of against my style."

"I'm glad," she said. "Because I wouldn't go. Right here in this house is where I always want to live."

We got a quilt and stretched out together on the living room floor and stayed there till plumb dark. I just couldn't quite get my mind made up to go home, and she didn't hurry me.

"Gid, I'm ready to have a baby now," she said. "I'm convinced you'll make a good daddy."

"Good lord," I said, sitting up. It was all shadowy in the room; she rested her head against my chest. We sure didn't get very far from one another that day. I guess she had been as lonesome as me.

“You’re a strange woman,” I said. “How come you don’t want your husband for its daddy?”

“Oh, Gid,” she said, “he wouldn’t make no good daddy. Not as good a one as you.

“You don’t really care, do you?” she said, looking up at me. I could barely see her eyes, but her voice was real serious. “I mean if me and you have a baby. Of course I’ll let on it’s Eddie’s, just you and me and the baby will know.”

I thought about it a long time. Here I was married to Mabel and her to Eddie. It was strange to think of a baby coming out of Molly, but I knew one thing, if one did I wanted it to be mine.

“No, I don’t care, sweetheart. I’d like for you to if you want to.”

She curled around me. “I knew you’d come to me sometime,” she said. And that was all we said that day. After a while I got up and dressed to go, and she walked out to my horse with me. We stood there awhile, looking at the Milky Way and the Big Dipper and all the rest of the summer stars. Finally I got on.

“I’ll just get over when I can,” I said. “Okay? I probably can’t stay this long ever time. I sure will miss you.”

“Okay,” she said. “Me too.”

I rode on home by moonlight; it was bright enough I seen a big old coyote loping into the brush ahead of me. I should have been thinking about a story for Mabel, I guess, but I was thinking about Molly instead, and what a tender sort of person she was. And yet she had something fierce in her, like Dad had in him. I saw her agin, all the ways she’d looked that day, hanging up clothes in the morning, with her shirttail out, and sitting on the couch that evening, without no shirttail atall. She had the most changing kind of face, for it always to be the same one. Riding across the League I run into Dad’s old horse, and he nickered. I sure did miss Dad.

Twenty-One

IT WAS JUST AMAZING HOW SEEING MOLLY EVER ONCE IN A awhile improved things for me. I begin to kinda take an interest in life agin. And I never seen a whole lot of her, either—I hardly ever got over more than once a week. Lots of time I was too busy, and other times, when I did ride over, I'd see Eddie's car and have to go back. There wasn't no sense aggravating him. But it didn't bother me too much if I missed seeing her one occasion or another. I knew that if I was a little patient, there would be a time when we could get together. Those times were worth the wait. Molly was awful good to me.

AND GOOD for me, too. In the meantime, between visits to her, I had the ranch to run, and Mabel to live with, and I began to see that I had better get busy and try to do a little better job of both than I had been doing. It wasn't fair to Dad and Mabel not to.

At first I was pretty worried that Mabel would find out I was courting somebody else, but that was just because I still didn't know Mabel too well. In those days she was so proud of herself I couldn't have convinced her I was in love with somebody else if I'd come right out and told her. Which I didn't. I was fond of Mabel, and a little sad for her, but not as torn up about marrying her as I had been. And I made her a pretty decent husband too. I got to understanding her a lot better as time went on. We never was much of a delight to one another, I had to admit that, but I know I treated her better after I took up with Molly. Mabel was just a combination of proud and scared; she never had anything, and she always thought she was entitled to everything.

It made me blue that I couldn't be more wholehearted with her, but I just couldn't. She wasn't the one. But anyway, she kept such a close eye on herself all the time that she hardly noticed me. She didn't have much notion of what was going on with me, and a good thing she didn't. After I got over my first blueness and began to treat her about half-nice, she thought I was plumb crazy about her.

"Well, I see you're beginning to learn how to treat a lady," she said one night. It was after supper, and we were sitting on the porch. I had complimented her on her cobbler, or something like that.

"I guess I ain't had much practice," I said.

"Well, you can get a lot on me," she said. "And don't think I won't tell you when you make a mistake. I ain't bashful about that." She scooted a little closer to me on the step.

I put my arm around her and hugged her and never said a word. It was dark, and we could hear an old hoot owl hooting somewhere in the pastures to the east. There wasn't no moon that night, but there was a good breeze from the southeast, and the country smelled good. We done had lilac in the yard. Life always seemed so complicated in the evenings. Mabel seemed perfectly happy, and I was sitting with my arm around her, about two-thirds melancholy. "Let's go in, honey," I said, "before the mosquitoes get to biting." "Well, you've got to kiss me first," she said. I did, and then we went inside and lit the lamps.

Twenty-Two

Early in June I spent a hell of a day. Mabel woke up in a bossy mood and practically chased me out of the house, so I done the chores and doctored a few sicklings and then decided I'd go to Antelope. That was where we got our mail, then, and I thought while I was there I'd hire somebody to come up and thrash my wheat. We had a pretty fair wheat crop and I was ready to get it thrashed; it was the last farm produce I ever intended to raise.

I rode old Dirtdobber that day, and I guess that was a mistake. He was the oldest horse on the place, and I never rode him nowhere except to get the mail. I think he was twenty-three years old. When I got to Antelope I tied him up and gave him a good rest, while I talked with the boys a little. I found an old boy with a thresher, said he'd be up after my wheat the next day. While I was fiddling around it come up a real mean-looking cloud in the northwest, and I figured then I'd do good to get home without getting wet. Besides which, the Montgomery Ward catalogue had come that day, and it was so much extra weight I didn't know if old Dirt would be able to carry it. He was particular about weight.

But I stuck the catalogue in my saddle pouch, and we headed out. If it rained like it looked like it aimed to, that old boy wouldn't have to bother about my wheat. But I was wrong about the rain, it never rained five drops. What it did was hail.

And I mean hailed. It started out the size of plums and moved up to pullet eggs, and before it was done there was hailstones on the ground bigger than anything our old turkeys ever hatched. Course me and Dirt were right out in the open when it started, and getting him to run was out of the question. I tried holding the catalogue over my head, and dropped it in about two minutes. Finally we got to a little old half-grown post oak, and I figured that was the best protection we would find. I unsaddled right quick and crawled under Dirt and then under the saddle too, and scrunched down tight. The first thing Dirt did was try to piss on me, but I wasn't worried about that, I was worried about my skull. I jobbed him a time or two to cut him off and damned if the old sonofabitch didn't jerk loose and step right on my hip and run off. So far as I was concerned it could hail him to death; I wasn't going after him. I got on the downwind side of the tree and hid as much of me as I could under the saddle, and stayed put. At least none of the big ones hit my head. My saddle got dents in it that never did come out. It hailed for a solid hour. Finally I didn't have to worry so much, I reached out and raked me up a kind of igloo and was pretty cozy. I had one less worry anyway, and that was the damn wheat crop.

When it quit the country looked like it was under a snowstorm. The sun came out in a little while and started melting it off, but some of the big piles didn't melt for two or three days. I was in a hell of a shape; Dirt had about halfway squashed my hip. I could hobble along, but carrying the saddle and blanket I couldn't make no time, particularly over that slippery hail. I guess Dirt had weathered it all right; I seen him about half a mile away, poking along toward home. "You old bastard," I said, "wait till I catch you." But all I could do was hobble on over to the Eldenfelders', they was a Dutch family that lived about half a mile away. I hated to run the risk of getting dog-bit—they had about fifty damn mean turd hounds—but it was the only place in hobbling distance. However, it turned out all right. They fed me a little rotten cowmeat and sent their big old dumb girl Annie to haul me home. A lot of the boys thought it was smart to get in Annie's pants, because she was willing and about a half-idiot, but I never fooled with her. She seemed kind of pathetic to me. The creek was up, so that was as far as she got me, but I gave her a dollar. "Bye-bye," she said. It's a wonder she could drive the wagon. I waded the creek and went on home. My hip was beginning to unsquash a little by then.

Old Dirt was in the barn when I got there, trying to kick in the door to the oatbin. The old fart had so many knots on him I didn't have the heart not to feed him.

But when I got to the house I wished I was back outside in the hailstorm. The ten or fifteen broken windowlights hadn't improved Mabel's humor. I was thinking I might get a good hiprub, but I could have staggered in on two wooden legs and she wouldn't have cared. I didn't see no signs of supper, and I guess I said the wrong thing.

"Hello," I said. "What's for supper, hail soup?"

"I'll hail soup you," she said, "going off and leaving me in a storm like that. Where you been all afternoon?"

"Well, I been coming home," I said. "It wasn't a very quick trip, I'll admit."

"I bet you was," she said. "I bet you was sitting down in the Antelope domino hall, losing some of your inherited money."

I let that pass.

"Where's the mail?" she said.

"Wasn't none but the catalogue, and I lost that in the hail. I guess we'll have to get them to send us another one."

She got so mad it tickled me.

"What kind of a husband are you?" she said. "We'll do no such thing. You just saddle up and trot back and find it; I want to do some ordering out of that catalogue before it gets too old."

"Why, you're crazy," I said. "Hell, it's beat to pieces by now, anyway. I imagine we can borrow one."

"We ain't going to borrow nothing," she said. "You go get it. You lost it."

I tried to grab her and hug her, hoping it would get her in a better humor, but she just stomped out to the bedroom, and I let her go. I got the milk bucket and milked, and when I got back, no sign of her. I cooked myself some bacon and eggs and ate supper. Then I washed the dishes, and still no Mabel. I went in the living room and did some figuring in my little daybook; I was thinking of buying three sections of land that joined us on the northwest.

About nine o'clock I heard her, and she came in in her bathrobe and nightgown, looking like she'd had a good nap. She was a shapely woman, too, when you caught her looking just right.

"Hi," I said, and she set down on my lap and kissed me and seemed fairly friendly.

"Where's the catalogue?" she said.

"Good lord," I said. "Ain't you forgot that yet? It's right where I dropped it, and that's where it's going to stay, as far as I'm concerned."

"Well, I knew you was ignorant but I never thought you was lazy," she said, and she jumped off my lap and went out the back door just boohooing. I would have swore she was crazy.

But I went out to get her; I didn't want her to run around barefooted and get on a snake. That would really aggravate her. When I came out on the backsteps she ran down in the storm cellar. It was pitch dark down there, and I went over and stood on the steps.

"Now, Mabel, come on out of there," I said. "There's no use in you taking on so over a damn catalogue. You'll get on a stinging lizard down there if you ain't careful."

"I hope I do," she said. "I hope they sting me to death, so I won't have to live with you."

I started down, and damned if she didn't grab a jar of peach pickles off the shelf and threw it; I heard it hit the steps below me and break. Then she threw two more, just whatever she happened to grab.

I thought what the hell, there wasn't no use in provoking her to ruin all the preserves.

"Okay," I said, "sleep down there if that's how silly you are." She didn't say nothing, so I went in and went to bed. There was a cot in the cellar, and it was a warm night; I didn't figure it would do her any harm.

Only I couldn't sleep worth a flip. I went back out twice more to try and persuade her, and all it did was cost me preserves. The last time I went was about three-thirty, and I just sat down in the kitchen and read the almanac till it got light. Then I went down in the cellar, and she was curled up on the cot asleep, peaceable as a baby. But the cellar steps looked like a cyclone had hit a jelly factory. I went in to cook breakfast, and I heard her hollering at me. So I went out.

"No, I ain't gone after the catalogue yet," I said.

"Could you carry me up these steps?" she said. "I'm barefooted and I'm afraid I'll cut my foot off on all this broken glass."

"No, I'm afraid to carry you, I might drop you and break your precious butt." I went and got a basket and a broom and the ashes shovel and cleaned up the mess, while she sat on the cot and watched. Then she came in and made coffee and never said another word about it. And for a day or two, she was sweet as pie.

Twenty-Three

One morning early in July a damn horse kicked a hole in the water trough, and while I was down patching it, getting wet up to my ears, I looked up and seen a horseback rider loping across the Ridge toward the barn. By god, if it wasn't Johnny, he'd come home, and he was riding the prettiest little sorrel gelding you ever saw. He called him Jack-a-Diamonds.

"Well, by god," I said, standing up to shake his hand. "Where'd you get that horse?"

"Bought him off a feller," he said. "How you been?"

"Oh, fair," I said. "How long you been home?"

"Since last night."

"You're walking just like a normal feller. You don't look crippled."

"I finally growed back together," he said. "This country sure looks good to me."

"Well, we had four inches of rain in May. Course we had that hail."

"Heard about that. See it smashed hell out of your wheat."

"What I get for raising it," I said. "Tie up your horse and stay awhile, I got to patch this water trough."

"I'll help you," he said, and he did. If he hadn't I wouldn't have got the damn thing patched by dinnertime. While we worked he told me a million funny stories; he was the same old Johnny. I was sure glad to see him back.

That night, of all the things, me and him and Molly went coon hunting, and had a hi-larious time. Johnny's dad had a new coon dog he was proud of and Johnny wanted some excitement, so he asked me if I wanted to go with him to try the dog out. I said sure, and after supper I told Mabel where I was going and met Johnny on the Ridge. We decided to go over and see if Eddie was home, and if he wasn't to take Molly. She was there by herself, peeling potatoes in the kitchen, and she put on an old pair of boots and was ready in a minute. Johnny had brought the dog with him across his saddle, and we all struck off toward the creek, walking. It was a hot night with plenty of moon, but we took a lantern anyway.

"I hope we don't get snake-bit," Molly said. She had been bit once and was afraid of snakes. Sure enough we killed three rattlers that night, but we didn't have any close calls.

We hadn't been out thirty minutes when the dog treed a big old fat coon in a live-oak tree. I didn't much want to kill him, because we'd have to lug him around all night, but we went ahead and done it. After that we got pretty excited, and the dog soon struck another trail. Johnny had the lantern and the gun, and I had the coon in one hand and Molly's hand in the other, so I could help her through the brush.

"I like this," she said. "I'm glad you'all came by."

Then the dog treed in the shaft of an old hollow oak, and from the squealing we heard it was a momma coon and two or three little ones. We never brought an ax, but the old tree was just barely standing, and me and Johnny pushed it over. Only no coons come running out.

"Now what?" Molly said.

"I'll stomp it open, I guess," Johnny said. About the time he said it the momma coon went scooting out the open end of the tree, right between Molly's legs. She jumped about three feet. I had the gun and couldn't shoot for Molly, so it was up to the dog, and he let the old momma get plumb away. He was a good dog for treeing, but he wasn't worth a shit for fighting. She got in the creek and he didn't have the backbone to go in after her.

"Don't you all kill the little ones," Molly said. "I want one for a pet."

"Sure," Johnny said.

We blocked up the open end and then Johnny stomped a hole in the old rotten wood. One little coon jumped right out into the dog's mouth, and that was all for him. I got down on my hands and knees and managed to grab another one by the neck and drag him out. He was nearly half-grown though, and I sure needed something to tie him with. Baling wire was what I needed, but that's the way, when you need baling wire you can't find it and when you don't need it you're tangled up in it.

"Do you think you can gentle him?" I said, holding him out so Molly could see.

"Probably not," Molly said.

Then Johnny yelled. He had kept his foot in the stomp hole, so the other little coon couldn't run out, only he discovered that his foot was stuck. I wasn't very worried.

"Pull your boot off," I said. "Or sit down or something."

"Hell no," he said. "If I was to sit down wrong, I'd break this hip agin and be laid up in the hospital another three months. My heel's stuck. See if you can stomp more hole."

Molly and me thought it was funny; we stood there and laughed. Only I didn't laugh long. The little coon that was in the log decided it was time to come out, and he did, right up Johnny's leg. Johnny yanked backward and fell a-spraddling. The coon went right over him and off, and the dog never seen it. I got so tickled I forgot I was holding anything, and the little coon I had whipped around and bit clear through the palm of my hand. When he turned me loose I was glad to do the same for him. I howled like a banshee.

So Molly didn't get no pet, and we went home with just one and a half coons and a cowardly dog, but we had fun anyhow. When we got to Molly's she bandaged my hand and we sat up in the kitchen, eating all the stray food and talking over old times. We were all in high spirits and Johnny told us a lot of stories about life on the plains. Finally me and him slept awhile on her living room floor, and about sunup she came in in her nightgown and bathrobe and woke us up and cooked the best breakfast I ever ate. We did her chores for her and about six o'clock rode off toward home, with Molly standing by the yard gate with a milk bucket in one hand, watching us go.

There was a big dew that morning, and the country looked as green and sparkly as it ever had in July. We stopped our horses on the Ridge and talked about the grass and the cattle for a while.

"Well, are you home to stay?" I said. "Did you quit your job?"

"Yep, I'm here for good," he said. "You need a hand?"

"Boy, you bet," I said. "If you want a job you can start today. And live in our bunkhouse and we'll board you if you want to."

"Fine with me if it's okay with Mabel," he said.

I said it was. We hadn't said two words about her.

"Course you might be ready to go in business for yourself," I said. "I wouldn't want to stand in your way if you do."

"I am in business," he said. "The cowboying business. You can have the ranching business; I don't want no part of it."

"Okay," I said.

"I'll go home and tell my old man and get my stuff," he said. "See you after while."

And him and old Jack-a-Diamonds went off along the Ridge west in a long easy lope, neither one of them carrying a care in the world. I just about envied Johnny, but I didn't quite. He was the most carefree, but I thought I had a few more good things than he had. I meant to swap him out of his horse, though. The sun was drying up the dew, so I got rid of Molly's bandage and went on home and ate another breakfast.

Twenty-Four

JOHNNY SURE MADE A GOOD HAND. ME AND HIM GOT things done in a day that I would have fiddled around with a week if I had been by myself. Besides, he was enjoyable to work with. At least most times. Sometimes he was the most aggravating feller I knew. Ever once in a while he acted like he still intended to try and court Molly some, but I didn't figure he'd get very far with that.

HAVING HIM to do the cow-work left me more time to get ambitious, and the land bug began to bite me pretty bad. I had already decided that land was something I'd never have enough of. So one day I buckled on my spurs and rode to Wichita to the bank and borrowed enough money to buy them three sections that joined me on the northwest. They were a good place to start extending. I had a deed drawn up and took it with me for the other feller to sign, and started home.

I rode hard that afternoon; the automobile was broke down or I would have gone in it. The weather was terrible—it was late August—and I didn't need no thermometer to tell me it was over a hundred degrees. When I crossed the Taylor place I decided to take the deed up and show it to Molly. I was proud of that deed, and I already knew Eddie wasn't there; I had looked that morning.

Molly was, though, ever inch of her, and she couldn't have looked better to me if she'd been Lily Langtry. I knocked at the back door and went on in, and she was just turning away from the stove. She had been putting up the last of her garden stuff.

"You're about as hot as I am," I said.

"I'm glad you come," she said. "Let's sit down and cool off."

I drank a couple of dippers of water out of the water bucket. She sat down at the table and I offered her a dipper full.

"I believe I will," she said, and she took the dipper and tilted her head back and drank. She had really been working: the arms of her shirt were sweated halfway down her side, and the tip ends of hair around her neck were wet. Her old shirt was plastered to her stomach. But she looked like the real thing to me; when she took the dipper down I leaned over and kissed her and she reached up to put her hands behind my head, so the dipper dripped water on my shoulder.

"You know why I'm glad you come?" she said. "I've been saving something to show you."

I grinned; I sure felt good. "What have you got I ain't already seen?" I said.

"This, Gid," she said, standing up. She grinned to herself and pulled the ends of her shirttail up and stuck her stomach out at me. It didn't look much bigger than it ever had, but it looked a little, and I got the message. Besides she grabbed me and hugged me.

"Don't that make you glad?" she said. "We've got one started. That makes me so proud. It's just what I've been wanting."

I didn't know what to say. It was okay with me, but I wasn't wildly happy about it, like she was. I was more excited about the deed.

"Why sure, Molly," I said, "if it's what you been wanting. And it's ours for sure?"

"It's ours for sure."

There was nothing else *to* say. She was happy enough to faint; she just sort of slid on me.

"Well, sugar," I said, after it was too late for it to have done any good, "I don't know about all this. You're so excited about it, we want to be careful and not jar it loose."

"This bed's just a puddle of sweat," she said, crawling over me. "I'll get some water and sprinkle us, so we'll be cooler." She brought in the dipper and sprinkled the sheets with me in them, and then sat down by me and caught my hand.

"It won't jar loose," she said. "I'm so glad the first one is yours. I wouldn't have wanted anybody else's to be the first."

"Honey, you're an awful strange woman," I said. "There ain't another like you in the world."

"That's okay," she said.

"See how this stretches the elastic," she said, sticking out her stomach agin when she started dressing. She had just got into her underpants.

"I thought it was supposed to make women less exciting," I said. "It sure hasn't you."

She flopped back on the bed and laughed a big one. I liked the way Molly laughed. "These sheets are still nice and cool," she said. I was done half-dressed but I lay back down a minute and grinned and kissed her.

"And you're my honey," she said. In a minute we got up and dressed. I showed her the deed, but it didn't impress her a snap's worth. But I must have impressed her a little; she wouldn't hardly turn loose of me that day.

"Gid, have you got time to see what's wrong with my windmill?" she said, "It just barely has been drawing lately."

"Sure, come on out with me," I said.

"I'll be out in a minute," she said. "I want to pin up this old hot hair." She raised her arms to pin it.

I got a pair of pliers and a couple of wrenches out of her tool box and climbed to the top of the pipe. It was just the sucker rod loose, and I tightened it in two minutes. But I didn't climb down, I rested a minute on the crossbars while I waited for Molly to come out. Dad was the only thing missing in life; I hated it that he had missed such a good year for cattle; it was just the kind of year he had always waited for. From where I sat I could see my new land.

I had my hand on the top of the pipe, and the damn rod went down and mashed my finger before I noticed. I damn near fell off, but caught myself. I had a blood blister to suck, and a big one. Some grayish clouds were building up in the northwest, so we might get rain.

Molly stepped out on the back porch, buttoning her shirt, with her hair pinned up high in a knot and her neck looking cool.

"Come on down." she said. "I'll get a crick in my neck looking up there."

"I'm surveying my new land," I said. "Except for your place I own everything west of here that I can see."

"You and your land," she said, "you ain't getting mine. Come on down here to me." She was shading her eyes and looking up.

So I climbed down. "I like to pinched my finger off," I said. "I better get on home before I get in more trouble."

She took my mashed finger and put it in her mouth and wet it; the finger still stung but I didn't much want to go home.

"You're supposed to kiss it," I said, "not slobber on it."

"I can't feel him yet," she said. "I ought to pretty soon."

"One of these days I'll repipe your windmill," I said, and then I remembered Eddie. Molly looked a lot thinner with her hair up on her head; it made her look cool and tender.

"I see you ain't interested in babies," she said. "Come with me to milk. It's cool enough now."

I got the bucket. The old brindle cow was already in the lot, waiting.

"Want me to milk?"

"No, she don't like strangers. You'd have to hobble her." So I put the feed in the stall and old Brindle went in. Molly got out her milking stool from under the trough and set down on it and went to milking. The old cow was an easy milker, but she kept switching her tail at flies and hitting Molly in the face. I got tickled.

"Here," I said. "I'll hold her tail." The old cow never noticed.

"If she ever steps on your foot you'll learn to wear shoes," I said. I squatted down by her and put my free hand on the back of her neck, where her skin was cool. I slipped my hand on under her shirt and rubbed her back and belly a little; a trickle of sweat slid along her ribs from her armpit.

"I wish I understood you," I said. "I never know just what you want from me. You'll make a good milker yourself." I felt in front and she grinned.

"I just want your loving and a little less conversation," she said.

We left old Brindle in the lot, eating prairie hay. I carried the milk bucket and she put her arm around my middle; we walked up to where my horse was tied. I set the milk bucket over in the yard and came back and kissed her bye. She poked her belly against me, but I got on my horse anyway, and she stood there grinning, fiddling with her shirttails.

"Aw, I'm glad, Molly," I said. "I just got this new land on my mind. I better go, I'm getting lonesome for you and I ain't even left yet."

"I guess I know what's good," she said. "Say hello to Mabel."

"I will, you say hello to Eddie." It was a kind of joke. If either of us actually did it, it was her; she was just that crazy.

"If I come by agin in a day or two, will you chase me off?" I said.

"That's one thing I've never been guilty of," she said. The little barn swallows come out and begin to flitter around, and she looked up at them. "I love the cool of the evening," she said.

I loped across the hill and left her standing by the fence, fiddling with her shirttails. It was strange riding off from Molly; I never done it in my life that I didn't want to turn and go back a dozen times before I got out of sight. She always stood right where you left her, as long as she could see you. I remembered her in the kitchen that afternoon, all sweaty and loving, drinking the dipper of water and her throat wet. I felt like Molly was just as permanent as my land. Old Denver wanted to tear out for the barn, but I held him to a lope and we got to the lots just as the sun was going down behind the Ridge.

II

RUIN HATH TAUGHT ME

Ruin hath taught me thus to ruminate,
That Time will come and take my love away.

SHAKESPEARE, *Sonnet 64*

One

JOHNNY CAME IN ONE AFTERNOON AND CAUGHT ME CRYING. I had been listening to Kate Smith.

"My god, cheer up, Molly," he said. "You're going to ruin the oilcloth."

"Sit down," I said. "I know it's silly." I got up and poured him a cup of coffee, and he blew on it awhile and didn't say anything, and finally he reached over and squeezed one of my hands.

"Now look, quit this stuff," he said. "It's a beautiful day. You ought to be out making a garden instead of sitting in here like this. What brought it on?"

"Oh, the radio," I said. "Listening to Kate Smith. Ever time I do that I get blue." And not because of her, because of the songs. "God bless A-mer-ica, land that I love . . ."—she always sang that. I just wanted the war over and my boys home. My boy home.

"Aw, quit listening to all this patriotic stuff," he said. "It's just depressing. And it don't do no good."

"You make me mad," I said. "It wouldn't hurt you to be a little more patriotic. You ain't gonna cheer me up talking that way. I just wish we knew something definite about Joe."

He rubbed my hand and drank his coffee.

"Well, I do too, honey," he said. "He was my boy too. But imagine he's dead; be better for us to face it. Missing over a year. We can't just sit here and quit."

He made me get up and go outside with him, and he was right, it was a real pretty day. Being outside cheered me up. We sat on the cellar awhile and he took his hat off and put his arm around me.

"I knew you'd smile sooner or later," he said.

"Look how tall my corn's getting," I said. "Three more weeks and I can cook you some roasting ears. Where's your boss today?"

"He's off trying to buy him another ranch for me to take care of," he said. "Gid's plain land-crazy."

"Well, you just let him go ahead." Johnny was always trying to slow Gid down. "Everybody's some kind of crazy." It was so clear we could see half the country. May was usually my favorite month.

"What kind of crazy are you?" Johnny said.

"Just plain crazy," I said. "I haven't got enough brains to be any other kind." Then he leaned over and kissed me; I figured he was getting about ready to. He'd had it in his mind ever since he came in.

"Well, Molly, I'm woman-crazy," he said, holding my shoulders and grinning his old reckless grin. He tickled me. I couldn't help loving Johnny, even when I wasn't much in the mood for him. Even when he was acting the soberest there was something about him that was like a boy; he never lost it, and it was one of the nicest things about him; when he was around I could have a boy and a man in the same person. Not like Gid at all—Gid never had been a boy; I guess his dad never gave him the chance. And that was why Jimmy was so much harder for me to raise than Joe. I never had any trouble handling Johnny and Joe.

"You want to help me tie up my tomato plants?" I said. "I might as well do that today."

"Well, now, you might as well not, either," he said. "I'd like to be treated like company for once, not like a damn hired hand. If I'm going to have to work, it had just as well be for Gid. He pays me."

"Pardon me," I said. "You was the one that mentioned gardening."

"Yeah, but you had the war blues then. Actually, why I'm here, I came a-courting." He kissed me agin; he was so funny.

"Why yes, honey, I'll marry you," I said when he quit. "Just let me go get my pocketbook so we can pay the preacher."

That always embarrassed him, even if he knew I was kidding. If there was ever a bachelor, it was Johnny McCloud.

"Aw hush," he said. "I'd just as soon marry an alligator."

It really got off with Johnny when I mentioned marrying; I should have quit doing it. I guess Gid kidded him about it all the time, and he was probably ashamed of himself for not wanting to marry me. If he had ever really asked me, I could have really turned him down, and he wouldn't have felt that way any more. I wouldn't have married agin anyhow; Eddie was enough husband for me. At least not Johnny. Gid I might have. But that was a different story.

"Well, I guess the tomatoes won't get tied up," I said, and took his arm. I wasn't too eager to go in the house with him then—for one thing, it was so pretty outside—but he was eager to go with me, so it was okay. I was the only woman Johnny had ever been able to count on, and I usually tried to give him what he needed—it wouldn't have been very loving of me not to.

He had a big ugly-looking blue spot on his hip where he said a horse had pitched him off against a tree stump, and I went in the pantry and got the liniment and made him lay back down while I rubbed some on it.

"You're sure nice to me," he said. "I'd have probably been a cripple years ago if it hadn't been for you."

"It don't take much to rub on liniment," I said. "You could have done that much already if you weren't so careless of yourself."

"It's so much more pleasant when you do it," he said. "You can rub my back a little if you just insist."

That was another difference in Johnny and Gid. Once Johnny got in a bed, no matter for what reason, he'd think of excuses to stay there for hours on end. Gid was just the opposite. You practically had to tie him down to keep him in bed ten minutes. I had been trying to break him of it for nearly twenty years; I hadn't made no progress, and in fact I'd lost ground. When we were both younger I could entice him to relax once in a while, but the older we got the less luck I had. Mostly, I guess, it was because Gid had so much energy he couldn't hardly stay still; but partly it was because he was ashamed of himself for being there in the first place, especially if it was in the daytime. At night he wasn't as bad, but then I never got to see much of him at night.

Not Johnny. He could lay around and enjoy himself for hours.

"Say, Molly," he said. He was lying there watching me; he was such a watcher it tickled me sometimes. "What'll you take to patch my britches pocket before I get them back on? I'm afraid I'll lose my billfold and all them valuables in it."

"I may not have any blue thread," I said.

"That's all right, I ain't particular."

I put my brassière on and patched them for him, while he dozed. His clothes were always just on the verge of being worn out; I think he just wore that kind when he visited me so there would be something for me to patch. I watched him sleep. Joe had his features to a T, and his eyes, and his recklessness; if he hadn't had the recklessness he wouldn't have got in no bomber crew to begin with. But that pleased Johnny. One day after Joe had already been reported missing, Johnny told me he'd rather have a dead hero for a son than a live coward.

"I'd rather have Joe than either one," I said, and I don't think he knew what I meant. Men don't think like women, or maybe it's that they don't feel the same kind of feelings. Gid had said practically the same thing to me when Jimmy got sent to the Pacific. And the boys were the same way, I guess. Joe actually enjoyed living over in England and flying in the bomber. I guess he had a million girl friends over there; I was always afraid he'd marry one of those English girls and bring her home to Texas and not know what to do with her. In his letters he never mentioned things like that. "How's the place, Momma?" or "What's Gid and Johnny doing?" or "Momma, I sure do miss your cooking, these army chefs sure can't cook like you. Why don't you send me some cookies?" Letters like that. Joe was the liveliest kid in the world, and the best natured. I waited till he was sixteen to tell him

Johnny was his dad—it had bothered Jim so much when he found out Gid was his. But it tickled Joe flat to death. I imagine he pretty well suspected it anyway, but when he grinned at the news I cried for half an hour I was so relieved. I doubt Johnny and him ever talked about it. They usually just talked about horses and ballplaying and rodeos, things they were interested in. They probably never even mentioned it. Things like that just didn't worry Joe like they did Jimmy.

Johnny was sound asleep. He was woman-crazy all right, at least where I was concerned, and he tickled me the way he let me know it. But he wasn't as crazy as he had been. One time years before he had come charging into the kitchen in such a hurry that he hadn't even seen me and knocked me flat on my back—it scared Jimmy to death. I guess the time was coming when Johnny wouldn't barge in on me in the afternoons, and I would miss that, mood or no mood. I put the needle in the pincushion and got back in bed and made him turn over so I could lay against him, under one of his arms. I never did doze off, I just lay and looked out the window and counted Johnny's pulse once in a while, for the fun of it. It looked like a cloud was building up in the south. Ever once in a while Johnny would grunt like a hog, just one grunt, and then be quiet agin. One time straightening out his leg he stratched me, so I jumped; he was the worst in the world about toenails. Once I gave him a pair of clippers and he kept them about two days and broke them trying to cut a piece of baling wire. The arm I was holding had his watch on it, and when it got to be six o'clock I got up right quiet and put on my dress and cooked supper. Steak and gravy and black-eyed peas was about all we had, but I had a few fresh onions from the garden, and Johnny loved fresh onions.

When I went back to the bedroom the room was full of shadows, except for the one west window where the last of the sunlight was coming in. I sat down on the bed and gave Johnny a shake.

"Get up if you want any supper," I said.

He opened his eyes and stretched. "Aw hell, you're done dressed," he said, and grinned.

"You heard me," I said.

"We ain't wrestled in a long time," he said. "You want to?"

"Not specially," I said. "I've lost my girlish strength."

"You never had none, you was just awful wiggly," he said.

I went on and set the table and he stomped around dressing and washing up for ten minutes before he ever showed himself in the kitchen.

"Boy, where'd you get them onions?" he said. "Have you milked?"

"No," I said. "You can milk while I wash the dishes."

"These dishes won't need washing," he said, and they didn't much.

He went to the barn with me but I did the milking. He let the cow in and made conversation, but milking was a little beneath his dignity. Gid would grab ahold and do anything, but Johnny was finicky about the things he worked at. A lot of that rubbed off on Joe, only I never let Joe get away with it. One time I sent him out to hoe goatheads, and when I went out to see about him he was playing with a stick horse and hadn't hoed a lick.

"What are you doing?" I said. "I thought I sent you out here with a hoe."

He had really worked his nerve up by that time. "Momma, go to hell," he said. "I'm riding. Cowboys don't hoe."

"I'll cowboy you, sonny," I said, and I did. Johnny, he laughed about the whole thing and just made Joe worse, so the next time he came loving up to me I told him a thing or two. "Go court your horse," I said, "cowboys don't fool around with girls."

"Aw, honey, now you ain't mad at me," he said, but he didn't get nowhere that day.

When I finished the milking Johnny opened the gate so old Muley could go out, and I started to the house with the milk bucket. He came up and put his arm around me and made me slosh some milk out on my foot, so I gave him the bucket to carry.

"I never was no hand at milking," he said. "Think of the time it's saved me."

The only time I ever got Johnny to do chores was the winter after Eddie got killed, when I come down with the flu so bad. Gid and him took turns with my chores until I got over it. Both the boys had it too.

It was a warm, pretty evening. I strained the milk and Johnny poured himself some coffee. I got a jar of plum preserves and opened it for him; he loved to drink coffee and eat plum preserves. After he had spit about a hundred seeds into his coffee saucer I took the jar away from him and put it back in the icebox.

"It's a wonder you haven't took sugar diabetes, as much sweet stuff as you eat," I said.

"It's a wonder I haven't tooken something worse than that from associating with old widow women like you," he said.

I walked over behind him and squeezed his neck a little. "I always get old after supper," I said. "In the afternoon I'm still young and pretty."

"I've noticed that," he said. "I wonder why it is."

We sat around awhile and then he put his hat on and we walked out to the back gate. There were plenty of stars showing, but there was a good bit of lightning back in the west.

"Well, I guess Gid's bought him another five sections by now," he said. "It's all I can do to keep him from working me to death. You'd think a man forty-seven years old would begin to slow down."

"Gid got a late start," I said. "He didn't really catch hold till after his dad died."

"He's making up for it."

"Tell him to come and see me," I said. "I don't get to see too much of him since they moved to town." And when he did come by he was in such a hurry I didn't get to talk to him long.

"He comes by often enough without me telling him to," Johnny said. "I'd just as soon not encourage the competition."

"How are him and Mabel making it?" I said.

"Oh, they're having trouble, Molly. But when ain't they? At least now they got a house big enough that they can kinda keep out of one another's way."

“I’m sorry,” I said. “Gid deserves better.”

“I think so too,” he said.

“We never heard the news tonight. I forgot about it.”

“We didn’t miss nothing,” he said. “You keep up with this war stuff too close.”

“Well, you’re an American,” I said. “Don’t you want to know what’s happening?”

“Not particularly,” he said. “When the Japs or the Germans cross the county line, then I’ll be interested.”

I didn’t say no more; it was a sore spot with us. There was no changing Johnny. But I think he was sorry he said it, because he knew it made me blue.

“I ’pologize, honey,” he said, patting my arm. “I didn’t mean to hurt your feelings. Sure enjoyed the meal.”

“I’m glad,” I said. I kissed him on the cheek and he got in the pickup and started off. Then he stopped and leaned out the window.

“Much obliged for patching them pants,” he said.

“You’re welcome.” He bounced on across the hill, hitting all the bumps. I could see the taillights bouncing. Johnny was a sorry driver and so was Gid. Joe and Jimmy could drive circles around either one of their dads. I stood by the fence until the taillights went out of sight. It seemed like I’d spent a lot of my life watching Gid or Johnny or one of the boys drive off across the hill. That was all right. I enjoyed being there where they could find me if they took a notion to come back—and they always had. After I watched the clouds awhile I decided it wasn’t stormy looking enough to worry, so I went in and went to bed.

Two

IT WASN'T BUT A FEW NIGHTS AFTER THAT THAT IT COME A real bad cloud. Just before I went to bed I stepped outside to look around, and it was as pretty a night as anybody could want—I could see ever star in the Milky Way. I went back in and read a piece or two in the *Reader's Digest* and went to sleep. When I woke up the wind was blowing a gale and the limbs of the old sycamore tree were thrashing against the roof. I got out of bed and made sure the windows were all down, and then went out on the back porch to see if I could tell anything about the cloud. The wind was out of the southwest and just about took my nightgown off. That was too much wind to sleep under, so I went back to the bedroom and got my bathrobe and a pillow. There was a cot with several quilts on it already made up in the storm cellar; I had learned long ago to have things like that ready.

I sat down at the radio a minute and tried to get a weather report, but all I got was static. Anyway, the way the sycamore thrashed was weather report enough. I put an apple in my pocket, in case I got hungry, and shut the back door good when I went out. Just as I stepped off the porch the big raindrops began to splatter me; there was an awful wind, and a big old tumbleweed came swooshing across the yard from the south and bounced right into me. In the dark I never seen it coming, and it scared me, and stung a little, but I got loose from it and went on to the cellar and shut the door after me. The sandstone steps felt cool on my feet; it was pitch dark. I had a kerosene lantern sitting on a table, but before I could work my way over to it I stumped my toe on an old pressure cooker that was sitting on the floor. I never could remember to throw it away, and I stumped my toe on it practically ever time I went to the cellar. From down there I could still hear the wind singing, but it didn't sound dangerous; nothing sounded dangerous from down in the cellar. I lit the lantern and looked through the quilts to be sure there wasn't no stinging lizard in them. The cellar was clean, and there never had been many stinging lizards down there, but it never hurt to look; not near as much as it hurt to get stung. Then I blew out the lantern and snuggled down in the quilts and ate my apple. It was a nice sweet one and smelled fresh, like it had just come off the tree that day.

When I got done I dropped the core under the cot. I had such a good taste in my mouth; it was one thing I liked about apples. Lately I had got so I always belched peaches, so I didn't eat them much, except in homemade ice cream. I felt nice and cozy and relaxed snuggled in the quilts, and I wasn't too worried about the storm. Where cyclones were concerned I was awful lucky. One time one went right between the house and the barn, and all it done was turn Dad's old wagon over; it never even hurt the chickenhouse.

I thought I would doze right off to sleep, but I didn't. I lay there wide awake. It began to rain real hard; I heard it beating against the tin door of the cellar. After I lay there thirty minutes or an hour I knew I was going to get real blue before the night was over, and in a little while I began to cry. I didn't even try to stop myself. At first I was just barely sniffing, but then all my feelings rushed up to my chest and my head and I heard myself crying over the rain on the door. I was crying so hard I thought I had fallen off the cot; when I was coughing and trying to get my breath I pulled back one of the quilts and felt the canvas with my hand, so I hadn't fallen. My breasts just felt like empty sacks. I turned the pillow over on the dry side and cried some more hard crying, and finally I quit and pushed the pillow off the cot and lay on my stomach with my head on my arms. I was all upset and knew I wouldn't go to sleep, but I didn't feel any more like I was going to die.

There was no cure for being upset that way; I just had to grit my teeth and wait for the feelings to die down. Being lonesome itself was just part of it—mostly I couldn't stand not having anybody to do for. I never was happy when I just had myself to do for, or even when I had somebody else wanting to do for me. That was nice, but that wasn't the main point about loving, at least not with me. The main point was having somebody I could let my feelings out on. And I couldn't do that very well at a distance, I needed to have somebody right around close, so I could touch them and cook for them and do little things like that. It was always men or boys, with me. I never knew a woman I cared for—not even Ma. Men need a lot of things they don't even know about themselves, and most of them they can't get nowhere but from women. It was easy to do for them, most of the time, and it made me feel so comfortable. A lot of times it wasn't easy, of course, but it still felt better to try. With Johnny and Joe it was easy; they were just alike and needed exactly the same kind of handling. With Gid it was sometimes awful hard because Gid was too honest; he never would fool himself or let nobody else fool him, even if it was for his own good. I tried it enough times to know it couldn't be done, especially if he was having hard times with Mabel. It had nearly always been hard with Dad, and with Eddie, and it was hardest of all with Jimmy, who was just Gid times two. At least Dad and Eddie liked themselves, even if they didn't like me, and I could figure out what to do from that. But Jimmy, he never liked himself or me, and that made life hell for him. And he hadn't changed. Wherever he was, over there in the Pacific, he was wishing he was somebody else's son besides mine. I never even put my hand on Jimmy, not even on his arm, after he found out that Gid was his daddy, and that I was still letting Gid and Johnny get in bed with me. Only I wasn't letting them come, I was wanting them to: Jimmy didn't know that, or didn't understand it, but if he had he would have just hated me more. I blame some of Jimmy's troubles on religion, but I can't blame them all on it; I have to blame most of them on myself. If I had married Gid instead of Eddie, Jim might have been a happy boy. But if that had happened, Eddie would have killed Gid, or Gid and Johnny would have fell apart, and there might not have even been a Joe. I don't know that I done very wrong. But I know that Jimmy's miserable; some of the time I am too. Four men and two boys were what I'd had for a life, and laying there on the cot I could picture every one of them, plain as day. But there wasn't a one of them I could get my arms around, and right then, that was what I wanted; I would rather have been blind and had the touch than like I was, with just the picture.

Everybody gets hard nights, though, I guess. It wasn't the first time I'd ever felt sick with my feelings, and wasn't girl enough to think it would be the last. When you lay around feeling cut off from folks, crazy things go through your mind. I would see men's hands and faces and other parts of them, sometimes even their stomachs, Eddie's or Johnny's or Gid's. Probably if I had gone on and married Johnny, it would have been good for both of us, but he wouldn't have done it, even if I had really wanted to. He was too responsibility-shy. Besides it would have made Gid feel terrible; he had wanted to marry me all his life.

Once I almost decided to marry Gid—I guess I was just jealous of Mabel. We were in my bedroom.

"If you've got the guts to quit her, I'll marry you," I said. "If you don't, I wish you'd quit wishing out loud."

That was when Gid was having terrible times at home, and when I said that he looked like he was about to split in two.

"Honey, you know it ain't a matter of guts," he said. "If I didn't have that much guts, I wouldn't be here now. But I don't believe in divorcement—it ain't right. If Mabel wants to do it, she can. I ain't going to."

"If it was conscience, you wouldn't be here," I said. "So I still think it's guts." I talked awful to Gid sometimes; I don't know why he didn't choke me. I would nearly drive him crazy.

"Well, let's just be quiet for a little while," he said. "Honey, I got to go in fifteen or twenty minutes."

That made me feel terrible, and I pulled him over to me. We had some rough times, me and Gid, a lot rougher than any I ever had with Johnny. Or with Eddie either. Nothing was rough with Johnny, and when things were bad with me and Eddie it was just because he plain enjoyed being rough and mean to women; I was hardly ever hard on him like I was on Gid. Sometimes I hated Gid, and I never felt that strong about Eddie one way or the other.

After I had cried enough, and thought about things enough, I finally did go to sleep. It wasn't good sleeping—I felt like I had fever, but I guess I would have slept all morning if Gid hadn't been good enough to come by and see about me. First thing I knew someone was banging on the cellar door. Down where I was it still pitch dark.

"I'm down here, I said. "You can open the door."

Bright sunlight fell on the steps and across the foot of the cot, and I seen Gid's old boots on the top step and knew it was him.

"Well, thank goodness," he said. "Can I come on down? I was scared you'd blown plumb away." He took another step, so I could see about to his knees.

I sat up and pushed the hair back out of my face. "My lord," I said, "I've overslept. What time is it, Gid? I bet the milk cow thinks she's forgot."

"Oh, it's not too late," he said. "About seven. I can get them chores for you. Can I come down?"

"Please come on down here," I said, pulling the quilts up around my middle. "Did the house blow away?" He came on down the steps, I seen his legs and his belly—he was getting a little bulge—and then all of him, standing there kinda grinning at me but looking like he had been worried. Gid was always my favorite; sometimes when I seen him the delight would shoot right through me, as sharp sometimes as a sting.

"Well, Molly, I sure was worried about you," he said. "I heard on the five o'clock weather report there was two tornadoes sighted out this way."

"Oh, sit down here," I said. "I'm all right." And when he sat down on the cot I couldn't keep from hugging him. He hadn't shaved that morning, and I felt the bristles on his face against my neck and his arms squeezing my sides; it made me feel good clear to the bottom. He was tense and tight as a drum. Gid always came to me tense. I held him and rubbed my hand on his neck and down his back, and in about two minutes he kind of sighed and let things loosen inside him.

"I don't know what I'd do if you was to blow away," he said.

"Hush," I said. "I won't." I made enough room on the cot that he could lay down by me; it wasn't comfortable, but for a few minutes it was okay; I felt like myself agin. Then Gid got embarrassed that I would think he came for bedroom stuff—as many times as he had come for that he still got embarrassed if he thought I knew it—and he sat up.

"Well, I never meant to come out here and go back to bed," he said, picking his hat up off the floor.

"I guess you're the silliest man alive," I said. "Maybe that's why I love you so much. When you were young I didn't think you were silly at all."

I got up too and slipped my bathrobe on and we went up the steps and outside. The yard grass was wet and cool against my bare feet, but it was a clear day, and the sun was drying things up fast. I guess it was the latest I'd slept in two or three years. There were a lot of broken limbs and leaves and tumbleweeds in the yard, and it had blown a few shingles off the roof, but I didn't see any serious damage. Gid went around the house, inspecting everything, but I felt too good to worry about wind damage; I stood by the cellar, yawning and stretching the kinks out of myself, soaking up the sun. Gid went in the house and got the milk bucket and came and stood by me a minute. He had a look on his face that meant he really wanted to spend the day with me but wanted to do fifty other things too.

"I'll go milk," he said. "I never ate breakfast in town, I could eat with you. I got a million things to do today."

I rubbed my head against his neck; it embarrassed him a little.

"Go on and milk," I said. "I'll get breakfast. But you needn't be planning on rushing off."

"I got to, Molly," he said. "I just wish I didn't."

I went in and cooked a big breakfast, eggs and bacon and biscuits and gravy, and pretty soon he came in with the milk. We sat down and ate.

"What do you hear from Jimmy?" he said, while we were drinking coffee.

"Nothing." And that was all he said during breakfast. I knew he was getting up his nerve to leave.

"Well, that was a good breakfast," he said, pushing back his chair. "I hate to eat and run, but I guess I better. I got many a mile to make today."

"Don't leave this morning, Gid," I said. "Just stay around here."

When I came right out and asked him, flat like that, he had to at least look at me. He was too honest just to dodge behind his hat.

"You need me to help you do something?" he said.

I could have slapped him for saying that. I needed him to help me live. "No," I said. "I just like to be around you."

It was like I had run a needle into his quick. He shoved his hands in his pocket and shook his head. He didn't say anything, and I sipped my coffee.

"I'm glad you do," he said, finally. "I'd like to stay a month. But you know what I'm up against. I've got a few more obligations than you have."

I felt miserable for being so hard on him, but I got harder in spite of it.

"Okay," I said. "Come back next time there's a storm."

"Aw, now be fair," he said, and I could tell he was trembling. "I got things I *have* to do; I'm a husband. Can't you understand that?"

"I understand you ain't going to stay," I said. "It's pretty plain what you don't want to do." Before I could finish saying it he had stepped over and yanked me out of the chair so quick I didn't even see his hand, grabbed my hair and yanked my head back so tears sprang out of my eyes, and my face was about two inches from his. But after he held me that way a minute his hands began to tremble.

"I'm sorry, Gid," I said, and we walked outside together and stood in the yard.

"I'm the most worthless white man alive," he said. "I'll stay a week."

"No, honey, go on and work," I said.

"You got some gloves? We might as well patch up them old corrals of yours."

We went down to the barn and he got out the tools, and we spent the whole morning patching on the lots, putting a new board in here and there and resting with one another and doing odds and ends and talking. We just piddled, and enjoyed it. Then I fixed him a big dinner and about two o'clock hugged him and sent him on. He was thinking about taking me in the bedroom but I didn't encourage him; if he had that day, he would have been down on himself for a month and wouldn't have come to see me all that time. If we held off, he'd be back in a day or two, when he felt easier, and and it would be better for him. Gid was a complicated person, but I had been studying him a long time, and I knew his twists. We had given one another a lot of good times, of one kind or another, since that summer I got pregnant with Jimmy. That seemed an awful long time ago. I guess the times we spent together, the good ones, not the bad ones—there were enough of them, too—were the best times either one of us ever had.

Three days later, about the middle of the afternoon, Gid came back over. I had been working in the henhouse all day and was sweated down, but I was still glad to see him. I wiped off my face and took him right in the house.

Three

One day about the middle of June a man from up around Vernon came by and wanted to sell me some alfalfa hay. I hadn't bought any alfalfa in three years and it sounded cheap enough, so I told him to go ahead and bring me ten ton; he said he'd be there with it the next day.

That afternoon about three o'clock I put on my overalls and got the hull fork and climbed up to see what I could do about cleaning out the loft. I didn't want the men to have to do it when they got there with the hay. It was a pretty hot day for that time of the year. I turned on the faucet at the water trough and washed my face and got a big drink before I climbed up. Working in the loft was like working in an oven.

I opened the loft doors at both ends, so there would be a little ventilation. There was plenty to do, I seen that. The loft probably hadn't been cleaned out since Dad built the barn. The wastage and chaff from all the hay we'd put up was about shin deep, all over the loft, and it was full of all kinds of mess that Dad had left around and I never had bothered: baling wire and hay hooks and buckets and whatnot. I got to poking around, and there was every kind of nest you could imagine in the old loose, dry hay. Rats' nests and mice nests and cats' nests and barn owls' nests and possum nests and probably even a skunk nest or two, if skunks can climb. Many a time, in the winter, I would go up in the loft and find a big old momma possum curled up in the hay, snoozing where it was warm.

There were fifteen or twenty rotten bales of leftover hay that wasn't good enough to feed, so the first thing I did was get a hay hook and drag those over and shove them out the north loft door; that way the milk cows could find them and eat what they wanted of them. I left one bale, to sit on.

Moving the bales was work itself, and when I got done I could feel the sweat dripping down my legs and down my sides. I drug my sitting bale over by the south door where I could get some breeze, and rested awhile. From the loft I could see way off south, to where Gid's fence line ran across Idiot Ridge. I wisht I could see more of Gid. I missed him when I didn't get to see him regular; but I guess he came over ever time his conscience would let him. I never had been able to talk Gid out of his conscience, or love him out of it, either; I had tried both ways. Me and Gid were in a situation where neither one of us could completely win, and I used to wonder why we let ourselves get that way. Maybe we didn't—I don't know that there are situations where you can completely win. Not where you can completely win something important.

A lot of medium-sized thunderheads were blowing around in the sky, so that patches of shadow would come over the pastures and sometimes right up to the barn. Then the clouds would go on north, and it would be bright and sunny till another bunch came along. When I had rested enough I got up and took the hull fork and went to raking the wastage out the loft door. The old stuff was so matted down that it made hard raking. I was always scaring out rats; most of them run along the rafters till they found a hole and went down into the saddlehouse or the oatbin. When Jimmy and Joe were little boys they used to take their rat terrier up in the loft and let him kill rats; it was how we lost that dog, actually. One day he ran a big rat out the loft door and went right out after it. The dog broke his neck and the rat got away. Joe come running up to the house, screaming; he was just heartbroken. It was the first time anything he loved had died. I picked Joe up and ran down to the barn and Jimmy had already carried the dog over by the post pile and was digging a hole to bury him. He was crying, but he wasn't hysterical. He had had one dog die of a rattlesnake bite. Joe couldn't understand why he was putting Scooter in the ground.

"We don't want the buzzards to eat him," Jimmy said, but Joe didn't know what a buzzard was. He had crying fits for three weeks after that.

I had raked out the east side pretty thorough and was trying to make a start in the northwest corner when my fork struck something that made a glassy sound, and, of all things, I fished up one of Dad's old whiskey jugs. It surprised the daylights out of me. No telling how long it had been back in that corner. It was still corked, and had whiskey sloshing around in it. Nobody had touched it since the day Dad set it in the corner.

I laid my hull fork down and picked up the jug and went back to my sitting bale. I felt real strange. Picking up the jug brought Dad back to me, and it gave me the weak trembles. Dad's beard and his hat pulled down over his eyes. When I pulled out the stopper and put my nose to the mouth of the jug, the strong whiskey fumes went right up my nostrils and made my eyes water. His eyes and his eyebrows and skinned-up hands and yellow fingernails and two broken-off teeth and the gray hair under his hat, around his ears. The whiskey smell was Dad's smell: I never got close to him in my life that I didn't smell it. The night Eddie and Wart brought him in out of the smokehouse they didn't even pull off his boots; Gid had to do it after he came.

For a while I sat by the bale, just holding the jug. It was brown, that thick glass kind. The outside was dusty, but the dust hadn't got through the stopper; it hadn't even rotted much. If I had drunk the whiskey, it would have made my tongue numb in a second. Twice in my life Dad had made me drink whiskey, and it scalded my throat both times. The first time I was just a little girl, three or four years old, and Johnny and his dad came over. The men were drinking. I don't know why they did it, but they caught us kids and made us each take a swallow of whiskey out of a tin cup. We cried and then ran off down to the pigpen together, me and Johnny; that was the day we got to be friends. That night Dad got me on his lap and teased me. "How'd you like that likker?" he said. "You want a little more? You can have some if you want it." Momma had done gone to bed. I hugged his neck big so he wouldn't make me drink any more.

The other time was years later, three or four years before he died. I had slipped off somewhere with Eddie while Dad was gone to Henrietta. Dad got back first, and when Eddie and me seen the wagon we knew he'd be mad. Eddie wouldn't come in with me; he let me off at the barn.

"Hell, he's your dad," he said. "You can handle him better than I can."

But I couldn't, really. When I went in the kitchen and told Dad where I'd been, he grabbed me and like to whipped the pants off me with his razor strap.

"When I leave you at home," he said, "I want to find you here when I come back."

My feelings were hurt and I hurt from the whipping too and wanted to go to bed, but Dad felt lonesome and sorry for himself and he made me sit up till midnight, keeping him company. We sat at the kitchen table and he poured me a big glass of straight whiskey and told me not to drink it too fast and not to leave till I drank every drop of it. I vomited half the night.

There was only one time in my life when I ever drank whiskey of my own accord, and that was the afternoon Eddie told me he wanted me to miscarry Jimmy. He didn't know I was pregnant by Gid, either; he thought it was by him. I cried and argued and argued with him about it.

"Shut up arguing," he said. "I told you before we started all this I never intended to have no kids. All the time I was growing up I had them little brothers and sisters of mine under my feet constantly, and I don't intend to fiddle with no more kids. They're just trouble. You should never have let it happen. If you don't get rid of it yourself, I'll take you to a man who'll get rid of it for you."

"What kind of a man is that?" I said. "And how do you know about him?"

"I done rung the bell a time or two before, in my life," he said. "It cost me fifty dollars, both times, but that's a damn sight cheaper than raising a goddamn kid. If you're smart though, you can save us that fifty dollars. Go horseback riding a lot."

"No, I want to have him, Eddie," I said. "I won't have any more, but I want to have this one." I was crazy about Gid in those days; he was all I could think about.

"I told you what you better do," he said, finishing his beans. "And you better do it, if you don't want no operation. Because I'll take you if I have to drag you, you can believe that, can't you?"

I could believe it. Eddie was just like Dad when it came to doing what he made his mind up to do. The only way to stop either one of them was to be stronger than they were, and I never was that strong, at least not physically. Once in a while I could stop them another way.

That afternoon I cried and cried. I could already feel Jimmy kick against my belly. Then I got one of Eddie's whiskey bottles and kept mixing it with water and drinking it till I guess I got drunk. My head felt like it had smoke in it, and everything in the house looked funny. I decided I would try to get Gid to run away with me, and if he wouldn't, I'd run away myself. I had fourteen dollars of Dad's money that Eddie had never found. I figured I would catch a train to Amarillo; that was where Gid and Johnny went when they ran away. I guess I was crazy. I changed clothes three or four times that afternoon, trying to decide what to wear to go see Gid. And I never had that many clothes; I changed into some twice. When Eddie came in I just had on an old cotton slip and was down on my hands and knees fishing under the sink trying to find a tow sack or something to use for a suitcase. I must have been drunk; I never knew Eddie was in the house till I felt his hips jammed against my behind and his hand around my middle. But I knew it was his hand; nobody's hand behaved like Eddie's.

"I'm glad I got me a wife that goes around half-naked," he said. "That's the most exciting kind."

I was crazy, I didn't even know what he was saying. "Eddie, have you seen a sack?" I said. "I need a good big sack." For a while he wouldn't even let me back out from under the sink; I couldn't even raise my head.

"Sack, my eye," he said. "You don't need no sack, sugar-doll," and his hand gave me fits and he got to wanting to kiss me; then he let me out. I couldn't get it out of my head that I was leaving; I wouldn't even know he was kissing me till he would quit for a minute. I had to vomit a lot that day too. When Eddie woke up he told me I could have the baby.

"I learned something today," he said. "It's more fun wallowing around with you when you're pregnant. I never knew that before. I wonder why it is?"

I was feeling so bad the news didn't penetrate to me till later.

"I guess it must be the tilt," he said. "The tilt's a lot better this way. I hope it keeps on improving, I like to have something to look forward to."

I guess it did, because it was him wallowing that made me start with Jimmy, when the time came. I never even tried to get him to quit; that wouldn't have worked with Eddie. The day the baby was born he left and didn't come home for three months, and that meant that Gid could come every day or two. I was happy. And Eddie liking the tilt so good made things a lot easier when Johnny got me pregnant agin, three years later. Otherwise Eddie would have either beat me to death or left me, then and there. Or both. If there was one thing Eddie never had much of, it was patience with me.

And Dad never either. Smelling the whiskey made me think of things about Dad that I hadn't thought of in years. He always felt the worst when he was the nearest sober; I guess it just took whiskey to make life look good to him.

One of the worst times I ever had with Dad in my life was the afternoon he told me and Richard about the facts of life. It was four or five years after Momma died; I was about seventeen. Except for one trip to town when I was a little girl, I had never been farther away from home than the schoolhouse. Eddie wasn't even in the country then, and since we were all too big for school, I didn't see Gid or Johnny more than a few times a year. Once in a while they would stop at the windmill for a drink of water. I had never even thought of having a boy friend—my brothers were the only boys I really knew.

And it was the same way with the boys—none of them ever had a girl friend till after they run away from home. Richard never, I'm sure; he only went to the schoolhouse two years. Me and Mary Margaret were the only girls he ever saw, and him and Mary Margaret fought like cats and dogs.

One evening I was rolling the flour to cook the supper biscuits, and Dad came in and sat down at the table. It was March or April, and the sand had been blowing; Dad's hair was full of grit, and he sat at the table and stratched his head. He never said a word to me. I started to ask him if he wanted me to give him a haircut; I gave all the haircuts my family had, as long as I had a family. Except for one burr haircut Joe got while he was in high school; it made me mad because he sneaked around so about it.

But Dad didn't want one. He was in a strange kind of mood, and I didn't bother him. I was getting ready to grease the biscuit pan when Dad went to the back door and yelled at Richard. In a minute Richard slouched in.

"Just leave them biscuits awhile," Dad said. "Come back here with Richard and me." They went off down the hall, and I wiped some grease off my thumb and followed them. They had gone into Daddy's bedroom and it was the biggest mess in the world. Dad never even let me make the bed.

"Shut the door," Dad said. He sat down on his bed and pushed back his hat. He sat there about ten minutes, just thinking, and I wanted to get back to my biscuits.

"What did you want, Daddy?" I said. Me and Richard were just standing there. Except Richard wasn't impatient. He never was.

"I guess Richard's old enough for me to show him a few things," he said. Neither one of us had any idea what he was talking about. Finally he grinned at Richard.

"Take your pants off," Dad said. It didn't surprise Richard; I guess he thought he was going to get a whipping, was all; he took off his overalls. It had been cold and he still had on his long johns.

"My god them's dirty underwear," Dad said. "Take them off too."

"Aw, it's cold," Richard said, but he started unbuttoning, anyway. In those days me and Richard and Mary Margaret all slept in the same bed—just Shep got to sleep by himself—and I had seen Richard pee a million times, so he never thought of being embarrassed just because of me. I was just a little bit embarrassed—not so much that as worried, because Dad was acting so strange. Richard was cold-natured and got goose bumps all over his legs.

"Now, Molly, get your clothes off a minute," Dad said.

I had been about to giggle at Richard's goose bumps, but that surprised me. "Why do I have to?" I said. I knew better than that. Dad looked at me for the first time since he'd come in.

"The next time you ask me why when I tell you to do something, you'll get a real tanning," he said. But he wasn't mad, he was just warning.

"What all did you say take off?" I said.

He was cutting himself some tobacco then. "Ever stitch," he said. "I need to show Richard about women, and you're the only one around. Hurry up."

That was the first time I ever felt funny being around a boy. I took my pants and shirt off, but I sure did want to keep my underwear.

"I'm cold too," I said. "Ain't this enough, Daddy?"

"I'm gonna warm you in a minute," he said. "I told you what to take off."

I still had on long johns too, only the legs were cut out of mine. I went ahead and took them off and stood there naked, holding my underwear in front of me. Dad never looked at me, but I felt awfully embarrassed; it was a strange feeling. Then Dad noticed I was holding my underwear and he snatched it out of my hands and threw it down on the floor. That made it worse.

"All right, now, Richard, looky there," Dad said, nodding at me. "That's how they look." Then he looked me up and down himself, a real long look. "Molly's a real pretty gal," he said. "You're lucky to get to see such a pretty one. She's a damn sight prettier than her momma ever was."

"What am I supposed to look at?" Richard said. "All I see is Molly, and I know her anyway." If it had been anybody but Richard, I would have been even worse embarrassed. There wasn't no harm to Richard.

Dad laughed. "You ain't looking good," he said. "Come up here by her and squat down where you can see. See where that hair's growing on her?"

I didn't know what to do with my hands. I knew Dad didn't want me to cover myself up with them. Finally I held them behind me. Richard had squatted down by me and was really looking.

"Oh yeah, that's where she pees," he said. "I see that. Why's all that hair grow there? It's on me, too, but not as much."

"That's to make it hard to get into," Dad said. "The thing to remember about it is that's where you make babies, right up in that crack."

"It don't look like a big enough place," Richard said. "I'm still cold without my pants."

"Stand up here," Dad said. "You can just stay cold. You ain't much of a boy, anyhow. Make him stiffen up, Molly, so I can tell him how it works."

I knew what he meant, or thought I did, and I didn't move. I didn't want to touch Richard.

"Take ahold of him," Dad said. "He don't know the first thing."

"No, I don't want to," I said. "Richard don't want me to, either. He understands it, he's seen the bulls."

"You're the contrariest damn girl I ever saw," Dad said. "Do like I told you."

Richard's was hanging there, about arm's length away, but I knew

I wasn't going to touch it, not even because Dad said to. In a minute I started to cry, and tears were running down my chest and stomach.

"I'll give you something to cry about," Dad said, and stomped out. I knew he was going after the razor strap, and I couldn't think of anything to do, I just stood there crying. But the minute Dad left Richard's got stiff. When Dad got back it still was. Richard and me were both surprised.

"Well, did she help you?" Dad said, when he seen it.

"Naw, it just done it by itself," Richard said. "I'm sorry. I never meant for it to." He was as embarrassed as me.

"Why, hell," Dad said, "that's what I've been trying to get you to do. Now you see, when it's like that it fits the crack in Molly. And most of the time it makes a baby, so you got to be careful where you shove it."

"You mean if you don't put it in you don't have no babies? Then why do people have babies anyway?" Richard said. Richard had a hard time understanding it. But I did too. I just stood there wishing it was over.

"Because it feels so good when it's up in there," Dad said "You'll feel it some day."

Richard perked up at that; he loved to feel good. "Oh," he said. "Then can I try it with Molly right now? I'd like to know just how it does feel."

Dad hit him across the behind with the razor strap.

"No, and get your pants on and get out of here," he said. "I've shown you all you need to see. You don't never do it with your sister; not never. And you better remember that."

I reached to pick up my underwear, but Dad shoved me back away from it.

"I'm going to have a little talk with you," he said, and Richard left.

"Why didn't you do what I told you to?" he said.

I tried to think of a good answer, but I couldn't. I didn't know why, actually.

"I don't know, Daddy," I said.

"Do you want me to whip you with this razor strap?" he said, standing up.

I shook my head. But I knew he was going to.

"If I brought that boy back and told you to do it agin, would you mind me this time?" he asked.

I thought about that a long time. From the way Dad looked I knew about all I could do was take up for myself. Besides, I didn't want to touch Richard.

"No, I wouldn't," I said, "I sure wouldn't."

"I'll make you think wouldn't," he said, and I got the worst whipping he ever gave me. But I never did say I would, and he finally quit. He would always quit if I took up for myself long enough. Sometimes it was real hard to do, and it was hard then.

OF COURSE Richard was a pest after that. Dad had got his curiosity aroused, and he soon forgot the part about not doing it with his sister. He pestered me for two solid years. But he wasn't no danger; he was just a nuisance. I could always fight Richard off.

Dad always expected his kids to mind him without asking no questions, and whenever I got in trouble it was always for not minding, or for asking questions first. But I still thought he was an awful good daddy, and that's what Johnny and Gid could never understand. They never liked Dad; neither did Eddie. But all they seen was his rough side. Dad never went around making over me, but I could tell he liked the way I fixed things and took care of him. It used to make me blue that I was the only one he had to love him. Momma and him wasn't suited for one another; Dad was rougher on her than he was on any of us. The boys all hated him because he worked them so hard, and Mary Margaret couldn't stand him.

Him and Eddie did manage to tolerate one another, I guess because they both liked to drink whiskey. Likker was the only thing Dad ever gave away; mostly because he liked company when he drank. And Eddie liked free likker. He took advantage of Dad that way.

Once Dad even told me that if I got married, to marry Eddie.

"He ain't much count," he said. "But at least, by god, he'll treat you like a wife ought to be treated. He won't pussyfoot around with you, I'll tell you that."

That may have been part of the reason I married Eddie. We hadn't never been considered respectable, and he hadn't either. Eddie and Dad were a lot alike; they never tried to get ahead like most men do. They spent their time trying to enjoy themselves, and a lot of the time they were miserable anyway. All Eddie's folks were living in Arkansas, and he never had a soul to look after him or take up for him.

I had liked Johnny ever since I knew him, but I never took marrying him serious. He wasn't the marrying kind, and we both knew it. So it was between Gid and Eddie. I liked Gid better, and there were times when I stayed upset for days, trying to make up my mind to marry him. Sometimes I wanted to so bad I could taste it. But I thought Eddie needed a wife the worst—I was dead wrong about that. And then I thought I was too wild and bad ever to suit Gid; I was afraid if I married Gid everything I did would disgust him—and I was dead wrong about that. I married Eddie, and everything I did disgusted *him*, and nothing I did ever made Gid stop caring for me. I'm more like Gid, in the long run, than I am like Dad or Eddie, but I was years and years finding that out.

I wasn't just sorry for Eddie, either; I was crazy about him sometimes. I was just crazy about him, about the way his hair was always shaggy and curly on the back of his neck. That may have been what I liked best about Eddie; it may have been why I married him, silly as that is. He never got a haircut and I was always dying to put my hand on the back of his neck.

But thinking about old times never got no loft cleaned out. I finally stoppered the bottle and got up, and then I pushed the sitting bale out the loft door, so I wouldn't be tempted to sit down and daydream no more. It was four-thirty or so, and cooling off, and by the time I got the west side of the loft raked it was six or after, and milking time. I stood in the loft door and wiped the sweat off my neck and face with my shirttail and watched the milk cow come up. When I got down I hung the jug on a nail in the saddle shed, with the whiskey still in it. It was good and aged, there wasn't no use pouring it out. While I was milking Johnny drove up in his pickup and I talked him into staying for supper with me. He wasn't very hard to persuade.

Four

I HADN'T GOT A CAR TILL 1941. BESIDES BEING EXPENSIVE and dangerous, I thought they was just plain ugly. I couldn't understand why so many people took such an interest in them. Both the boys were big car-lovers, of course: the first hundred dollars Jimmy ever made he spent on an old rattletrap Hupmobile. He run it for three years and sold it to Joe for fifty. From that time on they were both on the road constantly, going somewhere. I just let them go. Them driving didn't worry me like me driving. They grew up in a time when cars were the thing, and they knew enough about them to handle them okay.

After I had driven two years I got so I could wrestle the car to town and back without any serious danger, unless the road was slick or I met somebody in a narrow place. Gid and Johnny had taken me to Wichita and advised me when I bought the car. It was a Ford, a black one. We looked at about fifty, and it was the one Gid said I ought to get. I was enjoying the company, and I didn't care. Johnny was in a hi-larious mood that day.

"I wisht you'd get that red convertible," he said. "A widow like you needs a car like that to haul her boy friends in."

"I wouldn't mind it," I said. "I think I'd like one open, so I could climb out if I needed to."

"You'd need to if I was with you," he said. We had stopped to drink coffee and Johnny had drunk beer instead. It was old watery café coffee, so I wisht I'd drunk beer too. I was feeling good that day. We all were.

Gid was solemn as a judge though until we got the car bought.

Spending that much money, even if it wasn't his, always made Gid sober. Just to tease him I made them take me around to the Cadillac place, and I even got out and went in. They had the nicest salesman we met, too; I would have just as soon bought one of his cars. But Gid rushed me off.

"Whew, I'm glad to get out of there," he said. "He'd have sold you a limousine in another ten minutes."

"Well, I guess if I had wanted it I'd have bought it," I said. "It's my money, you know."

"I know," he said. "But it won't be long."

After we bought the Ford he loosened up a lot and we went to a big cafeteria and ate lunch. Johnny cut up with all the waitresses; it's a wonder they let us stay. Gid was just cutting up with me.

"Well, we got that done, we can enjoy ourselves," he said.

After dinner they flipped a coin to see who would drive me home in the new car, and Gid won. Johnny didn't care. He took off in Gid's car, and I bet he went right to some beer joint and tanked up.

Gid had on new boots and a new gray shirt that day, and he looked fine and handsome. He was just getting rich then; anyway he had a lot of confidence in himself. It was before Mabel made him move to town.

"Well, since we're here," he said, "let's just make a holiday of it. You want to go to a picture show?"

"I guess so," I said, "I'm just with you."

So we went and he bought some popcorn and we sat right in the middle of the theater, and Gid put his arm on the seat behind me, so that when I leaned back I could feel it against my shoulders and neck. It was such a comfortable feeling, and once in a while he would put his hand against my neck or my hair. Nobody else made me feel comfortable that way. I don't remember what the picture was, or what it was about. I never can remember picture shows; most of them are so silly, anyway. When we came out of the dark show the sun was so bright I could hardly see, and he had to practically lead me down the street to the car. It was a shiny, new-smelling car then; after I'd hauled chicken feed in it for a month or two it smelled different.

Gid drove, and we rode out of Wichita toward Scotland, into the open country. I took off my neck scarf and unpinned my hair; the bobby pins were hurting my head. It was nice to get out in the country agin; so far as I was concerned, Wichita Falls was the ugliest place on the earth.

"Drives like a good car," Gid said. "Just stiff. You bounce it over them old dirt roads awhile and it'll get broke in."

"It better be good," I said. "I intend for it to last me the rest of my life."

My hair itched from being pinned up all morning, and I combed it out while Gid drove home. It was early fall. The boys had both volunteered in August, and they were still in boot camp. After that Jimmy got sent to New Jersey and Joe to California. All the way across the country from one another.

"Well, I guess the boys are doing okay," I said. "The worst thing they've complained about is the cooking."

"Oh, have you heard from both of them?" Gid said.

"No, just from Joe." We were past Scotland, over in the dairy-farming country; I began to notice milk cows grazing in the pastures. "But he said Jimmy didn't like the cooking either."

Gid was looking blue.

"Don't get depressed, honey," I said. "We've had such a good day. There's nothing we can do about him now."

"Well, I wish we could think of something," he said. "I wish we could make it up to Jimmy someway, whatever we done wrong."

Gid's little girl Sarah was six years old then, and Jimmy had been on his mind a lot longer than she had. She was a cute little girl, but you could sure see her mother in her.

"You know we can't," I said. "We'd have to do over our whole lives. We just have to hope he'll outgrow hating us for it."

"Oh, he don't hate us, I don't guess, does he?" Gid said. He couldn't stand to think that. I had lived with Jimmy, and got so I could stand it long ago.

"Oh yes," I said. "He does. I'm just surprised he hasn't killed us."

"The army might change him," he said. "He might be a little more tolerant when he comes back."

I was looking at my comb. There were some hairs stuck in it, and the sun through the windshield was turning them golden. I was wondering how I would have been if I had been a blond; even worse, I guess.

"It won't change Jimmy," I said. "Any more than it would have changed you. We could have changed him if anybody could, and we didn't."

I had begun to cry. He wanted me to scoot over by the wheel, but I wouldn't do it. I sat by the door till after we turned off on the dirt road, and all Gid could do was pat me on the knee with his hand and try to watch the road.

When we got about a mile off the highway, out with the pastures on both sides of us and no cars anywhere, he stopped and pulled on the emergency brake—it squeaked, and it still squeaks—and took out his handkerchief and moved over by me and wiped my face. I took his hat off and laid it in the back seat; he done had some gray in his temples.

"You oughtn't to cry," he said. His handkerchief was plumb damp; I took it and put it in my purse, so I could wash and iron it for him. I looked out the window when he hugged me. I had my knees up in the seat, and he pulled back my skirt a little and rubbed his hand down the calf of my leg.

"If it was Mabel, she'd have on stockings," was all he said. In a little while he drove on and I scooted over by him and finished combing out my hair. It was such a pretty afternoon, so cool and sharp and clear.

When we got home I let Gid know I wanted him to come in with me, but he was ashamed from thinking about Jimmy, and wouldn't do it. Gid's car was there and Johnny's pickup was gone, so he had beat us home.

"You don't have to go," I said. "Nobody will come."

But he stood on the back porch and kissed me and wouldn't come in the house. It was me he was ashamed of, someway. He wasn't very often, but when he was it hurt me like a nail.

"You can stay," I said.

"I know I can," he said. "But, Molly, I better not."

I turned and walked off from him, into the cold house; one of the few times in my life I walked away from Gid like that. I guess he left; when I came out to milk he was gone. It made me feel terrible, because I knew he was mad at himself and in the awfulest misery, but there was nothing I could do about it but wait till he came to see me again. It was two months, two of the worst ones I ever spent. But he came back, and I made it up to him. Then for maybe six months he came every day or two.

THE NIGHT we got the car, though, Johnny came, and for once in his life he wished he'd stayed away. I was sick of myself and sick of ever body that night, and it was a lot more than Johnny could handle. I would wake him up and say terrible things to him. Finally he got his clothes and left. In three or four days I went over and found him and apologized, and it was all right.

Who needed to have been there that night was Eddie. He would have really thought I was nasty if he could have spent that one with me. I would have run him off too, or else he would have laid me out with a poker. Maybe that was what I tried to provoke Johnny into doing. Eddie might have done it; he wasn't scared of being mean.

OF ALL the boys and men I loved, Jimmy was the one I completely lost. His eyes and the way he went about things was Gid to a T; everybody knew it, and that made it worse. Eddie was dead before Jimmy got big enough for it to show, so it never bothered him. Actually it didn't bother Gid too much; he was proud of Jimmy, and couldn't help showing it. Mabel thought I was so trashy anyway, she was probably glad to have Jimmy and Joe for proof.

But it broke Jimmy. He was too smart to try and fool. Maybe the boys made fun of him—he and Joe both had lots of fights. Joe never minded them. Jimmy did. Jimmy was crazy about me till he was eight years old. Then he wasn't sure about me from then till he was thirteen. When he was thirteen I told him Gid was his daddy; then he was sure about me, and he hated me. He had been the most loving little boy; for eight years I couldn't turn around without him being around my neck, and when the coin turned he was just that hard a hater.

When he was ten or eleven his teachers at school started him going to church. There was a man teacher that liked Jimmy a lot—his name was Mr. Bracey—and for a long time he drove out ever Sunday and got Jimmy and took him to church and Sunday school, and then brought him home. He never even asked to take Joe—it was always Jimmy—but Joe didn't care. He probably wasn't in a church five times his entire life. And in the long run, Mr. Bracey done Jimmy more good than harm. I never was mad at him, even after Jimmy told me what he done. I never told Gid about it.

But it was the church people that really turned Jimmy into a hater; the more he took to religion, the more he turned against me.

When I told him Gid was his daddy, he didn't bat an eye. We were sitting at the table.

"I'm never going to call him Daddy, though," he said.

"I didn't mean for you to. I just wanted to tell you."

"I'm not ever going to call him anything," he said, and he didn't. Gid tried his best to get Jimmy friendly with him; he offered to take him cowboying and fishing and lots of places, but Jimmy wouldn't go. When he was real little he idolized Gid, but after he found out, Mr. Bracey was the only daddy he had.

Jimmy was the only person I ever saw I couldn't have a little effect on. Even Dad I could help a little, and even Eddie. But I might have been a stone so far as Jimmy was concerned.

He had friends, though. Him and Joe were always close brothers, in spite of being so different, and Jimmy had plenty of other friends, too. He went out for all the teams, mostly just to keep from coming home and doing chores, but he made them all. They tell me he was an awful good player; the whole town bragged on him. He was twice as good as Joe; he went out too, but he never took it seriously, and was just medium. I never went to any of the games Jimmy was in, because I knew he didn't want me too. I did see Joe play a few times.

Jimmy and me only talked about things once. He had been off to a religious camp one summer and they convinced him he was going to be a preacher. I didn't have much to say about it—I kept thinking about how much his granddaddy would have said. Gid didn't like it, but he never said a word about it. Johnny kidded Jim a little, but it was all right. Jimmy liked Johnny in spite of himself, and Johnny's kidding never made him mad.

But one Sunday night Jim come in from church. I guess he was eighteen or nineteen then, and I was sitting in the kitchen shelling peas. It was summertime, and I got up and fixed him a glass of iced tea. He tolerated me enough to drink it. I guess his resistance was down that night; he started asking me questions.

"Have you ever been to church in your life?" he said. "I just want to know."

"Oh yes," I said. "I used to go to camp meetings."

"Don't you like it in the Lord's house?" he said, looking at me through Gid's very eyes.

I didn't know what to say, except no, because I didn't, really.

He kinda looked down his nose.

"The minister says I ought to bring you to church so he could try and save you," he said. "But I don't think I will. You wouldn't go anyway."

I tried to grin, but it was hard. "No, I wouldn't go," I said.

"Molly, you don't believe in salvation, do you?" he said. Once in a while he called me just by my name, I guess to hurt me. He didn't like to call me Mother. But I couldn't stand him calling me Molly, as if he were just my friend.

"Jimmy, if you can't call me Mother don't call me anything," I said. "I mean that. Honor your father and mother, ain't that in the Bible?"

He didn't say a word; looked at the sugar in the bottom of his tea glass. His forelock fell down in his eyes and I kept wanting to reach out with my hand and brush it back out of his face.

"I don't guess I do believe in church salvation," I said.

I went on snapping the little peas and shelling the big ones, and he sat across from me a long time without saying a word. When I looked up from my fingers he looked me in the eye. He was like Gid; he always looked you in the eye when he hurt you.

"You committed adultery and fornication," he said. "That's about as bad as a woman can get." When he said it, though, he sucked at the corner of his mouth, and looked like a little boy trying not to cry.

"You don't know how ashamed I am of you, Momma," he said. "I'm so ashamed of you I can't tell you."

I let the peas alone. "You're telling me, Jim," I said. I would have given the best touches of my life to have been able to hold Jimmy then. I probably would have died right there if it would have taken what was bothering him away, but I knew nothing that easy would happen. He couldn't say any more, and I was choked up so I couldn't talk. We just sat.

"Fornication and adultery is what you did, Momma," he said.

I guess what he wanted was for me to deny it, to tell him I hadn't really done neither one, and that everything the preacher said about me was wrong. I sat the peas on the table.

"Jimmy, those are just two words to me," I said. "Even if they do come out of the Bible."

"But you did them," he said. "In this house we're living in, too."

"I wasn't saying I didn't," I said. "And I wasn't saying I'm good. I guess I'm terrible. But words is one thing and loving a man is another thing; that's all I can say about it." And that was true. The words didn't describe what I had lived with Gid, or with Johnny, at all; they didn't describe what we had felt. But Jimmy hadn't felt it, so I couldn't tell him that and make him understand.

"There's such a thing as right and wrong," he said. Like his daddy used to say.

"I guess so," I said. He wanted me to argue, and I just couldn't. I felt too bad and worn out. I wanted to cry and never shed a tear.

He finally got up and went to the door. "Yes, but there is," he said. "And if you live unrighteous, you'll end up turning on a spit in hell." He sounded like a little hurt boy trying to convince himself. It was silly to think of turning on a spit the way I felt; I couldn't be seared no worse than I was. In a little while I went on and shelled the peas.

Him and Joe left for boot camp about two weeks apart. Johnny and me took Joe to the train in Wichita, and I would have taken Jimmy, but he wouldn't let me. He hitchhiked, and he walked the three miles over to the highway, too; he wouldn't even let us take him that far. When he was out on the front porch ready to go I gave him twenty dollars but I didn't try to kiss him. He said good-by and walked out of the yard and off across the pasture without ever looking back. Just before he went over the Ridge he shifted his suitcase to the other hand.

I sent him a lot of cakes and cookies. He probably wouldn't like them, but maybe his buddies would.

Five

WHEN I STARTED THINKING ABOUT JIMMY I ALWAYS ended up thinking about Eddie. One morning out gathering the eggs I got him on my mind. It was funny, and Jimmy never would have understood it, but if I really done them two things he accused me of, I done them with Eddie, and he was the one I was married to.

I guess it really was the way the hair on the back of his neck was so shaggy that I liked best about him. A lot of times I felt completely crazy when I was around him, and I didn't care what I did. That's why he never liked me very well and was mean to me. He wanted somebody that acted real respectable to play like they was his wife while he went on and did what he pleased.

But I guess it was a good thing I married him. I read in the paper about these sex fiends who are always killing people because they can't get enough woman, and it wouldn't have taken very much of a push to make Eddie one of those. In fact, when he would be after me three or four times a day I thought he was one, and I told him so. It made him so mad he would almost choke me, because he thought I was to blame. He thought I was always stirring him up on purpose. And I did once in a while; but not no four times a day. He didn't really like me very much.

"You're a nasty bitch," he used to say. He said it so many times it finally quit bothering me. And the less I let things like that bother me, the meaner he got. Lots of times when one of his hounds was in heat he'd grab me and drag me out in the back yard and make me watch while all the dogs fooled around with her. I soon quit fighting that too;

it didn't bother me that much to have to watch. I don't guess it really bothered me at all.

"Looky there, sweetie," he said. "Why, she's just like you, ain't she? Just the same. What do you think about that sight?"

I wouldn't answer, or wouldn't say much. "It's just dogs breeding; it ain't too unusual," I said. Once in a while he would be fiddling around with me and make me mad.

"Well, honey," I said one time, "I didn't know you like to watch so much. I feel sorry for you. Let's go in and move the mirror over by the bed, so you can watch us." I knew how to take up for myself where Eddie was concerned.

What I said surprised him, but he couldn't back out. "All right, by god, let's do," he said. We went in and moved the mirror. I liked to drove him crazy that day. Eddie had to feel that he was the most exciting man that ever went in me, and when I didn't let him feel that way, he squirmed. That day we moved the mirror I lay there and laughed and giggled at him for fifteen minutes, and I could have been a feather pillow for all the good he was doing. He knew it, too. Every time he looked in the mirror I was grinning at him. I guess that was one of the times I hated him because I had married him instead of Gid. That was the time he squeezed my hand so hard he broke my next to littlest finger.

"I'm tired of your goddamn laughing, let's see you cry a little," he said, and squeezed it. But I wouldn't cry, either, I just looked at him, and he got up and dressed and went to Oklahoma and was gone six weeks. About the time he came back I got pregnant with Jimmy.

Our times weren't always bad though, mine and Eddie's. I was only mean to him four or five times, when I couldn't help it. He would come in sometimes when I was washing dishes and grin at me and untie my apron and stand there behind me, fiddling with my hair or rubbing my neck or back or sides or front till I would finally turn around and kiss him, and leave soap on his shirt.

I never seen but one of his girl friends; she was a redhead. She was at his funeral, and she came in with Eddie's sister Lorine. Lorine didn't mind letting me know that the redhead was the girl Eddie ought to have married. They never brought Eddie home after he was killed; he was buried in Chickisha, Oklahoma, where Lorine lived. I went up there on a train; it was the longest trip I ever made in my life; it was right in February, cold and rainy. Eddie looked nice. I didn't think the redheaded girl was too pretty, and she didn't act very kind. I rode all night on the train, back to Henrietta; it was a pretty sad trip for me. I kept seeing my face in the train windows; I couldn't see out at all. It was hard for me to believe Eddie was dead; I kept thinking I would feel his hands on me agin. When I got off the train in Henrietta it was after sunup, and Johnny and the boys were there waiting; I had left them with him, and they stayed in a little hotel; it was the first time the boys had ever been away from home. Johnny looked tired—I guess they had run him ragged—but I was so glad to see him. When they saw me the boys were too timid to say anything, but Johnny came up and put his hand on my forehead; his hand was so cool.

"Molly, you've got fever, honey," he said. "You've worried yourself sick."

"I sure don't like to travel," I said. I squatted down so the boys would see I wasn't mad at them, and they came and hugged my neck. Johnny bought them some doughnuts for breakfast; they hadn't ever had any before. Neither had I, I don't guess. While we ate he fixed the tarp over the wagon; it was drizzling rain. We had plenty of quilts and he fixed us a good pallet and me and the boys curled up and slept nearly all the way home. The boys were just worn out from missing me. They didn't let me out of their sight for days. Just before we got home I woke up and got on the seat with Johnny. He tried to make me wrap up, but the misty rain felt good. When we seen the house up on the hill, I cried till we got to it. That night I woke up in the bed and Johnny was asleep and snoring, with his arm around me. I kept imagining Eddie, but it would never be Eddie agin. I cried till the hairs on Johnny's arm were all wet, but he never did wake up.

I HAD the eggs gathered and was changing the chickens' water when Gid and Johnny drove up in Gid's car. They never got out but sat by the back gate with the motor running, watching me. I knew they wouldn't be staying no time, or they would already be out of the car and in the kitchen, so I went on and fixed the water. Gid was in a hurry somewhere and Johnny had just managed to stall him a little while by coming by to say hello to me.

"Boy, I'm sure having a scrumptious dinner today," I said when I did get over to the car. Gid still had his gloves on and his hand on the steering wheel.

"Well, I hope you've got a big appetite, so you can eat it all," he said. "We've got two days' work to do before dinnertime. How are you?"

"Except for being short of company, I'm fine," I said. "You look awful prosperous today."

"Hell, he is," Johnny said. "Who wouldn't be, hiring cheap help like me?"

I walked around to his side.

"That was dangerous," he said. "Didn't you know Gid had his foot on the footfeed? He might have run right over you."

"I ain't that bad," Gid said.

"I should have gone around behind," I said.

"No, you should have climbed over. He's just as apt to back up as he is to go forward."

They kidded with me a minute and said they would see me in a day or two; then they left. I got a little blue, because I knew some day I would have to show Gid the letter from Jimmy. It would nearly kill him. But the war would be over some day, and there wasn't much hope of getting out of it.

Gid never understood much about sex stuff, or at least I didn't think he did. Maybe I didn't understand it, or was wrong about it. I guess we were just raised different. Except for that one time with Richard, Dad never mentioned it—and then he hadn't been talking to me, anyway. Momma died when I was still pretty young, but she wouldn't have said anything about sex if I had got up one morning with triplets. It just wasn't nothing Momma would have talked about. Whatever ideas us kids had about it, we come up with on our own. I guess I just didn't have the background for thinking it was especially wrong; by the time I was eighteen or nineteen I would just as soon have had a baby as not.

Gid and Johnny were the boys I started out liking, and they weren't really go-getters in that respect. I guess their folks had thrown a scare into them. Then Eddie came along, and he knew just exactly what he was after and how to go about getting it. I didn't have no idea atall how to stop him, or even that I was supposed to stop him. Besides, Eddie was exciting. But I hadn't seen him five times when he got me down where I couldn't get up, and then it wasn't exciting, it was just plain hurting. I yelled to beat the band. It didn't matter to Eddie. And he hurt me ever time, for six months or a year; I couldn't see why a woman would ever want anybody to do her that way. But then I kinda begin to see one reason why: it was because a man needed it, and had it all tangled up with his pride, so that it was a sure way of helping him or hurting him, whichever you wanted to do. I hadn't been doing nothing atall for Eddie; just letting him have a good time. He was really nasty about it and I thought I'd quit him. Only before I did I started getting where I enjoyed it as much as he did; then I got so I enjoyed it more than he did. And that's when he quit caring anything about me: because he didn't want me to like it—not for my sake—he just wanted me not to be able to help liking it if it was him doing it. But of course I could help it, and by that time anyway Gid and Johnny had got a whole lot bolder, and I seen where it could really do wonderful things for a man if a woman cared to take a few pains with him.

I guess for a while I must have been pretty exciting to Eddie. It was after Joe was born that he completely quit caring about me. He still fooled around with me a lot, but he quit paying any attention to whether I liked it or not. He done what he pleased, and when he got done he stopped. One day I was just laying there watching him, and he said so.

"Well, there ain't but so much peaches and cream in any one bowl," he said.

"That's right," I said. "And when they're all eaten up you don't have nothing left but a dirty dish."

I think Eddie just married me to show up Johnny and Gid.

GID WAS just the opposite of Eddie. He thought I was nice and pure and he was nasty and bad—it shocked him to death to find out he wasn't my first boy. He just couldn't believe sex was right. I don't guess he left my bedroom five times in his life that he wasn't ashamed of himself—in spite of all I done. I had to be careful where I touched him or he would jump like he was electrocuted. But he was the thoughtfulest man I knew, and took the most interest in me. He just wasn't able to understand that I loved him and wanted him to enjoy himself—he got it in his head, but he never got it in his bones.

Old Johnny did though. He had more pure talent for enjoying himself than Gid and Eddie put together. He could enjoy himself and pat me on the shoulder and sleep for a week, and I loved that about him. The right or wrong of it seldom entered Johnny's mind.

I ALWAYS wished I had known Gid's daddy better. I think he could have straightened me out on a lot of things that it took me years to learn by myself. He had the highest standards of any man I ever knew—to this day Gid worries because he can't live up to those standards of his dad's.

One evening three or four months before he died me and him had a little talk. We were sitting at his kitchen table; Gid was out doing chores. I went over there a few times and cooked supper; they had had to batch for so long I felt sorry for them. Mr. Fry was in pain a lot of the time. I think he liked me, but I was always a little scared of him.

"Well," he said. "Some have to take and some have to give, and a very few can do both. I was always just a taker, but I was damn particular about what I took, and that's important."

"Why, Mr. Fry," I said. "Look at all you've give Gid."

"Oh yeah," he said. "A good ranch he ain't old enough to want and a lot of advice he ain't constructed to use.

"Them biscuits smell good," he said. "Let's get a head start on old Gid."

He buttered himself four biscuits. But I still had my mind on what he said.

"I don't guess I've ever done much of either one," I said.

"Aw hell," he said. "You could take a million dollars' worth, if you would. But instead you'll give out twice that much to sorry bastards that don't deserve it. And they won't put much back. I'm glad you and Gid won't marry. You'd smother him in sweetweed and he'd loaf the rest of his life. Misery makes a man work."

I was embarrassed, and he went on and ate his biscuits.

"Anyway, it ain't hurt your cooking," he said, and he looked up and gave me one of the longest looks I ever had in my life. I remembered that look a hundred times, whenever Gid or Jimmy looked at me across a table; they both had Mr. Fry's eyes.

"Molly, if I was just ten years younger I'd take your whole two million myself," he said. "The rest of the pack could go hungry. Gid would probably be the first one starved."

I couldn't say a word. My legs trembled, and I was glad they were under the table. I was looking at his hands. Finally he took a match out of his pocket and whittled it into a toothpick. I thought when I seen him in his coffin that if he had been ten years younger he would probably have done just what he said.

Six

On the last day of July I went into town to get some groceries and my mail, and to buy a war bond. Old Wash ington at the feed store had some new kind of chicken feed he wanted to sell me, and I stood around there talking to him about one thing and another till the middle of the morning. I never did buy the feed; I had more eggs than I knew what to do with anyway. I bought the war bond though—it was about the only patriotic thing I knew to do. When the war started they made me a plane spotter and gave me a lot of materials on what to look for, but no airplanes ever came over except the oil company's Piper cub, flying the pipelines. Once in a while a big one would go over at night, but I couldn't tell anything about it.

I stopped in the drugstore a minute and drank a four hundred, and then went to the post office. My *Good Housekeeping* had come, and a new *Reader's Digest*, and the rest of the box was full of sale circulars of one kind and another. When I pulled all them out, the letter dropped on the floor. I threw all the circulars in a wastebasket before I picked it up. Then I went over to the counter and opened it and read it, and my mouth felt dry, it felt like my lips were chapped. People kept going by me to get their mail; I don't know who; they were just like shadows. Finally Old Man Berdeau, the postmaster, came out and tacked some kind of notice on the bulletin board, and then he came over to me and offered me his handkerchief. I didn't think I was crying, but I was.

"I'm mighty sorry, Mrs. White," he said. "I guess they're going to get all the boys before it's over."

It was a month before I remembered to give him back his handkerchief. I walked out and started to look for Gid. I knew he had built a new house on the west side of town. On what they called Silk Stocking Avenue; he said they ought to call it Mortgage Row. People in cars kept stopping and offering me rides. I don't know what I said to them. I knew the house by Gid's car setting in front of it; then I seen him way at the back, digging postholes; he was putting up some kind of pen. He looked so surprised when I came running up to him; I put my face against his chest, so I couldn't see anything. I could smell the starch on his shirt and the sweat under his arms when he put them around me.

"They killed my last old boy," I said.

"Molly, would you like to go in?" I looked at his house a minute, it was a big ugly brick house.

"Let's go home," I said.

He took me to his car and put me in the front seat. "I've got to go in a minute," he said. I was hoping he wouldn't bring Mabel out, and he didn't. We went off.

"Stop at the post office a minute," I said. "I left my magazines." He went in and got them; Mr. Berdeau had put them up.

When we crossed Onion Creek I scooted over by him. "What's life going to leave me?" I said. And when we stopped at the back gate I noticed the car wasn't there. It was still parked at the post office, with the groceries in it.

I didn't really see Gid till we were sitting at the kitchen table. I had drunk my coffee but his was getting cold in the cup, and I reached out and put my hand on his wrist. When I saw the look in his eye I was ashamed of myself for being so selfish.

"Drink your coffee," I said.

And I quit grieving for Jimmy; it was strange to feel myself quitting, but I couldn't have cried any more right then if I had wanted to. I didn't really think about him agin that day, and when I did the next day it was not me losing Jimmy I thought about, it was Jimmy losing his life and never getting to have it.

Gid was there with me, at the table; I had never in my life been able to think of two men at a time. One would always crowd the other out.

"Stay here tonight," I said.

That afternoon we sat on the porch, in the glider, and Gid talked more than he ever had in his life. He told me about his business, and his trouble with Mabel, and a lot of other things. It was a hot day, and we could see the heat waves rising off the pastures. I had a hold of one of Gid's arms.

"We're the ones should have got married," he said, during the afternoon. I didn't say anything. I never did like to think about how much better things might have turned out if we hadn't acted like we did. We *did* act like we did, and some bad things happened, but others would have happened if we had acted some other way.

We did the chores and I cooked us a little supper and we turned on the lights and sat in the living room, and there wasn't much to do.

"Let's play dominos," I said. So we got out the card table and the dominos and played for three or four hours; neither one of us was sleepy. I got a lot of good hands and won more games than Gid.

"Domino," he said, and I laid down my hand and shuffled for a long time. Gid had asked to see the one letter Jimmy wrote, and I had lied about it and said it was lost. Actually I had hidden it in a shoebox. I felt dry inside and out when I lied to Gid—he was so trusting and it was so easy to do. And part of me wanted to show him the letter; if I had he never could have left me again. But thank God I didn't.

"Well," he said. "Maybe you'll locate it one of these days. We can't do nothing staying up."

It was hot that night; no breeze at all. I told Gid he ought to take his undershirt off, but he didn't. He went right off to sleep. I got up three or four times during the night to sprinkle the sheets with water. I couldn't get cool; I was dripping sweat. Once Gid woke up and raised up on his elbows a minute and seen I was awake.

"We've covered a lot of miles together, haven't we?" he said, and then went back to sleep. He always slept on his stomach. We had covered a lot of miles together—and we had covered a lot when we weren't together, too, I thought. Tomorrow night I would just have the moon and an empty bed. I put my hand on his neck and there was sweat in the little wrinkles of his skin.

I guess I slept a little; Gid was pulling on his Levi's when I woke up.

"I'll go get the chores," he said. "You stay here and rest."

"I can stay in bed the rest of my life, if I want to," I said. And I got up and cooked while he tended the animals. We didn't have much to say that morning. I went in to town with him so I could get my car. When we got to the post office I leaned over and kissed his cheek.

"Many thanks for staying," I said.

"Why, Molly?" he said. "He was the only son we'll ever have."

As soon as I got home I went to the hall closet and got the letter out of the shoebox and took it to the trash barrel and read it agin.

Dear Molly:

This is just a note to tell you I won't be home after the war, so don't you'all look for me. If I never see Texas agin it will be too soon as there are lots of other parts of the world I like better.

Joe wrote me that you was afraid I would marry some Filipino girl and bring her home without telling you. Don't worry, I am not going to marry no girl, Filipino or otherwise. I'm not very religious no more, this war has caused that, and I don't take after girls any more, I take after men. I have a friend who is rich, and I mean rich, he says if I will stay with him I will never have to work a day, so I am going to. I guess we will live in Los Angeles if we don't get killed.

Jimmy

I hope his rich friend loved him. He was a cruel boy, but I guess I had it all coming. After I burned the letter I went and got the basket and gathered yesterday's eggs.

Seven

I GUESS GID TOLD JOHNNY, BECAUSE HE CAME OVER RIGHT after dinner that day that I burned the letter. I was glad to see him; he was just the one I was in a mood for. We sat on the glider awhile too.

"Did you see Gid?" I said. "How did you think he looked?"

He kinda grinned. "He's taking it hard," he said, "because he decided not to work this afternoon. That's unusual. The last time Gid took an afternoon off was the day Sarah was born."

"It could have been worse," I said. And in two minutes I had told him about the letter. Telling him didn't make me feel any better—it just made me feel disloyal to Jimmy. But I had to tell it.

"That's terrible," Johnny said. But the surprising thing was, Johnny was in a good mood. He tried to act solemn and sad, but he just wasn't—Jimmy had never been close to him. Once in a while he would grin to himself about something.

And I guess I was a bad mother to the end, because I began to feel good too. It was such a relief, somehow, that Johnny wasn't really sad. Johnny could still sit there and enjoy life—I guess I had thought everybody would stop enjoying it forever because my sons were dead.

"You know what I'd like to do this afternoon?" he said. "I'd like to gather up a pretty woman like you and go fish that big tank in the southwest corner. We ain't fished that tank in nearly a year."

"That's right," I said. "It was last September, wasn't it, that we went down there?"

"Well, you're the pretty woman I had in mind," he said. "Do you want to go?"

"Did you know I'm forty-three years old?" I said. "That's about too old to be thinking about pretty."

"Why, I'm older than that, and I think about it all the time," he said, "Besides, I know a lot of young pullets that ain't thirty yet who'd trade looks with you this afternoon."

"It's because I've had you to keep me fresh," I said, and I smiled too. It felt good to really smile.

"I'll get us some worms," he said. "You get your fishing clothes on."

I packed the old picnic box with some bacon and eggs and potatoes and the coffeepot and part of a mincemeat pie I had left over in the icebox. I thought we might just stay out and have supper by the tank if we felt like it.

"Well, I didn't know we was going camping," he said, when he saw me putting the box in his pickup.

"I just put in a skillet and some stuff to eat in case we don't catch nothing," I said. "I thought we might have a fish fry and do a little night fishin'."

"I got enough worms to catch half the fish in the ocean," he said. "Look at them big fat grubs." We put the poles in, and a few quilts to sit on, and left.

THE TANK was still as a mirror, and the fish weren't biting much. "I guess they don't want to risk getting yanked up in this heat," Johnny said. We spread the quilts at the south corner of the tank dam, under three cottonwood trees. The trees made pretty good shade.

And Johnny couldn't resist shade. Before we'd been there an hour he was sound asleep on the quilts, and I was left to do the fishing. I didn't mind. We just had three poles, and they weren't much trouble to watch. In the summertime I usually did my sewing while we fished. Johnny's shirt had a rip in the shoulder, and I sewed it up and patched one of his socks while he slept. The tank and the country around it were just as still: there wasn't even enough breeze to stir the cottonwoods. I watched the water and sewed and fished a little, and couldn't keep much on my mind. Since Jimmy was dead, I could imagine that we had been closer that we were, and I let myself make up a lot of little scenes that never happened, where we were having fun together. Later I got to believing a few of them. I made up that Gid and I had married, and one fall he and Jimmy and me went to Dallas to the Fair. I never had been to the Fair, but Jimmy and Joe both went once, and Joe tried to bring me home some cotton candy; he didn't have much luck. Johnny slept two hours and I only caught four fish worth keeping: three nice little cat and one good-sized perch. I quit on worms and tried a little bacon for bait, but had no luck. I was feeling too lazy to go catch grasshoppers. When fish don't bite you might as well leave them alone.

About five I woke Johnny up, because I knew when he slept too long he always felt sour and sluggish.

"Supper ready?" he said.

"I just do the catching," I said. "You get to do the cleaning."

"I believe I'll swim a little, first," he said. "You want to come in?"

I didn't think it would fit too well with the day, for me to go in, so I said I would just dunk my feet. Johnny and I swum together a lot in the summertime, usually. I sat on the dam and cooled my feet down by the four fish, and he swum the tank a time or two and came out spluttering. He looked so cool I wished I had swum after all.

"Let's have a little target practice," he said, and he got his twenty-two out of the pickup and threw three cowchips out in the water and we shot at them till we had used up a box of shells. I had shot that gun so much I could shoot it nearly as well as he could.

THEN WE dug out a little place not too far from the water, and I laid the fire and got out the supper stuff while he cleaned the fish. The sun was easing on down and it turned the water gold when you looked across it. Five of my old cows came to drink on the other side of the tank and stood and looked across at us and bawled. I guess they were hoping I had a little cowfeed for them, but they never came on around. I greased the skillet and cooked the fish and some of the bacon and made the coffee, and we put the potatoes where they would bake. I had forgot to bring any pepper, but it was a pretty good supper, anyway. The sun went into the mesquites over west of us, and just a few streaks of light got through and struck the water. Then it was gone and there was just the afterglow, and the killdees and bullbats were swooping down over the water.

"You ever eat a killdee?" Johnny said. "They don't make two mouthfuls." We seen some crows going to roost. The dam's shadow began to stretch across the water.

"My potato didn't get quite done," I said.

"Now if you ask me," he said, "this is the good life." He was leaning back on one elbow drinking his second cup of coffee.

"It is good," I said. "I wish the boys could have lived some on it."

"They did, some of it," he said. "At least Joe did. I reckon old Jim was the one missed out."

"Reckon they'll ever find Jody?" I said.

"No, I don't imagine."

Mine would just be scattered, I guess. Dad was buried in Decatur, where his ma had lived, and Eddie was in Chickisha. I forget the name of the place where they buried Jim, and Joe was nobody knew where. I felt calm and rested, but pretty sad.

Johnny moved over by me. "What would you think if I was to steal a kiss from a pretty forty-three-year-old woman who's lost her boys?" he said. "She can cook the best fish I ever ate."

That was a funny speech, coming from Johnny. His voice kinda trembled. I smiled and leaned back against him.

"I guess you would just be kissing her because you feel sorry for her," I said.

"I guess that wouldn't have nothing at all to do with it," he said.

We kissed once and sat by the tank listening to the bullfrogs. There wasn't much moon that night, just a little sliver. We heard a snake get a frog, and the frog squeaked a long time. That sound always made me wince. Johnny turned on the pickup lights so we could gather up the stuff.

WHEN WE got to the house he helped me get the stuff in, and I figured he would stay all night. But he kissed me agin at the back gate, and went on.

"Aw, I'm too rambunctious," he said, when I asked him why. "You got too much on your mind to have me around. I'll be over in a night or two."

"Well, I hope so," I said. I hadn't had a bath in three days, so I went in and took one. The bed was empty and there wasn't no moon either, but I went right to sleep. I guess Johnny knew I was completely worn out.

Eight

ONE DAY THE LAST OF AUGUST I CLEANED OUT THE CELLAR. I had preserves and canned goods in there going back ten years or more. Some of it I had put up when the boys were little and we were real poor; I thought we had better keep as much stuff on hand as we could, in case of a hard winter. But I put up so much we never could use it all, and ever year we would wind up a little farther ahead of ourselves. Half of it had probably spoiled. I was the only one left, and I knew I couldn't ever eat half of the good stuff, much less the bad. What looked bad I threw away, and what looked good I stacked in the smokehouse, so I could get Johnny to haul it into Thalia and give it to some poor folks there.

After I got the stuff sorted I set what was left of the jars off on the floor, so I could wash the shelves. Even as cool as the cellar was, it was a hot, dusty job. About halfway through I climbed out and started to the house to get a drink, and there was Gid, standing in the yard waiting for me. He looked all tense.

"Why, hello," I said. "How long have you been standing out here in the sun?" It was only the second time he had been by since the day we heard about Jimmy.

"Just a few minutes," he said. "You look like you been working."

"Cleaning out the cellar," I said. "Can you stay for dinner?"

"I don't imagine," he said. "I just wanted to talk to you a little while."

But that was just what he thought he wanted, I knew that the minute I seen him. Gid had come to me keyed up like that too many times for me not to know what he was needing. I wisht I hadn't been so hot and dusty.

"Well, come on in," I said. "I'll at least get some ice tea down you while we talk."

But I didn't have no intention of fixing him any. I knew Gid too well. If I made him sit around and talk when he didn't want to talk, he would just get self-conscious, and get ashamed of himself, and that would spoil things for him before he ever touched me. The only way with Gid was to keep him from having to face what was on his mind until he was already in the bed. When I could manage that, he loved it. He loved it as much as Eddie or more; but it was just very seldom that he could let himself go.

When we went into the kitchen he was walking right behind me, and I turned real quick so that he ran right up against me. He kissed me without thinking, and I knew I had him for once, so I could forget it too. I wisht I could have gone to the bathroom and washed off a little of the dust, but it didn't really matter. Gid was loose, and that was the main thing; unless he was, neither of us could be.

I slept awhile—I didn't usually—and when I woke up Gid was sitting by me on the bed, washing my face and neck with a washrag.

"You had dust on your eyelids," he said. "I didn't mean to wake you up."

"I'm sweaty," I said. "Let me get some ice tea, I already got some made."

I went and got two glasses and brought them back to the bedroom. He was still sitting on the edge of the bed holding the washrag, but he had put his pants on.

And he had the saddest look on his face. I didn't know why; I felt so happy. I handed him his tea and crawled back on the bed.

"What's the matter, hon?" I said.

He pitched the washrag on the bedside table and didn't say anything for a minute. He squeezed one of my feet.

"I was just thinking about you," he said. "I guess I'm still crazy in love with you, after all these years. What I come out here for today was to tell you I wasn't going to do this any more. I guess I'm sad because it was our last time."

"Oh now," I said. I smiled, but it hurt my stomach, and I wanted to grab him and hold him. Gid had never said anything like that before, and I knew the instant he said it that he meant it, and that he would stick by it. And I knew I oughtn't to say a word: the more I said, the more we would lose. But I loved him, so I fought anyway.

"Well, it just about kills me when I think of it," he said. "But it has just got to be that way, Molly."

I waited a minute. "Gid," I said, "it ain't one bit of my business, but I've always wanted to ask you, and I might just as well. Do you and Mabel ever do this?"

He kinda twisted his mouth. "Oh yes, of course," he said. "Three or four times a year, I guess. But Mabel don't have nothing to do with what I just said."

"Well, Gid," I said. "That ain't very much. If she don't care to give it and I do, what's the harm in letting me? Why make it hard on both of us? Don't you know I need to be able to give somebody a little something?"

He didn't say anything; he still had one hand on my foot.

"Are you ashamed of me, too?" I said.

"Ashamed of you 'too'?" he said. "Who's good enough to be ashamed of you?"

"Jimmy was ashamed of me," I said. I didn't feel happy at all, any more.

"Who I'm ashamed of is us," he said. "The both of us. And Jimmy's part of the reason I made up my mind like I have."

"Why is it you're ashamed and I'm not?" I said. "Am I just sorry? I always thought really caring about a person made a difference in what was right and wrong."

"I don't know," he said. "I was raised to believe that what we done is wrong. The Bible says it's wrong. The churches say it's wrong. The law says it's wrong. And I've always believed it was wrong—except when we did it. But any no-count bastard can get around something that way. Lots of people think stealing's wrong, except when it's them stealing. But if this here's wrong, it's wrong when we do it too, now ain't it?"

My leg was trembling. I knew I had come to the wall, and I don't know why I even argued, but I had to.

"Gid, I'm just me," I said. "I ain't the law, and I ain't the church. All I say is, if it's wrong, then let's go ahead and have the guts to be wrong. We can't but go to hell for it, and that would be better than doing without you."

"We could do a lot worse than that," he said, and he put his head in his hands. "We could have another Jimmy. You ain't too old. And I've got a little girl now that's got to be thought of too. We ruined one child's life and we could ruin another. That's worse than any going to hell."

There wasn't one word I could say to that.

"Molly, you could marry Johnny," he said. "He's always loved you too."

"Johnny don't want to marry," I said. "And I don't either. You know you've always been my mainstay."

"Then why did you marry that sorry bastard you married?" he said. He'd been wanting to say it twenty years. "Why didn't you marry me? It's just about ruined my life, Molly!"

It *had* just about ruined his life, and I was to blame. And Jimmy's too, and I was to blame for that. And Gid was going to quit me. That was the way.

"I wish I knew what all was involved in this loving somebody," he said. "Mostly a lot of damn heartbreak, I know that."

"I know we've done at least a little something that was good," I said. "Please don't quit me, Gid."

"Oh, I'll be by," he said, "whenever I can risk it."

That was what finally made me cry. "Well, good-by then, damn you," I said, "because you can't ever risk it, not even if I am forty-three. I've liked it, even if you haven't, and I ain't ashamed of it, even if you are."

"What about Jimmy?" he said.

"Jimmy's dead. You quitting me won't make nothing up to him."

"Molly, it ain't quitting," he said. "We got to do it. Don't you know this is killing me? I never quit nothing in my life."

"If you can think of a prettier word for it, fine," I said. "You're the one that has clothes on."

Things were just a blur, but I reached out for him and he got up and put his shirt on. "I don't have much pride where you're concerned," I said, but he left, and I laid on the bed and cried for a long time.

Nine

Gid kept his word. I knew he would. He never loosened the reins on himself agin. It was over ten years before he ever touched me, and then it was just a pat on the shoulder.

Right after he quit me I couldn't stand to think he would actually make it stick. I was determined I'd bring him back the next time I saw him, whatever it cost me, or him. I knew I could make him come back; I had ways I had never had to use.

But I didn't lay eyes on him for two months, and when he finally did come I knew in five minutes that I wouldn't do what I had planned to do. It was October when he came; I was in the kitchen; and he knocked and came in with a coyote puppy. He had brought me one or two to raise before that.

"Well, I killed his momma, Molly," he said. "You want to raise him?"

"Of course," I said. "I'll get him a box."

And when we had the puppy fixed I walked to the gate with him. Only I stopped inside the fence and didn't go to the car, the way I usually did.

It would have been easy to have touched Gid, that day; he was just starving for somebody to. But it wouldn't have been loving him much to have tricked him into doing something he had suffered so much to quit doing. And the two months had really told on Gid, I guess worse than they had on me. If he really wanted to quit that bad, I thought I would do better to help him keep his word. If he broke it, it would just be that much more agony for him. But I don't know; never will know. The way he looked before he drove off, I think he was wanting me to help him break his word. Those things are awful complicated. Or more likely it was both he wanted: me, on the one hand, and to do what he thought was right on the other. I never will know which one he wanted the most. I don't imagine he knew himself. But when he drove off and I went back in, I thought he had sure been right about the heartbreak.

THAT LAST day, when he asked me why I married Eddie instead of him, I didn't have no answer for him. I thought about it a lot after that—too much, I guess—but I never came up with an answer for myself either. Not one I could be sure was right. There may not have been no one answer, but if there was, I didn't know it. I guess that said something pretty bad about me, that I didn't know why I married who I did, I knew an awful lot of little things about myself, what I liked to eat and smell and do. And I knew some bigger things than that—about giving and taking, and the things Mr. Fry had talked about the one time we talked. But marrying Eddie may have been the most important thing, for all of us, that I ever did. I didn't know why I done it, and I don't know what good it would have done me if I had. Knowing wouldn't have made it any less done.

For a month or so after Gid quit me, I like to have run Johnny ragged. He came over a lot. Sometimes I wouldn't let him in ten feet of me, and other times I went to the other extreme. I wasn't in very good control of myself. Finally one night at the supper table he brought it up.

"Well, I guess I better tell you off, Molly," he said. "You been getting me mixed up with up with Gid, lately, and it's about to get me down. You know me and him are different fellers. It ain't fair to me for you to pretend I'm him."

I was so ashamed I couldn't say a word. We sat for several minutes.

"You're right," I said finally. "I'm sorry, Johnny. Don't hold that against me, will you?"

"Of course not," he said. "Now that you've quit. I couldn't hold anything against such a good cook."

"Gid's changed his way of thinking about me," I said. "I guess you knew that. It made me pretty miserable."

"Not as miserable as it made him," he said. "I've been thinking he'd probably kill himself. But since he's made it this long, I guess he'll probably survive."

I let him know I appreciated his patience, and his finally speaking up. It made me feel a lot better after he had. I felt calm for the first time since Gid left the bedroom that day.

"Now see," Johnny said. "Me and you may not kill nobody over one another, but we're comfortable. We've always been comfortable, and I want us to keep on being that way."

"I don't know," I said. "I might kill a person or two for you. It would depend on who." That made him feel good. He knew I probably meant it.

But I guess Gid was still heavy on my mind, because I had to talk about it.

"Johnny," I said. "What do you think about this we do? Is it right or is it wrong?"

"Well, it's enjoyable," he said. "I ain't gonna bother to look no farther than that."

But that wasn't answer enough, just then.

"You quit worrying," he said. "That's the kind of thing Gid has to worry about. There's no need in you worrying about it too."

"But you know I've done it with him, too," I said. "Do you think it's wrong for me to do it with both of you all these years?"

"Of course not," he said. "Gid's even more crazy about you than I am, and he deserves a little enjoyment too. Only he's so crazy he reasons himself out of it.

"After all, we raised a son," he said. "And a good one. You and Gid had bad luck with yours, but that's life. The stars were just set wrong for Jim. I never lost a night's sleep in my life from being ashamed, and I don't intend to start."

"You're right about it," I said. "In a way, you are. I never lost much sleep over it, either, not till lately. I just wish Gid agreed with us."

"Oh no," he said. "That wouldn't be Gid. Somebody's got to take an interest in the right and wrong of things."

All the same I would always miss Gid, even if Johnny was right.

About nine o'clock I woke up and he was pulling on his boots.

"You ain't leaving tonight, are you?" I said.

"Oh, of all the stupid things," he said. "I left my damn milk cows in the lot; I just now remembered. If I don't go turn them out, there's no telling what they'll get into. I hate to leave."

"Oh, it's all right if that's all it is," I said. I got up and put on my nightgown and got a flashlight and walked out to his pickup with him.

"I guess you'll be barefooted the day you die," he said.

He had just half-thrown his clothes on; one of his sleeves was flopping, and I made him wait till I buttoned it at the wrist.

"You come back when you can," I said. "Now that I'm straightened out on who you are."

"Don't you worry," he said. "You won't hardly know I ain't living here."

It was a beautiful warm night and I walked around to the porch and sat on the glider awhile, in just my nightgown. I didn't feel very sleepy; I heard a coyote, back off toward the Ridge. The moon was just rising; it was full, and I sat and watched it, a big old gold harvest moon, barely up above the pastures. My hair was down, but I didn't have no comb, and I didn't feel like going in the house. While I sat there my menfolk begin rising with the moon, moving over the pastures, over the porch, over the yard. Dad and Eddie, they was drunk, had whiskey on their breath. Jimmy was looking away from me, thinking of school. Joe, he was laughing, and Johnny was lazing along, grinning about something. But Gid was looking at my face, and wishing he could put his hands on my hair.

III

GO TURN MY HORSES FREE

But, Lord Christ! when that it remembreth me
Upon my yowthe, and on me jolitee,
It tickleth me aboute myn herte roote.
Unto this day it dooth myn herte boote
That I have had my world as in my tyme.
But age, allas! that al wole envenyme
Hath me biraft my beautee and my pith.
Lat go, farewell! the devel go therewith!
The flour is goon, ther is namoore to telle;
The bren, as I best kan, now moste I selle. . . .

The Wife of Bath

Oh lay spurs upon my breast, my rope and old saddle tree,
And while the boys are lowering me to rest, go turn my
horses free.

TEDDY BLUE, from *We Pointed Them North*

One

I HAD JUST DROPPED A POST IN A HOLE AND WAS TAMPING the dirt around it with my shovel handle when I looked up and seen Gid hot-footin' it for the lots. He never said a word to me—he just struck out. Well sir, I thought, we'll both go. I knew he had some cold beer on ice in the water can, and I thought I'd help him siphon off a little. When I got there he was plopped down in the shade of his new GMC pickup, swigging on the first can. I opened me one and sat down and rested my back against the rear wheel and settled in to listen. Gid had pitched his hat on the running board and set his beer can down between his legs, so he'd have both hands free to wave. I seen the sun had blistered his old bald noggin agin, right through the straw hat. He had the hailstorm on his mind. Molly had come out that morning and argued with us a little about the fence line, and for some reason arguments with Molly always made Gid think of that hail.

"I'd been over at Antelope, getting the mail," he said. "Old Dirt-dobber thought the cloud was just threatening, but I knew better. You can't fool me when it comes to hail."

"Hell no," I said. "Nothing simple as weather could fool you."

"The Montgomery Ward catalogue had come that day," he said. "I yanked it out of my saddle pouch, and then I took down my lariat rope. 'Run, you old bastard,' I said, and I keewawed him between the ears with that rope. It broke him into a lope he was so surprised."

"Watch out, Gid," I said. "You're going to knock that can of beer over if you don't."

But he didn't give a shit for beer when he got to talking. Gid never started talking till he was sixty years old, and then he never stopped. That hailstorm hit Thalia in the spring of 1924, and Gid hadn't forgotten it yet. None of the old-timers had—in the long run it done more damage to the people than it done to the windowlights or the wheat crops. I guess the worst was Old Man Hurshel Monroe getting his skull cracked outside the door of the bank. They say Beulah Monroe found the hailstone that conked him and kept it home in the icebox for nearly ten years, till one of her grandkids ate it for an all-day sucker. I've heard that so many times I probably even believe it myself.

"We made it to a little mesquite tree," he said. "Old Dirt was slowing down."

"I guess so," I said. "What a man gets for riding a twenty-two-year-old horse."

"So I got down and yanked the saddle off. Uuuups . . . !"

"I knew you'd spill it sooner or later," I said. "Half a can of good beer nobody gets to drink."

"You wasn't gonna get to drink it nohow," he said. "What difference does it make to you?"

"Your beer all right," I admitted. "Why open it if you ain't gonna drink it?"

"Why buy it if I ain't gonna open it?" he said, reaching in the water can for another one.

"Here," I said. "Let me pour this one out for you so it won't interrupt your story."

"Just shut up," he said. "I've emptied two cans of beer to your one."

"Why sure," I said. "In the first place you're older than me. And in the second place, I've always had to drink my cans. I never been able to afford just to pour them out."

He stopped and swigged beer till there wasn't much left in the new can. "If you worked as smart as you talked, you'd have something to show for your long life," he said. That was Gid—he thought my working for wages was a disgrace. But I got my pleasure out of doing what

I wanted to, not out of owning no damn mesquite and prickly pear. I told him that a hundred times, but he never did understand it.

"I figured old Dirt would stand," he said. "So I crawled under him and scrunched up under the saddle." He kept wiping his face with his shirt sleeve, and I knew the sweat was stinging his old nose, where it had blistered and peeled. "Shore hot," he said.

"Finish your story. It'll be sundown before we get back to work."

"About the time I got under the saddle I heard water falling on it. I thought it must have quit hailing and gone to raining, and then I smelled it, and it didn't smell like no rain water I ever smelled. I peeped out to one side and saw some of it trickling along the ground, and it didn't look like no rain water I ever saw. It was still hailing to beat the dickens, and all I could do was sit there thinking about it. Finally I raised up and jobbed him in the stomach with the saddle horn. 'Damn you,' I said. 'You could have waited a minute.'"

"Haw," I said. "That's pretty good. I'd have paid money to have seen that."

"I wouldn't laugh, if I was you," he said. "It wasn't nothing to be ashamed of."

"No, but it ain't much to brag about, either," I said.

He waved his beercan in my face. "You better not talk," he said. "Where was you when we had that storm? At least I was home where I belonged. I wasn't off in New Mexico living with no Indian woman."

"Neither was I," I said. "I knew you'd drag that in. I can tell what you're going to say before you even say it. For the nine hundredth time, I wasn't off in no New Mexico. I was right near Baileyboro, Texas. And I wasn't where no horse could weewee on me, that's for damn sure."

"Not on me! On the saddle!" Gid was very particular about that point.

"It's too hot to listen to you explain," Actually, when they had that storm, I had done been busted up in my horsewreck and was in the hospital. I wasn't even living with Jelly.

"When I jobbed him, he kicked me," Gid said, and he looked kinda sad, remembering. Contrary as he was, I could feel sorry for Gid sometimes. He was getting old, and he wouldn't admit it. Middle of July, hot as a firecracker, and the old fart wouldn't stretch out and rest for love nor money. Telling them old stories, getting himself in a stir, remembering them. I wish I could have talked some sense into him, sat him down and told him, "Now goddamnit, Gid, you're getting about old enough to slow down. It won't hurt you to take a little rest in the afternoons." But when it come right down to saying it, I just let him go. Making him mad would have done more damage than the advice was worth. Besides, I kinda got a kick out of hearing the stories agin myself.

"Put your hat on, Gid," I said. "You'll go off and forget it and take a sunstroke."

"That was the first time Dirt had kicked in ten years," he said.

"It surprised me. And then he run off."

"Did you cuss him?" I said.

"Yeah, but it didn't do no good."

"Why no, that don't surprise me," I said. "It don't do no good when you yell at me, either."

"Yeah, but you ain't a horse," he said.

"That's all right. Neither one of us can understand you when you yell. You don't talk plain."

"Bullshit," he said. "If you'd just get you one of them little invisible hearing aids, you could hear fine. Nobody's going to blame you for getting old."

Gid was the worst about that kind of remark I ever saw. "Who said anything about old?" I said. "You splutter when you yell; maybe it's them false teeth, I don't know. And the next time I wish you'd buy Pearl if you're going to buy beer. You let this get a little warm and it tastes like horsepiss."

He threw his beer can on the pile we were building up by the loading chute. "You know, Johnny, we're going to have to haul them cans off, one of these days," he said. "Cattle will get to where they won't load with all them tin cans shining at them."

I chunked one on the pile myself. It's nice to have a pile to throw a beercan at. A man can see he's been accomplishing something. "Leave them cans where they are," I said. "The pile's just now getting big enough it's easy to hit. Besides, we ain't gonna load no cattle recently."

"That's about the size of it," he said. And that can pile is still right where it was. We never got around to hauling it off, and I'm glad. It's kind of a monument.

"When are we going to get to work?" I said.

He had to strike five matches to get his stogie lit, and then it went right out. He just bought them to chew, anyway.

"Looks like you'd be willing to rest," he said. "I try to ease up on you in the heat of the day and you go to rearing and tearing. You have to sit on an old bugger like you to keep him from killing himself. I guess you just want to prove you can still work."

"Blame it on me," I said. "I'm handy."

"Now if you were able to work in weather like this, it'd be different. I seen you get the weak trembles yesterday, digging that corner posthole."

"It was hot yesterday," I had to admit. "Anybody that works hard can get too hot."

"Sure, sure," he said.

"Don't be sure, suring me," I said. "You had the weaves yourself a dozen times. You just had the crowbar to prop up on or you'd have gone down fifteen times."

"Aw," he said, "that's just your imagination. The sweat drips on my bifocals and I stumble once in a while, that's all."

"Of course," I said. "That must be it. That's why you're going to have that operation next month. Sweat's what does it."

"Making fun of a sick man," he said. "Let me finish my story."

I knew that story like a good preacher knows the Bible, but I listened anyway. I liked to hear what new lies Gid would put in.

"What happened," he said, "was old Dirt squashed my hip when he ran over me."

"No wonder you're so bunged up nowadays," I said. "You ought to have taken better care of yourself when you were young."

"There's a blister bug on your hat," he said. "You better get him before he gets you. What do you mean bunged up? I've got a crick or two, but I ain't feeble."

I caught the brim of my hat and flipped the blister bug halfway across the lot. "Them sonofabitches are going to take this country," I said.

"Yeah, them and the mesquite. And the government. I hope I ain't alive to see it."

"You won't be," I said. "The country ain't that far gone."

"Then it don't like much," he said. "Ten more years like this and it will strain a man to make an honest living in this country. He flipped about four inches of stogie over toward the can pile.

"It strains the ones that make an honest living now," I said, "but that don't affect the majority. What was the matter with that cigar?"

"Nothing. Good cigar. That little piece I threw away wasn't worth lighting."

"Kiss my butt," I said. "I guess if you laid down a dollar and they give you two bits change, you'd let it lay, like it wasn't worth keeping."

"That's right," he said. "It ain't worth keeping. Won't buy nothing."

"Now, Gid," I said. "Think a minute. That's a hamburger you'd be throwing away. That's five Peanut Patties."

"Think yourself," he said. "Who wants a goddamn Peanut Pattie anyway, much less five of them? You'd think a man your age would get over craving candy."

"Nothing wrong with Peanut Patties. They stick to your ribs." Everybody hurrahed me about my sweet tooth. But I've craved candy all my life, and I don't believe in doing without something just because a bunch of idiots thinks it's silly. Delaware Punch is another thing I like.

"And anyway we're letting the cool part of the day go to waste," I said. "I guess it'll be a hundred and ten tomorrow."

"We ain't gonna work tomorrow," he said. "I promised Susie I'd take her to see *Snow White*." Then he went back to his story. "I don't know how I survived," he said. "Finally the hail was piled up around me and the saddle like it was an igloo, I remember that."

I reached in and got my pocketknife and slipped the boot off my right foot. "You're gonna talk till suppertime I might as well trim my corns," I said.

"Poor bastard," he said. "I guess a man's feet give out first."

"Not mine," I said. "I've had sense enough not to use mine much. I just got a few corns."

"Mabel talked me into having Susie a pair of little boots made," he said. "Made outa javelina skin. Shore purty."

"I bet," I said. "And probably didn't cost over five times what they were worth. What'd you want to spend money on that javelina skin for?"

"Soft. Don't hurt a kid's feet so much."

"That's the way the whip pops," I said. "The first pair of shoes I ever bought felt like they was made out of tin."

"Mine did too," he said. "No wonder we're both cripples."

"What'd you do when it quit hailing?"

"Stood up," he said. "When I looked around I seen I wasn't but just across the peach orchard from the Eldenfelders' house. So I got me a limb for a crutch and hopscotched across the orchard."

"A man's taking his life in his hands, going up to a Dutchman's house on one leg," I said. "It's a wonder the dogs didn't rip you up."

"I thought about that," he said. "We was near neighbors, and the dogs knew me a little, else I wouldn't have gone up at all. I picked me up a pocketful of big hails, just in case."

"Just in case what? You couldn't hit a dog with a hailstone in fifteen throws."

"I don't know," he said. "I could always chunk good and straight.

Remember the time we played that baseball game in Thalia and I chunked that Methodist preacher they had playing second base. I chunked him good enough."

"Yeah," I said. "By god I do remember. I remember he got you down and beat hell out of you after the ballgame, too. You didn't chunk him hard enough."

"He surprised me," he said. "Got in the first lick. I didn't figure a preacher would hit a man without warning him."

"A preacher's got that much sense," I said. "He may not have much more." And there's a sad end to that story. The preacher waited a year or two and got in a hell of a last lick—he was the one married Gid and Mabel.

"Anyhow I didn't need the hails," he said. "The dogs come charging out all right, thirty or forty of them, but that little bitty old rat terrier they used to have was the only one actually went for my legs. The rest just stood around growling and showing their teeth."

"By god now, that took nerve," I said. "If you'd a fell, there wouldn't have even been a belt buckle left. I might not have ragged you so hard all these years if I had seen that. I admire a man with the kind of backbone you showed."

"Just shut up," he said. "I limped on to the house. That rat terrier give me hell, too. I meant to come over some day when the folks were gone and kick the shit out of that dog, but the coyotes got him first. Finally the old man heard the commotion and came out on the porch. He thought it was funny, me fighting that rat terrier with my peach limb. 'Get up steps,' he said. 'Dead cow's for dinner.' Only I didn't find out what he meant till it was too late."

"Find out whose cow it was, you mean?"

"Naw, how long it had been dead. I thought it tasted all right for Dutchman's cooking. So did old Wolf. 'Good-cow,' he said. 'Dead mit de lightnin' vee days ven we find her.'"

"Poison you?"

"No, it didn't hurt me. Wasn't as spoiled as some of the stuff you buy in grocery stores nowadays."

"Was Bartle home then?" I asked. I remember Bartle Eldenfelder; he was a fighting demon.

Gid had to stop and laugh when I mentioned Bartle. "No, he was gone," he said. "That bastard." He had to wipe the laugh tears off his cheeks. "Frank Scott come by my place one morning and said he was going to whip Bartle for dancing with his wife. I told him I hoped he'd eaten a big breakfast—it just made him madder."

"Who won?" I said. I had underestimated Frank Scott's fighting ability once myself.

"Bartle whipped him right off. Frank came dragging back by bleeding like a stuck hog. Said Bartle hit him with a hoe handle."

"That was about the time his wife left him, I guess. She told everybody. Frank hit her with a hoe handle, but nobody believed her, neither." But if he never, he should have. She was too pretty for her own good, and a whole lot too pretty for Frank's. Once I was taking her out the door at a dance and met Frank coming in. If he hadn't taken time to hit her first, I would have got whipped worse than I did.

"Anyhow, that's the story," he said. "After I ate the rotten cow Annie hitched up the wagon and took me home. I had to wade the creek."

"Okay now," I said. "It's what you and Annie did before you waded the creek that I been waiting all this time to hear. Just tell that."

Gid grinned a little. "I swear you got a filthy mind," he said.

"No, I just like to know the feller I'm working for. If I'm working for a sex maniac, I want to know about it."

"That ain't it," he said. "You just got the damn nostalgia. You wish you was young enough to have a shot at Annie agin yourself."

"You damn right I am," I said. "And kiss my butt. I was better off then than I am now, it don't take no college degree to know that."

"Maybe you were and maybe you weren't," he said. "I know one thing, them times were hard. You couldn't drag me back."

I just snorted. “Okay,” I said. “How about if I could show you Molly, looking like she looked in 1924. I don’t guess that would tempt you none.”

That hit him right on the sore spot; I knew it would. I stood up and brushed the dirt off my pants.

“Well, that might change my mind all right,” he said.

I was sorry I said it. I could remember how she looked in 1924 myself.

“You want me to bring the water can?” I said.

“Naw, we ain’t gonna work very long. Take a big drink.”

We started back down the fence row, with him a little in the lead. I stumbled and like to fell; memories had kept me from seeing the ground.

“She could make my mouth water.” I sad.

“I’d just as soon not think about it,” he said. “I’ll be glad when I get that operation. My kidneys shore do ache.”

“You don’t reckon Molly will really get upset about the way we run this fence, do you?”

“I don’t think so,” he said. “But then I never could predict Molly very well. Anything that’s connected with her dad she’s touchy about.”

When we got to the working place, Gid began to tamp the posts and I began to dig. The damn ground was so hard it took me half a dozen licks to get through the top crust, and then the sandrock started. I don’t know how long we worked, but after a while I looked up and seen the old red sun sitting right on top of Squaw Mountain, ten miles away. That brought her back too. When we were young it was an awful good picnicking place—there was supposed to be an Indian woman buried there, and me and Molly spent many an afternoon looking for her grave. Squaw Mountain was where the rattlesnake bit her. It wasn’t even coiled but it got her right in the fat part of her calf. She shut her eyes when I got ready to cut around the bite; I barely had the nerve to do it. “If you don’t I won’t be your girl,” she said, and I went ahead. While I was working the tourniquet she kissed me. "I'm still your girl," she said. I had the devil of a time getting her home.

"She's going down, Gid," I said. "Let's quit."

He leaned on his tamping bar a minute, looking at the sun. He was so hot he was sweating on the ears. "One more hole," he said. I dug it and he dropped the post in and tamped it while I took my sweaty shirttail out so the evening cool would get to my belly.

"That's a day," he said. He dropped the tamping bar and stood there leaning on the post, panting a little and glaring at me.

"What's the matter?" I said. "Wasn't that hole deep enough?"

He snorted through his nose. "You never have believed how bad that hailstorm was," he said. "Out in New Mexico, living with an Indian woman. Your old man never made a bushel of wheat that year."

"So what," I said. "He knew about hail when he decided to plant the stuff in the first place." But I guess I should have been sorry where it concerned Dad. The hailstorm turned Dad back into a poor man, and that turned him into a drunkard. But I guess if the hail hadn't, something else would have.

Gid picked up the crowbar and I shouldered my diggers, and we started back up the fence row.

"Nearly seven o'clock," I said. "Too many hours for an old-timer like you to work. You ain't no wild coyote any more."

"You're no young stud yourself," he said.

We made it to the lots and pitched our fencing stuff in the back of the pickup. Gid flipped a coin to see which one of us would drive, and he won. He was an expert coin flipper, or else the luckiest man alive. He never had to drive over once a month.

"Don't run over that rock," he said, after we started off.

"You just settle down," I said. "I'm driving this vehicle, now. Tomorrow, is it, you're taking your granddaughter to the picture show?"

"Tomorrow," he said. "*Snow White.* Get you in a good game of dominos."

I drove out of the pastures and onto the highway. "Pretty sundown," Gid said. "Looky how the sky's lit up. Looks like somebody set the world on fire."

"It wasn't neither one of us that done it," I said. But the sky was awful bright, over west of Thalia. The whole west side of the sky was orange and red.

"I wish we had time to go by and see Molly," he said. "Maybe we can day after tomorrow."

Two

THREE DAYS LATER, I MET GID ON THE ROAD. HE NEVER showed up in the morning, so after I ate my dinner I decided I'd go in to the domino hall and play a little. I didn't figure he was coming; but I just shouldn't have figured. Before I got halfway to town I seen his car, about two hills up the road, coming like sixty: I knew right then I'd made the trip for nothing.

Usually, when I met him on the road, he'd come flying over some hill and get nearly by me before he even seen the pickup, much less recognized it. I'd get to watch him go skidding by, cussing and talking to himself. I always just stopped my vehicle and waited: there wasn't no sense in both of us trying to back up in a narrow road, no better than either one of us could drive. Gid would grind into reverse and back he'd come, leaning out the window and spitting cigar and backing as fast as a six-cylinder Chevvy would back. Usually he would swerve off in the bar ditch a time or two, and run over a beer bottle or an old railroad tie somebody had thrown out to get rid of. Most of the time the damage wasn't serious. Some times were worse than others.

It had rained that morning, and I met him right at the top of the hill by Jamison Williams' goat pasture. The old claytop hill was a little slippery. Gid went somewhere down the south side of the hill getting stopped. I kept one foot on the clutch and the other on the brake and sat there on my side of the hill, waiting. In a minute I heard the gears grind, and then I seen the back end of the Chevvy come over the hill. I saw right off it was coming in sight too fast and too far to the west, so I pushed in on my clutch and rolled on down out of the way. It looked like what happened was Gid's hands were sweaty and slipped off the wheel. Anyhow, the Chevvy went into a slide and came sideslipping down the hill and kinda bounced the bar ditch and went through Jamison's fence and made a little dido and came back through another part of the fence and headed for the road agin. Only by then it was slowed too much to bounce the ditch, and it hit the soft dirt and turned over.

Well, when I seen that I jumped out of the pickup and ran over and yanked open the first door I came to and helped Gid out. The glove compartment had come open and he was practically buried in maps and beer openers and pliers and old envelopes; he kept that glove compartment about as full as Fibber McGee kept his hall closet.

"Are you hurt, Gid?" I said. The only thing I could see was a big skinned place on his nose. It didn't look deep, but the blood was dripping on his new gray shirt. "Is your nose broke?" I said.

"No, goddamnit!" he said. "Get to hell away if you can't do nothing but stand there asking questions."

"You must have bumped the windshield," I said.

"Hell, I bumped the whole damn roof," he said.

"Don't' talk," I said. "Sit down here a minute. You was just in a wreck, don't you realize that?"

But he went walking up the hill, bending over so his nose wouldn't drip on his shirt. He acted like he was going on to the ranch, afoot. "Hey," I said. "Don't go walking off that way. Your insides may be hurt,"

"I lost my cigar coming down here somewheres," he said. "I just got it lit and I don't intend to let it go to waste." Now if that wasn't consistent. I sat down on the Chevvy and he went on and found his cigar and came back.

"Get up from there," he said. "Get the pickup and chain and we'll drag this sonofabitch out."

I got up and looked around, and if it wasn't just my luck. When I jumped out of my pickup I plumb forgot about it and the bastard had rolled off in the east bar ditch and stuck itself tight as a wedge. Gid was moderately mad when he seen he had two vehicles not fifty feet apart that wouldn't neither one budge.

"Shit," he said. "Looks like you could have taken time to stop that pickup, Johnny. I guess if I was chasing a herd of cattle and my horse fell, you'd just bail off and let the horse and cattle go."

"I might," I admitted. "There ain't much telling what I'll do." A kid would have known better than to leave that pickup out of gear.

"I thought I heard you yell at me when you went through the fence," I said. "That's what made me in such a big hurry."

"Aw, you got to do something when you're running over a fence," he said. "I just yelled to be yelling. What do you think I'm paying you for?"

"Damned if I know," I said. "I haven't worked for you but thirty-eight years, you ain't had time yet to tell me what you wanted me to do."

"Well, it's not for driving into the domino parlor every day, that's for sure," he said.

"I thought I better come in and get the news," I said. "The country could have gone to war, for all I knowed."

"You got a radio," he said.

"Yes, but when I turn it on I don't get nothing but music or static. And most of the time I'd rather listen to the static."

"Okay," he said. "Don't stand out there in the road arguing with me all day. Let's dig her out."

"Which one?" I said.

"Yours. It wouldn't do no good to dig mine, it would still be wrong side up when we got it dug."

"Dig her out yourself, by god," I said. I thought the car wreck must have driven him out of his mind. "Why, there's a tractor at the Henrys', not two mile away. I can go get it and be back before we could get the shovel sharp."

"Dig her out, by god," he said. "I don't intend to borrow from the Henrys."

But just then a hundred or so of Jamison Williams' goats came out of a post-oak thicket and made for the hole in the fence. When Gid seen them coming it sobered him in a minute.

"Run," he said. "Let's stop up them holes or them bastards will be all over the country and we'll have to round them up."

And by god they would. Goats could hide in weeds and badger holes where it would take you a week to find one, much less a hundred.

"Get your rope," he said. "Maybe we can string it between the posts."

"I've seen eight wire fences that couldn't stop a goat," I said. "What good do you think a lariat rope would do?"

"Okay," he said. "You take the north hole and I'll take the south."

"Take it and do what with it?" I said. "You don't mean patch it, do you?"

"Goddamn, Johnny," he said. "Ain't you got any initiation at all! Have I got to tell you ever move to make?"

"If you mean go-ahead, I don't guess I got any," I said. "You whipped that out of me long ago."

He went trotting over to the south hole, no faster than I could walk. I guess he thought he was running. I walked on to my hole and stood there.

"Wave your hands and yell," he said.

"Gid," I said. "Why don't you try out for the Olympics? You were really picking them up and laying them down. I'd hate to think what would happen if something got after you someplace where there wasn't nothing to climb."

But he was mad enough to bite somebody, and I was the only one handy, so I shut up. We made what noise we could, and it kept the most of them from just walking right on through. But the old Chevvy had cut a pretty wide dido, and there was about thirty yards of fence between me and him. It wasn't exactly hole, but it wasn't no goat fence, either. Gid was yelling like the Choctaw nation, but one old billy went right on through. I thought Gid might call up an ambulance or the volunteer firemen, though. The old billy stood in the road blatting and trying to get the rest to follow him.

"Chunk that sonofabitch," Gid yelled. I couldn't find nothing to throw but a clod, and I missed with it. Gid was farther up the hill, where there was more sandrock, and he begin giving the old goat hell. Only about the fourth throw he led him too much and the sandrock went sailing right on through the rear window of the pickup and rattled around in the cab.

"Goddamn," he said. "Of all the places you could have stopped that pickup."

"Of all the places you could have thrown that rock," I said. "If it broke that bottle of screwworm dope I had sitting in the seat, I'm quitting you for good. I don't intend to ride along smelling that stuff for the rest of my life."

About then the rest of the goats decided to move. They spread out and come for the fence like a covey of quail. We did our best to turn them, but there wasn't no way, short of actually grabbing hold. I wasn't in the mood to wrestle no Jamison Williams goat, so I stood there and tried to get a count on the ones that went through.

Gid gave up the hardest of any man I ever saw. He grabbed a nannie and fought her around and got her turned and then let her go and grabbed an old billy. The minute he did the nannie whipped around like a bobcat and jumped the bar ditch and run down the road a ways and jumped the off bar ditch and went on through the barbed-wire fence into the brush and was gone. Gid and the old billy went to the ground. It looked like Gid was getting the worst of it, only sometimes Gid had more stubbornness to him than a billy goat. A lot more, actually. It ain't no exaggeration to say he was the stubbornest man I ever knew, except his dad. It ain't no miscompliment, either. He was determined that at least one goat was going to stay in Jamison's pasture, and by god one did. We tied him with our belts, and Gid sat on him.

Gid sure did look worn out. He looked so old all of a sudden it worried me. His hat had got mashed in the struggle and was laying off to one side; he leaned over to reach for it and the old goat hunched and over Gid went, on his face. It wasn't particularly funny, and I reached down to help him up, but he wouldn't move.

"I'll just stay down awhile," he said. "I ain't no good when I'm up noways. I can't even stay on a tied-down goat."

I remembered the time, up on the plains, when Gid had ridden eighteen wild horses in one day. Falling off the goat was a real comedown. He sat there on the ground, wiping his skint nose on his shirt sleeve. I handed him his hat.

"And take this handkerchief, too," I said. "You'll get infected wiping that nose on your shirt."

"Don't give a damn if I do," he said.

"Maybe it won't be so bad," I said. "Maybe Jamison's got those goats trained to come to a horn."

"Aw, you couldn't call them up with an elephant horn," he said.

I never knew there was such a thing as an elephant horn, but I didn't say so. I squatted down on my hunkers. The old billy thought he was plumb to the high and lonesome, since he'd got rid of Gid, and he went hunching along the ground on one side.

"If I had the money, I'd just buy them goats," Gid said. "Then we could let them go, and anybody found one would be welcome to it."

"We'll get 'em a few at a time," I said. "Jamison oughtn't to be in no hurry."

Jamison was the slowest white man either of us had ever seen, and pretty near the most worthless. He kept him a little herd of sorry Mississippi cows, that he let run loose on the road in the summertime. Ever evening his old lady and his boys would have to get out and gather them up. I've seen them many a time, moving the herd, Jamison poking along behind in his old blue Dodge, and Judith and the boys driving the cattle down the road afoot.

"Oh hell," Gid said. "He's slow, but he ain't dumb. He'll figure out how much to charge us for his fence. If you had just have stayed home a few more minutes, all this never this never would have happened."

"No, nor if you had started a few minutes sooner. Same difference. If you could drive worth a shit it wouldn't have happened anyway. Whoever heard of a grown man letting his car get out of control that way?"

"I have," he said. "It happens all the time."

I noticed he kept rubbing his elbow, like something was wrong with it. Finally I asked him about it.

"Why nothing's wrong with it," he said, and then he looked at it and winced. He rolled up his sleeve and it looked like a rattlesnake had struck him; his elbow was the size of a grapefruit. I guess the blood vessels in it had burst; it was about the color of an old inner tube.

"That beats all," I said. "Wrestling with a damn goat and your arm nearly knocked off. Look how black it's getting."

"It's that damn steering wheel knob," he said. "It's as dangerous as a snake. I seen it whipping around at me when I first lost holt of the wheel, but I thought I got out of its way. Reckon my arm's broke."

I figured so. He had done broke that arm three times. One time a whirlwind blew him off the barn roof, and one time a little mean Hereford bull knocked him down. Once I think he even broke it slamming a pickup door on himself.

"I hear a car," I said. "I'll flag them down and they can run you into a hospital. You better get it X-rayed. I'll stay here and dig that pickup out." Actually I meant to go on up to the Henrys' and get that tractor.

But Gid wouldn't even get up and walk out to the road. I never seen a man turn down as much good advice as he done.

"Let them go," he said. "I'll rest a minute, and help you dig."

"No sir," I said. "That arm needs tending to."

I went out to the road. And of all the people to be coming along just then, it had to be Molly. I knowed it was her before I even seen the car; she always went in to sell her eggs on Friday. And sure enough, it was her old Ford, the only car she'd ever had. We were humiliated for sure, one wrecked and one stuck, and I just turned my back to the road. As proud and contrary as Gid was, he wouldn't ride in with her if his jugular vein was cut.

THE WAY she drove, I thought she might go by without seeing us. The driver's seat on her old car was sunk in, and she had to drive with her chin way up in order to see at all. Usually she never looked to the sides of the road. Actually, I don't know that she did see us. She may have smelled us. Anyway, she threw the skids to the Ford, and if the hill had been about one degree slicker there would have been three cars in the ditch instead of two. I wish she had stuck it—it would have evened things up. Her and Gid was ever bit as bad a driver as one another; the only difference was that when Molly got in a tight place she slowed down, and when Gid got in one he speeded up. Anything fancy was out of their category.

But by pure luck she got stopped all right. Gid was still sitting there, feeling of his arm, and the old billy had hunched and floundered about thirty yards away. Molly had on her sunbonnet and her blue milking overalls, and an old pair of men's overshoes that had belonged to me at one time, so she didn't exactly look like Lily Langtry. But she would be a good-looking woman the day she died; she always kept enough of her looks to make me remember how much she had when she had them all. She stood there in the road, taking her own good time looking the situation over. She shoved Gid's car with her foot, to see if it would shake, and then she studied the car tracks on the hill awhile, trying to make out what happened.

Gid couldn't stand the wait. "Come on over here," he said. "We ain't ashamed to admit we had a wreck. We'll tell you all about it."

But she walked off up the hill a little ways, trying to get it settled for herself.

"Look at her," he said. "Hog on ice. She's too independent for her own good. Somebody needs to take Molly down a notch or two."

"I could spit on two fellers who've been trying it for forty years," I said.

"Yes, and I've accomplished it," he said, "and I'll accomplish it agin."

"I never knowed you was such an optimist," I said.

In a minute she came stepping across the bar ditch. She looked perfectly peaceful: it was the way she usually looked. Lots of times I'd go by her place and find her sitting at the kitchen table, looking rich as cream. Life had took different on Molly than it had on me and Gid. She rested her hands on her hips and looked down at him a minute before she said anything. She had tipped her bonnet off, and her hair was blowing around her face. It was getting a sprinkle of gray, but it was still mostly black, and as long and pretty as it had ever been.

"Well, you sure skinned your nose," she said. "You look like you had an accident."

Gid snorted.

"Oh no, it wasn't no accident," I said. "We set out on purpose to see who could make the biggest idiot of himself."

"It's hard to say who won," she said, grinning at me.

"I don't want a word out of you," Gid said. "As many times as I've pulled you out of ditches and off culverts."

"I know it," she said. "I don't claim to be a good driver. But I'm going to town after while, and what are you going to do?"

"Sit here till my nose scabs over," he said. "I don't intend to walk a dripping blood."

"Aw, get your hook and chain," she said. "I can pull the pickup out."

He had just been waiting for her to offer so he wouldn't need to ask.

"If you think your old hoopey can do it, we'll sure be glad to let you try," he said. He reached out a hand for me to pull him up, but when I took it and pulled he bellered like a bull. He had stretched out his sore arm before he thought, and I had to ease him back. Molly squatted down and rolled his sleeve back up and had a look at the elbow. He tried to wave her away with his good hand, but she paid it no mind.

"Quit flapping that hand in my face," she said. "You look snake-bit." His arm was hurting so he couldn't talk, but he held up his good arm and I got him to his feet.

"Let's go," he said. "You get the chain and she can pull you out." He wouldn't look at Molly; he was afraid she was going to take him up to her place and doctor him awhile. And before I had time to move he went across the road to the pickup and began fishing around for the chain himself.

Molly grinned. "He never will learn," she said, "and I'm glad. You better go find that chain if you can. He's liable to drop it on his foot and be down agin."

"I wish he would. If he had an arm and a leg out of commission, we could slow him down enough that he wouldn't really hurt himself."

I went over to the pickup to see what I could do. Gid had about half the stuff under the seat slung out on the road.

"Get out of the way," I said. "A one-armed man ain't got no business trying to handle a chain."

The chain was tricky to get out once you found it. It was between the hydraulic jack and a big pipe wrench that had got wedged in so tight a couple of years before that we couldn't move it. I had to be awful careful about moving that jack: with the slightest excuse it would have wedged itself, and the chain would have been gone for good. Damn the man that invented pickup seats anyway: you can't get nothing under them without skinning your knuckles, and then you can't get it back out if you do get it in. Gid was grumbling because I'd pushed him out of the way.

"That's how it is," he said. "I pay a fortune in wages, and then I'm the one gets ordered around."

I had managed to ease the jack past the seat brace, and I finally captured the chain. Molly came up about that time and Gid shut up like a terrapin shell.

"I wonder where all those goats will go," she said. "They were strung out clear back to the bridge."

"I hope the sonofabitches starve to death," he said. He had given up trying to do anything and was leaning against the fender. "I hope the creek gets up tonight and drowns ever one of them. A man that would own a goat would own a hound dog—they ain't no worse."

"Why, I think goats are okay," she said. "They probably make Jamison good money."

They went on that way, having a nice friendly dispute to settle their nerves, and I drug out the chain. Then I gathered up all the stuff Gid had drug out and stuffed what I could of it back. I was just getting ready to hook on the chain when I seen Jamison Williams coming over the hill riding his old fat blue horse.

"Looky yonder," I said. "Get your checkbook ready."

"Damn you," he said. "If you wasn't so slow, we'd be in town by now."

"He's riding old Blue-ass," I said. "We could outrun him on foot."

Molly got tickled, but she tried not to show it.

"Why Jamison won't hurt you," she said. "I've never seen him mad."

"Oh no," Gid said. "I ain't scared of him hurting me. It's his ideas I'm scared of. He'll have some crazy idea about how much that old rotted-out fence is worth to fix. You watch and see."

"Don't let yourself panic," I said. "Think up a good story to tell him. Say a hit-and-run driver knocked you through that fence."

"Naw," he said, "what's the use? Jamison's too dumb to lie to. It'll be all he can do to understand the truth."

Actually, Jamison managed that without much strain. He rode straight up to the hole and slid off old Blue-ass and came right over to Gid, sticking out his hand. Jamison was foolish about shaking hands. He tipped his hat to Molly and came and shook hands with me before he ever said a word.

"By god, Gideon," he said. "I see you run through my fence. These roads are slick, would you say?"

"A little slick," Gid said. When he was in a tight corner he got mighty scarce with his conversation.

"Well, Gid," Jamison said, "I wonder how long it will take you and Johnny to bring them goats back in? Judith don't like for them goats to run loose on the road." Which was a lie. Judith Jamison never cared. In fact, she might have been glad.

"Depends," Gid said. "How much are they worth to you, Jamison, by the head?"

"Well, you know, Gid," Jamison said, "You know how I knew them goats was out. By god, if that old one-eyed billy didn't come right up in the yard and butt that littlest boy of mine. He butted that boy good and hard and was after the dogs."

"Goodness," Molly said. "Why, they looked so gentle. You wouldn't think they'd hurt anybody."

"That's what I told my wife," he said. "It's too bad she can't shoot no better. She would shoot that good dog before she hit the goat."

"Probably should have used the shotgun," Gid said. "Rifles are a little hard."

"Well, you know, Gid, it was the ten-gauge she used. I don't know whether her shoulder's broke or not. I guess the doc can X-ray it when we take the boy in. He would butt him through the garden fence."

"These roads are pretty slick, Jamison," Gid said. "If I was you, I'd wait till they dried up a little before I went in. A man can get off in the ditch and wreck his car before he knows what's happening to him."

"I guess forty dollars apiece for them goats," Jamison said. "They got to be drenched if I keep them, and they ain't due to wool till September."

He tipped his hat to Molly agin and went over and began to climb on old Blue-ass. I watched that, because Jamison Williams getting on a horse was a sight not many people got to see. Jamison was a little short fart; he led old Blue over to Gid's car and got up the car so he'd have elevation and got on from there. Gid didn't get much kick out of that performance. He was in a fairly solemn mood.

"Forty *apiece*?" he said. He was trying to let on he thought that was too high.

"Why, you could have them for that, Gid," Jamison said. "There was eighty-six of them. If you don't want to buy them, you and Johnny just feel free to bring them in any time and leave them in the pen. Judith and the boys can take them back to the pasture after they milk." We found out later it was Judith's collarbone that broke. I guess we ought to be glad she didn't shoot one of the children.

"We'll get them back tomorrow," Gid said. "And I'll get crew out to fix your fence. Shore sorry all this happened. Send me them doctor bills."

"Well, Gid, such is life," Jamison said. "By god, this rain did us good. Just leave the goats in the pen. We don't mind helping our neighbors, me and the wife."

"Okay. You'll all come to see us," Gid said.

"Sure, sure. Go, Blue. By god, I hope that boy's stopped bleeding when I get home."

He turned old Blue-ass toward the barn, and off they went.

"Ain't that a sight?" Gid said.

"Get in and back her up, Molly," I said. "This chain ain't very long."

It didn't take long to get the pickup out, once I got her hitched to it. It's just a wonder she didn't pull it in two.

"Now you got about ten feet of slack," I said. "Go slow till the chain gets tight. Then give her hell."

"You reckon she can do it?" Gid said.

"You just stand back so the mud won't splatter on you," she said.

She gunned that old Ford like it was a B-36. I just braced myself; I knew what she was going to do. Directly off she went, and it like to popped my head off when she hit the end of the chain. But we sure came out of the mud. Gid gave a jump for the running board, but he wasn't close enough, so he got left. I went to honking for her to stop: the road was still so slick I was afraid to tap my brakes. I just sat loose in the seat and got ready to jump if it come to that. There wasn't no limit to how reckless Molly could drive. Once I was riding with her when she turned over a trailer with two sows and eleven shoats in it; a Greyhound bus passed us and honked. "He never needed to honk at me," she said. It took me half a day to gather those squealing bastards up.

For a change, I was lucky. We came to a corner, and when we got around it she felt a little jerk on the chain and remembered me. I was out of the pickup and had the chain unhooked before we quit rolling good.

"I'll be," she said. "I guess we left Gid."

"He's coming down the road." I hadn't looked, but I knew Gid that well. I was fixing to back up for him when I heard him holler.

"Just hold on," he said. "If you was to back up you'd run over me." He was red in the face as an old turkey gobbler.

"What's the matter with you?" he said to Molly. "I wish you'd been tied to a tree."

"You didn't need to walk," she said. He didn't bother Molly. "Now git in this car. We won't go to town, we'll just go back to my place. I want to work on this arm a little." She slipped up and got him by his sore arm, so he couldn't pull back, and led him right on over to the Ford without another word said. He knew better than to fool with her when she had the advantage. We stopped at the wreck a minute, so he could fish out a box of cigars. I bet it blistered him a little to have her drive him up the hill he'd just slid down.

MOLLY WAS still living on the old Taylor place, where she had lived her whole life. It was on a hill—some say the highest place in the county—and you could see it for miles and miles around. The first time I ever saw Molly was on that place; she was carrying a jug of the old man's whiskey up the cellar steps. It was the first time I had ever been visiting anywhere. All my folks were blonds, and I never will forget how surprised I was to see them black-headed Taylor kids. Pa and the old man sat on the back steps and drank whiskey out of the same jug for half an hour, and then they chased me and Molly down and made us drink a little. We cried and run off down to the pigpen together and made some mud pies out of the pigwallow and ate them, to get the whiskey taste out of our mouths. When we went back the old man thought of some more devilment: he sat a bucket on the fence and said he'd give me a dime if I'd shoot it off with his old twelve-gauge shotgun. I didn't know what a dime was, but I was crazy about guns. Pa steadied it for me so I don't guess I caught the whole kick, but I caught enough. I missed the bucket, too, so the old man wouldn't give me the dime; I never found out what one was till two years later. Molly took up for me and led me down in the cellar and showed me the still.

And she stayed right there and done all of her living right up on that hill. I guess she just never saw no reason to move around. Her old man and old lady were dead before she married Eddie, and all the other kids had left home. Eddie never had nothing but a pack of turd hounds and a pair of roughnecking boots from the day he was born till the day he fell off the derrick; their getting married was just a matter of finding a justice of the peace who was sober enough to talk. But it's still strange to think of her spending her whole life there on her hill. One night when we were younger and were laying up together, I was awake listening to the wind rattle the windowpanes, and I asked her about it.

"Ain't you curious to see the world at all?" I said.

"No," she said. "I'm doing just as much living right here and now as I could anywhere." And she hugged me and we went back to sleep.

Probably, in the long run, she was right. She done her share up on that hill. She was born there, and went to school what little she went over in the Idiot Ridge schoolhouse. The flu killed the old lady in 1918; the old man drank lye. Her oldest brother Shep, I don't know what became of him. Mary Margaret married a store clerk, and Rich got caught stealing saddles and sent to the pen; Molly said once he was out, but he never came our way. Eddie fell off that oil rig, and then the Germans got Joe and the Japs got Jimmy. All that time Molly stayed there and went on. Sometimes I wonder what will become of the old

Taylor place when Molly and the rest of us are gone. I can't imagine that hill without her. But I guess there ain't nothing that don't come to an end sometime.

When we got there she took us in the kitchen and fed us peach cobbler and coffee. Gid was quiet as a mouse. After a while she went out in the smokehouse and brought in some kerosene for him to soak his arm in.

He perked right up. "Oh, is that all?" he said. He couldn't get his sleeve up fast enough. I guess he thought she went after the dehorning saw.

"Yell if she gets too rough," I said. "I got to go outside. Smelling that kerosene ain't good for a healthy man."

I went out back and sat on the steps. You could see way off west, across Molly's land and a lot of Gid's. Her back bedroom was a nice place to wake up. The clouds to the west were peeling away like layers of gauze, and it wasn't long before the sun was shining on the wet mesquite. I could hear her and Gid talking through the screen door. It was childish, but it made me feel left out. I knew all about it. Old as they was, Gid was still halfway talking about leaving Mabel and coming to live with Molly, and she was halfway encouraging it. And it would have been a good thing for Gid and her both, I guess; it just made me feel a little left out. We had both hung around her so long. Course Gid ought to left Mabel. Living with her thirty years was no judgment, in my book. But she had a grandkid to hold over him. I got up and walked around to the garden, to see how the tomatoes and the roasting ears were holding out. I seen I was going to have to make it around for supper a little more often, if I was going to beat the blister bugs to what there was. Molly kind of expected me for a supper anyway, a lot of times.

When I came out of the garden the sun was so bright that I went around to the front of the house, where the shade was. In a little while Gid come out on the porch; he had about a half a bed-sheet wrapped around his arm, and he was grinning like a possum.

"I'm as good as new," he said.

Molly came out with three big glasses of buttermilk and a plate of cold cornbread. Nobody had much to say, so we sat quiet for a change, eating cornbread and buttermilk. Once in a while the conversation would kinda settle; I guess we were all thinking about old times. Finally I looked around and Molly and Gid were staring off across the pastures, not seeing anything.

"What time is it?" I said. They both jumped.

Gid fished out his pocket watch, but it was stopped.

"Shadows are pretty long," Molly said.

"Time we got on," he said.

"Aw, you'all stay for supper. I've got some fresh black-eyed peas shelled. We'll dress a fryer."

"I guess we can't," Gid said, sounding a little gloomy. He set his empty buttermilk glass down on the tray. His nose still looked raw and stingy.

Molly walked out in the yard and began to pick on the lilac bushes. "I don't see why you'all don't just sit a few more minutes," she said. "Supper won't takc no time."

"We'll have to put it off till some other time," Gid said. "We're much obliged."

"I don't want your much obliged," she said, kinda snappy. "I want you to eat with me."

Then we walked around the house and stood by the cellar a minute, the cellar Old Man Taylor had built. The sun was down and it was clouding up agin over in the northwest.

Gid said let's go and Molly tried one more time to get us to stay. She walked out to the pickup with us, looking down in the dumps. Gid bragged on her bandage a little, to try and perk her up.

"You'all come by and see me," she said.

"I'll be by," I said. "I might even get back tonight."

"I wish you would, if it ain't out of your way. I'll keep something on the stove."

"No, don't go to no trouble," I said. "No sense in you waiting up special. I might not get by till eleven o'clock, I don't know."

"Okay," she said. "Do as you please."

We told her good-by and I drove on out through the cattle guard, into the lane. Molly was still standing by her windmill, watching the world, or maybe just watching us.

"SHE'S GETTING lonesome in her old age," he said.

"Tell me where to go," I said. "I don't want to get blamed for taking you someplace wrong." He never had found out I wasn't no mind reader. Once when we was younger and got drunk I took him to a rodeo in Newcastle and it turned out he had paid his entry fee in one in Waurika, Oklahoma, a hundred and fifty miles the other way.

"Just take me home," he said. He was blue; he always got blue in the late evenings—had been for years. If I had to face Mabel, I wouldn't have had no fondness for sundown, either.

"Molly's been lonesome a good while," I said. "Her independent talk don't fool me."

"We're the only ones that ever go and see her," he said. "Wonder why she don't like womenfolk."

"Same reason I don't. They're silly as hens, all of them except her."

He turned it over in his mind for a while. It wasn't quite dark good, but all the lights were on in Thalia. Ever time we topped a hill I seen them flashing. The shower had cooled things off and the country smelled nice and green. Being in wrecks made Gid thoughtful.

"Molly's had a lot," he said.

"Yes," I said. "But I wouldn't call it no whopping success of a life."

"She's made mistakes," he said. "So have I and so have you."

"At least I ain't made the same ones over and over agin," I said.

"Why not? You might as well make them you're used to as to make new ones all the time. It don't do no more damage.

"Anyhow," he said, "I wish she wasn't lonesome."

We drove through Thalia. Two or three cars were parked in front of the picture show, and a couple more outside the domino hall.

"Television's got the picture show business," he said.

"No wonder. They quit making good shows. The last one I seen that was any count was *Red River*."

"Good night," he said, "that was years ago."

"So were a lot of good things," I said. Six or eight kids were scuffling and fighting on the courthouse lawn, under the mulberry trees.

"You don't keep up," he said. "*Shane* was made since then. So was *The Searchers*."

"Them was so-so," I said. "All the good movie stars are getting too old."

"I wish I had the energy them kids have," he said.

"You'd waste it," I said. "Just like they're doing."

We passed the drive-in eating place, and it looked like 90 percent of the cars in town were there. "Them things are what makes the money," I said.

"I know it," he said. "I hate a drive-in. Them jukeboxes are awful."

"Susie'll be right there in a few years," I said. "Right in the middle of it."

"I guess so," he said. "I reckon so."

I pulled up in his driveway and stopped. Gid opened the door but he kept sitting there.

"How'll we get those goddamn goats?" he said.

"I favor a thirty-thirty," I said. "The ammunition's cheap."

"But the goats ain't. We'll just get out there about daybreak and get them ourselves."

"I knew you'd decide on the hardest way."

"If you stop at the domino hall," he said, "tell Charlie Starton to get his wrecker and go get that car. You might show him where it is." What he meant was, be damn sure I didn't let that car sit out there all night.

"Okay," I said. "See you when it gets light. Any special horse? You got one that's good on goats?"

"Bring me any one you can catch," he said.

He was out, still holding to the car door. I began to back up. The only way to get loose from him was to drive loose. When I swung into the street my headlights shone on him, standing outside his door cleaning his boots.

Charlie Starton was standing on the sidewalk in front of the domino hall, smoking a cigar.

"What's the matter with Gid?" he said. "Can't he drive?"

I never cared to stand around having no conversation with Charlie Starton.

"His reflexes don't work too fast," I said. "Are you coming or ain't you?"

When there was money involved Charlie's reflexes worked awful fast. He followed me right out and winched up the car. I turned in at Molly's, but it was past ten, and she had gone to bed; I hated that. I hated to see Molly lonesome, and I had been counting on some cold supper besides. But it wasn't no go. I went home and fed the chickens and ate me a bowl of Post Toasties and went to bed.

Three

About two weeks later we met Molly at the feed store one morning. It was August then, and the country was drying up, so Gid wanted to feed his old cows a little. I was in town early and we thought we'd be the first customers, but Molly's old Ford was sitting by the loading platform.

"She's getting her chicken feed," I said.

Gid looked a little nervous. Him and her might have been having arguments, I didn't know.

Her and the feed-store hands were sitting in the back of the store on the sacks of dogfood, drinking coffee. Samuel Houston was petting his old mangy dog and telling a big windy. He didn't own the feed store, he just foremanned it: His boy T.I. and a crew of Mexicans did what little work got done.

Molly looked up and said hello to us, but Samuel H. never broke his stride.

"He caught me about two miles this side of the stop sign," he said. "Come walking up to the car with a big gun on his hip and a badge on his chest. 'I'd like to see your driver's license,' he said, like it was a friendly conversation. 'I'd like to see your funeral notice, you sonofabitch,' I said. 'Now, mister, don't use that foul language,' he said. 'What are you going to tell the judge when you have to show him this ticket?' 'I guess, by god, I'll tell him I run a goddamn stop sign,' I said. 'Now give it here, I got to get this feed unloaded this morning.'"

"Why, I'd have stomped that mother into the pavement," T.I. said. "Where he needed to be stomped." He might have, too. Once at a medicine show T.I. won what they said was a genuine white Mormon wife, only it turned out to be a genuine White Rock Hen. He stomped a little that night. His real name was Texas Independence.

"Why, hello, Gid," Samuel Houston said, "have you seen my dog? This here's the smartest dog I ever raised, and I call him Billie Sol. He can suck the eggs right out from under the hens without them even noticing."

Gid just looked impatient. "I hate to bother you fellers," he said. "But if it ain't too much trouble, I'd like about a dozen sacks of cottonseed cake."

The three Mexicans got the biggest laugh out of that. They led such easy lives sitting around that percolator, I guess they could get a big laugh out of anything.

"Oh, it's no trouble," Samuel H. said. "No trouble atall. That's what we're in business for. Sit down and help yourself to some coffee."

"No thank you," Gid said. "I believe we'll get the cake and get on. The longer we wait the hotter it will get."

"Then, by god, why go? A man can get too hot out working, if he ain't careful. It'll be cool agin this afternoon."

"Oh, sit down a minute," Molly said. "I got a favor to ask you."

But Gid was having a stubborn fit; he kept standing up fidgeting. Finally I got tired of standing and sat down.

"We'd sure like to get on," Gid said. "Maybe me and Johnny could just load the feed ourselves, if you'd show us where it is."

"Why sure, Gid," Samuel Houston said. "It's right over there in the corner. Just feel right at home. Show him where that cottonseed cake is, T.I."

T.I. yawned like he had just got up. "Sure," he said. "Why don't you let these boys help you pitch it in the truck? They don't mind."

I knew it would eventually come down to me helping load it. Gid would have soon handled a rattlesnake as a sack of cattle feed. He never lifted one except in emergencies. But as soon as I stood up and moved, the Mexicans grabbed the sacks and had the feed loaded in a minute and a half. And as soon as Gid saw that, he was perfectly happy to stay awhile; he felt like things were getting done.

Only he said the exact wrong thing, and Molly thought he said it to her.

"That's the stuff," he said. "We can get going in a minute now and get some work done. I wasn't raised lazy, like most people."

I don't know what possessed him to say it; maybe it was being nervous. And I don't know what possessed Molly to take it wrong; he never meant to aim it at her. But she sat her cup down and gave him the strangest hurt look.

The elevator boss drove up then, and Samuel and T.I. and the Mexicans jumped to get to work. Just us three stayed there, and it was real quiet. I tried my hardest to think of some conversation to kinda pass it all over, and I know Gid did too, but we couldn't come up with much. It was plain silly, but it was awkward as hell; five minutes of it would have made me sick.

But it never lasted over two. Molly broke down crying; I knew she would. "That wasn't a very nice thing to say to me, Gid," she said. She bent over with her head between her knees and we could only see her hair, and her head shaking. Then all of a sudden she straightened up and looked right at me. "Well, aren't you going to take up for me?" she said, and went to crying agin.

I didn't know what to say. None of it made sense. I guess she took it as something against her dad—she always tried to fool herself about him. Gid never could appreciate how hard some people worked to fool themselves.

She cried hard when she cried, but it didn't last too long. Gid was just flabbergasted. In a minute her back got still, and she looked up. The tears were dripping everywhere, but she was kinda calm agin, and nobody would have believed she had been so upset. I went over and filled her coffee cup and handed it to her. "Thank you," she said. She rested her elbows on her knees and bent over, sipping coffee, with the tears running off the corner of her mouth and dripping right in the cup. Gid couldn't stand it—he got up and fished out his handkerchief.

"Here, don't ruin that good coffee," he said.

She took it and kinda grinned at him. "What am I going to do with myself?" she said.

"Why, I'm terribly sorry, Molly," he said. "I never meant a thing by that remark."

"Oh, I know you didn't," she said. "It's silly. I don't know why some things upset me so. You ain't to blame."

But he was, really. At least he sure thought he was. We sat for about five minutes, all of us a little bit worried, drinking our coffee.

"I thought of something while I was crying," Molly said. "I hadn't thought of it in years. It was when all of us kids were at home, when we still used blackstrap molasses for all our sweetening. Daddy went in to Thalia and bought the winter groceries one day." She stopped and looked out the feedstore door, at the hot, dusty street and the houses of Thalia on the other side of it, with television serials sticking up on their roofs like I don't know what. She looked like she was looking through a telescope at something as far away as the moon. And I guess they was about that far away, them days. It takes a long memory to sit on a bunch of dogfeed sacks and call up Old Man Cletus Taylor riding off to Thalia in a wagon. I bet he had a whiskey jug on the seat beside him, too.

"When he come back, just before sundown," she said, "he had a big barrel of sorghum molasses sitting in the front of the wagon. Him and Shep went to unloading the flour and stuff, and the rest of us kids stood there looking at that syrup barrel. I couldn't hardly imagine that much syrup. It was the sweets for the whole winter. Pretty soon Dad and Shep came back and walked the barrel to the back of the wagon, so they could lift it down." Her talking quavered a little. "I never did know how it happened," she said, "but anyway, when they were lifting it out of the wagon, one of them lost his grip and it fell and busted open on the ground. The molasses stood by itself, just a second, and then it all spread out and began to run down the hill toward the chickenhouse. We all just stood there; we couldn't move for a minute. The first was when Richard stuck his toe in it. It ran real slow, and ants and doodlebugs got caught in it. There wasn't no way to scoop it up. Then we all begin to cry. Mary Margaret took it the worst. She held her breath and ran all the way around the house before anybody could catch her to pound her on the back; then she went over and began to bang her head on the cellar door. She was the worst to hold her breath and bang her head I ever saw. Even Shep was crying. Richard was the only one that showed good sense. He squatted down and stuck his finger in it and kept licking it up that way till after dark. I couldn't believe it. Nothing had hurt me that bad before. After a while Richard put a horned toad in it, and it got stuck. I went in the house and got in one of the woodboxes and wouldn't come out till after supper. Shep and Daddy argued over whose fault it was till Shep just finally left home, and Daddy stayed down in the cellar drinking whiskey nearly that whole winter."

"My god," Gid said. "That was a tragedy."

"Nothing will ever make me forget watching that sorghum run downhill," she said.

"What was that favor you wanted to ask?" Gid said.

"Oh, Old Roanie got out in the big pasture the other day," she said. "I can't get her back." Roanie was her milk cow. She was a wild old bitch.

"We'll come right on and get her," he said, standing up. Molly put up her coffee cup and got in her car, and we got in the pickup "You drive," he said.

"Don't worry," I said. "This pickup is the only means of transportation I have. I ain't anxious to let you under the wheel."

"I wish we didn't have to get that cow in," he said. "We just barely will have time to do the feeding."

"I'm glad to do it today," I said. "Another day or two and you'll be gone to have your operation, and I'd have to do it by myself."

"Molly needs to be married," he said. "She ain't able to run that place by herself. I never meant to get her so upset this morning."

"She's too touchy sometimes," I said.

"I had heard that molasses story before," he said. "That was awful. I can imagine just how them kids felt."

When we got to Molly's house she was just going in the back door. Had her mind on dinner. I went on down to the barn. Gid was out before I got stopped.

"Let's pen the old hussy and eat dinner and go," he said. "Which one you want, Chester or Matt?" Molly named her horses after *Gunsmoke.*

"Chester, I guess," I said.

"Goddamn," he said, trying to saddle up. "This old bastard's so big around it's like trying to saddle a whiskey keg."

He didn't get no sympathy from me. I had reared back to throw my saddle on and heaved and Chester had got one of his big front feet on the girt. It like to broke my back. I dropped the saddle, too.

"Well, I've shot my wad," I said, "I never will get up strength for another throw."

Gid got a big laugh out of it.

And at that the horses was easier than the cow. She was standing right in plain sight, down by the salt lick. The sight cheered Gid up.

"Well, looky there," he said. "This won't take no time. I was afraid the old bitch would be off in the mesquite somewhere."

"She may be yet," I said. "I can remember cattle closer to the gate than she is that ended up getting away. How about Mick and Big Shitty?" They were two old outlaw steers Gid had owned for about ten years. We chased them up and down Onion Creek all one summer and finally tricked them into the lot with some hay. We kept Mick, too. But Gid got careless and Big Shitty ran over him and a water trough and tore up three fences and got plumb away.

"Aw, she's just an old milk cow," he said. "You sickle around behind her thataway."

I did. Old Chester loped about as graceful as a roadgrader. At first old Roanie came along fine; actually, I just don't think she had noticed us. I think she just thought it was Chester and Matt by themselves. Molly just sooked her afoot; she might not have never seen men on horses before.

But when she figured things out, the race was on. She had her head down and her bag swinging from side to side, and she was covering country. I was closest and I whipped up: I knew if I let her get in the brush, it would be my fault from the conception to the resurrection. Chester had no idea what it was all about, but he done his best. We barely got her turned before she hit the brush; then she struck out south, just as fast, and Gid and Matt struck out to head her agin. It was the funniest sight I ever seen. Old Matt didn't no more care about that cow than if she was the moon, and when it come time to stop and turn her he just went right on into the brush. The brush went to popping and the cuss words come a-flying back. But I took in after Roanie; I didn't have no time to worry about Gid. Actually, she turned out to have about twice as much speed as Chester, and I was just hoping she'd stop for the south fence when I seen Gid and Matt come flying out of the brush ahead of me, hot on her trail. Them thorny thickets hadn't helped Gid's disposition, I knew that; he didn't have his hat any more, or all his shirt. But he had his rope down. Nobody in their right mind would try to rope off a plowhorse, but Gid would rope an elephant off a Shetland if he took a notion. He was whopping old Matt with the rope about every two steps, and Matt was going to the races. Gid came roaring over a little knoll, swinging his rope and yelling, and pretty soon he let fly and caught him a cow. It was where his troubles began. Any horse with a grain of brains would have stopped when Gid threw the rope: Matt wasn't in that category. Gid reared back on the reins—he seen his fix immediately—but Matt went right on. I guess he seen the old cow when he run by her, but he sure never dreamed him and her were connected. She was just landscape to him. Roanie got a big surprise. One minute she was headed for the high and lonesome, and the next minute Matt had got to the end of the rope and she was tearing up the land like a plow. Gid, he was just a spectator, but his sympathies were all with the cow. Finally Matt figured out he was dragging an anchor. When I rode up all three of them were panting.

"She's caught now," I said. One of her horns was broke, and her front leg stuck out sideways, about as useful as a dishrag.

"Why can't nothing go right?" he said. Not "Why can't I do nothing right?" And if I had done it, it would have been "What in the goddamn hell did you mean pulling a stunt like that?"

"One consolation," I said. "We won't never have to get her up agin."

But Gid was too blue to rag.

"Nobody's fault," I said.

"No, but I'll get blamed," he said. "And I'll furnish the new cow."

"Oh no," I said. "Molly wouldn't want you to do that. We were just being neighbors. Accidents happen sometimes."

"Mostly to me," he said. "Let's go. She'll stay till we get back."

"She won't be hard to track if she don't," I said. "Where did you lose your hat?"

His hand flew up to his head, and he turned a shade bluer. He hadn't missed it till then. Me and Chester sat on the hill and waited while he went and found it.

Of course Molly was as nice as she could be about it. If it fazed her at all, it didn't show. She had meat and beans and gravy on the table when we got there, and some roasting ears steaming in a big bowl. Sweat was dripping off the ice-tea glasses.

"I hate to lose her," she said. "But she was wild as a wolf anyway. I had to hobble her all the time." She wouldn't hear of Gid furnishing her another cow, and she wouldn't even let us go down and kill the old hussy for her. Gid was out of the talking mood, so we ate and loaded our saddles and left. Molly was standing on her back porch tying her sunbonnet strings when we left.

"I shore hate that," Gid said.

I knew he would have to get over it in his own time, so I never said nothing. Nobody could talk Gid out of feeling bad. When something happened to get his mind off things a minute he was all right, and along came one of Jamison Williams' kids to do it. He was running right down the road.

"My god, ain't he running," Gid said. "Take to the ditch, he don't see us. Get out of his way and let him go."

But when he got even with us the boy stopped right quick and went to crying. He stood there in the road crying, picking one foot and then the other out of the hot sand and cooling it against his trousers leg.

"Nelson drowned in the horse trough," he said. "Just now."

We grabbed him and went. Judith was sitting in the porch rocker, rocking and crying and hugging the boy so tight he couldn't have breathed if he had been in perfect health. "Oh St. Peter," she said, "he's drowned and gone." Gid jerked the kid away from her and turned him upside down, and I ran to the back yard and kicked the rain barrel over and got it around there. Me and Gid squeezed the boy over it till about half the horse trough ran out of his mouth, and finally he came to. Gid carried him back and gave him to Judith; she was still hysterical. I don't think she ever knew it was us that drained him; she might have thought it was St. Peter. Anyhow, we went on.

"What a day," he said.

When we got to the ranch it was done too late to feed. I unloaded the twelve sacks of feed while Gid was trying to make up his mind what to do.

"I don't never get nothing done any more," he said. "These old pens need rebuilding. And that damn fencing ain't finished. Why does a man even try?"

"I've often wondered," I said.

"Well, you damn sure don't ever accomplish nothing if you don't try," he said. "Let's sit down in the shade here a minute."

"Some people get rich without trying," I said. "Look at Pearl Twass. She used to go in the bushes with just about anybody, and now she drives around in a big Chrysler and send her kids off to fancy schools."

"Yeah, but that's just rich," he said. "That's just diamonds on a dog's ass."

"Maybe so. But Pearl don't go in the bushes so cheap any more."

"Now I got to organize," he said. "Before I go to the hospital. Wisht I never had agreed to this damn operation. No telling how long it will tie me up."

"I thought it was just a standard operation for kidney trouble," I said. "Like grinding your valves."

"Oh it is," he said. "But you never know. I'm pessimistic, I guess."

"Well, don't worry about the ranch," I said. "I've taken care of it for thirty-eight years. I won't lay down on the job now."

"That's what worries me," he said. "How well you've taken care of things. That's why nothing on this whole outfit works like it ought to."

"No, it's because you're too tight to buy good equipment," I said.

"Anyhow," he said, "and be that as it may, I'm going to draw you up enough orders to last you till I get back."

"Glad to have them," I said. "Then I'll at least know what not to do."

He wet his pencil and went to figuring, and I whittled some. The big white thunderheads were bouncing along on the south wind like tumbleweeds and the lot was a little dusty.

"I guess this will hold you for a while," he said, handing me four or five pages out of the little book. "I wrote them down so you wouldn't forget any. Don't lose them."

I gave them the once-over. "The first thing I need to do is lose these here," I said. "I ain't got no crew of Mexicans working for me."

"Just a few little chores," he said.

"I want to straighten one thing out," I said. "When Mabel took you off on that boat trip, I had a little trouble with your brother-in-law Willy. Now if he shows up this time trying to tell me what to do, he's liable to get his feelings hurt." Willy was the state representative from our district, and a fat-ass politician if there ever was one. Every year he'd show up at the town baseball games, passing out little old scrawny peaches. Once he offered me one. "You ain't too old to vote," he said. "I will be before I vote for you," I said. He shut up like I'd poured him full of alum.

"I never told you about him coming out," I said. "I didn't see no sense in embarrassing you."

"Well, by god, I like that," he said. "Willy trying to give you orders?"

"Just trying to get me to quit," I said. "Him and Mabel still think I'm a bad influence on you."

"That fat bastard," he said. "It's no wonder to me he'd try something like that."

"It ain't to me neither," I said. "I just wanted to tell you, so you wouldn't be surprised if he shows up at the hospital to tell you how nasty I was to him."

"I wouldn't care if you drowned him," he said. "Damn I wish Mabel wouldn't scheme around like that—she's behind it. Seems like the older I get, the less I know for sure."

"Well, don't lose no sleep over Willy," I said. "I just wanted to mention it."

"Just don't let him make you mad enough to quit," he said. He was so gloomy all of a sudden; he was practically planning his own funeral.

"I like that," I said. "We been friends sixty-five years. You don't think a fat-ass like Willy could run me off, do you?"

"Course not," he said. "I'm sorry."

We didn't say anything for a while.

"Molly takes her age pretty well," he said then, out of the blue. "I'm half a notion to quit Mabel and go live with her yet. I might have a few years' peace. If I live over this operation, I might just do it. You don't need to tell nobody though."

"Oh, I won't," I said, and he looked at me pretty close.

"Would that bother you much?" he said. "If I was to move in with Molly? I hadn't really thought about it from your angle."

"Why, it wouldn't bother me a bit," I said. "I think it would be good for both of you. Besides serving Mabel and Willy right." The part about it not bothering me was a plain lie, and he knew it; I kept whittling on my stick and didn't look at him.

"I guess it would though," he said, kinda sad. "We've kinda split her, haven't we? Anyhow it's just one of my crazy ideas. I doubt she'd want to do it anyway."

We sat there an hour, watching it get dark, and didn't say another word. He sure was lonesome for Molly. I was too. And neither one of us had the other fooled.

Four

I was sure right about Willy coming. About a week after Gid went to the hospital I was out one morning doctoring some puny calves, and I seen Gid's big Oldsmobile driving up to the lot. Willy got out and came toward me like I was the President. He was peeling off the glove on his handshaking hand.

"Put her there, Johnny," he said. "By god, it's been some time."

"I got screwworm dope on my hands," I said. "What can I do for you, Willy?"

"Oh, not a thing, not a thing," he said. "I was just in town staying with Mabel while Gid's in such a bad way. I thought I'd run out and see if I could be any help. To tell the truth, I could use the exercise."

"Aw, I've seen worse overweight men than you," I said. "One or two."

Actually he was just a fat tub of lard.

"Well, whatever you need doing, just show me. I wasn't raised on a dry-land farm for nothing."

"You wasn't?" I said. "I thought it was being raised on nothing on a dry-land farm was what caused you to go into politics. Or was it because you couldn't *raise* nothing?" I just came right out and got insulting when I talked to Willy. I didn't have no time to fool around.

"It's just like Mabel says," he said. "You don't try to get along with people. I came all the way out here at my own expense to see if I could be of some help, and you insult my ancestry."

"Get off the goddamn soapbox," I said. "There ain't no voters around. You know damn well whose expense you come out on—Gid's. It's just a pity he didn't throw away his car keys and cancel his charge accounts before he went in."

"Now you listen, McCloud," he said. "My sister and I have had about enough of you."

"Listen yourself," I said. "I've had a damn sight too much of you and your sister. Now you see this jar of screwworm dope? It's the blackest, shittiest-smelling stuff they ever put in a bottle. Unless you want about half a bottle on the front of that white shirt of yours, you better get in that car and skedaddle." I started around the feed trough, holding my bottle ready to throw. I would have thrown, too, if he'd opened his mouth, but he never. That's one quick way to get rid of a politician.

ONLY THE next day I ran into him agin, and he had me at a disadvantage. I had just stepped out of the domino hall.

"Well, I see you been working hard today," he said, "looking after my sister's interests."

"No, I been playing dominos all afternoon," I said. "If it's any of your business."

"Mabel's business is my business," he said. "And you're working partly for her. So I guess we ought to talk."

"My checks are signed Gideon Fry," I said. "He's the one I work for."

"That's why we need to talk," he said. "Of course you haven't seen Gideon since the operation. If you had interest enough to go see him, you'd know he won't be in any shape to give orders for a long time."

"Hell, he don't have to be in very good shape to give orders," I said. "Besides, I'm going to see him day after tomorrow."

"Well he's a very sick man," he said. "The doctors have told him he'll have to quit work completely. Now what do you think of that?"

"It don't surprise me," I said. "They're always telling him something like that. But he ain't quit yet, and even if he had I wouldn't take no orders from you or Mabel. You can take your orders and put them where the monkey put the peanut."

And that ended conversation number two.

THAT ONE worried me just a little, though. On my way home that afternoon I stopped by Molly's. She met me at the back gate.

"I was hoping you'd come by today," she said. "I've been wanting to talk to you."

"You know, I talk a lot better when I'm full," I said.

She grinned. We had black-eyed peas and turnip greens and beef for supper. And I had about half of a custard pie and the better part of a pot of coffee.

"I've got to get the weeds mowed around my barn," she said. "I nearly stepped on a snake yesterday."

"One nearly stepped on me today," I said. "He was a political snake."

"Willy Peters," she said. "I was down to see Gid yesterday."

"I was hoping you'd been," I said. "How was he?"

She looked a little worried, too. "He was still a little dopey," she said. "I never got to stay but about ten minutes."

"Willy said they told him to quit work," I said.

"Oh, they told him that ten years ago," she said. "They just tell him that on general principles. One of the nurses told me they found some kind of little old tumor, but she didn't know if it was malignant or not. I think Mabel was in the building somewhere, what made them run me off so quick. I hated to leave."

"Well, I'll be down and see him tomorrow," I said. "Maybe we'll get to talk awhile. Let's go out on the porch."

The chairs were done out there; we went out and sat down. It was dark and we sat quiet awhile, enjoying the south breeze. The white clouds were rolling over, and the moon was done up. I wished old Gid could have been there with us—he would have enjoyed the cool. I could just barely see Molly, rocking in the dark. I reached out and patted her hand.

"What ever become of that old glider?" I said. "Tonight would be a nice night to swing a little."

"Good lord," she said. "I gave it to some high-school kids who come out hunting scrap iron. I wish I had it back."

"Want to ask you something," I said. "Just out of curiosity. Gid mentioned to me once that he was kinda thinking about leaving Mabel and moving out here with you. You'all ever decide about it?"

Molly sighed and didn't say anything for a while.

"Oh, we've talked about it a lot, Johnny," she said. "But we haven't decided. Gid hates to lose little Susie. Besides, I don't know, they may take him off to the Mayo Clinic now."

"I'd make a bet they don't do that," I said.

"Well, I just wish he'd come on out here where he'd have a little peace," she said. "He's done without it all his life. I believe I could take better care of him than he's been getting."

"Well, I just wondered how you felt about it," I said.

"I guess it will come down to whether he likes me better than he does Susie," Molly said. "He's got such a conscience, you know. You got to convince him something's right or he won't touch it. Or else you got to trick him someway."

"Why hell, tricking him's twice the easiest," I said. "I can trick him nine times an hour, but I never have been able to convince him of nothing."

We sat there watching the night till almost ten o'clock. The whip-poorwills were calling all over the ridge.

"Bedtime for me," I said.

She walked to the pickup with me and told me to tell Gid hello for her. "Glad you came by," she said. "Come a little oftener."

She was standing by the running board, and I reached out and patted her shoulder. When I drove off I remembered a lot of the times when we was younger and I'd stayed the night. It wasn't that I wasn't welcome no more, either. We were just different. Use to we could chase around and have fun doing nearly anything. Now we both just got yawny. It seemed plain sad.

Five

I HAD WONDERFUL LUCK AT THE HOSPITAL—MABEL AND Willy had already left for the day, and Gid hadn't had no sedative. He had his bed cranked up so he could see out the window and watch the traffic. I knew the minute I seen him he wasn't in no danger.

"Country getting dry?" he asked. He was white as a bleached sheet, but he didn't seem weak. At least his voice wasn't.

"Some," I said.

"What do you mean, some?" he said. I could see he was primed for a long conversation.

"Just some," I said. "A rain wouldn't do no harm, but then I've seen it a damn sight dryer. We had a good shower down on the River country the day you went in."

"Just an inch, Molly said," he said. "That's already burned up."

"Now just back up," I said. "You've been lying here half-unconscious in an air-conditioned room for ten days, and you're trying to tell me how hot and dry it is?"

"I got eyes," he said. "I can see that lawn out there. They water it ever day and it's still dry.

"How's the cattle?" he said.

"They all died of blackleg and a whirlwind blew the windmill over," I said. "How's that for calamity? When you coming home?"

"Be out in two days," he said. "Don't tell nobody though. They think they're gonna keep me two more weeks." Gid was a great one for walking out of hospitals; he'd done it four or five times in his life.

"Glad to hear it," I said.

"Willy's been driving me crazy," he said. "Been bothering you?"

"Not much. I chased him off with some #62 screwworm dope. That the right tactic?"

"It'll do till I get out," he said.

"Molly said they want you to ease up," I said.

"Hell, don't they always?" he said. "If doctors had their way, the whole world would be sitting on its butt. But I'll tell you a secret. This is the last hospital I ever intend to go in. If I get to hurting too bad to live, by god I'll shoot myself, like Dad done. He had the right slant on this business, that's for sure."

"I better give you my present," I said. I had picked him up a good smooth cedar whittling stick, and I handed it to him. I didn't figure he'd hurt nobody with it. Once I give him a stockwhip, and the doctors and nurses like to ate me up. They figured he had weapons enough as it was.

But the stick tickled him to death. "Many thanks," he said. "Looks like a dandy."

About that time the door opened and a little red-headed doctor popped in.

"Well, how's the patient?" he said. We didn't say anything, and he went over and checked the charts. I knew he had come to run me out.

"Now you're coming along fine," he said. "How would it be if this gentleman left, so you could take a little nap?" He said it just a little timidly; I guess he had already had a run-in with Gid.

"It wouldn't be worth a damn," Gid said, popping the stick on the sheet.

"Well, you know a sick man needs lots of rest," the doctor said. He wasn't Gid's regular man. "I'm sure this gentlemen wouldn't mind leaving."

"What do you know about me?" I said. "I might not leave for love nor money."

"Get out of here," Gid said. "I've got some business to talk with this man. I'll sleep when I get sleepy, like I've done all my life."

"Hospital rules," the doctor said. "If he won't leave, we'll have to show him out."

"That'll be fine," I said. "Just bring a few pretty nurses to help you."

"You old cowboys seem to think the world revolves around you," he said. "We'll see about this." And he left; he was plenty mad.

Gid was popping his stick against the sheet.

"That makes me just mad enough to leave," he said. "Two days or no two days."

I didn't say a word. He looked out the window for a while.

"Bring the pickup around the side," he said. "I've had my craw full."

And twenty minutes later me and him was on the road to Thalia, and everbody but the FBI was after us. The doctors and nurses acted like it was Judgment Day. But Gid didn't pay them any mind. That Wichita hospital was nothing to the one he walked out of in Galveston one time. That time he chartered a private airplane and had himself flown home. I guess having money is right convenient sometimes.

"Now I guess you'll die," I said. "Only I'll get the blame for killing you, instead of the doctors."

"Oh, I'm all right," he said. "I'll have to be careful of my side for a while."

"Take you home?"

"Yeah, I reckon."

We drove about fifteen miles and he was feeling a little sore.

"No, by god, take me to Molly's," he said. "If I go home, they'll just knock me out and haul me back to the hospital. Take me out there. The doctor can come and see me, and you and her can help me fight off the ambulance drivers."

"Okay," I said. "Once you get strong enough to take care of yourself, I can cart you in to town."

"You know, I may never get that strong," he said. "Won't this surprise Molly?"

Myself, I figured that question was settled, if he didn't die before I got him out there. I figured he'd stay right there the rest of his life. Where that left me, I couldn't tell.

Six

Getting Gid out tickled us all. I came up the hill to Molly's honking, so I guess she thought the war was on agin. Coming over those country roads had bounced Gid up enough that I think for a while he was kinda wishing he had stayed where he was; but Molly ran out and we helped him in the house and got him installed in the big south bedroom, where he caught every breeze there was, and he picked up pretty quick. Molly asked him what she could get him, and he said fresh tomatoes, so she sliced him up a bunch fresh from the garden and brought them in to him. He ate tomatoes and drank coffee till he got his spirits back. Late that afternoon his regular doctor showed up and tried to get him to go back, but Gid wouldn't do it. The doctor had to come out and see about him every day for a while.

Just getting away from the hospital done Gid a world of good. There was a day or two when he didn't feel too spry, but in the long run he got better a lot quicker. Molly fed him good and watched after him and made him sleep a lot, and he didn't have Mabel or Willy always worrying him.

Of course I had a big run-in with Willy. I had been at the filling station, drinking a Delaware Punch. All the boys got a big laugh out of hearing about Gid. Then I ran into Willy on the sidewalk, and he motioned with his hand for me to stop.

"Willy, don't be waving me down," I said. "I ain't no motorcar."

"I guess you realize what a serious thing you done," he said. "Taking Gid out of everybody's reach."

"Whose reach?" I said. "The doctor was just out this morning and said he was improving fast."

"Well, out of the reach of the people who love him," he said. "Anyhow, when's he coming back?"

"When he gets ready, I guess," I said. "He told me yesterday he was going to start fencing agin next week. Does that ease your mind?"

"Not a bit," he said. "You know he ain't to work."

"Oh sure," I said. "I know it. But I ain't agile enough to stop him, are you?"

"Well, I just wanted to warn you," he said. "Just don't you get crosswise with the law. I got some friends who are judges."

"You'll probably need them," I said, and he left.

Molly and Gid enjoyed hearing about it. Gid was propped up in bed eating ice cream.

"I wish there was some way to run him out of the country," I said. "That's the damn trouble with democracy. You got to wait around and vote, and then the people are so stupid they put the scroungy sonsofbitches back in office."

"I don't like to hear that kind of talk," Molly said. She was democracy-crazy.

Gid handed Molly his ice-cream dish. "Uum," he said. "This is mighty nice. Only I got to get up from here and start getting a few things accomplished."

Molly frowned, but he never noticed; he was already planning. I knew right then he wouldn't be in bed much longer.

Molly done wonders, though. She fought him and argued with him and dominoed him and ice-creamed him and kept him down another week. She was working so hard keeping Gid down she was about to get down herself.

I didn't know what they had decided about him staying and living there. Molly wanted him to, that was plain as day, and I guess they must have talked about it. But never while I was there, which wasn't too often. Running the ranch kept me busy all day, and usually I got over about suppertime to see how the invalid was doing. The nights weren't too hot, and we all sat around on the porch and talked.

THEN ONE MORNING it come to a head. I was over helping Molly set up an owl trap in her chickenyard. We worked on it about an hour and looked up and seen Gid coming out the back door, all dressed and carrying his suitcase. Molly was just crushed; I guess she thought he was going to stay for good.

"Now where's he fixing to go?" she said. "He don't have to go nowhere."

I was kinda wishing I wasn't nowhere around.

But she grabbed my wrist before he got to us. "Listen," she said. "Now if I can't talk him out of going, you be sure and see he takes it easy on his work. Will you do that for me?"

"Of course I will," I said.

Gid had put his gear in the pickup, and he came over, looking proud of himself.

"Owl trouble," he said. "Can I help?"

Molly was all over him. "You sure can," she said, "you can go in out of this hot sun and get back in bed and stay there. That would help me a whole lot."

But Gid put up his bluff.

"Can't," he said. "I've got to get to working."

And we stood there. I kept on working on the trap. Molly was trembling and about to cry, I could tell. But Gid was determined.

"Don't think I ain't much obliged to you," he said. "But I've got to go to work, Molly."

She looked at me kinda funny. It was really tearing her. I was surprised to see she still had those terrible strong feelings, at her age. I never had felt things that hard, at any age.

"All right, go to work," she said. "But, honey, you don't have to leave, you can go to work and come back."

She had never called him honey in public, in all the years I'd known her, either. I was trembling a little too, from just watching, and I don't know what held Gid up.

"Yes I have, Molly," he said. "For right now, anyway. Just running off from a hospital like that ain't the right way to settle anything."

She was crying then, but neither one of us quite dared touch her.

"There never will be a way right enough for you," she said.

He said maybe there would. "And much obliged agin, for taking care of me."

I guess she thought Gid was sort of leaving her for the last time. "You're mighty welcome, Gid," she said. "God bless you." And she turned and went to the house, crying and snuffling.

"We better go if we're going," I said.

It upset Gid a good bit too. We were pretty quiet, driving to town.

"I wish I could have thought of a nicer way to leave," he said. "I hate to upset Molly."

"Well, Gid," I said. "My god, you ought to stay out there with her, if you want to. It's about time you pleased yourself a little, if you're ever going to. Or it looks that way to me."

"Well, I want to," he said. "And I may do it. In fact, I guess I intend to do it. But you can't just go off and do something like that on the spur of the moment, without making no arrangements. There's a right way and a wrong."

"And you're the only man alive that can tell them apart," I said. "Or maybe just the only one that bothers to try."

When I let him out at his house he told me to buy a keg of steeples. He said he'd be out Monday and we'd start steepling the fence. I never stopped by Molly's, going home. I couldn't think what I would say to her.

Seven

IT WAS A GOOD THING I GOT THE STEEPLES, BECAUSE Monday morning he was there before I got the milk strained. I stayed about that far behind the rest of the day.

"Are you ready?" he said.

"I'm bound to be readier than you are," I said. "I'm well, anyway."

"Shut up and let's go," he said. I sat the milk in the icebox and got my steepling hatchet. I had soaked it in water all night so the head wouldn't fly off and kill Gid.

The wires were done stretched; I had done that; so all we had to do was steeple. We didn't waste no time. I got off from him a hundred yards or so, and we started in. I guess I steepled forty or fifty posts before I thought to look around, and Gid wasn't nowhere in sight. It scared the sense out of me: I thought he'd passed out. I started running back up the fence row, but I wasn't used to running and I thought I was gonna collapse. If he hadn't of hollered, I'd have passed him right by. He wasn't over fifty yards from where he started steepling. There was a little shady shrub oak tree there and he was sitting under it fanning himself with his hat. I never saw a man so wet with sweat in my whole life.

"I didn't know you could run so fast," he said. "Where's the fire?"

"By god," I said, trying to get my breath. "It looks like it's underneath you." I had to sit down and get my breath.

"I just came out here to rest," he said. "I was getting too hot."

"My god, Gid," I said. "If you're sweating like that already, what you better do is sickle in to town and rest on some nice cool bed. It ain't good for a man in your shape to get that hot."

"Oh, I'm all right," he said. "You're more give out than me, just from that run."

"I may be out of breath," I said. "But I ain't sweated down from steepling no ten or fifteen posts."

"It was more like a hundred and fifty, the way my arm feels," he said. "But it's just sweat. Must have been them drugs they gave me. I never sweated this much before."

"Hell of a note," I said. "Why don't you let me hire a Mexican or two, to finish this fence? They work a lot cheaper than doctors."

"I never asked for no advice," he said. "I guess I know when I'm able to work and when I'm not."

"I doubt very seriously that you do," I said. "But I can't do much about it."

"You can get to steepling," he said.

And that was the way it went, the rest of the week. Gid couldn't work but thirty minutes at a time without having to rest, but he wouldn't quit. The whole week he was just up and down. I finally just let him alone about it. I guess he just had so much sweat to get out of his system. After we finished the fencing we spent a week spraying the cattle and getting them shaped up. He finally got where he could work an hour or two at a stretch, but he wasn't the hand he used to be.

I ASKED him once if he'd been by to see Molly, and he said he had. Mabel was off on a vacation in Colorado and had Sarah and Susie with her, so Gid was batching. I imagine he seen Molly a lot. I never asked him what they decided about living together, and he never said. I knew he wouldn't do nothing till Mabel got back; that would make him feel too sneaky. He didn't much want to talk about it, and I couldn't blame him particularly, so very little was ever said.

One morning he came out looking kinda blue—he had got it into his head to fix the windmill that day. It was the mill on the old Fry place, where I was living. I had used it for years and years, without no particular trouble except a worn-out sucker rod now and then. But he had done ordered a new set of pipes and a new running barrel, and everything: a man was going to bring them out from town that morning. It looked like a hell of a hard day's work, and I tried to head him off.

"Just think a minute, Gid," I said. "It's the first of September. In another month it'll be cool, and that mill won't be half as hard to fix."

"I know it'll be a little hot," he said. "But we'll just fix it anyway, while we got the time. We might be doing something else in another month. Let's go get the sucker rod out."

The sucker rod in itself wasn't much of a job, and we had it out in no time. The job was going to be lifting that old pipe out and lowering the new pipe in. I never had been much of a pipe hand, and the old stuff was corroded at the joints. It had been in long enough to be petrified.

While we were waiting for the man with the pipe to come, we sat in the shade of the waterhouse and told some old windmilling stories we saved up for days like that. I had had an uncle get killed on a windmill, and I was scared of them as I was of a rattlesnake. I told Gid about it.

"It was a steel mill," I said. "Lightning struck it while he was up working on it. Electrocuted him."

"They're dangerous," he said. "If it's a wooden mill, the dam frames are apt to break and let you fall. Remember Clarence Fierson? He got his neck broke falling off one."

"Yeah, I remember," I said. "Went around with his neck in a brace for years. Lucky at that."

Pretty soon the pipe man came and the hard work began. It was all we could do to carry the new pipe over to the windmill where we needed it. Gid got as hot as a pistol, and I wasn't cool, myself.

"I don't believe we better fool with this stuff," I said. "You'll strain your operation, lifting this shit. I can barely hold out myself."

"You want to work on the mill or on the ground?" he said.

"I'm trying to think what will be the best for you. If you get up there you'll get dizzy and fall, and if you stay down here you'll get all the heavy lifting."

"Shut up about me," he said. "I ain't collapsed yet, and I been windmilling all my life. You stay down here."

He began to unscrew this and unscrew that, and in a little while it was too late to back out, we done had the thing torn into. We spent the rest of the morning unscrewing the old rotten pipe and lifting it out.

When dinner time came we were both give out. I went in the house and fried us a little steak and made some tea, and for dinner we had steak and bread and about a gallon of iced tea apiece. We were too tired to tell any windmill stories, too. Gid flopped down on the living room couch, and I got me a pillow and stretched out on the floor. We couldn't get ourselves moving agin till two o'clock.

"Godamighty," I said, when I finally sat up. "I sure hate to go back out there."

"Yeah, them pipes will be hot," he said. "Hot and heavy."

"I can't figure you out," I said. "As much money as you got, and you're still fighting a goddamn windmill. Why do you do it, Gid?"

"Sometimes I wonder myself," he said.

We got up and went back to work. The sun was just a blur in the sky it was so hot, and the new pipes would fry an egg. It was all we could do to keep ahold of them, gloves or no gloves, and we had to cut threads in three or four joints. That took half the afternoon. Then Gid got back up in the mill and we raised the pipe and let it down in the well, a foot at a time. Once Gid lost his grip and I thought the whole shebang would go to the bottom, but I managed to slow it with my pipe wrench till he could get another hold. Finally we got the pipe run and he came down to rest. We were both wringing wet.

"Well, we're nearly done," I said. "It'll be cool in another hour. I'm kinda glad we done her, now."

"Me too," he said, mopping his face. "One thing about it, when we get this bastard fixed this time, me and you oughtn't to have to ever lay a hand on it agin. It ought to last at least twenty-five years."

"So ought we," I said. "We might get to fix it agin. We're better windmillers than I thought we were."

"A man has to be experienced like us before he has enough know-how to fix one of these things."

"Watch out now," I said. "I fixed a lot of them while I was getting the experience, and you did too. Besides, it wasn't the know-how I was worried about, it was the do-how. Two weeks ago you were flat of your back eating soup."

"Laying around in bed's what like to ruined me," he said.

We put the sucker rod in, but it liked about a foot coming up to where it was supposed to connect. So we had to go down to the barn and get another piece and replace it. The barn was beginning to make a shadow and the big heat was over for the day. Gid went up and made the connection and came back.

"Turn her on," he said. "I want to see the water run."

I turned the mill loose and a little south breeze caught the wheel. Pretty soon the old rusty water began to pour out of the hydrant, and we stood there waiting for the stream to get clear. It was still and hour to sundown, but we were two tired cowboys, I don't mind to admit. Gid was squatted down watching the water run, and I was propped up against a standard with my shirttail out, letting my belly cool. Pretty soon the rusty water washed out and the water came out of the faucet good and cold and clear. Gid stuck his mouth to the faucet and drank awhile, and then caught his breath and drank some more.

"Be careful you don't founder," I said, "drinking so much cold water."

"Sure good water," he said, leaning back on his heels. "I remember when me and Dad had that well dug. It sure has been a good well."

Then we heard water splashing behind us. We looked up and seen it was the overhead pipe, the one that went to the storage tank. We had forgot to connect it.

"I'll get it," I said. "Just take a second."

"No, go on and get you a drink," he said. "I left my pliers up there anyway."

"You're the derrick hand," I said, and went to drinking. I took about three good cool swallows and heard him yell: he had just hit the ground. I guess he lost his grip, or else his foot slipped, but he couldn't have been over three or four feet up the ladder when it happened. It didn't look like he hit very hard, either, and I seen him start to get right up, he even got his hand on a rung. Then he hesitated, and I thought one of his legs might be broke.

"Wait, Gid," I said.

I got to him and eased him down on one elbow and he never acted the least bit hurt or wild, but I don't believe he recognized me at all.

"Well, boys, he threw me agin," he said. "I'll ride him yet."

It made the hair stand up on the back of my neck for a minute. But I wasn't really worried. I thought he was just out of his senses for a minute. He had gone out of his head that way several times. He tried to get up but I held him.

"Let me up, boys," he said. "I ain't hurt."

"Okay, now, Gid," I said. "Just lay a minute and get your breath."

He minded me. "That bastard threw me, Johnny," he said. He had quit fighting to get up and lay there, looking real weak. I think that scared me the most.

"Here," I said. "Where do you think you are? You just fell off the ladder a couple of feet. That you're talking about was a long time ago."

I knew just exactly what he was thinking. When we was young there was a horse called Old Missouri, that everybody tried to ride. Dad owned him, God knows why. One day, he threw Gid six times. He never threw me but once, because I never tried to ride him but one time. But there never was a horse that Gid couldn't wear down eventually, and he finally got so he could stay on Old Missouri.

"I've been throwed harder," he said.

He went on like that for a while, and I didn't try to stop him. I figured he'd come out of it in a few minutes. But he looked weak as a fish, and I finally decided to take him on it—getting him in the car was a real job. I stretched him out on the back seat and went back and turned off the faucet at the windmill. Gid's doctor was in Wichita, but I struck for Thalia, it was closer. I started out slow, trying to miss the bumps, but I finally let that go and concentrated on speed.

When I come to the highway I stopped a minute and Gid opened his eyes and looked at me. He seemed perfectly sensible.

"What you reckon Molly's doing?" he said. "I must be slipping." Then he went off agin. "Sounds like I hear a train," he said. "Let's me and you go to the Panhandle. I'm tired of this country."

It made me sad to hear him talk that way, when it was forty years too late and him out of his mind. I begin to let the hammer down on his old Chevvy.

And then, by god, he come completely out of it. "That god-damn old windmill," he said. "Did you turn it off?"

"Last thing I did," I said.

"Well, it won't take long to make that connection," he said. "My damn side hurts. I wish I'd woke up a little sooner, I'd had you take me over to Molly's, I ain't sick enough to go to town. Maybe this time I'd have sense enough to stay there where I belong. Why don't you just take me back? I'd kinda like to see her."

"Aw, we better let a doc look at you first," I said. "I can run you out there tonight or in the morning."

Then he looked out the window, I guess: he said what he always said when he looked at the country in that part of the summertime: "The country's too dry, I sure do wish it would rain. My grass is just about gone."

I didn't say nothing to that, but I was relieved he was back in his senses. I was trying to pass a Dutchman; he was pulling a load of hay.

"Oh me, Johnny," Gid said. "Ain't this been a hell of a time?"

"It sure has, Gid" I said. The sun was near enough down to be right in my eyes, and I needed all my concentration just to drive. I thought Gid said something else, to me, to Molly, to somebody, and then he didn't say no more and I was hoping he had dozed off to sleep. But when I caught the red light by the courthouse in Thalia, and had to stop, I looked back at him and knew right then that Gideon Fry was dead.

Eight

At the clinic they said he couldn't have been dead over ten minutes, or maybe fifteen. But I guess to Gid ten minutes was just as final as ten years. A bloodclot done it, they said. Some people blamed me for bumping him over them old roads. But I don't think it would have made any difference. I couldn't have gone off and left him there on the grass by the windmill, while I drove twenty-five miles in and the doctor drove twenty-five miles back. The doctor at the clinic said the fall had started internal bleeding.

The meanest, hardest part of it all, for me, was going off that night and leaving Gid at the hospital. They wheeled him away somewhere on a stretcher, and when I asked the doctor what I could do, he said, "Nothing." I called Buck, Gid's son-in-law, and he told me which funeral home to have Gid sent to; I asked him if he knew where Mabel was, and he give me her hotel number in Colorado Springs. When I got her I said, "Well, Mabel, I've got some pretty bad news for you." "What's happened to him?" she said. "He fell off a windmill," I said. "The fall never hurt him but it caused a bloodclot and the bloodclot killed him, Mabel. He died about an hour ago." "The Lord help us," she said. "Are you sure? What am I going to do?" They said she got hysterical after she hung up.

After that, things was kind of out of my hands; there wasn't no reason for me to stay. But I couldn't hardly go. It didn't seem right to just go off and leave him there. I kept wondering which jobs around the ranch he wanted me to get done in the next day or two. But I finally seen there wasn't nothing I could do but go. None of the hospital people paid any attention to me, and I hated the smell of the place.

I DROVE out to Molly's then, and broke it to her. She came out in the yard to meet me, it was done way after dark, and I told her about it and she cried, there by the yard gate. She was awful broke up. After a while we went over to the ranch and she drove Gid's car back to town for me and I followed in the pickup. We left it at Buck's. When we got back to Molly's she had quit crying for a little while.

"Well, come on in, let's make some coffee," she said. "You'll stay here with me tonight, won't you?"

"Of course," I said.

It was a sure sad night for us, but we didn't say fifteen words. We drank a good bit of coffee.

"You know, the night we got the word about Jimmy, me and Gid played dominos," she said.

"You want to play some tonight?" I said.

"Oh lord no," she said. "I'd rather not."

It was the first time I'd spent a whole night with Molly in three or four years, maybe longer than that. She went in the bathroom and put on her white nightgown and I got in bed. I held her hand and we both lay there awake for an hour and a half, on our backs. Once in a while Molly sniffled, but she wasn't crying much.

"Well, he was some feller," I said. "I don't expect to ever see another like him. You know that saddle he gave me? That's the most expensive saddle ever made in the Thalia saddle shop. Me and him had a big fight the day he give it to me. Over you, I guess."

I guess it was worse for Molly. Him and her had associated so much there, in the house, right there in that same bedroom we was in, there was no telling what all she was remembering. I guess he was all over the room, for her.

"Gid was my favorite," she said. I finally went to sleep, I don't know whether she did or not.

In the morning, when I woke up, an unusual thing happened. I had turned over during the night and I had my arm across Molly's middle and my face was in her hair. When I got my eyes open she was looking right square at me. There were dark circles under her eyes, but she had just the trace of a grin on her face. For a minute I didn't know why, and then I noticed myself. As old as I was, too, and on a morning like that. And Molly had done noticed, that's why she was watching me. At first I was plumb embarrassed.

"Well, I swear," I said. I didn't know what else to say.

But she grinned, and squeezed my hand. "That's the first time I've ever seen you embarrassed," she said. "I've had to wait sixty-two years."

"Well, it ain't because of that." I said. You've caused that many a time. You've stayed too pretty. It's because of Gid I'm embarrassed."

"I don't want you to be," she said. "That's nature, she ain't no respecter. I don't want you to be embarrassed even if we're a hundred years old." Then she grinned a sad grin; for a minute she reminded me of herself when she was twenty years old. "And you better not waste it, either," she said.

"You're an unusual woman," I said, rubbing her side. "Only it ain't much to waste. If old Gid can't, then by god I won't neither, how's that?"

"About as foolish as something he'd say," she said. "Only thank god you won't stick to it like he did." And she rolled over and hugged me and cried for an hour, at least. I had to get up and hunt a box of Kleenex.

Nine

A WEEK AFTER THE FUNERAL I STOPPED BY MOLLY'S house; she never heard the car come up. She was out in the garden, and I walked around the house and stood by the gate a minute, watching her. The garden was just about gone. When I walked out she was down on her knees, pulling onions and putting them in her apron.

"You're getting a little deaf," I said. "A person could sneak up on you."

She grinned, happy and jolly as could be. "Hold these onions for me," she said.

"Let's go sit in the kitchen, where it's cool and there's something to eat," I said.

But she took me to the porch, instead. "You can eat here, what there is," she said. "Cold potato pie is all there is, and you don't like it. I didn't figure you'd come tonight."

"I just like two kinds of pie," I said. "Hot and cold. Go get me some."

We ate a little pie and rocked awhile and she brought out some coffee.

"Well, I'm all packed," I said. "I guess I'll move tomorrow." They had fired me, of course—I was going back to the old McCloud place, three mile off. It wasn't a very long move.

"They didn't allow you much time," she said.

"Aw yeah," I said. "They said no hurry. But it don't take much time to move what little I got."

We talked a little while, about Gid and the will and one thing and another. Gid had left me the old pickup and a thousand acres of land—

he couldn't stand for me not to increase my holdings by at least that much. So I was set pretty for my old age—I done had two sections I inherited from Dad. That thousand acres sure burned Mabel and Willy; they thought the pickup would have been enough. He just left Molly his dad's old pocket watch. I guess he knew Mabel would have gone to court if he had left her anything more. Molly was plenty satisfied.

After a while the new moon came up, about the size of a basketball, and the conversation petered out. I could see Molly's face, and she looked tired. I was too. I gave her my pieplate to take in the house, and when she came back we walked around to the pickup together. The moon was so bright we could see the chickens roosting on the chickenhouse.

I had something big on my mind and I didn't know how to get it up. It just seemed like I better ask Molly to marry me, for the sake of all our old times, but I didn't know whether she'd much want to, and I didn't even know if I much wanted to, we got along so well like we were. Finally I came out with it; I was standing with my arm around her.

"Well, Molly, what would you think about us marrying?" I said.

"I'd think we ain't the kind, honey," she said, "but thank you a whole lot for asking."

It was kind of a sad relief. "It's a damn strange time for me to do it," I said. "I could have asked you forty years ago."

"We lived them pretty good," she said. "It ain't as important a question as a lot of people think."

"Don't you miss Gid?" I said. "I never thought I'd miss such a contrary so-and-so so much."

"Oh yes," she said.

"Molly, just for curiosity," I said. "Do you think you and him would have taken up together for good, if he had lived?"

She put one of her hands in my hip pocket and pulled out my handkerchief to see if it was clean. She had to smell it. This one wasn't, and she kept it so she could wash it.

"We'd decided to," she said. "I guess we decided about thirty times. And I think in about another year I would have got his conscience quiet enough and his nerve worked up so he could have come out and stayed."

We thought about it a minute.

"You know I think he worried about you as much as he did Mabel," she said. "He kept saying it wouldn't be fair to you if he moved out here." She gave me a long look. "I got sick of him wanting to be so fair to you," she said, "and I even got sick of you being around for him to worry about. You may have noticed."

"No," I said. "But I imagine it's true."

"Johnny, when it came to him, I just never cared to be fair, " she said.

"I don't blame you none."

When I got in the pickup she leaned in and kissed me on the cheek. "I'll take you in to a ballgame one of these cool nights," I said.

"I wish you would," she said. "I ain't been to a half a dozen games since Joe quit playing."

I started to drive off, but she had ahold of my arm. "I'll have a better supper tomorrow night," she said. "Just because we ain't marrying don't mean you're free to miss a night. You're welcome here every night, all night, when you feel like putting up with me."

"I'll be here in time to carve the beef," I said, and drove off. I felt pretty blue driving down the hill, and kinda wished I had stayed that night. But sometimes you can't get around being lonesome for a while.

I TOOK my time driving home on those old bumpy roads. When I got back to the house I put the pickup in the garage and shut the doors. I had me some Delaware Punches in the icebox and I got one and went out on the screened-in porch. Over at Molly's I had been a little sleepy, but the drive had woke me up.

The porch was cool, and the night was real quiet. I set my Punch bottle down and stepped out in the yard to take a leak. I could hear an oil rig working way over in the Dale, but except for that and a few crickets the night was perfectly still. When I got through I didn't much want to go in, so I walked around the old Fry place for a while, watching that white moon circling out over Gid's pastures. It was strange how I never knowed till Gid died just how used to him I was.

"You old so-and-so," I said. "You wouldn't listen. I offered to go up and fix that thing, but no sir, you had to do it yourself."

"Aw, you couldn't have fixed it if you'd a gone," he said. "You never was no hand with pipe."

"Hell no, a cowboy ain't supposed to be," I said.

"That's all right. Who made the fortune, and who worked for wages all his life?"

"You might have made the fortune," I said. "But I'd just like to know what good it did you. Working like a Turk. Which one of us was satisfied?"

"Hell, that's easy," he said. "Neither one. We neither one married her, did we?"

Talking to myself. Gid was off in the Great Perhaps. I looked around at the house and down toward the barn. One man's whoop is another man's holler, anyhow. At least Gid was stubborn about it. I remembered one election day, when I gave him hell. Me and Molly had the first shift. The bloom was really on the peach, as far as she was concerned. She wore a blue dress with white dots on it and never wore nothing on her hair. About two weeks before that I had got to spend my first whole night with her. We was there an hour by ourselves, and kissed and walked around and had the best time: I pumped my hat full of water so she could get a drink. Then Gid come and talked her into staying with him after I was supposed to leave. Only he had old Ikey for a partner and had to scheme around someway to get rid of him, I don't remember how he finally done it. It tickled me. He thought he'd have Molly to himself for two hours or so. I left about the time Ikey did and circled around and intercepted him; he was riding that old crippled mule. "Ikey, you ought to be ashamed of yourself," I said. "Living in a free country where they let you vote. And the first time the government gives you a little job you let somebody send you off on some damn errand. If you know what's good for you, you'll turn that mule around and get back up there where you belong." I broke me off a good-sized mesquite limb and handed it to him. "See if you can get that mule in locomotion," I said. I guess he thought I intended to use it on him. "Yes suh, Mistuh Johnny," he said. "I sure get back. I didn't inten' to leave in de fust place." So poor Gid got about twenty minutes. I guess it was kinda mean, really—nobody gets enough chances at the wild and sweet. But he would have done the same thing. There's just two things about it that I really regret. One was not being there to see the look on Gid's face when he heard that crippled mule clomping up, and the other is forgetting to bring a Kodak that morning, so I could have got a picture of Molly while she was sitting in her blue and white dress on the schoolhouse steps.

THREE GRAVESTONES

GIDEON FRY
1896–1962

MOLLY TAYLOR WHITE
1900–1976

JOHNNY MC CLOUD
1898–1985

THE LAST PICTURE SHOW

THE LAST PICTURE SHOW is lovingly dedicated to my home town.

One

Sometimes Sonny felt like he was the only human creature in the town. It was a bad feeling, and it usually came on him in the mornings early, when the streets were completely empty, the way they were one Saturday morning in late November. The night before Sonny had played his last game of football for Thalia High School, but it wasn't that that made him feel so strange and alone. It was just the look of the town.

There was only one car parked on the courthouse square—the night watchman's old white Nash. A cold norther was singing in off the plains, swirling long ribbons of dust down Main street, the only street in Thalia with businesses on it. Sonny's pickup was a '41 Chevrolet, not at its best on cold mornings. In front of the picture show it coughed out and had to be choked for a while, but then it started again and jerked its way to the red light, blowing out spumes of white exhaust that the wind whipped away.

At the red light he started to turn south toward the all-night café, but when he looked north to see if anyone was coming he turned that way instead. No one at all was coming but he saw his young friend Billy, headed out. He had his broom and was sweeping right down the middle of the highway into the gusting wind. Billy lived at the poolhall with Sam the Lion, and sweeping was all he really knew how to do. The only trouble was that he overdid it. He swept out the poolhall in the mornings, the café in the afternoons, and the picture show at night, and always, unless someone specifically told him to stop, he just kept sweeping, down the sidewalk, on through the town, sometimes one way and sometimes another, sweeping happily on until someone noticed him and brought him back to the poolhall.

Sonny drove up beside him and honked. Billy quit sweeping at once and got in the pickup. He was a stocky boy, not very smart, but perfectly friendly; picking him up made Sonny feel less lonesome. If Billy was out the poolhall must be open, and when the poolhall was open he was never lonesome. One of the nice things about living in Thalia was that the poolhall often opened by 6:30 or 7 A.M., the reason being that Sam the Lion, who owned it, was a very bad sleeper.

Sonny drove to the hall and parked and took Billy's broom so he wouldn't go sweeping off again. The air was so dry and dusty it made the nostrils sting and the two boys hustled inside. Sam the Lion was up, all right, brushing one of the snooker tables. He was an old man, but big and heavy, with a mane of white hair; cold weather made his feet swell and he wore his old sheepskin house shoes to work in in the wintertime. He was expecting the boys and barely gave them a glance.

Once they were inside, Sonny let Billy have the broom again and Billy immediately went over to the gas stove to warm himself. While he warmed he leaned on the broom and licked a piece of green pool chalk. Sam the Lion didn't particularly care that Billy licked chalk all the time; it was cheap enough nourishment, he said. Sonny got himself a package of Cheese Crisps and made room for himself at the stove, turning Billy's cap around backward for friendship's sake. It was an old green baseball cap some lady had given Billy three or four summers before.

"Cold in here, Sam," Sonny said. "It's nearly as cold in here as it is outside."

"Not as windy, though," Sam replied. "I'm surprised you had the nerve to come in this mornin', after the beatin' you all took. Anybody ever tell you boys about blockin'? Or tacklin'?"

Sonny ate his Cheese Crisps, unabashed. Crowell, the visiting team, had tromped Thalia 28 to 6. it had been a little embarrassing for

Coach Popper, but that was because the local Quarterback Club had been so sure Thalia was finally going to win a District Crown that they had literally jumped the gun and presented the coach with a new .12 gauge Marlin under-over at the homecoming game two weeks before. The coach was quite a hunter. Two of Crowell's four touchdowns had been run over Sonny's guard position, but he felt quite calm about it all. Four years of playing for Thalia had inured him to defeat, and so far as he was concerned the Quarterback Club had been foolishly optimistic.

Besides, he could not see that he had much to gain by helping the coach get new shotguns, the coach being a man of most uncertain temper. He had already shot at Sonny once in his life, and with a new under-over he might not miss.

"Where's your buddy?" Sam asked.

"Not in yet," Sonny said. That was Duane, Sonny's best friend, who besides being an All-Conference fullback, roughnecked the midnight tower with a local drilling crew.

"Duane's gonna work himself into an early grave," Sam the Lion said. "He oughtn't to play a football game and then go out and work all night on top of it. He made half the yardage we made."

"Well, that never tired him out," Sonny said, going to get another package of Cheese Crisps.

Sam the Lion started to cough, and the coughing got away from him, as it often did. His whole body shook; he couldn't stop. Finally he had to stagger back to the washroom and take a drink of water and a swig of cough medicine to get it under control.

"Suckin' in too much chalk dust," he said when he came back. Billy hardly noticed, but Sonny felt a little uneasy. He didn't like to be reminded that Sam the Lion was not as young or as healthy as he once had been. Sam the Lion was the man who took care of things, particularly of boys, and Sonny did not like to think that he might die. The reason Sam was so especially good to boys was that he himself had had three sons, none of whom lived to be eighteen. The first was killed when Sam was still a rancher: he and his son were trying to drive a herd of yearlings across the Little Wichita River one day when it was up, and the boy had been knocked loose from his horse, pawed under, and drowned. A few years later, after Sam had gone into the oil business, a gas explosion knocked his second son off a derrick. He fell over fifty feet and was dead before they got him to town. Sam sold his oil holdings and put in the first Ford agency in Thalia, and his youngest son was run over by a deputy sheriff. His wife lost her mind and spent her last ten years rocking in a rocking chair. Sam drank a lot, quit going to church, and was said to be loose with women, even married women.

He began to come out of it when he bought the picture show, or so people said. He got lots of comedies and serials and Westerns and the kids came as often as they could talk their parents into letting them. Then Sam bought the poolhall and the all-night café and he perked up more and more.

No one really knew why he was called Sam the Lion. Some thought it was because he hated barbers and always went around with a shaggy head of hair. Others thought it was because he had been such a hell-raising cowboy when he was young, but Sonny found that a little hard to believe. He had seen Sam mad only once, and that was one Fourth of July when Duane stuck a Roman candle in the pocket of one of the snooker tables and set it off. When it finally quit shooting, Sam grabbed the pisspot and chased Duane out, meaning to sling it at him. He slung it, but Duane was too quick. Joe Bob Blanton, the Methodist preacher's son, happened to be standing on the sidewalk wishing he was allowed to go in and shoot pool, and he was the one that got drenched. The boys all got a big laugh but Sam the Lion was embarrassed about it and cleaned Joe Bob off as best he could.

When he was thoroughly warm Sonny got one of the brushes and began to brush the eight-ball tables. Sam went over and looked disgustedly at the two nickels Sonny had left for the Cheese Crisps.

"You'll never get nowhere, Sonny," he said. "You've already spent a dime today and you ain't even had a decent breakfast. Billy, you might get the other side of the hall swept out, son."

While the boys worked Sam stood by the stove and warmed his aching feet. He wished Sonny weren't so reckless economically, but there was nothing he could do about it. Billy was less of a problem, partly because he was so dumb. Billy's real father was an old railroad man who had worked in Thalia for a short time just before the war; his mother was a deaf and dumb girl who had no people except an aunt. The old man cornered the girl in the balcony of the picture show one night and begat Billy. The sheriff saw to it that the old man married the girl, but she died when Billy was born and he was raised by the family of Mexicans who helped the old man keep the railroad track repaired. After the war the hauling petered out and the track was taken up. The old man left and got a job bumping cars on a stockyards track in Oklahoma, leaving Billy with the Mexicans. They hung around for several more years, piling prickly pear and grubbing mesquite, but then a man from Plainview talked them into moving out there to pick cotton. They snuck off one morning and left Billy sitting on the curb in front of the picture show.

From then on, Sam the Lion took care of him. Billy learned to sweep, and he kept all three of Sam's places swept out; in return he got his keep and also, every single night, he got to watch the picture show. He always sat in the balcony, his broom at his side; for years he saw every show that came to Thalia, and so far as anyone knew, he liked them all. He was never known to leave while the screen was lit.

"You workin' today?" Sam asked, noticing that Sonny was taking his time brushing the eight-ball table.

"The truck's being greased," Sonny said. On weekends, and sometimes week-nights too, he drove a butane truck for Frank Fartley of Fartley Butane and Propane. He didn't make as much money as his friend Duane made roughnecking, but the work was easier.

Just as Sam the Lion was about to get back to the subject of the football game they all heard a familiar sound and paused to listen.

Abilene was coming into town in his Mercury. Abilene was the driller Duane worked for. He had spent a lot of money souping up the Mercury, and in Thalia the sound of his exhausts was as unmistakable as the sound of the wind.

"Well, we barely got 'em clean in time," Sam said. Abilene not only had the best car in the country, he also shot the best stick of pool. Drilling and pool shooting were things he did so well that no one could decide which was his true vocation and which his avocation. Some mornings he went home and cleaned up before he came to the poolhall—he liked to be clean and well dressed when he gambled—but if it was too early for any of the nine-ball players to be up he would often stop and practice in his drilling clothes.

The Mercury stopped in front of the poolhall and Sam went over and got Abilene's ivory-banded cue out of the padlocked rack and laid it on the counter for him. When the door opened the wind sliced inside ahead of the man. Abilene had on sunglasses and the heavy green coveralls he wore to protect his clothes from the oil-field grease; as soon as he was in he unzipped the coveralls and hung them on a nail Sam had fixed for him. His blue wool shirt and gabardine pants were creased and trim.

"Mornin'," Sam said.

"Mornin'," Abilene replied, handing Sam his expensive-looking sunglasses. He once had a pair fall out of his pocket and break when he was bending over to pick up a piece of pool chalk; after that he always had Sam put the sunglasses in a drawer for him. Though he was the poolhall's best customer, he and Sam the Lion had almost nothing to say to one another. Abilene paid Sam two hundred and fifty dollars a year for a private key to the poolhall, so he could come in and practice any time he wanted to. Often Sonny would come in from some long butane run at two or three o'clock in the morning and see that Abilene was in the poolhall, practicing. The garage where the butane truck was kept was right across the street from the poolhall and sometimes Sonny would walk across and stand by one of the windows watching Abilene shoot. No one ever tried to go in when Abilene was in the poolhall alone.

"Let's shoot one, Sonny," Abilene said. "I feel like a little snooker before breakfast."

Sonny was taken by surprise. He knew he would not even be good competition for Abilene, but he went and got a cue anyway. It did not occur to him to turn down the invitation. Abilene shot first and ran thirty points off the break.

"Duane didn't go to sleep on you last night, did he?" Sonny asked, feeling that he ought at least to make conversation.

"No, the breeze kept us awake," Abilene replied. That was their conversation. Sonny only got to shoot four times; for the most part he just stood back and watched Abilene move gracefully around the green table, easing in his shots with the ivory-banded cue. He won the game by 175 points.

"You shoot pool about like you play football," he said, when the game was over.

Sonny ignored the insult and pitched a quarter on the felt to pay for the game. Abilene insulted everybody, young and old alike, and Sonny was not obliged to take it personally. Sam the Lion came over to rack the balls.

"I hope they hurry and get that truck greased," he said. "The way your fortune's sinking you'll be bankrupt before you get out of here."

"What'd our bet come to, Sam," Abilene asked casually. He busted the fresh rack and started shooting red balls. Sam grinned at Sonny and went over to the cash register and got five ten-dollar bills. He laid them on the side of the snooker table and when Abilene noticed them he took a money clip out of his pocket and put the fifty dollars in it.

"It's what I get for bettin' on my hometown ball club," Sam said. "I ought to have better sense."

"It wouldn't hurt if you had a better home town," Abilene said.

Sam always bet on the boys, thinking it would make them feel good, but the strategy seldom worked because they almost always lost.

Most of them only trained when they felt like it, and that was not very often. The few who did train were handicapped by their intense dislike of Coach Popper. Sonny was not alone in considering the coach a horse's ass, but the school board liked the coach and never considered firing him: he was a man's man, and he worked cheap. They saw no reason to hire a better coach until a better bunch of boys came along, and there was no telling when that would be. Sam the Lion went loyally on losing money, while Abilene, who invariably bet against Thalia, cleared about a thousand dollars a season from Sam and others like him.

While Sam and Sonny were idly watching Abilene practice, Billy swept quietly down the other side of the poolhall and on out the door. The cold wind that came through the door when Billy went out woke them up. "Go get him, Sonny," Sam said. "Make him put his broom up for a while."

Billy hadn't had time to get far; he was just three doors away, in front of what once had been the Thalia Pontiac Agency. He was calmly sweeping north, into the cold wind. All his floor-sweep had already blown away, but he was quite content to sweep at the curling ribbons of sand that the wind blew past him. A time or two in his life he had swept all the way to the Thalia city limits sign before anyone had noticed him.

When Sonny stepped out of the poolhall the black pickup that the roughnecks used was stopped at the red light. The light changed and the pickup passed the courthouse and slowed a moment at the corner by the poolhall, so Duane could jump out. He was a tall boy with curly black hair. Because he was a fullback and a roughneck he held himself a little stiffly. He had on Levi's and a Levi's jacket with the collar turned up. Sonny pointed at Billy and he and Duane each grabbed one of Billy's arms and hustled him back down the sidewalk into the warming poolhall. Sam took the broom and put it up on a shelf where Billy couldn't reach it.

"Let's go eat, buddy," Duane said, knowing that Sonny had put off having breakfast until he came.

Sam the Lion looked Duane over carefully to see if he could detect any symptoms of overwork, but Duane was in his usual Saturday morning good humor, and if there were such symptoms they didn't show.

"If you boys are going to the café, take this change for me," Sam said, pitching Sonny the dark green coin sack that he used to tote change from one of his establishments to the other. Sonny caught it and the boys hurried out and jogged down the street two blocks to the café, tucking their heads down so the wind wouldn't take their breath. "Boy, I froze my ass last night," Duane grunted, as they ran.

The café was a little one-story red building, so deliciously warm inside that all the windows were steamed over. Penny, the daytime waitress, was in the kitchen frying eggs for a couple of truck drivers, so Sonny set the change sack on the cash register. There was no sign of old Marston, the cook. The boys counted their money and found they had only eighty cents between them.

"I had to shoot Abilene a game of snooker," Sonny explained. "If it hadn't been for that I'd have a quarter more."

"We got enough," Duane said. They were always short of money on Saturday morning, but they were paid Saturday afternoon, so it was no calamity. They ordered eggs and sausage and flipped to see who got what—by the end of the week they often ended up splitting meals. Sonny got the sausage and Duane the eggs.

While Penny was counting the new change into the cash register old Marston came dragging in. He looked as though he had just frozen out of a bar ditch somewhere, and Penny was on him instantly.

"Where you been, you old fart?" she yelled. "I done had to cook ten orders and you know I ain't no cook."

"I swear, Penny," Marston said. "I just forgot to set my alarm clock last night."

"You're a lying old sot if I ever saw one," Penny said. "I ought to douse you under the hydrant a time or two, maybe you wouldn't stink of whiskey so much."

Marston slipped by her and had his apron on in a minute. Penny was a 185-pound redhead, not given to idle threats. She was Church of Christ and didn't mind calling a sinner a sinner. Five years before she had accidentally gotten pregnant before she was engaged; the whole town knew about it and Penny got a lot of backhanded sympathy. The ladies of the community thought it was just awful for a girl that fat to get pregnant. Once married, she discovered she didn't much like her husband, and that made her harder to get along with in general. On Wednesday nights, when the Church of Christ held its prayer meetings and shouting contests anybody who happened to be within half a mile of the church could hear what Penny thought about wickedness; it was old Marston's misfortune to hear it every morning, and at considerably closer range. He only worked to drink, and the thought of being doused under a hydrant made him so shaky he could barely turn the eggs.

Sonny and Duane winked at him to cheer him up, and gave Penny the finger when she wasn't looking. They also managed to indicate that they were broke, so Marston would put a couple of extra slices of toast on the order. The boys gave him a ride to the county-line liquor store once a week, and in return he helped out with extra food when their money was low.

"How we gonna work it tonight?" Duane asked. He and Sonny owned the Chevrolet pickup jointly, and because there were two of them and only one pickup their Saturday night dating was a little complicated.

"We might as well wait and see," Sonny replied, looking disgustedly at the grape jelly Marston had put on the plate. He hated grape jelly, and the café never seemed to have any other kind.

"If I have to make a delivery to Ranger this afternoon there won't be no problem," he added. "You just take the pickup. If I get back in time I can meet Charlene at the picture show."

"Okay," Duane said, glad to get that off his mind. Sonny never got the pickup first on Saturday night and Duane always felt slightly guilty about it but not quite guilty enough to change anything.

The problem was that he was going with Jacy Farrow whose folks were rich enough to make them unenthusiastic about her going with a poor boy like Duane. He and Jacy couldn't use her car because her father, Gene Farrow, made a point of driving by the picture show every Saturday night to see that Jacy's car was parked out front. They were able to get around that easily enough by sneaking out the back of the show and going somewhere in the pickup, but that arrangement created something of a courting problem for Sonny, who went with a girl named Charlene Duggs. Charlene had to be home by eleven thirty, and if Duane and Jacy kept the pickup tied up until almost eleven, it didn't allow Sonny much time in which to make out.

Sonny had assured Duane time and time again that he didn't particularly care, but Duane remained secretly uneasy. His uneasiness really stemmed from the fact that he was going with Jacy, the prettiest, most desirable girl in town, while Sonny was only going with Charlene Duggs, a mediocre date by any standard. Occasionally the two couples double-dated, but that was really harder on Sonny than no date at all. With all four of them squeezed up in the cab of the pickup it was impossible for him to ignore the fact that Jacy was several times as desirable as Charlene. Even if it was totally dark, her perfume smelled better. For days after such a date Sonny had very disloyal fantasies involving himself and Jacy, and after an hour's sloppy necking with Charlene even the fantasy that he was kissing Jacy had a dangerous power. Charlene kissed convulsively, as if she had just swallowed a golf ball and was trying to force it back up.

Of course Sonny had often considered breaking up with Charlene, but there weren't many girls in the town and the only unattached girl who was any prettier than Charlene was an unusually prudish sophomore. Charlene would let Sonny do anything he wanted to above the waist; it was only as time wore on that he had begun to realize that there really wasn't much of permanent interest to do in that zone. As the weeks went by, Sonny observed that Jacy seemed to become more and more delightful, passionate, inventive, while by contrast Charlene just seemed more of a slug.

When the boys finished eating and paid their check they had a nickel left. Duane was going home to bed, so Sonny kept the nickel; he could buy himself a Butterfinger for lunch. Outside the air was still cold and dusty and gray clouds were blowing south off the High Plains.

Duane took the pickup and went to the rooming house where the two of them had roomed since their sophomore year. People thought it a little strange, because each had a parent alive, but the boys liked it. Sonny's father ran the local domino parlor and lived in a room at the little hotel, and Duane's mother didn't really have much more room. His grandmother was still alive and living with his mother in their two-room house; his mother took in laundry, so the house was pretty full. The boys were actually rather proud that they lived in a rooming house and paid their own rent; most of the boys with real homes envied the two their freedom. Nobody envied them Old Lady Malone, of course, but she owned the rooming house and couldn't be helped. She was nosy, dipped snuff, had a compulsion about turning off fires, and was afflicted with one of the most persistent cases of diarrhea on record. The one bathroom was so badly aired that the boys frequently performed their morning toilet in the rest room of the Texaco filling station.

After Sonny got his delivery orders he jogged up the street to the filling station to get the truck, an old green International. The seat springs had about worn through the padding, and most of the rubber was gone from the footpedals. Still, it ran, and Sonny gunned it a few times and struck out for Megargel, a town even smaller than Thalia. Out in the open country the norther gusted strongly across the highway, making the truck hard to hold. Once in a while a big ragweed would shake loose from the barbed-wire fences and skitter across the road, only to catch again in the barbed-wire fence on the other side. The dry grass in the pastures was gray-brown, and the leafless winter mesquite gray-black. A few Hereford yearlings wandered dispiritedly into the wind, the only signs of life; there was really nothing between Thalia and Megargel but thirty miles of lonesome country. Except for a few sandscraped ranch houses there was nothing to see but a long succession of low brown ridges, with the wind singing over them. It occurred to Sonny that perhaps people called them "blue northers" because it was so hard not to get blue when one was blowing. He regretted that he had not asked Billy to ride along with him on the morning deliveries. Billy was no talker, but he was company, and with nobody at all on the road or in the cab Sonny sometimes got the funny feeling that he was driving the old truck around and around in a completely empty place.

Two

Sonny's next delivery after Megargel was in Scotland, a farming community fifty miles in the opposite direction. As luck would have it he arrived at the farm where the butane was needed while the farmer and his family were in town doing their weekly shopping. The butane tank was in their backyard, and so were nine dogs, six of them chows.

Besides the chows, which were all brown and ill-tempered, there was a German shepherd, a rat terrier, and a subdued black cocker that the farmer had given his kids for a Christmas present. When Sonny approached the yard gate the chows leapt and snarled and tried to bite through the wire. It seemed very unlikely that he could bluff them, but he stood outside the gate for several minutes getting up his nerve to try. While he was standing there five little teal flew off a stock tank north of the house and angled south over the yard. The sight of them made Sonny long for a shotgun of his own, and some ammunition money; all his life he had hunted with borrowed guns. The longer he stood at the gate the more certain he became that the dogs could not be bluffed, and he finally turned and walked back to the truck, a little depressed. He had never owned a shotgun, and he had never found a yardful of dogs that he could intimidate, at least not around Scotland. He sat in the truck for almost an hour, enjoying fantasies of himself carrying Jacy Farrow past dozens of sullen but respectful chows.

Just before noon the farmer came driving up, his red GMC pickup loaded with groceries, kids, and a fat-ankled wife. Some of the kids looked meaner than the dogs.

"Hell, you should just 'a gone on in," the farmer said cheerfully. "Them dogs don't bite many people."

Like so many Saturdays, it was a long work day; when Sonny rattled back into Thalia after his last delivery it was almost 10 P.M. He found his boss, Frank Fartley, in the poolhall shooting his usual comical Saturday night eight-ball game. The reason it was comical was because Mr. Fartley's cigar was cocked at such an angle that there was always a small dense cloud of white smoke between his eye and the cue ball. He tried to compensate for not being able to see the cue ball by lunging madly with his cue at a spot where he thought it was, a style of play that made Sam the Lion terribly nervous because it was not only hard on the felt but also extremely dangerous to unwatchful kibitzers, one or two of whom had been rather seriously speared. When Sonny came in Frank stopped lunging long enough to give him his check, and Sonny immediately got Sam the Lion to cash it. Abilene was there, dressed in a dark brown pearl-buttoned shirt and gray slacks; he was shooting nine-ball at five dollars a game with Lester Marlow, his usual Saturday night opponent.

Lester was a wealthy boy from Wichita Falls who came to Thalia often. Ostensibly, his purpose in coming was to screw Jacy Farrow, but his suit was not progressing too well and the real reason he kept coming was because losing large sums of money to Abilene gave him a certain local prestige. It was very important to Lester that he do *something* big, and since losing was a lot easier than winning, he contented himself with losing big.

Sonny had watched the two shoot so many times that it held no interest for him, so he took his week's wages and walked across the dark courthouse lawn to the picture show. Jacy's white Ford convertible was parked out front, where it always was on Saturday night. The movie that night was called *Storm Warning*, and the posterboards held pictures of Doris Day, Ronald Reagan, Steve Cochran, and Ginger Rogers. It was past 10 P.M., and Miss Mosey, who sold tickets, had already closed the window; Sonny found her in the lobby, cleaning out the popcorn machine. She was a thin little old lady with such bad eyesight and hearing that she sometimes had to walk halfway down the aisle to tell whether the comedy or the newsreel was on.

"My goodness, Frank oughtn't to work you so late on weekends," she said. "You done missed the comedy so you don't need to give me but thirty cents."

Sonny thanked her and bought a package of Doublemint gum before he went into the show. Very few people ever came to the late feature; there were not more than twenty in the whole theater. As soon as his eyes adjusted Sonny determined that Jacy and Duane were still out parking; Charlene Duggs was sitting about halfway down the aisle with her little sister Marlene. Sonny walked down the aisle and tapped her on the shoulder, and the two girls scooted over a seat.

"I decided you had a wreck," Charlene said, not bothering to whisper. She smelled like powder and toilet water.

"You two want some chewin' gum?" Sonny offered, holding out the package. The girls each instantly took a stick and popped the gum into their mouths almost simultaneously. They never had any gum money themselves and were both great moochers. Their father, Royce Duggs, ran a dinky little one-man garage out on the highway; most of his work was done on pickups and tractors, and money was tight. The girls would not have been able to afford the toilet water either, but their mother, Beulah Duggs, had a secret passion for it and bought it with money that Royce Duggs thought was going for the girls' school lunches. The three of them could only get away with using it on Saturday night when Royce was customarily too drunk to be able to smell.

After the feature had been playing for a few minutes Sonny and Charlene got up and moved back into one of the corners. It made Sonny nervous to sit with Charlene and Marlene both. Even though Charlene was a senior and Marlene just a sophomore, the two looked so much alike that he was afraid he might accidentally start holding hands with the wrong one. Back in the corner, he held Charlene's hand and they smooched a little, but not much. Sonny really wanted to see the movie, and it was easy for him to hold his passion down. Charlene had not got all the sweetness out of the stick of Doublemint and didn't want to take it out of her mouth just to kiss Sonny, but after a few minutes she changed her mind, took it out, and stuck it under the arm of her seat. It seemed to her that Sonny looked a little bit like Steve Cochran, and she began to kiss him energetically, squirming and pressing herself against his knee. Sonny returned the kiss, but with somewhat muted interest. He wanted to keep at least one eye on the screen, so if Ginger Rogers decided to take her clothes off he wouldn't miss it. The posters outside indicated she at least got down to her slip at one point. Besides, Charlene was always getting worked up in picture shows; at first Sonny had thought her fits of cinematic passion very encouraging, until he discovered it was practically impossible to get her worked up *except* in picture shows.

The movies were Charlene's life, as she was fond of saying. She spent most of her afternoons hanging around the little beauty shop where her mother worked, reading movie magazines, and she always referred to movie stars by their first names. Once when an aunt gave her a dollar for her birthday she went down to the variety store and bought two fifty-cent portraits to sit on her dresser: one was of June Allyson and the other Van Johnson. Marlene copied Charlene's passions as exactly as possible, but when the same aunt gave *her* a dollar the variety store's stock of portraits was low and she had to make do with Esther Williams and Mickey Rooney. Charlene kidded her mercilessly about the latter, and took to sleeping with Van Johnson under her pillow because she was afraid Marlene might mutilate him out of envy.

After a few minutes of squirming alternately against the seat arm and Sonny's knee, lost in visions of Steve Cochran, Charlene abruptly relaxed and sat back. She languidly returned the chewing gum to her mouth, and for a while they watched the movie in silence. Then she remembered a matter she had been intending to bring up.

"Guess what?" she said. "We been going steady a year tonight. You should have got me something for an anniversary present."

Sonny had been contentedly watching Ginger Rogers, waiting for the slip scene. Charlene's remark took him by surprise.

"Well, you can have another stick of gum," he said. "That's all I've got on me."

"Okay, and I'll take a dollar, too," Charlene said. "It cost that much for me and Marlene to come to the show, and I don't want to pay my own way on my anniversary."

Sonny handed her the package of chewing gum, but not the dollar. Normally he expected to pay Charlene's way to the show, but he saw no reason at all why he should spend fifty cents on Marlene. While he was thinking out the ethics of the matter the exit door opened down to the right of the screen and Duane and Jacy slipped in, their arms around one another. They came back and sat down by Sonny and Charlene.

"Hi you all, what are you doin' back here in the dark?" Jacy whispered gaily. Her pretty mouth was a little numb from two hours of virtually uninterrupted kissing. As soon as it seemed polite, she and Duane started kissing again and settled into an osculatory doze that lasted through the final reel of the movie. Charlene began nervously popping her finger joints, something she did whenever Jacy came around. Sonny tried to concentrate on the screen, but it was hard. Jacy and Duane kept right on kissing, even when the movie ended and the lights came on. They didn't break their clinch until Billy came down from the balcony with his broom, and began to sweep.

"Sure was a short show," Jacy said, turning to grin at Sonny. Her nose wrinkled delightfully when she grinned. She shook her head so that her straight blond hair would hang more smoothly against her neck. Duane's hair was tousled, but when Jacy playfully tried to comb it he yawned and shook her off. She put on fresh lipstick and they all got up and went outside.

Miss Mosey had taken the *Storm Warning* posters down and was gallantly trying to tack up the posters for Sunday's show, which was *Francis Goes to the Army*. The wind whipped around the corners of the old building, making the posters flop. Miss Mosey's fingers were so cold she could barely hold the tacks, so the boys helped her finish while the girls shivered on the curb. Marlene was shivering on the curb too, waiting for Sonny to drop her off at the Duggses. Duane walked Jacy to her convertible and kissed her good-night a timc or two, then came gloomily to the pickup, depressed at the thought of how long it was until Saturday night came again.

When they had taken Marlene home and dropped Duane at the rooming house, Sonny and Charlene drove back to town so they could find out what time it was from the clock in the jewelry store window. As usual, it was almost time for Charlene to go home.

"Oh, let's go on to the lake," she said. "I guess I can be a few minutes late tonight, since it's my anniversary."

"I never saw anything like that Jacy and Duane," she said. "Kissing in the picture show after the lights go on. That's pretty bad if you ask me. One of these days Mrs. Farrow's gonna catch 'em an' that'll be the end of that romance."

Sonny drove on to the city lake without saying anything, but the remark depressed him. So far as he was concerned Jacy and Duane knew true love and would surely manage to get married and be happy. What depressed him was that it had just become clear to him that Charlene really wanted to go with Duane, just as he himself really wanted to go with Jacy.

As soon as the pickup stopped Charlene moved over against him. "Crack your window and leave the heater on," she said. "It's still too cold in here for me."

Sonny tried to shrug off his depression by beginning the little routine they always went through when they parked: first he would kiss Charlene for about ten minutes; then she would let him take off her brassiere and play with her breasts; finally, when he tried to move on to other things she would quickly scoot back across the seat, put the bra back on, and make him take her home. Sometimes she indulged in an engulfing kiss or two on the doorstep, knowing that she could fling herself inside the house if a perilously high wave of passion threatened to sweep over her.

After the proper amount of kissing Sonny deftly unhooked her bra. This was the signal for Charlene to draw her arms from the sleeves of her sweater and slip out of the straps. Sonny hung the bra on the rear-view mirror. So long as the proprieties were observed, Charlene liked being felt; she obligingly slipped her sweater up around her neck.

"Eeh, your hands are like ice," she said, sucking in her breath. Despite the heater the cab was cold enough to make her nipples crinkle. The wind had blown all the clouds away, but the moon was thin and dim and the choppy lake lay in darkness. When Sonny moved his hand the little dash-light threw patches of shadow over Charlene's stocky torso.

In a few minutes it became apparent that the cab was warming up faster than either Sonny or Charlene. He idly held one of her breasts in his hand, but it might have been an apple someone had given him just when he was least hungry.

"Hey," Charlene said suddenly, noticing. "What's the matter with you? You act half asleep."

Sonny was disconcerted. He was not sure what was wrong. It did not occur to him that he was bored. After all, he had Charlene's breast in his hand, and in Thalia it was generally agreed that the one thing that was never boring was feeling a girl's breasts. Grasping for straws, Sonny tried moving his hand downward, but it soon got entangled in Charlene's pudgy fingers.

"Quit, quit," she said, leaning her head back in expectation of a passionate kiss.

"But this is our anniversary," Sonny said. "Let's do something different."

Charlene grimly kept his hand at navel level, infuriated that he should think he really had license to go lower. That was plainly unfair, because he hadn't even given her a present. She scooted back toward her side of the cab and snatched her brassiere off the mirror.

"What are you trying to do, Sonny, get me pregnant?" she asked indignantly.

Sonny was stunned by the thought. "My lord," he said. "It was just my hand."

"Yeah, and one thing leads to another," she complained, struggling to catch the top hook of her bra. "Momma told me how that old stuff works."

Sonny reached over and hooked the hook for her, but he was more depressed than ever. It was obvious to him that it was a disgrace not to be going with someone prettier than Charlene, or if not prettier, at least someone more likable. The problem was how to break up with her and get his football jacket back.

"Well, you needn't to get mad," he said finally. "After so long a time I get tired of doing the same thing, and you do too. You wasn't no livelier than me."

"That's because you ain't good lookin' enough," she said coldly. "You ain't even got a ducktail. Why should I let you fiddle around and get me pregnant. We'll have plenty of time for that old stuff when we decide to get engaged."

Sonny twirled the knob of his steering wheel and looked out at the cold scudding water. He kept wanting to say something really nasty to Charlene, but he restrained himself. Charlene tucked her sweater back into her skirt and combed angrily at her brownish blond hair. Her mother had given her a permanent the day before and her hair was as stiff as wire.

"Let's go home," she said. "I'm done late anyway. Some anniversary."

Sonny backed the pickup around and started for the little cluster of yellow lights that was Thalia. The lake was only a couple of miles out.

"Charlene, if you feel that way I'd just as soon break up," he said. "I don't want to spoil no more anniversaries for you."

Charlene was surprised, but she recovered quickly. "That's the way nice girls get treated in this town," she said, proud to be a martyr to virtue.

"I knew you wasn't dependable," she added, taking the football jacket and laying it on the seat between them. "Boys that act like you do never are. That jacket's got a hole in the pocket, but you needn't ask me to sew it up. And you can give me back my pictures. I don't want you showin' 'em to a lot of other boys and tellin' them how hot I am."

Sonny stopped the pickup in front of her house and fished in his billfold for the three or four snapshots Charlene had given him. One of them, taken at a swimming pool in Wichita Falls, had been taken the summer before. Charlene was in a bathing suit. When she gave Sonny the picture she had taken a ballpoint pen and written on the back of the snapshot, "Look What Legs!", hoping he would show it to Duane. The photograph showed clearly that her legs were short and fat, but in spite of it she managed to think of herself as possessing gazellelike slimness. Sonny laid the pictures on top of the football jacket, and Charlene scooped them up.

"Well, good-night," Sonny said. "I ain't got no hard feelings if you don't."

Charlene got out, but then she bethought herself of something and held the pickup door open a moment. "Don't you try to go with Marlene," she said. "Marlene's young, and she's a good Christian girl. If you try to go with her I'll tell my Daddy what a wolf you was with me and he'll stomp the you-know-what out of you."

"You was pretty glad to let me do what little I did," Sonny said, angered. "You just mind your own business and let Marlene mind hers."

Charlene gave him a last ill-tempered look. "If you've given me one of those diseases you'll be sorry," she said.

She could cheerfully have stabbed Sonny with an ice pick, but instead, to impress Marlene, she went in the house, woke her up, and cried for half the night about her blighted romance. She told Marlene Sonny had forced her to fondle him indecently.

"What in the world did it look like?" Marlene asked, bug-eyed with startled envy.

"Oh, the awfulest thing you ever saw," Charlene assured her, smearing a thick coating of beauty cream on her face. "Ouuee, he was nasty. I hope you don't ever get involved with a man like that, honey—they make you old before your time. I bet I've aged a year, just tonight."

Later, when the lights were out, Marlene tried to figure on her fingers what month it would be when Charlene would be sent away in disgrace to Kizer, Arkansas, to have her baby. They had an aunt who lived in Kizer. Marlene was not exactly clear in her mind about how one went about getting pregnant, but she assumed that with such goings on Charlene must have. It was conceivable that her mother would make Charlene leave the picture of Van Johnson behind when she was sent away, and that thought cheered Marlene very much. In any case, it would be nice to have the bedroom to herself.

Three

After he let Charlene out Sonny drove back to town. He was amazed that breaking up with her had been so easy: all he felt was a strong sense of relief at having his football jacket back. It was the jacket he had earned in his junior year when he and Duane had been cocaptains, and it had "Cocaptain" stitched across the front in green thread. He was proud of it, and glad to have it safely out of Charlene's hands.

When he got back to the square it was midnight and the town looked just as deserted as it had looked that morning. The night watchman's old white Nash was parked where it always was, and the night watchman, a man named Andy Fanner, was asleep in the front seat, his heels propped on the dash. As usual, he had his motor running and his windows rolled up; the town thought Andy a very likely candidate for monoxide poisoning and expected any morning to find him a purplish corpse, but he slept comfortably through hundreds of winter nights with no apparent ill effects. Sonny didn't share the general worry: he had ridden in the Nash and knew there were holes enough in the floorboard to provide ample ventilation.

He drove to the all-night café and started in, but when he looked through the window he saw that his father, Frank Crawford, was sitting at the counter, sipping defensively at a cup of coffee and talking to Genevieve Morgan, the night waitress. His father liked Genevieve and Sonny liked her too, but they couldn't both talk to her at the same time so Sonny returned to the pickup and backed down the street to the square to wait for his father to come out. Waiting made him a little uneasy; somehow he couldn't help begrudging his father the nightly conversations with Genevieve. She was a shapely black-headed woman in her mid-thirties whose husband had been busted up in a rig accident almost a year before. He was not yet well enough to go back to the oil fields, and since they had two boys and were paying on a house, Genevieve had to go to work. The waitressing job was ten at night to six in the morning, and she didn't like it, but in Thalia there were not many jobs open at any hour. When she took over the night shift Sam's business had improved enormously: half the truckers and roughnecks and cowboys in that part of the country would hit the café at night, hoping to make out with Genevieve. She was beginning to thicken a bit at the waist, but she was still pretty, high-breasted, and long-legged; men accustomed to the droopy-hipped plod of most small town waitresses liked the way Genevieve carried herself. Sonny liked it himself and had as many fantasies about Genevieve as he had about Jacy Farrow.

He hadn't been parked long when he saw his father leave the café and come walking up the empty street toward the square, shivering and shaking. All he ever wore was summer slacks and a thin cotton jacket, too short at the wrists. Sonny felt briefly guilty for not offering him a ride to the hotel. He would have, but his father would only try to give him ten dollars and that would make them both nervous. It would not be worth it to either of them to get in a money argument that late at night. Money arguments often upset them for hours. Frank couldn't help offering it and Sonny couldn't help refusing to take it. Sonny did not want it, nor could he see how his father could possibly do without it, as high as his prescriptions were. Frank Crawford was not the town's only drug addict, but he was the one with the best excuse: he had been high-school principal in Thalia, until his car wreck. One night he was coming home from a high-school football game and sideswiped a cattle truck. Sonny's mother was killed and Frank was injured so badly that six operations failed to restore him to health. He couldn't stand the strain of teaching, tried to learn pharmacy and failed, and finally had to settle for the job at the domino hall. He got through life on prescriptions, but the prescriptions didn't make him feel any better about the fact that his son was living in a rooming house rather than in a proper home.

Sonny was a little afraid his father might spot the pickup, but Frank Crawford had his chin tucked down and the cold wind made his eyes water so badly that he hardly even saw the street. He passed under the blinking traffic light and went into the hotel, and Sonny quickly started the pickup and drove back to the café. Five soldiers had just come out and were standing around their car flipping quarters to see who drove the next stint. Their car had Kansas license plates and the boy who lost the toss looked depressed at the thought of how far there was to go.

When Sonny went in Genevieve was back in the kitchen cleaning off the grill. He sat down at the counter and tapped the countertop with a fifty-cent piece until she came out of the kitchen to see who the customer was.

"Surprise," he said. "I guess I'll have a cheeseburger to go to bed on."

"You would," Genevieve said, far from surprised. She went back to the kitchen and slapped a hamburger patty on her clean grill. When the burger was ready she carried it right past Sonny and set it down at one of the red leatherette booths. Then she got a glass of milk for him and a cup of coffee for herself.

"If you'll sit in that booth I'll keep you company," she said.

Sonny was quick to obey. The steam from her coffee rose between them as he ate his cheeseburger. The window by the booth was all fogged over, but the misted glass was cold to the touch, and the knowledge that the freezing wind was just outside made the booth seem all the cozier. Genevieve sat quietly, her hands on the coffee cup; the warmth against her palms was lovely, but it made her a little too nostalgic for all the winter nights she had spent at home, sleeping against her husband. Then her whole body had felt as warm and comfortable as her palms felt against the cup.

"Your dad was in a few minutes ago," she said, raising her arm to tuck a strand of black hair back in place.

"Guess I just missed him," Sonny said quickly.

"Where'd you hide?" she asked, giving him a perceptive grin. Her teeth were a little uneven, but strong. Sonny pretended he hadn't understood her and tried to think of a way to change the subject. Charlene was the only thing that occurred to him.

"I guess you'll have to be my girl friend now," he said. "Me and Charlene broke up tonight."

"It was about time. I better take advantage of the situation while I can. Come on back in the kitchen and have a piece of pie while I do some dishwashing."

Sonny gladly went with her, but he was painfully aware that she was only joking about being his girl friend. He sat in a chair and ate a big piece of apricot pie while Genevieve attended to a sinkful of dishes. For a minute, lost in her work, she forgot Sonny completely and he felt free to watch her. Gallons of hot water poured into the sink and working over it soon had her sweating. Her cheeks and forehead shone with it; there were beads on her upper lip, and the armpits of her green uniform darkened. The errant strand of hair hung over her forehead when she bent to fish the knives and forks out of the water. As always, Sonny found himself strongly affected by her. Sweat, if it was Genevieve's, seemed a very intimate and feminine moisture. Even Jacy didn't affect him quite as strongly; beside Genevieve, Jacy seemed strangely diminished, and apparently Jacy knew it. She always made Duane take her to the drive-in rather than the café when they ate together.

When Genevieve finished her dishes she glanced over at Sonny and saw that he seemed rather melancholy.

"Honey, you shouldn't be down in the mouth about Charlene," she said. "You put up with her long enough. She didn't even have a good disposition."

"I ain't blue about her," Sonny said, handing her the pie dish.

When she asked him why he was blue, he shrugged, not knowing what to say. He was blue because he wanted her and knew he would never have her, but that wasn't something he could talk about. "There ain't nobody to go with in this town," he said finally. "Jacy's the only pretty girl in high school, and Duane's got her."

Genevieve squeezed out her gray dishrag. "I'd call that his tough luck," she said. "She'll bring him more misery than she'll ever be worth. She's just like her grandmother. Besides, I doubt Lois and Gene want her marrying a poor boy."

"What's the matter with them?" Sonny asked. "Why do they think everybody has to be rich?"

"Oh, I don't guess they do," Genevieve said. "I oughtn't to even talk about them. We were all good friends once. Gene and Dan roughnecked together when we first moved here and we all went to dances together. Lois' mother had disowned her and she and Gene were livin' in a little one-room place over the newspaper office. She couldn't even afford a flour-sack apron, much less a mink coat."

Genevieve untied her own apron, which was damp from having been pressed against the sink. She stared at the floor a moment, her look full of memory.

I'll always have a soft spot for Lois," she said. "Lois is some woman. Gene just never could handle her. Since he started making his strikes we haven't seen much of one another. When folks get rich all of a sudden it makes them feel sort of guilty to be around folks who've stayed poor."

"I hate people like that," Sonny said.

Genevieve sighed and got herself a fresh apron. "You oughtn't to," she said. "It's perfectly natural. I've always wondered what would have happened if Dan had bought the rig and made the strikes. They offered that rig to Dan first. In fact, Gene Farrow tried to get Dan to go partners with him on it, but when it comes to money Dan Morgan never took a chance in his life. If we had made the money we might be just as touchy about it now as they are. It can change people, you know."

Sonny looked at her curiously. He could not imagine Genevieve rich.

"Do you wish you all had made it?" he asked.

"Oh sure," she said, smiling tiredly. "I wish we'd made it."

Sonny handed her a ten-dollar bill in payment for the cheeseburger.

"Your dad give you this?" she asked.

He shook his head. "I never take money from him if I can help it. He needs all he's got."

Genevieve frowned, and Sonny nervously began popping toothpicks out of the toothpick machine. "It wouldn't hurt you to take a little something from him once in a while," she said. "You're the only boy I know who won't even let his own father give him money."

But Sonny had his mind on other things. "I hear Dan's goin' back to work soon," he said. "I guess you'll be quittin' work before long."

Genevieve slapped at his hand to make him let the toothpicks alone, but she was touched by the question. Of all the boys who had crushes on her, Sonny was her favorite. Also, he had the worst crush, and was the most vulnerable. She watched a moment as he walked over to the brightly lit jukebox and stooped to catch his reflection in the shiny plastic dome. He got out his pocket comb and began to comb his brown hair. He was so young and so intent on himself that the sight of him made her feel good about life for a moment; she almost wanted to cry, and since her husband's accident that was something she only dared do in moments of optimism.

"Honey, we got four thousand dollars worth of doctor bills to pay," she said finally. "I'll probably be making cheeseburgers for your grandkids."

Sonny shoved his comb back in his hip pocket. Four thousand dollars in debts was something he couldn't really imagine; it was a misfortune, of course, but somehow he felt lighter about things. He went back and got one more toothpick to show Genevieve he wasn't intimidated.

She ignored him and drew herself another cup of coffee. It was such a cold night that there probably wouldn't be any more customers until the bus came through at 3 A.M., and then it would only be the bus driver. The only time anyone ever got on or off in Thalia was when some soldierboy was coming home on leave or else going back to his base. The two hours before the bus came were the loneliest of the night.

"See you," Sonny said. "If I knew how to cook I'd stay and substitute for you."

Genevieve was idly peeling the polish off a fingernail, while her coffee cooled. "If you knew how to cook I'd let you," she said.

When he got within a block of the rooming house, Sonny killed his motor and let the pickup coast up to the curb. Sometimes just the sound of a pickup would waken Old Lady Malone. He tiptoed in, trying to miss all the squeaky boards. When Old Lady Malone woke up she always came slopping down the hall in her dead husband's house shoes to tell Sonny to be sure and turn out his fire. Then she frequently went in the bathroom and made bad smells for half an hour.

His room was discouragingly cold, and smelled dusty. Things always smelled dusty after the wind had been blowing for a day or two. He considered reading for a while, but there was nothing there to read except a couple of old *Reader's Digest*s and a few sports magazines. He had read them all so many times he had them practically memorized.

That morning he hadn't bothered to make his bed and the quilts were all in a heap. He undressed and snuggled under the heap, his mind returning at once to Genevieve. Not Genevieve at the café, though—Genevieve naked, just out of her bath, with the ends of her black hair dampened and drops of water on her breasts. In a room so dry, with the dusty air chafing his nostrils, the thought of Genevieve dripping water was very exciting; but unfortunately the fantasy was disturbed by his feet poking out from under the ill-arranged covers into the cold air. For a moment he attempted to kick the covers straight but they were too tangled. He had to get up, turn on the light, and made the bed, all the while somewhat embarrassed by his own tumescence. Like most of his friends he went through life half-convinced that the adults of Thalia would somehow detect even his most secret erections and put them down in the book against him. The chill of the room and his own nervousness were distracting, and by the time the quilts were spread right his only thought was to get under them and get warm. Before he could reestablish his picture of Genevieve naked he was asleep.

Four

THE ONE REALLY NICE THING ABOUT HIGH SCHOOL IN Thalia was that it gave everybody a chance to catch up on their sleep. Sonny and Duane habitually slept through their three study halls and were often able to do a considerable amount of sleeping in class. Working as hard as they did, school was the only thing that saved them. Occasionally they tried to stay awake in English class, but that was only because John Cecil, the teacher, was too nice a man to go to sleep on.

When they got to English class on Monday morning Jacy was already there, wearing a new blue blouse and looking fresh and cheerful. Mr. Cecil sat on his desk, and he also looked happy. He had on a brown suit and an old green tie that had been knotted so many times the edges were beginning to unravel. His wife Irene kept the family accounts and had decided the tie was good for one more year. She was a fat bossy woman and their two little girls took after her. Yet somehow, despite his family, Mr. Cecil managed to keep liking people. When he wasn't actually teaching he was always hauling a carload of kids somewhere, to a fair or a play or a concert. In the summertime he often hauled carloads of boys over to an irrigation ditch where they could swim. He didn't swim himself but he loved to sit on the bank and watch the boys.

"Well, I wonder what my chances are of interesting you kids in John Keats this morning," he said, when the class was settled.

"None at all," Duane said, and everybody laughed. Mr. Cecil laughed too—it was all in fun. The kids didn't hold it against him that he liked poetry, and he didn't hold it against them that they didn't. He read them whatever poetry he felt like reading, and they dozed or got other homework done and didn't interrupt. Once in a while he told good stories about the poets' lives; Lord Byron and all his mistresses interested the boys in the class a good deal. They agreed among themselves that Lord Byron must have been a great cocksman, but why he had bothered to write poetry they couldn't figure.

While Mr. Cecil was trying to decide what poetry to read that day Sonny got Joe Bob Blanton's algebra homework and began to copy it. For a year or two it had been necessary to threaten to whip Joe Bob before he would hand over his problems, but in time he began to want to be popular and handed them over willingly. That morning, to everyone's surprise, he held up his hand and got in an argument with Mr. Cecil over one of Keats's poems.

"I read the one about the nightingale," he said. "It didn't sound so good to me. It sounded like he wanted to be a nightingale, and I think it's silly of all these poets to want to be something besides what the Lord made them. It's criticizing the Lord."

Everybody snickered except Mr. Cecil. Joe Bob was sort of religion crazy, but nobody could blame him for it, considering the family he had. He was even a preacher himself, already: the summer before he had gone to church camp and got the call. Everybody figured Joe Bob had just done it to get a little extra attention from the girls at the church camp, but if that was it it sure backfired. So far as Brother Blanton was concerned the Lord's call was final: once you heard it you were a preacher forever. He started Joe Bob preaching sermons right away.

Mr. Cecil never quite knew what to do when Joe Bob got started. "Oh, I don't really think he wanted to be a nightingale, Joe Bob," he said. "Maybe he just wanted to be immortal."

Joe Bob was not satisfied with that either; he took out his pocket comb and slicked back his blond hair.

"All you have to do to be immortal is lead a good Christian life," he said. "Anybody can do it if they love the Lord, and you can't do it by writing poems anyway."

"Maybe not, maybe not," Mr. Cecil said, chuckling a little. "Here, now let me read you this."

He started reading the "Ode on a Grecian Urn," but the class was not listening. Joe Bob, having said his say, had lost interest in the whole matter and was doing his chemistry. Duane was catching a little nap, and Jacy was studying her mouth in a little mirror she kept behind her English book—she had been considering changing her lipstick shade but didn't want to do so hastily. Sonny looked out the window, and Mr. Cecil read peacefully on until the bell rang.

Civics class was next, a very popular class. Sonny and Duane had taken the precaution to sit in the back of the room, so they could cheat or sleep or do whatever they wanted to, but actually, in civics class, they could have done about as much if they had been sitting in the front row. Coach Popper taught civics—if what he did could be called teaching—and he could not have cared less what went on.

Not only was the coach the dumbest teacher in school, he was also the laziest. Three days out of four he would go to sleep in class while he was trying to figure out some paragraph in the textbook. He didn't even know the Pledge of Allegiance, and some of the kids at least knew that. When he went to sleep, he never woke up until the bell rang, and the kids did just as they pleased. Duane usually took a nap, and Joe Bob made a big point of reading the Bible. The only girl in class was a big ugly junior named Agnes Bean; the boys who didn't have anything else to do teased her. Leroy Malone, Old Lady Malone's grandson, sat right behind Agnes and kept the class amused by popping her brassiere strap against her back. Once he made her so mad popping the strap that Agnes reached under the desk, slipped off her brogan shoe, and turned and cold-cocked him with it before he could get his guard up. His nose bled all over his desk and he had to get up and sneak down to the rest room and hold wet towels on it until it stopped.

Another time, for meanness, the boys all ganged up on Joe Bob and stuck him out the window. They hung on to his ankles and let him dangle upside down a while, assuring him that if he yelled and woke up the coach they would drop him. Nobody was sure whether they really would have dropped him or not, but Joe Bob was sensible and kept quiet. The classroom was just on the second floor, so the fall might not have hurt him much even if they had dropped him.

After civics there was a study hall, and then lunch, a boring time. One year Duane and Jacy had been able to sneak off to the lake and court during lunch, but it was only because Lois Farrow was drinking unusually hard that year and wasn't watching her daughter too closely. Lois was the only woman in Thalia who drank and made no bones about it. That same year Gene Farrow gave a big barbecue out at a little ranch he owned, and all his employees were invited. Duane was roughnecking for Gene then and took Sonny along on his invitation. Lois was there in a low-necked yellow dress, drinking whiskey as fast as most of the roughnecks drank beer. She was also shooting craps with anyone who cared to shoot with her. That was the day that Abilene won over a thousand dollars shooting craps, six hundred of it from Lois and the other four hundred from Lester Marlow, who was Jacy's official date. Lois thought Abilene cheated her and wanted Gene to fire him on the spot, but Gene wouldn't. She cussed them both out, got in her Cadillac, and started for town, but the steering wheel got away from her as the Cadillac was speeding up and she smashed into a mesquite tree. Lois just got out, gave everybody a good hard look, and started to town on foot. Nobody stopped her. Gene Farrow got drunk and Abilene kept gambling. While he was rolling dice with Lester, Duane took Jacy over behind some cars and in excitement almost got her brassiere off. Sonny himself won $27 in a blackjack game, and he was not even an employee. That night somebody busted Lois' lip and blacked her eye; some thought Gene Farrow did it but others claimed it was Abilene. He had known the Farrows before they were rich, and he wasn't a man to put up with much name calling, and nobody but

Lois would have had the guts to call him names in the first place; if there was anything in the world she was scared of nobody knew what it was. She was a tall, rangy blonde, still almost as slim as her daughter, and she was not in the habit of walking around anyone.

If you didn't have someone to sneak off and court with, all there was to do at lunchtime was play volleyball. The one alternative amusement was watching the Melly brothers, George and Ed, who ordinarily spent their lunch hour jacking off in the boys' rest room. The Melly boys lived on a broken-down farm in the western part of the county, and had very few pleasures. Freshmen and sophomores got a kick out of watching them go at it, but it was really beneath the attention of seniors like Sonny and Duane.

As classes were being dismissed that afternoon Coach Popper announced that anyone interested in coming out for basketball should be in the gym in fifteen minutes. Basketball was not a big deal sport in Thalia; Sonny and Duane only went out because they were seniors and felt obligated. Also, the road trips were nice because the boys' and girls' teams rode on the same school bus. When all candidates were assembled in the boys' dressing room there turned out to be only nine boys there, not even enough for two teams. It was no real surprise: Thalia was generally conceded to have about the most miserable basketball team in the state. On a few spectacularly dismal occasions they had managed to lose games by over a hundred points.

The nine boys began to get into their jockey straps and shorts, and were rubbing foot toughener on their feet when Coach Popper came in from the equipment room. He wore a green fatigue jacket that he had swiped from the army and he was dragging two big sacks of basketballs. He was big and he was proud of it: two hundred and thirty-five pounds, at least half of it gut.

As soon as he got to the dressing room he stopped and took a quick tally. His countenance darkened.

"Goddammit!" he said. "Ain't there but nine of you little farts? Forty-six boys in this high school, ain't but nine come out? If this ain't a piss-ignorant place to have to coach. Where's Joe Bob, anyhow? The least that little piss-ant can do is come out for basketball."

"He's home jackin' off," Leroy said. "Or else he's readin' the Bible. That's all he does, one or the other."

"You all take ten laps and get out there and shoot some free throws," the coach said. "I'm going down to the church and get him. He ain't worth a shit but he's easy to find and I ain't gonna drive all over this county looking for basketball players. I ain't gonna hold no practice unless we got at least two teams, either."

He hitched his pants up over his big, sagging belly and went out the door.

All but two or three of the boys ignored the ten-lap command and began shooting whatever kind of shots came into their heads. The only one who actually ran all ten laps was Bobby Logan, the most conscientious athlete in school. Bobby liked to stay in shape and always trained hard; he was smart, too, but he was such a nice kid that nobody held it against him. He was the coach's special favorite.

When the coach came back he had Joe Bob at his heels. By that time all the boys were throwing three-quarter court peg shots, like Ozark Ike in the comics. Balls were bouncing everywhere. Once in a game Sonny had seen an Indian boy from Durant, Oklahoma actually make a three-quarter court peg shot in the last five seconds of play. It didn't really win the game for Durant, because they were already leading Thalia by about sixty-five points, but it impressed Sonny, and he resolved to start trying a few himself.

"Hey, quit chunkin' them balls, you little dumbasses," Coach Popper yelled. "Just for that we'll have some wind sprints."

Joe Bob was standing just behind the coach combing his hair. The coach happened to turn around and the sight made him so mad he grabbed Joe Bob's comb and threw it up in the stands as high as he could. "Get your skinny ass suited out," he said. All the boys grinned when Joe Bob went into the dressing room because while the coach was gone they had mixed a little glue in with the foot toughener. If Joe

Bob used any of the foot toughener he would probably have to keep his socks on for about three weeks.

The coach divided the boys into two teams and put them to running simple plays. He sat in a bridge chair with a blue towel around his neck and watched them, yelling from time to time. He had a little paper cup for his tobacco juice sitting by the chair. The loudest he yelled all afternoon was when a freshman who hadn't yet learned to dribble let a ball knock the cup over. They spent the last twenty minutes of practice running wind sprints up and down the gym. Joe Bob's feet were so badly blistered by that time that he had to hop the last two wind sprints on one leg. Some of the freshmen were no better off, and Coach Popper thought it was a hilarious sight.

"Tough it out, boys, tough it out," he yelled. "You got to be men like the rest of us, ain't none of you pretty enough to be women."

In the dressing room there was a great laugh when it turned out Joe Bob had used the foot toughener after all. The only reason he could get his socks off at all was that he had almost solid blisters and the blisters peeled loose a lot easier than the glue. When Coach Popper saw the sight he laughed till he cried. "You might try boilin' 'em off, Joe Bob," he said. "It wouldn't be no harder on your feet."

In fact, the coach made matters even worse for Joe Bob by horsing around and trying to grab his pecker.

"Look at that little worm there," he said, making a grab. "What kind of female you ever gonna get with that thing for bait, Joe? Wouldn't do for a six-year-old girl."

He kept laughing and grabbing, backing Joe Bob around the room until finally Joe Bob couldn't stand it anymore and ran to the showers with one sock still on.

"Another minute and I'd have had him bawling," the coach said jovially, sitting down to take off his tennis shoes.

It was all pretty funny, the boys thought, but when they came out of the shower something happened that wasn't so funny. Everybody was horsing around, popping towels and grabbing at one another's nuts, like they usually did after practice. Duane and Sonny and Bobby Logan were having a little three-way towel fight, and the trouble started when Duane caught Bobby a smacker on the hip. It was just a flat pop and didn't hurt Bobby at all, but the coach happened to be coming out of the shower about that time and for some reason it made him furious. He was naked except for a whistle around his neck, but he grabbed a towel and laid into Sonny and Duane. He let one fly at Duane that would have castrated him on the spot if it had landed. "I'll show you little fuckers some towel fightin'," he said. The boys were too surprised to fight back: they just retreated into a corner where there were benches and clothes hangers to block some of the coach's shots. His wet hair was down in his face and he was snorting and puffing like a mad boar hog.

In a minute or two he got over it, though, and threw the wet towel at Sonny. "No more goddamn towel fightin'," he said and went over and looked closely at Bobby Logan's hip. The freshmen were scared almost to death—one was so nervous he put his shoes on the wrong feet and wore them home that way, too scared to stop and change. The older boys had seen the coach flare up before and knew it was just a matter of surviving until he cooled off. The time he shot at Sonny it was because he thought Sonny had scared away a dove he was sneaking up on. Fortunately, Sonny was a hundred yards away and wasn't hit.

"I don't understand how Mrs. Popper's lasted," Duane said, as he was dressing.

"She ain't the healthiest looking woman in town," Sonny reminded him. Mrs. Popper's name was Ruth; she was a small woman, pretty but tired and nervous looking. No one saw much of her. At Christmastime she sometimes made Sonny and Duane cookies and brought them around. Sam the Lion had known her all her life and said that she had been lovely when she was young.

Jacy was waiting for the boys when they came out. "My folks are gone to Wichita," she said. "Let's go get a hamburger."

They got in the convertible and drove to the drive-in, a place called

The Rat-Hole. The boys were starved and ordered two hamburgers apiece; while they were cooking, Jacy and Duane smooched a little and Sonny cleaned his fingernails and looked out the back window. About the time their order came Abilene drove up in his Mercury and parked beside them. They all waved at him and he nodded in reply, barely moving his head. He was drinking a can of beer.

"You need a haircut," Jacy said, putting her hand lightly on the back Duane's neck. They were sitting very close together, and were feeding one another French fries when the Farrows' big blue Cadillac pulled in and parked beside them. Lois Farrow was driving. She had her sunglasses on, even though it was a cloudy day. Duane scooted back to his side of the car as quickly as he could, but the Farrows gave no indication that they even noticed him. In a minute Mrs. Farrow got out and walked around to Jacy's window.

"We're having supper at home tonight," she said. "As soon as the boys get through with their hamburgers you take them to town and get yourself home, you hear?"

Mrs. Farrow looked bored, even with her sunglasses on. For some reason Sonny felt scared of her, and so did Jacy and Duane. All three were nervous. Mrs. Farrow noticed Abilene sitting there and she calmly thumbed her nose at him. He gave her a finger in return and took another swallow of his beer. Lois went back to the Cadillac and the three kids hastily finished their meal, Jacy dripping tears of annoyance into her strawberry milk shake.

"She didn't have to look so hateful," Jacy said, sniffling. "I just wish my grandmother was alive. She'd see we got married even if we had to run away and do it."

Five

AT THE FARROW SUPPER TABLE AN HOUR LATER, LOIS AND Jacy politely ignored one another, while Gene made conversation with desperate good cheer. After supper, though, he gave up, watched Groucho Marx, and then got in bed and quickly drank himself to sleep. He just wasn't built to withstand the quality of tension Lois and Jacy could generate.

The one thing Lois envied Gene was his ability to drink himself to sleep quickly. He went to sleep on so little alcohol that he was never bothered with hangovers the next day, whereas Lois had to drink for hours before the liquor would turn her off. If she just had to sleep, she took pills.

When it was almost Jacy's bedtime Lois stopped at her door for a minute, knocked, and went in. Jacy had already showered and was sitting on the bed in pink pajamas, rubbing cleansing cream into her face. Occasionally, despite her precautions, Jacy got what she called a blemish, but she took great pains with her complexion and didn't have many.

"Go on, don't let me interrupt your facial," Lois said. She walked around the room, frowning. Almost every object in the room annoyed her; she couldn't decide whether Jacy simply had bad taste or had deliberately chosen ugly objects as a means of affronting her. There were five or six stuffed animals, all of which Duane had won for her at ball-throwing booths in the State Fair; they were grouped in one corner, around a large Mortimer Snerd doll, also a gift from Duane. One wall was mostly bulletin board, and every picture of Jacy or Duane that had ever appeared in the *Thalia Times* was tacked on it. In addition to the pictures there were football programs, photographs of Jacy as cheerleader (sophomore year) and as Football Queen (junior year), the menu of the junior dinner dance, the program of the junior play, and many other mementos. On the bedside table there was a framed picture of Duane, and on the wall, a framed picture of Jesus. Next to the picture of Duane was an alarm clock and a white zipper Bible, and on the other side of the bed was Jacy's pile of movie magazines, most of them with Debbie Reynolds on the cover. Debbie Reynolds was Jacy's ideal.

"Well, I guess you hate me tonight, right?" Lois said.

"Oh, Momma you know I love you," Jacy said, wiping the cream off. "But I love Duane too, even if you don't like it."

"Like it? Liking it or disliking it hasn't entered my head, because I don't believe it. Who you love is your own pretty self and *what* you really love is knowing you're pretty—I'm sure he tells you how pretty you are all the time so I don't doubt you're fond of him. Even your grandmother learned that much about you. And you are pretty, you ought to enjoy it. I'd just sort of hate to see you marry Duane, though, because in about two months he'd quit flattering you and you wouldn't be rich anymore and life wouldn't be near as much fun for you as it is right now."

"But I don't care about money," Jacy said solemnly. "I don't care about it at all."

Lois sighed. "You're pretty stupid then," she said. "If you're that stupid you ought to go and marry him—it would be the cheapest way to educate you."

Jacy was so shocked at being called stupid that she didn't even cry. Her mother knew she made straight-A report cards!

"You married Daddy when he was poor," she said weakly. "He got rich so I don't see why Duane couldn't."

"I'll tell you why, beautiful," Lois said. "I scared your daddy into getting rich. He's so scared of me that for twenty years he's done nothing but run around trying to find things to please me. He's never found the right things but he made a million dollars looking."

"If Daddy could do it Duane could too," Jacy insisted, pouting.

"Not married to you, he couldn't," Lois said. "You're not scary enough. You'd be miserable poor but as long as you had somebody to hold your hand and tell you how pretty you are you'd make out."

"Well you're miserable and you're rich," Jacy countered. "I sure don't want to be like you."

"You sound exactly like your grandmother," Lois said, looking absently out the window. "There's not much danger you'll be like me. Have you ever slept with Duane?"

It was undoubtedly the most surprising conversation Jacy had ever had!

"Me?" she said. "You know I wouldn't do that, Momma."

"Well, you just as well," Lois said quietly, a little amused at herself and at life. She never had been able to resist shocking her mother; apparently it was going to be almost as difficult to resist shocking her daughter.

"Seriously," she added. "There's no reason you shouldn't have as much fun as you're capable of having. You can come with me to the doctor sometime and we'll arrange something so you won't have to worry about babies. You do have to be careful about that."

To Jacy what she was hearing was almost beyond belief.

"But Momma," she said. "It's a sin unless you're married, isn't it? I wouldn't want to do that."

"Oh, don't be so mealymouthed," Lois shouted. "Why am I even talking to you? I just thought if you slept with Duane a few times you'd find out there really isn't anything magic about him, and have yourself some fun to boot. Maybe then you'd realize that pretty things and pretty people are what you like in life and we can send you to a good school where you'll marry some good-looking kid with the wherewithal to give you a pleasant life."

"But I don't want to leave," Jacy said plaintively. "Why can't I just stay here and go to college in Wichita?"

"Because life's too damn hard here," Lois said. "The land's got too much power over you. Being rich here is a good way to go insane. Everything's flat and empty and there's nothing to do but spend money."

She walked over to Jacy's dresser and picked up the big fifty-dollar bottle of Chanel No. 5 that Gene had given his daughter the Christmas before.

"May I have some of your perfume?" she asked. "I suddenly feel like smelling good."

"Help yourself," Jacy said, suddenly wishing her mother were gone. "Don't you have any?"

"Yes, but this is right here, and I feel like smelling good right now. Do you ever feel like doing anything right now?"

She wet her palms and fingertips with perfume and placed her hands against her throat, then touched her fingers behind her ears. The cool scent was delicious. She dampened her hands again, touched her shoulders, and then stooped and ran her palms down the calves of her legs.

"That's lovely," she said. Almost at once the perfume made her feel less depressed, and when she looked at Jacy again she noticed how young she was. Jacy's hair was pulled back by a headband, and her face, clean of makeup, was so clearly a girl's face that Lois ceased to feel angry with her.

"This is the first time in months I've seen your eyelids," she said. "You should leave your face just like that—it would win you more. Makeup is just sort of a custom you've adopted. All you really need right now is an eyebrow pencil."

Jacy looked blank and sleepy and Lois knew her advice was wasted.

"Okay," she said. "I'll let you alone. I probably confused you tonight and I do hope so. If I could just confuse you it would be a start. The only really important thing I came in to tell you was that life is very monotonous. Things happen the same way over and over again. I think it's more monotonous in this part of the country than it is in other places, but I don't really know that—it may be monotonous everywhere. I'm sick of it, myself. Everything gets old if you do it often enough. I don't particularly care who you marry, but if you want to find out about monotony real quick just marry Duane."

With that she left and walked down the thickly carpeted hall to her bedroom. As she walked through the door she heard her husband snoring; the only light in the room was the tiny orange glow of the electric blanket control. Lois sat down on the bed and rubbed her calves wearily. To kill the morning she had gone to Wichita Falls and spent $150; to kill the afternoon she had had three drinks and several rubbers of bridge at the country club. It seemed unjust that after all that work she should still have the problem of how to kill the night. She got up and went out in the hall, where she could see her wristwatch. It was only a little after ten.

After considering a moment she went to the kitchen and got a whiskey glass out of the cabinet. Bourbon was her night drink. She picked up the wall phone and dialed the poolhall and Sam the Lion answered.

"Hi, friend," she said. "How are you?"

"Hi, honey," Sam said. "I'm winterin' fairly well. How about you?"

"Oh, I won't complain," Lois said. "I wish you'd come and see me sometime. Has your number one customer left for the night?"

"No, he's here shootin'," Sam said. "I'll let you talk to him as soon as he finishes his run. You come and see me, you got a car."

In a minute or so Abilene took the phone. "Yeah," he said.

"Hey. Feel like a night off?"

"Depends on the salary," he replied.

"Well, drill hard," she said. "You're better at oil wells anyway."

She took her bourbon into the den and switched the TV on. A Claudette Colbert movie was just starting. She pulled her bathrobe around her and settled back in Gene's big leather chair to watch. From time to time she rubbed her calves. When the third commercial came on she went back to the kitchen and refilled her whiskey glass.

Six

After civics class Tuesday morning Coach Popper stopped Sonny in the hall. There had been an assembly that morning and the coach had on a necktie, an article of dress he seldom wore.

"Like your tie, Coach," Sonny said jokingly. It was a bright orange necktie and it stuck out from under the coach's shirt collar in the back.

"Purty, ain't it," the coach said distractedly. "Need you to do somethin' for me. Ruth's been sick the last couple of days and needs somebody to drive her to Olney to the doctor. She's afraid they might drug her or something so she wouldn't be able to drive home. If you'll drive her down and back I'll get you out of your afternoon classes."

Sonny immediately accepted the offer. He was for anything that would get him out of algebra class. The Poppers' house was only a couple of blocks from school and as soon as he finished lunch he walked over. He looked through the doorpanes before he knocked and saw that Mrs. Popper was ready to go. She was sitting in the living room, her purse in her lap.

"Oh hello, Sonny, what do you want?" she asked, when she came to the door.

"Coach said you needed a driver," he said. "I thought he told you I was coming."

Mrs. Popper looked disappointed but she tried hard to hide it. "No, he didn't mention it," she said. "I thought he was going to drive me himself. I guess he just couldn't get off."

She handed Sonny the keychain and he went and got the car out of their garage. It was a black '53 Chevy. When Mrs. Popper got in she had a Kleenex in her hand and was daubing at her eyes with it. Sonny felt like he ought to say something to cheer her up, but he couldn't think of anything. The Chevy didn't have much pickup but it ran smoothly once they got on the road. The wind was rustling dust in the dry bar ditches beside the highway.

"I'm sorry to be all this trouble," Mrs. Popper said. "You're very nice to drive me."

"It sure beats sittin' through algebra," he said.

Mrs. Popper smiled, but neither of them spoke again, all the way to Olney. Sonny watched the road, only glancing at her occasionally; she was looking out the window at the gray pastures. Her hair was brown with just a few traces of gray, and she wore it long, almost shoulder length. There was something about her that was really pretty. She was a little too thin, and her skin was too fair for the country she lived in: wind and sun freckled her on her cheekbones and beneath her eyes. Just before they got to the clinic she opened her purse and got out her lipstick, but she just held it a minute and put it back in her purse without using any.

While she was with the doctor Sonny sat in the waiting room of the clinic, reading magazines. There were lots of copies of *Outdoor Life* around, with good hunting stories in them. The only trouble was that the people in the waiting room made him so gloomy he could hardly read. A shaky old man sat next to him on the green waiting-room couch. He had had his voicebox taken out and had a little screen where it ought to be; every third breath he wheezed so loud that Sonny couldn't concentrate on his reading. Then a little boy came over and spat his bubble gum in the pot of a rubber plant next to Sonny. It was a pink, wet hunk of bubble gum and Sonny kept wanting to cover it with dirt. Across the room from him there was a farmer and his wife with an old old lady between them. They were very nervous, and Sonny knew why because he had seen them there several times before:

if they had to wait too long the old lady would start going to the bathroom right in her chair. It was very embarrassing, but then something about the waiting room was always embarrassing. When his father had still been getting regular shots Sonny had had to wait there often, and it hadn't changed a bit.

Finally the wheezing and the bubble gum and the old old lady got on his nerves so much that he went out and waited in the car. The coach was too tight to have a radio put in the car, so there was nothing to do but sit and look out the long empty street toward the west. Someone in a passing car threw out an empty ice-cream carton and the wind skittered it across the street to the far curb.

When Mrs. Popper finally came out she was walking so stiffly that Sonny thought they must have given her the drug after all; then when she got close he saw that she walked that way because she was crying. The wind blew her hair across her face and a few strands stuck to her wet cheek. She tried awkwardly to brush them back. Sonny got out and opened the door for her, wondering what he ought to do. He knew nothing at all about crying women.

He got in and drove back through Olney, thinking surely she would quit, but she didn't. She was not crying loudly, but she was crying.

"Would you like for me to take you to the hospital?" he asked. "I don't have to be back to school by any special time."

"Oh no," Mrs. Popper said, straightening up. She shook the tears out of her eyes so hard that two or three drops splattered on the dashboard. "I'm just scared," she said. "I have to have an operation tomorrow for a tumor in my breast."

The rest of the way home she sat quietly, but it wasn't really that she was just sitting, either. It seemed to Sonny that in some way she was pulling at him, trying to get him to say something to her. He would have been glad to say something to her, only he had no idea what to say. Even algebra class would have been better than what she was doing: nobody had ever pulled at him in such a strange way. It made him so nervous that he grew careless and let the car edge off the shoulder of the road. After that he concentrated very hard on his driving.

When they got to her house Sonny drove the car on into the garage. He got out, relieved that it was over, but Mrs. Potter kept sitting in the front seat as if she didn't know she was home or in her garage or anywhere. She wasn't crying, just sitting there. After a minute Sonny went around and opened the door for her.

"Oh," she said. "Thank you."

"Here's the car keys," Sonny said. "I guess I better go back to school."

"No, not yet," Ruth said. "If you can stand me for a few more minutes I'd like you to come in and have cookies and a Coke." She looked at him apologetically, but she didn't take the car keys.

Sonny knew he couldn't get out of going in. Somehow or other Mrs. Popper had got in control and he didn't know anything to do about it. Reluctantly he followed her through the back door and into the kitchen. The yellow kitchen linoleum was old and worn out.

"Just sit at the table," Mrs. Popper said. There was something wild in her face that made Sonny think of his father—when she smiled at him there was a pressure behind the smile, as if something inside her were trying to break through her skin.

"Would you like milk or a Coke?" she asked. "I'm really sorry I made you come in—you can go right now if you like. For a minute I was just scared to be alone."

Sonny said he would take a Coke. She got one, and set a plate of thin Nabisco cookies on the table with it. For a minute of two, watching him eat, she seemed to be getting all right, and then to his amazement and disgust she burst out crying again, loudly. She put her head in her arms and sobbed, her body shaking as if she had the heaves. Sonny was sure she must be crazy and he wanted to be away from her. He didn't even want to swallow the bite he had in his mouth. Mrs. Popper seemed to know what he was thinking; she looked up at him and tried to quit crying.

"You'll never forgive me, I know," she said. "You think I'm pitiable, you're disgusted. Go on away if you want to, you don't have to stay any longer."

"Thank you for the Coke," Sonny said hastily, taking her at her word. "Maybe you'll get to feeling better after your operation."

"Oh no, it's not the operation," she said, wiping her face with a yellow table napkin. "It's not the operation at all. The tumor probably won't be dangerous. It's just that thinking about it makes me so lonely I can't stand it."

"Well, I guess you'll be glad when basketball season is over," Sonny said, feeling a little more kindly toward her. "Coach probably doesn't get to stay home much during football and basketball season."

Mrs. Popper laid down her napkin and looked at Sonny as if she were seeing him for the first time. She quit crying and became completely calm. "My God," she said. "You don't know a thing about it, do you?"

Then she did a thing which he would never forget: she got up, came around the table, put out her hand, and traced her fingers down his jaw almost to his mouth. Her fingers were cool. She put her hand on his head for a minute, felt his hair against her palm and between her fingers, and then quickly reached down for one of his hands and pressed it against her cheek and throat. She held his hand there for a moment and then laid it back on the table as carefully as if it were a piece of china.

"I know I mustn't be that way," she said, and again it looked as if something were pushing at the inside of her skin. Sonny felt very confused, but no longer particularly scared or particularly anxious to get away. From the way she touched him and looked at him he knew she had thought about kissing him when she put her hand on his face. He didn't know what would have happened, because he had no idea how it would feel to kiss someone older than himself, someone who was married. But when he looked at Mrs. Popper's mouth he wished that she had gone ahead, or that he had done something. He was sure it would have been nice to kiss her, much nicer than it had been to kiss Charlene.

But Mrs. Popper went back to her own chair and looked at the splotch on the tablecloth her tears had made.

"Here I am wanting to tell you I'm sorry again," she said, smiling a little. "I know I've given you a bad afternoon. For ten seconds there I was ready to try and seduce you, I don't know what it means myself. I've never seduced anyone and I've never been seduced, but I've always liked the word. I thought if I was ever going to find out what it meant it had better be now."

She sighed. "I don't guess you can imagine being seduced by the wife of your coach. I'm not so terribly pretty and I don't think you even like me. It probably wouldn't be best for you to be seduced by a forty-year-old woman you don't even like. Do you have a girl friend?"

"I did have," Sonny said. "We broke up last Saturday night."

"Why did you break up?" she asked. "Do you mind talking? I wish I wasn't so avid. You don't really have to answer my questions if you don't want to."

"I was going with Charlene Duggs," Sonny said. Something had changed; he felt more comfortable with Mrs. Popper than he had all afternoon. "Charlene thought I got fresh with her, but I never did, really. I guess the reason we broke up was because we didn't like one another much to begin with."

"I shouldn't be sad about it, if I were you," Ruth said. "I know Charlene and I don't think she's nearly nice enough for you. Even I would be better for you than she would."

She put her fingers to her temples and smoothed back her hair. "Besides, she must be a dumb creature, not to appreciate you. I can't even imagine how it would be to be young and have someone like you get fresh with me."

Sonny decided she really was a little crazy, but he liked her anyway. He even wanted to compliment her in some way, say something that would make her feel nice.

"I already like you better than I ever liked her," he said, wondering if it was a wrong thing to say.

Mrs. Popper's face lightened—she looked glad that he had said it. They were silent for a moment and Sonny finished his cookies and Coke. There was no longer a reason for him to stay, but he kept sitting, hoping that Mrs. Popper might want to come around the table again.

She knew that was why he was staying, too, and she did stand up, but not to come to him. She went to the sink and looked out the back window a moment before she spoke. She was not crying, but her face was sad. "Maybe you better go on to basketball practice," she said. He stood up and she walked with him to the front door.

"I see you feel you've missed a chance," Ruth said, when they were at the door. She looked at him frankly. "You see, I'm very confused, even if I look like I'm not. That's why you must go. I've got on a great many brakes right now—what I was thinking about a while ago is nothing I've ever done except with Herman, and for a long time I haven't even believed a man could want me that way. I don't know if I believe it now, even though I see you do. But then I think it isn't really *me* you want, it's only *that* . . . sex. Not that there's anything wrong with you wanting that, it's perfectly natural. . . ." She was talking faster and faster, but suddenly she stopped.

"You must really think I'm crazy," she said. "I am crazy I guess."

"Why's that?" Sonny asked.

"What?" Ruth said, caught by surprise.

"I mean why do you feel crazy? I guess I shouldn't be askin'."

"Of course you should," she said. "I was just surprised you had the nerve. The reason I'm so crazy is because nobody cares anything about me. I don't guess there's anybody I care much about, either. It's my own fault, though—I haven't had the guts to try and do anything about it. It took more guts for me to put my hand on your face than I ever thought I had, and even then I didn't have enough to go on."

She shut the screen door and they stood for a moment looking through the screen at one another. Sonny hated to leave; in some funny way he had come to like Mrs. Popper and he knew that the minute he left she would go in the house and cry again.

"Maybe I never will know what seduce means," she said quietly. "Thank you for putting up with me. You don't need to tell Herman about the operation. I'll tell him when he gets home."

Sonny was trying to think of something appropriate to say that would let her know that he really liked her, but he couldn't think of anything that didn't sound corny. Ruth noticed, and to spare him further embarrassment she shut the living-room door. When she heard his footsteps on the sidewalk she began to cry.

Basketball practice was so far along that Sonny didn't bother to suit out, but he did check in with the coach. Joe Bob and one of the freshmen had done something wrong and the coach was sitting on his bridge chair watching them run punishment laps.

"Come on, run 'em," the coach yelled. "Be men. I don't want no sissies on this team. Quit flapping your hands, Joe Bob, you look like a goddamn goose."

Sonny slipped his shoes off and took some free-throw practice with the rest of the team. He expected the coach to ask about Mrs. Popper, but he just sat on the bridge chair, chewing tobacco and occasionally scratching his balls. When he did ask, after practice, it was not exactly about Mrs. Popper—he wanted to know if the doctor had given her any prescription.

"I don't think so," Sonny said. "We didn't get any filled."

"Good," the coach said. "Damn doctors. Every time she goes over there they prescribe her ten dollars' worth of pills and they don't do a fuckin' bit of good. I tell her to take aspirin, that's all I ever take. If she's got a sore place she can rub a little analgesic balm on it—that's the best thing for soreness there is."

He didn't say so, but analgesic was also free. The school bought it by the case and the coach took what he needed.

"She wasn't feeling too good when I left her," Sonny said, thinking the coach might be worried enough to hurry on home. Instead, the news seemed merely to disgust him.

"Hell, women like to be sick," he said. He was on his way to the showers, but he stopped long enough to grab a cake of soap from a passing freshman. "Ruth had rather be sick than do anything. I could have bought a new deer rifle with what she's spent on pills just this last year, and I wish I had, by God. A good gun beats a woman any day."

Seven

"I GUESS SHE JUST COULDN'T GET OUT OF IT," SONNY SAID, chalking his cue. It was Saturday night and Duane had just found out that Jacy wasn't going to be at the picture show that evening: she was going to a country club dance with Lester Marlow.

"She wasn't sheddin' no tears over the telephone," Duane said bitterly. "She may be getting to like country club dances, that's what worries me."

He was in such a terrible mood that the pool game wasn't much fun. Jerry Framingham, a friend of theirs who drove a cattle truck, was shooting with them; he had to truck a load of yearlings to Fort Worth that night and asked them to ride along with him, since neither of them had dates.

"We might as well," Duane said. "Be better than loafin' around here."

Sonny was agreeable. While Jerry went out in the country to pick up his load he and Duane walked over to the café to have supper. Sam the Lion was there, waiting for old Marston to bring out his nightly steak. Penny was still at work and Marston was hopping to get the orders out. Penny had taken to wearing orange lipstick.

The boys sat down with Sam the Lion and ordered chickenfriend steaks. "Sam, how's the best way to get rich?" Duane asked.

"To be born rich," Sam said. "That's much the best way. Why?"

"I want to get that way. I want to get at least as rich as Lester Marlow."

"Well, of course," Sam said, buttering a cracker. "You're really too young to know what's good for you, though. Once you got rich you'd have to spend all your time staying rich, and that's hard thankless work. I tried it a while and quit, myself. If I can keep ten dollars ahead of the bills I'll be doin' all right."

"How much do you think Gene Farrow's worth?" Duane asked. "How rich would I have to get to be richer than him?"

"How much cash you got?" Sam asked.

"Fifty-two dollars right now. Fifty-one after we eat."

"Then cashwise I imagine you're as rich as Gene," Sam said, looking suspiciously at his salad. Marston was always sneaking cucumbers into his salads, against strict orders. Sam the Lion regarded cucumbers as a species of gourd and would not eat them.

"I doubt if Gene could lay his hands on fifty dollars tonight," he added.

Both boys were stunned. Everyone thought Gene Farrow was the richest man in town.

"Why Sam, he's bound to have lots of money," Duane said. "Mrs. Farrow's fur coat is supposed to be worth five thousand dollars."

"Probably is," Sam said. "That's five thousand he don't have in cash, though. He's got lots of trucks and equipment and oil leases, too, but it ain't cash and there's no way of tellin' how much of it's his and how much is the bank's."

He broke a biscuit in two and wiped his gravy bowl clean. "There ain't no sure-nuff rich people in this town now," he said. "I doubt there'll ever be any more. The oil fields are about to dry up and the cattle business looks like it's going to peter out. If I had to make a guess at who was the richest man in town I'd say Abilene. He may not own nothing but his car and his clothes, but I've never seen the day when he couldn't pull a thousand dollars out of his billfold. A man with a thousand dollars in his pocket is rich, for Thalia."

Duane cheered up suddenly and began to go after his steak with good appetite. "Well that's all good news," he said. "Maybe if the Farrows go broke they won't mind my marrying Jacy."

Sam grunted his disagreement. "Penny, bring me a dish of that cobbler," he said. "Apricot. Nope, Duane, you're wrong. I don't know about Lois, but if Gene was to even think he was going broke he wouldn't want you to get within a mile of that girl. There ain't nobody snootier than an oilman who's had to sell one of his Cadillacs."

"Aw, Sam it's not him," Duane argued. "I get along with him all right. It's Mrs. Farrow who don't like me. I bet it's her fault Jacy's off with Lester tonight."

"Well, Lois has got a lot of judgment, maybe she's doin' you a favor," Sam said. "That little girl is goin' to be a hard one to please."

Talk like that made Duane huffy. "I please her well enough," he said. Sonny wished the meal were over. It was getting so Duane wanted to talk about Jacy half the time, and for some reason the conversations always left Sonny depressed.

Outside, after they had all finished, Sam the Lion slapped them on the shoulder. "Well, have fun in Cowtown," he said. "If I didn't have all these businesses to run I'd ride along with you. Ain't been to Fort Worth in fifteen years." The night was cold and sleety and he hobbled on back to the poolhall on his sore feet.

The boys walked over to the courthouse where they could wait out of the wind. While they were waiting they saw Lester and Jacy drive by in Lester's Oldsmobile. Jacy wasn't sitting very close to him but as they passed under the street light the boys could see that she was laughing at something. Her hair was rolled up on her head in a fancy way.

"You don't need to look so blue about it," Sonny said. "This time next year you'll probably be married to her. Look at me, I ain't got no date either."

"Yeah, but you ain't in love," Duane said.

Finally Jerry's cattle truck screeched up to the stoplight, jam-packed with Hereford yearlings. When it stopped they all began to bawl and shove around and shit through the sideboards. The boys ran over and climbed up in the high cab—Jerry whanged the truck in gear and they were off.

"Break out the beer," Jerry said. "There's two six-packs there on the floor somewhere."

Sonny found an opener in the glove compartment. When he popped into a can the cold beer spewed all over him, its smell filling the cab. "The coach would have a shit fit if he knew we were breakin' trainin'," he said happily. For a moment Mrs. Popper crossed his mind—what would she be doing on a Saturday night?—but it was so much fun to be going down the road in a high, bouncy cattle truck that he soon forget her. All he and Duane had to do was drink beer and watch the fence posts and the culverts whiz by; before the first six-pack was finished their troubles were forgotten and they were happily reminiscing about old times in Thalia High School, reliving all the ball games they had played and the fights and adventures they had had. Jerry Framingham enjoyed the conversation: most of the kids he had graduated with were in the army and he seldom had any company at all on his cattle hauls.

Sonny and Duane found that they were a little out of shape for beer drinking. By the time they reached Fort Worth they were both fairly drunk, and the anecdotes they were telling seemed so funny to them that it would sometimes take them three or four miles to quit laughing. One classic story simply broke them up: it was about the time they had persuaded Billy to come out for football, although he wasn't even enrolled in school. Billy knew nothing about football and hadn't thought it at all strange when they put his shoulder pads on backward, daubed foot toughener in his ears, and made him wear a jockey strap for a noseguard. When he trotted out on the field with his jockey strap on his nose the whole team had hysterics and Coach Popper laughed so hard he almost ruptured himself.

Jerry Framingham was not drunk and thus did not become uncontrollably amused when he heard such stories retold—in fact the boys' laughter seemed to irritate him a little. "You drunk bastards can't do anything but laugh," he said.

Jerry's turn came later, after they had unloaded the cattle. They were having a beer or two in a honky-tonk on North Main and Jerry talked them into putting up five dollars apiece toward a fifteen-dollar whore he knew about. They could all three have easily found five-dollar whores, but Jerry insisted on flipping to see who got the more expensive one, and he won the flips. The whore was in a dinky little North Main hotel. Sonny and Duane walked around outside, freezing their tails, while Jerry went up to have fun. They stepped inside a cheap dance hall a few minutes to warm up and watched a lot of sideburned stockyard hands dance their skinny girl friends around the room.

As soon as Jerry was done and they were back in the truck the boys went to sleep. Jerry was somewhat weakened himself and on the home side of Jacksboro he pulled the truck off the road and went to sleep himself. About four in the morning Sonny woke up, practically frozen to death. Jerry and Duane were both mashed on top of him, trying to keep warm, and the door handle was about to bore a hole in his back. The windshield was completely sleeted over. Sonny pushed around until he woke the others up and he and Jerry got out and scraped the sleet off the windshield with an old Levi's jacket. While they were doing that Duane crawled over and vomited in the bar ditch. Coming back from Fort Worth was never as much fun as going.

While they had rolled around trying to sleep they had kicked the heater wires loose, so the rest of the trip home was miserably cold. The café looked like the most comfortable place in the world when they finally pulled in. Genevieve was sitting at the counter reading an old paperback of *Forever Amber* that everyone who worked at the café had read several times. When she saw what bad shape Sonny and Duane were in she put it away and fixed them some toast and coffee; as soon as they ate a little they dozed off and slept with their heads on the counter while she filled the coffee maker and got things ready for the morning business. Asleep they both had the tousled, helpless look of young children and she kept wanting to cover their shoulders with a tablecloth or something. When Marston came in she woke them up. She put on her heavy blue coat and the boys stumbled outside behind her, trying to keep their eyes open. The cold air snapped them out of it a little. Genevieve had an old gray Dodge that was hard to start and by the time she got it to kick off the boys were wide awake.

"What do you think about a woman that would make her daughter go with Lester Marlow?" Duane asked, remembering that he had a grievance.

"I don't know much about Lester, but if I had a daughter I don't know that I'd want her going with either one of you boys, the way you all cut up," she said, treating the whole matter lightly. She pulled up in front of their rooming house and raced her motor, so the old car wouldn't die.

The boys got out, thanked her, waved as the car pulled away, its exhaust white in the cold air. "Well, at least we got to go *somewhere*," Sonny said, picking up a beer can somebody had thrown out on the lawn. Fort Worth, after all, was a city, part of the big world, and he always came back from a trip there with the satisfying sense that he had traveled. They flipped to see who got the bathtub first and he won.

Eight

THE FIRST BASKETBALL GAME OF THE SEASON WAS WITH Paducah, a town well over a hundred miles from Thalia. It was the longest trip of the year and usually the wildest: in Paducah they played basketball as if it were indoor football, and they had everything in their favor, including a gym so small that the out-of-bounds lines were painted on the wall. The Paducah boys were used to the gym and could run up the walls like lizards, but visiting teams, accustomed to normal-sized courts, had a hard time. Every year two or three Thalia players smashed into the walls and knocked themselves out.

This time it happened to Sonny, and in the very first minutes of play. Leroy Malone managed to trip the gangly Paducah center and while the center was sprawled on the floor Sonny ran right along his back, in pursuit of the ball. Just as he was about to grab it somebody tripped *him* and he hit the wall head first. The next thing he knew he was stretched out beside the bench and one of the freshmen players was squeezing a wet washrag on his forehead. Sonny tried to keep his eyes closed as long as he could—he knew Coach Popper would send him back into the game as soon as he regained consciousness. He feigned deep coma for about five minutes, but unfortunately the coach was experienced in such matters. He came over and lifted one of Sonny's eyelids and saw that he was awake.

"Possuming," he said. "I thought so. Get up and get your butt back in there. We're forty points behind and it ain't but the second quarter."

"I think I got a concussion," Sonny said, trying to look dangerously ill. "Maybe I ought to stay out a little while."

"Get up," the coach insisted. "We just quit football practice ten days ago, you ain't had time to get that out of shape. If you want to rest, by God go in there and foul out first. Knock the shit out of that forward two or three times—he's the one doin' all the scorin'. Hell, we come all this way, let's make a showing."

Sonny reluctantly got up and went back in. He managed three fouls before the half, but he was too weak to hit anybody very hard and none of the fouls was really satisfactory. The half-time score was Paducah 62 and Thalia 9. During the half the coach called them over for one of his little pep talks, this one very brief.

"You ten boys have got the shortest little peckers of any bunch of kids I've ever coached," he said sincerely. "By God, if you don't stomp some asses this next half I'll stomp a few tomorrow afternoon when we start practicing."

He scowled fiercely and strolled off to the concession stand to have some coffee.

In the second half things began to look really ominous. Sonny felt strangely lightheaded and went out on the floor not much caring what he did. Paducah defense had become virtually impenetrable: for one thing, they had started openly tackling whichever Thalia player had the ball. It seemed to Sonny that at last the time had come to shoot peg shots—there was not much chance of moving the ball down the court any other way. Whenever they tried, Paducah tackled them, tripped them, threw body blocks into them, or had the referee call fouls on them.

Actually, the refereeing was another very bad aspect of basketball in Paducah. Unusual as it was, Paducah had a male home economics teacher, a frail little man named Mr. Wean. The school board felt that teaching home ec was really too light a job for a man so they made Mr. Wean basketball referee. He had never managed to learn much about the game, but he was quite docile and called whatever the Paducah team told him to call. Also, he was in bad shape and couldn't possibly run up and down the court for forty-eight minutes. Instead of following the ball, he just stood on the center line and made all his calls from there.

After considering the matter for half a quarter or so Sonny concluded that peg shots were the only feasible tactic. He was simply too weak to dodge the blocks the Paducah boys were throwing. From then on, every time he got the ball he threw it at the backboard he was attacking. At the very worst it slowed down Paducah's scoring. The other Thalia players were quick to see the wisdom of such an offense and in five minutes they were all doing it. Whoever caught the throw-in after a Paducah score would immediately whirl and throw a full-court peg shot. The only one it didn't work for was Leroy Malone: the big Paducah center anticipated him, caught the ball, and threw a ten-yard peg shot right at Leroy's groin. It hurt so bad he later told Sonny he was unable to jack off for two weeks.

The groin shot drew such sustained applause from the Paducah bleachers that Sonny was angered. Mr. Wean had failed to see that it was a deliberate foul: indeed, Mr. Wean was seeing less and less all the time. Thalia's peg-shot offense confused him—he had to keep turning around and around to keep up with the ball. After a while this made him so dizzy that he simply stopped and stood facing the Thalia goal—most of the Paducah team was down there anyway, catching the peg shots and throwing them back. Mr. Wean felt that he had somehow got involved in a game of ante over, and he didn't like it. He had a fat wife and all he really wanted to do was stay in the home ec classroom and teach young, small-breasted girls how to make pies. Instead he was standing on the center line, sweating and wishing the quarter would end. Suddenly, Sonny had an irresistible urge to chunk somebody. He unleashed a flat, low peg shot that caught Mr. Wean squarely in the back of the head and sent him sprawling.

The Thalia bench, boys and girls alike, arose with shrieks and cheers, their jubilation all the more noticeable because of the moment of total silence in the Paducah bleachers. The shot instantly made Sonny a celebrity, but it also scared hell out of him and his teammates who were on the floor at the time. They rushed over and tried to help Mr. Wean up, but his legs were like rubber. He had to be dragged off the floor. Paducah's assistant football coach was called in to referee the rest of the game—by the time he got his tennis shoes on, the hometown bleachers had recovered from their shock and were clamoring for Sonny's blood. He knew his only hope was to foul out immediately and get to the bench. While he was trying to decide on the safest way to foul, Coach Popper came to his rescue and took him out.

"Good lick," the coach said. "Nobody but a queer would teach home ec anyway."

From there on things were dismal for the Thalia five. Duane fouled out before the quarter ended, leaving no one but Joe Bob and the freshmen to play the fourth quarter. Paducah was ahead 88 to 14. Coach Popper got so mad at the freshmen that he couldn't see; he almost strangled himself tugging at the towel around his neck. He sent Sonny in again but Sonny quickly threw a couple of light body blocks and fouled out. That left Joe Bob and the freshmen to do the best they could. For the remainder of the game they never once managed to get the ball into their end of the court. As soon as they threw it in, the Paducah players took it away from them and made another goal. In five minutes the score was 110 to 14 and Coach Popper called time out. A huddle was in order.

"I tell you," the coach said philosophically, "let's just forget about winning and try to hold the score down. We're gonna get beat over a hundred points if we ain't careful. Oaks, you throw the ball into Joe Bob and Joe Bob, as soon as you get it lay down with it. That way they'll have to tie it up and jump for it every time. That'll slow 'em down a little."

The tactic worked fine the first time it was tried. Joe Bob swallowed the ball and Paducah had to tie it up to get possession. It took them about forty seconds to score. Thalia tried it again and three Paducah players gang-piled Joe Bob as he went down. He had to be carried off.

The freshman who shot his free throw for him was so scared he barely got the ball halfway to the basket.

Joe Bob's injury left the four freshmen alone on the field for the last few minutes of the game. None of them wanted to swallow the ball and get gang-piled so they did what they could to cooperate with Paducah. The final score was 121 to 14.

"Well, hell, at least my B team got some experience," Coach Popper said. "Might as well look on the bright side. Let's go to the bus."

Basketball defeats weighed very lightly on the coach: football was the only sport that really counted. Ten minutes later he was flopped down in his bus seat, sound asleep.

The boys sat in a stupor for the first twenty miles or so, trying to get used to feeling safe again. Besides, Old Lady Fowler, the girls' coach, was still awake and they could not start to work on the girls until she dropped off. She went to sleep as they were pulling out of Vernon, and from there on it was dog-eat-dog.

The four little freshmen had no chance with the girls and had to get what amusement they could out of tormenting Joe Bob. They crowded him in a seat, took his underpants off, and threw them out the window. Joe Bob was too weak from the gang-piling to fight back, and he might not have bothered anyway. He lost so many pair of underwear that his mother bought them wholesale. He was the only boy on the team who wore his regulars, rather than a jockey strap: Brother Blanton wouldn't hear of him wearing anything so immodest.

"What if you got hurt and were taken to a hospital wearing a thing like that?" Brother Blanton said. "Our good name would be ruined."

Most of the kids had seen Joe Bob's underwear often enough to be thoroughly bored with it. The freshmen attracted no notice at all, and soon went to sleep.

Sonny started the return trip sitting by Leroy Malone, whose balls were so sore that the mere thought of girls made him writhe. After a little bargaining Sonny managed to switch with the kid in front of him, which put him next to the pretty but prudish sophomore he had

had his eye on. Knocking Mr. Wean down gave him so much status that he was able to hold the girl's hand almost immediately. Martha Lou was her name. By the time they reached Electra she was willing to let him kiss her, but the results were pretty discouraging. Her teeth were clenched as tightly as if she had lockjaw, and even Sonny's status couldn't unlock them. His only reward was a taste of lipstick, in a flavor he didn't much care for.

The only real excitement on the bus ride home involved Jacy and Duane, the star couple. That was usually the case. None of the other kids excited one another much. There was a fat blonde named Vida May who would feel penises, but the teachers knew about her and made her sit so close to the front that it was dangerous to fool with her even when the teachers were asleep.

Jacy and Duane, as a matter of course, were sitting in the very back seat. Duane didn't like the back seat much because there was a little overhead light above it that the bus driver refused to turn off. The bus driver's name was Wilbur Tim and he wasn't about to trust any kids in a totally dark bus. One time years earlier his wife Jessie had found two prophylactics when she was sweeping out the bus, and it just about sent her into hysterics. She was the apprehensive type and went around for months worried sick that some nice little girl had got pregnant on her husband's bus. After that Wilbur installed the light.

It was a small bulb that didn't really give any light, just a nice orange glow. Jacy loved it and wouldn't sit anywhere else, despite Duane's protests. She thought the light was very romantic and suggestive: everyone in the bus could tell when the couple in the back seat were kissing or doing something sexy, but the light wasn't strong enough for them to see too clearly. Courting with Duane when all the kids on the school bus could watch gave Jacy a real thrill, and made her feel a little like a movie star: she could bring beauty and passion into the poor kids' lives.

Because Jacy enjoyed them so much, the kissing sessions in the back seat had become a sort of regular feature on basketball road trips. All the kids watched, even though it made them itchy and envious. Jacy, after all, was the prettiest girl in school and watching her get kissed and played with was something to do on the long drives home. The element that made it really exciting to everyone was the question of how far Jacy would go. Once Duane got started kissing he was completely indifferent to whether he had an audience or not: all he wanted was more. The dim light made it impossible to tell precisely how much more Jacy allowed: everyone caught shadowy glimpses, and occasionally a gasp or a little moan from Jacy indicated that Duane was making some headway at least, but no one ever knew how much or what kind.

Only Jacy and Duane knew that he was making a great deal of headway indeed. Jacy would kiss and play around any time, but she seldom got excited past the point of control unless she was on the school bus, where people were watching. Being in the public eye seemed to heighten the quality of every touch. On the bus seat she never had to feign passion—she was burning with it. It was easy for Duane to get his hands inside her loose uniform and touch her breasts, and she loved it. Also, since she was in shorts, it was easy for him to do even more abandoned things to her. She loved to have him slide his hands up the underside of her legs, and sometimes she would even get to the point where she wanted him to touch her crotch. It was a matter that took very delicate managing, but if Duane's hand were cupped against her at the right time so she could squeeze it with her legs, something nice would happen. That was not for the audience, however: she didn't want the kids to see that. When the moment came near she would try to get Duane to crowd her back in the corner, so they couldn't be seen so well. Sometimes it worked beautifully. The younger and more naïve kids were sure Duane went all the way; the juniors and seniors knew better, but felt he must be going a pretty significant distance, anyhow. Every trip added to Jacy's legend. The following day at school she would be on every tongue. Some of the girls said bitter things about her, but the boys took notice when she walked by. The only one seriously discommoded by bus-seat sessions was Duane, who frequently ached painfully by the time the bus reached home. He didn't like it, but he supposed such frustration was something he would simply have to bear until they were married.

Just before the bus got back to Thalia Coach Popper woke up and looked around. Most of the kids were asleep by that time, Jacy and Duane among them, but Jacy had gone to sleep with her legs across Duane's and when the coach saw that he was infuriated. It would put him in an awful spot if Lois Farrow somehow found out he had let her daughter go to sleep with her legs across Duane's. Gene Farrow was on the school board, and an incident like that could cost a coach his job. He stormed back and shook Jacy until she was awake enough to stumble down the aisle to the front seat, where she stayed the rest of the way home.

When all the kids had been delivered to their houses the coach got to thinking about it and began to cuss. There was no end to the trouble a couple of silly-ass kids might cause, particularly if one of them was Lois Farrow's daughter. Lois Farrow was the one person in Thalia who didn't give a damn for the fact that he was football coach.

Wilbur Tim dropped him off at his home, and he stomped inside, still angry. When he turned on the light in his bedroom closet it woke Ruth up. She had just had her breast operation a few days before and was still taking pain medicine. As he was taking off his shoes she sat up in bed.

"Herman, could you bring me a pain pill?" she asked. "It's hurting a little and I'm too groggy to get up."

"You sound goddamn wide awake to me," the coach said, fed up with women. "I bet if I let you you could lay there and talk for two hours. Get up and get your own pills, I ain't no pharmacist."

After a moment, Ruth did. She was dizzy and had to guide herself along the wall, holding her sore breast with one hand. She had washed that day and her white cotton nightgown smelled faintly of detergent. The coach ignored her and flopped on the bed. So far as he could tell, it had not been enough of an operation to make a fuss about. The scar on her breast was barely three inches long. He had cut himself worse than that many times, usually when he was hurrying through a barbed-wire fence to get to a covey of quail. The only thing that worried him about Ruth was the chance that they hadn't removed all the tumor and might have to operate again, in which case there would be no end to the expense. The cheapest and most sensible thing would have been for them to take the whole breast off while they were at it. The breast wasn't doing Ruth any good anyway, and if they had taken it all that would have been the end of the matter. He had told them so, too, but the doctor had ignored him and Ruth had gone off in another room and bawled. A woman like her would try the patience of a saint.

The next day at basketball practice the coach gave Duane a dressing down in front of the whole squad. He told him if he ever again so much as sat with Jacy on a basketball trip he would give him fifteen licks with a basketball shoe. A basketball shoe was the only thing the coach ever whipped boys with, but since he wore a size thirteen that was enough. He also told Duane to run fifty laps around the outside of the gym, and at that point Duane rebelled.

"I ain't runnin' no fifty laps all at one time," he said. "I'll do ten a day."

"You'll do fifty right now or check your suit in, by God," the coach said. "If you check it in you don't need to come out for track or baseball, neither. We can get along without you."

Duane went to the locker room, took his suit off, and left. It was just what the coach had hoped for. Any mess the boy got into with Jacy Farrow could no longer be laid at his door. It put him in such good spirits that he worked the boys until seven o'clock that night. The next day he commandeered a sophomore, and the team had ten players again.

Nine

In Thalia, winter was always duller than summer, at least for the boys. In the winter it was too cold to sit around on the square and think up meanness to do—if they wanted to sit around they had to do it in the café, and that cost money. When the square became empty because of the cold, the town seemed emptier than ever.

A senior year was supposed to be exciting but with winter setting in Sonny's suddenly began to look very dull. When Duane quit basketball, the game became a sort of tiring chore that Sonny went on with because he didn't have a legitimate excuse to quit. Thalia lost every game by thirty points or more. Even teams that were as bad as they were beat them thirty points on sheer morale. No team had less in the way of morale than Thalia.

Besides that there was his work. It was an unusually cold winter, and the demand for butane was high. Often, after practice or after a game, Frank Fartley would be waiting for Sonny at the gym and Sonny would have to spend half the night driving over the dark, ice-rutted roads looking for a farmhouse with an empty butane tank. Sometimes he could only find them by the mailboxes, usually old-fashioned Sears and Roebuck models stuck on posts beside the road.

Sonny took to drinking coffee to stay awake, and Genevieve didn't approve. "You've got to get you another job," she told him one time. He had come stumbling into the café at two-thirty in the morning, half-frozen. The heater in the old International only worked about half the time.

The trouble was, there weren't any other jobs, and Genevieve was scarcely in a position to give that kind of advice. Her husband was not improving as rapidly as he had been—it looked like it would be summer before he got back to work. The strain had begun to tell on Genevieve: her uniform no longer fit so snugly at the shoulders, and often she was so tired she couldn't sleep even when she had the time.

Everybody seemed to have the winter doldrums, including Sam the Lion. He was taking daily naps for his heart condition and his cough was still just as bad. Duane's grandmother took the flu and was in the hospital two weeks; everyone expected it to carry her off but all it did was destroy what was left of her mind. Since he didn't have basketball to wear him out, Duane had taken to working a double shift. It was cold work, but it paid, and he could count on having Saturday nights off to spend with Jacy.

The strange conversation Jacy had had with her mother threw Jacy temporarily into a state of uncertainty. For a time she had been convinced that she knew exactly what her mother wanted of her, and exactly how to get around it; but since the conversation she hadn't been so sure. It seemed incredible that her mother would actually give her license to sleep with Duane. For a day or two she was rather tempted, just to see what sex felt like, but then she decided that would merely be walking into her mother's trap. Advice like that was bound to be a trap.

For a time the conversation had the effect of inhibiting Jacy drastically. After she and Duane had concluded they were in love she had taken to allowing him considerable freedom with her body. She had even let him feel inside her panties on a few occasions, but when her mother told her to go ahead and sleep with him she immediately put a stop to that. She felt she had to if she were going to protect their love from her mother's subtle treacheries. Besides, the only times she really enjoyed letting him touch her there was on the school bus.

She even tried to quit letting him take off her brassiere, but Duane complained so bitterly about the loss of that privilege that she finally let him start doing it again. There were a few awkward dates, but in time Jacy became rather proud of herself for the mature way she was handling the situation. She could let Duane kiss her and play with her breasts and yet remain quite cool about it all, protecting them from his passion and her own. Her mother was outwitted and Duane had as much fun as was good for him. Sometimes in church she felt a little like a martyr because of the effort it cost her to keep the two of them morally upright. Her grandmother would have approved if she had been alive and known about it—her grandmother had been had been a woman of virtue.

Besides, sexual intercourse was supposed to be painful at first, and she knew Duane wouldn't want to hurt her until it was absolutely necessary. There was a time and a place for everything, as her grandmother had always said.

The week before Christmas there was a big county wide dance held at the American Legion Hall, an annual affair that everybody looked forward to. About the only people that stayed away were the hardshell Baptists and a few of the smaller, eccentric denominations who, like the Baptists, believed that dancing was sinful. In the old days, before the church women of the town had organized, eggnog had been served at the dance, and the men who couldn't tolerate dilution brought their whiskey bottles inside and kept them in their coat pockets while they danced. But when the church women finally organized, they saw to it what drinking was done, was done outside.

This year Lester Marlow was one of the first people to arrive at the dance. He stood around the almost empty hall for an hour, practicing looking rakish and devil-may-care. Lester was temporarily a celebrity in Thalia by virtue of the fact that, only the night before, he had lost a record amount of money to Abilene in an all-night nine-ball game. He had come out the loser by some $820, winning only 11 of 181 games, but that fact did not dismay him at all. Instead he felt almost legendary for having lost so much, and as he strolled around the silent dance floor he continually adjusted the hang of his cashmere sports coat. He wanted to look like the sort of fellow who was ready to accept all risks.

He had not bothered to bring a date, but had a plan involving Jacy that he meant to put into effect at the proper time.

Half an hour later, when Jacy drove up in her convertible, Lester was waiting at the curb, bourbon flask carelessly in hand.

"Why hi, Lester," Jacy said nervously. She knew Sonny and Duane would be coming along any minute.

"I hear you lost some money last night," she added. The sum *had* been impressive.

"Duane coming?" Lester asked at once. Jacy nodded. Any other time Lester would have taken the nod as final, but he had had enough whiskey to be able to set aside his normal caution.

"You know Bobby Sheen, in Wichita?" he asked. "He's going to have a midnight swimming party tonight in his indoor pool. A lot of kids from the club are going to be there. I guess you heard about the last one: his folks were gone to Miami and everybody swam naked. I was there and it was really something. I don't know what they'll do tonight, but his folks are gone again and it's probably going to be pretty wild. If you want to run over there with me after the dance, why don't you? Bobby has great parties."

Lester was smart enough to leave it at that. He rakishly took another sip of bourbon and went back into the dance. Just as he was walking away Sonny and Duane rattled up. They parked the pickup and immediately got in Jacy's car. Duane had noticed Lester talking to her and asked about it.

"Oh, he just wanted to tell me about losing all that money," Jacy said, a little on edge. She had been all primed to enjoy the dance, but Lester's invitation upset her timing a little and Duane came along before she could think things out.

In a few minutes Sonny got out of the car and went in the dance to see what Mr. and Mrs. Farrow were doing. They were on the sponsoring committee and Jacy felt she and Duane probably ought to go in separately unless her father was already drunk enough not to notice them.

While Sonny was reconnoitering Jacy made a quick decision: clearly she would have to go to the swimming party with Lester. It took a rich, fast crowd to go swimming naked, and Jacy always prided herself on belonging to the fastest crowd there was, moral or immoral. Indeed, for a rich, pretty girl like herself the most immoral thing imaginable would be to belong to a slow crowd. That would be wasting opportunities, and nothing was more immoral than waste.

Then too, when word got around that she had gone swimming naked with a lot of rich kids from Wichita Falls her legend would be secure for all time. No girl from Thalia had ever done anything like that.

It was clear that she had to go: the only problem was Duane. He had the night off and was expecting to devote it entirely to her—if she left him at eleven o'clock to go somewhere with Lester it would make him so mad he might even break up with her, and that was to be avoided. She quickly decided that her best bet would be to spend a couple of hours being extremely nice to him, so he would be too much in love with her to be mad when she left. If he was mad anyway she would have to blame it all on her mother—that always worked.

She turned to Duane and started to kiss him, but then stopped and looked at him fondly a moment. "I love you so much tonight," she said. "I wish we could stay together all night."

As soon as they settled into the kiss Jacy turned so that one of her breasts nudged Duane's hand. He was astonished, but not too astonished to take advantage of what was offered him. He pulled her brown sweater out of her skirt and slipped his hand beneath it. Her belly was warm but the brassiere was a cold barrier. It was frustrating to come up against the stiff, cold material when Jacy's warm breasts were just underneath. Duane had experienced that frustration many times before, but it was nothing Jacy usually cared to help him out with; anyway he could hardly expect her to undress right in front of the Legion Hall. Then Jacy broke the kiss with a soft sigh. "Wait a minute," she said. "I don't want to go in right now—let's get in the back seat a few minutes." As soon as they had she edged both her bra straps off her shoulders. Duane slipped the bra down a few inches and her breasts were free. She didn't seem to mind that the tight straps more or less imprisoned her arms. She kissed Duane lingeringly while he touched her breasts and nipples.

Sonny came out to report a minute or two later, meaning to tell the two that it was perfectly safe for them to come in together. Lois and Gene were at the other end of the hall, and both fairly tight besides. When he got to the car and saw what Jacy and Duane were doing, he hated to interrupt, but he wanted to let them know about Jacy's parents. Finally he rapped on the windshield a time or two and went hastily back inside.

Duane was annoyed that Sonny had even knocked. He was deliriously caressing Jacy's bosom, and gladly would have given up the dance for another hour with Jacy in her present mood. For her part, Jacy was quite ready to go in, though she was careful not to show it. The evening ahead would require delicate timing, and it would be unwise to allow Duane too many goodies right at the beginning. She straightened up and smiled at him, her arms still imprisoned by the bra straps.

"We better go in while we can," she said, turning so her back was toward him. "Would you put my bra back on? I can't manage it without taking off this sweater."

Her request was a perfect touch. She had never even used the word "bra" in Duane's presence before, and her willingness to let him put the garment on her added a quality of intimacy to the proceedings that more than compensated for the interruption. He reached under her sweater from behind and slipped the straps up over her slim shoulders—when her arms were free she raised them and let Duane put her breasts back in their cups. When he had the bra hooked he held her a moment, feeling very tender and protective.

A square dance was in progress as they entered the hall and Gene and Lois were dancing. All the men loved to square dance with Lois Farrow because if she was in a good mood she was tolerant of a little free-and-easy feeling around. She might be heavier at the waist than she had been once, but she was still a much prettier woman than most of the men saw at home, and they hovered around her.

During the course of the evening Jacy noticed that more people at the dance paid attention to her mother than to her—an annoying fact that she had never noticed before. Her mother was the belle of the ball, and she wasn't. She could tell by the men's faces that they found her mother very attractive, and the same men hardly noticed her at all. Lois was wearing a loose white dancing dress with a low neckline; her hair was combed out long and shook about her shoulders as she danced. Jacy noticed, too, that her mother was wearing some sort of very brief, fashionable bra. The men could see her breasts move as she danced. It wasn't that Lois' breasts were overly large or indecently exposed, exactly; it was just that they were shaped right and exposed just enough to excite the men in the hall. The more she saw the men watching her mother the more annoyed Jacy became. Not only were the respectable men like the bankers and the doctor watching her mother, but the unrespectables were, too: the farmers and oil-field hands and filling-station men. When her mother danced their faces lit up; when she danced they didn't even notice. It was very insulting. Jacy decided that the next day she would point out to her mother that high-necked dresses would be more becoming for a woman her age. She could say it had to do with facial structure and all that, but it might not work. Her mother knew a good bit about facial structure too.

Jacy was somewhat let down to discover that she had fewer admirers among the male community than she had supposed. A close count revealed that she had only two admirers who really counted: Lester and Duane. Sonny admired her extravagantly, but he had no money and had not been in the backfield, so he really just didn't count. Of course almost all the sweaty little sophomores admired her, but they counted even less than Sonny.

Since there was clearly nothing she could do about her mother, Jacy turned her attention back to the swimming party and guided Duane back to the farthest, darkest corner of the Legion Hall, where the couples most in love always danced. In that corner it was possible to dance very close, and an hour or so of really close dancing fitted in perfectly with Jacy's plan. She had known for a long time that boys had erections on dance floors, at least when they danced with her—apparently it was just one of the little commonplaces of life that pretty girls had to put up with. It had never occurred to her that such a phenomenon could be useful until she began laying plans to get away to the swimming party, when she concluded that the thing to do was make Duane simply delirious with love. If he were delirious, and convinced she was on the verge of giving herself to him, then he couldn't be too mad when she made ready to leave. The quickest way to convince him was by dancing as close as it was possible to dance; so grimly Jacy did it, pressing herself right against him. It was so creepy it almost set her teeth on edge, but the effect on Duane was very strong indeed.

"Let's sneak out to the car a minute," he said, his breath hot in her ear.

Jacy knew that wouldn't be sensible. Much better to hold out the promise of a brief trip to the car after she had his reaction to her leaving. Then if he just had to be pacified some way, she could let him put his hand inside her panties. After all, he *was* very sweet, and had given her a fifty-dollar wristwatch for Christmas.

"I'll go talk to Mother a minute." She said. "Maybe I can talk her into letting me stay out a little later tonight."

She left the dance floor and found her mother in the front foyer, but the circumstances were extremely surprising. Abilene had just come in the door and her mother was kissing him, right there in the Legion Hall. Not only was it a shock to Jacy, but even more of one to the short, pretty brunette Abilene had come in with. Lois was kissing him right on the mouth, and though he seemed a little flushed he was not trying to make her quit. Even when her mother broke the kiss she kept her hands locked around Abilene's neck.

"Merry Christmas," she said, glancing at the brunette, whom she had not noticed. The girl was angry, but she was shorter than Lois and much younger and didn't quite know what to do with her anger.

"Uh, this here's Jackie Lee French," Abilene said. "Jackie Lee, this is Lois Farrow, my boss's wife."

"Hello, Jackie," Lois said.

"I don't have to talk to her," Jackie Lee said, turning angrily to Abilene. "I think she's just awful. What do you mean kissin' her like that, I'm embarrassed to death. I ought to slap her face."

"You can't even reach it, honey," Lois said, smiling at her. "Is your name really French or is that just something you like to do?"

Jackie Lee was absolutely stunned. Her mouth fell open. Nobody had ever talked like that to her before—she was the star barmaid in the tavern where she worked, and all the cowboys and airmen treated her very much like a lady.

Abilene made an amused face and took Jackie Lee by the elbow. "I never come here to referee no fight," he said, moving toward the dance floor. Jackie Lee went with him, holding her butt in indignantly.

Lois snorted in amusement. "I know what I did wrong," she said. "You're supposed to have mistletoe." When she noticed Jacy she snorted again and went into the coatroom. She had a flask of bourbon in her coat pocket and took a neat nip, fishing in her purse for some Kleenex. The dancing had made her sweaty.

"My goodness, Mother," Jacy said. "you oughtn't to behave like that. What would Daddy say if he saw you?"

"Nothing," Lois replied. She took another nip and put the cap back on the flask. "He wouldn't say a damn thing and there's no reason he should. Kissing one another at Christmas time is a custom among civilized peoples. Beside, why are *you* lecturing *me*? What have you been doing bank in that dark corner for the last hour, telling secrets?"

Jacy was taken aback. For a moment she couldn't think how to reply. "I was just coming to ask you something," she said finally. "Lester wants me to go with him to a swimming party in Wichita Falls. Is it okay if I go?"

"Sure," Lois said. "Have a good time. And let's you and me just leave one another alone so far as men are concerned, okay? We compete about enough things as it is."

After Lois went back to the dance floor Jacy decided her feelings were hurt and stayed in the coatroom, sniffling a little. It seemed to her her mother had no sense of responsibility at all, and it was very confusing. Then she grew angry, jerked the bourbon flask out of her mother's coat and took a tiny sip of whiskey in defiance. Like mother, like daughter, people would say if they saw her. She put the flask back and hurried in to Duane before the tears could dry on her cheeks. "Oh I'm just sick," she said. "Mother says I have to go to a swimming party with Lester. I can't get out of it now. It's all her fault and I could just kill her."

Ten minutes later she and Duane were in the front seat of the pickup, kissing. The pickup was parked in a darker place than the convertible. Duane had been furious and it had taken all Jacy's coaxing to get him out of the Legion Hall without some kind of scene taking place. Even when they got to the pickup he kept wanting to go back in and drag Lester out and fight him. Jacy quickly saw that she would have to go to desperate lengths to keep him with her. She sprawled across his lap, kissing him, and she didn't bother to cross her legs and trap his arms with her own, like she usually did. He could dimly make out her white, half-exposed legs in the dark cab. When he touched her lightly above the knee she didn't stop him. Wildly encouraged, he at once forgot Lester and leapt to the attack: he put his hand right on the warm slick band of silk that passed between her legs. She still didn't stop him! It was a miracle of generosity!

Jacy thought so too. She had never left herself quite so wide open before and she hoped Duane appreciated it. After a few nervous minutes of tracing his fingers delicately along the edges of her panties he got up enough nerve to slip his hand inside a leghole and touch the real place, which was surprisingly slippery. He had not really expected to arrive at that destination that evening and he was not quite sure what to do next. Jacy gave no clues. She quit kissing him and pressed her face tightly against his neck, not exactly sure if she liked what was happening or not. She was determined to go on with it a few minutes, though: it would never do to go to a naked swimming party in total ignorance of such matters. Once in a while Duane hit on the right spot and she couldn't help gasping and squirming a little, but most of the time he seemed to be fumbling around in a rather pointless way and that made her impatient. She went a little out of it for a few minutes, waiting for Duane to hit the right spot and quivering with pleasure when he did. It was not until he took his hand away and tried to lay her down on the seat that she realized she had pacified him quite enough. He was actually trying to get on top of her! It was terrible of him to try such a thing when her head wasn't completely clear—it was hard enough for her to finish the evening in the proper tone without him doing that.

"No, no Duane, I've got to go," she said, "Lester will be coming any minute."

She struggled up, gave Duane a quick kiss to show she wasn't mad at him, and then got herself out of the pickup and into Lester's Oldsmobile. She wanted a minute or two to calm down before Lester came out—the dancing and the courting had left her wet with sweat, and she wasn't even sure but what she smelled.

To her great annoyance, Duane got out of the pickup, his hair all tousled, and stood right on the porch of the Legion Hall, obviously waiting for Lester. After all she had given him, it was infuriating! When Lester came out he bumped right into Duane and Duane grabbed him. They had words, that was clear, but Lester managed to shake loose and came on to the Olds. The sleeve of his sports coat was torn.

"What'd he say?" Jacy asked.

"God he's mad," Lester said, panting. He was visibly scared, but he did his best to make light of it. "He called me names, hoping I'd hit him."

"Oh, he's so silly," Jacy said. "I don't know what I'm going to do about him. He's just so crazy about me he doesn't have good sense."

"I'm not saying anything against Duane, but that's a roughneck for you," Lester said. "They never are very sophisticated about these things."

The farther he got from the scene the easier it was for Lester to believe he would have come out well in a fight with Duane. His emotions became mixed, and so did Jacy's. It occurred to her belatedly that it wouldn't have been so bad if Lester and Duane *had* fought over her. At the very least it would have taken a few people's minds off her mother.

They rode to Wichita in silence, each of them thinking out the kind of fight scene they wished had taken place. Lester imagined that he had fought to a standstill, contemptuous of pain, while Jacy saw it differently: Lester would win by dishonorable means, like kicking Duane in the groin, and she would weep on the sidelines. Then she would go and comfort Duane and drive away with him, contemptuous alike of money and parental displeasure, content to be ruined for love.

It seemed a pity to her that Lester hadn't had the guts to start the fight.

THE SHEEN home, where the party took place, was a two-story, twenty-room mansion near the Wichita Falls country club. When they drove up several sports cars were parked in the long curved drive.

"This may be the wildest thing yet," Lester said, smiling at Jacy a little nervously.

No one answered the doorbell, so they went on in. Lights were on and there were girls' coats and boys' coats and glasses and liquor bottles all around, but no people. A Dave Brubeck album was lying next to the phonograph.

Once they opened the basement area it was obvious from the yelling and splashing where everyone was.

"Yep, they're naked," Lester said when they arrived downstairs. He left Jacy in the ping-pong room a minute and peeked into the pool. She found the prospect of walking into a room full of naked city kids somewhat frightening, but she determined to do it and look delighted, whatever she might feel. She let Lester hold her hand when they walked in, and that was something she didn't permit very often.

At first it was not especially startling, because all the Wichita kids were in the water, having water fights and cutting up. You couldn't see what ordinarily you were not supposed to see. There were about six boys and six girls, most of them kids Jacy knew slightly from dances at the country club. One rather famous rich girl was there—her name was Annie-Annie and she was black-headed and notoriously wild. She was only seventeen and had been sleeping with boys for years. Her boy friend was Bobby Sheen, the kid whose parents owned the house. He was a very good-looking boy and had owned the first Ford Thunderbird in that part of the country.

"Hey, look," he yelled, when he saw Lester and Jacy. "New victims."

To Jacy's embarrassment all the kids immediately stopped their water fights and swam right over to the side of the pool where she and Lester were standing. Bobby Sheen made a big show of jumping out of the water and shaking Lester's hand, just as if he had been properly dressed.

"Hi, Jacy," he said, grinning and sluicing the water off his hair with one hand. "Glad you made it to the party. We're dressed informally, as you see."

That brought a big laugh from the kids in the pool, and Bobby cocked his leg in acknowledgment. Jacy laughed too, though a little thinly. She was trying not to look at Bobby's penis, or at anybody's penis.

Annie-Annie got out of the pool too and walked over to them. She was a tall, willowy girl, very graceful. Having her out of the water embarrassed Jacy almost as much as having Bobby out. Streams of water dripped off Annie-Annie's breasts and ran down her stomach into her black pubic hair. She didn't even bother to dry herself, and Jacy thought that most indecent. Letting drops of water shine in one's pubic hair was certainly not a ladylike thing to do.

"You two will have to join the club," Annie-Annie said. "We're the Senior Nudists, and we'll let you join if you want to."

"Sure," Lester said. "How much does it cost? I'll pay for both of us."

"Oh it doesn't cost money," Annie-Annie said, grinning and still dripping. "You just have to be initiated. You walk out on the diving board and take all your clothes off, while we watch. You all willing?"

"Sure," Lester said, not looking at Jacy. "We were just fixing to get undressed anyway."

When he asked Jacy if it was okay, she nodded. She didn't know what else to do. She certainly wasn't anxious to go out on the board and take her clothes off, but she couldn't very well stand around with them on while everybody else was naked.

"I'll go first," Lester said.

All the kids got out of the pool and sat on the edge, kicking their feet in the water. One little kid surprised Jacy no end. He was by far the youngest, littlest kid there; he had freckles and a burr haircut and looked about thirteen, and he had on a green diving mask. While they were all waiting for Lester to untie his shoes the kid walked right past Jacy to get a towel. What surprised Jacy was his penis, which stuck straight out. It wasn't very big or anything but it certainly was sticking out and Jacy thought it was just awful that he would walk around with it like that. A couple of the other girls giggled.

"That's my little brother Sandy," Bobby Sheen said. "Don't pay any attention to him—he's not in the club. He just likes to swim under water with his mask on and look at girls while he fiddles with himself. If he gooses you or anything tell me and I'll make him go to bed."

When Lester got out on the diving board, Jacy expected everybody to yell and whistle, but instead they just sat quietly on the side of the pool, watching. The room was so quiet that they could hear the gentle slap of water against the tile poolside. Lester had expected yelling too, and the silence unnerved him. He decided that speed was of the essence, and his disrobing was incredibly speedy. He peeled off his shirt, yanked down his pants and underwear at the same time, and in a second was in the water. Jacy was amazed at how quickly he did it. He swam over and pulled himself up on the side with the others, no longer the least embarrassed.

When Jacy saw how unselfconscious he had become she grew terribly annoyed with him for having gone first. If he had offered to let her be first, like a gentleman should have, she would be sitting calmly on the side and it would be over with. But everybody in the room was watching her and there was simply nothing to do but bluff it out.

"Goodness, I hope I don't fall off this thing," she said, when she got on the diving board. Diving boards always looked a lot higher up when you were on them.

"Sandy will fish you out if you do," Annie-Annie said.

Sure enough, that hideous little Sandy had slipped into the pool again and was swimming around like a frog about ten feet from the diving board. He had his mask on. Jacy decided she was with the most brazen bunch of kids she had ever seen, and she didn't like one of them.

She took her shoes off first, and then pulled her sweater off over her head. It was not as easy for her to undress fast as it had been for Lester. Once the sweater was off the question was whether she should take her skirt off first and then her bra and panties, or her bra off first and then her skirt and panties. She decided the skirt should come off first and she got out of it without looking up. It was embarrassing to have to reach back and unhook a bra in front of so many kids, but she had so much off already that she couldn't afford to dawdle. It seemed as though she had been out on the board about thirty minutes, as compared to five seconds for Lester. Once she got the bra off she started to yank her panties down and jump, but just as she bent over to slide them down Sandy frogged right under the board and peered up at her through his goggles. Jacy lost her balance and had to sit down very quickly to keep from falling in. At that all the kids burst out laughing and whistling and pointing at Sandy, who was becalmed just beneath her, his tiny little mast sticking up out of the water. It was plainly degrading. Angrily Jacy jerked the panties off her ankles and dropped them right on Sandy's mask.

Instantly the crowd became hers: they all began to laugh *at* Sandy, who frog kicked off toward the shallow end of the pool. Jacy let herself off the board and swam to the poolside to much acclaim—two boys helped her up on the side.

For an hour she swam and giggled, and the longer she stayed with them the more she came to like the crowd. They seemed like the wildest, most intelligent kids she had ever seen, and she determined then and there to throw in her lot with them. Before the night was over she could stand by the pool talking to some boy or other and feel perfectly at ease—the drops of water shining in her pubic hair soon ceased to disconcert her and began to seem rather becoming. At last she could even look at boys' penises without embarrassment.

Only one thing upset her: her new wristwatch, Duane's Christmas present. She had forgotten to take it off when she jumped into the pool. The kids all pooh-poohed her and told her not to worry so much about a fifty-dollar watch and she saw that they were right. It was just a wristwatch, and she could always make it up to Duane some other way.

Ten

JACY AND LESTER HAD NOT BEEN GONE FROM THE DANCE ten minutes before word got around that they were going to a swimming party where everyone would be naked. The reason word got around so fast was that Lester told several of the younger kids about it just before he left. He told them he and Jacy were going to swim naked, just like everybody else. It was almost past belief, but when the kids saw him actually drive away with Jacy they instantly believed it and began to talk about it. Nothing wilder had ever been heard of in Thalia—it was even wilder than actually making out, because that was customarily done in the dark and nothing much could be seen.

In no time there were groups of excited boys standing around, speculating about the look of Jacy's breasts. They even had a hot argument over whether or not blond girls really had blond hair underneath their panties. Some of the younger, illiterate kids thought that all women had black hair in that particular place, but the better-read youths soon convinced them otherwise by reference to the panty-dropping scene in *I, the Jury,* a book the local drugstore could never keep in stock.

The news about Lester and Jacy did not surprise Sonny much. He knew that any time Lester came to Thalia he was likely to end up taking Jacy somewhere, and since he had heard for years that Wichita kids were always having orgies it was only natural that sooner or later Lester would take Jacy to one. The worst thing about it was that it would depress Duane something fierce.

While he was waiting for Duane to get the news, Sonny wandered into the refreshment room. There had been a big table full of plates of cookies, with a huge bowl of punch for the kids and the grown-ups who didn't drink. All the punch was gone and the only cookies left were a few rubbery, inedible brownies. Empty paper cups were strewn all around and a lady in a black dress was bent over picking them up and putting them in a big wastebasket. It was Mrs. Popper. The school teachers' wives always fixed the refreshments for the Christmas dance, but somehow Sonny was surprised to bump into Mrs. Popper just then. Coach Popper never came to dances, and especially not to Saturday night dances. He would not have missed *Gunsmoke* for all the dances in Texas.

"Hello, Sonny," Mrs. Popper said. "Want to help me pick up these cups, since you're not dancing? I'm tired."

She looked tired, too—at least her face did. She was not wearing any makeup and had apparently just come down to do her part with the refreshments.

"Sure, be glad to," Sonny said, picking up a cup. The punch had been a sweet, grape mixture and the rims of the cups were sticky. Sonny gathered about twenty and went to drop them in the wastebasket.

"I guess you still haven't found a new girl friend, have you?" Mrs. Popper asked quietly. Sonny was very startled. He had forgotten she knew about his old girl friend.

"No ma'am, but I'm looking hard," he said.

"Are you?" Ruth said, even more quietly. "It seems to me that if you were really looking hard you might look at me."

Surprised, Sonny did look at her, and remembered that they had become a little fond of one another the afternoon he had driven her to the hospital. He remembered wishing they had kissed, and when he looked at her mouth he wished it again, a very strange wish to be having in the refreshment room of the Legion Hall, during the Christmas dance. But there was something fresh about Mrs. Popper's mouth, as if what was left of the softness and beauty she was said to have had as a girl still lingered there. Sonny was mute. Suddenly he wanted Mrs. Popper and he didn't have the slightest idea what to do about it. He was simply mute, and his silence filled Ruth with despair. She waited a moment, hoping he would say something; when he didn't she felt something slip out of line inside of her and she turned away, holding the wastebasket full of dirty cups. She was afraid she might cry. Sonny saw the look of sadness come in her face and realized he had to say something if he wanted anything to happen between them.

"I'll help you carry that out to the trash barrel," he said.

Then it was Ruth's turn to be mute—mute with relief. They went out the back door together and walked to the group of barrels at the edge of the alley. When they had dumped the cups into one of barrels, Ruth hesitantly came close to Sonny and then came very close. Her cheek was warm against his throat, and he smelled the thin, clean smell of her perfume. For a minute they were too silent—Sonny looked over her head, beyond the town. Far across the pastures he saw the lights of an oil derrick, brighter than the cold winter stars. Suddenly Mrs. Popper lifted her head and they kissed. Their mouths didn't hit just right at first and she put her fingers gently on each side of his face and guided his mouth to hers. The touch of her cool fingers startled and excited him and he pulled her to him more tightly. Her breath was warm across his cheek. Near the end of the kiss she parted her lips and teeth for a moment and touched him once with her tongue. Then she took her mouth away and for several minutes pressed her lips lightly against his throat.

"You're not as scared as you were the first time I wanted to do this," she said.

It was true: Sonny didn't feel at all scared, though his legs were trembling just a little from excitement. He liked to feel Mrs. Popper's lips moving against his throat. This had been the first time in his life when kissing someone had been as pleasant as he imagined kissing should be. It was never that pleasant with Charlene.

"Maybe we're going to have something, after all," Ruth said. "Will you drive me to the hospital again next week, if I arrange for Herman to ask you?"

"You bet," Sonny said. "The sooner the better, as far as I'm concerned." He bent down to find her mouth and Ruth put her hands on his cheeks again. They kissed slowly and luxuriously. At first the kiss was as soft as the first one had been, but then Ruth discovered that Sonny had awakened and was thrusting at her, not so much with his mouth as with himself, wanting more of her. He kissed so hard her head was pushed back and when she opened her eyes for a moment she was looking straight up, toward the stars. Sonny tried to get even closer to her, pulling her against him with his arm. In years nothing had thrilled her so much or touched her so much as he did, simply by wanting her—the rush of her blood made her almost dizzy. She took his tongue into her mouth and touched it lightly for a second with her tongue and the edges of her teeth. Then she took her face away quickly, pressing it against his neck again.

"I'm going home now," she said. "This is no place to dawdle. Tuesday we'll do this more. I really want to do it more, don't you?"

"You bet," Sonny said, bending to kiss her neck. He didn't want to talk—what he wanted was more of the delicate, delicious sensations her mouth had given him. It seemed to him it might just be best if he said so.

"I want to kiss you one more time before you go home," he said.

"Goodness," Ruth said. "Okay." She lifted her hand and traced the edges of his lips with one finger before she kissed him. Again, when they kissed, he pressed against her with an insistence that thrilled Ruth: it was if he were trying to find her very center, her deepest place. While they were kissing, a car turned into the other end of the parking lot and the lights arced in their direction. It was simply some teenagers turning around, but it scared them and they broke apart immediately.

"In three days I'll see you," Ruth said, picking up the wastebasket.

Sonny felt it wouldn't do for him to follow her in, so he walked around the building and entered at the front door. When he came in Duane was standing by the coatroom, obviously furious. Leroy Malone and two or three other boys were standing there too.

"I guess you heard the news," Duane said. "My girl's gone swimming naked with Lester Marlow. That's about the damnedest thing I ever heard. It's enough to make a man go get drunk."

"I guess Mrs. Farrow forced her into it," Sonny said.

"Let's go get drunk," Leroy suggested. "I know where we can steal a couple of bottles of vodka—I saw a man put two in his car just a minute ago."

The suggestion had much appeal, and Sonny immediately seconded it. Getting drunk would be the only way to save Duane from a gloomy night, and besides he felt a good bit like getting drunk himself. Kissing Mrs. Popper had left him excited and confused.

Leroy swiped the vodka and the three of them drove to the poolhall, which generally stayed open until one or two o'clock on Saturday nights. A good many of the younger kids trailed up also, hoping to get a swallow or two of vodka.

They all bought Cokes and took them back to the john one at a time and spiked them. None of them were used to vodka and it was not long before it began to have an effect on their behavior, not to mention their pool shooting. They shot so badly that it took them thirty minutes to finish an eight-ball game.

"Boys, from the way you all are shootin' a feller would think you were drunk," Sam the Lion said innocently, breaking them all up.

Leroy Malone was very inventive when it came to pestering Billy, and when eight-ball began to get tiresome it occurred to him that it might be fun to get Billy drunk. He drew Sonny and Duane aside.

"Let's take Billy somewhere and get him drunk," he said. "Think how funny he'd be drunk."

The boys were not against it. Anything for mischief and adventure.

They grabbed Billy and waltzed him outside. Several of the younger boys got wind of the plot and tagged along.

"We could go on down to the stockpens," Leroy suggested. "There's a blind heifer down there we could fuck. She belongs to my uncle. There's enough of us we could hold her down. It'd be as good a place as any to get Billy drunk."

The prospect of copulation with a blind heifer excited the younger boys almost to frenzy, but Duane and Sonny, being seniors, gave only tacit approval. They regarded such goings on without distaste, but were no longer as rabid about animals as they had been. Sensible youths, growing up in Thalia, soon learned to make do with what there was, and in the course of their adolescence both boys had frequently had recourse to bovine outlets. At that they were considered overfastidious by the farm youth of the area, who thought only dandies restricted themselves to cows and heifers. The farm kids did it with cows, mares, sheep, dogs, and whatever else they could catch. There were reports that a boy from Scotland did it with domesticated geese, but no one had ever actually witnessed it. It was common knowledge that the reason boys from the dairy farming communities were so reluctant to come out for football was because it put them home too late for the milking and caused them to miss regular connection with the milk cows.

Many of the town kids were also versatile and resourceful—the only difficulty was that they had access to a smaller and less varied animal population. Even so, one spindly sophomore whose father sold insurance had once been surprised in ecstatic union with a roan cocker spaniel, and a degraded youth from the north side of town got so desperate one day that he crawled into a neighbor's pig pen in broad daylight and did it with a sow.

"I say a blind heifer beats nothing," Leroy said, and no one actively disagreed with the sentiment. They all got in the pickup and headed for the stockpens, eight or nine of the younger boys shivering in the back.

The stockpens were a mile or two north of town, surrounded by mesquite. When they got there all the boys in the back piled out and went to locate the heifer, but Sonny and Duane stayed in the cab a minute and took a final drink of vodka to warm them up. They gave Billy a Coke that was about a third full of vodka and he drank it happily.

"We better slow him down," Duane said. "If he gets too drunk he may want a turn at the heifer. I doubt old Hank Malone would want an idiot screwin' his livestock."

Sonny got out, not saying anything. It bothered him when people called Billy an idiot. Billy didn't seem *that* much dumber than other people, and he was a lot friendlier than most.

When they got to the lots Leroy was sitting on the fence watching the younger kids chasing the scared, sightless heifer around the dark pen.

"They're after her," he said. "They'll get her in a minute."

The little heifer didn't weigh over three hundred pounds and in a few minutes the boys cornered her by the loading chute and wrestled her to the ground. She struggled for a while but finally gave it up and lay still. A freshman was sitting on her head and her frightened breath raised little puffs of dust from the sandy lot. Sonny, Duane, and Leroy got off the fence and went over to watch. Billy had climbed up on the fence, but he didn't know what was going on and just sat there sucking the empty Coke bottle.

"You boys are holding her wrong," Leroy said in a superior tone. "Ain't you ever fucked a heifer before? You little piss-ants must be virgins. Let her up on her knees."

The younger boys thought that was bitter news: the heifer had been trouble enough to get down. Leroy was a senior, however, and they respected his authority. When they let her up she almost got away, but there were nine of them and they managed to hang on and stop her.

It had come time to decide who went first, and the younger boys, nearing exhaustion just from holding the heifer, pressed for a decision. It would be one of the three seniors, of course.

"You all decide," one of them pleaded. "We can't hold her all night."

At that point Sonny surprised everyone, even himself, by suddenly withdrawing from the competition.

"You all help yourselves," he said hastily. "I drunk too much, I think I'm gonna have to puke."

It was the best excuse he could think of. When he agreed to come to the stockpens he supposed he would naturally be a participant, but the moment he saw the little blind heifer he knew he didn't want to. It had something to do with Mrs. Popper, though he was not certain just what. It didn't seem right to kiss Mrs. Popper and still fiddle around with heifers, blind or not blind. Not only did it not seem right: it no longer seemed like fun. Kissing Mrs. Popper even once was bound to be more fun than anything he could possibly do with the skinny, quivering little heifer. He suddenly felt like he had graduated, and it was an uneasy feeling. He knew Duane and the other boys would think it awfully strange of him not to take a turn, so to fool them he went off in the mesquites and pretended to be sick.

When he came back to the fence the orgy in the lot was in full progress. Duane was attacking the heifer, and Leroy, who had already finished, was helping hold. Two or three of the younger boys had their pants down and were parading lustfully around the lot. One sophomore was in something of a predicament because, by an unexpected stroke of luck, he had actually made out with a girl that night, a pig from Holliday who had come to the dance. As a consequence of that success the boy was feeling somewhat enervated and was attempting to restore himself by beating his member against a cold aluminum gate. When the freshmen started in on the heifer it was even more hilarious: many of them were too short to reach the target comfortably and had to struggle on tiptoe.

Then in the midst of it all the heifer finally broke loose and went dashing across the lot with one of the freshmen hanging furiously to her tail. Sonny was just as glad. Somehow it wasn't as exciting as it had been when he was a freshman.

"Look at ol' Billy takin' that in," Leroy said. "What we ought to do is buy him a piece. We could get the carhop for a dollar, if it was just Billy."

"Hell, if she's that cheap we ought to gone to her ourselves," Duane said. "I heard she was a five-dollar whore."

"Naw," Leroy said. "Anybody with five dollars can do better than Jimmie Sue. That heifer's got prettier legs than she has. She'd be okay for Billy, though. I've heard that idiots die when they're fifteen or sixteen—we oughtn't to sit around and let Billy die a virgin."

"I don't know if we ought to try anything like that," Sonny said. "What if it upset Billy and Sam the Lion found out about it? I'd just as soon not get crosswise with Sam."

"Aw don't be a chickenshit, Crawford," Leroy said. "It might do Billy good to get a little."

"Not if he gets it from Jimmie Sue it wouldn't," Sonny said, very ill at ease.

"You don't have to chip in if you're so stingy," Duane said. "Let's go on and get her."

Sonny quit arguing—he really didn't know how to argue against a whole crowd. He never had even wanted to before. They piled back in the pickup and he drove to the back entrance of the town's one little hotel. Leroy and Duane went up to make arrangements with Jimmie Sue Jones, the available girl, and Sonny sat in the cab with Billy, who was still sucking on the empty Coke bottle. It was almost the first time in Sonny's life that he had not been willing to go on and do whatever the crowd was doing. Before, it had always seemed like fun, whether it was getting drunk or screwing heifers, but he didn't think it would be any fun at all to make Billy do it with Jimmie Sue. Billy was in a perfectly peaceful mood, sucking on the bottle and glad to be along with all the boys, and it seemed a pity to disturb him.

In a minute the boys came out with Jimmie Sue, who was a sort of drive-in version of Penny, only dirtier. She had been car-hopping in Thalia for nine years and everyone in town was tired of her. She had been married once, to a mechanic with rat-tail sideburns, but he soon left her and went back to Bossier City, Louisiana, where he came from. The drive-in paid Jimmie Sue next to nothing and she seldom got tips, so she had to peddle herself when she could to make ends meet. She dyed her hair red and had no eyebrows except those she painted on in the morning, and she was so absentminded that sometimes she only painted on one eyebrow and went around like that all day. For Billy she didn't bother to paint on even one. When she got in the cab it immediately began to smell so oniony that Sonny had to roll his windows down. Jimmie Sue looked at Billy disgustedly.

"Why that thing's just a kid," she said. "You all oughtn't to woke me up for a thing like that. I ought to get at least two dollars."

"Hell no, you said a dollar and a half," Duane reminded her.

"Well, I'd just as soon it was an idiot as not," Jimmie Sue said, unpeeling a stick of chewing gum. "The only thing I draw the line at is Mixicans and niggers. I guess I told you about the time that nigger man in high heels stole my suitcase right out of the bus station, that time I went to Los Angeles. . . ."

It had been Jimmie Sue's one adventure. She saved her money and went to Los Angeles to work, but the very hour she arrived in the Los Angeles bus station a black man wearing high heels stole her suitcase and all her possessions. Jimmie Sue had never been so disappointed in all her life as she was with Los Angeles. She couldn't get a job and had to turn around and hitchhike back to Thalia, to keep from starving. Hitchhiking across the desert without any eyebrows proved a slow business, too. If it hadn't been for a carful of horny Mexicans she never would have got out of Needles, California, and bad as that was, Lordsburg, New Mexico was worse. Tired of eating dust, she let a Negro pick her up. By the time she got back to Thalia she had nothing good to say about minority groups.

Billy looked at her with mild curiosity, but was obviously neither disturbed nor excited by her presence in the cab. Sonny drove back over the narrow, one-vehicle road that cut through the mesquite to the stockpens.

"You all just get that thing out while I get ready," Jimmie Sue said. "This ain't the ideal dressin' room."

Billy was happy to get out: he wondered if they were going to sit on the fence and watch the boys chase the cow again. To his surprise, no sooner was he out than six or seven of the boys grabbed him and unceremoniously threw him down on the cold hard ground. They took off his shoes, pants, and underwear. Groups of boys were always taking his pants off, and that alone wouldn't have bothered him. It was having them off so late at night and at the stockpens that puzzled him. Also his legs were cold.

"All right," Jimmie Sue said. "Let the stupid little thing in."

"Wait a minute," Duane said. "There's a flashlight there in the glove compartment. We want to show him where to go."

He got the flashlight and flashed it over Jimmie Sue, who was laying back in the pickup seat, as spraddle-legged as the narrow pickup would permit her to be. All the boys looked, and for a moment, paused in amazement. None of them had realized quite how fat Jimmy Sue was until the flashlight played over her huge hams and flabby stomach; nor had they considered how unappetizing the female anatomy could be when presented in its most unappealing light. They were all quiet for a moment, staring. It was only after they had looked for a while that they began to feel a little stirred up. Jimmie Sue was so ugly it was almost exciting—it was as if they were finally being shown the nasty things parents and preachers had always whispered about. It wasn't exactly what they had expected, because they persisted in thinking about it in terms of pretty girls, movie stars like Elizabeth Taylor, but it was precisely what they had been taught to expect, and after the shock wore off it was exciting.

"Shove that thing in here with me," Jimmie Sue said. "I never hired out for no peep show."

The boys shoved Billy in, more or less between Jimmie Sue's legs, and tried to shut the door. They couldn't get it completely shut but there were so many of them there was not much chance it would come open.

Billy grunted with surprise and tried to back out, but he was trapped.

"Why this is the dumbest thing I ever saw," Jimmie Sue said. "It don't even know what to do."

The boys flashed the light long enough to see that Jimmie Sue had managed to catch Billy with her legs, but she yelled at them to turn it off and they did. Apparently Billy got close enough to the object of it all that he caught on, because he stopped pushing backward and in a moment the pickup began to rock a little from side to side. Everybody yelled encouragement.

"Quit that yellin' and get hold of this thing," Jimmie Sue said irritably. "He ain't in."

The flashlight was brought into play again and it was discovered that Billy, cramped as he was had completely missed his natural target and was poking energetically at a deep wrinkle in the folds of Jimmie Sue's stomach. Duane and Leroy laughed until they could barely stand up, but the younger kids were more fascinated than amused. None of them had ever seen so strange a sight, and they made no effort to correct Billy's aim. Jimmic Suc was getting madder by the minute.

Sonny stood by the rear end of the pickup, determined not to look. It wasn't that he thought Billy would mind him looking—it was just that he didn't really want to look. Jimmie Sue was uglier than Charlene, and the pickup would smell like onions for weeks.

"Why goddamn you, you little thing!" Jimmie Sue yelled furiously. "Now look what a mess you made!"

Sonny knew from the tone of her voice that it was time to get Billy out, so he hurried around to the door. The boys still had the flashlight on and were cackling and giggling: Billy had reached the end of his journey while still in the wrinkle, and Jimmie Sue was pounding at his face, trying to back him out of the pickup. Sonny managed to scatter the crowd enough to get the door open and help Billy out, but calming him down was something else. He was scared and confused and shivering, and Jimmie Sue had bloodied his nose. Sonny helped him get dressed and even found the empty Coke bottle for him, but Billy no longer wanted it.

"Well, now I know idiots is just as bad as Mixicans," Jimmie Sue said. "Don't you wake me up for that crazy thing no more. I wouldn't mess with him agin for less than three-and-a-half."

By the time they got back to the poolhall the front of Billy's shirt was all covered with blood. Sonny couldn't get the nosebleed completely stopped. He knew Sam the Lion was going to be furious, and he didn't blame him: it was no way to treat Billy. He wished he had known how to stop the whole business, but the only possible way would have been to offer to fight if they didn't let Billy alone, and he couldn't very well offer to fight when his own best buddy was one of the crowd. If Lester and Jacy hadn't run off to the swimming party none of it would have ever happened.

As soon as the pickup stopped Billy jumped out and ran in the poolhall. It was officially closed, but they could all see Sam the Lion inside, reading a newspaper he had spread out on one of the tables. All he was really doing was waiting for Billy to come in. They lived in a plain little three-room apartment above the poolhall, and Sam never went to bed until Billy was in safe.

Billy ran right on past him, up the stairs, and Sam left his paper and followed him. The boys waited nervously outside, wondering if they would be able to narrate the episode in such a way that Sam the Lion would see the humor in it. Sonny knew they couldn't and waited miserably for Sam to come down, but the boys who thought they might strutted around on the sidewalk talking with great bravado. Duane was sleepy and lay down in the cab of the pickup and went to sleep. The boys could have left, but none of them really wanted to go home until Sam the Lion came down and bawled them out. His bawling them out would relieve their minds of whatever minor guilt feelings they had about Billy, and would leave them free to enjoy the celebrity of having participated in such an event.

Finally the light went out in the upstairs apartment and Sam the Lion came down. He opened the door and stood quietly a minute, looking at the boys. Sam the Lion was not the type who yelled and cussed about the pranks boys pulled. They could not see his face, but the light from the poolhall touched his white mane of hair.

"Who's got his underwear?" he asked, after a minute.

Sonny had them, and it put him on a terrible spot. He had been so anxious to get Billy back in his pants that he had forgotten to put the underwear on him—he picked them up later and stuffed them in his pocket. For a moment he was tempted to say nothing and pretend the underwear was lost—if he pulled them out and handed them over it would make him seem more of a participant than he had been. Sam didn't withdraw the question and the other boys began to look at Sonny nervously, so he took the underwear out of his pocket and awkwardly handed them over.

"When I was helpin' get his pants on I couldn't find them," he said. "I just forgot to hand them to him."

"Who went and bloodied his nose?"

"Jimmie Sue Jones," Leroy said. "We thought he was getting tired of being a virgin so we chipped in and bought him a piece. Jimmie Sue got mad about somethin' and gave him that nosebleed."

"Jimmie Sue?" Sam said, startled. "You what?" He had supposed it was just a simple case of the boys taking Billy's pants off, something that happened all the time. When he realized what Leroy said he was stunned, and sat down in the doorway of the poolhall.

Sonny became really worried. "Is Billy all right?" he asked. "We're sorry, Sam."

"He went to sleep," Sam said, a little absently. "Did he want to go with Jimmie Sue?"

"Not hardly," Leroy said. "He didn't even know what he was supposed to do."

Sam scratched his ankles for a minute and then stood up again. He didn't look particularly mad, just tired and discouraged.

"Boys, get on home," he said. "I'm done with all of you. I don't want to associate with you anymore and I don't want Billy to, either. Scaring an unfortunate creature like Billy when there ain't no reason to scare him is just plain trashy behavior. I've seen a lifetime of it and I'm tired of putting up with it. You can just stay out of this poolhall and out of my picture show and café too."

With that he closed and locked the door and went upstairs to bed. The boys were thunderstruck. They had been prepared for Sam to rage and storm and instead he had simply closed the door and locked them out. No one knew what to say. They stood on the cold sidewalk a minute, confused.

"We're his best customers," Leroy said. "He can't run us off, can he?"

Sonny and the other boys knew very well he could. It made Sonny feel a little sick. They all crawled back into the pickup and Sonny delivered them to their homes. Duane didn't fully wake up until they were back at the rooming house, and when Sonny told him what Sam the Lion had done he though it was hilariously funny. Since he had been lying down and Sam had not seen him it was clear to Duane that he was not included in the banishment.

"Good thing I went to sleep when I did," he said. "I'd hate to have to eat at that drive-in all the time."

He went in and contentedly went back to sleep, but Sonny stayed awake and reread most of an old copy of *Outdoor Life*. Duane taking the news the way he had made the evening even more depressing, and it had been depressing enough as it was.

Kissing Mrs. Popper had been the only good thing that happened all night, and Sonny had no idea what would come of that. It occurred to him that at least it would be something exciting to think about in bed, so he turned the light off and tried it. Her face and the touch of her lips were fresh in his mind and it worked pretty well, though occasionally, before he finished, a few old images of Jacy and Genevieve slipped in. Jacking off was an old game, monotonous, but a good way to get to sleep when all else failed.

Eleven

When Sonny kissed Mrs. Popper outside the Legion Hall it seemed to him that a whole spectrum of delicious experience lay suddenly within his grasp. No kisses had ever been so exciting and so full of promise, neither for him nor for Ruth. She felt as if she were finally about to discover something she had somehow missed discovering twenty years before. Neither of them foresaw any great difficulties, just the minor difficulty of keeping it all secret.

Both, in fact, were so excited that they longed to talk about it to someone, but that they couldn't do. In Thalia sex was just not talked about. Even Genevieve would go to considerable lengths to keep from calling a spade a spade. Everything acknowledged the existence of sex: babies were born now and then, and things to prevent them were sold at the drugstores and one or two of the filling stations. The men told dirty jokes and talked all the time about how they wished they had more pussy, but it didn't really seem to bother many of them so long as the football team was doing well. The kids were told as little about sex as possible and spent most of their time trying to find out more. The boys speculated a lot among themselves and got the nature of the basic act straight when they were fairly young, but some of the girls were still in the dark about it when they graduated from high school. Many girls simply refused to believe that the things the boys peed out of could have any part in the creation of babies. They knew good and well that God wouldn't have wanted any arrangement of His to be *that* nasty.

The only thing everyone agreed on was that the act itself could only be earthly bliss. Once the obstacle of virginity was done away with, mutual ecstasy would be the invariable result. One or two of the bolder girls knew differently, but they didn't want to be thought freaks so they kept quiet about their difficulties.

When Sonny and Ruth met again, the Tuesday after the dance, they both expected things to be simple and wonderful, and they were both disappointed. For one thing, they both felt compelled to go through with the unnecessary trip to the doctor; both of them were nervous and tense and they rode to Olney in silence. They dusty air had given Ruth a sniffle, and Sonny could see the bluish shadows under her eyes. The wait in Olney was short, but on the way back they found themselves even more at a loss for conversation than they had been coming. Ruth could not imagine what had possessed her to think she could bring off such a thing as a love affair. They each concluded that they were not as appealing in the daylight as they had been in the dark, so they sat looking out their separate windows at their separate sides of the road. There was little in the leafless winter landscape to cheer them.

It was only when Sonny drove the Chevrolet into the dimness of the garage, with Herman's lawn tools and hedge shears hanging neatly on the walls, that they regained some hope. They both realized they were about to miss the chance they had been counting on. Sonny reached for Ruth's hand and she quickly scooted over toward him and they kissed. The kiss was awkward but warm and they didn't think of moving apart—for several minutes they let their mouths and faces touch.

Both would have been just as happy to stay in the garage all afternoon, but they felt obligated to complete the experience, and for that they had to go in the house, where things were not so good. The wallpaper in the bedroom was light green, and blotched in places. It was the bedroom where Ruth and Herman had spent virtually all their married nights: on one wall there was a plaque Herman had been given for taking a troop of Boy Scouts to the National Jubilee. Two or three copies of *High School Athletics* lay on the bedside table.

"Are you sure he won't come?" Sonny asked. The room seemed full of the coach.

"You know he won't," Ruth said. "He's just starting basketball practice."

She took his hand again and they kissed standing up. Neither of them really believed what she said: as they kissed both of them kept imagining the coach walking in. They were so conscious of him they hardly felt the kiss, but Ruth was determined to go on however dangerous it was, even if Herman did walk in.

They were unable to think of a smooth way to undress—it would have been better to do it while they were still kissing, but neither of them was expert enough for that. Ruth had on a dress and a slip, both of which had to come off over her head. Sonny could not even get her bra unhooked with the dress still on. Both of them wished for something to say, something that would break the tension, but neither could think of anything. Finally they simply broke apart and hurried about their own undressing. Ruth got her dress off, but when she bent to pull the slip over her head one of the straps caught on a bobby pin—for an awkward moment she could not get the slip loose. Her face was hidden in the silk. Sonny moved to help her, but just as he did she tore it loose and looked up at him with a wry smile, as if to comment on her awkwardness. They took their undergarments off at the same time, both of them choked with embarrassment. Ruth glanced at Sonny's body, curious and a little frightened. He was two or three steps away from her and for a moment they did not know how to get to one another. Sonny was too self-conscious about his erection to move. Finally, with another wry smile, Ruth sat down on the bed and he sat down with her. When she lifted her arms to embrace him he saw the small scar on her breast. They fell over in an embrace but in a moment scrambled up again: the room was cold and they needed to be under the covers.

When they were covered and warm they felt better and kissed again with pleasure. They were amazed at the feel of one another's skin, but in a minute or two they began to be nervous again. It seemed to them they must have been lying there kissing for half an hour at least. Ruth touched her hand to Sonny's throat and chest now and then, but other than that she didn't move. He felt very unsure: it occurred to him that perhaps his experience was inadequate. There might be some way of doing it that was especially suitable to ladies, some way he knew nothing about.

Ruth had her eyes closed and was waiting trustfully for a beautiful thing to happen to her. She knew that Herman knew nothing about the beautiful thing, or that if he did he had no interest in giving it to her. But she supposed Sonny would know: she would only have to wait and receive it. His body was very warm against her. It was only when she opened her eyes and looked at him that she remembered how young he was and realized he didn't know what to do.

"It's all right," she said, opening her legs. Sonny gratefully moved about her, but there was another long moment of awkwardness when they tried to join. Sonny was not absolutely sure of the target, and when he found it Ruth could not at first accommodate him easily. When he moved she gasped and Sonny's face was so close to hers that he could not tell whether she felt pain or pleasure. She said nothing, so he kept moving—in a moment it became easier and pleasure made him move faster and more surely.

For Ruth the discomfort was only momentary, but even once it ceased she could not manage to cross over into pleasure. The bed had begun to squeak. As Sonny moved more confidently it squeaked louder, and Ruth could not help hearing it. She would never have imagined it could squeak so loudly. Soon the squeaking drove all hope of pleasure from her mind. The noise made her fearful that someone outside the house might hear it; anyone walking on the sidewalk in front of the house could hear it, she was sure.

In a few moments she was near panic: she was convinced that everyone in Thalia could hear the squeaking bedsprings. If all the cars stopped, if the housewives came to their doors and listened, they could all hear the squeaking bed and would know what she was doing. It was a horrible bed; she felt it had betrayed her. No one could receive a beautiful thing with such a squeaking going on beneath her. She tried to lie very still, but Sonny's movement went on, and the sound was constant. Finally she began to cry, and when the tears dripped down her cheeks and wet Sonny's neck he realized that something was wrong after all. He raised his head and saw that Ruth's eyes were flooded with tears. She was ashamed that she had stopped him and quickly hooked her arm over his neck so he wouldn't raise up and see her face again. Sonny felt she must want him to stop but his body didn't want to and in a moment he went on, hearing the springs only as a faint background to his pleasure. Soon he finished and lay still upon her.

As soon as the squeaking stopped Ruth felt better. She kept her arms around Sonny, holding him so he could not see her face and now and then wiping the tears out of her eyes with the back of one hand. Once Sonny became still it was very pleasant to have his body upon hers—he was so warm and young, almost like a child. She had always wanted a child more than anything, but Herman wouldn't hear of it—he didn't want the expense. On the rare occasions when he took his pleasure of her he was always careful to wear a condom, even though they made Ruth's bladder hurt. Having Sonny upon her was very different, and deeply pleasant. She ran her hands up and down his back, and when she felt composed again lifted her arms so he could raise his head.

"I'm sorry I cried," she said. "I guess I was just scared."

"Aw, he isn't going to come," Sonny said, no longer worried. "They're runnin' plays right now, I bet."

"No, not scared of that," Ruth said, touching his mouth softly with her fingers. "I was scared I could never do this, I guess. I wanted to be wholehearted about it, but I wasn't."

She was silent a moment. "Do you know what it means to be heart-broken?" she said. "It means your heart isn't whole, so you can't really do anything wholeheartedly."

Sonny wanted to leave, but he didn't think he should, quite so soon. Mrs. Popper was sad, but at least she seemed calm and she kept touching him softly with her hands. He kissed her lightly and her cheeks were warm; then he stretched and drew the covers back a little, so he could see more of her body. She was very slim and small-breasted, her arms a little too thin. When Ruth saw he was looking at her she grew frightened. She had never considered her body attractive, and she was afraid that if Sonny looked too long he would not want to be with her anymore. She turned on her side and curled toward him, her head on his thighs. Her shoulder bones stuck out, making her look even thinner. Sonny rubbed her back a minute and then got out of bed and quietly dressed. When he sat down on the edge of the bed to tell her good-bye she was on the verge of tears again.

"I was right the first time, wasn't I?" she said hopelessly. "I'm too old and ugly for a young man like you. I don't know how to do this anyway and maybe I'm too old to learn. I can't do anything without crying about it—how could you like me?"

"I like you," Sonny said awkwardly—actually he was not sure. All her crying upset him and made him nervous about himself, and she was certainly not as pretty as a movie star or as pretty as Jacy. Still, he did like her some. Since they hadn't got caught he had begun to feel elated about the whole thing. It was an adventure to have slept with somebody's wife. He didn't know if he would tell anybody or not, but it was sort of a feather in his cap, nonetheless.

Ruth sighed. "If you like me then you decide what to do about me," she said. "I'm not going to chase after you anymore. If you really like me you figure out how to come and see me—I sure don't want you to drive me to the doctor. I think right now you just like what you can do with me. That's fine, but now that you've found out women think you're good looking you'll probably want to go do it with somebody younger and prettier. I wouldn't blame you one bit."

Suddenly she wanted him to leave. She had become embarrassed about her body and didn't want him to see her naked anymore. She stayed curled up on the bed, her breasts and loins hidden from him.

"Track starts pretty soon," Sonny said. "I just won't go out. I can sneak up the alley and in the back door."

He sounded like he really wanted to, and Ruth changed back to hoping. What if he did only want her for sex? It was more than anyone else had ever wanted her for. Suddenly she felt like doing something a little wanton and she sat up and kissed him, her naked breasts against his shirt. Sonny liked that, and when he left he looked back through the doorway and saw her, still naked, bending over the bed to strip away the sheets. It would be well worth giving up track to come and see her, even though the coach would rage and storm at losing his only decent hurdler.

THE SECOND TIME Sonny came, Ruth wanted to tell him that the squeaking bedsprings bothered her, but she didn't quite have the nerve. She really wanted them to lie down on the floor, but she was afraid if she told Sonny he would think her depraved or something. She knew men were curious when it came to women's desires. Nothing revolted Herman more than to think that she was enjoying him that way. Once or twice in their marriage she had felt something good, but when she began to move or wiggle beneath him to make it feel even better it made Herman furious. "Lay still," he said. "What kind of woman do you think you are, anyway?" After that she lay still, and if she happened to feel something a little good she didn't let him know. Herman was so heavy that most of the time she just felt mashed.

She had not really expected Sonny to come again; when he slipped inside the back door she was filled with delight, and determined not to make any mistakes that might scare him away. They were both still very nervous, and the bedsprings bothered Ruth even more than they had the first time. They were almost too much. She felt something a little good but the springs kept her from concentrating on it; every time she felt it the grinding of the springs drove it away, and finally she simply endured them, waiting for the quiet lovely time when he was still, dozing on her body.

Sonny knew something was wrong because Ruth's body was cold and her arms and legs were tensed—she was trying to hold herself in such a way that the springs would be silent. She managed not to cry, but it took a long time for the tension to drain out of her—she was so tense that even the aftermath was not so enjoyable. Neither of them spoke—they simply had no words. Ruth was not sure she wanted him to come anymore; it was not working out at all like she had imagined. But when she felt a little better she began to stroke his back and to play with the shaggy hair at the back of his neck, and she decided she did want him again. Something about it was good, even if much was bad.

ON HIS third visit she gathered up her nerve and told him, as they were undressing, that the noise of the bedsprings bothered her. She asked if they could lie on a quilt on the floor. Sonny was mildly surprised, but it was okay with him. When Ruth saw that he didn't think it was wrong of her to want it all to be nice she was so relieved she couldn't speak. She walked to the hall closet, naked, and got an old blue quilt that she and Herman had quit using years ago.

They spread the quilt on the floor by the little gas stove and sat a moment watching the flicker of the blue gas flames as they touched one another. They still couldn't talk, but they had ceased to be nervous, and they quit trying to conceal their loins from one another. For Ruth the quiet was wonderful. All she could hear was Sonny's breath and her own and she knew no one in the street could hear them breathing. She realized too that Sonny was enjoying her keenly and that made her glad. He was in no hurry and Ruth had moments of pleasure that were stronger than any she had ever known before. She discovered that Sonny didn't mind at all if she moved: in fact, he liked it. She became excited enough that her breath was ragged, but it was all still new to her and she could not pull the moments of pleasure together into one that was complete. For her the beautiful time was still afterward. Sonny was still inside her when he went to sleep, and Ruth found that lovely. It was almost as if he were a child inside her, and she put her calves over his legs to keep him there. When he finally came out she slipped upward on the quilt so that his warm cheek was against one of her breasts. It was so lovely that she wanted it not to change. That day, for the first time, she was regretful when he had to leave.

By THE time Sonny had paid her a half-dozen visits he was everything to Ruth: he was what made the days worth confronting. The thought that he might quit coming filled her with terror. The thought of going back to the existence she had had before he came was too much to face.

Sonny allowed her to love him, though it was strange to him and he had to get used to it slowly. They were soon able to spend four or five hours a week on the old blue quilt. Ruth learned a great deal about Sonny and also a great deal about herself. After the first weeks she did nothing that would frighten him. She learned that he liked to be naked around her—it gave him a sense of adventure. She gladly let him, often mending his shirts or patching his pants after they had made love. She discovered that she had no particular modesty about her loins, only about her breasts, which seemed to her too small. Also she was afraid the small scar might disgust Sonny, since apparently it disgusted Herman. She took to wearing one of Herman's old hunting shirts while they talked. Sonny didn't like for her to wear anything while they were making love, but she always put it on afterward. She learned gradually how to play with him and how to tease him. One day she got a brush and comb and showed him a way to comb his hair that she felt was more becoming. Sonny was delighted. She would have liked to cut his hair for him, but there wouldn't have been time.

She soon made terms with lovemaking itself, though for a time they were not the best possible terms. She thought that once they relaxed with one another the beautiful thing would happen, the whole moment toward which all the sharp little individual moments tended. She had read about it, she expected it, she longed for it, and came very close to it, but it eluded her. For a week or two she was sure, every time, that it would happen. Once or twice she came so close that she was desperate for it to happen, and when she missed it after all her agitation was very intense. The violence of her excitement surprised Sonny and disturbed him a little: despite her weeping spells he thought of her as a quiet, rather timid woman. Her movements were sometimes so strong and unexpected that he was thrown off balance—once when she missed she was beside herself with disappointment. "Oh please," she said. "Please keep going." Sonny was already gone, but she continued to struggle against him until they were both soaked with sweat; he could not call himself back, and she gave up.

After that Sonny didn't come back for three days and Ruth was fearful she had ruined it all. When he did come she was so thrilled and relieved that she resolved not to seek the moment if it was going to put everything else in danger. If he would keep coming, keep wanting her, that would be enough. They sat on the blue quilt and she opened his shirt and rubbed his chest with her palm. When she looked past him, at the green wallpaper and Sears and Roebuck furniture she realized that she had lived for years in a room that was terribly drab.

Sonny was hesitant about making love, worried that he could cause Ruth disappointment again. "No, look," she said, taking his hand and kissing his palms and fingers. "Nothing was your fault. You have to remember that I've been lonely for a long time. Loneliness is like ice. After you've been lonely long enough you don't even realize you're cold, but you are. It's like I was a refrigerator that had never been defrosted at all—never. All these years the ice has just been getting thicker. You can't melt all that ice in a few days, I don't care how good a man you are. I didn't even realize it, like I didn't realize till just now how ugly this room is. I don't know, maybe at the center of me there's some ice that never will melt, maybe it's just been there too long. But you mustn't worry. You didn't put it there." She moved her hand up to his shoulders.

The talk of ice and refrigerators meant little to Sonny, but he was relieved that she wanted him to make love to her again. That day she was very warm and amenable, but much calmer—calmer than he had ever known her. He recognized that in a way she had withdrawn from the struggle, but his own pleasure was so strong that he merely felt grateful, not responsible. She saw to it that he didn't feel responsible, and for herself, had no difficulties except at the very end—then, for a wistful, regretful moment, she felt like crying.

AFTER THAT, for more than a month, she concentrated on making Sonny welcome. He came often, sometimes just to make love, sometimes staying to drink some hot chocolate or to let her mend his clothes. He tolerated the chocolate and the clothes mending, but Ruth knew very well that what they did on the quilt was what he really liked, what he enjoyed doing with her. It thrilled her that that, of all things, would be what made a person want to come and see her. She expected, almost from day to day, that he would tire of her, and when she saw him coming in the door wanting that same thing of her, she was always happy for a moment.

THEN, IN March, things changed. Sonny came in one day and repeated a story about Coach Popper, one he had just heard. The week before the coach had taken the track boys to a meet in Forth Worth. Bobby Logan was sharing a room with the coach and in the middle of the night the coach mistook Bobby for Mrs. Popper and kissed him on the ear. All the boys thought that was pretty hilarious, and Sonny repeated the story to Ruth because he thought it might get her to talking about the coach a little. He could not help being curious about their life together. She told him that the coach seldom touched her, but Sonny could hardly believe that. The coach was so hairy and horny looking that the boys all supposed he kept after her all the time. Around the gym and the practice field the coach gave the impression that he was an inveterate woman chaser. "Find 'em, fool 'em, fuck 'em, and forget 'em," he was often heard to say. Sonny had the nagging feeling that the reason Ruth couldn't come with him was because the coach's tool was bigger and better. Time and again the coach had pointed out to one boy or another the ignominy of having an insufficient tool.

"Why hell yes, Joe Bob," he would say. "A feller can get along with false teeth and a glass eye and hearing aids and even a hook or a wooden leg if he has to, but there ain't no known substitute for a big dick. I guess you're just out of luck."

When he told Ruth about the ear-kissing incident he half expected her to be flattered that her husband would miss her so, but instead she looked miserable and forlorn. They had already finished lovemaking and she was so dispirited by the news that she neglected even to cover herself with the flannel shirt.

"I don't care," she said, tears seeping out of her eyes. "I don't care who he likes. If he wants to play around with little boys and they think it's funny why should I care? I just get tired of everybody thinking he's such a mighty man just because he coaches football. I'm the one they think is nothing, just his mousy wife, and they're right, I am mousy. I might not have been if I hadn't been ignored for twenty years. Now I'm forty and I don't have any children and I can't even do . . ." sniffed, "I can't even do sex."

Sonny was stunned. He had never been so surprised.

"Why did you stay with him?" he asked finally. Then it was Ruth who was dumb. It was a question she had avoided for years.

"I wasn't brought up to leave a husband," she said in a small voice. "I guess that's why. Or maybe I was just scared to."

"But how did you come to marry him?" Sonny asked, still curious.

"Because my mother didn't like him, I guess," Ruth said. "I was fooled too. I was twenty years old and I thought hairy-chested football coaches were about it. I've paid for my own bad judgment."

There the conversation stalled—Ruth was too depressed to talk, and Sonny was confused. It seemed to him that Ruth must think the coach was queer or something, and the coach was the last man that anyone would accuse of such a thing. A few of the boys thought Mr. Cecil must be—they knew he got some kind of a kick out of watching them all swimming and horsing around naked at the irrigation ditch—but Mr. Cecil was much too much of a gentleman to do anything out of the ordinary, and nobody knew for sure about him. To suspect the coach of being that way was entirely too much—he didn't even mention the conversation to Duane. In fact, he had never told Duane he was sleeping with Mrs. Popper because he was afraid Duane would make fun of him for sleeping with an older woman.

It was that night, after that conversation, that things began to change for Ruth. She dreamed she was having a baby. She had had such dreams for years, but usually they were vague and fragmentary, but this one was vivid. It was not just a baby she had, though; it was Sonny. He was removed from between her legs, and afterward lay at her breast.

The next day Sonny came, and while they were spreading the blue quilt on the bedroom floor Ruth remembered the dream. It was very vivid in her mind as she undressed. She lay quietly, her eyes closed, as Sonny began, but almost before she knew it she became excited, so much so that she could not be still. She thought of the dream again, hoping the excitement would die before she became completely possessed by it, but insead of dying it became keener. Because of the dream, pleasure took her over: with her eyes shut she could pretend she was giving birth. Sonny was inside her but in truth she was bringing him out—it was that which excited her. She grabbed his hands and put them on her thighs, so that he would force them wider. She was filled with a strength that she had not suspected and held him with her thighs, just at the entrance, just connected, both of them struggling, until she was finally seized, rent by what she felt. Then she took Sonny back to her, her heart was pounding, her eyelids fluttering; she almost fainted with the relief of delivery. For half an hour she slept, not moving, and Sonny lay on top of her, not knowing if he dared move. He had no doubt that Ruth had broken through, but her success was as strange and almost as frightening as her failures. The strength she had called up amazed him: for minutes she had held him with just her thighs, his arms pinned to his sides so tightly he could not get one free. Yet, sleeping beneath him, she might have been a girl, so still and at peace she seemed.

When Ruth awakened she did not want Sonny to leave. She felt entirely comfortable, and she wanted to touch him, play with him, have his hand on her. After that, she never used the dream again, but she kept it in her mind as a safeguard, and even though she still sometimes missed, having the dream was a great reassurance.

In the weeks after Ruth's breakthrough the two of them became very close and comfortable. Once Sonny quit worrying about her response or lack of response, he found her much more pleasant to be with, and there were even afternoons when he visited her, not to make love but just to talk, hold hands, or watch television.

Only one problem arose, and that was one they had been expecting: the town knew about them. A couple of the housewives who lived along the alley compared notes, and in a few days the town knew. Sonny worried about it a lot, Ruth hardly at all.

"What do you think the coach would do if he found us?" Sonny asked one day. Ruth was sitting on the quilt combing her brown hair. She had decided to let her hair grow longer.

"Probably shoot us both," she said lightly. "He's always glad to have an excuse to use his deer rifle."

Sonny mused on that and decided she was right. "What do you think we ought to do about it?" he asked.

"I don't know," Ruth said, puckering her mouth at him happily. "Why don't we buy a new quilt? This one's about had it."

The next day she got one, for sentimental reasons also blue.

Twelve

One night in mid-March Sonny woke up too early—around 3:30 a.m. The first thing that occurred to him was that Sam the Lion would be asleep. Sam the Lion had made his decree of banishment stick, and, though Sonny had endured it as best he could, he had about reached the point where he could endure it no longer. It occurred to him that if he got dressed and went down to the café Genevieve might let him sit and talk awhile. A cold March norther was blowing and the warm blankets were hard to leave, but the chances were he would have to leave them in an hour or so anyway, to make an early butane run.

Genevieve was sitting in one of the booths, reading an old issue of the *Ladies Home Journal*. To his immense relief she looked delighted to see him.

"Come on in here," she said, "I'm not going to throw any bottles at you."

"Could I have a cheeseburger?" he asked quickly. One of the worst parts of the penalty had been eating at the drive-in, where the cheeseburgers were half raw and the tomatoes soggy.

"You can have two if you want them," she said, and she made him two while he sat nervously in the booth. When she brought them in he swallowed the first one in only five or six bites.

"Quit eating so fast," Genevieve said. "You've lost weight. Even if it was a terrible thing to do to Billy, I'm on your side."

Sonny was grateful. "I couldn't talk them out of it," he said. "It was Leroy's idea."

"Where was Duane?" she asked.

It was a ticklish question. Duane had gone right on using the café and the poolhall, just as if he hadn't been along. It was a sore spot with the other boys, and a few of them wanted to tell Sam the Lion about Duane's part in it. Thinking about it made Sonny uneasy.

"He was there," he admitted. "Just don't tell Sam."

"I figured he was," Genevieve said quietly. "He just didn't have the decency to own up and take his punishment. He probably got just as big a kick out of it as Leroy did."

Sonny was embarrassed and kept eating the cheeseburger. Nobody had ever criticized Duane in front of him before—for no reason that he could think of life was becoming more complicated.

"Well, I won't say no more about it," she said. "That's between you and him. But you've got to make up with Sam, that's for sure. I won't have you eating at that drive-in anymore. He misses you and he'll make it up if you do it right. He knows you too well to think you really went out of your way to upset Billy."

"How's Dan?" Sonny asked.

"Coming along. He's well enough to be contrary."

Sonny began to relax. The café was just the same: the jukebox, the booths, the high-school football schedule pinned on the wall. Genevieve cradled the coffee cup in her hand and stared at the frost-smoked windows.

"I've gotten into something else," Sonny said tentatively. She was the only person he could think of that he might be able to talk to.

"Got a new girl friend?" she grinned, and then she suddenly remembered the gossip. Until that moment she had not taken it at all seriously.

"I guess I have," Sonny said. "Not a girl friend, a lady friend. It's Mrs. Popper." He didn't know whether he was glad to have the secret out, and Genevieve was not sure at all that she was glad to have received it.

"Ruth Popper?" she said, amazed. "How do you mean, Sonny? Have you been flirtin' with her like you do with me, or is it different?"

"It's different," he said. "It's . . . like in a movie."

She saw that he was watching her face, dreadfully anxious to know what she thought about the news.

"I don't know what to think about you," she said. "Quit lookin' at me that way. This is an awful small town for that kind of carrying on, I can tell you that. You can't sneeze in this town without somebody offerin' you a handkerchief."

"Coach Popper don't care nothin' about her," Sonny said. "I don't see why he should care."

"He cares about himself, though—and about what people think of him. He owns a lot of guns, too."

Sonny looked so young and solemn and confused that after a moment it all amused her and she chuckled. He looked far too confused to be into anything wicked.

"All right," she said. "I won't say no more about it. You're a man of experience now, you don't need my advice anyway."

Sonny didn't know about advice, but he was glad to have her approval, however he could get it. He had some pie and chatted about lesser things until the streets outside were gray with a cold dawn. Genevieve got up to tend to the coffee maker.

"I better go on," Sonny said. "Sam's going to be coming any time."

"You stay," Genevieve said, not even turning around.

Sonny didn't like the idea, but he didn't have long to worry about it. In a few minutes the café door opened and Sam the Lion and Billy stepped inside. Sam had on his old plaid mackinaw, his khakis, and his house shoes. When he saw Sonny he opened his mouth to say something but Genevieve cut him off.

"Don't say a word," she said. "I won't have him eating at that drive-in no more. He can apologize like a civilized person and you can listen to him."

When Billy saw Sonny his face brightened and he went right over and sat down by him. He had forgotten all about the bad night, and didn't remember anything bad that Sonny had done. Sonny turned his baseball cap around backward for him.

"I'm sorry," Sonny said, when Sam the Lion came to the booth.

"Scoot over," Sam said, a little embarrassed. "If Billy can stand you I can too." He sat down by Sonny and ordered his sausage and eggs. Sonny was so relieved that he couldn't think of anything to say, and Sam the Lion was so relieved that he couldn't keep quiet. There was the basketball team to talk about, a disgraceful, hapless basketball team that hadn't come within thirty points of winning a game. Sam the Lion gave it hell, and continued giving it hell as the café filled, as the cowboys and the truckers came in, blowing on their cold hands. Soon smoke was rising from a dozen or more cups of Genevieve's coffee. Sam the Lion poured his in a saucer and went on talking while the two boys, not listening, happily ate their breakfasts.

Thirteen

IT WAS IN THE EARLY SPRING, WHEN SONNY WAS REALLY beginning to get in touch with Ruth, that Duane really began to get out of touch with Jacy. He forgave her for going to the nude swimming party in Wichita, but somehow they were never as comfortable with one another as they had been before that happened. The thing that bothered Duane most was that, instead of going to Wichita less and less, Jacy was going more and more. It got so he was lucky if he spent one Saturday night a month with her. Time after time she drove off to Wichita with Lester Marlow, always, she said, because her mother insisted. Duane raged and stormed, but he never quite got up the guts to have it out with Lois. Instead, he decided to concentrate on getting Jacy to marry him as soon as they graduated. He knew she had her application in to several fancy girls' schools, and he realized that if she got away to college he would have seen the last of her. His only chance was to marry her sometime during the summer, while she was still at home.

Jacy, however, had put aside all thought of marrying Duane. She had convinced herself that that would be a very selfish thing to do. Her parents, particularly her father, would never stand for it: he would have it annulled, Duane would lose his job and would probably be in the army before the summer was out. It would clearly be unfair of her to put Duane in such a position. If she sacrificed what she felt for him, he could keep his job and stay out of the army several months longer. It was the sort of thing he would thank her for someday.

The truth was, Jacy had been very strongly affected by the nude swimming party. Unknown to anyone but herself and Lester she had been back several times to exactly the same type of party. All the Saturday night trips were of her own arranging, but she told Duane they were her mother's doings. Duane was too naïve to understand her wanting to mix with kids like herself, kids who had money and lived recklessly. It would save everyone misery to let him think it was her mother's fault.

Jacy had begun to be very attracted to Bobby Sheen, the leader of the wild set. He was not especially handsome, but he combed his hair in a rakish fashion and he was always merry and lustful. It was rumored that he and Annie-Annie made love four times a week, sometimes in curious ways. He had an air of absolute confidence, as if he were ready for anything and could do anything that might be demanded of him. At first Jacy didn't give herself much of a chance with him, supposing that he and Annie-Annie would soon get married; but then she danced with him one night and took hope. He got erections while dancing with her, just like other boys did.

A week or so after that she thought it was really going to happen between Bobby and herself. After one of the naked swimming parties the boys and girls paired off and went to bed in various bedrooms of the huge Sheen house. Jacy had to share a bed with Lester Marlow, but that was all right; the first time it had happened she made it quite clear to Lester that sharing the bed was all she intended to do. Anything more intimate was out of the question. Lester had red pubic hair, which seemed to her ridiculous. After this particular party Lester and Jacy both went to sleep, as usual, but somebody woke Jacy up by kissing her. It was Bobby Sheen, and he didn't have any clothes on. When he saw she was wide awake he quietly motioned for her to follow him, and she did, trembling a little. Fortunately she had on some green pajamas, so it was not too immodest.

Bobby led her down the carpeted hall to an empty bedroom and the minute he got her through the door he unbuttoned her pajama top and began to play with her breasts. He was merry and confident about it all and it didn't occur to Jacy to stop him. There was a huge double bed in the room and once they got on it Bobby undressed her completely. Jacy was excited and decided to cast caution to the winds. She let him get between her legs and was prepared to let him go all the way, but he stopped wanting to. He started to and did something that hurt a little before he stopped, looking at her with disbelief.

"Are you a virgin?" he asked.

"I guess so," Jacy admitted miserably. "But I don't want to be."

Bobby made a face of mock-horror, as if he had discovered a leper in his bed.

"What a letdown," he said, but with his usual good cheer. "I'm sorry I woke you up. Why don't I give you the name of a gynecologist? There's no point in being messy on Momma and Daddy's bed."

"Okay," Jacy said, eager to be agreeable. She was not sure what having the name of such a person committed her to, but she was willing to try anything Bobby recommended. The look on his face made her realize that it was absolutely ridiculous for her to be a virgin: she was probably the only one in the whole house. That thought was so mortifying that she sat up and reached for her pajamas, prepared to go ignominiously back to bed. Bobby, however, was not all that discouraged.

"Don't run off," he said cheerfully. "I was just surprised. If you're not sleepy we can still play around a while."

Jacy was not sure what that involved either, but she dutifully lay back down. "What about Annie-Annie?" she asked.

"That bitch sleeps like a horse," Bobby said.

Jacy was quite shocked to discover all that "playing around" involved. Bobby Sheen knew amazing things to do, things she would not have put up with one second if it had been anyone other than him. As it was, she was determined not to show her ignorance and just let him do whatever he pleased. Him doing things was okay, but when he wanted her to do things to him she was so nervous and shaky that she got goose bumps all over. Bobby couldn't help giggling.

"Don't boys have cocks in that town you live in?" he asked, laughing.

Jacy was at a loss for an answer. For days she could not get the evening off her mind. It seemed to her she had come off very badly with Bobby. He didn't call her for any dates afterward, and every other boy who had ever been near her had promptly called her for dates. The only conclusion possible was that Bobby found her backward and country, and if there was anything she hated and loathed it was to be thought backward and country. It was clear that she was going to have to get rid of her virginity. She gave the matter much thought and came up with a plan that seemed to have multiple advantages. The week after graduation the senior class was going on what was called their senior trip. For four years the class had saved up money for it, and had given bake sales, conducted scrap iron drives, and done all sorts of other chores to make the money. They were going all the way to San Francisco and back on the bus and it would take every bit of the money they had made. She and Duane would thus be together practically all the time for a whole week, and it occurred to her that if she let Duane sleep with her sometime during the trip it would solve all kinds of problems. For one thing, it would *make* the senior trip. She and Duane would be regarded as extraordinarily daring, and all the kids would talk about them all the way home. Also, if she slept with Duane a time or two it would make it that much easier for her to break up with him after the senior trip was over. Duane would have something beautiful to remember, and he wouldn't be able to say she had promised him anything she hadn't delivered.

Then when she got back from the trip she would no longer be a virgin and could set about taking Bobby Sheen away from Annie-Annie. If she could get him in love with her before the summer was over she might forget about the girls' school and go to S.M.U., where Bobby was going. They might even pledge related fraternities.

The one flaw in the whole plan was Duane. It occurred to her that he might not want to break up with her even if she let him sleep with her before breaking the news. He was dead set on their getting married in the summer, and he was a very stubborn boy. She decided that the best thing to do would be to make an ally of Sonny—she knew

Sonny would do anything she wanted him to if she played up to him the least little bit. If Duane got ugly and wouldn't quit trying to go with her she could then date Sonny a few times. Duane would never in his life excuse that.

The senior play was rehearsing at that time and Sonny and Jacy both had parts. In order to strengthen her hold over him Jacy started giving Sonny a ride home every night; often, at her suggestion, they would ride out to the lake and sit and talk a while before going home. Jacy mostly wanted to talk about Duane, about how much she wanted to marry him but how frightened she was that it would never work out, her parents being set against it like they were. Sonny tried to listen, but mostly he just looked. Jacy had a way of leaning forward so she could hook a finger inside her blouse and straighten her bra strap, a movement that always made him ache with desire. Even the flash of her white teeth as she popped her chewing gum—even that could cause discomfort. Once in a moment of emotion she reached out and they held hands for a little while. "I tell you I don't know what I would do if I didn't have you to talk to, Sonny," she said affectionately.

At such times Sonny could hardly keep from wishing that Duane and perhaps Ruth too were out of the picture Jacy was everything he wanted. She had always seemed infinitely more desirable than Charlene or the other girls, but she had also begun to seem cool and simple and lovely in contrast to Ruth, who had begun to disturb him a good deal. Once Ruth found pleasure her need for him rapidly increased and her sensual appetite had become, if anything, stronger than his own. At first he had found it delightful—he had never imagined that he would ever in his life have as much sex as he wanted. By the time he had visited Ruth almost daily for a month he was forced to admit to himself that it might even be possible to have more than he wanted. Ruth lost all caution, all concern for what the townspeople might think. All she wanted was Sonny, and he began to feel strangely washed out and restless. He ceased to eat particularly much, or to sleep particularly well. Despite almost daily sex he had erotic dreams at night and would often wake up to find himself painfully engorged.

As he grew more tired and less certain of himself, Ruth seemed to grow fresher, more self-possessed, and more lovely, though it was only at odd, oblique moments, lying beside her or coming into her room, that he noticed that she was lovely. Instead of drooping about the house as she had once done she acquired grace and animation and moved about as active and lithe as a girl. She even repapered the bedroom, much to the coach's disgust.

Sonny found he could not keep a consistent feeling about her two days or even two hours in a row. At one moment, during lovemaking, seeing her become avid, sweaty, almost frenzied, he felt as he had the first day with her in the car, as if he were being pulled by some force stronger than his own. A few moments later, an hour later, he would see her, her face calmed, lit from within, her eyes wide and soft, and feel completely happy with her. He simply could not understand what had happened to her. When she touched him, drew him into her, it was not that she was trying to have him exactly—she was insisting that he have her. She was not saying "You're mine," she was saying "I'm yours," and that was almost more troubling. She was completely focused on him; the rest of her life had ceased to matter.

Her hair had grown longer, and he loved to smooth tendrils of it back behind her ears. But he wasn't sure that he wanted any person to be his: it made him too responsible.

"You're my love, I can't help it," she would say, if he brought the matter up. And she would go on brushing her hair, completely at peace with herself because of him.

One night he almost gave way to an impulse and spoke of Ruth to Jacy, but he didn't because he realized just in time that it would mean the end of his talks with Jacy. She wanted to talk about her problems, not his. Because of their talks she began to fill his fantasies again, and the fantasies made a fitful background to his afternoons with Ruth. Somehow he was sure that passion with Jacy would be more intense and yet less strained than it sometimes was with Ruth. With Jacy things would be sharper and better timed, and would never be blunted by anxiety or bad balance or anything.

To Ruth, that period of her life later seemed a little insane, but insane in a good way. She remembered little about it, just Sonny's person. Occasionally it occurred to her that people were probably talking, or that she ought to go to the store or somewhere, but none of those things seemed immediate. Sonny was the only thing immediate.

Later, when time was passing much more slowly, she told herself that she had not planned well—she had not thought to save anything. She had held nothing back for the morrow, but it was because she did not suppose she could afford to think about the morrow.

It was not until an evening in early May that the fact of a future was brought home to her. Sonny had come that afternoon, and all had gone well. Three hours later, while Herman was finishing his supper, Ruth went out into the backyard and began to take some clothes off the line. It was just dusk, a soft spring dusk, and as she was unpinning Herman's stiff, unironed khakis a car went by on the street. Idly curious, she glanced around to scc who was passing and saw Sonny and Jacy, on their way to play practice in Jacy's convertible.

She only glimpsed them as the car passed between her house and the next, and all she saw really was the glint of spring sunset on Jacy's gold hair. She did not even see Sonny's face, did not know whether he looked happy or glum to bc with Jacy, but the glimpse ruined her content. For a moment or two she had to hold onto the clothesline—it was as if she had been struck a numbing blow across her thighs. Her legs felt so unsteady that she could hardly move down the line to the next stiff pair of pants. Sonny had never mentioned Jacy to her: she had glimpsed the very beginning of something. Duane and Jacy might have broken up. As she dragged the sheets off the line she felt a sudden panic, silly but nonetheless terrifying. She was sure that Sonny was in love with Jacy and would never come to her house again. She would have wept, but the dread that seized her was too dry. It was as if she had suddenly been faced with her own end, an end too dry and commonplace to cry about. When all the clothes were piled in the basket she stood in the yard a minute, under the empty lines, her only comfort the soft evening air. She could not stand the thought of going into the tight, hot kitchen, where Herman was eating black eyed peas, but the next moment a thought came to her and she grabbed the clothes basket and hurried in. Herman had finished the peas and was eating a bowlful of yellow canned peaches, one of his favorite desserts.

"Herman," she asked, "have Duane and Jacy broken up? I thought I saw her go by just now with someone else in the car."

The coach looked up with mild interest. "Hope so," he said. "Nothin' I'd like better than to see them two bust up. I might get a couple of good baseball games out of Duane if they would."

Ruth took heart and took out the ironing board and sprinkler bottle. Life came back into her legs; she decided the spasm of dread had been irrational. Even so, considering it calmly, it was clear that in time she was bound to be hurt, and badly so. She was twenty years older than him, and he would not keep wanting her forever. Sooner or later he would leave and she would have to get over him, but she was so relieved to know that it was going to be later—not for a week, at least, and perhaps not for a month or even a year—that she resolved not to care. As she ironed she indulged herself in the pleasant fantasy that she was in Sonny's room, doing the ironing for him. She nursed a strong secret wish to go to his room sometime, to be with him where he lived rather than where Herman lived.

The coach finished his peaches and lay on the couch for a couple of hours, watching television while Ruth finished ironing. When the late news came on he turned the set off: news bored him. He straggled lazily into the bedroom to undress, and found that Ruth was there ahead of him, sitting on the edge of the bed rubbing hand lotion into her hands. She had her shoes off and was barefooted. It seemed to the coach that she looked younger than a woman her age ought to look: her ankles were slim, and even her face looked young. He didn't know it, but she had managed to sustain her favorite fantasy all the way to the bedroom and was pretending to herself that she was undressing in Sonny's room. All the coach knew was that she irritated him. She went to the closet to hang up her dress and even the lightness of her walk irritated him. He sat down in the rocker to pull off his sweaty socks, remembering that she had mentioned Jacy and Duane.

"Who was it you seen with Jacy?" he asked, stirred by his dislike of the girl.

"I didn't get a good look at the boy," Ruth said, a little surprised. "It was Sonny Crawford I think."

The coach grunted. He stood up, emptied his pockets onto the dresser, and pitched his pants through the bathroom door in the general direction of the dirty-clothes hamper. It was a warm night and the room seemed a little close to him. He threw up a window and stood in front of it a minute, idly scratching his testicles and enjoying the nice south breeze.

After a minute he stretched out on the bed, but for some reason he couldn't get Jacy Farrow off his mind. It was little twats like her that ruined young athletes, so far as he was concerned. If it hadn't been for her, Duane would have come out for track and they might have won a track championship. As he lay on his back, still scratching himself, he thought how nice it would be to hump a little rich girl like her until she got so sick of it she would never want to see another boy, much less bother one. That would be a smart piece of coaching, but hard to bring off.

While his thoughts were running in that direction he happened to glance over and notice Ruth—or at least he noticed half of her. She was undressing behind the closet door, but the strong breeze had blown the door open a bit wider than usual and Ruth was half exposed, the line of the door bisecting her body. The coach saw one leg, one breast, one shoulder and the side of her head as she turned and reached into the closet to take her gown off the hook. Ordinarily the sight of Ruth's body gave him a feeling of mild distaste: his own mother had stood five-eleven and had worked just as hard as men worked nearly every day of her life. Nothing seemed more pathetic to him than a skinny woman, Ruth especially, but when he glanced at the closet he was not thinking of Ruth at all but of Jacy Farrow. He was thinking that if he ever got Jacy into the right corner he would pay back all the little pusses who had kept his boys stirred up over the years. The thought of administering such a lesson had him a little excited—his underwear developed a sizable hump. Ruth stepped out from behind the door, lowering the gown over her body, and the coach looked at her again. Something told him he would never get Jacy into the right corner, but Ruth was right there and she was just like a girl anyway. She had kept *him* stirred up at one time—if she hadn't he would have stayed a bachelor and had the money to take some real hunting trips. He could have gone to Alaska, even. She deserved a prod as much as Jacy; no woman who had done a proper day's work moved as lightly as she moved.

Ruth's mind was still elsewhere—she was unaware of the state her husband was in. It was not a state she had expected him to be in again. She sat down on the bed with her back to him and rubbed her calves a minute before stretching out. While she was sitting there the springs squeaked and Herman got out of bed; she supposed he had forgotten to go to the bathroom.

"Turn off the light in there, please, when you're done," she said. Light from the bathroom made a bright patch on the floor of the darkened bedroom.

Then she turned to lie down and noticed with a start that Herman was not headed for the bathroom at all. He was at the dresser, his underwear bulging out ludicrously. The sight stunned her, as it always had: all their married life Herman had announced his arousal by going to the dresser and rummaging in the sock drawer until he found the prophylactics. While she watched he found a package and strode into the bathroom to make himself ready.

She knew that she was supposed to use the time while he was in the bathroom to prepare herself for wifely service, but she suddenly felt as if her whole body had become stiff as a plank. She had been thinking how nice it would be to spend a whole night in Sonny's room, but when confronted with Herman's intention all thought seemed to leave her. She merely lay on the bed, not thinking at all.

When Herman came out he switched off the bathroom light, so that the bedroom was dark. He lay down heavily and without hesitation rolled himself onto Ruth, only to roll back a moment later, chagrined.

"What the hell?" he said. "You done asleep?"

In her paralysis Ruth had forgotten to do what she was supposed to do on such occasions: lift her nightgown and spread her legs. Those two actions were all that Herman required of her in the way of sexual cooperation. She raised her hips off the bed and pulled up the gown, and when he was satisfied that the obstruction had been removed the coach rolled back onto her and after a couple of badly aimed thrusts, made connection. Once he struck the place he went at it athletically.

Ruth clenched her fists at her sides. Her chest and abdomen felt crushed, but it crossed her mind that she had crushed herself. What was crushing her was the weight of all the food she had fed Herman through the years, all the steaks, all the black-eyed peas, all the canned peaches. It was particularly the canned peaches: she had never until that moment realized how much she hated them. It seemed to her that pyramids of cans of slimy peaches piled on her abdomen. After a moment the weight became intolerable and she moved a little, to try and ease it. She moved from side to side and stretched her legs, to try and escape it. Herman sweated easily and his sweat was already dripping down her ribs, but what bothered her was the weight of the cans. As she kept moving, trying to lighten the weight, she became aware of a distant pleasure. She began to writhe a little, in order to adjust the weight of the pyramid and intensify the pleasure—she flexed her legs and raised the lower part of her body a little, trying to get the weight right on the throbbing nerve.

Her movements annoyed the coach a great deal. When he started he had not even been thinking of her, but of Jacy, and thinking of Jacy had been very enjoyable. At first Ruth had acted perfectly decent, but just when it was getting nicest she began to writhe and wiggle and even started going up and down against him. The coach was too surprised and outraged to speak, and anyway he had got to the point where he needed to hold onto Jacy in his mind. He tried to beat Ruth down with his body, so she would be still again, but his efforts had the opposite effect: the harder he tried the more she moved. He couldn't slow her down at all, and he couldn't stop himself.

For a minute, with pounding heartbeats, they were running a hundred-yard dash with each other on equal terms. Neither knew how close the tape was, neither was sure of victory, but the coach crossed first. He recaptured Jacy for a second and desperately burst across, gasping with exhaustion and pleasure. Ruth was just at the turn. The weight was terribly sharp for a moment and then the coach's heavy surge burst the pyramid and left her gasping, free of all weight.

For his part the coach wanted badly to be gone on his side of the bed. Quickly he withdrew, but to his amazement and shame Ruth would not let him. She grasped him, put him back, would not have him leave, and he was too tired and surprised to fight. Except for the working of their lungs the two were still. In time, when their breath became quieter, the room was totally silent. The coach did not try again to withdraw, for fear he couldn't. When he did in the natural fashion he quickly rolled onto his side of the bed.

Ruth was away, in a misty, drowsy country, but even there she felt a little worried and a little sad. She had not meant it and could not understand how she had done it, given Herman something she thought was only for Sonny. It was as if her body had betrayed a trust and responded to the very man who had neglected it most. Perhaps she was not safe, not even from Herman. Hearing his exhausted breathing in her ear she had had a moment of sympathy for him as a person. She had felt for him a little bit. Perhaps she was no longer safe from anyone?

The coach knew good and well he wasn't safe. His body wanted to sleep, but his mind was far too agitated. He would never have imagined his own wife would grasp him: it was something worse than shameless. He didn't want to remain in the same bed with her and considered going to the couch. Still, Ruth was the one who had beslimed the bed: she ought to go. The messiness of the female body had never been more offensive to him. If he even moved his leg he touched a wet spot. Disgusted, he got up and went in the bathroom to clean himself. The bright light made him blink.

When he came back to bed, Ruth was dozing. She knew he was offended, but it didn't touch her. She felt pleasantly sleepy and had overcome her mild distress at being suddenly accessible. If Herman was going to insist on his connubial rights, then all the better that she could finally enjoy it.

The coach stood over her in the dark, mad, but vaguely uneasy too. He had never dreamed Ruth had such wildness in her, and he was not sure how to get at her.

"Ain't you gonna change them sheets?" he asked sourly.

"Hum? No. Why?" she asked drowsily.

"Well by God," he said, walking distractedly around the bed. "You're a fine one, ain't you. If my mother was alive and knew how you acted she'd have your hide. I've always heard women got nasty in their old age but I never thought it would happen to no wife of mine."

"Didn't you like it, Herman?" Ruth asked, still sleepily. She was near enough asleep that she could be a little mean.

With a grunt the coach lay down and turned his back on her. Like it! It was fine come-off. What could a man say to a damn woman?

Fourteen

"KEEP AN EYE ON THEM CORKS, BILLY," SAM THE LION said, getting to his feet. "I've got to go water the grass a little."

The corks bobbed undisturbed in the brown water of a large stock tank, and Billy, also undisturbed, sat by the water's edge, watching them. Sonny was stretched out on his stomach in the Bermuda grass along the base of the tank dam. The May sun on his back was so warm that it made him drowsy, and he was almost asleep, content to leave Billy in full charge of the three fishing poles.

Sam the Lion took a long time to water the grass, but he finally came back, grumbling and buttoning his pants.

"Be nice to be able to piss," he said. "If I last another year I'll be dribblin' it on my shoes. I'd almost be willing to be young again if I could take a real piss. Looks like we ain't gonna catch much today."

"We never do," Sonny said. Once every year or two the pretty spring weather would tempt Sam the Lion to get out and, as he put it, get a little scenery. The rest of the time he was content to get his scenery from the pretty calendars the local foodstore put out.

When the urge for the outdoors came on him he would get Billy and the three fishing poles, enlist Sonny as a driver, and take the boys year after year to the same tank, perhaps the worst stocked fishing tank in the whole country. Once in a while they caught a perch or two, but always such undernourished specimens that old Marston refused to cook them.

"Hell, Sam, you wouldn't have nothing but two ounces of fried bones if I did cook them," he maintained.

Sam the Lion didn't much care, and neither did the boys. Billy loved to sit on the bank and watch the rings in the water or the dragonflies that skimmed along the surface. He was always surprised and a little disconcerted when Sam the Lion grabbed one of the poles and actually pulled up a fish. When he looked into the water he saw no fish, and he was never really sure where they came from.

After a while Sonny got tired of dozing and got up and walked along the tank dam a little way. It was a beautiful afternoon, a good day not to be doing anything—the sky was very blue and the pastures were green with spring grass and mesquite. In a moment he himself had the urge to water the grass in the way that Sam had, and he walked to the edge of the dam to do it. He felt warm and well and was faintly pleased by the spurt of his own water, even stretching himself a little to see if he could send a stream all the way to the foot of the dam. He didn't quite make it, but it was a high sloping dam and he came close enough to be fully content with his own range.

It was only as he turned around and was buttoning himself that he noticed that Sam the Lion had observed his little game. It embarrassed him just a little, but it did something much stranger to Sam the Lion. Sam began to snort, always a sign that something was affecting him powerfully, and then he began to laugh his loud, solid, rich laugh, something he did so rarely that both boys were startled. He sat by the water laughing, running his hands through his hair. Tears began to run down his face so freely that Sonny was not sure what was happening, whether Sam was laughing or crying. He pulled his handkerchief out of his hip pocket and began to wipe his face but no sooner had he done that than he burst out cussing and got up and stomped around furiously on the Bermuda grass.

"Goddammit! Goddammit!" he cursed. "I don't want to be old. It don't fit me!"

Then, seeing that the boys were scared, he became embarrassed and sat back down, still sniffing and snorting. He looked at the water and blew his nose and for a minute tried to pretend that nothing out of the ordinary had happened. But both boys continued to stare at him and he gave it up and tried to explain.

"I'll tell you what it was, son," he said, looking at Sonny a little ruefully. "Seein' you pissing off the dam reminded me of something. I used to own this land you know. It's been right at fifty years since the first time I watered a horse at this tank. Reason I always drag you all out here probably—I'm just as sentimental as anybody else when it comes to old times. What you reminded me of happened twenty years ago—I brought a young lady swimming here. It was after my boys were already dead, my wife had lost her mind. Me and this young lady were pretty crazy, I guess. She had all the spirit in the world, and we had some times. We come out here swimmin' one day without no bathin' suits and after we got out of the water I walked off up there to piss. She was always on the lookout for something funny and she offered to bet me a silver dollar I couldn't stand on the top of the dam and piss into the water. I took the bet and gave it a try but I never came no closer than you did. That lady's still got the silver dollar."

He was quiet, looking at the water.

Sonny had never known Sam the Lion except as an old man, and he was surprised and a little awed by the story. He wanted to ask who the woman was, but he didn't have the nerve.

"What became of the lady?" he asked.

"Oh, she growed up," Sam the Lion said, a tone of regret in his voice. "She was just a girl then, really."

"How come you never married her?"

"She was done married," Sam said gravely. "She and her husband were young and miserable with one another, but so many young married folks are that way that I figured they'd work out of it in time. I thought they'd get comfortable when they got a little older but it didn't turn out that way."

"Is growin' up always miserable?" Sonny said. "Nobody seems to enjoy it much."

"Oh, it ain't necessarily miserable," Sam replied. "About eighty percent of the time, I guess."

They were silent again, Sam the Lion thinking of the lovely, spritely girl he had once led into the water, right there, where they were sitting.

"We ought to go to a real fishin' tank next year," Sam said finally. "It don't do to think about things like that too much. If she was here now I'd probably be crazy agin in about five minutes. Ain't that ridiculous?"

A half-hour later, when they had gathered up the gear and were on the way to town, he answered his own question.

"It ain't, really," he said "Being crazy about a woman like her's always the right thing to do. Being a decrepit old bag of bones is what's ridiculous."

It had rained the week before and there were deep ruts in the dirt road. Sonny drove as carefully as he could, but Sam the Lion scratched his head and watched the speedometer nervously, convinced that they were proceeding at a reckless speed.

"Did you know about me and Mrs. Popper?" Sonny asked suddenly, feeling that if he was ever going to talk about it the time was at hand.

"Yeah, how is Ruth?" Sam asked. "I haven't had a close look at her in years."

"Sometimes she's okay," Sonny said. "Sometimes she doesn't seem to be too happy."

Sam snorted. "That's probably the understatement of the day," he said. "I figured her for a suicide ten years ago—people are always turning out to be tougher than I think they are."

"I don't exactly know what to do about her," Sonny said hopefully.

Sam the Lion laughed almost as loudly as he had on the tank dam.

"Don't look at me for advice," he said. "I never know exactly what to do about anybody, least of all women. You might stay with her and get some good out of her while you're growing up. Somebody ought to get some good out of Ruth."

They pulled onto the highway and in a few minutes the fenceposts were going by so fast that Sam the Lion could hardly see them. He breathed as little as possible until they hit the city limits sign—then Sonny slowed down and he relaxed.

"Say, was Duane along that night you all got Billy in the mess?" he asked. "I've been wondering about that lately."

Sonny was caught off guard and was completely at a loss to answer. He automatically started to lie, but because it was Sam the Lion the lie wouldn't come out. He decided it wouldn't hurt to tell the truth, but the truth wouldn't come out either. First the lie and then the truth stuck in his throat, and right in the same place.

"I see," Sam said. "Watch out, that's Old Lady Peters backing out of her driveway up there. She thinks it's still 1930 an' she's just as apt to back right in front of you as not."

He gripped the door handle tightly, prepared to leap out if necessary, but Sonny had seen the old lady blocks before he had and calmly, out of habit, swerved wide around her and coasted them safely up to the poolhall door.

Fifteen

THREE DAYS AFTER THE FISHING TRIP, DUANE GOT SO frustrated that he beat up Lester Marlow. Jacy and Lester had gone to Wichita together three Saturday nights in a row, and Duane could stand it no longer.

"I don't care if it ain't Lester's fault," Duane told Sonny. "Maybe if he has a couple of front teeth missin' Mrs. Farrow won't be so anxious to have Jacy go with him."

Sam the Lion overheard the remark and gave a skeptical chuckle. "The only person who'll profit by that sort of reasonin' is Lester's dentist," he said. "Maybe Jacy likes to go with Lester."

That was an incredible thing to suggest. Duane and Sonny were both flabbergasted.

"You don't think she *wants* to go with that fart, do you?" Duane asked indignantly.

"Well, Lester ain't entirely unlikable," Sam replied, not at all flustered. "I don't know Jacy well enough to know what she wants, but you've been blaming her mother all this time for something that might not be her mother's fault. If I was you I'd investigate."

Duane stormed out of the poolhall, mad as he could be. He didn't want to investigate, he just wanted to whip Lester, and about midnight that night, as Lester was passing the courthouse, Duane waved him down. Sonny was the only other person to see it.

"I know you're mad," Lester said, as soon as he got out of the car, "but you needn't be. All I've done is take her to dances. I've never even kissed her."

It was a shameful admission, but true: Jacy gave Lester absolutely nothing in the way of intimacies. She didn't have to.

"You took her to a naked swimming party," Duane said. "Don't tell me you didn't kiss her."

"I didn't," Lester said, but at that point Duane hit him on the mouth. Lester swung a half-hearted blow in return and found himself sitting down—at least he found himself getting up, and he could only assume he had been knocked down first. The fight was well started and things were easier for him: he couldn't feel himself being hit, and after three or four more licks Duane bloodied his nose and stopped fighting.

"That's just a taste," he said. "Don't you take her anywhere else!"

Lester said nothing, and Duane and Sonny walked away. Not saying anything was something of a triumph, Lester thought. He had made no promises. He went across the street to the filling station and ran some water on his nose, thinking that in a way he had been ganged up on. Sonny had been there. It could even have been that he was not knocked down fairly—Sonny could have tripped him. On the way back to Wichita he concluded that Sonny probably did trip him, and instead of going to his home he drove out to a place on Holiday Creek where some of the wilder boys often gathered on Saturday nights. A lot of boys were there, sitting on the fenders of their cars drinking beer, and when they saw how bloody Lester was they were briefly impressed. What happened? they wanted to know.

"Couple of roughnecks beat me up," Lester said stoically. "You know, Crawford and Moore, over in Thalia. It was about Jacy Farrow. I would have done okay if one of them hadn't tripped me."

"Those motherfuckers," one of the boys said. "We ought to go over there and pile their asses."

"No," Lester said gallantly. "I don't want anybody fighting my fights."

"Aw, hell, it'd be somethin' to do," a boy said. "Besides we can get the Bunne brothers to do the fighting." The Bunne brothers were local Golden Gloves champions, a welterweight and a light-heavy. They enjoyed fighting, in the ring or out.

Lester didn't try again to discourage them, but for himself he decided it would be best not to go back to Thalia. The boys took that in stride—they didn't really like Lester much and were just as glad he stayed in Wichita. The nice thing about his getting beat up was that it gave them an excuse to drive to Thalia and watch a fight.

The Bunne brothers were located at a Pioneer drive-in, trying to make some girls in a green Pontiac. The welterweight was named Mickey, the light-heavy, Jack. They were glad to get a chance to go fighting: the girls were just a punch of pimply virgins who had run off from a slumber party in Burkburnett. A couple of boys elected to stay and work on them, but that still left seven raring to go. They piled in a second-hand Mercury and headed for Thalia, driving about eighty-five and laughing and talking. Saturday night had taken a turn for the better.

After the fight with Lester, Sonny and Duane walked over to the café to have a cheeseburger. Duane really wanted sympathy, but Genevieve was not inclined to give him any.

"No sir," she said. "There wasn't any point in your bullyin' Lester—it ain't his fault you can't make you girl friend behave."

"You're as bad as Sam." Duane said bitterly. "Why Jacy would marry me tonight, if she had the chance."

Sonny got up and put a couple of nickels in the jukebox, hoping a little music would ease the tension. It didn't seem to help much, so after a few minutes the boys left and drove out to the Y, a fork in the road about five miles from town. The fork was on top of a hill, and when they got there they sat and looked across the flat at the cluster of lights that was Thalia. In the deep spring darkness the lights shone very clear. The windows of the pickup were down and they could smell the fresh smell of the pastures.

They only sat a few minutes, and then drove back to town. When they pulled up at the rooming house the Wichita boys were there, sitting on the fenders of the Mercury.

"There's the Bunne brothers," Duane said. "That damn Lester must have sent 'em."

Both of them were badly scared, but they didn't want the Wichita boys to know that so they got out as if nothing were wrong. For a moment no one said anything. Sonny nervously scraped his sole on the pavement and the sound was very loud in the still night.

Mickey Bunne came cockily over and broke the silence.

"Hear you men beat the piss out of Lester," he said.

"I beat the piss out of him," Duane said quickly. "Sonny wasn't involved."

"That ain't the way Lester tells it."

The other boys got off the fenders and began to edge around.

"He probably lied about it," Duane said. "I didn't hit him over five times, anyway. I told him to stop going with my girl."

Mickey moved a step closer. "He said you both whipped him."

"You don't really think it would take two of us to whip Lester, do you?" Sonny asked. "All he had was a bloody nose and a busted lip. If we'd both fought he wouldn't have been able to drive home, much less tell lies about it."

The Wichita boys were momentarily silent, even Mickey. What Sonny said was obviously true: it didn't take two people to whip Lester Marlow, and he hadn't been damaged much, anyway. Most of the boys didn't feel particularly unfriendly to Duane and Sonny, but that didn't matter. There had to be a fight. The Bunne brothers wouldn't go home without a fight. Fortunately Mickey Bunne was quick-witted and saw right away what tack to take.

"Who whipped him don't matter," he said. "We don't like you country boys tellin' us who to go with and who to leave alone. We like to screw country girls once in a while.

Duane was getting a little nervous. "I didn't tell him not to screw country girls," he said. "I told him not to bother Jacy. He can fuck the whole rest of this town for all I care—I'm just tired of him botherin' Jacy."

Mickey grinned. "Lester don't bother her," he said. "She laps it up. I seen her naked one time myself, out at Bobby Sheen's. She ain't bad lookin'. Who she really likes is Bobby Sheen—him and her played around all one night. I guess she's about as much ours as she is yours. I may want to go with her myself some time, you can't tell."

That was too much for Duane: he hit at Mickey, and the fight was on. It was not too bad for Duane, although Mickey beat him handily and knocked him down once. Duane was so mad he didn't really feel the pounding he took. He was fighting for his girl, after all. Sonny was the one who suffered most. He wasn't mad at all, and he wasn't fighting for anyone in particular. Besides that, he didn't like to fight and didn't know how, whereas Jack Bunne liked it and knew how very well. It made for a painful beating.

Fortunately the Bunne brothers knew when to quit. They were not looking for trouble, just for excitement. Sonny and Duane were both standing when they quit, although Sonny wanted very much to sit down. He had a pain in his ribs.

"Well let's go, men," one of the boys said. "The deputy sheriff's liable to come drivin' by."

"We ain't broke no laws," Jack Bunne said, not even winded, but the boys all went on and piled in the Mercury. They whooped and laughed as the car pulled away.

"Motherfuckers," Duane said wearily.

Sonny walked over and sat down on the curb. One of his ears was paining him severely, and he had caught at least a couple of hard licks in the rib cage. Duane came and sat down too. They were both too winded and depressed to say anything. It was enough just to sit. The town was very quiet. From the west, far out in the pastures, they heard some hounds, so far away that their braying sounded as thin as the yapping of puppies.

"Why don't we just take off an' go someplace," Duane said. "I'm sick of this town. You're the only friend I got here, except Jacy."

"You mean go and stay gone?" Sonny asked.

"No, just for a day or two. We could go to Mexico and get back by sometime Monday."

"Reckon the pickup would make it?" Sonny asked, welcoming the prospect.

They got out their billfolds and counted their money. Saturday had been payday, and between them they had almost a hundred dollars.

"We can make it on that," Duane said. "Let's go clean up."

A few minutes later Sonny vomited all over the bathroom, but once he got the mess cleaned up he felt much better. His ear was not throbbing so badly. They put on clean Levi's and shirts and doctored themselves with aspirin, convinced they would both survive. The pickup didn't have much gas in it and they had to stop in town and wake up Andy Fanner, who had a key to one of the gas stations.

"Why you boys or-tant to go all that way," Andy said cheerfully. "The water's buggy in Mexico."

"We'll just drink beer and tequila," Duane said.

"You need-ernt to tell me," Andy said sagely. "I been there. You get the clap you'll wish you hadn't drunk nothin'. Where you goin', Laredo?"

The boys looked at one another. They hadn't planned that far ahead; they were just going to Mexico.

"Which is the best place?" Sonny asked.

Andy wasn't positive and he didn't have a map, so they went back to the café and got one out of the glove compartment of Genevieve's old Dodge. They took it inside to read it.

"Good lord," Genevieve said, when she saw their skinned-up faces. They explained, and she sat down in a booth with them. "You all can just have the map," she said. "I ain't going far enough away that I need to worry about getting lost, I don't guess."

"Let's go all the way to Matamoros, since we're goin'," Duane suggested. "I've heard it's about the wildest."

"Matamoros suits me," Sonny said, gulping his coffee. They could hardly believe such an adventure was before them, and they wanted to get away before something happened to stop it.

Genevieve, however, was a little dubious. She followed them out to the pickup to see them off. The streets were empty, the streetlights shining palely. The stoplight blinked red and green all to itself.

"This pickup don't look so good," she said. The boys were so eager that it made her strangely sad. "Have either of you ever been that far away before?"

"Austin's the farthest I've been," Sonny said. It was the same with Duane, and Matamoros was almost twice as far as Austin. It made them all the more eager, but to their amazement Genevieve suddenly began to cry about something, right there on the street. Sonny had been just about to start the motor when she put her elbows on the pickup window and wiped away the tears with her hand. Both boys were stricken, afraid they were going to miss the trip after all.

"Why don't you boys take my car?" Genevieve sniffed. "You'll never make it in this old pickup."

They were astonished. It was an unprecedented offer. Women were clearly beyond all understanding.

"Naw, we better go in this one," Sonny told her softly. She was looking off down the street—he had never noticed before, but she seemed lonesome.

"We might wreck yours, an' then where would we be?" he added.

"Okay," Genevieve said, hardly paying attention. Something made her breasts ache. "Wait just a minute."

She went in the café and got a ten dollar bill out of her purse. After she had wiped her eyes with a Kleenex she took the money outside and handed it to Sonny.

"Hide that somewhere," she said. "Use it when you don't have anything else to use. I'd like for you to get back in time for your graduation."

Both boys assured her that the money was quite unnecessary, but she pressed it on them anyway. "Sam's up there sitting on the curb," she said. "Guess he can't sleep. You might go say good-bye to him."

The boys were glad of anything that would prolong the ecstasy of departure a few more minutes. Sonny backed solemnly into the empty street and turned toward the poolhall. Sam the Lion was sitting on the curb, scratching his ankles. Sonny drove right up in front of him and leaned out the window.

"Better come go with us," he said. "We're headed for the Valley."

Astonished, Sam got up from the curb and came over to the pickup. He peered at the boys curiously.

"Going to the Valley tonight," he said. "My God." He was touched by the folly of youth and stood with his foot on the running board a moment.

"I guess the town can get along without us till Monday," Sonny said.

"I reckon," Sam said lightly. "If I was young enough to bounce that far I'd go with you. Need any money?"

"No. We got plenty."

"You can't tell," Sam said, fishing out his billfold. "Better take ten dollars for insurance. They say money kinda melts when you take it across a border."

The boys were too embarrassed to tell Sam that Genevieve had given them some already. They took the bill guiltily, anxious to be off. Sam stepped back to the curb and the boys waved and made a wide U-turn in the empty street. Genevieve was still outside the café and they waved at her too as they went by. She watched them, hugging her breasts. When they got to the stoplight it was red and they stopped, even though there wasn't another moving car within fifteen miles of them. The light winked green and the pickup turned the corner and sped out of sight.

Genevieve went over and kicked lightly at the front tire of her Dodge—to her the tire always looked low. The boys had made her remember what it was to be young. Once, before they had any kids, she and her husband Dan took off one weekend and drove to Raton, New Mexico. They stayed in a motel, lost twenty dollars at the horse races, made love six times in two days, and had dinner in the coffee shop of a fancy restaurant. She had even worn eye shadow. Romance might not last, but it was something while it did. She looked up the street and waved at Sam the Lion, but he was looking the other way and didn't notice her and she went back into the empty café, wishing for a few minutes that she was young again and free and could go rattling off across Texas toward the Rio Grande.

Sixteen

All day the boys alternated, one driving the other sleeping, and by late evening they were in the Valley, driving between the green orange groves. It was amazing how different the world was, once the plains were left behind. In the Valley there were even palm trees. The sky was violet, and dusk lingered until they were almost to Matamoros. Every few miles they passed roadside groceries, lit with yellow light bulbs and crowded with tables piled high with corn and squash, cabbages and tomatoes.

"This is a crazy place," Duane said. "Who you reckon eats all that squash?"

They drove straight on through Brownsville and paid a fat, bored tollhouse keeper twenty cents so they could drive across the bridge. Below them was the Rio Grande, a river they had heard about all their lives. Its waters were mostly dark, touched only here and there by the yellow bridge lights. Several Mexican boys in ragged shirts were sitting on one of the guardrails, spitting into the water and chattering to one another.

A few blocks from the bridge they came to a stoplight on a pole, with four or five boys squatting by it. Apparently someone had run into the light pole because it was leaning away from the street at a forty-five-degree angle. As soon as Sonny stopped one of the boys ran out and jumped lightly onto the running board.

"Girl?" he said. "Boy's Town? Dirty movie?"

"Well, I guess," Sonny said. "I guess that's what we came for."

The boy quickly got in the cab and began to chatter directions in Tex-Mex—Sonny followed them as best he could. They soon left the boulevard and got into some of the narrowest streets the boys had ever seen. Barefooted kids and cats and dogs were playing in the street, night or no night, and they moved aside for the pickup very reluctantly. A smell of onions seemed to pervade the whole town, and the streets went every which direction. There were lots of intersections but no stop signs—apparently the right of way belonged to the driver with the most nerve. Sonny kept stopping at the intersections, but that was reversal of local custom: most drivers beeped their horns and speeded up, hoping to dart through before anyone could hit them.

Mexico was more different from Thalia than either of the boys would have believed. The number of people who went about at night was amazing to them. In Thalia three or four boys on the courthouse square constituted a lively crowd, but the street of Matamoros teemed with people. Groups of men stood on what, in Thalia, would have been sidewalks, children rushed about in the dust, and old men sat against buildings.

Their guide finally ordered them to stop in front of a dark lump that was apparently some sort of dwelling.

"This couldn't be no whorehouse," Duane said. "It ain't big enough to have a whore in it."

Not knowing what else to do, they got out and followed their guide to the door. A paunchy Mexican in his undershirt and khakis opened it and grunted at the guide. "Ees got movies," the boy said.

They all went inside, into a bedroom. Through an open doorway the boys could see an old woman stiriing something in a pot, onions and tomatoes it smelled like. An old man with no shirt on and white hair on his chest sat at a table staring at some dominoes. Neither the old man nor old woman so much as glanced at the boys. There were two beds in the bedroom and on one of them three little Mexican boys were curled up, asleep. Sonny felt strange when he saw them. They looked very helpless, and he could not feel it was very polite for Duane and him to barge into their room. The paunchy man immediately brought up the subject of movies. "Ten dollars," he said. "Got all kinds."

He knelt and drew a tiny little projector out from under the bed and took several rolls of eight-millimeter film out of a little bureau. The boys looked uncomfortably at one another. They either had to pay and watch the movies or else refuse and leave, and since they had driven five hundred miles to see some wickedness it was pointless to refuse. Duane handed over a ten dollar bill and the man stuffed it in his pocket and calmly began to clear one of the beds. He picked the sleeping boys up one at a time, carried them into the kitchen, and deposited them under the table where the old man sat. The little boys moaned a little and stirred in their sleep, but they didn't wake up. The paunchy man then put the projector on their bed and prepared to show the movies on a sheet hung against the opposite wall.

"I don't like this," Sonny said, appalled. "I never come all this way just to get some kids out of bed. If he ain't got a better place than this to show them I'd just as soon go on."

Duane was of the same mind, but when they tried to explain themselves, the guide and the projectionist both seemed puzzled.

"Ees okay," the guide said. "Sleepin' away." He gestured at the three little boys, all of whom were sound asleep on the dirt floor.

Sonny and Duane were stubborn. Even though the little boys were asleep, it wouldn't do: they couldn't enjoy a dirty movie so long as they were in sight of the displaced kids. Finally the projectionist shrugged, picked up the projector, and led them back through the hot kitchen and across an alley. The guide followed, carrying the film. Above them the sky was dark and the stars very bright.

They came to what seemed to be a sort of long outhouse, and when the guide knocked a thin, middle-aged man opened the door. He had only one leg, but no crutch, the room being so small that he could easily hop from one resting place to the next. As soon as they were all inside the guide informed the boys that it would cost them five dollars more because of the change of rooms: the one legged man could not be put to the trouble of sitting through a pornographic movie for nothing. Sonny paid it and the projectionist plugged the projector into a light socket. An old American calendar hung on the door, a picture of a girl in mechanic's overalls on the front of it. The one-legged man simply turned the calendar around and they had a screen.

"You mean they're going to show it on the back of a calendar," Duane said. "For fifteen dollars?"

The light was turned off and the projector began to buzz—the title of the picture was *Man's Best Friend*. It was clearly an old picture, because the lady who came on the screen was dressed like ladies in Laurel and Hardy movies. The similarity was so strong that for a moment the boys expected Laurel and Hardy to come on the screen and do dirty things to her. As the plot unfolded the print became more and more scratchy and more and more faded; soon it was barely possible to tell that the figures on the screen were human. The boys leaned forward to get a better look and were amazed to discover that the figures on the screen *weren't* all human. One of the actors was a German shepherd dog.

"My God," Duane said.

They both immediately felt the trip was worthwhile, if only for the gossip value. Nobody in Thalia had ever seen a dog and a lady behaving that way: clearly it was the ultimate depravity, even more depraved than having congress with Negro whores. They were speechless. A man came on and replaced the dog, and then the dog came back on and he and the man teamed up. The projectionist and the guide chuckled with delight at this development, but the boys were too surprised to do anything but watch. The ugliness of it all held them spellbound. When it was over they walked to the pickup in silence, followed by the guide and the projectionist. The latter was making a sales pitch.

"Lots more reels," he said. "Got French, Gypsy, Chinese lesbians, all kinds. Five dollars a reel from now on."

The boys shook their heads. They wanted to get away and think. The guide shrugged and climbed in beside them and they drove away, leaving the fat man in the middle of the road.

"I hope he puts them kids back in bed," Sonny commented.

"Boy's Town now," the guide said happily. "Five hundred girls there. Clean, too."

They soon left the downtown area and bumped off toward the outskirts of Matamoros. A red Chevrolet with Texas license plates was just in front of them, throwing the white dust of the dirt road up into their headlights. Soon they saw Boy's Town, the neon lights from the larger cabarets winking red and green against the night. At first it looked like there were a hundred clubs, but after they drove around a while they saw that there were only fifteen or twenty big places, one on every corner. Between the corners were dark, unlit rows of cribs. The guide gestured contemptuously at the cribs and took them to a place called the Cabaret ZeeZee. When the boys parked, a fat policeman in khakis walked up and offered to open the door for them, but the guide chattered insultingly to him and he shrugged lazily and turned away.

The boys entered the cabaret timidly, expecting to be mobbed at once by whores or else slugged by Mexican gangsters, but neither thing happened. They were simply ignored. There was a large jukebox and a few couples dancing, but most of the people in the club were American boys, sitting around tables.

"The competition's gonna be worse here than it is in Thalia," Duane said. "We might as well get some beer."

They sat down at one of the tile-topped tables and waited several minutes before a waitress came over and got their order. She brought them the first Mexican beer they had ever tasted, and they drank the first bottles thirstily. In their tired, excited state the beer quickly took effect—before they knew it they had had five bottles apiece, and the fatigue of the trip seemed to be dropping away. A fat-faced girl in a green blouse came over, introduced herself as Juanita, and with no further preamble squeezed Sonny intimately through his blue jeans. He was amazed. Though responsive, he felt the evening would bring better things than Juanita, so he politely demurred. Juanita went around and squeezed Duane the same way, but got the same reply.

"Texas ees full of queers," she said, swishing her buttocks derogatorily as she walked away. The boys contemplated themselves over the beer bottles, wondering if they had been seriously insulted.

As the night wore on Sonny gradually set his mind on a slim, black-headed girl who spent most of her time on the dance floor, dancing with boys from Texas A & M. There were a good many boys from Texas A & M in the cabaret.

"I thought Aggies was all irresistible cocksmen," Duane said. "What's so many of them doing in a whorehouse?"

In time Sonny approached the girl, whose name was Maria. She cheerfully came to the table with him and downed three whiskeys while he was having a final beer. Between drinks she blew her warm, slightly sticky breath in his ear and squeezed him the way Juanita had.

"All night party?" she asked. "Jus' twenty-five dollars. We can leef right now."

It seemed ungallant to haggle with such a confident girl, so Sonny agreed. It turned out he owed eight dollars for the drinks, but it didn't seem gallant to haggle about that either. He paid, and Maria led him out the back door of the Cabaret ZeeZee into a very dark alley, where the only light was from the bright stars far above. The place she took him didn't even have a door, just a blue curtain with a light behind it. The room was extremely tiny. The one light bulb was in a socket on the wall and the bed was an old iron cot with a small mattress and a thin green bedspread.

In the room, Maria seemed less perky than she had in the club. She looked younger than she had inside. Sonny watched her unzip her dress—her back was brown and smooth, but when she turned to face him he was really surprised. Her breasts were heavy, her nipples large and purplish, and she was clearly pregnant. He had never seen a pregnant woman naked before, but he knew from the heavy bulge of her abdomen that she must be carrying a child. She tried to look at him with whorish gaiety, but somehow it didn't work: the smile was without life, and showed her gums. When he was undressed she splashed him with coolish water from a brown pitcher, and scrutinized him with such care that an old worry popped into his mind. Perhaps his equipment was too small? He had worried about that when he first began to go with Ruth, and had even tried to find out how large one's equipment was supposed to be, but the only two reference works in the high-school library were the *World Book* and the *Texas Almanac,* neither of which had anything helpful on penises. Gradually it had ceased to worry him, but with Maria he had begun to feel generally hesitant.

"But aren't you going to have a baby?" he asked, not sure that the question was proper.

Maria nodded. "Two already," she said, meaning to reassure him. Her heavy breasts and large grape-colored nipples were not at all congruous with her thin calves and girlish shoulders.

Sonny lay down with her on the cot, but he knew even before he began that somehow twenty-five dollars had been lost. He didn't want to stay in the room all night, or even very much of it.

Two minutes later it came home to him why Ruth had insisted they make love on the floor: the cot springs wailed and screamed, and the sound made him feel as though every move he made was sinful. He had driven five hundred miles to get away from Thalia, and the springs took him right back, made him feel exposed. Everyone in town would know that he had done it with a pregnant whore. Suddenly he ceased to care about the twenty-five dollars, or about anything; the fatigues of the long trip, down from the plains, through the hill country and the brush country, through Austin and San Antone, five hundred miles of it all pressed against the backs of his legs and up his body, too heavy to support. To Maria's amazement he simply stopped and went to sleep.

WHEN HE awoke, he was very hot. The green counterpane was soaked with his sweat. It was not until he had been awake a minute or two that he realized the sun was shining in his face. He was still in the room where Maria had brought him, but the room had no roof—the night before he had not even noticed. It was just an open crib.

He hurriedly got up and put on his clothes, his head aching. While he was tying his shoes he suddenly had to vomit, and barely made it past the blue curtain into the street. When he had finished vomiting and was kneeling in the white dust waiting for his strength to come back he heard a slow clop-clop and looked up to see a strange wagon rounding the corner into his part of the street. It was a water wagon, drawn by a decrepit brown mule and driven by an old man. The wagon was entirely filled by a large rubber water tank wrapped in ragged canvas; as the wagon moved the water sloshed out of the open tank and dripped down the sides of the wagon into the white dust. The old man wore a straw hat so old that it had turned brown. His grizzled whiskers were as white as Sam the Lion's hair. As he stopped the mule, three or four whores stepped out of their cribs with water pitchers in their hands. One passed right by Sonny, a heavy woman with a relaxed face and large white breasts that almost spilled out of her green robe. The whores were barefooted and seemed much happier than they had seemed the night before. They chattered like high-school girls and came lightly to the wagon to get their water. The old man spoke to them cheerfully, and when the first group had filled their pitchers he popped the mule lightly with the rein and proceeded up the street, the slow clop-clop of the mule's feet very loud in the still morning. When he passed where Sonny was kneeling the old man nodded to him kindly and gestured with a tin dipper he had in his hand. Sonny gratefully took a dipper of water from him, using it to wash the sour taste out of his mouth. The old man smiled at him sympathetically and said something in a philosophic tone, something which Sonny took to mean that life was a matter of ups and downs He stayed where he was and watched the wagon until it rounded the next corner. As it moved slowly up the street the whores of Matamoros came out of their cribs, some of them combing their black hair, some with white bosoms uncovered, all with brown pitchers in their hands and coins for the old waterman.

Sonny found Duane asleep in the front seat of the pickup, his legs sticking out the window. Three little boys were playing in the road, trying to lead a dusty white goat across into a pasture of scraggly mesquite. The goat apparently wanted to go into the Cabaret ZeeZee. A depressed looking spotted dog followed behind the boys and occasionally yapped discouragedly at the goat.

Duane was too bleary and sick to do more than grunt. His hair was plastered to his temples with sweat. "You drive," he said.

By some miracle Sonny managed to wind his way through Matamoros to the Rio Grande—in daylight the water in the river was green. The boys stood groggily under the customs shed for a few minutes, wondering why in the world they had been so foolish as to come all the way to Mexico. Thalia seemed an impossible distance away.

"I don't know if I can make it," Sonny said. "How much money we got?"

They found, to their dismay, that their money had somehow evaporated. They had four dollars between them. There was the money that Sam and Genevieve had given them, hidden in the seat springs, but they had not planned to use that.

"I guess we can pay them back in a week or two," Sonny said. "We'll have to use it."

When the customs men were through the boys got back in the pickup and drove slowly out of Brownsville, along the Valley highway. Heat waves shimmered above the green cabbage fields. Despite the sun and heat Duane soon went to sleep again and slept heavily, wallowing in his own sweat. Sonny drove automatically; he was depressed, but not exactly sleepy, and he paced himself from town to town, not daring to think any farther ahead than the next city limits sign.

Soon the thought of Ruth began to bother him. In retrospect it seemed incredibly foolish that he should drive a thousand miles to go to sleep on a pregnant girl's stomach, when any afternoon he could have a much better time with Ruth. The thought of her slim, familiar body and cool hands suddenly made him very horny and even more depressed with himself. It occurred to him that he might even be diseased, and he stopped in a filling station in Alice to inspect himself. Duane woke up and exhibited similar anxieties. For the rest of the day they stopped and peed every fifty miles, just to be sure they could.

There was money enough for gas, but not much for food, so they managed on Cokes, peanuts, and a couple of candy bars. Evening finally came, coolness with it, and the boys got a second wind. The trip ceased to seem like such a fiasco: after all, they had been to Mexico, visited whorehouses, seen dirty movies. In Thalia it would be regarded as a great adventure, and they could hardly wait to tell about it. The country around Thalia had never looked so good to them as it did when they came back into it, at four in the morning. The dark pastures, the farmhouses, the oil derricks and even the jackrabbits that went dashing across the road in front of them, all seemed comfortable, familiar, private even, part of what was theirs and no one else's. After the strangeness of Matamoros the lights of Thalia were especially reassuring.

Duane was driving when they pulled in. He whipped through the red light and turned toward the café. Genevieve would be glad to see they were safely back.

To their astonishment, the café was dark. No one at all was there. The café had never been closed, not even on Christmas, and the boys were stunned. Inside, one little light behind the counter shone on the aspirin, the cough-drops, the chewing gum, and cheap cigars.

"It ain't a holiday, is it?" Sonny said.

There was nothing to do but go over to the courthouse and wake up Andy Fanner—he would know what had happened.

Andy woke up hard, but they kept at him and he finally got out of the car and rubbed his stubbly jaw, trying to figure out what the boys wanted.

"Oh yeah, you all been gone, ain't you," he said. "Gone to Mexico. You don't know about it. Sam the Lion died yesterday mornin'."

"Died?" Sonny said. After a moment he walked over to the curb in front of the courthouse and sat down. The traffic light blinked red and green over the empty street. Andy came over to the curb too, yawning and rubbing the back of his neck.

"Yep," he said. "Quite a blow. Keeled over on one of the snooker tables. Had a stroke."

Soon it was dawn, a cool, dewy spring dawn that wet the courthouse grass and left a low white mist on the pastures for the sun to burn away. Andy sat on the fender of his Nash and told all about the death and how everybody had taken it, who had cried and who hadn't. "Good thing you all got back today, you'd 'a missed the funeral," he said. "How'd you find Mexico?" Sonny could not have told him; he had lost track of things and just wanted to sit on the curb and watch the traffic light change.

Seventeen

Sonny was embarrassed that he didn't have a suit to wear to the funeral—all he had was a pair of slacks and a blue sports coat that was too short at the wrists. No one seemed to notice, though. The graveyard was on a rough, gravelly hill, where the wind was always blowing. Sonny was able to quit being embarrassed because of Mrs. Farrow, who cried all through the graveyard ceremonies. She stood at the edge of the crowd, the wind blowing her long hair, and her cheeks wet; when she walked back to her Cadillac to drive away she was still crying and wiping her eyes with her gloves.

It was because of her crying so much that Sonny learned she had been the woman who watched Sam the Lion piss off the tank dam. That night at the café Sonny asked Genevieve about it and she didn't hold back.

"Sam's gone and Lois never cared who knew," she said. "Everybody knew but Gene. She and Sam carried on for quite a while. Lois was just crazy about him. She would have married him, old as he was, but he wouldn't let her leave Gene."

A few weeks before Sonny would not have believed it, but the world had become so strange that he could believe anything. Genevieve was wiping the counter with a gray washrag.

"Sam was quite a man, you know," she said. "And Lois was just beautiful when she was young—I always envied her her looks. She was prettier than her daughter ever will be, and nine times as wild. She had more life than just about anybody in this town."

Sonny didn't tell her about the bet at the tank dam, but he thought about it a lot, just as he thought about many of the things Sam the

Lion had done. Some of them were very strange things—the will he left, for instance. He left the poolhall to Sonny and Billy; he left the picture show to Old Lady Mosey and her nephew Junior Mosey, who was the projectionist; he left the café to Genevieve, five thousand dollars to the county swimming-pool fund, and strangest of all, a thousand dollars to Joe Bob Blanton. No one knew what to make of it, not even Joe Bob. People thought it was a damned outrage, but that was what the will said.

Two weeks after the funeral the seniors left for San Francisco, on their senior trip. Sonny was glad to go. It seemed to him he had jumped up and gone to Mexico on the spur of the moment and had never quite managed to get back to Thalia, really. The town had become strange to him, and he thought it might be easier to return to it from San Francisco.

The bus left Thalia at midnight and when dawn came was crossing the Pecos River, a dry winding rut cutting through the naked flats of West Texas. Most of the seniors had cut up all night and worn themselves out, but Sonny was awake, and just tired enough that his memory could do what it pleased. The sky was completely cloudless, a round white moon hanging in it. He had not thought of Sam the Lion much since the funeral—in Thalia it was no good thinking about him—but for some reason the bitter flats of the Pecos brought him to mind and Sonny remembered the way he used to slop around the poolhall in his house shoes, complaining about the ingrown toenail that had pained him for years. A bronc had stomped on his foot once, and the toenail had never recovered. Sam the Lion, the horsebreaker, pissing off the tank dam while Lois Farrow watched—it was too much to be thinking about on the way to San Francisco, and his eyes kept leaking tears all the way to Van Horn.

They got to San Francisco in the middle of the night and checked into an expensive cheap motel on Van Ness Avenue, not far from the bay. Duane and Jacy were full of secret plans about the Thing they were going to do, and all the boys were itching to go bowling or find whores. The first day there the room mothers kept them all herded together and saw to it that they rode a cable car, visited the Top of the Mark, and went across the Golden Gate bridge. All the Californians looked at them as if they were freaks, whereas it seemed to the kids it was the other way around. The room mothers were scandalized by the number of bars in the city and kept everyone in a tight group to protect them against lurking perverts.

The second day was unscheduled and most of the boys spent it on Market Street, looking at dirty magazines and talking to girls and sailors in the cheap sidewalk lunch counters. Sonny and three other boys wandered into a bar between Market and Mission and were met by a tall black-headed girl named Gloria who offered to let them take pictures of her naked. The bar itself was plastered with pictures of Gloria naked, a great inducement to photography. Unfortunately her fee for the privilege was twenty dollars and none of the boys could afford it.

The major event of the trip occurred on the afternoon of the second day in San Francisco when Jacy finally allowed Duane to seduce her. The girls were all supposed to accompany the room mothers to the De Young Museum that afternoon, but Jacy cleverly got out of it. She was rooming with an obliging little girl named Winnie Snips, and she got Winnie to tell the room mothers that she had taken to her bed with menstrual cramps. No one ever doubted the word of Winnie Snips. She was valedictorian, and just unpopular enough that she was glad to do anything anyone wanted of her.

After the girls and the room mothers left, Sonny stationed himself in the lobby of the motel so he could give the alarm if the party got back early. It was an ugly lobby full of postcard racks and it depressed him a little to sit in it. The only senior who bothered with postcards was Charlene Duggs who sent about a dozen a day to an airman boy friend of hers in Wichita Falls. She wanted everyone to know how much in love she was, but she didn't have much to say and just wrote "Gee, I miss you, Love and kisses, Charlene" on every card. When

Sonny thought about Jacy he got even more depressed, but Duane was his friend and a scheme of such daring had to be supported.

As it turned out, Sonny's depression was nothing at all compared to the one Duane had to cope with in the seduction chamber upstairs. The glorious moment had arrived, and was going to be just perfect: they could even see the bay and a part of Alcatraz through the window. "I love you," Duane said, as soon as they had kissed a few times. "I love you too," Jacy said, breathing heavily. It was the way things were done. Then she let Duane take absolutely all her clothes off, something she had never done before. For some reason, being naked with him was different than being naked around a bunch of Wichita kids. She caught him looking right at the place between her legs, and that seemed rather discourteous. Still, there was no backing out, so she stretched out on the bed while Duane undressed. He had been in a state of anticipatory erection for at least half of the 1,800-mile drive, and could hardly wait to get his socks off. They kissed again for a moment, but both supposed speed to be of the essence and Duane soon rolled on top. Jacy sucked in her breath, preparing to be painfully devirginized. For a moment or two she did feel something that was hard and slightly painful, but it wasn't nearly as painful as she had expected it to be and in a moment it ceased to be hard at all and became flexible and rather wiggly. It certainly wasn't hurting her, but it wasn't going in, either. It sort of tickled, and kept sliding off into her pubic hair. Curiosity got the better of her and she opened her eyes. Duane had a very strange look on his face. He was horrified at himself, unable to believe his member should betray him—not then, of all times.

"What's wrong, honey?" Jacy asked, wiggling slightly. She couldn't stand to be tickled.

"Um," Duane said, a little choked. "I don't know."

He held himself above her, embarrassed to death but hoping beyond hope that his body would come to its senses and enable him to go on. He hoped for two or three long minutes, while Jacy offered her intimate of intimates, but his body continued to register complete indifference. Duane didn't have the faintest idea what to do: no emergency had ever been more unlooked for.

After a time Jacy felt a rising sense of exasperation.

"Well get off a minute," she said. "You might get tired and fall on me."

Duane complied, too disgraced to venture speech. He sat hopelessly on the edge of the bed, looking out at the bay. Jacy sat up and shrugged her hair back across her shoulders. Obviously they were faced with a crisis. The situation had to be salvaged or they would be the laughing stock of the class. Suddenly she felt furious with Duane. She looked with vexation at the offending organ.

"It was Mexico," she said. "I hate you. No tellin' what you got down there. I don't know why I ever went with you."

"I don't know what happened," Duane said glumly. He got up and crept reluctantly back into his clothes, but Jacy stalked about the room, indignantly naked and not giving a damn.

"What'll we say," she said. "The whole class knows what we were going to do. I just want to cry. I think you're the meanest boy I ever saw and my mother was so right about you."

"I don't know what happened," Duane said again. He really didn't. He started for the door but Jacy stopped him.

"Don't go out there yet," she said. "We haven't had time to do it—Sonny would know. I don't want one soul to know."

Duane sat back down on the bed and Jacy went into the bathroom and cried a few real tears of anger. It seemed to her Duane had been a monster of thoughtlessness to put her in such a position. She didn't want to touch him again, ever, and it angered her to think she would have to go on pretending to be his sweetheart for the rest of the trip. It would never do to let the class think they had broken up over sex. In fact, she would have to be even more loving with him in public, so everyone would think they were having a warm, meaningful affair.

When she thought they had been in the room long enough she went out and told Duane to leave.

"You better not tell one soul, either," she said. "You just pretend it was wonderful. And wear your slacks when we go to supper tonight—I think we're going someplace nice."

She stood naked, hands on hips, conscious that her nudity embarrassed Duane a little, and thoroughly pleased that it did.

"Well, I'm sorry," he said again. "I don't know what happened."

"If you say that one more time I'll bite you," Jacy said.

When Winnie Snips and the other girls piled into the room an hour later, pale with curiosity, Jacy was sitting in a well-rumpled bed with only her pajama tops on, staring out at the bay. The evening fog was coming in.

"Oh gee," Winnie said. "Tell us about it, Jacy. What happened?"

Jacy looked languorously around at them, calm, replete, a little wasted even.

"I just can't describe it," she said. "I just can't describe it in words."

The very next day, to Duane's immense relief, the seduction happened after all. Jacy insisted he take her for a walk to show everyone how much they wanted to be alone, and while they were walking down Geary Street, holding hands in case anyone from the class should see them, Duane suddenly felt himself return. They were just outside a cheap hotel, and without hesitation he seized his chance.

"Come on," he said. He had Jacy in the lobby of the hotel before she even knew what he meant. An old lady in a blue-flowered silk bathrobe registered them without comment and took five dollars from Duane. In the creaky cage of an elevator he kissed Jacy hungrily and fondled her breast, conscious that all was still well below. Jacy was skeptical and didn't return the kiss, but there *was* something rather adventurous about being fondled in an elevator—Winnie Snips would faint if she heard of such a thing.

Their room was tiny, with green walls, an old-fashioned bed, and a narrow window that looked across Geary Street to a one-story nightclub with a dead neon sign outside. Duane wasted absolutely no time—he was taking no chances with himself. He was out of his clothes by the time the door closed, and he tugged Jacy toward the bed, pulling rudely at her skirt. She shrugged loose and went to the window to undress at her own pace.

"If you can't wait you can jump out this window," she said. "I don't think it will work anyway."

Duane was not certain it would either, and waited nervously. The room was chill and Jacy had goose bumps on her breasts. As she lay down she looked at Duane casually—men were certainly strange. All she really expected was something tickly, but Duane surprised her horribly. He didn't tickle a bit, but instead he did something really painful. At first she was too startled to move, and then she yelled out loud. Someone in an adjoining room kicked the wall indignantly. "Quit, quit," she said—it was intolerable. Duane was much too thrilled to quit, but fortunately he didn't take long. Jacy was at her wit's end as it was.

She got gingerly out of bed, meaning to take a hot bath, and discovered that the little room didn't even have a bathroom in it, just a lavatory. "There must be one down the hall someplace," Duane said, but she wouldn't let him go look for it. She felt strange and wanted to leave. All the way back to the motel she kept glancing over her shoulder, expecting to see a trail of blood on the sidewalk behind her. Duane was walking happily along, infuriatingly proud of himself.

"Oh, quit prissing," Jacy said. "You needn't think I'm going to take you back just because of that. I don't think you did it right, anyway."

"Sure I did," Duane said, but he wasn't really positive, and he brooded about it during the remainder of the trip. They did it twice more, once in the motel in San Francisco and one in Flagstaff, Arizona, on the way home. Duane was confident he was doing it right, but for some reason Jacy didn't swoon with bliss. She only allowed it twice more because she thought Bobby Sheen would like it if she had a little more experience. The whole business was far from delightful, but she supposed that was probably because Duane was a roughneck. In Flagstaff it went on much too long and she got exasperated and told him off once and for all.

"You never will learn," she said. "I don't know why I went with you so long. I guess we have to keep on being sweethearts until we get home, but that's gonna be the end of it. We'll just have to think of something big to break up over."

Duane just couldn't understand it: he was more dejected and more in love than he ever had been. Jacy was bending over to slip her small breasts back into their brassiere cups; she had never looked more lovely, and he could not believe she was serious about breaking up. He tried to talk her out of it, but she went over to the motel dressing table and combed her hair thoroughly, looking at herself in the mirror and paying absolutely no attention to him.

The rest of the way home, across Arizona, New Mexico, Texas, he tried to think of ways to make her realize that they had to stay together. He was sure her disaffection would only be temporary. Jacy was thinking how glad she would be to get home. She had even decided there was no point in making a big production of breaking up: she was sick and tired of the seniors. As an audience they were not worth bothering about. When the bus finally pulled into Thalia late one June afternoon she didn't so much as tell Duane good-bye. She was tired and went right over to her parents' Cadillac while her father got her bags. Lois was watching her shrewdly.

"I see you got enough of him," she said quietly. "That's that."

"I'm just not interested in saying one word about it, if you don't mind," Jacy said.

Watching them drive away, Duane felt a little sick at his stomach. He realized Jacy had meant what she said: she was really done with him. It was very confusing to him because he had always thought you were supposed to get whoever you really loved. That was the way it worked in movies. It was all he could do to carry his suitcase to the pickup.

Sonny had merely endured the return trip, sitting in the back of the bus watching the desert go by. He had paid Duane and Jacy as little attention as possible, and it was not until he and Duane got in the pickup in Thalia that he noticed his friend was depressed.

"What's the matter?" he asked, surprised.

"Nothin'," Duane said.

Sonny knew better. "Well what is it?" he persisted. "You feel bad?"

For a moment Duane considered telling the truth, but then he decided not to.

"I'm worn to a frazzle," he said. "That California's hard on a person."

They were living over the poolhall, Billy with them, though Genevieve had kept him while the seniors were gone. Returning to the poolhall was a little strange, particularly since Sam the Lion wasn't there. If he had been there they would have shot some pool and had a great time telling him all about the trip. It would have picked everyone's spirits up. As it was, the poolhall was quiet and empty, and there was not a great deal to do.

Eighteen

While the seniors were in California a great scandal rocked Thalia. All the mothers were agreed that it was the very worst thing that had ever happened in the town: John Cecil was fired from his teaching job for being a homosexual.

The scariest thing of all, the mothers thought, was that it was just by a happenstance that he was found out. If it hadn't been for Coach Popper's vigilance and his interest in the welfare of the children, nobody would have know about Mr. Cecil, and a whole generation of young innocents would have been exposed to corruption.

The gist of the matter was that Mr. Cecil had persuaded Bobby Logan to take a summer-school course in trigonometry, in Wichita Falls high school. Mr. Cecil was going to summer school himself, at the college there, so he drove Bobby over to his class every day. That seemingly innocent arrangement was enough to arouse the coach's suspicions. He had been planning to have Bobby work out in the gym every day during the summer, so he would be in good shape when football season came. It was a pleasure to work with a fine young athlete like Bobby, and when Bobby told him about the trigonometry class he was angered.

"Why goddamn," he said. "You mean you're gonna sit in a damn schoolhouse all summer when you could be workin' out? What kinda shit is that?"

Bobby was a little embarrassed. "I'll have to have trig to get in a good college," he said.

"Trig my ass," the coach said. "I can get you a scholarship anywhere and you won't need to know a fuckin' thing."

He raged on, but Bobby was determined, and that night, thinking it over, it came to the coach in a flash: Cecil was a queer.

He didn't say anything to Ruth about it because it wasn't a thing to talk to women about. The next morning he happened to be standing around the filling station and he mentioned his suspicion to some of the men. They were sitting on piles of old tires, chewing tobacco and discussing masculine matters, and all of them agreed with the coach right down the line.

"Hell yes," one said. "Whoever heard of a man teachin' English. That's a woman's job."

"Oughta see the school board about it," the coach said sternly. The idea got quick support.

"By God, if you don't I will," Andy Fanner said. "I got two boys in that school."

"Well, I tell you, men," the coach said, squaring his shoulders with purpose. "I hate to cost a man his job, but if there's anything I hate it's to see a goddamn homasexyul messing around with a bunch of young kids. I got too much respect for the teachin' profession to put up with that."

It turned out the coach didn't have to say a word to the school board. Some of the men went home and told their wives and the wives called the school board president even before they began to call one another. The school board president was a Pontiac salesman named Tom Todd. When Tom was fourteen years old he had been seduced one night at a family reunion by a male cousin from Jonesboro, Arkansas, and he had felt guilty about it ever since. He went right into action and that very night they got John Cecil before the board and fired him.

All Mr. Cecil could say was that he hadn't done anything to Bobby, or to anyone else. He was stunned and guilty looking though, and the board knew they had their man. They didn't question Bobby Logan because his father didn't want him to know what homosexuality was yet. If it had already happened to him his father preferred that he didn't realize it.

Mr. Cecil went home and tried to explain to his wife what a terrible mistake had been made. "Why I've never even touched one of my students," he said.

"Oh, they wouldn't have fired you if you hadn't," she said. Then she screamed and ran across to the neighbor's house and then screamed again and ran back and got the two girls. She didn't return that night, but the next morning she got some of her stuff and headed for Odessa in Mr. Cecil's car. Her sisters lived in Odessa.

Ruth Popper found out about it the night Mr. Cecil was fired. The coach was in an unusually good mood that night and was propped up in bed reading an old issue of *Sports Afield*—there was a fishing story in it he had read at least fifty times.

Ruth could not sleep with the light on, and was reading the *Reader's Digest.* She lay flat on her back, and Herman noticed.

"Prop up if you're gonna read," he said. "It ain't good for your eyes to read laying down."

She obediently tucked a pillow under her head, and as she did, noticed that Herman was looking at her in a very satisfied way. Suddenly, to her complete surprise, he reached under the cover and rubbed her in rough, husbandly fashion.

"I guess tonight there's a lot of women in this town glad they ain't in Irene Cecil's shoes," he said. "I feel awful sorry for Irene."

"Why?" Ruth asked. "I've always felt a little sorry for John."

"You would," the coach said, abruptly removing his hand. "I guess you'd like to be married to a queer. The school board fired him tonight. Me and some others fellers found out about him an' took some action. He'll never teach in this part of the country again."

Ruth didn't credit her hearing. "What did you say?" she asked.

"Why didn't you know it, honey," he said, gruffly condescending. "I could tell that feller was queer as a three-dollar bill—been thinking it for years. Reason I never spoke up sooner was because I never noticed him actually botherin' with any of the kids. When I saw he was after

Bobby, I knew it was time to put a stop to it. That's one boy I don't intend to see messed up."

He farted gently into the sheets and went contentedly back to his fishing story.

Ruth wanted not to be there; not to be anywhere. She wanted to hug her knees with shame. Then gradually the shame was replaced by a dull, hot feeling inside her that soon filled her completely. Before she even recognized it as anger it had taken possession of her, and with no warning she swung her feet around in the bed and began to kick Herman furiously and as hard as she could. She kicked the magazine he held clear across the room and her bare heels caught him in the ribs and groin. The coach was so surprised he didn't know what to do. He tried to catch her ankles but he couldn't seem to and she continued to flail at him with her feet until he hastily got out and stood uncertainly by the bed, not sure what was happening to his wife.

"Here, now, here," he said. "You gone crazy? What's the matter with you?"

"You!" Ruth yelled, sitting up in bed. She was beside herself and meant to pursue him out of the house. "You're the matter," she said, her voice shaking. "You fat . . . you fat . . ." she didn't know what to call him. Looking around wildly, she saw the open bathroom door. "You fat turd!" she finished, a little lamely.

The two of them were both stunned. Quiet fell on the room. Ruth was panting, but since the coach had got beyond the range of her heels she had lost the urge to chase him. He would have liked to sit back down on the bed, but Ruth looked too strange and dangerous for him to risk it. He knew it would mean a fight if he got near her, so he stood where he was and scratched himself nervously. He would never have believed his own wife could look so dangerous.

"I never done nothin'," he said finally. "What if I did fart?" It was the only thing he could think of that might have made her mad.

"Oh, Herman," Ruth said. Her legs were trembling and all the strength had gone out of her.

"You got John Cecil fired."

"But he's a goddamn queer," the coach said righteously." He needed it."

"Then how about you?" she said. "Who roomed with Bobby in Fort Worth, John or you? You think I don't know about things like that? Now you've ruined John's life."

The coach's mouth fell open. He felt tired and went over and sat down on the couch, fumbling with his undershirt.

"Why Ruth, you don't think nothin' like that," he said. "Nobody in this town would believe that. I'm the *football coach*!"

"Don't yell at me," she said. "I know what you are."

Herman looked at her solemnly. "I sure don't know what to think about a wife like you," he said, not at all belligerent.

"We're even," she said. "I don't know what to think about a husband like you, either. Marriage is a bad joke, isn't it."

She saw that she could rip him wide open if she said the right mean things, but she didn't really have the energy and it didn't seem worth doing.

"What are we going to do?" he asked.

"You're going to sleep on that couch from now on," she said, throwing his pillow across the room.

"Hell I am," the coach said, getting up. "Hell I am." But he picked up the pillow and stood holding it.

"You are," Ruth said, switching off the bedside light. "There's some sheets in the bathroom."

"Goddammit, I ain't gonna sleep on this couch," Herman said. "It's gonna take more than your kicking to keep me out of my own bed."

"I'll do whatever it takes," Ruth said. "Maybe I'll call the school board and get a few things off my chest."

Her calm voice infuriated the coach, but it frightened him, too. She was clearly an unstable woman. He felt like kicking hell out of her, but instead he went and got some sheets and made a bed on the couch, feeling like a martyr. She didn't deserve it, but the manly thing to do would be to give her a night to cool off. It seemed to him that his mother must have been the last good woman who had ever lived.

The next day Ruth went to see John Cecil, hoping to comfort him. It occurred to her that he might be hungry, so she took what was left of a banana-nut cake she had baked the day before and walked over to the Cecils' house. The porch was dusty and the morning paper lay in the flower bed where the newspaper boy had thrown it. John took a long time to answer her knock.

"Hello, John," she said. "Can I come in?"

He looked tired and a little sick, and she felt silly for bringing the rich cake. He had on a long-sleeved shirt with the sleeves rolled up unevenly.

"I'll just put this on the cabinet," she said awkwardly, moving past him with the cake. She got to the kitchen just in time to see a little pot of asparagus boil over—John had put too much water in the pot. "Oh, goodness," he said. She turned the burner off and he sponged off the stove. Curiously, the event seemed to lift his spirits a little.

"That's exactly the kind of bachelor I make," he said.

He pulled up a kitchen chair for Ruth to sit in and they looked at one another directly for the first time since she had entered.

"What are you going to do, John?" she asked. He seemed such a kind man, and she realized at that moment that they had lived three blocks apart for fifteen years without really becoming friends.

He shook his head, rubbing the back of his neck with both hands. "I'll just have to do what I can for Irene and the girls," he said. "I've got a friend who runs an Indian reservation in New Mexico—maybe he'll let me teach out there. If that don't work out I guess I can go back to Plainview and work in my brother's grocery store. When you've messed up your life the way I've messed up mine it doesn't much matter."

"But *you* didn't mess it up," Ruth said. "My husband messed it up.

I'll never forgive him for it. If anybody needed to be fired for . . . what they fired you for, it was him."

John Cecil looked at her with astonishment. "Oh, you don't mean that, Ruth," he said, after a moment. "Why Herman's the football coach."

She saw that he didn't believe her, and knew that Herman had been right. Nobody, not even John Cecil, would believe her, and in truth she didn't even know for sure herself what Herman was. She just felt sad and uncertain and wanted to cry.

"But you've even got two kids," she said. "We don't have any kids, and we never will."

John chuckled. "It's kind of amazing to me that me and Irene had the girls," he said. "I guess it just don't take much enthusiasm for people to have two kids."

Suddenly Ruth wanted to be home, away from John Cecil. His sadness was so heavy that just being with him made her feel the weight, made her own limbs seem heavier. She made an excuse and left quickly, glad to be outside.

The next day John Cecil left Thalia for good, to go back to Plainview to his brother's grocery store. The job on the Indian reservation hadn't worked out.

When Sonny returned from the senior trip, Ruth and he discovered that they were famished for one another. The first afternoon he stayed so long that, while they were dressing, the coach's pickup drove into the driveway. It was something they had dreaded and been frightened of for months, but just then they felt so calm and comfortable with one another that they were not even scared. Besides, the coach customarily spent ten or fifteen minutes carefully putting away his fishing equipment. Sonny quietly finished dressing and went in the living room, so he could go out the front door as the coach came in the back. Ruth, wearing only her panties, folded the quilt and took it to the cedar chest in the hall closet, where it was kept. She was still a little excited, still a little warm. She picked up her dress and went into the living room—the late sun was filtering through the Venetian blinds and Sonny was peeping out of one window, watching the garage. Ruth came up behind him, slipped her arm around his waist and rubbed his stomach. When he realized she was still almost naked he turned with a smile and lifted her breasts. She put the dress on and Sonny buttoned it in back.

"I love you," she said. "You must treat me right from now on."

He didn't reply, but when they heard the back door open he kissed her lightly and walked blithely away, down the front sidewalk.

Herman was in the kitchen, poking around in the cabinet trying to find some Mercurochrome to put on a skinned hand. He could never find things like that when he needed them. Ruth stood in the door a moment, watching him fumble in the cabinet, and her mood was so good that she felt a moment of fondness for him. All he really needed of her was an occasional small kindness.

"I'll find that," she said. "How was fishing?"

For three weeks she continued to make his bed on the couch, and he accepted it, bewildered. Every night he thought he would think up a way to get his supremacy back, but every night the task proved too much for him and he decided it wouldn't hurt Ruth to have one more night to cool off.

In fact, he needed only to wait. Ruth found that she didn't like to sleep alone. She slept better with a body next to hers, even if it was Herman's. For a night or two she fought with herself, determined to keep the advantage she had gained, but she just felt more and more restless and decided finally that it was a silly way to keep an advantage. The next evening, when she was changing the pillowcases, she put Herman's pillow back on the bed. Without a word being said, he came too.

Nineteen

Summer shaped up very well for Sonny, but very badly for Duane. The first thing Sonny did was quit his job with Frank Fartley. He then hired on as a roughneck with Gene Farrow. He liked driving the butane truck better, but doing it full time gave him no chance to be with Ruth, whereas if he roughnecked at night he could count on spending the whole afternoon with her. Coach Popper was away fishing almost every day. Ruth was becoming happier every day, and was a lot more fun to visit than she had been. She and Sonny both lived for the afternoons.

Duane, unfortunately, had no one to make his days worthwhile. True to her word, Jacy had cut him off cold. Once in a while he saw her driving through town, her sunglasses on, the top of her convertible down, her bare arms tanned from all the hours she spent lying around the country club pool in Wichita. Such glimpses made him ache with desire, but ache was about all he could do. He spent most of June futilely trying to get her to talk to him on the phone—usually she just hung up, but the few times she didn't hang up were even worse.

"Why don't you go back to Mexico," she said once. "I guess girls are just easier to please down there."

"Just go with me once more," he kept saying. "Just one more time. You can at least see me."

He was convinced that if he were actually in her presence for a few minutes all her craziness would go away and they could be in love again.

Jacy knew how he felt, and repeatedly refused to see him. The whole town knew he was desperate to get her back, which suited her fine. After a month had gone by she put a stop to the calls.

"You find somebody else to pester," she said. "I've got a new boy friend now and I can't be talking to you."

"Who?" Duane asked, confused. The blow was unexpected.

"Lester Marlow," Jacy said. "I guess I've just been wanting to go with Lester all along and didn't realize it."

Duane hung up, went downstairs, and threw three pool balls against the back wall of the building as hard as he could, knocking out three big hunks of plaster and scaring Old Man Parsons almost to death. Old Man Parsons was a retired hardware salesman who looked after the poolhall during the day.

That night Duane told Sonny that he was leaving town—he had already packed his suitcase.

"There's not a goddamn thing to stay for," he said. "I'm goin' to Midland. All the roughnecks say you can get a job out there anytime. Jacy's goin' with Lester, why not leave?"

Sonny had no answer. Late that night he and Duane and Genevieve had coffee and pie together and Duane caught the three o'clock bus out. The prospect of setting out into the world had already taken Duane's mind off his problem. He was speculating about what sort of wages he could draw in Midland. Sonny felt okay about it, figuring to see Duane back in Thalia as soon as Jacy got off to college. When they walked Duane to the bus in the warm summer night they all felt good. Sonny and Genevieve stood on the curb in front of the café and watched the bus pull out. Soon all they could see of it were the red taillights, far out beyond the city limits sign.

"Wouldn't mind goin' someplace myself," Sonny said.

"Well, Uncle Sam will see you get your chance," Genevieve said, stretching her arms.

Abilene's Mercury was parked in front of the poolhall. Sonny was ready to go home, but he hated to go through the poolhall while Abilene was practicing. Finally he went in and had another cup of coffee with Genevieve, waiting to hear the Mercury roar away.

When Jacy heard about Duane leaving town she was a little bit upset. His calls had not been all that annoying—sometimes when she was bored the calls picked her up a little. It was true that she had started going with Lester more or less officially, but it was certainly no deep love affair. She was getting ready to be deeply in love with Bobby Sheen, and she regarded Lester as a necessary stepping-stone. Only by going with someone in Bobby's circle could she keep herself constantly before his eyes, and she knew that if she kept herself constantly before his eyes he would soon realize that she was more beautiful than Annie-Annie. Jacy knew quite well that she was prettier than Annie-Annie, but at the same time it worried her a little that Annie-Annie always managed to look extremely sexy. The only thing Jacy could figure was that the sexy look was something Annie-Annie had acquired with experience, and there was certainly no reason why she couldn't get just as much experience as Annie-Annie had. Lester Marlow was exactly suitable for such a purpose: he adored Jacy and was completely manageable. She still thought red pubic hair was a little ridiculous, but some things had to be accepted if one was to become a woman of the world.

The Wichita kids called sexual intercourse "screwing," so Jacy took to calling it that too. Lester's parents were in Colorado for the summer, so she and Lester could screw whenever they wanted to—Lester was always willing and usually more or less able. In a week or so Jacy managed to become completely unshy about the whole business, and even worked out a sort of routine. She slept until noon, got up, ate some peanut butter, called Lester to see if he was home, put on shorts, sandals, a blouse, and her new sunglasses and drove to Wichita. The drive always made her sweat a little and it was pleasant to walk into Lester's big cool house. Lester would always be there looking slightly nervous.

"Hi," Jacy would say. "Want to screw?" That was the favored approach among the Bobby Sheen set. Lester wouldn't have dared not to want to, so Jacy would go up to his parents' bedroom, the room with the biggest, most comfortable bed. There she would peel off her clothes and wait for Lester to peel off his. The screwing itself was pretty athletic—Jacy had never been very big on athletics, but she knew good and well she could learn to screw if she put her mind to it. Fortunately, Lester had a good attitude: he would do exactly as directed. When they were finished they usually drove over to the country club and lay around the pool with Bobby Sheen and Annie-Annie and all the other kids, most of whom had been screwing too. One day Bobby Sheen offered to rub suntan oil on Jacy's back and legs and she knew she was making progress. He rubbed the oil on in a very sexy way, she thought.

From time to time it occurred to her that she had really run Duane off too soon. He wasn't quite as manageable as Lester, but he was really a good bit sexier, and she discovered that some of the girls thought there was something pretty romantic about sleeping with roughnecks. She could probably have got another month or so of good out of Duane, but that she hadn't didn't really worry her: Bobby Sheen was the main objective, and if for prestige reasons it became necessary to have a roughneck in love with her there was always Sonny. He was very available, and just as nice as Duane.

Once, just to show that she wasn't snobbish, she called Sonny up and invited him to have a hamburger with her. It was a pleasant summer evening in early July and they decided to drive to Wichita and eat. Jacy drove, her hair blowing across her face. She had on a white silk blouse with the ends tied together in a knot across her stomach—an inch or two of her midriff showed between blouse and shorts.

"Do you ever hear from Duane?" she asked, sighing. "I really feel bad about that."

"I had a postcard," Sonny said. "He's makin' three-twenty a month. Said he bought a car."

"Well, I guess I'll always be a little bit in love with Duane," Jacy said. "We just had too much against us. It wasn't easy having to be the one to break up."

Talking about it made Sonny uneasy. In fact, just riding with Jacy made him feel a little disloyal. He still thought of her as Duane's girl.

They ate hamburgers, drank milk shakes, and rode slowly back to Thalia, looking at the millions of summer stars. Jacy let Sonny out at the poolhall and went on home, realizing only after she got there that she had enjoyed the evening. Dating no one but Lester Marlow was really tiresome. Except for not being rich, Sonny was more her type of boy. The thought of screwing Lester one more time was utterly boring, but she didn't really feel like she could push things with Bobby Sheen. She decided that in a day or two she would call Sonny again and perhaps go to the lake with him to find out if she liked to kiss him. It would be nice once more to go with somebody she liked to kiss.

The very next day, Bobby Sheen seduced her. Annie-Annie had gone to Dallas to buy her college wardrobe, and Jacy had skipped Lester and gone straight to the club to swim. Bobby asked her if she wanted to go to his house to play some records and that was it. They spread towels over the seats of his MG and wore their wet bathing suits to the house. As soon as they were inside Bobby slipped her straps down so he could play with her breasts. Jacy tried to concentrate and do everything right but it was actually pretty arousing, screwing Bobby Sheen, and she couldn't keep her head clear. He was about five times as athletic as Lester and when she thought it over later she was pretty sure she came, which was what one was supposed to do. At any rate, she went to sleep and didn't wake up until six o'clock. She found Bobby downstairs. He had on Bermuda shorts and was eating a peanut butter sandwich while he watched the news on TV.

"Peanut butter?" he asked absently, when he noticed Jacy. She didn't want to eat, she wanted to sit in his lap, but she saw he was really watching the news and made herself refrain. They had come home in his car, she had no way to leave. During the commercial Bobby got up to fix himself another sandwich. "Oh, you're afoot, aren't you," he said. "As soon as the news is over I'll run you back to the club."

He was quite cheerful and relaxed, but Jacy was a little surprised that he didn't take on over her more than he did. For the next four or five days she hung around the club pool almost constantly, expecting to hear that Bobby and Annie-Annie had broken up; she was sure that as soon as that happened Bobby would call her for another date.

The next Sunday morning Jacy was in the kitchen peeling an orange when her mother came in from the bedroom to get more coffee. On Sunday mornings Lois always lay in bed and drank coffee until the coffee pot was empty. Gene was gone—he always spent Sunday morning inspecting his leases.

"Honey," Lois asked, "don't you know that Sheen boy in Wichita? Bobby Sheen?"

"I sure do," Jacy said. "Why?"

"He got married yesterday to some girl named Annie Martin," Lois said. "It's in the paper this morning. I knew I'd seen them around the club. They got married in Oklahoma a couple of days ago and it just now made the paper. You know her?"

Jacy walked into the bedroom and found the article. It was just a tiny article with no picture, the kind the paper always ran when kids of prominent families ran off and got married without their parents' consent.

When Lois came into the bedroom with her coffee, Jacy was sitting on the bed crying bitterly.

"He's the luh-ast one," she said. "I'll just be an ol' maid."

Lois set her coffee down and got her daughter a box of Kleenex. She had seldom seen Jacy so upset, and least of all over a boy. Her tears were ruining the newspaper, and since she hadn't finished reading it Lois gently pulled it away.

"Oh, honey," she said. "Don't cry like that. That's the way it is you know. Win a few, lose a few. That's really the way it goes, all through life."

Twenty

About a week after Bobby Sheen got married, something totally unexpected happened to Jacy, and it was led up to by an event so startling that everyone in Thalia almost went mad with surprise. Joe Bob Blanton was arrested for rape!

It was one of those days when it seemed to Christian people that the Lord must have lost all patience with the town. It was a wonder he hadn't simply destroyed it by fire, like he had Sodom, and since the heat at midafternoon that day was 109 degrees He could easily have done so simply by making the sun a little hotter. A few degrees more and the grass would have flamed, the buildings begun to smoke, and the asphalt streets to melt and bubble.

Joe Bob didn't rape Jacy, of course, but the general confusion that followed his arrest made possible what did happen to her. Joe Bob didn't actually rape anybody, but very few would have believed that at the time.

"That poor kid's downfall started the day old man Blanton got the call to preach," Lois Farrow said, but she was the only one who took that view. No one else thought of blaming Brother Blanton for his son's disgrace, and still less did they think of blaming Coach Popper or the school board president or San Francisco or Esther Williams, the movie star. They were all quite willing to put the blame squarely on Joe Bob himself.

Joe Bob was a seventeen-year-old virgin. For years he had been tormented by lustful thoughts. When he was only fourteen Brother Blanton slipped into his room one night and caught him masturbating by flashlight over a picture of Esther Williams. Joe Bob had torn the picture out of a movie magazine one of their neighbors had thrown away. Of course Brother Blanton whipped him severely and disposed of the picture; he also told Joe Bob in no uncertain terms what the sequel of such actions would be.

"Joe Bob," he said, "have you ever been through the State Hospital in Wichita? The insane asylum?"

"No sir," Joe Bob said.

"Well, sometime I'll take you," Brother Blanton promised. "There are three or four hundred men over there, pitiful creatures, rotting away, no good to their families or to the Lord or anybody. I don't know about all of them, some of them may have come from broken homes or been alcoholics, but I'm sure most of those men are there because they did just what you were doing today. They abused themselves until their minds were destroyed. I don't want to scare you now. You're young, you haven't hurt yourself much, and the Lord will forgive you. I just want you to know what will happen if you keep on with this kind of filthiness. You understand, don't you?"

"Yes sir," Joe Bob said.

He understood, but he soon discovered he was just too weak to stop. He kept right on playing with himself, all through high school, in the face of certain insanity. His father hadn't told him how long it took for a mind to be destroyed, but he never doubted that his would be, sooner or later.

In the summer of his junior year, when he got the call to preach, he thought there still might be hope. If he preached, girls might like him, and if they did he might be able to overcome his vices and lead a normal life. The hope was very short-lived. The very night he preached his first sermon he succumbed to the vice again. Besides that, he found he did not really like to preach. He didn't have anything to say, and he soon decided he must have heard a false call: he could always get the Lord off his mind, but the only way he could get girls off his mind was by jacking off. In San Francisco he had been with the boys who wandered into the bar where Gloria was, and the thought of Gloria haunted him for weeks. By the time he got back home he had decided to resign himself to eventual insanity, and he ceased to make any effort to curb his self-abuse. If the Lord spared him until he got through college that would be enough to ask.

Joe Bob might have got through the summer all right if it had not been for the scandal caused by Mr. Cecil's dismissal. That set the town on its ear so that it made things hard for all sinners. The church ladies decided the time had come for some widespread soul-saving. If a homosexual was teaching English in high school, there was no telling what state of degeneracy the ordinary populace had fallen into. Ruth Popper herself was known to be sleeping with a high-school boy. They decided to have an All City Revival, and they didn't waste any money bringing in a slick traveling evangelist who would have charged them three hundred dollars. There were six active preachers in the town, plus Joe Bob and a few old ones that were retired, so the ladies decided to put aside denominational differences and make do with the native preaching stock.

Everybody but Joe Bob thought it was a fine idea. He didn't because it meant he would have to preach two sermons.

"Yes sir," Brother Blanton told him. "We've all got to get out there and preach our hearts out if we're going to get this town back on the right track."

Joe Bob agreed, but he was afraid he could preach his own heart completely out in just a minute or two. During the winter his ministerial flame had burned very low—he was not even confident that he himself was saved. He knew that he harbored hatred in his heart for about three-quarters of the boys of the town, and that was surely not a Christian attitude. He had no idea what he could say that might prompt anyone in the congregation to rededicate their life to Christ, and so far as he knew, getting people to rededicate their lives was the only point of a revival.

He worried about it for two weeks, and it turned out his worries were fully justified. Joe Bob had to preach the last sermon in the first go-round of preachers, which meant that he had to preach on a Thursday night, the worst possible night to preach. The first wave of revival spirit had had time to ebb, and the second wave had not yet begun to gather. The revival was held in the local baseball park under the lights, and when Joe Bob got up to preach there was just a sprinkle of a crowd, old faithfuls from all the churches in town, people so habituated to churchgoing that they never missed a sermon, no matter how dull. Joe Bob was dressed in his black wool suit, the only suit his father would let him preach in. The night was sweltering. For days Joe Bob had racked his brain, trying to come up with a sermon, but the only moral advice he could think of was that people ought to read the Bible more. That was his theme, and he sweated and stammered away at it for twenty minutes.

"When I say back to the Bible I don't mean just a chapter here and there," he tried. "I mean the *full* Gospel, the *whole* Bible, *all* of it! Ever bit!"

He kept working that point over desperately, hoping somebody, at least one person, would come down and rededicate his life. Finally, to his great relief, the Pender family got down out of the stands and came. It was not much of a triumph, because the Pender family rededicated their lives regularly, several times a year, but it was better than nothing. The Penders lived in a cabin down on Onion Creek where they shot squirrels and farmed sweet potatoes. Every two or three months, when things got boring, they came to church and rededicated their lives, hoping thereby to move the community to charity. They were a generally scruffy lot—in fact old man Elmer Pender spat tobacco juice right on home plate as Joe Bob was calling for the closing hymn.

Because of the Penders, the first sermon was not a total disgrace, but Joe Bob still had the second one to preach. That one was scheduled for a Saturday night, only one night before the revival was due to end. Hysteria would be at its height, and Joe Bob knew he would need something more potent that the Full Gospel to exhort on that night.

On the next-to-last night of a revival it would be a black disgrace not to get twenty or thirty rededications.

All week he brooded about the final sermon. He knew good and well there was no way he could get out of it, and as the week wore on the only way he could get it off his mind was by abusing himself. By Saturday morning he was in a serious state. He stayed in his room until noon and abused himself twice. Then he talked his father into letting him use the family Plymouth, on the grounds that he needed to go off and commune with nature in order to get inspiration for his sermon. Nature that day was about as hot as the place Joe Bob was supposed to be saving people from. He drove out to the lake and sat staring at the water for a couple of hours, thinking how much he didn't want to preach that night. Finally he tired of staring at the bright sun-whitened water and drove into town to get a Coke. That move turned out to be his downfall.

The facts of it almost passed belief. Nobody in Thalia would have supposed that Joe Bob could get in so much trouble in Thalia, Texas, right in the middle of a hot Saturday afternoon. Sonny heard about it almost as soon as the news got out. The sheriff happened to be in the poolhall shooting a quiet game of snooker when Monroe, his skinny deputy, came bursting in, white as a sheet.

"Sheriff, Johnny Clarg's little girl has kinda been kidnapped," he said. "They seen the preacher's boy putting her in his car about an hour and a half ago, in front of the drugstore."

"What the hell?" the sheriff said, taking aim at a red ball. "Maybe Joe Bob gave her a ride home—be doing her a favor, hot as it is. Why should Joe Bob want to kidnap Molly Clarg?"

"Don't ask me," Monroe said. "She ain't at home, though. Miz Clarg's all upset—she's done looked everywhere for 'em. They was seen drivin' out of town toward Olney. Miz Clarg's afraid Joe Bob might be goin' to mo-lest her or something."

At that the sheriff quickly slapped his cue into a rack. He was getting beat anyway, and a sex crime called for immediate action.

"Some of you boys might come with us," he said. "If that's the way it is, no tellin' what we'll find."

In all, three cars set out on the search. Brother Blanton was in one, with his wife and some good church deacons. Mrs. Clarg was in another, with a deputy and some of her friends, and the sheriff and several men were in the lead car. Sonny was with the sheriff.

Fortunately, no particular searching was required. It was clear to everybody that Joe Bob had taken Molly out to an old lovers' lane, three or four miles south of town.

"Boys, I don't know what to think, but I fear the worst," the sheriff said, wiping his sweaty face on his shirt sleeve. He drove like sixty, roaring over the rattly cattle guards as if they weren't there. If they hadn't been lucky and encountered Joe Bob on an open stretch of dirt road the sheriff might well have plowed right into him and killed Molly and several other people. When they spotted him Joe Bob was on his way back to town, but he was coming reluctantly, at a speed of five miles an hour. He stopped instantly when he saw the three cars coming toward him.

The sheriff quickly got out of his car and rolled down the cuffs of his shirt sleeves, while Joe Bob sat in the Plymouth, looking miserable. Everyone but Brother Blanton and his wife got out of the cars and stood looking indecisively at the Plymouth. After a moment Mrs. Clarg became hysterical and ran over to the Plymouth and yanked Molly out. Molly was five, and had been sitting quietly in the front seat eating a lemon all-day sucker Joe Bob had given her. When her mother yanked her out everybody noticed that she didn't have her panties on.

"Get him, ain't you goin' to?" Mrs. Clarg cried. "He's the one done it, here's my little girl, why don't you get him. If my husband was here he'd kill him dead."

At that the sheriff and Monroe leaped in and pulled Joe Bob out of the car.

"What'd you do to that child?" the sheriff said. "We all know you done somethin'."

Joe Bob started to say something but he was too scared and nervous to get it out. Instead he collapsed, and they carried him to the sheriff's car and rushed him back to Thalia.

Sonny volunteered to drive the Blantons' Plymouth into town. Seeing Joe Bob so scared depressed him and he drove slowly. Molly Clarg's panties were lying in the car seat—no one had noticed them, but Sonny supposed they were evidence so he left them there. By the time he got back to town the poolhall was full of men, all of them talking about the crime. It was generally agreed that Johnny Clarg would go to the jailhouse and kill Joe Bob as soon as he came in off his rig.

Then Monroe came in with news that the doctor had said Joe Bob hadn't actually done anything to Molly. Apparently he had just given her the lemon all-day sucker as a bribe to get her to take her panties off, and that was all he had done. It was kind of a letdown.

"Never had the guts," Andy Fanner said. "Preacher's boy."

"Well, the sheriff figures he might have mo-lested her a little bit," Monroe said. "It stands to reason."

"I've thought for years the boy was that kind," Coach Popper said, when he found out about it.

At any rate, Joe Bob had found the one method available to him for getting out of his second revival sermon. He spent that night and many others in jail, but in a way, what *did* happen at the revival that night was his triumph. His disgrace made possible the greatest upsurge of religious feeling the town had ever known. Brother Blanton insisted on preaching his son's sermon, and what he said did it. He rose above calamity and got right out there on home plate to lay matters on the line.

"Good people," he said, "I guess today I've suffered about the worst shock that can come to a man of God. My own son sits in jail tonight, sick with corruption. This very afternoon he was caught in an act of carnal trespass, a thing so foul it's almost unspeakable. How that tears my heartstrings I can't say, but what I want you to know tonight is that

I've come through. The Lord has held me up. I've not lost one bit of faith. As for Joe Bob, I've given him up to the Lord. I've prayed to the good Lord this very night that they'll send my boy to prison. Yes, to prison! Sometimes in this life things just don't work out, and I believe it is God's merciful will that Joe Bob go to suffer with the murderer and the thief. It will be a hard thing but a just thing, and I know Joe can count on God's help."

At that Brother Blanton broke down, stretched his arms to the crowd, and began to cry. "Oh, my friends," he said. "If only you would take heed from my trouble. If only you would listen and realize that Jesus Christ is the only answer. If only you would come down tonight, just come down and pray with me and let all of us rededicate our lives right now to the pure way, the righteous way. . . ."

The crowd was overcome by Brother Blanton's self-sacrifice. They flocked down, weeping and hugging one another, the women all slapping at their faces with damp powder puffs, trying to keep their makeup from running completely off. The Penders even came again, Elmer, Lee Harvey, and Mag, the three of them swept away by the general fervor.

There was one strange moment though, right at the start of the sermon: Lois Farrow walked out. As soon as Brother Blanton said he hoped Joe Bob would go to jail, Lois left the stands, got in the Cadillac, and drove away. A lot of tongues clicked—most people thought Lois needed saving worse than anyone in town. Even Brother Blanton felt a momentary irritation when he saw her leaving. Saving a soul as far gone as hers would have really gained him some heavenly credit.

What Lois did after she left was even more unusual: she went down to the jail and made Monroe let her play checkers with Joe Bob. It almost passed belief, but she sat right in the cell and played Joe Bob three games, two of which Joe Bob won. He was not feeling too bad, really. Getting out of the sermon had taken a big load off his mind.

Jacy stayed home from the revival and spent the evening watching television. While *Gunsmoke* was on, her Daddy and Abilene came in.

She could hear them in the kitchen, drinking and talking about some drilling problem. After a while Abilene came into the room with a whiskey glass in his hand and stood looking at her.

"Hi," she said. "Where's Daddy?"

"Gone to bed."

"Want me to turn the TV off?" she asked. She was never quite sure what Abilene expected of her.

"Naw, I'm going to the poolhall soon as I finish this drink," he said, leaning against the doorjamb. She was in shorts and her legs were stretched out on Gene's footstool.

"Wish I could go to a poolhall," she said, with a small pout. "I've always wanted to. It's terrible the things girls aren't allowed to do."

"Why hell, come on," Abilene said. "No problem there. I'll show you the poolhall. I got my own key."

He had always thought of her as a prissy kid, but her legs convinced him he hadn't been watching close enough.

"Aren't there people there?" she asked.

"If there are they'll be upstairs asleep," he said. "They won't bother us."

"Okay, I will go then." She felt a little nervous, but she knew he would be irritated if she backed out. She stepped out into the night in front of him. Just getting in the Mercury was exciting: it was the most famous car in that part of the country, and the seat covers smelled of tobacco and beer. Abilene kept it very neat. There was nothing vulgar in it, no dice hanging from the rearview mirror, but there *was* something on the dashboard that fascinated Jacy. It was a tiny, expensive-looking statue of a naked woman. A magnet held it to the dashboard, and as the car moved the statue wiggled provocatively. The woman had a gold stomach and tiny little bloodstones for nipples. Jacy tried not to stare at her.

When they stopped in front of the poolhall Abilene took a comb from behind the sun visor and slicked his hair back a little. The building itself was very dark. Abilene went in first and turned on a little light behind the cash register; he looked at her so inscrutably that Jacy began to be nervous. After he locked the door he got his special cue out of its drawer.

He pulled the light string above one of the snooker tables and the fluorescent tubes blinked on and spread bright light over the green felt and the neat triangle of red balls. As Jacy watched, Abilene put the jointed cue together and glanced appreciatively down its polished length. The cue had an ivory band just below the tip. Jacy was fascinated. She had never been in such a male place before, and it was thrilling.

After he had carefully chalked his cue, Abilene took a white cue ball out of one of the pockets and rolled it slowly across the table. Then he nudged the ball gently with his cue and it went across the table and came back, right to the end of the cue. Abilene smiled, and Jacy came over and stood beside him, so that she could see better. He handled the cue as lovingly as if it were a part of his body.

"Can I see it a minute?" she asked.

Abilene held it out to her a little reluctantly, clearly unwilling to let it leave his hand. Jacy held it awkwardly, trying to sight along it as expertly as he had. When she leaned over the table and playfully attempted to shoot the cue ball Abilene stepped in and took the cue away.

"I don't let nobody shoot with this one," he said. "There's plenty of others to shoot with, if you just want to practice."

Jacy pouted a little, not really interested in the other cues. She sat down on a bench and watched Abilene as he got ready to shoot. She had never seen a man who was so absolutely sure of himself. He put the white cue ball in the center of the table, sighted quickly, and then with a quick hard thrust of his hips sent the white ball ramming into the tight triangle of red balls. There was a sharp crack, and the red balls scattered and rolled all over the table, a few of them bumping together with soft little clicks. Abilene began to shoot them into pockets, moving lightly and purposefully around the table. The cue was never still. Sometimes he held it up and rubbed a little more chalk onto the tip, or propped it briefly against his hip as he contemplated a shot, but most of the time he didn't contemplate, he just moved rapidly and smoothly from shot to shot.

Jacy began to bite a hangnail on her thumb. She had never seen anything like what she was seeing. Sometimes Abilene seemed to be teasing the red balls across the table, nudging the white ball softly and gently and barely easing the red ball into the pocket. Sometimes he was quick with one stroke and slow with the next, and sometimes, as if excited or annoyed, he suddenly shot a ball very hard, ramming it into a pocket with a quick disdainful thrust of the cue. The balls made a solid thonk when they were whammed into the pockets. Abilene was totally absorbed in the table full of balls, and Jacy became almost as absorbed in the lovely movements of the cue. When all the balls were gone Abilene racked them and quickly broke again. The hard crack of the cue ball affected Jacy strangely. She felt a trickle of sweat roll out of her armpit and down her ribs. She was vaguely aware that she wanted something, but she couldn't take her eyes off Abilene long enough to think what. He took his time with the second rack, moving around the table more slowly, now lifting the cue and dropping it, withdrawing it and shoving it forward, drawing out every stroke. Jacy was almost annoyed that he had forgotten her—she squirmed a little on the bench, feeling sweaty. She wanted to run and grab the cue away from him, so he would realize she was there. But she merely sat, and he kept shooting until only the cue ball and one red ball were left. That one he shot terribly hard, without caution, thonking it into one of the corner pockets. The sound made something happen in Jacy, something like what used to happen when she and Duane courted on the basketball trips.

Abilene must have known it happened. He laid the cue gently on the green felt and the next minute was kissing her, one hand rubbing her shorts. Jacy found she had no muscles left—she was limp, leaning back against the wall. But when he stepped back a little her hand followed and caught his wrist. Abilene shook her hand off and went and got an old pair of overalls that were hanging on a nail near the door of the poolhall. He turned off the light by the cash register and then carefully spread the overalls on the snooker table before he switched that light off too. When he came back to Jacy the hall was dark except for the rows of light coming through the south windows from the lampposts along the street.

"Come on, stand up," he said. When she did, he urged her out of her clothes, waiting impatiently, and when the clothes were strewn at her feet, he ran his hands down her sides, grinning a little, not at the thought of her but at the thought of her mother. "Be sure you got them overalls under you," he said, when he helped her up on the table.

In a moment he was above her and Jacy pressed her hands against the hard muscles of his arms, not sure of anything. Then he moved and she was sure again, sure it was hurting, sure he was too much. She stretched her arms above her head and caught her fingers in the corner pockets, sucking in her breath. She wanted to tell him to quit but he was ignoring her, and before she could tell him it changed; she was no longer hurting but she was still ignored. He was just going on, absorbed in himself, moving, nudging, thrusting—she was no more than an object. She wanted to protest that, but before she could she began to lose sight of herself, lose hold of herself. She was rolled this way and that, into feelings she hadn't known, hadn't expected, couldn't avoid. She lost all thought of doing anything, she was completely lost to herself. He played her out as recklessly as he had played the final ball, and when he did she scattered as the red balls had scattered when the white one struck them so hard. She spread out, diffused, almost unconscious. Abilene said nothing. Jacy didn't know anything until she realized he had left the table and was not touching her anymore.

In a minute she got up too and tried to find something of herself. It was all new, and it was going to be wonderful. Abilene was going to be in love with her, and he counted for more than Bobby Sheen or any of the boys at the club. The only thing that worried her was that he kept ignoring her. He didn't even help her find her clothes. But it was such a romantic situation, screwing in a poolhall, that surely being in love would follow. When they got back in the Mercury she tried to make him say something to her.

"What a night," she said. "I never thought anything like this would happen."

"Yeah," Abilene said. They pulled into the Farrow driveway and he glanced at her. She leaned over and kissed him but he turned his face away. Jacy got out, very puzzled, and walked across the yard. When she was halfway across, Abilene raced his motor and made his mufflers roar, so that anyone in the neighborhood who was awake would know what car was in the driveway. Then he backed out and left.

It was not until she stepped in the back door that Jacy realized her mother was home and would have heard the mufflers.

Lois did hear them—she was in the den in her bathrobe and slip, having a light drink and watching a Spencer Tracy movie on the Late Show. When she heard Abilene's car she got up and went to the kitchen, wondering what he wanted at that time of night. She had not even realized that Jacy was out until they met in the kitchen. Jacy's hair was tangled and she was barefooted, her slippers in her hand. She looked scared and very confused, and in a moment a couple of tears leaked out of her eyes—she had just realized that Abilene wasn't going to be in love with her at all. It was a terrible disappointment. She was too upset to keep quiet.

"Oh, he's awful," she said. "Why do you fool with him, Mama? Daddy's a nicer man than him, isn't he?"

Lois could only shake her head. She sat her glass down and with a Kleenex ruefully wiped Jacy's wet face. "He sure is, honey," she said. "Your daddy's a very nice man. I ought to have given Abilene hell, instead of him."

At that moment she didn't feel capable of giving anyone hell, or anything else, either. What Abilene had done hit hard, and her legs felt weak. She freshened her drink and went back to the den to sit down, but the movie was just a blur. For a minute she felt like crying, but she felt too insignificant to cry, too valueless. When she went back in to get another drink, Jacy was sitting morosely at the cabinet reading an article on lipsticks in an old fashion magazine.

"Go to bed, honey," Lois said. "Or come and watch television with me. Brooding's no good."

Jacy didn't feel like going to bed, so she obediently followed her mother into the den and they looked at Spencer Tracy for a while. In a few minutes Jacy began to cry again. She was sitting on the floor and she moved back against Lois' legs and put her face in her mother's lap. Lois stroked her hair.

"I don't know what I'm going to do," Jacy said, looking up. "What do *you* do about it, Mama? Life just isn't the way it's supposed to be at all."

"You're right," Lois said, smoothing back the hair on her daughter's temples. "It isn't the way it's supposed to be at all, but what I've done about it hasn't worked very well. Maybe we better work out something different for you."

Twenty-One

Her disappointment with Abilene left Jacy very depressed. It was only the middle of July and she couldn't leave for college for six weeks, but she just couldn't stand the idea of staying in Thalia that much longer. She had slept with two of the most interesting men in the whole area, and neither one of them had fallen in love with her or even shown any particular interest in sleeping with her again. Screwing in the poolhall had been wild while it lasted, but it was hardly going to keep her from rotting with boredom for the rest of the summer. It would have helped if she could have told somebody about it—if the story got out that she had slept with Abilene on a snooker table she would have been a legend in Thalia forever, but she couldn't think of any way to publicize it. Neither Abilene nor her mother were going to, that was for sure, so the whole thing was just wasted. It was disgusting.

The more she thought about matters the more annoyed she was at Duane for leaving town so soon. Things would not have looked quite so dull if he had stayed around. She was not about to start up again with Lester.

One morning while she and Lois were eating a listless breakfast, Jacy gave vent to her irritation.

"I'll be so glad to get to Dallas," she said, "I don't see how people keep livin' in this town. There's not one thing to do."

"Well, there is *one* thing to do," Lois said, chewing a section of orange. "The problem is finding a man to do it with who isn't either dull or obnoxious. Right now I guess Ruth Popper's got about as good a setup as anybody."

Jacy was amazed. "Ruth Popper," she said. "You mean you would like to do that with the coach, Mama? Why I think he's the most horrible man around here. He's even worse than Abilene."

"I didn't say anything about him," Lois said spitting the orange seeds into her hand. "I wouldn't let that tub of guts come within fifteen feet of me. Ruth's been sleeping with Sonny Crawford for about six months now, didn't you know? I don't know Sonny very well but he's reasonably good looking and he's young. If I didn't have anything better than Herman Popper, Sonny would look awfully good."

"What?" Jacy said. "Are you kidding me? Sonny sleeping with Mrs. Popper? Why that's the silliest thing I ever heard of. She's forty years old."

"So am I honey," Lois said. "It's kind of an itchy age. You want the rest of this orange?"

Jacy was just flabbergasted—life was crazy. She didn't want the orange, and she didn't like the idea of Sonny sleeping with Mrs. Popper. That wouldn't do at all. She had always considered Mrs. Popper mousy, and besides Sonny had always wanted to go with her, not with someone forty years old. It was unflattering of him to sleep with Mrs. Popper.

It did end her boredom, though. She decided then and there that she would stop that romance and stop it good. She would go with Sonny for the rest of the summer, and he would never give Mrs. Popper another thought. He was reasonably good looking, like her mother said, and going with him wouldn't be too unpleasant. It would make August pass a lot quicker. Necking with him might even be fun, but she made up her mind right away that she wasn't going to let him screw her. She had had quite enough of that for one summer—it didn't really work out. She was nostalgic for the days when boys necked with her and wanted her desperately and didn't get her. That was better than actually screwing, somehow. When she got to college she could start screwing again and there it would probably be altogether great. Fraternity boys were gentlemen and would fall right in love with her when she let them screw her.

That very evening Jacy called Sonny and told him she was bored and lonesome; why didn't they go to Wichita and eat Mexican food? Sonny was eager, and the very thought of someone eager perked Jacy up. She took a long bath, shaved her legs and armpits, perfumed herself, and did her hair in an Italian way that made it look casually disarrayed. She wore a sleeveless dress and a sexy bra that left the tops of her breasts uncovered.

When Sonny went to pick her up he was not sure exactly what might happen. Jacy was relaxed and at ease and chattered away about one thing and another. They left Sonny's pickup in the Farrows' driveway and went in the convertible. One of Jacy's arms was stretched out on the top of the seat, almost touching Sonny's shoulder. Before they got to Wichita she scooted over next to him, close enough that he could smell her perfume. The wind whipped a few strands of her hair against his neck. On the way back, after the meal, she rested her arm lightly against his shoulder.

Sonny was in a quandary. He didn't know if he was still honor-bound to treat Jacy as Duane's girl, or if he could treat her as if she were free. Duane might decide to come back any time, but of course there was no guarantee that Jacy would go with him if he did. It was confusing, and having her so close to him made Sonny feel a little bit disloyal.

"Let's go to the lake," Jacy suggested, when they were back in Thalia. "I haven't been there in a long time."

It was exactly what Sonny wanted to do, but as he drove there his uneasiness increased. The thought of Ruth popped into his mind—they had seen each other that very afternoon, and had had an ardent, sweaty, good time. It was more sweaty than was usual because the Poppers' air conditioner had broken down and the coach had gone off fishing without fixing it. After their lovemaking Ruth and he had showered together, to cool off. He had stood behind her and watched the streams of water sluice off her shoulders, her back, her small hips. Driving to the lake, it occurred to him that in a way he was bound to Ruth, but with Jacy sitting close beside him, light-voiced, her hair fragrant, her arm cool, it was hard to keep Ruth in mind. He had wanted Jacy for years, and had fantasized just the sort of situation he was approaching. The lake was very still, but the crickets were singing and bullfrogs croaked loudly in the south channel, where the water was shallow.

For a moment, after stopping, Sonny sat still. Any move would put Jacy in his arms and involve him in two disloyalties, but Jacy was very close to him, so close that he could hear her breath, and soon he was unable to think about anything but her. When he turned, Jacy closed her eyes and they kissed for a long time. She was delighted. It was thrilling to bestow oneself upon someone young and worshipful. It made her feel like a generous, experienced, worldly woman, and feeling that way did something for her that Abilene and Bobby couldn't do. It was the way life was supposed to be, and because it was so nice she rewarded Sonny with all the little amorous flourishes she could think of, nibbling his lower lip and now and then slipping her tongue into his mouth. She could not really believe all those stories about Mrs. Popper—he seemed too hesitant and inexperienced. She would be the one to teach him about love and passion. That thought excited her even more, and when his hand touched her bare throat she sat back and with a wanton shrug undid the front of her dress. She rested her head against the back of the seat and smiled at him when he lifted her breasts out of the shallow cups of the bra. To Sonny it seemed a little incredible that he was holding those particular soft breasts in his hands at last. He held them and fondled them for quite some time, and not only that night but almost every night for the following two weeks. Jacy's breasts were his, her mouth was his, indeed almost all of her was his. She shivered, smiled, kissed his fingers, nibbled at his throat, even let him touch her panties on occasion, but when he grew bold and began to want to go all the way, she diverted him with her mouth or her breasts and told him it wouldn't do.

"Not here," she said huskily. "I'm too old for screwing in cars. I like beds."

Sonny was surprised at her language, but encouraged. He suggested they go to Wichita and get a motel room, but Jacy quickly thought her way out of that.

"I would, but I'm afraid to right now," she said. "I think my folks are watchin' us. They know I don't want to go to college and they think we're goin' to run off and get married." Sonny was surprised, but not entirely persuaded and Jacy nuzzled at his ear. "We'll do it when it's safe," she said. "I don't like to be in a hurry."

Until that night it had never occurred to Sonny that he could marry Jacy, but the idea was not long in taking hold of him. He began to think about it practically all the time.

Nothing at all was said about Ruth. Jacy never let on that she knew anything about him and Ruth, and Sonny didn't mention it. After the first date with Jacy he did not once go back to Ruth's. He could not have faced her. At times he missed her, and he often missed making love to her, but he did not go back. Sometimes in the middle of the night he would wake up and feel nervous and ashamed. Late at night he could not help facing the fact that he had treated Ruth shamefully and probably hurt her very much. He didn't understand it, but he knew Ruth loved him. It was unreasonable, but she did; she had put herself at his disposal, and he had left her. It wasn't right and it made him feel terrible, but at the same time he knew he wasn't going to quit going with Jacy. He was being unfair to Ruth, but what he felt for Jacy was beyond fairness. He had a chance to have something he had always wanted, and he wasn't going to pass the chance up.

He and Ruth would soon have had to quit anyway, he told himself. She was old. Her brown hair was not free of gray. Seeing Jacy at close range had made him realize how old Ruth really was. Ruth's thighs were a little thin, and when she sat up her breasts sagged, not much but some, enough to notice. It didn't make much difference, and yet it did. Jacy's body was fresher and smoother, and it even smelled a little better.

All the same, he hated being the cause of Ruth's suffering. The only way he knew how to handle it was just not to go near her, or to say anything to her, or to try to justify what he had done.

To Ruth, his absence spoke very clearly. She knew at once what it meant. Three days after he quit coming a neighbor of hers named Fanny Franklin mentioned that she had seen Sonny with Jacy Farrow. "They better get that girl off to school before she marries one of these roughnecks," Fanny said happily. She knew all about Ruth and Sonny, though she had never mentioned it, and it gave her a good bit of satisfaction to break such news to Ruth.

For a day or two Ruth spent much of her time sitting listlessly in front of the television set, not crying, just sitting. She didn't despair. Sonny had always wanted the Farrow girl—it was natural he would go with her if he got the chance. Still, she thought he might continue to come and see her once in a while, if only for sex. Even if he only did that it would be okay. She just needed to be with him a little while, from time to time.

When he had not come for two weeks, Ruth was forced to conclude that sex with her did not mean that much to him, and then she did despair. She knew he would never come, not ever again. If she saw him at all it would be on the street, and he would do his best to avoid her. She looked in the mirror often, and it told her more plainly than ever that she was old. She hated being old and despised Jacy Farrow for being young. Before long she began to despise Sonny too. The afternoons were long and hot and unrelieved and she would have forgiven him in a minute if he had come through the door. She could not do anything in the afternoons for wondering if he would come, and she could barely handle her disappointment when he didn't. At first she didn't cry, but later she cried a great deal and it only made her look older and uglier.

All the neighborhood women began to come to see her, friendly and smug, but she herself scarcely ever went out—she only went to the grocery store. At times she felt dizzy and almost feverish. She discovered that she missed Sonny sexually, as well as in other ways. From time to time she tried playing with herself, but it didn't work very well. One night in a moment of bitterness she grasped Herman and tried to get him to play with her, but he jerked himself angrily away and she didn't try again. If Sonny was not coming back, there was no point in her wanting sex anymore. It was a door she might just as well close.

The nadir came one day in the grocery store, when she bumped into Jacy. Ruth was in an old dress, her hair was dry, and she had not bothered to put on makeup. Jacy was in shorts, tight at the thighs. Her legs were tanned and her hair shone. They passed one another in front of the pork and beans. Jacy had on sunglasses, but she took them off when she met Ruth.

"Why hello, Mrs. Popper," she said, grinning with delight. "Haven't seen you in the longest time. I thought you must have left town for the summer."

When Ruth got home she began to tremble. She carried the blue quilt across the hot yard and stuffed it in the garbage can. She could think of no reason why anyone should desire her or want to know her or touch her, and she did not expect to touch or make love to anyone she cared about as long as she lived. It was a terrible feeling, knowing she would never really touch anyone again. She lay on the bed all afternoon staring dully at the wallpaper and wishing there were some simple way to die. She tried to remember herself when she was young, tried to recall one time in her life when she had been as attractive as Jacy, but she couldn't think of one. It seemed to her she had always been old. There was no relief in blaming Sonny, because what was there to blame him for? Jacy was exactly the type of girl with whom boys were supposed to fall in love. She herself was just the football coach's wife.

Twenty-Two

One Saturday morning Sonny came in from his tower and found Duane in the apartment, asleep on the couch. While Sonny was taking a shower he woke up and came groggily into the bathroom.

"How you doin', buddy," he said. "It's a real drive from here to Odessa, especially if you don't start till after you get off work."

"Where's your car?" Sonny asked.

Duane took him downstairs and proudly showed him the car—it was a second-hand Mercury, nice and clean. "Thirty-eight thousand miles on her," Duane said. "Runs like new. I like to drive it so much I thought I'd run home for the weekend."

Sonny was a little relieved. For a few minutes he had been worried that Duane's trip home might have something to do with his relationship with Jacy. Fortunately she was in Dallas that weekend, buying her college clothes.

Duane looked almost the same, except that he was browner. He wore shirts with the sleeves cut completely out, and his shoulders and upper arms were tanned almost black.

"You don't know what sun is till you live out on that desert," he said. "Them folks in Odessa don't even know it's a desert, they think it's God's country." He smoked a lot more than he had, but he was out of school and not in training, and it was natural.

The poolhall was always full of people on Saturdays. It was almost football season and football was what everybody wanted to talk about. The men were glad to see Duane and asked him what kind of football teams they had way out in West Texas.

"Wish you was back here, Duane," several said. "We could use a good fullback this year."

Such talk made Duane feel fine. He had always been very proud of being in the backfield.

When it began to get dark Sonny and he decided to drive to Wichita and drink some beer. They put on fresh Levi's and clean shirts and drove over in Duane's Mercury. He insisted that Sonny drive it.

"Handles wonderful," Sonny said. "Quite a change from that pickup."

They started the evening at a place called the Panhandle Tavern, out on the Burkburnett highway. It was a good place to drink beer, but then nearly any place was. When they left there they stopped in at the big Pioneer drive-in and watched a steady stream of teen-age boys and girls circling around one another in their cars. Finally they went on to Ohio Street and drank in a big roomy bar the size of a barn. There were a lot of airmen there, dancing, playing shuffleboard, guzzling beer. Duane and Sonny drank and idly watched the dancing.

It was pleasant for a while, and then for some reason it began to go wrong. An edge came into the evening. Sonny felt it long before anything was said. He kept drinking beer, but he didn't get high, the way he should have. He should have been comfortable with Duane, too—after all, they were best buddies—but somehow he wasn't comfortable with him at all. The pretty girls on the dance floor reminded both of them of things they didn't really want to remember.

"Still screwin' that old lady?" Duane asked casually.

"Yeah, ever now and then," Sonny said. It seemed to him the best thing to say. Duane hadn't mentioned Jacy all day, but Sonny knew he must have been thinking about her.

"Seen old Jerry Framingham last week," he said. "He came through going to Carlsbad with a load of goats. Said he thought you and Jacy had been going together a little."

"Yeah, we have," Sonny admitted quickly. "Once in a while we come over here and eat Mexican food or something. She's been kinda bored, waitin' for school to start."

He didn't look at Duane but he could tell that something was wrong. Instead of looking at Duane he looked around the room. There were jars of pigs' feet on the bar. Bunches of glum airmen stood around with beer glasses in their hands. There was a jukebox, a Schlitz sign, and a clock that said Lone Star Beer underneath it.

"Way I heard it what you probably been eatin' is pussy," Duane said, his voice shaky and strained. "Not old lady Popper's, either."

"It ain't true," Sonny said. "Whoever told you that didn't know what he was talkin' about. Sure, I been goin' with Jacy, why not?"

He couldn't keep down a pulse of irritation with Duane for having kept so quiet about the matter all day. He had kept quiet about it too, but then it wasn't his place to bring it up.

"I never said I blamed you for it," Duane said. "I don't blame you much. I just never thought I'd see the day when you'd do me that way. I thought we was still best friends."

"We are," Sonny said. "What are you so mad for? I never done nothin' to you."

"I guess screwin' my girl ain't nothin' to you," Duane said stiffly.

"I haven't screwed her, but she ain't your girl anymore, anyway. Hell, you don't even live here anymore."

"Don't make no difference," Duane insisted. He was beginning to seem drunk. "She's my girl and I don't care if we did break up. I'm gonna get her back, I'm tellin' you right now. She's gonna marry me one of these days, when I get a little more money."

Sonny was astonished that Duane could be so wrong. He knew Duane must be drunk.

"Why she won't marry you," he said. "She's goin' off to school. I doubt I'll ever get to go with her agin myself, once she gets off. I never saw what it could hurt to go with her this summer, though. She's never gonna marry you."

"She is, by God," Duane said. "Don't tell me she ain't. She'll never let you screw her, that's for sure. Hell, I was just seein' how honest you was, I knew Jacy wouldn't let you screw her. You ain't that good a cocksman. You never even screwed Charlene Duggs, all the time you went with her."

Sonny didn't know what to say. He was amazed that Duane would bring up such a matter. It was unfair, and the more he thought about it the madder he felt.

"Course I didn't," he said. "You know why? Because you and Jacy had the pickup all the time on Saturday night. Nobody could have screwed her in the time I had left."

"I could have," Duane said smugly. "I could have screwed her in five minutes."

Sonny knew that was true, but because it was true it seemed even more unfair of Duane to bring it up. Suddenly, for the first time in his life, he felt like hitting Duane.

"You know why you could," he said, almost choking. "The only reason you could have was because you was in the backfield. I was in the fuckin' line. That's the only reason Jacy went with you as long as she did, because you was in the backfield."

"That's a lie, you chickenshit," Duane said. "What are you talkin' about? Me an' her was in love."

"You was, she wasn't," Sonny said confidently. "Just because you was in the backfield. She likes me as good as she ever liked you. I'll stay all night with her one of these nights, too—she's done promised."

"You won't either," Duane said, furious.

"Why shouldn't I? She's done told me you couldn't even do it that time in San Francisco. What about that?"

Duane couldn't take that. He came out of his chair and slammed Sonny in the face with the beer bottle he had in his hand. It knocked Sonny backward, but he was soon up and at Duane. It was too much to take, saying he couldn't have screwed Charlene, just because he was in the line. Sonny couldn't see too well, but it didn't matter because in a minute they were both rolling on the floor anyway, punching and kicking at one another. The barmaids and the airmen calmly got out of the way and the boys rolled over against the bar, whacking at one another and bonking their beads on the brass footrail. They got up and slugged a minute on their knees but before they could get to their feet the cops were there. The next thing they knew they were out on the curb, each handcuffed to a cop. One of Sonny's eyes was hurting and he had to hold his hand over it, but otherwise he didn't feel too bad. He and Duane stood beside one another at the police desk, and to their surprise were no longer particularly mad.

"Don't know what happened," Duane said. "Never meant to hit you with that bottle. Reckon we got enough money to pay our fines?"

They did have, barely, and in a few more minutes, without knowing exactly what had taken place, they were on the sidewalk again, walking back up Ohio Street. They walked past the bar where they had had the fight and one of the barmaids waved at them, tolerant, jolly, and apparently amused. It deflated the boys a little bit. Theirs must not have been much of a fight, as fights went on Ohio Street.

"My damn eye sure hurts," Sonny said. "Run me up by the General Hospital—maybe they can give me a shot or something. It's a wonder we didn't tear up that bar."

"I guess they get worse fights than us in there ever night," Duane said unhappily. "When it comes to Jacy I guess I'm just crazy."

By the time they got to the hospital Sonny's eye had swollen shut and was paining him terribly. The momentary good feeling that he had had at the police station was entirely gone, and he was a little scared. It was nice that he and Duane were not going to be enemies for life, but he was still scared. When a doctor finally took a look at his eye he immediately ordered Sonny a hospital room.

"You're not leavin' here tonight," he said.

"You could lose the sight in that eye if we aren't careful, and you might lose it even if we are. In the morning we'll have to have a good look at it."

“Damn,” Duane said nervously. “Why’d I have to have that bottle in my hand?”

“Aw, they’re always tryin’ to scare you,” Sonny said. “It feels like it’s just swole up.”

Duane was really worried, and it made him so nervous and stiff that Sonny was almost glad when he left. He had a shot that made him sleep, and the next day the eye was hurting so badly that he had several more shots and was just in a sort of daze all day. He knew his father was there some of the time. The day after that he had some kind of operation, and when he woke up his father was there, shaking a little but not too badly. It was the first time they had seen one another since graduation night, when Sonny had reluctantly accepted fifty dollars as a graduation present.

“Son, must have been some fight,” Frank said.

“Oh, just me and Duane. He gone back to Odessa?”

“Yeah, he had to. Tried to see you yesterday, but they wouldn’t let him. He said to tell you he was awful sorry.”

“Well, it’s over now,” Sonny said. “I might have done it to him if I’d been holding a bottle. What’d they say about my eye?”

“They don’t know yet,” Frank said. “You didn’t lose all your sight in it, but I guess you might lose some.”

Sonny found it was not so bad having his father around. Frank didn’t say much, just sat in the room. He seemed comfortable and Sonny was too. There was only one awkward moment in the three days Frank stayed. It came one night when Sonny was eating supper.

“Son,” Frank said, “reckon it would work out if we put the poolhall and the domino hall together? The building’s big enough, ain’t it?”

It was, but the whole idea made Sonny nervous. “I don’t think it would do too well,” he said. “The men who play dominos wouldn’t want a lot of kids in there shooting pool and making racket.”

Frank said that might be so, and didn’t mention it again.

Sonny was in the hospital eight days. He got lonesome, but it was just about as bad when visitors came. Genevieve came one afternoon and brought Billy, who was scared of the hospital and didn't know whether to sit down or stand up. Sonny was so used to seeing Genevieve in her waitress uniform that she looked strange to him in her regular clothes. She came right out and asked about his eye.

"How is it, really?" she said.

"I don't know," Sonny said honestly. "It wouldn't surprise me if I was one-eyed when they take the bandages off. Duane caught me a good hard lick."

"Well, it was awful of you two to fight. You knew he joined the army, didn't you? His mother told me two or three days ago."

Sonny hadn't known it, and was very surprised. For the first time he really wondered about his eye. He had always planned to go to the army too, and it occurred to him that if he was one-eyed the army wouldn't take him. He had never supposed he would be unable to make the army.

The next afternoon the nurse brought in a note.

"A lady's down in the waiting room," she said.

The note just said: "May I come in and see you a little while? Ruth."

Sonny looked at the nurse, who was young and friendly.

"Could you tell her I'm asleep?" he asked.

"Sure I could. But you're not asleep."

"If I go to sleep right now will you tell her I'm asleep?"

The nurse did as he asked, but Sonny was blue anyway. He would not have minded seeing Ruth, but he felt bad whenever he thought about her and he was afraid that if she came up something bad might happen. In a way he wanted to see her—indeed, the more he thought about her the more lonesome he became for her—but it seemed like seeing her would only make everything worse.

The next to last day he was there, Jacy came to see him. She wore a sleeveless green dress and looked a little sad. As soon as the nurse left the room she came to the bed and kissed Sonny for a long time.

It surprised him and he embarrassed himself a little by getting a hard-on.

"Oh, I was so worried," Jacy said. "I just had to see you. When do you get out?"

"Tomorrow," Sonny said. "Why?"

"I want us to get married," Jacy said, her dewy mouth close to his. "I really do. Whenever you get out, just as soon as you want to."

Sonny was stunned. "Get married?" he said. He thought he must be having a dream.

"Do you want to?" she asked.

"Oh yeah, yeah," he said. "But ain't you goin' to college?"

"No. I don't care about that. I love you and that's more important. My folks won't like it, but we can run off."

It was an inspiration she had had as soon as she heard about the fight. Sonny was so dear, to fight for her. Running off with him would make her whole summer, and the fact that she did it even though he only had one eye would knock everyone in Thalia for a loop. It would be a lot wilder than Bobby Sheen and Annie-Annie—they were both rich and healthy. She would be running off with someone poor and sort of mutilated. Of course her folks would catch them and have it annulled, but at least she could show Sonny how much she was willing to sacrifice for him.

Jacy sat on the hospital bed and they kissed some more and talked about how wild it would be being married. Life seemed almost too crazy to be true.

The next day they unbandaged Sonny's eye. It wasn't that he couldn't see anything out of it, it was just that all he could see was fog. It was like being inside a cloud. He could tell when people moved around, but he couldn't tell who they were until they spoke.

"Could be a lot worse," the doctor said. "We'll see how it responds before we do anything else."

They gave him a black patch to wear over his eye and told him to come back weekly for checkups, but Sonny hardly listened. Marrying

Jacy was all he could think of, and he thought about it on the ride back to Thalia, while his father drove.

As soon as they got home Sonny took the extra eye patch the doctor had given him and showed Billy how to wear it. Billy was tickled to death. Because Sonny did it, he thought seeing out of only one eye was a great way to see, and from then on he wore the spare eye patch whenever he went out to sweep the town.

Twenty-Three

JACY WAS DEAD SERIOUS ABOUT GETTING MARRIED: THE DAY after Sonny left the hospital they drove to Wichita and got the license. They had to wait three days, so to be doing something Sonny quit his roughnecking job and arranged for a new job pumping leases, something he could do with one eye. The rest of the time he just stayed around the poolhall thinking about sleeping with Jacy. The prospect helped take his mind off his eye.

Jacy spent the three days imagining the effect her marriage would have on her parents and on the town. Everybody was curious about Sonny's eye, which made it absolutely the ideal time to run off with him. Her folks would simply have a fit. Probably they would call the police and have them arrested and torn out of one another's arms, but at least they would have been married and everyone would know it.

Friday afternoon, when it actually became time for them to run away, she wrote her parents a quick note:

> DEAR MAMA AND DADDY—
> I know this is going to be a shock to you but I guess it can't be helped. Sonny and I have gone to Oklahoma to get married—I guess it will be in Altus. Even if he is poor we are in love. I don't know what to say about college, I guess we'll just have to talk about that when we get back. We are going to Lake Texoma on our honeymoon and will be home Monday. I guess I will live at the poolhall until we find someplace else to live. Even if you don't like Sonny now I know you will love him someday.
> JACY

She left the note on the cabinet, propped up against a box of crackers. Gene found it when he came in from work three hours later. Lois was in Wichita that day and returned late. When she came in, Gene was pacing the kitchen floor, obviously distressed. He handed her the note.

"Oh, goddamn her," Lois said. "I can't believe it."

"Well, we got to get going," Gene said. "I want to catch 'em. Even if we can't get 'em before they marry we can sure as hell get 'em before they go to bed. That way we can get it annulled with no trouble."

"Why bother?" Lois said. "I suppose we could get it annulled anytime—that's what money's for. Why don't we just let her do the getting out—you know she won't stay with Sonny ten days. I just hate to think of what she'll do to him in that length of time. If we don't get that little bitch off to college she's going to ruin the whole town."

Gene was so upset he couldn't take what Lois said. He turned and slapped her, but it was a light, indecisive slap.

"You just change your clothes," he said, shoving her in the direction of the bedroom. "I said we're going to get 'em and by God that's all there is to it. What do you mean calling my daughter a bitch? You're her mother, ain't you?"

"I don't see what that has to do with it," Lois said, but she didn't feel like arguing. She felt sorry for Gene, and pity always made her feel wretched. She already had visions of a horrible scene somewhere in Oklahoma. She stood in the doorway and heard Gene call the highway patrol and ask them to stop Jacy's car. When he hung up he seemed to feel better. A man should react to such an event in a certain way, and he was doing what he should.

"I won't have her living over no poolhall, not even for ten days," he said. "Hurry up and get changed, and don't call my daughter a bitch again."

"No promises," Lois said. "You know what she's doing as well as I do, Gene. She doesn't give a damn about Sonny, she just wants to hurt us and get a little attention while she's doing it. What is that but bitchery?"

"Well, she comes by it honest," he said, looking his wife in the eye. "I know right where she gets it."

Lois merely nodded. "I'm sure you do," she said. She obediently went into the bedroom and put on more somber clothes.

Sonny and Jacy, meanwhile, were off on the realest of adventures: running away to get married. Jacy had an expensive suitcase and enough clothes to last her a week, while Sonny, who owned no suitcase, had a canvas overnight bag and an extra pair of slacks hung on a hanger in the back seat. They were in the convertible, and Jacy drove. Sonny didn't yet trust himself to drive on the highway with one eye.

Jacy was wearing a lovely white dress she had bought at Neiman's the week before, to wear to fraternity parties. She had some new sunglasses, and drove barefoot. It was great fun to be running away to get married—both of them were delighted with themselves. All Sonny had to do was lean back and watch Jacy and imagine the bliss that was going to be his in only a few hours. It was a bright, hot day and there were drops of sweat on Jacy's upper lip. Neither of them minded the heat, though. They stopped in Lawton and had milk shakes, probably the last milk shakes they would ever have as single people. Both of them were hungry and they sucked up every milky drop.

Then they went on to Altus, a popular place for getting married. It was late afternoon when they arrived—Sonny stopped at a filling station and asked where they might find a justice of the peace. "Why there's one right up the road," the attendant said. "What part of Texas you all from?"

They told him and drove on. It turned out to be absurdly simple to get married. The justice of the peace lived in an old unpainted frame house and came to the door in his khakis and undershirt.

"Been having myself a little snooze," he said. "What part of Texas y'all from?"

He surveyed their license casually, got a pencil, licked the point, and filled in what he was supposed to fill in. Sonny would have preferred him to use a fountain pen, since pencil erased so easily, but he didn't say anything.

"I better go get Ma to witness," he said, belching. "I guess I could put a shirt on too, if I can find one."

"Get many marriages up here?" Sonny asked, to be polite.

"Not as many as I'd like," the J.P. said. "Not like I used to when we was a Christian country. Used to be people feared God, but not no more. I don't marry half as many kids as I used to—fornication don't mean nothing anymore. Kids nowadays fornicate like frogs, they don't never think of marryin'. What decent ones is left is mostly hifalutin' kids, church weddin's and recepshuns and such as that. Ma! Got some customers."

An old woman wearing a sunbonnet and gray work gloves came in from the backyard. She was a thin little woman and looked tired, but she nodded politely. "Pardon this getup," she said. "I was out getting' the last of my black-eyes. Garden's just about gone for this year. What part of Texas you all from?"

The old man had wandered out, but he came back into the living room buttoning a khaki shirt over his belly. He stuffed the shirttail unevenly into his pants and shuffled over to an old pigeonhole desk to find his service.

"Y'all don't mind if I read this, do you?" he asked. "I ain't got a memory worth a damn."

They didn't mind him reading, but Jacy did mind him standing so close to them. He had a body odor that almost made her gag, but he winked at her with mild lechery and seemed to think she found him attractive.

"Wouldn't mind marrying you myself, honey," he said. "You got more meat on you than Ma has."

"Don't be sassing, now," his wife said. "You can wait till I get this sunbonnet off before you start."

He read the service heavily, sometimes stopping to trace his place with a forefinger. When he asked about rings Sonny shook his head. “She’s marryin’ a cheap skate, Ma,” the J.P. said.

When it was over Sonny gave Jacy a quick kiss, but she wanted a long romantic one so they kissed for almost a minute while the old lady wandered off to start shelling her black-eyed peas. As soon as they quit kissing the J.P. came over and placed a wet kiss of his own on Jacy’s cheek—it made her furious. Sonny gave him a ten dollar bill and he stuffed it in his pocket contemptuously.

“Yeah, a cheap skate,” he said. As they left he followed them out on the porch. “Hell, you’ve got a collaspable,” he hollered, when they were getting in the car. “Used to be collaspables were twenty dollar weddin’s ever time. Y’all got any fornicatin’ friends down in Texas tell ’em to cut it out and come up here to see me. I’ll set ’em right with the Lord as cheap as the next man.”

“Why he’s just awful,” Jacy said. “I never dreamed they let people like him do marryin’.”

“Anyway, we’re man and wife,” Sonny said, barely able to believe it. At the first stop sign they kissed again and wiggled their tongues enthusiastically. Jacy was for going to Lake Texoma to spend their wedding night, and Sonny was agreeable to anything.

They left Altus in a high good mood and drove back to Lawton, where they stopped to eat. In Lawton, for some reason, Jacy began to feel a little depressed. A strange thought occurred to her. They were in the parking lot of the restaurant where they were going to eat, so they kissed for a while, as newlyweds should. While they were kissing Sonny got excited and fondled her in a place in which he was very interested. It was all right for him to do it, of course, but a little later, while she was in the rest room of the steak house, it occurred to her that maybe her parents wouldn’t have the police arrest them after all. Maybe they would just wash their hands of it and go on watching television. It might even be that they thought she ought to *live* with Sonny, since she had married him.

That was a very sobering thought: to think that they didn't love her enough to want to keep her from living over a poolhall.

Thinking about it took away her appetite, and though she tried to appear gay she really only picked at her fried shrimp. They ordered beer with the meal and drank it self-consciously. It occurred to Jacy that even if her folks sent the cops they might miss them in the dark, or they might even get to the motel before the cops started looking. The thought depressed her more and more.

Sonny noticed that marriage was making Jacy a little nervous, but he supposed it was just worry over her parents. He was sure she would calm down once they got to Lake Texoma. But the strange thing was, the closer they came to the lake, the more nervous she became. He scooted over next to her and patted her leg, but that just seemed to make her more edgy.

When Sonny scooted close to her Jacy really began to feel funny. She realized suddenly that she just didn't want a wedding night with him at all—she had been wrong to think she did. She didn't know whether she even wanted to kiss him anymore or not. Kissing someone who just had one eye was kind of creepy.

Then, just outside Madill, a cop stopped them and everything changed completely. Jacy ceased to feel the least bit nervous.

"What part of Texas y'all from?" the patrolman asked, holding out his hand for Jacy's license. He flashed a flashlight in their faces.

"Newlyweds, ain't you?" he said, when they told him where they were from.

They admitted it.

"Well, better follow me in," he said. "I think somebody's lookin' for you."

"But we ain't done nothin' wrong," Sonny said. Ain't we got a right to get married? How can you arrest us, just like that?"

"I ain't arrestin' you," the patrolman said, peeling a stick of chewing gum. "I just want you to come with me, till we find out. I don't have no idea what you've got a right to do."

"I guess we better follow him, honey," Jacy said. She turned to Sonny and kissed him promisingly. "I'll just be heartbroken if my folks have done this," she added, kissing him again lightly as she put the car in gear.

The patrolman led them to a jailhouse in Madill. He didn't put them in a cell or anything, but they had to sit in the jail for almost two hours and that was almost as depressing as being in a cell. Jacy realized she was tragically in love, and clung to Sonny tightly. They even got in some nice kissing, but in a way it was depressing, at least to Sonny. Jacy's folks were in Lawton and were coming after her. He couldn't figure out the justice of it.

"I thought anybody had the right to get married," he said, several times. The patrolman had gone on about his business. There were only two people besides themselves in the whole jail: one was a prisoner and the other was a redheaded jail-keeper named Elmer.

"Well you might have the right and you might not," Elmer said. "I couldn't say. I ain't gonna hold no gun on you, but if you leave you'll just get caught agin. You might as well wait here as anywhere. If you're thirsty we got a Coke machine you're welcome to use."

While they were waiting the sheriff came in, a fat, white-headed man. He took one look at them and concluded they didn't have any right to do anything.

"Kids, we really oughta lock you up," he said. "Running off from home, making your parents chase all the way up here. I don't know what the world's coming to."

Sonny didn't either, but he knew one thing for sure: he was never going to get to sleep with Jacy. They would never be together in an actual bed, not for a whole night or even part of a night. Somehow his whole life had worked out to keep that one thing from happening, and it was the one thing he wanted most of all. He was not at all sure he would ever get to make love to anyone he cared about, much less to Jacy. In the hot little jail lobby, sitting on the one bench, he couldn't even remember why he had ever thought he *would* get to sleep with her.

It disappointed him terribly and made him feel a little sick and very tired. About ten o'clock Elmer let the one prisoner come in and watch the late movie with him on the jail's old Magnavox TV. That was what they were all doing when Lois and Gene arrived. Sonny was so tired by then that he wasn't even scared of Gene, even though Gene started yelling at him the minute he stepped through the jailhouse door.

"You're fired, you whelp!" he said. "What do you mean, runnin' off with my daughter, tellin' her she's gonna live over a poolhall?"

He would have gone on, but Elmer cut him off.

"Just take him out in the yard to bawl him out, Mister," he said. "I can't hear this movie if you bawl him out in here." It was a Randolph Scott movie, and they had all been sort of enjoying it.

As they went out the door Jacy clung to Sonny, crying bitterly. Mrs. Farrow said nothing at all, but Gene was still mad as cats.

"I'll bawl him out all right," he said. "Think I worked like a dog all my life so my daughter could end up over a poolhall?"

"We was gonna get another apartment," Sonny said, though they had not actually given the matter much thought.

"I bet you was," Gene said. He grabbed Jacy by the arm and jerked her away from Sonny. "Where's your car keys, hon?" he asked.

Snuffling, Jacy fished in her purse and handed them to Lois.

"It's a hell of a note," he said.

"Oh shut up and take her home," Lois put in wearily. "I'm tired of this."

"You bet I will. You take her car. So far as I'm concerned Sonny can walk."

He led Jacy to the Cadillac, got in, and spun the big car off, throwing up dust in the unpaved road that ran by the jailhouse. Lois and Sonny were left standing in the jailyard, by a little cedar bush. It was very quiet all of a sudden, the moon white overhead.

"I would like to apologize for all this, Sonny," Lois said. "It wasn't my doings. So far as I'm concerned you have a perfect right to anything you could get out of Jacy, but I can tell you right now that wouldn't have been much."

Sonny didn't know what to say. He felt awfully tired, and Lois noticed it.

"You're welcome to ride back with me," she said. "In fact I'd enjoy the company. I can understand how you might not want to, though. If you don't just say so and I'll give you some bus money."

Mrs. Farrow didn't seem so bad, and Sonny was much too tired to enjoy the thought of waiting for a bus. "I believe I'll ride with you," he said.

They started back over the same road that Sonny had just driven with Jacy. Mrs. Farrow drove fast, but there was no sign of the Cadillac ahead of them.

"Gene's probably driving ninety," she said. "I bet he's telling Jacy it was all my fault and his, for not loving her more or something."

Sonny didn't know whether he napped or not, but soon they were almost back to Lawton. The wind whipped Mrs. Farrow's hair about her face just as it had Jacy's, when they were driving up. To the west, toward the plains, there were low flashings of lightning and the rumble of thunder. Somewhere over near Frederic it was raining. Sonny noticed that Mrs. Farrow had a little flask that she drank from now and then.

"Here," she said, holding it out to him. "Have a little bourbon—you can have the rest of it, in fact. I've got to drive. It might pick you up."

Sonny took the flask and sipped from it. The whiskey was very sharp on his tongue, but he kept the flask and continued to sip, and after a time he felt a vagueness spreading through him that was almost comfortable. He was surprised to find Mrs. Farrow so likable.

"Not much of a wedding night, is it?" she said. She grinned at him, but it was not an insulting grin.

"No, not much of one," he said.

"Let me tell you something you won't believe, Sonny. You're lucky we got her away from you as quick as we did. Even if you had got to a motel room she'd have found some way to keep from giving it to you. God knows how, but Jacy would have thought of something. You'd have been a lot better off to stay with Ruth Popper."

Sonny was startled. "Does everybody know about that?" he asked.

"Of course," Lois said. "It sounded like a good thing to me. You shouldn't have let Jacy turn your head."

"She's prettier," Sonny said. "I guess I shouldn't have though. I don't guess I can go see Mrs. Popper any more."

"I shouldn't imagine. I wouldn't have you back if you'd left me for Jacy, but then you never know. I'm not Ruth."

They turned south out of Lawton. The bourbon was going down easier and easier. In the west the lightning flashes were closer together, and in the moments of light they could see heavy clouds low over the plains.

"I hope we don't have to put this damn top up," Lois said. She found herself moved by Sonny's youth. He held the bourbon flask very carefully and looked almost comically young. Giving way to an impulse, she reached over and touched his neck. It startled him a great deal.

"Didn't mean to scare you," she said. "I guess I just felt motherly for a second. Or maybe I felt wifely, I don't know. It's strange to have a married daughter who wouldn't go through with her wedding night."

Sonny looked at her curiously and she smiled at him, an honest, attractive smile, as she kept stroking the back of his neck lightly. He drank more bourbon and watched the intermittent lightning yellow the plains. He felt as though life was completely beyond him.

In a little while they crossed Red River, the slap of their tires echoing off the old stone bridge abutments. The water in the channel was shallow and silvery.

"Anyhow, I know why Sam the Lion liked you," Sonny said, and it was Lois' turn to be startled.

"Sam?" she said. "Who told you he liked me? Genevieve?"

Sonny nodded. Lois was silent for a moment. "No, it was more than that," she said. "He loved me, honey."

They were silent almost to Burkburnett, but Sonny noticed that Lois kept wiping her eyes with the backs of her hands.

"I get sad when I think about Sam for long," she said in explanation, her voice unsteady. "I can still remember his hands, you see. Did you know he had beautiful hands?"

They passed by Shepherd Field, with its flickering, rotating airplane beacons and its rows of dark narrow barracks.

"I think he was the only man in that whole horny town who knew what sex was worth," Lois said, her voice a little hoarse. "I probably never would have learned myself if it hadn't been for Sam. I'd be one of those Amity types who thinks bridge is the best thing life offers womankind. Gene couldn't have taught me, he doesn't know himself."

Then they were coming down on the lights of Wichita.

"Sam the Lion," Lois said, smiling. "Sam the Lion. Nobody knows where he got that name but me. I gave it to him one night—it just came to me. He was so pleased. I was twenty-two then, can you imagine?"

Then suddenly her shoulders began to shake and she did a strange thing. She wheeled the convertible off the highway in a screech of brakes and stopped on the hill across from the auction barn. She scooted across the seat and grabbed Sonny's arms, tears running down her face.

"But you know somethin'," she said, her whole body shaking. "It's terrible to only find one man your whole life who knows what it's worth, Sonny. It's just terrible. I wouldn't be tellin' you if it wasn't. I've looked, too—you wouldn't bu-lieve how I've looked. When Sam, when Sam . . . the Lion was seventy years old he could just walk in . . . I don't know, hug me and call me Lois or something an' do more for me than anybody. *He* really knew what *I* was worth, an' the rest of them haven't, not one man in this whole country. . . ."

She lay against Sonny's chest and cried very hard, her face hidden.

He put his arms around her and waited. He felt so tired that he could be calm through anything. After a while Lois' body quit heaving. She slipped her hand inside his shirt and touched his chest, and when she finally sat up her face was quite calm. In fact there was something almost gay in her face.

"Hey," she said. "I like you. I don't know if you know what I'm worth or not, but I sure like you and I should like you to have a nicer wedding night than Jacy could ever have given you. I'll take you someplace right now and we'll see to that. Okay? You're not scared of me, are you?"

"No," Sonny said, though he was. But he was glad to go with her, scared or not; he would have gone with her anywhere, just to see what she would do next, what crazy thing life would bring next. Lois got back behind the wheel and drove to a big motel on the Henrietta highway, one Sonny had passed many times. He had certainly never dreamed he would be going into it with Jacy's mother, on his wedding night.

Lois paid for a room and got the key. They were right at the back of the court, and she had a little trouble getting the key in the lock. "Gene and Jacy are home now, wondering why we're driving so slow," she said. She went in and Sonny followed her. She turned on a small bed light and raised her hands to her throat to unclip a black necklace she wore.

"We'll let 'em wonder," she said. "I'll tell them we had a flat and had to get it fixed in Lawton. It's amazing how many good excuses there are."

She was undressing, gracefully and without embarrassment, but she stopped a moment to set the bed lamp on the floor. Her breasts were bare—she was the first full-breasted woman Sonny had seen naked.

"I like a little light but I don't like it in my eyes," she said.

With the lamp on the floor the room was mostly in shadow. As Sonny hesitantly undressed, Lois came and stood quietly by him, smiling, occasionally reaching out to stroke his shoulder or arm or chest.

"Shy young men are lovely," she said, smiling. He thought her breasts were what was lovely. When they lay on the bed he quickly reached to caress her, but Lois caught his hands and held them for a moment in the valley between her breasts. She raised up on one elbow, her face just above his, and touched him lightly with her lips before she spoke.

"No, no, now," she said. "You're scared to death of me. Your muscles are all tight." She put her hand on his arms, then on his thigh muscles. Sonny knew they were tight.

"You're scared of me because I'm Lois Farrow," she said. "I'm rich and mean, all that. What everybody thinks of me. But that's not true for you. I may be that way with a lot of men because that's what they want and deserve, but it's still not true. Sam . . . the Lion knew I wasn't any of that, and I want you to know it too. See my hand? It's not like that, and hands are what's real. Put yours right here on my throat."

Sonny did—her throat was warm, and she lowered her face and kissed him. After a while she took his hand off her throat and played with his fingers, kissed them. She kissed him and played with him until he began to play too. He relaxed and became as serious and playful as she was. She seemed really glad to be with him, crazy as it was. What surprised him most was the lightness of her movement—her body was heavier than Ruth's, yet she seemed weightless, so light and easy that they might have been floating together. He came right away, without remembering her at all, and it was only a little later, when he did remember, that he wondered if he had come too soon. She seemed secretly pleased, even delighted, and she took his hands again. They played a little more—Lois continued to touch him lightly with her lips or her fingers.

"You've got a big inferiority complex you ought to cure yourself of," she said.

A little later she spoke again. "It's not how much you're worth to the woman," she said quietly. "It's how much you're worth to yourself. It's what you really can feel that makes you nice."

Dressing, she looked at her watch. "God, it's two," she said. "I guess

I better tell them we had a flat and had to *walk* to Lawton." She giggled a little and raised her arms to lower her slip over her head. "The excuse never sounds quite so good afterward," she added lightly. She walked over and asked Sonny to button her dress, and then watched him strangely while he put on his shirt.

"Your mother and I sat next to one another in the first grade," she said. "We graduated together. I sure didn't expect to sleep with her son. That's small town life for you." She grinned and stroked his chest again as he buttoned his shirt.

"What will we be?" he asked, when she stopped at the poolhall to let him out.

"Very good friends for a long time," Lois said. "Even I couldn't get away with taking on my daughter's ex-husband on a regular basis. They'd have me committed. Why do you look so sad? You're fine, Sonny."

"I was just thinking of Mrs. Popper," he said. "I guess I treated her terrible."

"I guess you did," Lois said.

He sat in the car a moment longer and then looked at her gratefully. He started to speak but Lois slipped partly across the seat and covered his lips with her palm. When he closed his mouth she took her palm away and kissed him.

"Don't ever say thank you to a woman," she said. "They'll kill you if you do. You let the ladies say thank you."

Twenty-Four

THE NEXT MORNING SONNY WOKE UP FEELING IN LOVE with Lois Farrow, but by the time a long week had passed he was back to missing Jacy and wishing he had been able to stay married to her. One night at the café Genevieve told him Lois had asked her to tell him they had taken Jacy to Dallas and would stay there with her until school started. The news did not improve his spirits.

"What do you think about it all?" he asked Genevieve.

"I don't know about it *all*," Genevieve said, "but the one thing that stands out nice and clear is that Lois' little girl took you for a nice ride. Boys in this town don't seem to have much sense when it comes to girls like her."

While they were talking all the football boys trooped into the café, laughing and cutting up. They were making a big thing of how sore and bruised they were—the first workout had been that afternoon. They played the jukebox and sat around talking about what a horse's ass the coach was. Sonny felt left out and even more depressed. He had always been on the football team and had done the same things they were doing after workouts, but suddenly he wasn't on the team and the boys didn't even notice him, he might have been out of high school ten years.

After a while he went over to the picture show and watched a funny movie with Dean Martin and Jerry Lewis. The movie took his mind off things, but afterward, when he was buying a bag of popcorn from Old Lady Mosey, he got another disappointment. She told him they were going to have to close the picture show sometime in October.

"We just can't make it, Sonny," she said. "There wasn't fifteen people here tonight, and a good picture like this, Jerry Lewis. It's kid baseball in the summer and school in the winter. Television all the time. Nobody wants to come to shows no more."

Sonny said he would be sorry to see the place go, and it was true. He went outside and sat on the curb, waiting for Billy to get through sweeping out. Since Sam's death Billy had grown nervous and restless, and was only really happy when he was with Sonny. If Sonny wasn't there to meet him after the show, he would go sweeping off somewhere and be lost half the night, so Sonny had got in the habit of being there. He and Billy would go walking together, Billy carrying his broom and occasionally sweeping at a leaf or a paper cup someone had thrown out. Sometimes they walked as far as the lake. Sonny would sit and watch the water while Billy swept the dam.

Once a week Sonny went to Wichita to have the doctor look at his eye, but the doctor seldom told him anything new. "Looks like sometime this fall I'll have to send you to Dallas. Better be saving your money. If the doctor down there decides to operate it'll cost you plenty."

So far as Sonny was concerned the Wichita doctor was costing plenty himself, but for once money was not too big a worry. His pumping job paid him enough to live on and he was able to put what the poolhall brought in in the bank. The pumping job was a lonely kind of job, but that was okay: he was not in the mood for people anyway. He spent his mornings bumping over the country roads in the pickup, going from one lease to the next, checking the rod lines, greasing the pumps and motors. Often he took Billy with him—Billy loved to go. When dove season came around Sonny bought a shotgun, an old L. C. Smith .12 gauge singleshot; occasionally, to Billy's surprise, he would take a shot at a dove or a jackrabbit, but he seldom hit anything.

He thought about Ruth a good deal, always painfully. After football season started he thought about her even more—Coach Popper's name was on every tongue. It looked like Thalia was finally going to win the district, and opinion was divided as to whether the team owed its success to the coach's coaching or to Bobby Logan's quarter-backing. Sonny felt strangely reluctant to go to the games, and stayed home from the first three or four. He felt a little guilty about not going, but somehow he just didn't want to.

Finally, in early October, the game with Chillicothe came up and Sonny broke down and went. It was a game that seemed likely to decide the conference crown—custom demanded that every male in Thalia go. At first Sonny enjoyed himself, and regretted having missed so many games. The night was cool and clear and the grass on the football field looked greener and softer than it ever had when he played. The assistant coach asked him and Jerry Framingham to run the first-down chain, and they accepted. When the band played the Thalia school song it was a little thrilling: it touched something in Sonny and made him feel as though he was part of it again, the high school, football, the really important part of life in the town.

It would have been better if he had never felt that way, because as soon as the game started he realized he was not part of it at all. Bobby Logan was part of it, and Coach Popper was very much part of it. He strode up and down the sidelines, scowling fiercely at the referees—everyone knew the coach was there. Even the linesmen were part of it, even the freshmen and sophomores on the bench—at least they were suited out. But Sonny wasn't part of it, and neither was Jerry, who had been out of school so long that he was used to not being part of it. Sonny couldn't get used to it. He kept wishing he was out on the field playing. Running the chain, measuring first downs, that was nothing: he might have been invisible to everyone but the referees. He was an ex-student—nothing. A feeling came over him sort of like the feelings he used to get in the mornings, only the new feeling was worse. Then he had felt like he was the only one in town, but standing on the sidelines, holding the chain, he felt like he wasn't even *in* town—he felt like he wasn't anywhere.

As the game went on the feeling became worse, even though Thalia was winning. Bobby Logan was quarter-backing beautifully: he got

Thalia a seven point lead and they still had it when the fourth quarter began to run out. The whole town began to believe that Thalia had won the conference, and Sonny began to believe that he was not there. The people in the stands were wild, their eyes glazed, they saw nothing but the boys on the field. When the game was over and Thalia had won, it was chaos. The cheerleaders, the band, and a mob of high-school girls rushed out of the end zone to greet the dirty, victorious heroes. The girls hugged the boys and clung to them as they walked off the field. The Quarterback Club, the local gamblers, farmers, lawyers, well-wishers of all sorts crowded around Coach Popper to congratulate him, strewing the green, cleat-torn grass with cigar butts and chewing-gum paper.

Jerry Framingham was as excited as the rest of them: he was going off with some of his truck-driving buddies to get drunk, so Sonny was left to carry the chain back to the football bus. The boys were all crowded around the bus, hugging and kissing the girls who met them on the field. Sonny put the chain with the rest of the equipment and walked back through the crowd to his pickup, feeling like he had been completely erased. People he had known all his life were all around him, but they simply didn't see him. He was out of school.

Back at the poolhall, Billy was gone, sweeping somewhere, probably, and the poolhall was dark and empty. Sonny began to cry. Every minute or two he would think how silly it was and would stop for a little while, but he couldn't stop completely. He was out and could never get back in. He would have got drunk but there was no liquor. The only person who could have made him feel real was Ruth, and he couldn't go to her. Or Lois, but he couldn't go to her either. Or Sam the Lion, but he was dead. Finally he went to hunt for Billy and found him down by the jail. Billy, it turned out, was able to bring Sonny back. They started walking together and Sonny felt okay again. He had started talking to Billy almost as he would have talked to Duane, sometimes even more freely than he would have talked to Duane, and though Billy never answered he was always friendly. Feeling like he wasn't there had made Sonny think about Ruth, and when he really thought about her he felt ashamed of himself. He realized that for years she must have felt like she wasn't there; he was probably the only person who had ever made her feel she *was* there, and he had quit her without a word and left her to feel the old way again. It would have been a bad way to behave even if it had got him Jacy, but it hadn't, and it had probably left Ruth feeling hopeless. He had just begun to realize how hard it was to get from day to day if one felt hopeless.

As they walked, Sonny took off his eye patch and let Billy wear it. They walked north from the jail, past the Masonic lodge and the Jehovah's Witness church. To the south, back toward the drive-in, they could hear horns honking as people celebrated Thalia's victory. Once in a while a dog barked at them as they walked by, but most of the dogs in Thalia knew Sonny and Billy and didn't give them any trouble. They circled past the cemetery and Sonny waited in the road while Billy swept the cattleguard. They didn't often pass the cemetery, because Billy knew that Sam the Lion was there somewhere and he was always reluctant to leave. For once Sonny did not particularly mind. Billy swept the cattleguard and got it very clean—from the pastures to the north they heard the moan of a coyote and when Billy was satisfied they walked on, past the rodeo pens and back to the dark poolhall.

Twenty-Five

A WEEK BEFORE THE PICTURE SHOW CLOSED DOWN DUANE came home from boot camp. He drove in on Sunday morning and word soon got around that he was leaving for Korea in a week's time. Sonny learned that he was home Sunday night, when he and Billy were having a cheeseburger in the café.

"Wonder where he is?" he asked. "He hasn't been to the poolhall."

"I kinda doubt he'll come," Genevieve said, frowning. "His conscience is hurting him too much about your eye. I think he's gonna stay at the rooming house this week."

"Well, maybe he'll come in," Sonny said. "There ain't much to do in this town. I couldn't live in it a week without going to the poolhall, I know that."

"I think it's all silly," Genevieve said. "Why don't you go see him? Be a shame if he goes to Korea without you all seein' one another."

Sonny thought so too, but he was nervous about going to see Duane. He kept hoping Duane would show up at the poolhall and save him having to make a decision; but Duane didn't. So far as anyone knew, he spent the whole week watching television at his mother's house. A couple of boys saw him out washing his Mercury one afternoon, but he never came to town.

As the week went by, Sonny got more and more nervous. Several times he was on the verge of picking up the phone and calling—once he did pick it up, but his nerve failed him and he put it back down. If Duane didn't want to be bothered there was no point in bothering.

Friday night there was a football game in Henrietta, but Sonny didn't go. He heard the next morning that Duane had been there drunk. All day he considered the problem and finally decided that he would go see Duane at the rooming house and let the chips fall where they may—it couldn't hurt much to try. If Duane didn't want to see him all he had to do was say so.

About five-thirty, as it was beginning to grow dark, Sonny got in the pickup and drove to the rooming house. Duane's red Mercury was parked out front. A norther had struck that afternoon and sheets of cold air rushed through the town, shaking the leafless mesquite and rattling the dry stems of Old Lady Malone's flowers. Sonny rang the doorbell and then stuffed his hands in his pockets to keep them warm.

"H'lo, Mrs. Malone," he said, when the old lady opened the inside door. The screen door was latched, as always. "Duane here?"

"That's his car, ain't it?" she said, edging behind the door so the wind wouldn't hit anything but her nose and her forehead. "He's here if he ain't walked off."

She shut the door and went to get Duane. Sonny shuffled nervously on the porch. In a minute, Duane opened the door and stepped outside.

"Hi," Sonny said, finding it hard to get his breath because of the wind. "Thought I'd better come by and see you before you got off."

"Glad you did," Duane said. He was nervous, but he did look sort of glad. He was wearing Levi's and a western shirt.

"Want to go eat a bite?" Sonny suggested.

"Yeah, let me get my jacket."

He got his football jacket, the one from the year when the two of them had been cocaptains, they got in the warm pickup, and drove to the café. Conversation was slow in coming until Sonny thought to ask about the army, but then Duane loosened up and told one army story after another while they ate their hamburger steaks. It was pretty much like old times. Penny waited on them—she had had twin girls during the winter, put on twenty-five pounds, and was experimenting that night with purple lipstick. Old Marston had died in February of pneumonia—he had gone to sleep in a bar ditch in the wrong season. Genevieve had hired a friendly young widow woman to do the cooking.

"Guess we ought to take in the picture show," Sonny said. "Tonight's the last night."

"A good thing, too," Penny said, overhearing him. "Picture shows been gettin' more sinful all the time, if you ask me. Them movie stars lettin' their titties hang out—I never seen the like. The last time I went I told my old man he could just take me home, I wasn't sittin' still for that kind of goings on."

"Yeah, we might as well go," Duane said, ignoring her. "Hate to miss the last night."

They went to the poolhall and Sonny got his football jacket too. Then they angled across the square to the picture show and bought their tickets. A few grade-school kids were going in. The picture was an Audie Murphy movie called *The Kid from Texas,* with Gale Storm.

"Why hello, Duane," Miss Mosey said. "I thought you was done overseas. Hope you all like the show."

The boys planned to, but somehow the occasion just didn't work out. Audie Murphy was a scrapper as usual, but it didn't help. It would have taken *Winchester '73* or *Red River* or some big movie like that to have crowded out the memories the boys kept having. They had been at the picture show so often with Jacy that it was hard to keep from thinking of her, lithely stretching herself in the back row after an hour of kissing and cuddling. Such thoughts were dangerous to both of them.

"Hell, this here's a dog," Duane said.

Sonny agreed. "Why don't we run down to Fort Worth, drink a little beer?" he asked.

"My bus leaves at six-thirty in the mornin'," Duane said. "Reckon we could make it to Forth Worth and back by six-thirty?"

"Easy."

Miss Mosey was distressed to see them leaving so soon. She tried to give them their money back, but they wouldn't take it. She was scraping out the popcorn machine, almost in tears. "If Sam had lived, I believe we could have kept it goin'," she said, "but me and Jimmy just didn't have the know-how. Duane, you watch out now, overseas." Outside the wind was so cold it made their eyes water.

Sonny insisted they go in the pickup. He knew Duane would go to sleep on the way back and he didn't want the responsibility of driving the Mercury. The wind shoved the pickup all over the road, but the road was still a lot better for their spirits than the picture show had been. Rattling out of Thalia reminded them a little of the time—it seemed years before—when they had gone to Matamoros. As soon as they reached a wet county they stopped and bought two six-packs of beer. The cans spewed when they were opened and the smell of beer filled the cab.

By the time they crossed the Lake Worth bridge they had gone through a six-pack and a half and were feeling okay. Soon they came to the Jacksboro highway bars and Sonny pulled off at a place called the Red Dot Tavern. Inside, a lot of tough-looking boys with ducktails were playing shuffleboard, and a couple of women with dyed hair were sitting at the bar with their middle-aged sweethearts. The ducktails looked at the boys belligerently, but no direct challenges were offered.

"All we can do here is get drunk and get whipped," Duane said. "Let's see what the prospects are on South Main."

They drove slowly around the courthouse—the only courthouse they knew that had a neon American flag on top—and parked far down Main Street, where the bars were. The wind whipped around the big granite courthouse and cut right down the street, as cold as it had been in Thalia. The boys went in a hash house and had some chili and crackers to fortify themselves, then let the wind blow them down the street to a bar called the Cozy Inn, where a three-piece hillbilly band was whomping away. One middle-aged couple was dancing, and a few more were sitting in the booths or at the bar. The barmaid, a friendly old woman in her mid-fifties, wiped off their table with the end of her apron and then brought them some beer.

"Where you boys from?" she asked. "Thalia? Ain't it windy up there? I wouldn't live that close to the plains for nothin'. My oldest sister lives out in Floydada."

In a few minutes the band ended its set and the three young musicians straggled off to the rest room to relieve themselves.

"Maggie, you sing us a couple," one of the older customers said.

The barmaid didn't much want to, but the other couples took up the cry and finally she went over and picked up a guitar, shaking her head and deprecating herself.

"I ain't much of a singer," she said, but she strummed a minute or two and sang "Your Cheatin' Heart." Everyone thought she was real good, the boys included. Her voice was rough but strong—it filled the Cozy Inn better than the three sideburned young honky-tonkers had. She sang like she meant every word; it was not hard to believe that she had run afoul of a cheating heart or two somewhere in her life. After that she sang "Making Believe," and would have put the guitar down and gone back to the bar if Duane hadn't gone up and stopped her. He liked her singing.

"I'm goin' off to Korea tomorrow, ain't no tellin' when I'll get to Fort Worth agin," he said. "Sing one more."

"Why sure, if that's the case," the woman said. "Both my boys was in the service. I was right proud of 'em."

"These is for the soldier boys," she announced, not wanting the rest of the crowd to think she was singing out of vanity. She sang "Filipino Baby" and everyone applauded loudly; encouraged, she finished with "Peace In The Valley" and went back to the bar to draw someone a Pearl. Sonny felt suddenly depressed. The old barmaid had reminded him that he wasn't in the army. It seemed a fine thing to be going off to Korea and Sonny wished very badly that he could go. When the band came back the boys left and stood on the cold street a minute, both slightly wobbly from the beer.

"We sure ain't findin' no women," Duane said. "Want to look some more or do you want to take the easy out?"

"It's too cold to prowl much," Sonny said.

With no more ado they turned up the street toward the easy out, a whorehouse called The New Deal Hotel. It was about the nicest whorehouse in that part of the country, but a little expensive on that account. Since it was Duane's last night the boys decided to splurge. When they got to the hotel a bunch of high-school boys from Seymour were standing on the sidewalk shivering, trying to get up the nerve to go inside, It was easy to tell they were from Seymour because of their football jackets.

"Yep, it's a whorehouse all right," Duane said. "You boys coming up?"

"How much do they charge?" one boy asked, his teeth chattering. "We're afraid to go up for fear we ain't got the money."

"They start at about ten bucks," Duane said, and the boys' faces fell. They had been hoping for five.

Sonny and Duane went on in and up the green-carpeted stairs, leaving the Seymour boys to count their money. The madame was a quiet, polite woman who looked and dressed like the saleswomen in a Wichita Falls department store. Sonny's girl was a polite, thin-nosed brunette from Corsicana, named Pauline. Everything was splendidly comfortable in the New Deal: the rooms were warm, the beds wide and clean, the carpets good. The girls were pleasant, but so efficient that afterward it seemed to Sonny that he and the girl had barely touched. Before he was even thawed out he and Duane were going back down the green stairs, each ten dollars poorer and neither much less horny.

They Seymour boys were all gone, the streets almost empty. While they were walking back to their pickup the city street-sweeper chugged by and Sonny remembered Billy and hoped Miss Mosey had seen he got home out of the cold.

"Well, I guess the next piece I get will be yellow," Duane said philosophically.

By the time they got back to the Lake Worth bridge, he was asleep.

Sonny didn't care—he enjoyed the drive, and was in no hurry. With the wind blowing against him he couldn't make much time, but he didn't need to. North of Jacksboro he stopped the pickup and got out to take a leak, and Duane woke up and followed suit. It was about five o'clock when they pulled into Thalia. The posterboards in front of the picture show were naked. It seemed to Sonny it would have been better to have left *some* posters up, even the posters to *The Kid from Texas*.

"Got about two hours till bus time," he said, when they were at the rooming house. "Want to go down and have some coffee?"

"Yeah," Duane said. "Wait till I go in and get my gear."

In his uniform Duane looked a lot different. When he got back in the pickup he casually handed Sonny the keys to the Mercury. "Here," he said. "Why don't you look after that car for me?"

Sonny took the keys, embarrassed. "Your Ma don't need it?" he asked.

"I wouldn't want her drivin' it, no better than she can drive. You might help her run the groceries home, if you have time."

Sonny didn't know what else to say. In the warm café they both got a little sleepy and ended up playing the jukebox to keep awake. Genevieve wasn't there. Her husband had gone back to work in August and she had hired a girl named Etta May to work the night shift.

When the bus pulled up out front, both boys were glad. Sitting and waiting was hard on the nerves. The bus driver came in to have a cup of coffee and Sonny and Duane walked across the street to the yellow Continental Trailways bus. The wind made their eyes water, and took their breath—they had to turn their backs to it. Duane leaned his dufflebag against the front of the bus.

"Hear anything from Jacy?" he asked suddenly, since there was just two minutes left to talk.

"No, not a thing. She hasn't been back to town since August. I guess she just stays in Dallas all the time."

"I ain't over her yet," Duane said. "It's the damnedest thing. I ain't over her yet. That's the only reason me and you got into it, that night. Reckon she likes it down in Dallas?"

"It's hard to say," Sonny said. "Maybe she does. Reckon you and her would have got it all straightened out if I hadn't butted in?"

"Aw no," Duane said. "They would have annulled me too, even if we had. You all never even got to the motel?"

"No," Sonny said.

The bus driver came out of the café and hurried across the street, tucking his chin into his shoulder so his face would be out of the wind. Duane picked up the dufflebag and he and Sonny shook hands awkwardly.

"Duane, be careful," Sonny said. "I'll take care of that Mercury."

"Okay," Duane said. "See you in a year or two, if I don't get shot."

He got on and waved quickly from the window as the bus started up. A ragweed skated across the dusty street and the bus ran over it. Sonny put his hands in his pockets and walked back across the street to the pickup, not feeling too good. It was another one of those mornings when no one was there.

Twenty-Six

Of all the people in Thalia, Billy missed the picture show most. He couldn't understand that it was permanently closed. Every night he kept thinking it would open again. For seven years he had gone to the show every single night, always sitting in the balcony, always sweeping out once the show was over; he just couldn't stop expecting it. Every night he took his broom and went over to the picture show, hoping it would be open. When it wasn't he sat on the curb in front of the courthouse, watching the theater, hoping it would open a little later; then, after a while in puzzlement, he would sweep listlessly off down the highway toward Wichita Falls. Sonny watched him as closely as he could, but it still worried him. He was afraid Billy might get through a fence or over a cattle-guard and sweep right off into the mesquite. He might sweep away down the creeks and gullies and never be found.

Once, on a Friday afternoon, Miss Mosey had to go into the theater to get something she had left and she let Billy in for a minute. The screen was disappointingly dead, but Billy figured that at least he was in, so he went up into the balcony and sat waiting. Miss Mosey thought he had gone back outside and locked him in. It was not until late that night, when Sonny got worried and began asking around, that Miss Mosey thought of the balcony. When they got there, Billy was sitting quietly in the dark with his broom, waiting, perfectly sure that the show would come on sometime.

All through October, then through November, Billy missed the show. Sonny didn't know what to do about it, but it was a bad time in general and he didn't know what to do about himself either. He had taken another lease to pump. He wanted to work harder and tire himself out, so he wouldn't have to lie awake at night and feel alone. Nothing much was happening, and he didn't think much was going to. One day he went to Wichita and bought a television set, thinking it might help Billy, but it didn't at all. Billy would watch it as long as Sonny was around, but the minute Sonny left he left too. He didn't trust the television. He kept going over to the picture show night after night, norther or no norther—he sat on the sidewalk and waited, cold and puzzled. He knew it would open sooner or later, and Sonny could think of no way to make him understand that it wouldn't.

One cold, sandstormy morning in late November Sonny woke up early and went downstairs to light the poolhall fires. Billy was not around, but that was not unusual. Sonny sneezed two or three times, the air was so dry. One of the gas stoves was old and he had to blow on it to get all the burners to light. While he was blowing on the burners he heard a big cattle truck roar past the poolhall, coming in from the south. Suddenly there was a loud shriek, as the driver hit the brakes for all he was worth—the stoplight was always turning red at the wrong time and catching trucks that thought they had it made.

Sonny went back upstairs and dressed to go eat breakfast. He couldn't find either one of his eye patches and supposed Billy must have them. It was the kind of morning when a welding helmet would have been a nice sort of thing to wear. The sky was cloudy and gritty, and the wind cut. When he stepped outside Sonny noticed that the big cattle truck was stopped by the square, with a little knot of men gathered around it. The doctor's car had just pulled up to the knot of men and the old doctor got out, his hair uncombed, his pajamas showing under his bathrobe. Someone had been run over. Sonny started to turn away, but then he saw Billy's broom lying in the street. By the time he got to the men the doctor had returned to his car and was driving away.

Billy was lying face up on the street, near the curb. For some reason he had put both eye patches on—his eyes were completely covered.

There were just four or five men there—the sheriff and his deputy, a couple of men from the filling stations, one cowboy, and a pumper who was going out early. They were not paying attention to Billy, but were trying to keep the truck driver from feeling bad. He was a big, square-faced man from Waurika, Oklahoma, who didn't look like he felt too bad. The truck was loaded with Hereford yearlings and they were bumping one another around and shitting, the bright green cow-shit dripping off the sideboards and splatting onto the street.

"This sand was blowin'," the trucker said. His name was Hurley. "I never noticed him, never figured nobody would be in the street. Why he had them damn blinders on his eyes, he couldn't even see. What was he doin' out there anyway, carryin' that broom?"

"Aw, nothin', Hurley," the sheriff said. "He was just an ol' simple-minded kid, sort of returded—never had no sense. Wasn't your fault, I can see that. He was just there—he wasn't doin' nothing."

Sonny couldn't stand the way the men looked at the truck driver and had already forgotten Billy.

"He was sweeping, you sons of bitches!" he yelled suddenly, surprising the men and himself. They all looked at him as if he were crazy, and indeed, he didn't know himself why he had yelled. He walked over on the courthouse lawn, not knowing what to do. In a minute he bent over and vomited by one of the dusty, stunted little cedar trees that the Amity club had planted. His father had come by that time.

"Son, it's a bad blow," he said. "You let me take care of things, okay? You don't want to be bothered with any funeral-home stuff, do you?"

Sonny didn't; he was glad to let his father take care of it. He walked out in the street and got Billy's broom and took it over to him.

"Reckon I better go try to sell a little gas," one of the filling-station men said. "Look's like this here's about wound up."

Sonny didn't want to yell at the men again, but he couldn't stand to walk away and leave Billy there by the truck, with the circle of men spitting and farting and shuffling all around him. Before any of them knew what he was up to he got Billy under the arms and started off with him, dragging him and trying to run. The men were so amazed they didn't even try to stop him. The heels of Billy's brogans scraped on the pavement, but Sonny kept on, dragged him across the windy street to the curb in front of the picture show. That was as far as he went. He laid Billy on the sidewalk where at least he would be out of the street, and covered him with his Levi's jacket. He just left the eye patches on.

The men slowly came over. They looked at Sonny as if he were someone very strange. Hurley and the sheriff came together and stood back a little way from the crowd.

"You all got some crazy kids in this town," Hurley said, spitting his tobacco juice carefully down wind.

By the time Sonny got back to the apartment Genevieve was there. She was crying but when she saw Sonny she made herself quit. She stayed for about an hour, made some coffee, and tried to get Sonny to cry or talk or something. He wouldn't. He wandered around the apartment, once in a while looked out at the gritty sky. Genevieve saw it was going to take some time.

"Sonny, I got to go to the café," she said. "People keep eatin', come what may. Come on down when you feel like it. Dan'll be glad to pump your leases for you when he comes in this afternoon."

Sonny didn't know what he would feel like doing that afternoon, so he didn't say anything. When Genevieve left he turned on the television set and watched it all morning: it made a voice in the room, anyway.

About the middle of the afternoon he began to feel like he had to do something. He had the feeling again, the feeling that he was the only person in town. He got his gloves and his football jacket and got in the pickup, meaning to go on out and pump his leases, but no sooner had he started than he got scared. When he passed the city limits signs he stopped a minute. The gray pastures and the distant brown ridges looked too empty. He himself felt too empty. As empty as he felt and as empty as the country looked it was too risky going out into it—he might be blown around for days like a broomweed in the wind.

He turned around and drove back past the sign, but stopped again. From the road the town looked raw, scraped by the wind, as empty as the country. It didn't look like the town it had been when he was in high school, in the days of Sam the Lion.

Scared to death, he drove to Ruth's house. It was broad daylight, mid-afternoon, but he parked right in front of the house. The coach was bound to be in school. Sitting in the driveway was the coach's new car, a shiny red Ford V-8. The Quarterback Club and the people of the town were so proud of his coaching that they had presented him with the car at the homecoming game, two weeks before.

Sonny went slowly up the walk, wondering if Ruth would let him in. He knocked at the screen, and when no one answered opened the screen and knocked on the glass-paneled front door.

In a moment Ruth opened it. She was in her bathrobe—that was about all Sonny saw. He didn't look at her face, except to glance.

"Hi," he said.

Ruth said nothing at all. She was surprised, then after a moment angered, then frightened.

"Could I have a cup of coffee with you?" Sonny asked finally, lifting his face.

"I guess," Ruth said, her tone reluctant. She let him in and he followed her through the dark, dusty-smelling living room to the kitchen. They were awkwardly silent while she made the coffee. Neither knew what to do.

"I'm sorry I'm still in my bathrobe," Ruth said finally. "It gets harder all the time to get around to getting dressed."

But then, as she was pouring the coffee, anger and fright and bitterness began to well up in her. In a moment they filled her past the point where she could contain them, and indeed, she ceased to want to contain them. She wanted to break something, do something terrible.

Suddenly she flung Sonny's coffee, cup and all, at the cabinet, then she flung her own, then flung the coffee pot at the wall. It broke and a great brown stain of coffee spread over the wallpaper and dripped down onto the linoleum. Somehow the sight of it was very satisfying.

"What am I doing apologizing to you?" she said, turning to Sonny. "Why am I always apologizing to you, you little . . . little bastard. For three months I've been apologizing to you, without you even being here to hear me. I haven't done anything wrong, why can't I quit apologizing. You're the one who ought to be sorry. I wouldn't be in my bathrobe now if it hadn't been for you—I'd have had my clothes on hours ago. You're the one that made me quit caring whether I got dressed or not. I guess just because your friend got killed you want me to forget what you did and make it all right. I'm not sorry for you! You would have left Billy too, just like you left me. I bet you left him plenty of nights, whenever Jacy whistled. I wouldn't treat a dog that way but that's the way you treated me, and Billy too."

Sonny was very startled. He had never thought of himself as having deserted Billy. He started to say something, but Ruth didn't stop talking long enough. She sat down at the table and kept talking.

"I guess you thought I was so old and ugly you didn't owe me any explanations," she said. "You didn't need to be careful of me. There wasn't anything I could do about you and her, why should you be careful of me. You didn't love me. Look at me, can't you even look at me!"

Sonny did look. Her hair and lips looked dry, and her face was paler and older than he had remembered it. The bathrobe was light blue.

"You see?" she said. "You shouldn't have come here. I'm around that corner now. You ruined it and it's lost completely. Just your needing me won't bring it back."

Sonny didn't know. Her eyes seemed like they had always seemed, and having her so mad at him was suddenly a great relief. He saw her hands, nervously clasped on the table. The skin on the backs of her hands was a little darker, a little more freckled than the white skin of her fingers. He reached out and took one of her hands. She was startled, and her fingers were stiff, but Sonny held on and in a moment, disconcerted, Ruth let him hold her hand. Their hands knew one another and soon warmed a little.

When Sonny wove his fingers through hers Ruth looked at him cautiously and saw that he was still and numb, resting, not thinking at all. He had probably not even heard the things she said, probably would not remember them—he was beyond her hurting. It was as if he had just come in and they had started holding hands. She would have to decide from that, not from all the things she had said, nor even from the things that had happened, the pain and humiliation of the summer. What if he had valued a silly young girl more than her? It was only stupid, only the sort of thing a boy would do.

She could forgive him that stupidity, but it was not about forgiveness that she had to decide: it was about herself, whether she could stand it again, whether she wanted to. Even if the springs in her would start again it would only be a year or two or three before it would all repeat itself. Something would take him from her and the process of drying up would have to be endured again.

"I'm really not smart," she thought, and with the fingers of her other hand she began to smooth the little black hairs at the back of his wrist. "I'm not smart, and if I take him back again it will all be to go through again."

She didn't know whether she was brave enough to accept it, but she turned his hand over and traced the little lines in his palm, traced them up to the wrist. She pressed the tips of her fingers against the blue veins at his wrist, and followed the vein upward until it went under the sleeve of his shirt. It irritated her that her fingers wanted to go on, to go up the arm to his elbow and over the smooth muscle to the hollow of his shoulder. All at once tears sprang in her eyes and wet her face, her whole body swelled. She knew she was going to have the nerve, after all, and she took Sonny's young hand and pressed it to her throat, to her wet face. She was on the verge of speaking to him, of saying something fine. It seemed to her that on the tip of her tongue was something it had taken her forty years to learn, something wise or brave or beautiful that she could finally say. It would be just what Sonny needed to know about life, and she would have said it if her own relief had not been so strong. She gasped with it, squeezed his hand, and somehow lost the words—she could not hear them for the rush of her blood. The quick pulse inside her was all she could feel and the words were lost after all.

In a moment she felt quieter. She put his hand on the table and stroked his fingers with hers. After all, he was only a boy. She saw that the collar of his shirt was wrinkled under his jacket.

"Never you mind, honey," she said quietly, reaching under the jacket and carefully straightening out the collar. "Honey, never you mind. . . ."